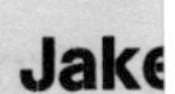

Jake Arnott was born in 196

novel, *The Long Firm*, was first published by Sceptre in 1999 to huge public and critical acclaim, and in 2004 was made into a widely-praised television series by the BBC. *He Kills Coppers* and *truecrime* followed to equal acclaim in 2001 and 2003.

The Long Firm

'One of the smartest, funniest and most original novels you will read all year. It is a gloriously accomplished re-creation of the city in the era of the Kray twins . . . as sharp and lethal as a Savile Row lapel.' John Tague, *Independent on Sunday*

'This is pulp fiction so polished as to be immaculate' James Harkin, *New Statesman*

'*The Long Firm* manages to hook you from the first. It is compulsive reading, powerful writing with an evocative feel for the bleaker side of the Swinging Sixties' Dominic Bradbury, *The Times*

'Outstanding . . . Arnott's recreation of the decadent, dangerous atmosphere of the times is immaculate. His prose is as smooth as a seersucker suit, as sweet as a purple heart. Suck it and see.' Robert MacFarlane, *Observer*

'Gripping . . . slumming it doesn't get much better than this' Mark Sanderson, *Time Out*

'As polished as a brass knuckleduster . . . This is strong-arm stuff, which zings with an authentic low-life argot and grips the reader with its head-in-a-vice portrait of the ugly glamour of the era.' *Sunday Times*

'One of the most impressive first novels I've read in years.' Simon Shaw, *Mail on Sunday*

'Terrific – highly entertaining, cleverly plotted and deftly characterised . . . a tremendous read.' John Preston, *Sunday Telegraph*

'Both exciting and funny. It takes the clichés of the genre and makes them sexy and freshly interesting' Robert Potts, *Observer*

'Makes *Lock, Stock and Two Smoking Barrels* seem like *Listen with Mother*. A must-read.' Terry O'Neill, *Elle*

He Kills Coppers

'Easily as good as, if not better than, the superb *Long Firm* . . . a stylish tour-de-force, Arnott's taut lucid prose moving the reader effortlessly from the 1966 World Cup to the 1980s and the age of Thatcher's Boot Boys and the Battle of the Beanfield. Smashing.'
Julia Bell, *Big Issue*

'Brilliant . . . You won't be able to put it down.'
Mark Sanderson, *Sunday Telegraph*

'A wonderful mix of period detail and atmosphere, this is a fine, evocative novel' Stuart Price, *Independent*

'A fine piece of work that can only increase Arnott's reputation further.' Jim Driver, *Time Out*

'Arnott's tough and streetwise novel packs a powerful punch'
Simon Shaw, *Mail on Sunday*

'Incendiary stuff.' Neil O'Sullivan, *GQ*

'It propels Arnott even further into a league of his own.'
Christopher Fowler, *Independent on Sunday*

'Set mainly in 1966, the summer when England won the World Cup, *He Kills Coppers* impressively evokes both the innocence and the precariousness of that time . . . Arnott is a writer of many shades and, as in his debut, *The Long Firm*, shows his penchant for combining challenging storylines with strong storytelling.'
Max Davidson, *Sunday Telegraph*

'Gritty and absorbing' *Mirror*

'Much more than a gripping adventure, it's a faultless chronicle of changing mores and, as a study in crime and punishment, it superbly plays the sins of Porter against the dubious morality of his pursuers. Touching, darkly humorous, essential reading.'
Ally Fogg, *Big Issue in the North*

truecrime

‘His fictional (or, more accurately, factional) characters bristle with authenticity . . . It should be read as a matter of urgency’
Erwin James, *Guardian*

‘Funny, fast, witty and brutal . . . Whenever he’s got a new book out I drop everything, knowing that the next couple of hours are going to be pure gangland bliss.’ David Bowie

‘*truecrime* brings [Arnott’s] trilogy into the 1990s, and it blows the gaff sky high . . . the most expansive, ironical and funny novel of the series.’ David Isaacson, *Daily Telegraph*

‘Arnott pinpoints with devastating accuracy how today’s world leads to the survival of the shallowest. His ear for low-life patois is as sharp as ever and the narrative proceeds at a cracking pace.’
Michael Arditti, *The Times*

‘The prose is as hard, stylish and memorable as our antihero himself.’ *Arena*

‘Probably the most astringent satire yet on what was probably the slimiest of decades, the Nineties.’
Mark Simpson, *Independent on Sunday*

‘A fast, stylish and unexpectedly angry book that ultimately rails against the crime-as-glamour period it details.’
Andrew Holmes, *Scotland on Sunday*

‘[An] incredibly accurate social history of Britain in the Eighties and Nineties . . . A superb, profound and thoughtful response to the *Lock, Stock* generation.’ Ally Fogg, *Big Issue in the North*

‘Arnott’s satire is right on the money.’ Peter Guttridge, *Observer*

‘Chilling, funny and caustic . . . he manages to pull off the difficult trick of satirising a decade while maintaining realism through careful and sometimes brilliant detailing’ Peter Watts, *Time Out*

JAKE ARNOTT

the long firm trilogy

SCEPTRE

The Long Firm © 1999 Jake Arnott
First published in Great Britain in 1999 by Hodder and Stoughton
A division of Hodder Headline

He Kills Coppers © 2001 Jake Arnott
First published in Great Britain in 2001 by Hodder and Stoughton
A division of Hodder Headline

truecrime © 2003 Jake Arnott
First published in Great Britain in 2003 by Hodder and Stoughton
A division of Hodder Headline

These three books first published as *the long firm trilogy* paperback in 2005
by Hodder and Stoughton, a division of Hodder Headline

A Sceptre paperback

1

A CIP catalogue record for this title is available from the British Library

ISBN 0 340 89732 5

Typeset in Sabon by Palimpsest Book Production Limited,
Polmont, Stirlingshire
Printed and bound in Great Britain by
Mackays of Chatham Ltd, Chatham, Kent

Hodder Headline's policy is to use papers that are natural, renewable and recyclable products and made from wood grown in sustainable forests. The logging and manufacturing processes are expected to conform to the environmental regulations of the country of origin.

Hodder and Stoughton Ltd
A division of Hodder Headline
338 Euston Road
London NW1 3BH

JAKE ARNOTT

The Long Firm

SCEPTRE

What's a jemmy compared with a share certificate?
What's breaking into a bank compared with founding one?

Bertolt Brecht, *The Threepenny Opera*

1

The White-Hot Poker

'You know the song, don't you? "There's *no* business like *show* business".' Harry gets the Ethel Merman intonation just right as he heats up a poker in the gas burner.

'"Like no business."'

Turning the iron slowly, sheathing it in blue flame.

'You know?'

I nod with enough emphasis to cause the chair I'm tied to to edge a little across the room. This only brings me closer to Harry. The gas roars softly. Blue flame looking cold. Poker looking hot. Glowing now, already brighter than the fire that feeds it. Getting red hot, white hot.

'Well what if there *was* a business like show business. *Like* show business. You know?'

Nod nod edge edge.

'There is, Terry. There is.'

I can feel the heat of it on my cheek now as he points it at my face. I feel sick.

'You know what it is, don't you?' Harry asks in a hoarse whisper. 'It's what I do.'

'Harry,' I croak.

'Shh,' he insists. 'You'll have a chance to talk. Don't worry. You'll want to tell me the whole story. But first the show. I'm going to show you something.'

My brain is throbbing with terror. I've got to think. Work out how all of this happened. Put it all together and find a way out. Think. Remember.

Johnny Remember Me.

The Casbah Lounge. Pine panelling, tattily upholstered benches around the walls, a fish tank embedded in the central partition. Sipping bitter black espresso. Boys sitting or standing around in groups clattering transparent glass cups and saucers. Looking. Checking out who was in the place. Checking out who other people in their group were checking out. And checking out who was being checked. Dull eyes twitching, slightly glassy from speed and coffee and cigarettes.

'Johnny Remember Me' wailing mournfully from the jukebox. Last year's hit still haunting. Strange girl's voice calling out of the echo-chamber wilderness.

My first year in London. I had to start somewhere. A crummy bedsit in Westbourne Grove. Working as a messenger in an advertising firm. I'd escaped suburbia, that was the main thing. I found places that I could go. A handful of theatrical pubs and seedy coffee bars. The Casbah Lounge was one of them.

A group of Earl's Court queens there with cheap polari sophistication. Vada this, vada that. Casual bitchiness judging anybody's fleeting object of affection.

Then he came in. Thick set in a dark suit and tightly knotted tie. Looking out of place amidst all the loud clothes the young homos were sporting. Standing out sombre and heavy among the bright shirts and hipster slacks from Vince or Lord John. He looked around the coffee bar, negotiating all the signals, all the brief flashes of eye contact with a weary frown as if his imposing presence was a burden. He looked clumsy and awkward, intimidated for all his toughness. All the looks, the staring. In places he was more used to, spielers, drinking clubs, heavy boozers like the Blind Beggar or the Grave Maurice that level of eyeballing would have seemed an affront, a prelude to combat. Here, he had to get used to the fierce looks and learn a new way of staring. He had to come off guard in order to make contact.

He had dark, oil-slicked hair, a battered face that made him look older than he was. An extra tuft of hair joined his eyebrows so they furrowed in a single line. You couldn't say he was pretty. Handsome, in a brutal sort of a way. Impressive. Something about him I found rather attractive. Something dangerous. The style he had in the way he held himself, holding himself up against any embarrassment. The way he looked. Like he meant it. It inspired some arch glances amongst the queens. *Get her*, someone murmured.

As I looked over he caught my stare. His face tightened and drew back a touch. I smiled and his frown narrowed for a second then opened up. A lopsided grin brought out the crease of a scar in his right cheek, then thinned out to a sad smile as he continued to scan the room.

His gaze moved into a more professional line of vision and a flurry of communication flashed from one face to another. *Trade*, another voice muttered coldly. *Johnny Remember Me*, howled the jukebox. Someone coughed significantly and went over. As I watched the casual intensity of the negotiations the man seemed to look over at me. I turned away thinking not so much that it was rude to stare but that it was bad for business. I didn't want to interfere. So I looked at the fishtank. Huge carp mouthed silently. A stream of silvery bubbles trailed to the surface.

Someone nudged me. The queen had returned, a faint smile on his lips. He nodded petulantly at me

'He wants *you* dear.'

The poker throbs with heat and light. Harry blows on it and a few tiny sparks fly off and quickly die in the cold air of the lock-up. He plunges it back into the brazier.

'You stupid fucker,' he says. 'Thought you could have me over, didn't you?'

I start to say something. Harry slaps me hard across the face.

'Shh,' he hisses at me again. 'I know, I know, you want to explain it all. But I ain't interested in some story you'll come up with. I want the truth. The whole truth. And by the time I've finished with you by Christ I'll get it.'

Harry comes up close to me. My head is twisted to one side from the slap, one cheek still sore from the blow. He grabs my jaw and forces me to look directly into his stare.

'You've been a naughty boy, Terry,' he whispers into my face. 'We need to teach you a lesson.'

Breaking a person's will, that's what it was all about. He'd explained it to me once. Harry didn't like to do business with anybody that he couldn't tie to a chair. He liked to break people. Sometimes it was a warning, sometimes punishment. Always to make one thing very clear. That he was the guvnor. That's what all the violence was for. That was the point of it. That was the one gruesome detail that was missed out in the trial. All the press reports, the TORTURE GANG BOSS headlines. All the lurid stories to tease the punters. The beatings, the pliers, the black box for giving electric shocks. They all missed the point. He liked to break people.

'But how can you tell?' I'd asked him back then. 'Don't people just fake it?'

And Harry had laughed. A little spasm of knowledge.

'Oh, you can tell,' he had assured me softly. 'They become like children. Crying and that. Calling for their mummies.'

The Casbah Lounge. That's where it all began. I walked across the floor, nodded at the man and we went out together into the night air. He had a big black Daimler parked outside. A driver awaiting instructions. He held the door open for me. I felt flash. And completely reckless.

I'd never done it for money before, never even thought about renting it. I was a nice boy from the suburbs, passed the eleven plus and everything. But I'd always been drawn to trouble. Ended up getting expelled from Technical High School. I left home, left a semi-detached life for the longed-for city. I craved some sort of excitement. I think carrying around the secret that I was a homo had something to do with it as well. That part of me didn't really exist until I moved down to London.

We got into the back of the motor together. The man nodded to his driver. As we pulled away I felt a sudden surge of trepidation in my stomach but I tried to ignore it.

'Harry,' he whispered as introduction, taking my hand in his.

'Terry,' I responded.

'Hello, Terry,' he breathed huskily, stroking my leg.

I remember us pulling up somewhere off Sloane Square. Harry had an expensive flat in Chelsea. He poured us both a large brandy and showed me his photograph collection. Harry with Johnnie Ray, with Ruby Ryder, Tom Driberg MP, Sonny Liston. Pictures of him looking stern faced next to film stars, singers, boxers, the great and the good.

Then we had sex. He fucked me up against a full-length mirror. My breath misted the glass but I could make out his reflected face clenched in need as he came into me. Afterwards we had a smoke and he spoke softly. His voice lost some of its gruffness and took on a high-pitched almost child-like tone.

'You're a nice-looking kid,' he whispered.

'Thanks.'

'I ain't very pretty am I?'

He touched his battered face sadly.

'Oh, I don't know,' I replied, not quite knowing what to say.

He drew a finger across his brow.

'And me eyebrows join. I look like a bloody werewolf. You know what my Aunt May told me? What it means if your eyebrows join?'

I shrugged.

'It means you're born to hang.'

The next morning he saw me off, casually handing me a five-pound note. He said he'd like to see me again. He was a businessman, he claimed, and a club owner. He invited me to a party at his club, The Stardust in Soho.

'What do you think I'm going to do with this?' Harry asks, waving the poker in front of me. 'Eh?'

I squirm about a bit against the ropes that tie me. Tony Stavrakakis stands behind me. It was him that had secured me to the chair. The big Greek rests a heavy hand on my shoulder to stop me from moving about too much and to concentrate on what was going on. Harry fiddles with the brazier thing. I don't want to think about it. I don't want to think at all. I want to break down and blubber uncontrollably. To give in and give up the truth that Harry would insist upon. I want to break. But Harry's right. You can't fake a thing like that.

'Show business is in my blood, Terry. Did I ever tell you about my grandad? Billy Sheen. The Canning Town Cannonball they called him. Champion bare-knuckle fighter he was. But he wasn't just a fighter, he was a showman as well. Had a strong singing voice and did a strongman act in the music halls. He could leap out of a barrel, break a stack of house bricks with his bare hands. But you know what the climax of his act was? Licking a white hot poker. Yeah, that's right. Has to be white-hot mind. Just red hot and it'd shrivel your tongue off and no mistake. He learnt it off this big black fellah doing it before a crowd on Mile End Waste. And he taught it me.'

Harry laughs and moves the poker in the flame again.

'You watch this carefully now,' he insists.

He brings the metal to the tip of the flame, its hottest point. At the same time he moves his lips and tongue, making spit in his mouth.

'Have to make sure your gob's good and wet too. Hard to do if you're scared. Nothing like fear to make your mouth dry. Nah, you have to make sure your mouth's good and wet and the poker's white hot. Then you can't go wrong.'

He chews and sucks, moving his tongue to the front of his mouth as he watches the poker glow. Tiny bubbles of sputum dribble at the corner of his mouth and his tongue darts out to draw them back in again.

'You watch carefully now.'

The Stardust. Harry was out front, flanked by two huge doormen, greeting people. He grabbed my hand with both of his. Gave me a wink as I passed through into the club.

'Glad you could come, Terry. Get yourself a drink, I'll see you later.'

The Stardust. Not exactly my scene. Mostly an older crowd, overdressed and out of style. Heinz and The Wild Boys were performing that night. I went to the bar and ordered a rum and Coke. A modernist kid to the left of me in a two-piece tonic mohair. Three-buttoned single-breasted jacket, narrow lapels, flap pockets, from Harry Fenton's no doubt. He wore his hair *en brosse*, in a french crew. He nodded at me. I felt shabby standing next to him. I want some of that, I thought to myself. Something more than that.

Bleached-blond Heinz was dragging his backing band through a medley of Eddie Cochran songs.

'Pretty, ain't he?' said the mod kid.

'Yeah,' I shrugged. 'I guess.'

'Shame about the voice. Still, Joe Meek's so in love with him he's convinced he's going to be big.'

He nodded at a tall quiffed man sitting at the main table watching the performance intensely. Joe Meek, record producer, famous for his ice-rink-in-space electric organ sound. He'd had a big hit with 'Telstar' by The Tornadoes.

'Joe should stick to instrumentals,' muttered the modernist as the blond singer crooned 'C'mon Everybody' slightly off key. 'So should Heinz for that matter.'

Harry had come into the club with his entourage. He beckoned me over with a jerk of his head.

'Come over and join us,' he said and led me to a large table.

The party was an assortment of celebrities. Along with Joe Meek there was a boxer or two, someone from television and Ruby Ryder the film actress. Equally famous and with their own brand of glamour were the people pointed out with names like Alibi Albert and Jack the Hat. 'Faces', Harry referred to them as. And as it turned out that was what Harry was. A face. *Mad* Harry, I was slightly disconcerted to learn, was his also known as. Every so often a flashbulb would go whoosh and the main group would go into a fixed expression for a second. Showbiz eyes and teeth. Underworld jaws and suits.

I was introduced to Joe Meek. Being the official young person present, he was keen for my opinion on Heinz. I hesitated.

'Love the peroxide riah,' I declared with genuine conviction.

'It's great ain't it?' Joe had a high-pitched west country accent. 'Got the idea from *Village of the Damned*. You know, those spooky kids from outer space.'

He was as tall and thick set as Harry but his movements had a kind of jerky thinness to them. He had big farmboy hands that fluttered at you. I didn't have the heart to tell him that I didn't think Heinz was going to work. The dyed hair, the shiny jacket with silver piping. Wonderfully camp. Woefully out of date. Something new was happening. The Beat Boom, people were calling it. Rock and Roll, well, that was for the die-hard leather crowd and Heinz certainly didn't impress them. Apparently in Birmingham a gang of rockers had chucked tins of beans at him. Rhythm and Blues, that was what everyone was talking about. Something new was happening but Heinz definitely wasn't it.

Heinz finished to polite applause. He came over to the table grinning awkwardly. Joe fussed around him for a while and then chatted, wide-eyed manic, to Harry. Pupils like sharpened pencil leads. Pilled on amphetamine, no doubt about it. Blocked, we called it. They talked business. Management. Heinz sat between them and they furtively eyed him like confection as they talked. Harry was drawn to Tin Pan Alley, a way of breaking into legitimate show business. Maybe thinking of becoming the next Larry Parnes or Brian Epstein. And why not? He was a homosexual Jewish wide boy just like them. But maybe a bit too wide. Not quite smooth enough. Harry would never look right in a camel-hair coat somehow. He was too much of a performer to be a successful impresario. You could never see him in the background. Too conspicuous, too much of an act himself. In fact all the faces seemed to have more confident a turn than any of the showbiz lot. The gangsters were the real stars at The Stardust.

I got drunk. I wasn't used to boozing. I staggered into the gents, splashed some cold water in my face and dried it on the towel machine. Jack the Hat was handing over a huge bag of pills to the modernist child.

'Fancy a doob, mate?' he called over to me.

I rejoined the party with a purple heart melting on my tongue. Around the table stories were being offered up. Showbiz secrets and behind the scenes gossip swapped for tales of fixed fights and doped dogs. Frauds and rackets and heavier jobs were alluded to as all the tricks of the trade seemed open for discussion. Like conjurers taking apart an illusion confident that their public was elsewhere. The audience, the punters. The mugs.

One of the villain's women got up and gave us a song to much encouragement. She had a clear sad voice. You could see that she had been pretty once but now looked a bit washed out. As she sang 'Cry Me A River' without accompaniment I wondered what kind of a life it would be being the woman of one of these hard-faced men.

When she'd finished there was applause and banging on the tables. Everyone was far gone by now. Music started up and Jack the Hat got up and danced on the table. I could hear Joe Meek next to me bawling about the record industry in the mod kid's ear over the noise.

'They're trying to steal my sound! The rotten pigs! I'm still the bloody guvnor!'

Jack the Hat was starting to strip off and two of the boxers tried to gently coax him down off the table. Harry came up and put his arm around me.

'Enjoying yourself?'

I nodded. Actually I was. It wasn't a trendy scene but there was something altogether furtive and exciting about The Stardust. It reminded me of that bit in Pinocchio where all the bad boys bunk off school and go to Playland where they don't have to do any work and can just fuck about all day. As a child I'd always longed for that sort of cheap utopia. When the funfair came to our local common every year, I'd be drawn to the cheap thrills of the waltzer and the dodgems. I spent as much time simply gazing at the gypsy lads as they casually hopped amidst the spinning machinery, collecting fares. Showing off. Danger and glamour. Greased-back pompadours and muscled arms marked with tattoos and stained with engine oil. I'd always fancied the rough boys who ran the fairground rides. The Stardust scene seemed a version of the playland I'd dreamt of as a child and I wanted to be a part of it. I'd conveniently forgotten that, in the story, all the lazy boys are turned into donkeys in the end. I should have been warned.

Anyway, the speed had sobered me up. Given me confidence. When the party was over and people began to stagger out of the club, Harry asked me to go back with him and I said yes.

At the door a bloke in a heavy overcoat came across and muttered something in Harry's ear. They whispered gruffly to each other in the doorway.

'All right, I'll deal with it. Terry,' Harry said, turning to me, 'Jimmy will drive you to my flat. Wait there for me. I won't be long.'

He nodded to a sandy-haired man who was waiting outside. I recognised him as Harry's driver from the night we met at The Casbah. Harry said a few words to him, turned and winked at me and then went off into the night.

From the back of the Daimler I saw Jimmy's eyes slotted in the rear-view mirror.

'All right son?' he asked with a little nod of the head.

There was a weary edge to his voice.

'Yeah,' I replied. 'I guess.'

Jimmy unlocked the door of the flat and held the door open for me. He wrinkled his nose in an obliging sneer.

'Make yourself at home,' he said. 'Harry might be a while.'

Then he was gone and I was alone in Harry's flat.

I poured myself a large brandy and looked through Harry's record collection. Judy Garland, Dorothy Squires, some opera and Winston Churchill's Wartime Speeches. On the coffee table was *A History of Western Philosophy* by Bertrand Russell and a well-thumbed edition of *Physique Pictorial*. I collapsed into the leather-buttoned chesterfield and flicked through the magazine. The speed had begun to wear off and I started to feel drowsy from the brandy. A second glass sorted me out and I fell into a light sleep on the sofa.

I woke up with a start to find Harry standing over me still in his overcoat. He prodded me gently with his foot.

'All right?' he whispered.

He had a slightly crazed look about him. His face twitched with the strange distracted playfulness that a cat displays when it's just killed a mouse.

'Where have you been?' I asked rubbing my face awake.

'Shh,' Harry ordered with a finger in front of his mouth. 'Never you mind.'

I sat up and he grinned at me.

'Come on,' he said softly, taking my arm and leading me into the bedroom.

When I next woke up it was eleven o'clock.

'Shit,' I said sitting up in the bed.

'What's the matter?' asked Harry blearily.

'I'm late for work.'

'Fuck them.'

'I should phone in sick or something.'

'Nah. What you want to work for them for? Phone them up and tell them to stuff their job.'

I laughed.

'You could work for me,' Harry suggested.

'Oh yeah? Doing what?'

Harry grinned slyly.

'You could make yourself useful round here. Look after the place for me. Look after me a bit and all.'

Harry pulled me back under the covers and nestled up close to me.

'What do you say?' he asked, with a big sloppy grin.

'All right,' I said.

And that's how it happened. I chucked in my job. Harry looked after me. I became kept.

He bought me things. We went shopping for clothes. Harry disapproved of Carnaby Street. 'Too cheap, too lairy,' he insisted. Instead he took me to Blades in Dover Street. There Rupert Lycett

Green combined bespoke tailoring with the latest tight silhouette style and colourful cloth. He paid for me to have a couple of suits made up there. And a Pierre Cardin off the peg from Dougie Millings in Great Pulteney Street.

Harry's taste was more conservative. He had his suits made at Kilgour, French & Stanbury in Savile Row. Charcoal-grey wool or dark-blue chalkstripe. But I persuaded him to go for a two piece. Waistcoats were out and the watch chain he sometimes wore looked far too old fashioned. And we got the tailor to taper his cut a little so that he looked slightly taller and less thick set than he actually was.

We bought hand-made shirts from Jermyn Street. Turnbull & Asser, Harvie & Hudson. Ties from Mr Fish in Clifford Street.

I was spoiled rotten. I got to know about *haute couture*. And that wardrobe was an essential part of the way that Harry operated. Being so well dressed was the cutting edge of intimidation. A sort of decorative violence in itself.

And I got to meet the main faces on his firm. Jimmy Murphy, who had driven me to Harry's flat. Tony Stravrakakis who was generally known as Tony the Greek or Bubble, and Jock McCluskey, a huge Glaswegian. Also Manny Gould, Manny the Money, a little bloke with round glasses who dealt with accounts such as they were. There were many other minor faces he could call upon to go in plenty handed when needed. But generally Harry liked to keep things small and tight. The fewer people he had to trust or pay off the better.

Harry's queerness seemed to be something that the firm accepted. Not that they had much choice. He'd often berate them with his opinion that hanging around with women made you soft. My status was less secure. But, of course, I was a threat to nobody. At that time I simply belonged to Harry as far as they were concerned. I suppose, for the most part, they treated me as they treated the many women who were connected to members of the firm. I got the impression that Jimmy Murphy didn't exactly approve of me, though. Nothing was said directly, just the occasional glance or comment.

Anyway I was on the firm in a more or less unofficial capacity. Sometimes called upon to deliver messages and packages or to find out information. Other times when Harry was calling on someone I'd go in ahead to let them know that he was on his way. Smooth the way as it were. Harry disliked awkwardness or anything 'unnecessary'.

Like a true gentleman he was never rude or brutal by mistake. I knew that Harry had other boys who did similar things and more but I had to live with that.

I even had my own little racket for a while. Joe Meek was paying Harry to help get his singles into the charts. It was simple enough. There were about sixty or so chart-return listed shops in London whose sales the Hit Parade was based on. You could buy a hundred copies to get it into the charts, buy a few more the following week to push it up a bit more, then get on to the deejays to say it's in the charts and give them a backhander so they'd give it airplay. I was put on to the job, being the firm's official young person. The only problem was some shops, if you bought, say, ten, they wouldn't mark it down because it looked like an obvious fix. It was then that I'd persuade them what was good for business. I'd learnt how to put on the casually threatening manner from Harry though I often took Big Jock McCluskey with me for good measure. Also, every other record company was up to the same thing so we'd try and target other record fixers, muscle in on them, even get them to buy Joe's records instead of the ones they were supposed to be fixing. It was a minor league racket, for sure, but I have to say I got a real kick out of throwing my own weight about for once. I could see the attraction in leaning on people, the aura of power that it gave you. It was a thrill, something almost sexual about it. Once, I vada this kid in a listening booth as I'm walking out of a record store on Shaftesbury Avenue. He's gaping at me through the glass and it's obvious he thinks that I'm a bit tasty like. So I give him a wink and wait for him outside the shop. I act all tough and he loves it. We end up back at his flat in Bloomsbury. It was the first time I'd had sex with someone my own age in weeks.

I'd take all the records back to Joe's recording studio on the Holloway Road and he'd hand over a wad of cash. I'd get a percentage and the rest would go to Harry. Sometimes I'd take a load of pills round as well. Amphetamines. Joe was mad for them.

But my main job was to be with Harry. For sex and for companionship. Harry liked to go out to smart restaurants, to the racetrack, to the opera even. There were so many flash places that I went with him where we were treated with almost grovelling respect. So many people who hid their fear by looking pleased to see him.

Then there were nights at his club, parties at his flat where boys were served like canapes to his queer friends in high places. More often than not descending into a clumsy orgy. Harry would never get involved himself. He enjoyed the organising side of it. Manipulating things.

There was an attractiveness that went with the fierceness. He drew people to him. He had a sort of threatening charisma that made you want to be close to him, an aura that you could feel safe within. A bit like those fish that swim right up close to sharks, you felt protected being in his slipstream. I remember him saying that, in a fight, the best first move is always to go in close rather than back away. If you give space to your opponent, he'll have room to take a proper swing at you. 'Always be near to them but make sure they're far away from you.' It was advice that I took to heart.

There were things that I kept from him. I kept the bedsit in Westbourne Grove without telling him. If the worst comes to the worst, I thought, at least he doesn't know where I live. And, of course, our backgrounds were very different. He used to joke that I'd 'been to clever school'. I'd left all my safe suburban upbringing behind me. I didn't really keep in touch with my parents, for obvious reasons. But this baffled Harry. 'Your poor old mum,' he'd berate me. 'I bet she worries about you.'

I remember once him taking me to a Boys' Club in the East End that he patronised. It was for a boxing tournament that he had donated the trophy for. He was sort of a guest of honour. I tried not to wince as I watched wiry adolescents with huge upholstered fists clumsily batter away at each other.

Harry chuckled darkly when he noticed my unease.

'Bet you never been in a real fight, have you Terry?' he goaded.

And he was right. I was soft. A hundred playground humiliations played back in my mind. *Sissy. Poof.*

After the final bout Harry went back to congratulate the scrawny little lad who had won.

'Well done, Tommy,' he said, ruffling the blond curls of the young fighter.

Tommy blinked, still half dazed from combat and slightly shy of Harry's obvious affection. His grey-blue eyes looked far older than my own. I felt awkward standing in this makeshift dressing room that stank of youthful sweat and stale liniment. Something I couldn't ever really understand or be part of.

But I loved the image of it all. Harry's masculinity. Being fancied by such a tough and dangerous man. The danger of it. It seemed so real compared to my privet-hedged experience of life. There was something sexy about it. Though the sex itself was really quite gentle. I know in some of the trial reports they made him out to be some sort of sadist but I don't think he was really into that. That was just business.

But then there was the waiting. I never really knew what he was up to. A lot of his work was done at night. I was expected to be there for him at all hours at his flat. Sometimes he'd never turn up. He'd be away somewhere or simply staying over at his mother's house in Hoxton. There would be no explanations. I was expected to understand this part of Harry's life and yet be completely ignorant of it at the same time.

One night he and Jimmy Murphy came to the flat at four in the morning covered in blood. They looked wild eyed.

'What the fuck's happened?' I cried.

'Nothing,' replied Harry. 'Nothing's happened. Help us get out of our clothes.'

'What?'

'You heard me. Undress us. We mustn't touch anything in the flat.'

I reached out a hand to unbutton Harry's jacket and touched a clot of blood and tissue. I recoiled.

'What have you done Harry?' I gasped.

Harry lost his patience and slapped both sides of his hand against both sides of my face. I fell onto the hallway floor. I touched my cheek and a smear of blood came away on my fingertips. Somebody else's blood.

'Do what you're told and don't ask any stupid questions,' Harry ordered softly.

I looked up at Harry glowering down at me and Jimmy Murphy with a faint smirk on his lips.

'Look at that.'

Harry pointed with the toecap of his boot. At first I thought that he was going to kick me and I started to curl up. Then I saw where he was pointing with his foot. There was a mark on the hallway floor where I'd put my hand out as I'd fallen and smeared the blood and stuff from Harry's coat onto the polished tiles.

'Look,' he said. 'Fucking forensic all over the floor. Get up,' Harry ordered. 'Go and get a bowl of water and clean this mess up.'

I picked myself up off the floor. This was the first time Harry had laid a finger on me. And he'd done it without losing his temper, that's what was really chilling about it. How calm he could be with violence. Up until then I hadn't really thought about the real nastiness of what Harry did. The ugliness behind all of his charm. What lurked behind the scene in all of his rackets. I kept my head down and sloped off to the kitchen.

'And put some Savlon in it,' Harry called after me. 'I don't want fucking germs all over the flat.'

'Watch.'

Harry stands with his legs slightly apart. One foot slightly in front of the other. Back foot slightly turned out. His weight is on his back foot, his centre of gravity lowered as if squaring up to something. Like a boxer. Or a showman.

He heats up the poker once more then brings it out of the brazier in an arc. Displaying it. Bringing it slowly down in front of his face like a fire-eater or sword swallower.

His eyes are wide and bright. Tiny images of the glowing metal burn in each one. His tongue, wide and drooling, unfurls to his chin. He looks demonic.

He holds this mask of expression as he brings the poker up close. His face reddened with heat and concentration. Cords of sinew stand out in his neck. Veins bulging out on his forehead. Then he licks it. Drawing it down slowly and tossing back his head. There's a short sizzle. Like a drop of water in hot fat. *Shh*. A nimbus of saliva vapour disperses above his head as a drop of sweat goes cold on my neck.

Tony Stavrakakis gives a slow heavy laugh of appreciation, slapping me absently on the shoulder. Harry breaks his showman poise and sighs.

'See? Nothing to it.'

He puts the poker back into the flame and wipes his mouth with the back of a hand.

'Right then,' he says, looking over at me with a grin. 'Now it's your turn.'

Then came Harry's black moods. His evil brooding moods. It was

Jimmy who warned me the first time. He knew the signs. The signs that Harry was 'going into one' as the firm phrased it. A slow but sure descent into half madness. The Mad Harry nickname didn't simply refer to his gameness, his readiness to have a go whatever the odds, although it was a convenient reputation for obtaining money by extortion. There was more to it than that. Turns out Harry was certified insane in a prison hospital psychiatric wing when he was doing time in the fifties. Diagnosed manic depressive. The manic side could often be expressed in violence and action. Sometimes he'd flare up and throw stuff about the flat. Sometimes he'd lash out at me. But I think he found ways of channelling that side of his nature. Putting the frighteners on people and that. It was what he was good at.

But the depressive side hit him really badly. He would sit brooding, filled with all kinds of horrors. Morbid thoughts. He would listen to his opera records. His eyes wet and bulging as divas shrieked their arias of distress. Then he'd get out his LP of Churchill's wartime speeches and play them over and over. He seemed soothed by the gloomy voice offering nothing but blood, toil, tears and sweat.

The anti-depressants helped. But they also made him drowsy and a bit puffy about the eyes and face which of course he hated. And he had this Harley Street shrink that he saw. Thing was, Harry was paranoid that anyone outside the firm might find out about his mental illness. A sign of weakness to his enemies, I suppose, but also he did have a terror that he might get committed and locked up in a mental home. So no one was to know. He couldn't go to this doctor's place in case anybody saw him and the doctor couldn't come around to the flat for the same reason. So the doctor was picked up in the Daimler and Jimmy Murphy drove around the West End as Harry and this shrink had a consultation in the back of the limo.

The paranoia got more and more intense. Harry was liable to lash out at anyone or anything. As word got around the firm that the boss had 'gone into one' they generally stayed away. It was left to Manny the Money to bring over the takings of all the various businesses and rackets in a huge suitcase. They went through it together, arranging different piles of money all over the bed. Once I saw Harry grab the little man by the throat, convinced that some of his money was missing.

'Where is it, you little fucker?' Harry hissed as he asphyxiated Manny.

Somehow Manny managed a shake of the head and his habitual shrug. When Harry finally released him he merely straightened his tie, pushed his glasses back onto the bridge of his nose and began counting out the takings again. He knew that the best way to respond to Harry's outbursts was to not respond at all. Just wait for it to come to an end. And indeed this was the best way to deal with him. Just to wait for him to calm down and hope that you lived that long.

I was the closest person to him during this time. Long brooding silences would be punctuated by his morbid reflections. Doping himself with brandy and handfuls of anti-depressants he'd talk of violence, boastful confessions of how he'd hurt people. Awful stories. It was then that he'd told me that he liked to control people by breaking them physically and mentally. It made me sick to the stomach to hear him talk like that. When I complained that he gloated over causing pain he took a knife and drew it slowly and deliberately across the back of his hand. He cut himself quite deeply and I had to get a crooked doctor that the firm used to come over and sew up the wound.

Once he held a loaded revolver to my head.

'When I go, you're coming too,' he said softly as he cocked the hammer.

I closed my eyes and counted in my head, trying not to move at all until I felt air on the spot made by the pressure of the barrel. I opened my eyes. Harry had wandered off into the bathroom. I traced around the little circular dent in my temple.

And yet, despite all the delirium, this was the time that I really got to know Harry. He was vulnerable, not a big tough guy any more. For once his guard came down and a frightened little child peeped out at me. He was ill and needed looking after. I'd never felt that kind of responsibility to another human being before. And no matter how difficult it was I couldn't help feeling emotionally protective towards him. It was a practical sort of affection. I cared for him because, quite literally. I cared for him. I didn't really have a choice about it and so sensitive feelings that hadn't really occurred in our relationship before just sort of happened. He needed to be held, to be reassured. A soothing voice to calm him. There. There. There.

And then, quite suddenly, he came out of it. He started doing exercise to get rid of the fat he'd put on during his illness. We went down to The Stardust for the first time in weeks. The firm started having proper meetings again and Harry got involved in all his big plans once more. He was back to his old self and he treated me. He bought me clothes and took me out. It was as if to compensate for how he'd been in the last few weeks though the period of depression was never mentioned directly. He talked of getting away for a while. Of going on holiday to Greece or Morocco. Everything seemed happy once again. But I found it hard to adjust to his recovery. His illness had seemed more real than anything else. I resented the cheeriness that people greeted him with, as if nothing had happened. And, I suppose, I started to resent Harry too.

One day a smartly dressed woman came to the flat. She was a shoplifter, a 'hoister' as Harry would put it. Harry didn't usually fence but this woman stole to order. She specialised in thieving *haute couture* from the fashion houses of Knightsbridge and Bond Street. She had Harry's mother's measurements so she could lift whole outfits for him to spoil his dear old mum with. It was worth all the effort, not just for the money Harry paid but also for the protection he could offer should she ever need it.

'Ooh!' Harry cooed as this hoister woman held up a silk blouse by Tricosa. 'That's lovely!'

I suppressed a giggle. Harry could be quite camp at times but it was best not to draw his attention to it unless you were sure that he was in a good mood. As it happened he was. The woman had brought over a whole bundle of stuff and Harry thought that now was as good a time as any to go and visit Mother. He handed me the clothes and the keys of his brand-new Jaguar Mark II and I went out and put them carefully on the back seat as he paid the woman off. When I came back up to the flat Harry was getting ready to go. He called me into the bathroom.

'Why don't you come with me?' he said, looking at me through the mirror.

I shrugged. It wasn't something he'd ever suggested before. And I suppose it was then that I got to thinking, not without a certain amount of dread, that Harry was beginning to see me as a permanent fixture. Part of his life that he could take home to Mum.

We drove out east. Past the Angel and up the City Road to Shoreditch and Hoxton. Harry nodded moodily at the familiar scenery and pointed out a weed-covered bombsite. There was a council sign posted on it: Temporary Open Space.

'That's where our house was. Where I was born.'

He sighed.

'Bombed to fuck.'

Mrs Starks was an immaculately dressed wiry little woman. She was taking tea with Harry's Aunt May in the front room of her terraced house when we arrived. She made a fuss over Harry as soon as we were in the door. He got out all of the hoister's ill-gotten wares and there was a shrill fuss made over the clothes as they were laid out on the sofa, not least by Harry himself.

'He spoils me, he does, May,' said Harry's mother.

'He's a naughty boy,' replied Aunt May coming over and stroking his forehead. 'Born to hang, that's what he is.'

'Hello dear,' his mother said to me warmly as we were introduced.

I wondered what she knew.

'I'll put the kettle on, make a fresh pot,' I suggested wanting to appear useful.

'What a nice boy,' I heard her comment as I went into the kitchen with the tea things.

While I was in the kitchen a middle-aged man shuffled in.

'*He's* here then,' he muttered.

He was swarthy looking with greying curly hair. He wore a collarless shirt with braces. A copy of *The Morning Star* was under one arm.

'I'm the old man,' he announced. 'Don't suppose he's mentioned me.'

And it was true, Harry had never talked of his father. He'd often spoken of his mother without any paternal reference. I'd somehow assumed that he was dead or permanently absent.

'There's some biscuits by the breadbin,' came Harry's voice from the doorway. 'Hello Dad,' he added flatly, noticing his father.

'Son.'

They nodded at each other cautiously.

'How's business?' inquired Starks the elder.

'Oh,' Harry shrugged. 'You know.'

'Yeah, I know,' he turned to me and shrugged. 'Still, it's a shame my only son turned out a gonnif.'

'I make a good living. You and Mum see enough of it.'

Harry's father grunted and turned his head to me again.

'He was a bright kid. Could have got an education, done something with his life.'

'Well maybe if you had been around a bit things might have been different. You were on the run half the time.'

'Yeah, but that was on principle. The Party was against the war so I had to avoid the call up.'

'The Party was against the war up until 1941. We didn't see you till VJ Day.'

'I was a pacifist. I wasn't going to fight in no capitalist war.'

'Yeah, but you ran a capitalist spieler, didn't you?'

'I suppose you blame me for your criminal tendencies.'

'No Dad. Fact is we all learned to run rackets in the war. The black market, everyone was in on it, one way or another.'

Now Harry turned to me.

'I was the youngest spiv on Shoreditch High Street,' he said proudly, then turned back to his father. 'Just lay off with all that principled pony.'

'Yeah, well, you can come back here with all your bourgeois trappings, just don't forget where you're from.'

'Well, Dad,' replied Harry, wearily, 'I don't suppose you'll ever let me. Now come in through and have a nice cup of tea and we can pretend at being happy families for a while, eh?'

'Mum liked you,' said Harry as we drove back west.

The words chilled me. There was a cold feeling right down in my guts. I realised then that I had to get out, that I would have to leave him. I'd never really thought about how long me and Harry would last but I certainly didn't fancy myself as part of the family. Perhaps I was scared of the prospect of going through his madness again.

But fear prevented me from coming up with any properly thought-out way of leaving. It would have been stupid to confront him. I didn't rate my chances in a showdown with Harry. So I resorted to guerrilla tactics. I could niggle him, wind him up, it wasn't difficult. I somehow figured that if I got up his nose enough he would tire of me altogether.

I would undermine him. Harry hadn't managed to lose all the weight he'd put on during his depression. All the booze and lack of exercise had taken its toll. And the anti-depressants. As he sighed at himself in the mirror I would hold back from reassuring him that he didn't look so bad.

I started to affect an indifference to the sex that we had together. I got into the habit of sneaking out into the bathroom and wanking off before spending the night with him just to make sure that my boredom seemed genuine. Then I'd deliberately go through the motions in a way that reduced it to just a functional level. Robbed of any illusions it became an empty pleasure for Harry. And I knew that that was not what he wanted. Nobody does, let's face it.

And I stopped keeping the flat in the kind of order that Harry insisted upon. He hated mess and so I just let the housework go until it became too much for him.

'Look at this fucking place!' he finally exploded at me. 'It's a fucking dump!'

I let him stomp about the flat a bit, picking up clothes and papers that had been strewn about the drawing room.

'Well?' he demanded.

'Well what?' I replied a bit cockily.

'Well, are you going to tidy this pit up?'

I shrugged and let out a long sigh and started to collect up some of the debris in a listless way. And he snapped. He came over and clouted me across the ear and I went down on the carpet.

'Behave yourself!' he bellowed.

I acted all hurt, which wasn't difficult with a thick ear.

'You can't treat me like this,' I sobbed. 'I'm not your bloody slave.'

I looked up at him from the floor as he seethed above me. I had to be careful. I wanted to goad him enough into saying something reckless but not so much so he'd kick the shit out of me.

'It's not fair, Harry,' I whined at him.

He stared down his nose at me, nostrils wide with anger like a double-barrel shotgun.

'Well if you don't like it, you can piss off,' he declared and with that I got up off the floor and walked to the door.

'Terry!' he called after me. 'Come back here!'

But I was gone. I didn't look back once. That was it, I thought, finish.

So I went back to the bedsit in Westbourne Grove. I'd never officially given it up nor told Harry where it was. He'd never asked. To be honest I didn't expect that I'd be able to get back into it. I hadn't paid rent in nearly three months and my landlord wasn't known for his leniency. Tenants in arrears were likely enough to be called upon by his heavies and a couple of alsatians for good measure. I was surprised to find that my key still fitted the lock and my possessions, meagre as they were, hadn't been tampered with. Two dingy, damp rooms in a run-down Victorian terrace. Its squalor reminded me of the luxury I had briefly been familiar with. I put a shilling in the meter and tried to make myself at home. The unaired rooms smelt of cat's piss and sour milk but it was my own place, at least for the time being, and Harry didn't know where I lived. Or so I thought.

I'd scarcely taken anything with me when I'd walked out of Harry's. Just the clothes I was wearing, a Rolex watch he'd bought me and a bit of spending money that I had in my wallet. And I had no work to go to. Thoughts of the leisurely life that I'd almost got used to hung around in my head, mocking me. I'd have to get some kind of dreary job again. I'd go back to being the sort of person that villains would ridicule whilst they preyed upon them. A mug.

And I couldn't understand why the landlord hadn't sent anyone around about the rent. Stories I'd heard from other tenants about his rent collectors were far from reassuring. He wasn't likely to have merely forgotten one of his godforsaken slum dwellers. He was the type that got rich from counting every penny. Waiting around to be knocked about and thrown out in the street started to drive me crazy. I figured that I had nothing to lose by meeting my fate head on.

I pawned the watch Harry had given me and sold my Dansette gramophone player to a junk shop on Golborne Road. A few weeks' rent and some bluffing might hold some sway. I'd learnt from Harry that a direct approach with as much front as possible could often get results.

The estate agent's office was in Shepherd's Bush. The clerk on the lettings desk ran his finger down a ledger and frowned up at me.

'There's no rent owing on that address,' he informed me.

'What do you mean?'

He smiled coldly at me.

'You have an arrangement with Mr Rachman.'

This threw me. I'd been all geared up to plead my case. Sudden relief, then sudden uneasiness. I got flustered.

'What do you mean, *arrangement*?' I demanded.

The clerk turned the ledger around so that I could read along the row that he had his finger on. There was my name, the address, and RENT FREE written in red ink across the payment columns.

Just then Rachman himself came out of his office in the back. One of his heavies loomed behind him. Rachman was short, fat and bald. He looked over at the desk sourly.

'Is there a problem here?' he hissed in a thick Polish accent.

The clerk pointed at the ledger and Rachman walked up and leaned over. The heavy stayed where he was but stared at me morosely.

'Hm,' mused the Pole looking to where the clerk's grubby finger now smudged the page. 'No problem at all.'

Rachman smiled at me with dead eyes.

'You see, many of my properties I let without financial remuneration. To my friends, you understand. And friends of friends. Mr Starks has proved to be a very useful friend to have. Don't you agree? You will give him my best regards when you see him next, won't you?'

I grinned and nodded at Rachman and got out of the estate agents as soon as possible. It was midday. I went into the first pub I came across and tried to drink away some of the fear and paranoia. Had I been followed? Had he known for some time about the bedsit? Whatever. I'd underestimated the scope of Harry's power and the booze didn't calm me down any. They closed for the afternoon and I staggered back to Westbourne Grove. To where he knew I was.

Two days later, sure enough, a knock came on the door. It was Jimmy Murphy. He cocked his head towards the street.

'Come on,' he said. 'He's in the motor.'

I got into the back of the Daimler. Harry scarcely acknowledged me and didn't start to talk until we'd been moving along for a while.

'You shouldn't have walked out like that,' he said softly. 'It was out of order.'

'I'm sorry.'

Harry shrugged.

'Well maybe I was a bit out of order myself,' he said.

We looked at each other properly. Harry gave a sad little smile and cupped my cheek with an open palm.

'So are you going to come back and behave yourself?'

'I don't think that would be a good idea Harry.'

His hand dropped from my face and he sighed. He sat back and let his head rest against the leather of the seat, his face turned from mine, gazing out of the window.

'I'm sorry Harry.'

He shrugged against the upholstery.

'Yeah, well, that's the way it goes I suppose.'

He turned to give me a little sneer.

'You're nothing special,' he hissed.

He leant forward and told Jimmy to drive back to my place. We sat in silence as we went around a block. Then, when we were back on Westbourne Grove, he spoke again.

'So, what, you working?'

'No.'

Harry nodded thoughtfully.

'You want a job?' he asked.

'What kind of job?'

'One of my businesses. Needs an assistant manager. You've been to clever school, should be able to handle that. What do you say?'

'What kind of business?'

'Electrical goods. Wholesale, retail.' Harry sniffed. 'Legitimate.'

Dominion Electrical Goods occupied a warehouse on Commercial Road. I had to get the tube right across the city. Westbourne Park to Whitechapel on the Metropolitan Line. Manny the Money met me there and showed me around the office. Mr Pinker, the manager of Dominion Electrical, wasn't in.

'He's off sick,' little Manny muttered.

Manny went through my duties. It was simple. Signing delivery notes and filing invoices. Manny would come in from time to time to keep the books up to date but all the records needed to be kept in their proper box files. Now Manny wasn't involved in Dominion in an official capacity. Turned out none of the firm was. This he made clear and that Jimmy Murphy would come in every so often to keep an eye on things.

Mr Pinker wasn't in the next day. Or the day after that. It was just me and a couple of labourers who genially sat around playing cards until a lorry arrived and there were fridges to shift. There wasn't much for me to do. It struck me that this was the sort of job I might have ended up doing if I'd stayed on at school. Except that, with Harry involved, there was bound to be some sort of angle.

Jimmy came around and we had a cup of tea in the office. He brought out a hip flask and gave us both a shot.

'Everything all right?' he asked.

I nodded.

'No visits or phone calls?'

I shook my head.

'Right,' he said, getting up and draining his laced tea. 'Keep up the good work. I'll see you.'

And he left.

With time on my hands I started to think about what was really going on. I tried to work out what the angle was. Every aspect of a legitimate business seemed in order. We weren't doing much trade, that was for sure, but there's no law against that. I'd thought at first that the warehouse must be fencing for lorry hijacks. I'd heard gossip amongst the firm in the past of how they dealt in gear knocked off that way. The jump up, they called it. But deliveries at Dominion were nothing of the sort. All the paperwork seemed in order, invoices properly made out and everything. The only thing I could think of was that this was a legitimate business funded by dodgy money. That would make sense after all.

Harry came in with Jimmy at the end of the week. He looked around. He seemed happy enough with how things were going. He asked me how I was getting on.

'Fine,' I replied. 'We haven't done much trade, though.'

'Yeah,' said Harry vaguely. 'We'll have to do something about that. In the meantime keep it all kosher. Know what I mean? Anything else?' he asked as he made for the door.

'Just one thing,' I said. 'This Mr Pinker. He hasn't been in at all.'

Harry grinned and looked over at Jimmy.

'Well,' he said. 'If you do see him, let us know.'

And both him and Jimmy Murphy laughed.

That little shared joke got me thinking. Mr Pinker was the set up. The joke was on him. I guessed that he was some straight businessman that they were taking for a ride. That he was the mug. But that didn't stop me, in the last couple of hours of Friday afternoon, from searching the office for more clues before I locked up for the weekend.

There didn't seem to be anything of interest though. Minutes of an annual general meeting revealed that Sir Paul Chambers DSO was on the board as a non-executive director. A meticulous treasurer's report obviously compiled by the diligent Manny Gould. Everything looked in order. Then, when I'd just about given up I found an envelope at the back of the bottom drawer of the filing cabinet. Central Registry of Births, Deaths and Marriages was stamped on it. I took it out and laid it on the desk. I fished inside and pulled out a long form. It was a birth certificate. James Nathaniel Pinker was written in the column headed Name, if any. Under when and where born was scrawled: Eleventh March 1929, 304 Fore St., Edmonton. It made no sense, except to confirm that my as yet invisible boss actually existed. I slipped my hand under the flap of the envelope again and came out with a similar form. Except that this was a death certificate. It too bore the name James Nathaniel Pinker. He'd died of meningitis on the Ninth of June 1929. All his paperwork was in order. Delivery note and final demand. The manager of Dominion Electrical Goods had only lived for three months.

I put the birth and death certificates back in the envelope, shoved it into the filing cabinet, locked up the warehouse and went back to Westbourne Grove. I spent the weekend getting drunk and trying not to think about Mr Pinker or Dominion Electrical Goods. I was getting a good wage, I had a rent-free flat, I knew that even thinking about what was really going on would only get me into trouble. So I tried to block it all out with booze. Two bottles of gin but I was still haunted by my boss the dead baby.

The next week reminders of unpaid invoices started to pile up. We continued to get deliveries. There was hardly space left in the warehouse to put all the stuff. Harry came in on the Wednesday.

'Seen Jimmy?' he demanded tersely as he strode into the office.

I shook my head.

'Right,' he went on, beckoning me out of the office. 'I need to do a bit of shopping.'

He wandered about the crowded showroom. He pointed out a couple of fridges, a cooker and three television sets.

'I'll take all of them,' he said, peeling some notes off a wad.

'You're going to pay for them?' I asked.

'Course I'm going to pay for them,' he frowned at me. 'And I want a proper receipt and all.'

I got the labourers to load up the stuff in the van. Harry gave the driver a list of addresses. He tapped one of the TVs and nodded at me.

'Put this one in the back of the Daimler.'

I lugged it out to where the motor was parked. Tony Stavrakakis was leaning against it having a smoke. He helped me heave it into the boot. Harry came out and opened the back door of the limo. He looked over at me.

'Come on,' he said.

I got in the back beside him and Tony the Greek pulled away. There's something soothing in the smooth motion of a limousine at cruising speed, something comforting about being driven around in a big powerful car. Harry always seemed most at ease in the back of a motor. It was an intimate space for him. He'd used it as a consulting room and no doubt a confessional as well. It was the place we'd first met and where we'd finally split up. I suddenly thought of all those times in between when we'd be all dressed up and chauffeured off somewhere flash.

Harry gave me a sideways look and patted me absently on the leg.

'All right?' he asked.

There were so many questions that I wanted to ask Harry but just then I didn't want to say anything awkward. I didn't want to spoil the moment. There were some things that I really missed about being with Harry. So I just smiled.

'All right,' I replied.

Our destination was Willow Nook Old People's Home in Stepney. Harry went in and spoke with the matron then we carried the telly in through to the lounge. A few wrinkled inmates gaped at us with yellowed eyes. Perched on high-backed chairs that lined the room they looked like lizards sunning themselves.

'Look at all these coffin dodgers,' Harry muttered under his breath as we put the television in place.

A podgy, red-faced man came into the room and went around leaning over and smiling at the inmates.

'Look at that silly cunt,' Harry muttered again. 'Shaking hands with all these half-croaked fuckers.'

'Who's he?' I asked.

'Benny White. Local councillor. Second-rate politician, thinks he's fucking important. Still, he has his uses.'

'Harold!' the councillor declaimed across the room. 'What a fine gesture. Local business putting something back into the community.'

Harry shrugged as Benny White rubbed his podgy hands together. A reporter and a photographer arrived ushered in by the matron. The councillor drew himself up in front of the gathering and gave a little speech.

'Isn't this lovely,' he began. 'Look at this, ladies and gentlemen, a magnificent new television set!'

There was a muted response. A bit of orchestrated groaning from the senile assembly. Harry beamed beside the TV set. The reporter who had been scribbling away in shorthand came over.

'All right Joe?' asked Harry. 'Got all you need?'

'Yeah, sure,' he replied. 'Just the photo.'

'Course. Let's get this over with. Benny!' he called over.

The councillor came over and a few pictures were taken of them shaking hands over the television with the matron and one of the better-looking inmates in the foreground.

Driving back, Harry asked me how the business was going.

'Everything's fine,' I lied.

Harry nodded thoughtfully.

'There are a few things I'd like to know about, though,' I ventured, thinking about my dead baby boss.

Harry touched my arm in a placating fashion.

'Of course Terry,' he assured me. 'We'll talk,' he promised. 'In the meantime, as I've said, keep everything kosher.'

They dropped me back off at the warehouse.

'And when you see Jimmy,' Harry said in parting, 'tell him I want to see him.'

I read the story in next day's *East London Advertiser*. A HELPING HAND was the headline with a photo of Harry, the TV set and the councillor. *Benjamin White, councillor for Stepney East, launched his 'Old Folk's Appeal' today and one of the first to make a donation with a gleaming new television set was local businessman – Harold Starks . . .*

'All right Terry?'

It was Jimmy Murphy. I held up the paper for him to look at and he nearly pissed himself laughing.

'Charity,' he said scathingly. 'Yeah, Harry's big on that. Good for public relations, he says.'

'He's looking for you, Jimmy,' I informed him.

'Yeah, yeah,' he replied as he sat down on my desk.

'So,' he announced, pulling out a hip flask from his jacket pocket. 'How's it going?'

'Well,' I replied and pointed to the pile of invoices on my desk. 'There's all these unpaid bills, what am I supposed to do about them?'

Jimmy took a slug from his flask and sighed.

'Don't worry about them,' he said and passed me the curved metal bottle. I took a swig myself.

'So what am I supposed to do? Pay them?'

'Mr Pinker will sort them out when he gets back.'

'Mr Pinker?'

'Yeah.'

'When he gets back?'

'Yeah,' Jimmy took back the flask. 'What's the matter?'

'Jimmy, I know about Mr Pinker.'

'What you mean?'

'I know he's dead.'

Jimmy laughed lightly at me.

'Oh yeah,' he said casually. 'That.'

There was a pause in which we both looked around the office.

'Jimmy,' I said. 'What the fuck is going on?'

'Don't you know?'

'No, of course I don't know.'

'You mean you haven't been told?'

'Haven't been told what?'

'What a long firm is.'

'What?' I implored.

'A long firm,' replied Jimmy, screwing the cap back down on his hip flask. He got up off the desk and made for the door.

'Don't worry,' he said as he walked out. 'You'll find out soon enough.'

* * *

Harry holds the poker up in front of me.

'You've seen how it's done. Now you can have a go.'

I start to hyperventilate. As I shunt about in the chair its rubber feet squeal against the concrete floor.

'Hold him down, Bubble,' Harry whispers to Tony Stavrakakis and the big Greek puts both of his heavy hands on my shoulders.

'The thing is, Terry,' Harry goes on, 'it's a question of trust. You've got to trust me now so that we can do this right. And if you can trust me enough to do that, well, maybe I can trust you and all. It's all a bit medieval, I suppose. Trial by Ordeal. You know, the punishment itself sorts out whether you're guilty or not. If it goes wrong, well that's proof of a sort. It would be a shame, but then, if you do lose your tongue—'

He smiles over at the big Greek.

'Well, you won't be able to grass, will you?'

The warehouse was becoming ridiculously crowded. There was scarcely any showroom space any more and walking through the building was like going through a maze the walls of which were cardboard boxes stacked high and filled with all kinds of electrical goods. One of these walls had nearly collapsed and I was helping the labourers to make it safe when Harry arrived team handed. Most of the firm was with him, Manny, Jimmy and Tony Stavrakakis. They looked around and muttered to each other a bit.

'We're having a board meeting,' Harry announced. 'We'll be in the office.'

'You want me to come up?'

'Nah. Carry on with what you're doing. We won't be long.'

We restacked the boxes and I realised that with all the shifting around I'd lost track of a lot of the stock. I'd left the clipboard with the stock list on it in the office so I went upstairs to fetch it. I was about to rap on the frosted glass door when I realised that I could hear the firm talking. I carefully pressed my ear against the door jamb and listened.

'. . . so we're all ready then?' It was Harry's voice. 'We hit the floor next Wednesday.'

'And the kid?' came Tony's Cypriot accent. 'He doesn't know nothing?'

'That's right,' Harry replied. 'And let's keep it that way. Don't want him worrying his pretty little head this stage in the game.'

'What if he has to take the fall?' asked Manny. 'He won't be any trouble to us, will he?'

I could barely hear Harry's deep chuckle.

'Nah,' he said. 'And we can make sure of that when the time comes. At the moment him knowing nothing is our best cover. So, let's get going.'

I heard them all getting up to come out of the office so I tiptoed down the stairs as quickly and silently as possible.

'Right,' said Harry coming up to me. 'We're having a closing-down sale. Next Wednesday.'

He grinned at me.

'Everything must go.'

Jimmy had the clipboard I had gone to fetch in his hand. He nodded at Harry.

'Right,' Harry continued. 'We'll be off now. Jimmy's staying behind to do a stock check with you. Why don't you come for a drink tonight?' he asked, all full of affable charm. 'At the club.'

Jimmy and me spent the afternoon going around the warehouse and ticking off stock. When we had finished on the fridges he glanced sideways at me.

'So,' he said. 'You worked it out yet?'

'What?'

'What the scam is.'

I shrugged.

'Are you going to tell me?' I asked.

Jimmy smiled and took the hip flask from out of his jacket pocket. He unscrewed the metal bottle and took a shot. He gave a sharp sigh and smiled again.

'Well that depends son,' he said. 'That depends. You see I'd be doing you a favour, see? I'd expect a favour in return. Know what I mean?'

'I'm not sure.'

I felt myself being drawn into a dangerous game. I was already out of my depth but my curiosity was getting the better of me.

'What do you mean, a favour?'

Jimmy handed me the flask and I took a swig. The whisky burned the back of my throat and I coughed. Jimmy tapped the clipboard.

'What I mean is, we could be a bit clever with these figures. It could be worth our while.'

'Well, I don't know.'

'Look, do you want to know what a long firm is or not?'

I hardly dared to say anything but my head nodded automatically. Jimmy took back the flask and screwed the top back on.

'Right,' said Jimmy, giving me a satisfied glare. 'You owe me. Right?'

The scotch glowed in my empty sinking stomach. Jimmy started to explain it all.

'A long firm's a good racket. Simple, see? All it needs is a bit of capital and a legitimate front. You found out about Pinker, didn't you?'

'Yeah.'

'Well he's dead but his birth certificate is still valid. You see, they keep records of births and deaths in different files. That's the beauty of it. So if you get hold of a birth certificate of someone who died when they were a kid, no one's going to know from it that they're really dead. There, you've got yourself a front man. You can get all the essential documents you need from a birth certificate. Driving licence, passport, bank account. With a bank account set up you can open a business account. Register a firm at Companies House. Bribe a few influential faces on to the board as non-executive directors. Rent a warehouse, get some tasty-looking stationery printed with all your friends in high places prominent on the letter heading. Deposit some cash into your business account, move it about a bit so it looks like you're trading. And you are, at first. Buy in a load of gear wholesale, pay on the dot for the first delivery then work up a bit of credit. Delay payment on all the stuff that comes in after that until you've got a warehouse full. Then, bosh, hit the floor.'

'Hit the floor?'

'Grand slam. Everything must go. Cut rate, strictly for cash. Sell the whole lot off in a single day. Make a withdrawal from the business account the same day and then disappear. The whole operation's been fronted by someone who died years ago so you can't be traced. You can make ten grand, twenty grand, who knows?'

'Right,' I said, trying to take it all in.

'Thing is Terry, nobody knows for sure how much the scam will bring. Everything moves so quickly when you hit the floor. You're selling in quantity and for cash so there's bound to be some leeway. Harry isn't going to be anywhere near the warehouse on the big day. He can't afford to be associated with this set up.'

'Wait a minute.'

'I know what you're thinking. But it's not like we'd be having him over in any big way. He won't know, for fucksakes. A couple of grand. Three or four maybe.'

'I don't know.'

'Listen, you reckon everything's going to be all right if you just keep your head down. You're scared of what Harry might do if he found out. Right? Well, yeah, you've got good reason to be. But what do you think you're doing here in the first place?'

'What do you mean?'

'I mean, you walk out on Harry Starks, next thing you know he gives you a cushy little job like this. That was quite a liberty, you know, walking out like that. He was choked.'

It was embarrassing hearing this from Jimmy and I think he knew it. I couldn't look at him.

'Right choked he was,' he went on. 'You think he'd just let it pass? You think he'd just forget about it and give his old boyfriend a job just for old times' sake? Hasn't it ever occurred to you that you've been set up?'

'What?'

'Whose signatures are they on all those invoices and delivery notes? If this little racket is ever investigated, who's the one person they can finger for it? You, that's who. You're the mug here, Terry, and no mistake.'

'Harry wouldn't.'

'Harry wouldn't what? Let you take the fall? Do me a favour. And what are you going to do about it? You ain't going to grass him up, are you? He'll make sure of that. He always does. It's what he's good at. And you aren't going to grass me up to him neither. So it's up to you son. I'm taking a piece of this scam and if you're in, you can have your fair whack.'

'And if I'm not?'

'Then you keep fucking quiet about it.'

Jimmy brought his face up close to mine and hissed halitosis and whisky fumes at me.

'Otherwise I'll fucking do you, nancy boy!'

* * *

It seemed such a long time since I'd been to The Stardust that I was surprised that the doorman recognised me. He nodded me through with an expectant grin. As I went downstairs into the nightclub I felt none of the charm that I'd once associated with the place. It was just a tacky dive. I guess I'd grown old in the past few weeks.

I got myself a drink and looked out across the room. I clocked a few faces I vaguely remembered. Harry was at his usual table, holding court. He casually waved over at me. I drained my gin and tonic, straightened my tie and wandered across.

'Terry,' Harry announced amiably, indicating a chair opposite him. 'Have a seat.'

There was a young man sitting next to him. He wore an expensive mohair suit and his blond hair was cut in a short college-boy style. Harry's new boy, I assumed. My replacement. The new boy looked at me shiftily, trying to affect some sort of professional sneer. I gave him a fierce stare and he looked away. He was pretty enough, I thought, and convincing in his role of Harry's kept boy. He looked to be doing a better job of it than I ever managed. He had a cheap haughtiness, an eagerness to be spoiled that I'm sure Harry fell for.

'So, how's it all going?' Harry asked.

I glanced across the table. The new boy was looking disdainfully bored. I kind of hoped Harry would give him some spending money and send him away but maybe he was part of the night's proceedings. A gesture to show me what had been between us was all passed. It certainly reminded me of how expendable I was. It was then that I resolved not to tell Harry anything. Maybe I felt some spite at him for casually showing off his new boyfriend as he was setting me up to take the fall for the long firm. But mostly I figured that, if Harry knew that I knew, things would be a lot more dangerous for me. It would mean telling him of how I'd snooped around behind his back. I decided that I'd go along with Jimmy's plan. I deserved to get something out of all this, after all, given the risk I was taking. So I resolved to play dumb. Looking over at the new boy, I realised that that was another thing he was better at than me. I shrugged.

'It's all going fine, Harry,' I lied.

'So we're all ready for the big day?'

I nodded.

'Right. Well, as you know, I won't be there on the day. I'll be otherwise engaged. Remember, I'm not officially connected with

Dominion Electrical Goods. I'm like a silent partner. Silent,' he repeated, putting a finger to his lips. 'You understand?'

'Sure.'

'Right, well Jimmy will be there but Manny will be coming around later to pick up the takings. Jimmy's going to be organising security, can't be too careful with all those takings. But it's Manny that looks after the money. You clear about that?'

'Yeah.'

'Good. Don't worry, it'll all go fine. I'll explain it all later. You'll get a bonus and everything. OK?'

'Yeah.'

'Good. You're a good kid.'

Harry leant over the table to give me a friendly pat on my cheek. I involuntarily flinched away from his heavy hand. The new boy watched and sniggered. Harry frowned.

'Relax,' he said. 'Have another drink.'

I had plenty.

I spent the next few days getting the warehouse ready for the big sale. There were huge gaps in the stock check that me and Jimmy Murphy had done. I tried to cover them up amongst all the paperwork in the office hoping desperately that I could maintain my assumed ignorance of everything.

The last thing to do was to put up signs on the outside of the building. CLOSING DOWN SALE. LAST FEW DAYS. EVERYTHING MUST GO. I tacked them up on the shopfront with a sense of doom. They reminded me of those signs you see religious nutcases carrying about. You know, THE END IS NIGH, stuff like that.

The big day. I was as nervous as fuck. Jimmy arrived with a couple of heavies I'd never seen before. Freelancers. Harry wanted to keep any connection between him and the long firm to a minimum. But we needed some sort of muscle, just in case. The amount of money expected to change hands that day would be tempting for any outside team to heavy into. Jimmy gave me a wink, implicating me. I sighed heavily.

'Don't worry, son,' he assured me. 'It'll soon be over.'

And things did move fast that day. After weeks of doing very little trade we were suddenly very busy. It wasn't called a long firm for nothing. This sort of fraud required a lot of patience. A long wait and then a quick killing.

They came from all over town, our customers. Word must have gone out: a gravy train on Commercial Road. And it was well worth their while. They were getting goods at criminally low prices, it was like legalised fencing. And everyone got a receipt so no one could be accused of receiving stolen goods. Even though they were. Everything went dirt cheap but then we were getting a hundred per cent profit on everything we sold. Harry had a very pure sense of business.

They came in vans, lorries, high-sided pantechnicons. Even a flat-bed truck that we loaded up and tied down with a tarpaulin over it. And everyone got their receipt. As I signed them I was reminded that each one was evidence against me. That I had been set up by Harry. And so I could feel justified in being part of Jimmy's scam. He would nod over at me at particular parts of the stock that we sold that he hadn't included in the stock check and I would destroy our copies of the receipts for that sale.

I can scarcely remember any really clear details of the day we hit the floor. Everything happened so quickly, what with all the activity, but I think the time passed swiftly also because I dreaded the end of it.

When we were cleaned out I took all of the money into the office. I paid off the labourers, gave them a bonus that Harry had suggested. They went off happy, no doubt to the nearest pub. I envied them as I set to work sorting out piles of cash on the office floor. I'd never handled so much money in my life before or since. The smell of all those fingered notes was vaguely disgusting. Jimmy peeled off some notes for his freelance heavies and they were gone too. Just me and him. We put the money we planned to take for ourselves to one side and counted it up. It was nearly three thousand pounds. Jimmy scooped it up and shoved it into a holdall. He took out his hip flask, had a slug himself and then passed it to me.

'We'll divvy up that later,' he said as I took a swig myself.

Manny arrived with a battered old suitcase, no doubt to carry the takings in to Harry. We counted through the takings together as Jimmy watched by the door. Manny was very systematic. He went through the original delivery notes to check all the stock that had been sold. He was completely in his element as we sorted through the piles of money. He seemed instinctively able to keep different columns of figures in his head as the day's takings were calculated. I noticed a frown growing on that little round head of his as he realised that some of the cash was missing. He was implacable, starting the count from the very beginning again as he noticed some of those columns in his mind just didn't add up. His formidable little head started to shake from side to side as deep down, on an almost unconscious level, it realised that something was wrong.

'Is this *all* the money?' he demanded, sniffing at the piles of notes on the floor.

'Yes, of course,' I replied, trying not to shake with the real fear that I felt.

'Then we must count it all again,' he insisted and got back down on his hands and knees.

I looked over at Jimmy who was feigning nonchalance. He shrugged back at me. Manny looked up, perhaps sensing something. His little eyes pierced through me. He stood up.

'Look,' he said. 'Maybe there's been some mistake. Something you've forgotten.'

He shrugged amicably.

'It's not too late,' he said reassuringly. 'Things move fast. Money gets lost in all the fast dealing of it. Just hand it over and there'll be no more said.'

Manny was moving towards me with a soothing smile on his round little face. I backed away and as I did so saw Jimmy come up behind him. I tried to say something but my mouth was dry. It was like pantomime. *Behind you*. I saw Jimmy take a cosh from out of his jacket pocket.

'Don't worry,' said Manny. 'We can work this all out.'

I stuttered something unintelligible and then Jimmy whacked Manny with his cosh, putting that troubled little mind to rest.

It was like slow motion. Manny's eyes rolled white in their sockets. He shrugged fatalistically then fell to the floor scattering piles of notes around the office.

Jimmy slapped the shot-filled leather cosh in the palm of his hand and looked down at Manny.

'Fuck,' he said thoughtfully. 'Fuck, fuck, fuck.'

I was down on my knees checking on Manny and trying to extricate the notes trapped under his heavy little frame. I was worried that Jimmy might have killed him but the little man seemed indestructible. Semi-consciously gurgling something that sounded like Yiddish. Jimmy moved swiftly then, gathering up the money on the floor and stuffing it into his holdall.

'What are you doing?' I demanded.

'Change of plan,' he announced. 'We're going to take the lot. Do a runner.'

I looked up at him and frowned.

'What?'

'We've got no choice now. We can take the fucking lot and go.'

'Go where?'

'I don't know. Over the water. Belfast. Dublin. There's enough here to get us sorted.'

He caught my stare.

'So, are you in?'

He looked down at me fiercely.

My hesitation was answer enough.

'Well, you ain't going to stop me are you?'

He'd finished collecting all the money. His cosh hanging out of his trouser pocket. He took it out.

'Turn around,' he said.

'Jimmy, no,' I replied but he poked me in the face with it so that I turned away and tensed up.

'You'll thank me for this,' he said and whacked me on the side of the head.

The blow caught my temple and I went down, blacking out as I hit the floor. I woke up grabbing hold of a five-pound note that Jimmy had missed underneath the desk. I was only out for a couple of minutes. I heard the warehouse door slam downstairs as Jimmy made his getaway.

'Fuck,' I groaned and closed my eyes again, my head throbbing with pain and trying to think what to do.

There wasn't much that I could do. I knew that I would have to face Harry about all this. I got up and felt the bruise on the side of my head. Jimmy was right of course, giving me a whack was doing me a favour in a way but I knew that it wouldn't be nearly enough. I tried to think of what to say without giving too much away of my own guilt. It seemed pretty hopeless. Manny was still prone on the floor. He had got a much worse whack than I had. Jimmy had really taken a proper swing at him. So I sat him up against the desk and phoned Harry.

Harry answered and demanded to speak to Manny. I had to tell him that Manny was unable to come to the phone. There was a pause, then Harry said that he was coming over. His voice was cold and matter of fact. I was scared shitless.

He arrived with Tony Stavrakakis. He didn't even look at me at first but went over to Manny and tried to talk to him. Manny was still slumped down against the desk, muttering incoherently. Harry crouched down and slapped the round head a while until he realised it was a waste of time.

'Jimmy,' he finally said, looking up at me.

'He's gone,' I replied, rubbing my face, trying to make as much as I could of my own wound.

'And the money?' he demanded.

'Gone,' I said, mournfully.

Harry stretched his legs and stood upright. He nodded thoughtfully and looked over at Tony the Greek. He sighed and shook his head. He tutted, tongue against teeth. As if ticking off all of the bad things that had happened. All of the bad points. Tick, tick, tick.

'Well, Terry,' he said calmly, his voice soft as if to indicate disappointment rather than anger. 'We need to have a little chat. Don't we?'

Harry made some phone calls as I sat with my elbow on the desk cradling my dazed head. The doctor that the firm used came over to check on Manny. And Jock McCluskey arrived with a minor face I didn't know the name of. He briefed them to go after Jimmy. They were both armed.

'Right,' said Harry as the doctor led a semi-conscious Manny out of the office. 'Let's get out of here.'

He cocked his head at me sharply.

'You're coming with us.'

I was made to get into the boot of the Daimler. By the time we arrived at our destination I was sick with fear and petrol fumes. It was a lock-up garage beneath the arch of a railway bridge. Harry unlocked a padlock and we went inside.

A light was flicked on. The bare bulb revealed an almost empty room. There was a table to one side with some bottles and old chip wrappers scattered on it. A brazier with a gas canister stood by the arched end wall. In the middle of the cavernous space was a wooden chair. It looked lonely, sat there all on its own. A few lengths of rope lay curled around its legs.

'Take a seat,' Harry insisted.

As I sat down he went over to the table and picked up a bottle of Johnny Walker.

'Fancy a drink?' he offered and I nodded.

He poured the scotch into a chipped mug and passed it to me. It was about half full. I drank it down in two or maybe three quick gulps. Harry then took the mug off me and nodded at Tony. The Greek started to tie me to the chair.

'Right. Let's get started.' Harry bared his teeth at me in a grin. 'Showtime.'

'So, now it's your turn, Terry,' Harry says, heating up the poker again. 'Trust me.'

He smiles at me playfully as if the whole thing is a childish dare.

'Now, we want to get this right, don't we? Don't want to burn your tongue off. You're going to need that later to tell us the whole story. Open wide. Give him a hand, Bubble.'

Tony pulls me head back by its hair. My jaw hangs open. Harry holds the poker over the flame until it's white hot. Then he advances, pointing it at me.

Panic. A spasm of breathing. I'm panting like a dog. Can't speak.

Please, Harry. Don't Harry.

'Come on. Stick your tongue out.'

I do as he says. My mouth feels so dry. He holds the poker in front of my nose. Heat and light press against my face. Harry gently draws it down. It slides against my tongue with a rasping hiss. A whisper of steam stings my eyes. I feel only the pressure of the luminous metal. No heat. But I'm sure that it's searing into me, burning my tongue from out of my head. I black out for a second.

I come to suddenly. A numb, gaping mouth heaving out heavy sobs. My tongue is still there. I lick at my lips to make sure. Swooning with relief I feel a lovely warm feeling in my cock. I realise that I'm pissing myself. Through the tears, I see Harry nodding at me. There's piss running down my legs.

'There, there,' he says, patting me on the shoulder. 'That's it. It's all over now.'

I continue crying as Harry walks over and tosses the poker back into the brazier and turns off the gas. Then comes back over to me. Tony's let go of my hair and Harry strokes it back into place using his splayed fingers as a comb.

'It's all right,' he says, softly. 'You can tell us all about it.'

And I do. I tell him everything. I try to tell him everything at once but he gets me to start at the beginning, occasionally stopping me and asking questions. And it all comes out. All of it. The whole truth.

Tony unties me and Harry pours me another drink. This time the scotch burns against my swollen tongue. I cough most of it out down my front.

'I'll tell you what happens now,' Harry says, reading my mind. 'You can go now. We're quits. You don't talk to anybody about anything. You've had a taste of what will happen if you do.'

And that was it. I never saw Harry again, though years later, what with the trial and that, he became quite famous, or rather, infamous. As I left he peeled off a few notes at me. About fifty quid. As if to remind me that I owed him. I got a taxi back home. Next day I got a rash of tiny white blisters all over my tongue. Made it difficult for me to talk. Not that I had any inclination to.

2
Dissolution Honours

A nation is a collective enterprise; outside of that it is mostly a gambling space for the opportunism and adventurism of power.

Wole Soyinka

1964

Monday, 2 November

To the House of Lords for Ceremonial Introduction. Black Rod leads the way, his ebony shaft of office surmounted by a golden lion rampant. The Garter King of Arms carries the patent conferring my imminent status of Lord Thursby of Hartwell-juxta-Mare. Flanked by two peers I approach the Woolsack.

Always had a craving for preposterous ritual & you don't get much better than this. Teddy Thursby taking his seat in the Upper House. Joining the lords temporal, the lords spiritual. I'm wearing all the gear of course. Ermine, knee britches, silver buckled shoes, silk stockings. Try to move with processional rhythm. The slow gentle dignified sway. But it's hard not to swagger a bit.

Ceremonial introduction is so solemn & ridiculous. Useless, stupid, bloody beautiful ritual. So calm and soothing. I love it. Maybe it's the High Church upbringing. But then I always played that up a bit. Went through a big Anglo-Catholic phase at Oxford. Dead give-away, I suppose. Still, it always pays to send out the right signals, the right codes. That way you can make your intentions known whilst still remaining discreet. And that's what I've always been. Discreet.

Present the patent & the writ of summons to the Lord Chancellor. Sign the Test Roll, take the Oath, kiss the book. The strange purity of detail. Each tentative, futile gesture an escape from the everyday.

Feel like a new boy again. Like my first day in Parliament back in 1924 when I took my seat in the Commons. There had been ceremonial introduction then as well. No dressing up though. I remember other rituals equally important if slightly less formal. Chips Channon showing me round the Members' lavatories. 'The most important rooms,' he had announced with mock solemnity, vainly trying to affect a sparkle in those deadly dull eyes of his.

That was forty years ago. I've had some success, I suppose. Never lived up to my potential though. Early days held such promise. That stupid scandal back in the thirties. Failing to declare a business interest. Misleading the House. Had to resign from Cabinet & I never got a government post again. Became the flamboyant backbencher instead. Glad to be out of it now, to tell the truth. All those years of service & all I've got to show for it is a measly life peerage. Kicked upstairs. Some wag said that it was entirely appropriate, given my reputation, that I should be given a peerage in Sir Alec's Dissolution Honours List. Oh well, I'm a fucking Lord now. I can lord it about a bit.

Met Tom Driberg in the Lobby afterwards. He congratulated me. Genuine warmth there, I'm sure of it. Always felt a sort of cross-bench camaraderie with old Tom. Pure disinterested brotherly, or rather sisterly, affection. Nothing physical you understand. Shared interests. He's High Church too, of course. And we both have a taste for a bit of rough. He always wants to go down, mind you, being a socialist. I suppose he sees fellatio as an expression of democracy. He once confided his conviction that ingesting young & vigorous semen counters the effects of ageing. He was quite serious about it. I replied that it was probably the closest he'd ever get to transubstantiation. I'm not averse to it myself but I usually like to maintain a proper posture when mingling with the masses, rubbing my honourable member up against the constituency. Mutual masturbation, I think, is the tedious technical term. I hate these modern definitions. Makes everything sound coldly medical rather than deliciously sinful. There's an ancient word that far better describes my pleasure. *Slicklegging*.

Of course I've always been more discreet, which isn't saying much when it comes to Driberg. Don't know how he's managed to get away with it all these years. I've always been very careful, furtive perhaps, but then that's in the very essence of pleasure in slicklegging. I've always acted with caution. Never caught wet handed as it were.

'How are you celebrating?' Tom asked.

I shrugged. I hadn't gave it much thought. All that ceremony seemed enough. Frankly, I'm a bit too broke at the moment to throw a proper party. A few drinks in White's later on perhaps. Tom suddenly looked at me conspiratorially.

'Well, you must come to a party tomorrow night, Teddy,' he insisted. 'I think you'll find it interesting.'

He writes down an address & presses it into my hand with an implicative smile.

'Be there around ten,' he said.

I went back to Eaton Square & picked up my mail. A few telegrams of congratulation. One from the constituency association. Won't have to deal with that dreary lot any more. Two ominous-looking letters. One from Ruth, one from the National Provincial Bank.

Sir,

Can I remind you that the borrowing on your account is creeping ever upwards and that the overdraft is now about £1,000 higher than a year ago.

I feel sure that you are as concerned as I am about this. It is not merely a question of credit squeeze or of the absence of security – this borrowing is costing you something in the region of £150 per annum in interest. Is it not possible to re-budget and reverse the trend? Otherwise, without some assurance of an improvement in this situation I would feel compelled to seek the advice and guidance of my head office.

Yours faithfully,
George Budgen
Manager.

Teddy,

I really have had enough of you avoiding facing up to our situation. I'd much rather talk to you directly but I doubt if we'd be able to manage that with any civility so I am forced to write.

I am sorry that our marriage has turned out so very badly. I feel that I have played my part well enough but I am constantly undermined by your behaviour and your extraordinary mode of life.

It has always been me that has had to make compromises in order to maintain your precious veneer of respectability but I no longer feel that I can go on in this way.

A final break between us would probably be for the best but I realise what effect a separation would have on you professionally and socially, so I will agree to continue with the charade under certain conditions.

As soon as you are in a position to do so, I would like the sum of £250 paid into my account at Chase National Bank on a Banker's Order each month. I want a separate provision made for me financially. I'm sick of having to deal with your increasingly irate creditors and of never being sure whether the cheques I write will be honoured or not.

For my part, I will be with you occasionally at Hartwell Lodge, say, the first Sunday of each month so that we can go to church together. Also I agree to go with you to such functions in London and elsewhere that will serve to keep up the facade of happily married life in our new roles of Lord and Lady Thursby.

For the rest of the time we can be free of each other. You can be free to carry on with your selfish and dissolute lifestyle and I can be free of any useless expectations of your duty as a husband.

Ruth.

Well, with all the pomp & circumstance over it's back to ghastly fucking reality, I suppose. I suddenly felt completely deflated. Pour myself a large gin & start to make dreary calculations. Incoming: no MP's salary, odd bits of journalism beginning to dry up (no one interested now I'm no longer the flamboyant backbencher), expenses for attendance in the Lords (but the less time spent at that Darby & Joan club the better), BBC work poorly paid & notoriously slow in actually coughing up. Outgoing: my 'selfish and dissolute lifestyle', as Ruth calls it. Could make some economies there I suppose though I'm loath to do so. And that bitch wants £250 a month! Just where she thinks I'll find that kind of money is beyond me. Ungrateful cow. I never asked anything of her. Though, on reflection, that could be seen as the root of our problems. Repairs on Hartwell Lodge. Dry rot, wood beetle, estimated costs £2,000. Get up and pour myself another gin.

Depressing that I should have to be thinking of how I can balance the books on the very day of my glorious investiture. Maybe I could write a book. Get an advance on the royalties and pay off a few debts. What about, though? Still too young to be writing my memoirs even though I am almost as old as the century. The obvious thing, of course, would be to sell the house. Hartwell Lodge. The baronial seat of the first (& last, let's face it) Lord Thursby. No, it would never do. Besides, I love it too much even though its Tudor foundations are falling to bits.

Get rotten *fou* brooding over such matters. And so to bed. Gin melancholia well & truly set in.

Tuesday, 3 November

Johnson in the White House with a landslide. Yanks obviously had no stomach for this Goldwater creature & I can't say I blame them.

Evening & I'm off to this 'party' Tom D. mentioned yesterday. Find the slip of paper he handed me with that salacious grin of his in my pocket. A Chelsea address & a name. Harry Starks. The name means nothing. Sounds Jewish. Still, Tom's contacts always hold some strange promise.

Arrive about ten thirty. Shown into a large, rather over-furnished drawing room by a blond-haired young man. Some sort of a houseboy maybe. A hideous stone fireplace had been constructed around the chimney breast & a bar, complete with optics, had been built into a connecting wall but apart from that there hadn't been too much vandalism. There were a few quite agreeable pieces of furniture that one would guess had been here when the present occupier had moved in but, my goodness, the place was stuffed with all manner of junk. Boxing & horse-racing memorabilia, African & Oriental kitsch, trashy porcelain figurines & lots of gilt-framed photographs. Each one showed a heavy-set man with slicked-back hair caught in stillness with any number of what one would call, I guess, 'showbusiness personalities'. Next to each professional smile, the man, whom I guessed must be our host, held an equally professional stare. Defiant & direct yet shyly cautious, as if superstitious of the camera & somewhat wary of being identified. A lonely expression amidst the cheap & flashy glamour, looking out from the glossy surface as if in search for something more.

The blond boy brought me a gin & tonic & I looked around the room. Quite a crowd. A close-knit group of men with battered faces who looked like retired boxers or doormen. A few flashy-looking types, someone I'm sure I recognise from the television, more sombre men mingling with them, & lots of young men. Boys. I caught sight of a clerical collar. I saw our host talking with Tom Driberg. An imposingly powerful-looking man. His Savile Row suit gave him an air of savage nobility. It was a dark-blue chalk stripe just like my own.

Tom caught my eye & beckoned me over.

'Harry,' he said, 'let me introduce you to Lord Thursby.'

His joined-up eyebrows raised as one. I could see he was impressed. Probably took me for full-blooded aristocracy instead of just a kicked-upstairs life peer. There's a strange sort of bond between the lower-class tearaway & the upper-class bounder. A shared hatred of the middle classes I suppose. He shoved out his hand, adorned with chunky rings & a big gold wristwatch.

'I'm honoured, your lordship.'

I grinned. It was the first time I was referred to by my title since the ceremony.

'Call me Teddy,' I insisted & took his strong grip.

'Harry,' he grinned back & I just knew we'd get along.

'Harry does a lot of charity work in the East End,' said Tom.

'Really?'

Harry shrugged.

'Boys' clubs, that sort of thing,' he explained.

His own sort of *noblesse oblige*, I suppose, with its optional *droit de seigneur* one imagines.

Two of the boys were setting up a film projector & a screen at one end of the room. One of the pugilists had assumed the role of major domo, arranging the seating, giving orders to the other boys & glancing over to Harry, who appeared to be directing everything from afar whilst still engaged in conversation with me.

'Come on Teddy,' he said with a wink, gently taking my arm & leading me to a seat. 'The entertainment's about to begin.'

The party slowly got seated as the room was darkened. The film was a series of vignettes. Short scenes of innocent depravity. An old-fashioned, almost prelapsarian quality about them. More like drawing-room farce than any of this modern art-house pornography. There was as much emphasis on costume as on nudity in their erotic content. Dressing up was as important as undressing. Master & footman were depicted amidst the golden age of Edwardian romanticism complete with chaise longue & french windows. Sailors on shore leave wrestled with each other in playful brutality. Even a scene with leather boys, despite its bondage & mild sadism, had a naive quality to it, a child-like *nostalgie de la boue*.

Gasps of delight & muttered comments of approval from the room as the film proceeded but also other sounds that indicated that what was on screen was merely dumbshow for the main drama of the evening. There was already some groping in the darkness. The celluloid clattered to an abrupt end leaving a bright white square on the screen. Two of the boys started undressing each other. The beam of the projector caught their tight little bodies in a harsh chiaroscuro. Wanton flesh outlined with charcoal-thick shadow. One boy knelt to take the other's cock in his mouth.

Harry distributed the boys among his guests as largesse. They went into service or were themselves served. One of the businessmen was on his knees in front of the broken-nosed major domo. Some of the party were content in their role of audience. Touching themselves as they looked on. They also serve, those who watch & wait.

A young lad was propelled towards me by our host & we found a quiet corner in one of the bedrooms. He leant back against the wall with a lazily arrogant look on his tough little face as we indulged in a little slicklegging. I grabbed at his crotch & kneaded it through the cloth.

'Get your cock out,' I ordered softly as I undid my own fly.

I spat on the palm of my hand & rubbed our cocks together vigorously, coaxing some languid groans from the hoarse-voiced youngster.

'You naughty boy,' I muttered harshly as I brought the two of us off. 'You naughty, naughty boy.'

I gave a strangled cry of delight & relief as my mind darkened & sperm spilled out through my hand onto the front of my trousers. The youth gave an indolent sort of grunt then was off, no doubt to continue in his duties. I pulled out the handkerchief from my top pocket & wiped myself off. Felt a sense of calm & no little exhaustion from my exertions. Takes it out of you at my age. From every part of the flat could be heard the strange sounds of sexual indulgence. I felt drained & in need of refreshment. A gin & tonic would do the trick,

I thought. Wandered out through the gloom of the bedroom. Nearly tripped over Tom Driberg, honourable member for Barking, on his knees, energetically sucking away.

Wednesday, 11 November

I got a call from Harry in the week suggesting that we meet for a drink. So I invited him to White's. I knew he'd be impressed, not just because it was London's oldest & most prestigious club. It retains a touch of aristocratic raffishness that has all but vanished from the rest of clubland, a quality that I instinctively knew Harry would be drawn to. Just as I was drawn to his own kind of style. Such a change from the dreary businessmen, the constituency-party Tories I've been used to dealing with. Boring me to death in the Hartwell Conservative Club. I suspected even then that Mr Starks wasn't exactly, shall we say, kosher despite his Yiddish name. He was dangerous, but that was part of his charm.

I saw him catching his own reflection in the huge mirror on the stairway as I showed him around. Seeing himself framed by its baroque elegance he permitted a wistful smile to play across his lips. We walked through the collonaded entrance into the games room. Harry walked over to the billiard table. He seemed drawn to it, reassured by its familiarity.

'White's is one of the few clubs in London with a billiard table,' I explained.

He looked absorbed as he gently fingered the green baize.

'I used to have a billiard hall,' he declared. 'Well, I was part owner. The bloke who ran it offered me a partnership. He was having a spot of bother.'

Harry grinned over at me.

'Fancy a game, Harry?' I asked.

'No thanks, Teddy,' he replied, slapping the side of the table. 'Solid enough things, billiard tables. Still, so easy for the felt to get ripped.'

Harry caught my eye with a blank stare. A well-practised look. One that can intimidate & yet draw one in at the same time.

'Let's have a drink,' I suggested breezily & we walked through together. Harry leant back in his leather armchair, taking a sip of brandy & soda, casually surveying the fixtures & fittings.

'Nice place,' he commented. 'Wouldn't mind joining myself.'

I smiled, hoping that he was joking. The club has a two-year waiting list & Harry's background wouldn't exactly support an application. I had a vague horror of him making White's some sort of offer. Then he frowned with the thick line where his eyebrows joined. He took another gulp of brandy & sighed sharply.

'So, Teddy,' he said.

I could tell he enjoyed the familiarity just as he savoured the formality. The combination was irresistible.

'I was wondering if we could talk business.'

'Business?' I countered with a casual cautiousness.

'Yes, business. I have a proposition. I wonder if you'd be interested in becoming involved with a new company I'm starting up. As a director.'

'Well, I'm a bit tied up at the moment, Harry. Otherwise.'

'Oh, I don't mean that you'd be involved in an executive position, Teddy. I wouldn't expect you to take part in the day-to-day running of it. Just, you know . . .'

He shrugged.

'The occasional board meeting?' I suggested helpfully. 'Turn up to the annual general meeting. That sort of thing?'

'Yes,' he replied with a smile. 'That sort of thing.'

Friday, 13 November
To Bristol to record *Any Questions?* With me on the panel – Dingle Foot, Tony Crosland & Violet Bonham-Carter. Excellent dinner before the programme.

One of the questions was 'What do you think will be the effects of a more permissive society?' I replied that the twenties had been a bit of a wild party but we'd got away with it then because we didn't ask anybody's permission. Much laughter and applause.

Tuesday, 17 November
Have officially been made a director of Empire Refrigeration Ltd. Appointment confirmed with a cheque for £2,000 brought around to my flat in person by one of Harry's boys. And it wasn't only the money that was delivered by hand.

So, I'm out of a hole financially, for the time being at least. I can keep the bank & Ruth off my back for a while. Things are looking up. Harry's desire for legitimacy definitely has its possibilities for me. The name Lord Thursby is bound to look good on his letter headings. His strong-arm stuff can get him respect but friends like me can get him respectability.

Saturday, 21 November
By way of reciprocation, Harry takes me to his club. 'It ain't exactly White's, Teddy,' he explained. The Stardust is located at the unfashionable end of Soho, south of Shaftesbury Avenue, virtually in Chinatown. A nice enough place, I suppose, if a little on the kitsch side. Still, if its decor lacked the bohemian charm of some other Soho haunts, this was more than made up for by the real danger of some of its clients. A photographer was on hand, of course, to record my visit. And so I finally enter Harry's gallery of 'personalities', grinning with bow-tied & puffy-faced affability next to a stern Harry & a coloured boxer.

Monday, 23 November
Today I joined the board of Victory Electrical Goods. Took rather a shine to the young man that Harry sent around. His name is Craig. Good-looking in a rough sort of way that I find irresistible. Trouble written all over him of course but something shy & vulnerable about him as well. A nervous sensitivity. After some very satisfactory slicklegging we have a little chat. Turns out he's got nowhere permanent to stay. Suggested that he could stay with me. I would pay him to keep the place tidy, do the odd job here & there. He seemed taken with the idea but said that he'd have to check with Harry first.

Friday, 27 November
To Hackney Dog Track with Harry. Rather jolly. Must confess that I enjoy slumming it just as much as Mr Starks relishes a taste for high society. Exciting to be amongst hard men & tough little boys.

Harry suggested that he start paying me a monthly fee. 'As a business consultant', he explained. Occasionally I'd be asked favours. An introduction or merely my presence at a meeting or a business lunch. I agreed. He also gave the OK for Craig to move in.

A lucky night. I came away with £30 winnings.

Monday, 30 November
The Albany Trust are lobbying me for my support in advocating homosexual law reform. Said that I agreed with them in principle but I have to be careful in involving myself in anything that might cause people to draw any unfortunate conclusions.

Repairs have started on Hartwell Lodge.

Thursday, 3 December
Craig has moved in. Meagre possessions, poor boy. Just two battered suitcases in the spare room. Embarrassing moment when, seeing him looking with interest at my bookshelf, I started to talk about various volumes & he meekly confessed his illiteracy. Promised to help him to learn to read. He appears as interested in matters of taste & breeding. He is always trying to glean bits of knowledge of etiquette or culture. Has a particular curiosity in the curios and *objets d'art* in the flat & seems to have a passing knowledge of antiques.

Monday, 7 December
Lunch with Harry at the Lords. He loves all the pomp & circumstance of the place, of course. Harry's charm is that there is absolutely nothing bourgeois about him. Instead he exudes a rough feudal charm. He refers to his neighbourhood, indeed his whole milieu, as his 'manor'. I wonder if he had played at being a pirate lord as he scrambled about the bombsites of his childhood just as I had done in the more salubrious landscape of my own youth.

He is fascinated by the world of privilege. A patriotic desire to be part of a really big racket, I suppose. He wants a piece of the action. He actually asked my advice on how one got on to an honours list. 'I wouldn't want a peerage,' he confided to me. 'A knighthood would suit me.' I think its martial aspect appeals to him, the notion of nobility of arms. He has a great admiration for upper-class men of action like Lawrence of Arabia or Gordon of Khartoum. Empire heroes and explorers he no doubt read of in picture books. And in his own way he sought to emulate them, to find some respectable and gentlemanly way to demand money with menaces. Some way of jumping the counter of middle classness straight into aristocracy.

Wednesday, 9 December
Managed to have a civilised telephone conversation with Ruth. She is very content with the new arrangements by which she will be financially provided for. So she should be.

The repairs to Hartwell are now in full swing. 'The place is like a building site, Teddy,' she said, which conjured up delicious images of sweating workmen for me. We have decided not to have Christmas at Hartwell Lodge due to the state of the place. She is going to friends and so I will be able to spend the time with Craig. We agreed that I will come down for a weekend some time in the new year once all the repair work has been completed. I have also resolved (to myself) to get her out of the way some time later, so I can host a 'party' there.

Saturday, 12 December
Took Craig to see Olivier's *Othello* at the Old Vic. Larry a frightful old ham affecting some ludicrous West Indian accent. Craig enjoyed himself. Thought L.O. very talented. 'He could be in the Black and White Minstrels,' he said.

Tuesday, 15 December
Dinner at Quaglino's with Harry. First really serious chat about business. Present arrangements are fine but there are opportunities to expand. To be honest I'm worried about the precarious nature of Harry's entrepreneurial activities. I dread being embroiled in some sort of ghastly scandal. Harry wants legitimacy & the way to this is in doing business on a grand scale. And so we can both benefit from this approach.

We went through the facts together. Harry's various business concerns have accumulated capital which has been constantly moved around in order to avoid the attentions of the Inland Revenue & other interested parties. Now is a time for expansion, I argued. A big project to invest in. Preferably overseas.

Harry was enthusiastic at the notion of founding a business empire. The adventure of it appeals to him. Some way of making a mark on the world. He has an atavistic sense of economics. Dull commerce bores him. He has a desire to conquer, to carve something out for himself.

'Maybe I could get a Queen's Award for Industry, Teddy,' he commented drily.

Saturday, 19 December
Worried about Craig. He went out the night before last and I saw nothing of him until he rolled back into the flat late tonight filthily drunk. We had a row. He has been, of late, lazy & derelict in his duties. When I diplomatically pointed some of this out he became obstreperous. 'I'm not your bloody servant, you know,' he snarled at me with a beery breath then slunk off to bed.

I can understand that the inequality of our respective status can make him insecure & even bitter towards me. But I did so much hope that we could get on without class resentment rearing its ugly head.

Monday, 21 December
The Commons tonight voted overwhelmingly (355 to 170) to abolish the death penalty for murder. Given the size of the majority it does not look like the Lords will try to frustrate this decision. This is the last important business of Parliament this year.

Friday, 25 December
Christmas. Craig went over to Bethnal Green to see his mother during the day & then back here for the evening. We had a pleasant evening together. Talked about ways that we could get on better. Craig was very sweet, apologising for his bad behaviour etc.

1965

Friday, 8 January
To the Colony Casino Club in Berkeley Square with Harry. One of the many new casinos that have opened up since the new gaming laws. Lots of overdressed Americans in the place. Apparently the film actor George Raft was present but I'm not sure who he is anyway. Harry introduced me to a charming New Yorker called Dino Cellini. 'It's an honour to meet ya, Lord Thoisby,' he said in that cartoon Brooklyn drawl. All wonderfully Runyonesque. He & Harry then went off in a huddle but not before H. had handed me a big stack of chips to play with.

Haven't played roulette since Monte Carlo in the twenties. It all took me back rather. I'd gambled recklessly back then. A young man's vice. Squandering one's inheritance to order to fuel one's own ambitions. *Faîtes vos jeux*. Had a winning streak then lost it all by the end of the evening.

Friday, 15 January
A sort of eager solemnity in the Smoking Room. News is that Winston is v. ill. A stroke or something. Still, the old bugger made 90 only last month.

Saturday, 16 January
Craig has gone & done his disappearing act once more. Left the flat in an utter mess. And we had planned to spend time together this weekend. Really it is too much. Felt quite depressed. Had enough of waiting around so I went out to the Colony Casino again. Found out that by using Harry's name I can have an account with them. Lost about £500. Felt cathartic though, somehow.

Sunday, 17 January
Still no sign of C. so I cleaned up the flat myself. Found a holdall of silverware under his bed in the spare room. His interest in antiques obviously more professional than I'd imagined. Worst fears realised. I've a thief living under my roof.

Tuesday, 19 January
Craig rolled in late, drunk. Confronted him about the silverware. He got very indignant & finally quite tearful, saying that he'd had a rotten life, never had a chance, etc. I ended up comforting him, but saying that he really must start to behave.

Thursday, 21 January
Awful day. The police turned up at the flat. That is to say a thuggish little man with beady eyes calling himself Detective Sergeant Mooney. Wanted to interview Craig but Craig wasn't in. So instead he started to ask me all sorts of impertinent questions about our 'domestic arrangements' etc, making all sorts of ghastly insinuations. When I asked him if he knew who I was he just nodded with a nasty smile & replied, 'Oh yes, I know all about you.' The upshot is, of course, that the grubby little policeman wants money. £200 pounds! Laughed in my face when I suggested payment by cheque. I'll have to see Harry. Haven't got that sort of cash to hand at the moment. Also, things as they are with Craig cannot go on. He'll have to go.

Friday, 22 January
Went to see Harry at his Mayfair flat. Told him about yesterday's unpleasantness. He seems to know this Mooney fellow. 'He's known for the fit up,' H. commented. 'Don't worry, I'll straighten things with him.' Felt relieved & thankful but when I said, 'Thanks, Harry, I owe you for this,' Harry gave me a rather fearsome grin and said v. softly, 'I know, Teddy, I know.'

Sunday, 24 January
Had it out with Craig. Asked him to leave. Terrible scenes, him shouting and becoming abusive. Then he went all quiet & just started packing. Left very quickly, muttering 'You'll regret this' on his way out. Queen Anne carriage clock & some silver candlesticks seem to have left with him. *C'est la guerre.*

Felt v. depressed. Nursed a bottle of gin & listened to home service. News came on that Winston has finally croaked. Strange morose feelings about it. Not grief for him so much as a sort of mourning for my own failed career. I was one of the few people that stood by him in the wilderness years & yet when that undeclared assets business came about he froze me out. Can't blame him for that, I suppose but I always felt a slight sense of betrayal.

Couldn't stand moping about any more. Brooding about the past. Went out to the Colony to play the tables for a bit. Always gets me out of myself. Of course, by the time I got to the casino I was absolutely rotten *fou*. Have to watch this. Can't even remember how much I lost.

Saturday, 30 January

Winston's big send off. Full State junket at St Paul's. Wanted to avoid the whole thing to be honest but Harry insisted that I go around to his for drinks. Turns out he was holding some sort of wake for the old bugger. Harry's a big Churchill fan, of course. Got all of his LPs. I became the guest of honour, having known him personally. Was able to regale the assembled group of villains & 'personalities' with some anecdotes. Told of how, when W. was holding forth at the Oxford Union back in the twenties, F.E. Smith had heckled him, hissing, 'Shut up, Winston. It's not as if you've a *pretty* voice.' Harry was in a more reverent mood, though. Proposed a toast. 'To the last great Empire man,' he announced. 'We shall not see his like again.' All of the East End lot quite dewy eyed. One thing the Socialists will never fathom. The deep loyalism of the genuine working classes.

Saturday, 6 February

Repairs completed on Hartwell Lodge so I travelled down to Hartwell-juxta-Mare by train. Good to get out of London for a couple of days. The Lodge is back to its former glory, I'm glad to say. How I've missed it! It's such a strange hybrid of architecture. A Tudor end that had been built in the 16th century & a Georgian half added about 200 years later. Wonderfully secluded with a belvedere on top that gives a simply marvellous view of the coast. I wish that I could have it for myself.

Ruth & I dined agreeably enough. She still retains a sharp sense of humour, tinged though it is with bitterness. But as the day wore on to gloomy darkness things began to get awkward. We both had a lot to drink & it released the venom. I've never approved of women getting drunk. Especially Ruth. It makes her all the more ugly.

'You've never cared about me, Teddy,' she slurred at me. 'It gets so fucking lonely out here.'

'Then why don't you divorce me?' I countered.

'That's what you want, isn't it? Well I'm not going to give you the pleasure.'

'You mean that you stay married to me just to spite me?'

'Is that what it does, Teddy? Spite you? Our little arrangements, all I've put up with. Oh, no, you won't get rid of me so easily. I'm Lady fucking Thursby now.'

'Then you should start behaving like her.'

'Don't you start lecturing me about behaviour. I know what you've been up to.'

'Now Ruth, don't be tiresome.'

'I've heard all about you and your *friends*.'

She used the word as if it were a curse.

'I've heard,' she went on, 'that you're in with some sort of thug. Been seen at the dog track together, importuning young men.'

'That's a damned lie!' I protested loudly.

She let out a hideous, eldritch shriek of laughter at this.

'Oh, Teddy,' she continued, hatefully. 'You're such a fucking joke. You and your precious discretion. You think anyone's taken in by your ridiculous façade? Everyone knows you for what you are.'

I said that I'd had quite enough of this & got up to leave the room.

'I didn't marry a man,' she called out after me. 'I married a boy. I wonder if you'll ever grow up before you die?'

Sunday, 7 February

To St Matthew's at Hartwell-juxta-Mare for Mass. Ruth & I play at being Lord & Lady Thursby for the benefit of the parish. All teeth & smiles. Try to ease myself into the tranquil gloom of the village church. The solemn, calming ritual. Harbouring murderous thoughts towards my wife hardly puts me in a state of grace though. Go through the motions. Have a chat with the vicar afterwards, shake hands with a few dimly recognised parishioners.

Catch the afternoon train back to London. Nagging fears of gossip. I dread any kind of scandal.

Friday, 12 February
Went to Leicester Square Odeon for a charity showing of *Lawrence of Arabia* that Harry had organised. His favourite film, apparently. At drinks in the interval Harry all misty eyed & sombre. Some wag, a famous comedian or pop star or something, one of Harry's 'personalities' had secreted sand into his shoe from a fire bucket & proceeded to pour it out theatrically at the bar. 'Bleeding sand gets everywhere!' he declared in a loud South London twang to much laughter. But Harry was not amused. For once he was entirely unimpressed by all the showbiz types crowding out the bar & foyer. He turned his back on the frivolity & muttered darkly to me, 'Lawrence was a real man. He faced adversity with real bottle. And he was bent, like me.'

Harry feels an obvious attraction to the television-age celebrity that he often surrounds himself with but is really drawn to a deeper sense of fame.

Within him dwell dreams of high renown & adventure. We spoke of Arab culture & Harry talked about N. Africa. He had been in Tangiers in the fifties when he'd worked for Billy Hill, the king of the racecourse gangs.

Monday, 15 February
Lords debate on overseas aid. Afterwards talked to Lord Chilvers about Africa. Tony Chilvers is a newly ennobled captain of industry with plenty of ideas. We talked about the situation in Rhodesia. Both agreed that if Smith strikes out on his own the Tory party could be split in its response. Then he went on to the newly independent black states. 'The thing is Teddy,' he told me, 'we want to make sure that they don't turn commie. All of their nationalist intellectuals tend to look to the Soviet Union as an example of development and industrialisation.' He went on to talk about theories of growth, 'conditions for economic take-off' etc. I was a bit lost but then he started to tell me about the opportunities for investment. Especially in Nigeria, apparently. Huge country, rich in resources, wanting to modernise. He knows of many schemes that promise generous dividends.

I suddenly thought of Harry & his considerable ill-gotten capital. Such a venture would surely appeal to his strange imperial vision. It seemed ideal. The new government in Nigeria is, by all accounts, unstable & already rife with corruption. I said that I'd be interested in such an enterprise & knew of potential investors. Tony Chilvers promised to introduce me to a prospect.

Wednesday, 17 February
Miserable grey day. Sunk into gloom. Coming down with the 'flu I fear. Feel old and lonely. I miss Craig for all his faults. News on the wireless – Gambian independence. Africa again. Coincidence or a sign that this investment idea is meant to be.

Thursday, 18 February
Stayed in bed all day, feeling ghastly. Plenty of medicinal scotch. Horrible feeling of being alone with one's illness. Who will look after me when I am old & infirm?

Saturday, 20 February
Feeling much better. Went for a bit of a stroll amongst the drizzle. Spoke to Tony Chilvers on the telephone. Arranged a meeting with some Nigerian fellow. Colony Casino in the evening. Won £1,200!

Sunday, 21 February
Phoned Harry to mention African idea. Seemed v. keen. Also mentioned recent illness & H. said, 'If I'd have known I'd have sent one of the boys around to nurse you better.' 'Well, now you come to mention it,' I joked, 'I haven't made a full recovery.' 'Right then,' he said & put the phone down. At around six, a blond-haired youth appeared! Gave him a drink & we quickly got on with the slicklegging. Very brusque and methodical but felt that was all for the best. Didn't want to feel in any way engaged emotionally, what with all the awful consequences that stemmed from my attachment with C. Went to bed feeling wonderfully sated.

Tuesday, 23 February
Invited over to Tony Chilvers's huge modernist mansion in Kingston-upon-Thames to meet this African chap. Expected a much older man.

John Ogungbe looked like he was still in his twenties. Short & lithe in a tightly cut fashionable suit with an open-necked silk shirt. He wore dinky little slip-on crocodile-skin loafers. His hair was cut short to his scalp which, with his well-defined bone structure, prominent mouth & flat nose, accentuated his skull. As if the skin had been stretched tightly over his face with some economy. He is very striking.

We shook hands & his thick lips peeled to reveal an impressive set of teeth. But as he gave me this flashing white smile I noticed that his eyes remained impassive, cautious. They were yellowish & slightly bloodshot.

John has come from Nigeria to London to study engineering. Since qualifying he has divided his time between here & there & has been involved in various building schemes. He is determined, he tells me in great earnest, to use his education to improve the lot of his own people. We talked of development & I tried to make all the right noises.

His current project is to build a township near Enugu in southern Nigeria. The plan is to construct 3,000 houses & a shopping precinct. He has secured government approval but lacks enough investment to get started. He wasn't disappointed when I told him that I don't have that sort of capital at my disposal. He said that he thinks that my title & status will be of use in attracting support for the scheme. And that I might be able to help him find potential investors in London.

Tony gave us lunch. John Ogungbe asked us what we thought about Ian Smith and the Rhodesia situation. We were both v. diplomatic & rather skirted around the issue. Tony changed the subject & bewailed the fate of business under a Labour administration. Apparently Wilson is planning to introduce a Corporation Tax in the budget. Gave serious warnings to J. Ogungbe against Nigeria embracing socialism. Also invited me to join a special group looking at party policy on overseas aid that the Advisory Committee on Policy has set up. I accepted.

Wednesday, 24 February

Went to see Harry at his flat. Explained to him what had been discussed yesterday. Suggested that he meet with John Ogungbe & he agreed. I thought of arranging some sort of civilised luncheon at White's or somewhere but Harry had his own ideas.

'Why don't you invite him to my club?' he proposed.
'The Stardust?'
'Yeah, why not? He can be guest of honour.'
'Are you sure that's a good idea, Harry?'
I was determined that we should make a good impression. I dread any vulgar behaviour from Harry. Of course, I couldn't say this to him. He could get so touchy.
'What's the matter with my club?' he retorted indignantly.
'Nothing Harry. It's just that . . .' I sighed. 'We need to be on our best behaviour.'
Harry laughed heartily at this.
'Don't you worry, your lordship,' he said. 'I'll behave myself.'

Thursday, 25 February
1922 Committee have approved new system for choosing the next leader – a vote by MPs. Sir Alec is bravely hanging on but only a matter of time before he will have to announce resignation.

Saturday, 27 February
At The Stardust Club with John Ogungbe as guest of honour, Harry fussing about as host, trying maybe a little too hard to make our guest feel welcome. But he managed to invite a few of his business friends who he thought might be interested in investing some money into the scheme. Of course there were the inevitable photographs.
Mr Starks & Mr Ogungbe eye each other up a little suspiciously at first. I could tell that Harry found John attractive, not just as a business proposition. When I first introduced them he slyly winked at me as if in complicity. There was something over-friendly in Harry's manner that worried me. Not sure about Harry's feelings about race. I knew that he was touchy about his own Jewishness but I didn't quite know whether he himself harboured prejudice in other areas. He seemed completely unabashed about talking about colour though. He quickly turned the conversation to boxing. I suspect that this is the one area where Harry has contact with blacks. He reeled off a list of coloured pugilists as if John might know them personally, readily conceding their superiority. 'White boys just ain't hungry enough any more,' he lamented. I wasn't sure if this concession covered for an overall feeling of superiority that he might have. I feared that he might say something uncircumspect.

John Ogungbe appeared to enjoy himself. He laughed loudly at all of Harry's jokes and oft times gave that glazed-eyed grin I'd first noticed on meeting him. Harry was very taken with him.

'What a find, Teddy,' he confided to me. 'He's the son of a chief, you know.'

We all got very drunk. Harry's strategy was to entertain lavishly, if a little crudely. Not being sure of Ogungbe's proclivities, Harry had made sure that there were some pretty boys on hand as well as a few available tarts. When John showed an interest in one of the women Harry made sure that the lucky girl went home with him.

Sunday, 28 February
Dreadful hangover. Felt sullied & spiritually dissipated. Went to Evensong at All Saints in Margaret St. It's Quinquagesima. The service had a marvellously calming effect upon me. Felt grateful to have a moment of peace for one to pray quietly to one's Redeemer. 'Bow, stubborn knees, & heart with strings of steel, be soft as sinews of the new-born babe. All may be well.'

Monday, 1 March
Ogungbe appeared at my flat in Eaton Square quite out of the blue.

'Harry was quite taken with your scheme,' I told him. 'And with you, if you don't mind me saying.'

Ogungbe grunted & nodded. Much more sullen now.

'He tells me you're the son of a chief.'

Ogungbe laughed sharply.

'My father worked on the railways. I gave him that chief story because I knew it would impress him. I also told him that I had six wives but he didn't seem so interested in that.'

I couldn't help laughing myself.

'He's something of a tribal chief himself, isn't he?' he suggested mischievously.

'What do you mean?'

'Come on. I'm not stupid. You think I haven't worked out where he gets all his money? And that whore the other night. She told me plenty.'

'I hope that this doesn't put you off doing business with him.'

Ogungbe laughed again.

'Don't worry. I know all about the British sense of fair play. You think we Africans are innocent natives? We know how things operate. We've had it done to us for long enough. We've learnt from it.'

I'm less enamoured by this new Ogungbe that was sitting opposite me in my drawing room. I'm not sure of what the proposed business deal would entail & what would be its consequences but I didn't like the thought of him having the upper hand. Despite this I arranged for a proper meeting to go through the scheme.

Friday, 5 March

Meeting at Ogungbe's offices in Euston. A large table laid out with architects' plans & engineering drawings. He even had a little model of the scheme. He went through the whole thing in detail.

Harry sat with Emmanuel Gould, who takes care of his finances. Little Manny sat quietly, intently blinking through his round spectacles as Ogungbe laid out all the plans in front of us. Harry, by contrast, was agitated and enthusiastic. Pointing at things & eagerly asking questions.

The conversation moved on to money & then Manny took an active part. The initial investment was to be £25,000 & then further payments as construction was undertaken. In the long run, a profit of over £200,000 could be realised from the project. Manny stroked his chin & looked cautiously over at Harry who nodded almost absently. A company would be set up to oversee the investment. I had my doubts about the whole thing but then it wasn't my money. I just hoped that my name on the letter heading of this new firm would bring me a handsome commission.

Then everyone stood up & shook hands. Harry hovered over the model of the township and rubbed his hands together.

'What's it going to be called?' he asked.

'That's yet to be decided,' replied Ogungbe.

'Tell you what,' Harry went on, gazing down at the tiny blocks of flats. 'We could call it "Starksville".'

Ogungbe gave Harry his impassive grin. As he looked over at me his yellowy eyes glared.

Monday, 8 March

West African Developments came into being today with me nominally on the board. Drinks around at Harry's to celebrate. After initial euphoria H. looked a bit grim faced. 'I'm putting a lot into this, Teddy,' he said. 'I'm going to have to call in a few favours.'

Thursday, 11 March
Terrible news. Harry has been arrested. One of his boys came around to tell me the news. Apparently he has been charged with 'making an unwarranted demand with menaces'. Horrible sinking feeling. This could ruin me. Need to make sure that I can distance myself from any unpleasantness.

Friday, 12 March
Visit from Manny Gould. The latest is that Harry has been refused bail and is on remand in Brixton prison. Manny made all sorts of reassuring noises about it being a 'very flimsy case'. I'm not so sure. Told Manny that my reputation wouldn't allow me to be caught up in all this & the little Yid just shrugged and said, 'Well, if Mr Starks goes down, so might you, your lordship. And we want to avoid that now, don't we?' He insisted that I made sure that the Nigerian project went ahead as planned. 'Business as usual,' he said. 'That's the order of the day.'

Saturday, 13 March
Very depressed about how things have turned out. Oh, why have I allowed myself to get caught up in all this? Feeling strangely reckless. Went to the Colony Casino & played the tables as if tempting the fates. Bumped into one of Harry's cohorts. Seemed casual about the whole business. 'I wouldn't worry,' he said with an affable grin. 'People can be got at.'

Monday, 15 March
Went to see J. Ogungbe at his Euston office. He was very perturbed about the Harry situation. I reassured him that West African Developments would be able to fulfil their commitment to the project. 'That's good, Teddy,' he said. 'We have an agreement, after all, and if it were to fall through I would hold you personally responsible.' He's off to Nigeria this week to oversee the start of construction on the scheme.

Thursday, 18 March
Harry's application for bail to a judge in chambers turned down.

Friday, 26 March
Bad week for the Tories. Liberals win Roxburgh, Selkirk & Peebles by-election. If we can't win seats in the Borders where can we win them? Knives out for Sir Alec. *Daily Telegraph* running a front-page story suggesting there could be a leadership contest before Easter. With Sir Alec goes the last of the old school, I fear. *Après?* – the inevitable rise of the grammar school boys.

Wednesday, 31 March
Judge Griffith-Jones at the Old Bailey turned down another application for bail. They were going to take it to the Lord Chief Justice, apparently.

Friday, 2 April
Manny came around to see me to persuade me to support Harry's application in the Lords. I am extremely reluctant to do this but once again oblique references to my being implicated etc. M. suggested that I should table a question along the lines of asserting the rights of an individual in being held in custody for such a long period without trial. Eventually agreed to do what I could. Didn't really have any choice. Feel quite sick about the whole business.

Wednesday, 7 April
House of Lords. A bit unsteady on my feet as I asked the question. Had a few drinks beforehand. Dutch courage. My question v. badly received. Challenged as to whether I held any kind of brief for Mr Starks. Denied this vigorously, saying that I have always fought for the right of any person not to be held without trial. Catcalls. Viscount Milburn declaring that 'such a question has no place in being asked here'. Felt thoroughly humiliated by the whole thing, though managed to maintain a posture of righteous indignation throughout. Application denied in any case. Trial date has been set for April 15.

Thursday, 8 April
To Little Venice for lunch at Diana Cooper's. She was as charming as ever but confessed that she felt awfully depressed at getting old. 'I feel posthumous, Teddy,' she confided to me. Made me conscious

of my own decline, too. All the other guests were of a younger generation. Some television presenter & new friends that D. had made in the neighbourhood. We talked of Duff and reminisced about Philip Sassoon's weekend parties at Trent Park in the '30s. Like a dream of another world.

Thursday, 15 April
Good news as to opening day of Harry's trial at Old Bailey. Key prosecution witnesses failed to turn up. Judge ordered adjournment.

Friday, 16 April
Prosecution case against Harry has completely fallen apart. Judge threw the case out of court. *Evening Standard* reported Harry's comment leaving the Old Bailey: 'It's a case of police harassment, pure and simple.'

Big celebration at The Stardust in the evening. Lots of now familiar faces. And 'personalities'. Film actress Ruby Ryder & radio comedian Gerald Wilman. Wilman very camp. Told a funny story about a repentant homo actor being caught *in flagrante delicto* with a hotel bellboy. 'I'll turn over a new leaf,' the queer thespian declared. 'Just once I've got to the bottom of this page.' Also noticed Detective Sergeant Mooney amongst the gathering greedily quaffing the champagne. Harry very grateful about my support. 'You've been very staunch, Teddy. I appreciate that.' Showed his gratitude in the form of a new boy for me to take home. Feel tremendous relief (in more ways than one!).

Friday, 16 April
Good Friday. Away for a weekend at Hartwell Lodge. Went to St Matthew's at Hartwell-juxta-Mare for the Mass of the Pre-Sanctified. Gave thanks for how things have turned out this week.

Saturday, 17 April
Fine spring day. Went for a walk with Ruth along the coastal path. Wild flowers in bloom everywhere. Sea air marvellous. Good to be out of London for a spell. Good to be away from all this business with Harry. It really has been too much. Must try to maintain a safe distance from his intrigues in the future.

Monday, 19 April
Board meeting of West African Developments. Harry had initial report on the progress of the township project from Ogungbe. It all sounded a bit vague to be honest. Harry seemed pleased enough though. Passed around some photos of workmen digging out the foundations & grinning for the camera with relish. Grandiose illusions – they were carving out the footings of his new empire. Mentioned the matter of my commission. Harry said that this would be paid once the scheme had started to realise some return on investment. Not what I had in mind.

Tuesday, 20 April
Craig turned up on my doorstep late last night. It had been raining & he was all wet & dishevelled in a rumpled and dirty suit with the collar turned up. He looked terrible. 'I was just passing,' he muttered & managed a mirthless smile. Should have told him to get lost, really. But he looked desperate & I feared some sort of scene in the street. So I invited him in & he stood in front of the fire in the drawing room as I poured him a brandy. He shivered & mumbled something about 'needing to get back on his feet'. Let him stay over in the spare bedroom. When he left this morning I slipped him a five-pound note.

Saturday, 24 April
V. warm day. Went for a stroll. Saw a pretty youth on the King's Road with long hair, frilly shirt & bell-bottomed trousers. Reminded of Oxford days & the dandy style we wore in those days. Oxford bags – trousers flared out to 28 inches in bright hues. Quite as outrageous as any of this 'swinging' style. Young people always think that they've found something new. Had wistful thoughts of when one was young & fashionable & desired. Now I'm just a flabby-faced old buffer in a bow tie. Playing the Lord.

Wednesday, 28 April
Craig turned up again, looking a good deal smarter. Said he wanted to borrow some money. I gave him twenty quid and told him not to worry about paying it back. I can hardly convince myself that this is the end of it though.

Wednesday, 5 May
In the Lords for a debate on the Finance Bill. Saw Tom Driberg in the Smoking Room later, eager for gossip & making none too oblique references to Mr H. Starks. I chided him that gossip should, by its nature, be confined to talking about others, not oneself. When parting he suddenly became serious. 'Be careful, Teddy,' he said. Sudden paranoia. Driberg urging caution is not a good sign.

Tuesday, 10 May
Craig at my flat again. No good deed ever goes unpunished. Talked of some 'business' plan of his. Some fairy story about setting up a car-hire firm. What he wants is someone to invest in it.

'Maybe you'd like to put some money into it,' he suggested.

'I'd like to help,' I tried to assure him. 'But, you see, all my money's tied up at the moment, I'm afraid.'

'Well, maybe you could get one of your friends interested.'

'Craig, please.'

'Look, Teddy. The thing is I need some cash. Someone I know, a journalist, he says he could pay me quite a lot of money. A human-interest story, he calls it. Says I'd make a very good subject. Plenty of colour, if you know what I mean. Well, I told him, I'm not going to rat on my friends, am I? I wouldn't do a thing like that, would I Teddy? Not unless I was really desperate.'

'How much do you want?'

'Five hundred pounds.'

'And that would be the end of it?'

'Yeah.'

'Look, I'll need some time to get the money.'

'Of course, Teddy. There's no hurry. I'll give you till the end of the week.'

Wednesday, 11 May
Went to see Harry about the Craig business. I didn't know what else to do. He was in an ugly mood. Worried about the Nigeria project. He'd heard nothing for weeks & is seething with suspicions of treachery. He's not the most well tempered of men, I must say. And there are rumours of psychopathic tendencies.

I finally got around to mentioning C.'s blackmail & I really wish I hadn't. Harry went into barely controlled rage.

'I thought I told that little slag to lay off,' he spat out, pacing about his flat. 'Well he's asking for it now.'

I tried to placate him.

'Maybe just a warning,' I suggested.

'He's had his fucking warning. You leave this to me. You won't have to worry about that little fucker.'

Then he returned to his brooding & I made my excuses & crept out.

Friday, 14 May

Went to White's. Saw Evelyn Waugh there, looking grim in a loud dogcheck suit. I asked how he was. 'Toothless and melancholic,' was his reply. He had all his teeth removed apparently & dentures have proved v. unsatisfactory. 'These false snappers ruin my appetite for solid food,' he said, looking like he was compensating with liquid intake. He appeared utterly desperate. 'I'm a wreck, Teddy,' he told me. 'I hardly sleep though I'm full of dope. I get up late, try to read my letters, have some gin, try to read the paper, have some more gin. Then it's lunch time.' He gave a ghastly smile, his mouth an empty rictus. Eyes cold, unblinking, vigilant.

Came home with an overwhelming sense of decay. My generation is dying out. All the Bright Young People of the twenties have become old and hideous. In my own decline I'm left with an abiding sense of failure – a wasted political career, a rotten marriage, constant worries about money, scandal, blackmail. I've utterly failed to resist temptation, I've given in to beastly lusts. The flesh is weak & going flabby. I feel resigned to the slow surcease of life, clinging on to some hope of redemption yet wallowing in a descent into final decadence. This is my fate & I must bear it with all the courage I can muster. Mine are dissolution honours, after all.

Monday, 17 May

Meeting of the group Tony Chilvers is chairing on party policy on overseas aid. Bit of a talking shop really, full of dreary types going on about 'modernising the party'. There's all manner of small groups meeting about new policy. Any recommendations go to Shadow Cabinet via the Advisory Committee on Policy. The chairman of the ACP is Ted Heath – obviously building a power base for the inevitable leadership contest.

Spoke to Tony after and he asked how the Nigeria project was going. I said something vague about problems in communication. I really have no idea what's happening.

Friday, 21 May
Constant jabber about the direction of the party. Lots of talk about the need for new policies & 'modernisation'. An obsession with becoming 'classless' which merely means middle class. Classless in the v. worst sense. Indistinct. One particularly gruesome comment: 'We must become the party of the consumer' – which brings to mind bodily function rather than any real political vision. The Blasted Heath, needless to say, is behind most of this 'reform'. Manoeuvres, more like. Reggie Maudling will run against him for the old school, I hazard. A scholarship boy, but at least with some ballast.

Wednesday, 26 May
Harry invited me over. There was boxing on the television broadcast from America & Harry was having a little party. When I arrived I recognised some of the people from the first of Harry's 'parties' that I had attended & there were quite a number of young pugilists. From a Boys' Club boxing team, apparently. Lots of masculine & youthful energy as we crowded around the screen. Harry v. partisan for one of the fighters, Sonny Liston, an acquaintance, he proudly announced, passing around a photograph of them together at The Stardust Club. I rather favoured his opponent, Cassius Clay, a good-looking fellow Harry dismissed as a 'mouthy coon'. Anyway, the whole thing was over in the first round! Clay floored Liston in about two minutes, standing over him arrogantly, refusing to retire to a neutral corner & delaying the count. The room filled with catcalls of disappointment & indignant comments. Discussion followed as to whether the fight was fixed. Then we all had more drinks.

The brevity of the evening's entertainment after all the anticipation charged the atmosphere. Harry was animated. He has a tremendous manic energy & charisma. A noble savage demeanour that is such a palliative to the dull mediocrity that seems to be taking over everywhere. Something atavistic about him. He confirms one's worst fears but in a way this is somehow reassuring.

We all started to get drunk & the horseplay began. Starting with demonstrations of boxing moves & combinations, some light sparring between the younger boys, moving on to more erotic play. I had thought of asking Harry about the Nigeria business but I know he's worried about it & I didn't want to spoil his mood. Instead H. brought up a subject that I'd much rather forget. Craig. He became part of the banter.

'Had an accident, didn't he?' Harry asked in mock innocence. 'What was it Frank, fell down the stairs or something.'

'Something like that,' replied one of the older men laconically.

'Or slipped on the soap,' Harry went on. 'Was that it?'

'Yeah, could be.'

'Slipped on the soap and fell down the stairs.'

Laughter. I suddenly felt sick. Somebody was plying me with brandy & I didn't refuse. Harry came up to me & whispered in menacing mockery.

'See? I can get things sorted for you.'

Then the business started in earnest. Older men pawing at the youths. Harry kissing greedily at a boy with bright red hair. I had no stomach for it. I felt horribly drunk. Completely *fou*.

I got up & staggered towards the door. Harry noticed & pushed the redhead in my direction.

'Go on,' he ordered. 'See to his lordship. He'll only want wanking off.'

Before I knew it the boy was guiding me into one of the bedrooms & was starting to roughly knead at the crotch of my trousers.

'Whatsmatter?' His voice high pitched. 'Can't get it up?'

Harry had followed us in.

'He can't get it up,' the youth observed, shrilly.

I swayed in the spinning room.

'Get him on the bed,' Harry ordered tersely.

They both heaved my flaccid body onto the awful softness of the mattress.

'Get his clothes off,' Harry hissed sharply.

I felt a tugging at my vestments. My shoes thudded onto the floor. I lay helplessly inebriated. More muttered orders at the doorway. Suddenly the darkened room was filled with light. My eyes smarted. The red-haired boy pulled off my remaining clothes then stripped himself & got into bed with me. There seemed to be many people in the room now. Low cackles of laughter & underbreath comments.

Whispered directions from Harry. The naked youth stuck his cock rudely in my mouth to the sound of soft clicks & ratchets. Someone was taking photographs.

Thursday, 27 May
Woke up late in the afternoon in my own bed with no idea how I got there. Strange feeling of lethargy throughout my body & thick drowsiness in my head. Was I drugged last night? Awful recollections of shame, humiliation & most of all fear. Quite glad to be in a state of sedation.

Monday, 31 May
Detective Sergeant Mooney turned up at my flat again. Something deeply unsettling about this man. All of the physical threat of H. Starks but none of the charm. His beady little eyes were always darting about, taking everything in. I asked him what his business was.

'I was hoping that we might co-operate, sir.'

'Yes, yes,' I replied impatiently. 'How much do you want?'

'Oh, it's not money I'm after, your lordship,' he retorted, as if affronted.

Then he got to the point. Influence. That's what he was after, & offering a 'reciprocal arrangement' as he called it. I asked him to explain.

'Well, if I start by the way I could bring my influence to bear in a way that could be of benefit to you. Now, there's a whiff of scandal in the air regarding connections that you have with some, shall we say, rather colourful characters. There's still a great deal of sensitivity about any kind of intrigue involving sexual immorality. Remember all that Profumo business. In no time you've got the gutter press stirring things up. Nobody wants that. I've got a pal in the Criminal Intelligence Branch. There's an increasing concern about organised crime. Apparently, they've been asked to investigate an alleged connection between a peer of the realm and a well-known figure in the criminal underworld. Racy stuff, wouldn't you say? If the tabloids ever got hold of it.'

I groaned audibly. Mooney's little eyes gleamed.

'But if I was to use my influence . . . convince my friend at C11 that it's all nonsense and hearsay. As I've said, no one wants a scandal like this. It only makes the general public lose faith with the establishment. Gangsters are always trying to cultivate friends in high places. They think that it gives them an air of respectability. I could suggest that you're merely a dupe in all this. Persuade them to drop the inquiry. And in return, you could use your influence for me in a certain matter.'

'And what would that be?'

'Well, I'm in a spot of bother myself. Years of keeping London's streets safe to walk along and I'm being accused of impropriety. That's the thanks I get. Left-wing trouble makers taking advantage of the British system of justice and sense of fair play.'

'What's happened?'

'I arrested some demonstrators who were making a nuisance of themselves outside an embassy. Now they say I planted evidence on them and tried to force them to make untrue statements. Turns out one of them belongs to some sort of civil liberties group. A diabolical liberties group, more like. Making accusations. The British Police Force is the envy of the world. Any other system would have them rounded up and shot.'

'So what do you want me to do?'

'Well, they're demanding a police inquiry. If you could use your influence.'

'I'm afraid that I don't actually have very much influence on the affairs of state.'

'Well, every little helps. But I was thinking that maybe you could have a word with your friends in the press. An article about trouble makers trying to blacken the name of authority, that sort of thing. Everyone knows that these people are always just stirring up trouble. Something that might put me in a favourable light and counter some of these scurrilous accusations. I've brought some of my press clippings. They might be useful.'

He handed me a sheaf of grubby newsprint.

'Well, I'll see what I can do.'

He finished his drink and got up to leave. We shook hands. Mooney's palm was cold and clammy.

'I suggest,' he added as I showed him out, 'that you don't mention our little arrangement to Mr Starks. He might take advantage of the situation.'

Thursday, 3 June
Lunch with the editor of *The News of the World*, obvious choice for what Mooney wants & I've done some articles for them in the past. I fed him the story. A plot by subversives to discredit the forces of law & order. One of Mooney's cuttings mentioned personal courage in breaking the Ricardo Pedrini racket in 1962. We talked the story into shape – a dedicated & courageous fight against crime & vice in Soho, extolling an impeccable service record & hinting that sometimes unconventional methods bear fruit. British police the best in the world etc., trouble makers just want to undermine authority. He agreed to run it & quite out of the blue asked if I was interested in doing a weekly column. Bluff stuff. Old values in a modern world, that sort of thing. Said that I was definitely interested.

Saturday, 5 June
Have agreed to do column for N.O.T.W. Not exactly intellectually challenging but it means a weekly income & opportunities to get other bits of journalism. Feel that this is really what I should be concentrating on. A chance to air forthright views with a detachment gained from being out of the rat race of politics. And regular money might help to keep me out of trouble.

Suggestions for name of column – *Points of Order* (a bit dull), & *Entitled Opinions* (which I hate – a cheap joke against the peerage).

Monday, 7 June
Board meeting of West African Developments. Latest progress report from Ogungbe extremely vague – no sense of when actual construction is to commence. Harry manically optimistic about it all, though. The whole project seemed to represent something v. important to him & so he refused to accept any possibility of failure. Ambition. It's dreams we believe in, after all. Much talk of drastic measures to be taken unless there was more clarity about the scheme. 'We'll fucking sort it out,' he said, his usual business acumen hopelessly inapplicable in these circumstances. V. glad not to have any of my own money invested in this.

Sunday, 13 June
First column published – *Being Reasonable*. Bringing a bit of respectability to what is, I have to say, a very trashy rag. Elsewhere

in the paper news that some pop group have been all given MBEs in the Queen's Birthday Hons. Just shows how dreadful things have become.

Monday, 14 June
Called to an emergency meeting at Harry's flat. All his cohorts there. H. seemed to be delegating all sorts of tasks & activities to his gang. V. animated again, apparently in a good mood but difficult to tell. His temperament is so unpredictable.

'Right then,' he said, slapping his hands together. 'That ought to keep you lot occupied. Make sure that you behave yourselves. Don't get involved in anything unnecessary. All right?'

Grunts & nods all round.

'Right then, Teddy,' he said, looking over at me for the first time. 'It's all sorted.'

This unknown certainty made me feel uneasy.

'Er, what's all sorted, Harry?'

'I've decided what to do about this African business.'

'Really? Well that's good.'

'Yes it is, Teddy, it is. We're going to go there. Sort it all out.'

'Ah,' I said. 'So when are you going?'

'We, Teddy. I said "we". Me and you.'

'Well, thank you for the offer but . . .'

'You don't want to come?'

'Well, much as I'd like to accompany you, I've er, other commitments. You know, business in the House, a column to write, that sort of thing.'

Harry smiled & shrugged. I forced a grin back.

'Suit yourself then. But since I'm sorting my affairs out you might want to look at this.'

He nodded to Manny who shuffled through his papers, fished out a handful of markers & passed them over to me. I stared at them blankly.

'Gambling debts,' Harry went on. 'From the casino you've been frequenting. I sanctioned your account, I own an interest in the place after all, but since I'll be away I'll no longer be able to act as guarantor. I'll have to hand them back and let the parties concerned deal with them themselves. They are, of course, debts of honour, and as such have no real legal binding. So I guess the people concerned will have to find their own ways of securing payment. Some of them are quite imaginative, I believe. And if that doesn't persuade you . . .'

He held out his hand to Manny again. The little Jew handed him a pile of glossy photographs. He waved them at me, shaking his head & tutting loudly.

'Naughty Teddy,' he taunted.

He held one up to my face. I flinched and looked away but not before I'd caught an awful glimpse of myself naked on the bed in a grotesque posture of supplication.

'Harry, please,' I begged.

'No. You listen. And listen good. This African business was your idea. Remember? I've poured a lot of gelt into this scam and I want to know what the fuck is going on.'

'But what can I do?'

'You can be with me. I don't know what these jungle bunnies are up to but I guess having a peer of the realm along for the ride might help putting them in their place.'

'When are you planning to go?' I asked wearily.

'In a couple of days. Manny's sorting out tickets. Hope your passport's up to date.'

I flapped the scraps of paper in my sweaty hands impotently.

'I don't really have any choice about this, do I?'

'No Teddy,' he replied brusquely. 'You don't.'

Friday, 18 June
Lagos
BOAC flight to Kano, in northern Nigeria, then connecting flight to Lagos. V. travel sick. Awful heat & closeness. Ogungbe met us at the airport. Took us for drinks at the Lagos Polo Club. The best club in town, he assured us. Faded colonial atmosphere which Harry loved but made me feel uncomfortable. Pre-Independence, Ogungbe explained, its membership had been, of course, mostly white but now its exclusivity was based on rank & means. Nigerian military and police officers, white civil servants & members of the diplomatic corps & businessmen of every colour and nationality. The ideal place to make business connections.

H. wandered out of the bar to watch a chukka of polo & Ogungbe took me to one side.

'Your friend is worried about the project,' he said softly.

'He is rather.'

'Try to reassure him. These things take time. There is a lot of, shall we say, bureaucracy.'

'You mean people to pay off?'

'The notion of a free economy in this new country of ours is an illusion. Officials on every level want their share.'

'So, how far has construction of the scheme developed?'

Ogungbe shrugged.

'Well there have been some delays. We've had to wait for the end of the rainy season to start work proper. And I've had to secure import licences for the building materials.'

'More "bureaucracy", is it?' I said scathingly. 'I suppose every petty official's got his hand out for the backsheesh.'

Ogungbe's yellowy eyes flared at me in indignation.

'Don't presume to lecture me, Teddy. Your people have taken plenty. And years of colonial rule have left us with no political or institutional framework to regulate growth. People who have struggled all their lives to earn a few pounds now find millions passing through their hands. What do you expect?'

I coughed.

'I'm sorry. It's just that this whole project, well, we want it to go smoothly, don't we?'

'Of course. You must try to reassure your friend Harry. It's very important that his investment in the scheme continues. Otherwise we could all lose out.'

'I'll do my best,' I replied.

Suddenly I felt hot & sweaty. Wandered out of the club room onto the veranda to get some air. Galloping hooves of polo ponies thundered across the field beyond.

Saturday, 19 June
Enugu
Morning flight from Lagos in a light aircraft. The plane bounced up & down in the air above the jungle canopy. Felt quite sick by the end of the journey. An official reception to greet us at Enugu as we dizzily staggered out onto the runway. A motorcade drove us through the town to the President Hotel where we were staying.

There, the regional minister, Dr Chukwurah, gave a welcoming speech & there was a party. All the local dignitaries lined up to greet us. One man, enthusiastically shaking our hands, said: 'Welcome Lord Thursby, welcome Lord Starks. It is a great honour.'

Harry laughed.

'It's just Mr Starks,' he explained.

'You're not Lord?' the man asked, unable to hide his disappointment.

'Well.' Harry smiled mischievously. 'I'm something like that. You can call me Harry.'

The man smiled & shook his hand again.

Dr Chukwurah announced that we would visit the project on the outskirts of Enugu the next day.

'But while you are in the city is there anywhere you would like to visit?'

Harry thought for a moment.

'Yeah,' he said. 'There is one place I wouldn't mind having a look at.'

'And what would that be?'

'The jail. I wouldn't mind having a look around your jail.'

Dr Chukwurah frowned.

'Really, Mr Starks?'

'Well,' Harry went on, 'I've a keen interest in criminology, see? One of my hobbies if you like. It certainly would be interesting to compare prison conditions here to those of back home.'

'Very well,' said Dr Chukwurah & motioned over to the Chief of Police.

'Harry, really,' I muttered chidingly under my breath.

He grinned back at me.

'You want to come too, Teddy?'

I certainly didn't. I need to take a rest. Exhausted from all this travelling. And this appalling heat.

'Suit yourself,' he replied & went over to where the police officers present were organising themselves into a guard of honour.

When he had gone, Chukwurah came over to me.

'Lord Thursby.'

'Call me Teddy, please.'

'Very well, Lord Teddy. I thought we might have a quiet word.'

He led me into an empty room away from the reception area.

'Lord Teddy, my government and particularly the government of this region are very keen to encourage investment from overseas in development.'

'Well, that's good.'

'Yes it is. But it is important to make sure that any expansion or economic growth is controlled and regulated for the benefit of the people. We don't want people coming over here trying to make, what the Americans would call, a quick buck.'

'Of course not.'

'Of course not, yes. What we want is long-term commitment otherwise such schemes are not viable. As a politician, I'm sure you understand.'

'I think so.'

'Ogungbe is a very ambitious young man. He has, as we say here, got a big eye. As such he is not to be trusted fully. And your friend Mr Starks with his keen interest in criminology . . .'

'I assure you Harry's intentions are entirely honourable.'

'I hope so. For both your sakes. I wouldn't want you to get out of your depth. You're a long way from home out here. Might I ask how much you have personally invested in this scheme?'

'Well, I've not exactly put any money into it myself. I'm more of a consultant to the whole enterprise.'

'A consultant? Yes. That's good. Well I hope you can maintain a certain objectivity in that role. If things don't turn out the way they seem. Now, let's rejoin the party, shall we?'

I agreed. I needed a drink. Jet lag & poor air conditioning made me light headed & a little nauseous. The booze didn't help but I needed something to stop my head from spinning. The party began to wind down. I made my excuses & went to my hotel room to lie down. I took off all my clothes & lay down in bed under a single sheet. Felt hot & sticky. The air around me was heavy with a humid dread. I got up, wetted a face flannel & rested it on my eyes. Slept fitfully, my mind crowded with half dreams. Confused thoughts made lucid with anxiety.

After a few hours there was a tapping on my door.

'Come,' I droned into the darkness.

It was Harry. He stood over the bed.

'Teddy?' he whispered.

'Yes?' I groaned, taking the flannel away from my eyes, blinking at the light.

'What a fucking hell hole,' he announced.

'What?'

'The prison. Makes the Moor look like Butlin's. I pity the poor bastards banged up in there.'

I groaned again & rolled over. Harry patted me on the shoulder.

'That's right Teddy, you get some sleep. Need to get up tomorrow to go and look at our investment. See how the natives are getting on with building Starksville.'

Sunday, 20 June

Next morning we rode in a motorcade to the outskirts of Enugu & the development. Dr Chukwurah made another speech & then motioned to me and Harry with expectation.

'Go on, Teddy,' Harry urged me. 'You're good at this sort of thing.'

I can't really remember my address. It all came out on cue. All the *thank yous, great honours, wonderful opportunities for a young country in the modern world* & all that crap. When you've been at this game as long as I have you don't even have to think. Which is just as well as my mind was racing with uneasy imaginings. The heat constantly getting to me. Head throbbing. Brain fever.

We stood before a large billboard announcing the development. There wasn't much behind it. A huge clearing had been hacked into the jungle. A few earth movers & dumper trucks were parked here & there. The foundations had been dug & various plots marked out with pegs & string. Ogungbe led us around the site with a copy of the plans in his hands. In a determined way he pointed out each section of the scheme as if conjuring an image of it before us. I looked down into the earthworks thinking of archaeology rather than construction. As if history had already left this pitiful site behind & moved on somewhere else. The earth a very red clay. Monsoon water in the trenches, its rustiness made me think of corrosion.

'Of course we haven't been able to start work properly because of the rainy season,' Ogungbe explained.

Harry frowned & nodded. Unconvinced.

'Yeah,' he said. 'But that's over now, isn't it?'

'Yes, just over.'

'So why haven't we started?'

'We're waiting for the cement.'

'Cement?' asked Harry, incredulously.

'Yes,' replied Ogungbe with a placatory grin. 'There's been a hold up. I'm going over to Lagos today to sort it out.'

We continued our tour. Harry sidled up to me.

'Cement,' he muttered disdainfully.

I shrugged, not knowing quite what to say.

'I don't like the look of this. Cement? What can be the problem with that. I know all about cement, Teddy.'

Monday, 21 June
Drove out into the bush to visit a tribal village. Treated to a display of ceremonial dancing. Strange ritual processions in huge raffia masks. Harry was quite absorbed by it. Plentiful supplies of palm wine that dulled my headache somewhat.

After the performance Harry was all smiles, mingling with the natives & showing off a few boxing tricks to the young men of the village. Seemed quite at home. Natives seemed drawn to his charisma. Surrounded by smiling piccaninnies. Looking like Kurtz.

Later, he was more stern and subdued.

'Where's Ogungbe?' he asked.

'He's already gone back,' I replied. 'He's flying back to Lagos tonight.'

'I've got a bad feeling about all of this,' he said. 'I think we should pull out.'

'Let's sort this out when we get back home,' I suggest.

'I think we've been had over, Teddy,' he said with a soft fierceness. 'And I don't like that. I don't like that one bit.'

The motorcade took us back to the President Hotel in Enugu. We were due to fly back to Lagos in the morning & get a connecting flight back home. Drinks in the hotel bar. Harry became involved in deep conversation with the Chief of Police. Dr Chukwurah took the opportunity to speak to me directly.

'I hope that your visit has been a success Lord Thursby.'

'Yes,' I reply cautiously. 'I think so.'

'And, no doubt, you'll be anxious to get back home.'

I nodded. You can say that again.

'And your friend Mr Starks. I hope he is satisfied with the way things are going.'

'Well . . .' I shrugged.

'If there are any discrepancies between your investment and the actual progress of this project I'm sure you realise that this is best dealt with by the proper authorities. I, for one, am keeping a close eye on Ogungbe so you mustn't worry on that account.'

'Quite.'

'But your friend Mr Starks. He strikes me as an impetuous sort of a fellow. It wouldn't be a good idea for him to involve himself in the internal affairs of this country.'

'Most certainly not.'

'I hope you can convince him of that. Well,' he said, raising his glass. 'Here's to a safe passage home. And if you do happen to find yourself caught up in any, shall we say, difficulty . . .'

He handed me a slip of paper surreptitiously.

'You can get in touch with me on this number. You might find it hard to get through. The telephone system here is a little primitive. But if you do find yourself in any trouble I advise you to persist.'

Tuesday, 22 June
Lagos
Flew back to the capital in the morning. Again tossed around in a light aircraft & I was sick this time. Too much palm wine & too little sleep. A constant state of anxiety. But some sort of relief as with my head between my knees, vomiting, I thought: at least we are going home.

Landed at the city airport & I found out that Harry had booked us into the Excelsior Hotel by Lagos Harbour. There were some delays in the connecting flight, he explained. We took a taxi & booked in. I went straight to my room & to bed. The air conditioning here was much better than in Enugu. I fell into a deep and thankfully dreamless sleep.

Wednesday, 23 June
Packed and ready to go but no sign of Harry. Not in his room. Boy at reception said that he'd gone out early this morning. I went back to my room & waited. What the hell is going on?

Thursday, 24 June
Still no sign of Harry this morning. Anxious thoughts only relieved by bouts of impatience & boredom. Started drinking after lunch.

Tried not to think about what might have happened. Sweaty hand nervously fingering the slip of paper with a telephone number on it. Decided to give it a bit more time. Went to my room and had a nap.

Woken about six by Harry.

'Where the hell have you been?' I demanded. 'I've been out of my mind with worry.'

'Just needed to find out a few things,' he replied casually.

I got dressed.

'When's our flight? I want to go home.'

Harry gave me a rather disturbing little grin.

'We ain't going home, Teddy,' he said. 'Not just yet.'

'What? Harry, this is intolerable.'

'We've got some unfinished business to attend to.'

'You might have. I've had enough.'

I picked up my suitcase.

'I'm going to the airport.'

Harry blocked my path.

'I'd advise against that, Teddy.'

'Get out of my way!' I seethe and tried to push past him. Harry wrenched the case from my hand & threw it onto the bed. Then he grabbed me.

'Get your hands off me you bloody hooligan!' I shouted in his face.

With an open palm he slapped my face. His nostrils flared a little but otherwise his expression was calm & measured. Cold. He threw me onto the bed and I crumpled into a ball, knocking my head against my suitcase. The bedsprings creaked a little. I was helpless. Like a child. Suddenly overcome with memories of prep school cruelty. The ghastly humiliations when one is small & utterly powerless. Being beaten. Wanting desperately to please the older boys. I started to sob.

'I want to go home,' I wailed.

Harry sat down on the edge of the bed & gently stroked the cheek he has struck.

'Shh,' he implored, softly, suddenly becoming an older boy even though he is half my age.

He waited for my sobbing to subside, patting my shoulder slowly. I felt sick to my stomach.

'Listen,' he whispered. 'We've been had over. Well and truly. But if these fuckers think they can get away with it, then they've got another think coming.'

'But what can we do? We're out of our depths here, Harry. Let's get home and try and sort things back there.'

'That'll be too late. We need to act now.'

'I really think we should walk away from this one, Harry. You know, put it down to experience.'

Harry's face suddenly darkened.

'You silly old queen. You think I can just walk away? Wipe my mouth and say, "Oh well, fifty grand down the drain"? What kind of a wanker do you take me for?'

He handed me a handkerchief & I wiped my face.

'So,' I ventured fearfully, 'what are you going to do?'

'Tomorrow,' he said, 'I've got something to show you.'

Friday, 25 June

Drove down to the docks. Harry in his element, looking along the waterfront & nodding as if in recognition. He had the driver stop by a quayside & he pointed out a group of cargo ships moored out in the bay.

'There's our cement, Teddy,' he announced.

I frowned & squinted at the distant ships.

'So what's it doing out there? Shouldn't they come into port to be unloaded?'

Harry grinned.

'Yeah, well, that's what you'd think, isn't it?'

'I don't understand. What's going on?'

'You'll see,' he replied & gave the driver an address to take us to.

We pulled up in front of a line of ramshackle bars that were built haphazardly between two large warehouses.

'Come on Teddy. There's someone I want you to meet.'

We got out & walked over to one of the fearsome-looking drinking dens. *Highlife Bar*, was garishly daubed in red paint over the entrance. The place was full of white merchant seamen, drinking noisily in groups. A few black men stood at the bar talking intently, staring sidelong at us as we walked in. Some tartily dressed Nigerian girls at a table in the corner looking bored. Harry nodded at the barkeeper, who looked up & cocked his head at a room in the back whilst polishing glasses & lining them along the counter.

A beaded curtain clattered gently as we went through into a grubby little room with a dirt floor. A swarthy-looking man was seated at a table drinking beer. He stood up and greeted Harry. The barkeeper came through with a bottle of cheap brandy & three glasses. He set them up on the table & Harry handed him a few notes. Harry poured us all drinks. He introduced us. His name is Rico.

'Salud,' he said, lifting his glass & draining it in one.

'Rico is the captain of one of the ships out there,' Harry explained. 'It didn't take me long to find our precious cement. And why it's still here and not in Enugu. Thanks to our friend here. Rico, why don't you tell Teddy what you told me?'

Rico nodded as Harry poured him another drink.

'Is simple.' Rico shrugged, taking a sip of brandy. 'We bring cement from Cadiz. This man he say bring it here to Lagos. He say bring but not unload. Stay in Lagos harbour for a month or so then take it back.'

'I don't understand,' I said.

'We make more money waiting in the harbour than we would by unloading. This man say there is problem with import licence. He probably sell licence to someone else. So is not possible to put into dock. Instead, we wait. Come ashore, have a few drinks, have fun with local putas. Then we go home.'

'I still don't understand. How can you make more money by not unloading the stuff?'

Rico laughed, showing a blackened front tooth.

'No comprende? Is old trick. Demurrage clause.'

'Demurrage clause?'

Rico explained it all in broken English. An agent for a company procures cement for a fixed price. The cement arrives at port but waits offshore & is never actually unloaded. The company issuing the purchase order is then liable for payment for all the time that the ships have been waiting to discharge their goods. This is the demurrage clause in the contract, a common procedure in shipping. If they wait long enough they end up getting more money than if they had actually delivered the stuff. Then they can sail off with the cement & sell it somewhere else. And the agent gets to keep the money from the original purchase order.

'You've got to admit, Teddy,' Harry commented, 'it's a brilliant racket.'

'Well yes,' I agreed. 'But in this case we're the ones that have been, how would you say? Had over.'

'Yeah. And we ain't the only ones. Are we Rico?'

Rico frowned.

'At first,' he said, 'I think, the longer we wait the more we get out of the deal. But then I hear nothing. My men are sick and tired of waiting around. They get drunk, get into trouble and I start to worry. I think maybe this agent man, he not honour his agreement.'

They started to talk more intently, their faces up close. I found myself being ignored. I took a sip of the brandy in front of me & winced. It was foul but I was glad to have something alcoholic to comfort myself with. Harry and Rico spoke softly, almost lovingly, of vengeance. This was what I'd feared most. I poured myself another glass of the vile spirit.

I looked towards Rico. Tattoos, scars, strong-looking oil-stained hands. He looked as capable of violence as I knew Harry to be. I couldn't quite follow what they were saying. Harry was giving brusque instructions quietly to Rico with a solemn grin on his face. Finally they leant back from each other & finished their drinks.

'Right,' said Harry as he got up from the table. 'Phone me at the hotel when you know. Come on, Teddy.'

We went back through the main part of the bar. An argument had started between a merchant seaman & one of the Nigerians. A glass was broken. We hurried out into the hot muggy night.

It was getting dark. On the waterfront we could see the lights of the cement ships out in the bay. Black water lapped against the sea wall. The sky was streaked with purple clouds. We stood in a pool of yellow light from a streetlamp on the quayside. Above us huge moths battered against its sickly glow. A whiff of sewage & gasoline hung in the humid air.

'You can always find what you want down at the docks,' said Harry.

'Harry . . . What on earth is going on?'

'We're going to sort out our business problems, that's all.'

'Wouldn't it be better to inform the authorities?'

Harry laughed.

'You've got to be joking.'

'I could try pulling a few strings with the Consulate.'

'It's too late for that. Look Teddy. You've got to trust me. All right? Don't you worry, we'll sort this out. Then we can fuck off home.'

'I'm not sure.'

'We've got to stick together. We're on our own out here. Sorry I knocked you about.'

He patted the cheek he had slapped. I sighed.

'That's all right, Harry. You're forgiven.'

And it was true. I bore him no malice. I just felt a sickening fear & a desperate longing to go home. Harry smiled at me.

'Thanks Teddy.'

He pulled me to him & hugged me. As he slapped me on the back I felt something hard digging into my stomach.

'What's that?' I asked.

'What?'

Harry pulled away from me, frowning.

'That.'

I tapped gently at his stomach with dread. Harry grinned & opened his jacket to reveal the butt of a pistol lodged in the waistband of his trousers.

'I told you, you can always find what you want down at the docks. I found something else, too.'

I closed my eyes & shook my head.

'Oh, God,' I muttered to myself.

'Cheer up, Teddy. Come on. I've got something else to show you.'

He led me to another bar. It was full of uniformed sailors & young black boys. There seemed to be a few women as well but on closer inspection this proved not the case. On a small stage a drag act was miming to some torch song.

'Come on.' Harry cocked his head at me as I hesitated at the doorway. 'The fleet's in town. Let's enjoy ourselves.'

Harry seemed to be indulging his own recklessness to the limit. Like my own predilection for gambling, I suppose. *Faites vos jeux*. I didn't have much choice but to go along with it. For the time being, anyway.

Drank a good deal though I didn't really feel the effect. My mind was racing too fast. We chatted with the sailors. Harry animated, laughing & joking with them. Making all sorts of suggestions. He persuaded a couple of them to come back to our hotel with us for a nightcap. We found our driver & went back to the Excelsior.

We went to my room & Harry produced a bottle of brandy. We had a few drinks together then Harry paired off with one of the sailor boys, gently leading him out of the room & along the corridor. I heard them giggling softly, like children.

The remaining jack sat on the bed looking languidly up at me, a cigarette drooping out of the corner of his mouth. I must confess, of all the services, I've always rather had a thing for sailors. Guardsmen are always greedy, asking for more money & threatening to turn nasty. But there's an almost innocent generosity about sailors. Perhaps it's just that the short bursts of shore leave mean that they've got plenty of money & vigour & very little time to spend either. There's something wild & abandoned about them, maybe something about being away at sea for so long that frees them from dreary landlocked virtues. And the uniform. Especially the trousers. The way that they taper up from loose bell bottoms into the tight crotch with its exquisite buttoned fly flap. Undoing this quaint device, seemingly designed for the very purpose of slicklegging, produces such a frisson of pleasure in itself. I rubbed the boy off as he lay back on the bed and groaned listlessly. I couldn't get a hard on myself. I was still too anxious & the booze hadn't helped. So I just watched as he went into little spasms of delight from my ministrations.

Went into the bathroom & washed my hands. Splashed some cold water in my face & looked up into the mirror. Puffy features staring incredulously back at me. I dried them on the towel & went back into the bedroom. The sailor had rolled over on the bed & was already snoring in a deep slumber.

Sat on the edge of my bed for a long time, trying to think everything through. I could hear Harry and his boy in the next room. I fished out the piece of paper from my jacket pocket & picked up the telephone.

Saturday, 26 June

Woke up this morning & the sailor had gone. Dreadful hangover & the heat oppressive. Harry insisted that we wait so I had some tea & a copy of *The International Herald Tribune* brought to my room.

Spent hours sitting on the bed sipping luke-warm tea & gazing at the paper. Not able to focus on anything for long. I was going out of my mind.

Finally Harry came into my room full of grim purpose.

'Right,' he ordered. 'It's the off. Let's get going.'

'Do I really have to come as well?'

'Of course. We've got to stick together.'

We went downstairs & Harry waved to our driver. Obviously being kept on a retainer. Harry had planned everything with his usual precision. But I don't think he noticed as we pulled away from the hotel that we were being followed.

We picked up Rico from a quayside then drove around the harbour crossing over to an island across a huge bridge.

'Where are we going?' I asked, nervously checking behind to see that we were still being tailed.

'We've found Ogungbe,' Harry replied.

'We make him give us our money,' Rico added darkly.

'Yeah,' Harry growled & stroked the gun in his waistband.

'Harry,' I croaked. 'I cannot abide violence. I'm just no good at that sort of thing.'

'Don't worry,' Harry said. 'We'll deal with that side of things.'

'But there's no need for me to come along. I'll only be a liability.'

'Oh no, Teddy. We need you. You see, me and Rico here, we'll do the hard stuff. We need you to do the soft stuff. Quiet persuasion combined with a lot of menace. Never fails.'

I was suddenly overcome with a surge of nausea. I wound down the window & puked onto the dusty tarmac. The driver sucked his teeth audibly. Harry patted me on the back.

'Yeah,' he said encouragingly. 'Better out than in.'

I turned my head to see that we were still being tailed by the car that followed us from the hotel. A hot wind flowed over the back of my head. I puked again. Only bile came up. I'd hardly eaten in the last twenty-four hours. My stomach groaned but I felt an odd sense of calm. Everything that was happening was now completely out of my control. All the danger that surrounded me was just some horrible gamble. Nothing was predictable. As I watched a line of nondescript office blocks file backwards in my field of vision I realised that this is how we travel. Looking backwards. Seeing what has just passed.

'Teddy,' Harry called to me. 'Are you all right?'

I slumped back into the car seat & wiped my mouth with a handkerchief.

'Yes. Just getting some air.'

We pulled up in front of a low-rise whitewashed concrete flatblock. Thought I recognised the design of the dwellings and wondered why. Then I realised that it was the same architecture on the plans for the residential part of the Enugu scheme.

Rico pointed out a flat.

'Are you sure that's the right number?' asked Harry.

Rico nodded. Harry leant forward & gave some instructions to the driver. Then he sat back in his seat & all was still for a while. Harry closed his eyes for a couple of seconds. His face became very calm, he breathed deeply a couple of times. Then his heavy lids slitted open. His jaw clenched and his mouth tightened. His face had become a mask.

'Let's go!' he hissed sharply.

All at once we moved quickly out of the motor car. Onto the street. We looked ridiculously conspicuous but Harry led us swiftly up to a doorway & banged heavily against it. Five seconds & then he banged again, harder. A few curious black faces gazed up from the street. Harry took a couple of steps backward & charged at the door, forcing it open with his shoulder. He rushed in & we followed. A half-dressed Ogungbe was trying to scramble out of a window at the back of the flat. Harry grabbed him & dragged him across the room.

'Not so fucking fast, Sambo!' he shouted.

He was using his fists on him now & kicking him into a ball of submission on the floor in front of us. Harry grabbed a chair and planted it in the middle of the room. He pulled out a few lengths of rope from his pockets & handed them to Rico.

'Tie him to the chair,' he ordered.

Rico pulled Ogungbe off the floor, seated him & proceeded to bind him in place. Harry rubbed at his skinned knuckles thoughtfully. He nodded at Rico who started to slap Ogungbe's face.

'Hijo de puta! You fuck me with your fucking demurrage clause!' he shouted.

Ogungbe's head twisted from side to side, trying vainly to avoid the blows. Rico stopped & looked towards Harry who nodded slowly. Ogungbe's screwed-up face loosened a little. Harry waited until he opened his eyes then he pulled out the gun, worked the action on it & then pointed it at the end of Ogungbe's nose. His yellowy eyes widened and went cross eyed towards the barrel.

'I say we kill this little bastard now,' he said coldly.

'No, please,' Ogungbe begged.

'Shut up!' he snapped.

He drew the pistol down Ogungbe's face. Forcing it against the lower lip he shoved it into his mouth. Ogungbe shut his eyes, his face trembling, sweat pouring down his brow. A muffled sound came from the back of his throat. Harry turned around & smiled at me. With his free hand he beckoned me over and nodded. *Your turn.*

I gently extricated the gun from Ogungbe's mouth & rubbed his bruised face.

'Now, now,' I said. 'There's no need for all this, is there?'

Ogungbe started breathing heavily.

'W-w-what do you want?'

Harry clouted him on the ear with the pistol. Ogungbe shrieked. He looked up at me plaintively.

'Make them stop,' he sobbed.

'Now, be reasonable John. They're very upset. And understandably so.'

Rico punched him in the stomach & he collapsed, groaning horribly, held up in the chair by his bonds. I somehow felt terribly calm amidst this violence. I had a part to play. I had to reason with him.

'Now John,' I continued softly. 'You owe these gentlemen money. It's only fair to expect that they want it back. Isn't it?'

Ogungbe's body started to shake. At first I thought that he was having some sort of a fit. He was panting like a dog. Then he lifted his head & we could see he was laughing.

'What's so fucking funny?' Harry demanded, moving towards him.

I held him back. I smiled at Ogungbe & cleared my throat.

'My friends here don't quite get the joke, Ogungbe. Maybe you'd like to explain it all.'

'Your friends thought that they could make plenty money out of stupid Africans. Think we're dumb natives. My country is a land of negative miracles. So rich in resources that are stolen from us and then sold back at a profit. We've learnt well from our colonial masters, our imperial gangsters.'

'Well, that's a fine speech, Ogungbe. But it doesn't really help. You see, we invested money in your scheme in good faith.'

'You wanted a quick profit from crooked money.'

Harry raised the gun again, pointing it at Ogungbe's temple.

'That's enough fannying around. Give us our cash back or I'll blow your fucking head off.'

Ogungbe flinched. I cleared my throat.

'I would suggest that you comply with my friend's demands,' I implored.

Suddenly there was the sound of people coming in through the broken front door. Everyone swung around. Three men in khaki fatigues rushed into the room with service revolvers drawn.

'Hold still, everybody!' the leading one shouted.

He waved his revolver at Harry.

'You! Drop your weapon!'

Harry let the pistol fall to the ground.

'Police?' he asked.

'Na so police. At all. We soza.'

Ogungbe laughed.

'Behold our country's glorious armed forces, gentlemen.'

The leader of the soldiers came forward and slapped Ogungbe hard.

'Shut up! You not get mouth. No more palaver from you. You think you clever. Go to England college. Learn big big grammar. Well, I go England college too. Sandhurst. Learn big big grammar too. Maintain military discipline at all times. Implement counter-insurgency tactics. And so on. We learn order. This country is a mess. Tiefman taking over everywhere. Chopping big big bribe from everyone. People like you. Soon soza take over. Restore order.'

'Thank you, lieutenant,' a voice came from out of the room.

Dr Chukwurah entered. He looked around the room, nodding.

'Well,' he said, smiling. 'Here we all are.'

He lit a cigarette & nodded over at me.

'Thank you for leading us to Ogungbe. I don't think we would have found him so quickly without you.'

Harry frowned at me.

'You?'

I shrugged back.

'So, we'll take over from here. You'll be escorted to the airport and put on the next flight home.'

'What about our fucking money?' Harry demanded.

Chukwurah took a sharp draw from his cigarette.

'You have caused quite enough trouble in our country already. And broken many of its laws. I'm sure that you've seen enough of our penal system not to want to hang around and face the consequences. All the assets of Ogungbe's little scheme will be confiscated by the proper authorities. Believe me, he's tried to embezzle as much from the government grant I secured for him.'

Chukwurah walked up to Ogungbe, flicking ash at him.

'You have a big eye, Ogungbe,' he said. 'And a long throat. But ambition and greed have got the better of you.'

He stubbed the cigarette out in Ogungbe's face. There was an awful scream. Chukwurah turned his head. He glared at us.

'Now, fuck off back to your own country,' he said.

Sunday, 27 June

Lagos Airport, 3 a.m. Long wait for the next flight home. Harry v. sullen. Dreams of his little empire, his place in the sun, all gone. Me v. relieved to be finally getting out of this god-forsaken place.

Yesterday, as we were being escorted back to our hotel to pick up our belongings, Rico was dropped off at the dockside. We looked out at the ships for the last time. Rico pointed out one that was listing badly in the water. He became agitated, cursing loudly in Spanish. They had been moored there for so long that moisture had got into the cement, solidifying it, adding more & more weight to the cargo. The ships were starting to sink.

3

Jack the Hat

Open the soap duckets. The chimney sweeps. Talk to the sword.
Shut up; you got a big mouth. Please help me up.
Henry . . . Max . . . come over. French-Canadian bean soup.
I want to pay, Larry. Let them leave me alone.

Dutch Schultz's last words

Soho Square. Park the cream and blue Mark II Zodiac and walk around to The Flamingo on Wardour Street. Mod club. Spade music blaring out below the pavement. R&B. Soul, they call it. Tip some hat brim at the doorman and slip him a note with a sly grin. In. Downstairs. Check the bag in the inside suit pocket. Pills. All kinds. Purple hearts, french blues, nigger minstrels, black bombers. Enough to keep all those mod boys and girls dancing all night to that spade music. Uppers, leapers, they call them. And sure enough there they all are leaping around on the dancefloor. Doing The Monkey or The Hitchhiker or whatever. But this mod thing is changing. Hair getting longer, clothes getting more lairy. Still a demand for the pills, though. That's the important thing. Keep some of the black bombers for myself. Keep me going. Keep me together.

New record starts. Needle scratch static. Engine noise. Rat-tat-tat gunfire. Car tyres squealing. Crash. A lairy spade voice mouths off. AL CAPONE'S GUNS DON'T ARGUE. Then this funny old beat starts jumping along with horns wailing over the top like sirens. All the mod boys and girls jerk about like spastics. Cagney moves. Shoulders shrugging, fingers pointing two-gun style. This ain't soul. This is something else. Funny rhythm, moving on an up beat like. The kids kind of stomp around to it. What the fuck is this? What have the spades gone and come up with now? No singing, just this Jamaican coon going *chicka, chicka, chicka*. And fannying on like he reckons he's a bit tasty. DON'T CALL ME SCARFACE. MY NAME IS CAPONE. C.A.P.O.N.E. CAPONE. Silly cunt. But it's catchy. *Chicka, chicka, chicka, chicka a boom a chicka*. Picks up on that black bomber buzz I've got inside. I do a little waddle myself as I cross over to the bar. A bird on the dancefloor checks the hat and grins. I dance around her a bit and give her the old leer.

Get to the bar and order a bacardi and Coke. Lean back and take it all in, pushing the hat back from my brow. Slow number now and suddenly all the young things find a partner and sway about a bit, the blokes grabbing at these tarts' arses as they stagger about the floor. Slow, mournful church-organ chords as a spade sings when a man loves a woman, she can do no wrong. Now this is soul. It's like some sort of hymn except this blackie's talking about love and all the trouble it brings. And I kind of well up. As if I've got anything to feel sentimental about. Maybe it's guilt thinking about what a bastard I've been with birds. Madge. That horrible accident in the motor. Shudder and remind myself it *was* an accident. Christ's sake, Jack, pull it together. Maybe it's just the booze. And the black bombers.

'All right Jack?'

It's Beardsley come over and I give him the nod. He's wearing some crap light-blue seersucker. Cut far too tight on him. Kind of eye-tie look. He's still into the mod thing. If anything his hair's shorter than usual. I'm wearing my check serge number. I cut enough of a dash with this crowd, I reckon. Could teach them a thing about dancing too. I wander over to the gents for the drop and expect him to follow in a decent enough interval.

Run some cold water in the basin and take off the hat to splash some in my face. It's steaming hot in this dive or is it just me? Check the mirror. Count the wisps of hair on top. Bald. No two ways about it. Bald. Old Jack is bald as a coot. Fucking joke. All these kids growing their hair long just as I'm losing mine. Diabolical. Put the hat back on. Get the angle right. Become the Hat. Jack the Hat.

Beardsley's here by now and I pass over the bag of pills and he hands me a wad. Slip it in the suit without checking.

'Might be a while before I get more of these.'

Beardsley shrugs and downs a couple of blues himself. I make to leave.

'Jack.'

Beardsley whispers. Serious.

'What?'

'I want a shooter.'

I make a face. Wide boy mod acting tough.

'You don't want a shooter.'

'Get me a gun, Jack,' he insists, folding another wad into my top pocket. I shrug, give him a pat on the cheek and push the notes down since they don't match the tie.

'All right.'

I get out of there pushing my way past all the jigging kids giving a few Cagney shrugs for good measure. Go round to The Stardust. Mad Harry's club. More my scene really. Not many people about. A few second-rate faces. Matt Munro on the jukebox.

Someone gives me the nod. Gets me a drink. Respect. I like that. Some wankers think I've lost it. But I'm still there. Jack the Hat. I down another bomber with bacardi surreptitious like, and there's Harry.

Grins as he sees me. Scar crease criss-cross smile lines.

Chicka, chicka, chicka.

DON'T CALL ME SCAR FACE.

'Jack, you lairy bastard.'

'Who you calling lairy? You big poof.'

Harry laughs. *He* can take a joke. We go back. Dartmoor. Did time in the Moor together in the fifties. And in Exeter. Harry saw me deck that screw in the exercise yard. Knows I've got bottle.

'You want to watch that, Jack. People have been known to get topped for mouthing off like that.'

Cornell, he means. Common knowledge Fat Ron topped George Cornell. Went a bit moody over a snide remark.

RONNIE KRAY'S GUNS DON'T ARGUE. DON'T CALL ME FAT POOF.

'Fat Ron's got no sense of humour.'

Harry laughs.

'Well, he is a bit touchy. You want to watch yourself there.'

'The Twins don't scare me.'

Harry knows I'm off their firm for the time being. Glad to be out of it, to tell the truth. Don't fancy being one of their cronies on a twenty-five quid a week pension, doing their dirty work. Fuck that. I'm a freelancer. That's me.

'Just don't push your luck.'

Chicka, chicka, chicka.

'I ain't afraid of nobody.'

Reach into my suit pocket for a bomber, pull out a bit of lint.

'Sure, Jack. Fancy a drink?'

Harry's got some sort of a proposition, I can tell. We grab a table and I wait for the spiel.

'Still pushing pills?'

Shrug.

'It's a living.'

'Well I've got something lined up. Need a bit of muscle.'

Nod and grin. A job. I'm your man.

'What?'

'The Airport.'

'Heathrow?'

Harry gives this Jewboy shrug.

'Heathrow, Thiefrow, whatever. The Richardsons out of the picture. It's up for grabs.'

The South London mob used to run the Airport. Now they're all sent down after that stupid gunfight in Catford. Charlie and Eddie Richardson, Roy Hall, Tommy Clark and Frankie Fraser. Best of that firm all wiped up. Shame about Frankie. He was in the Moor and all. Chinned the governor for the kicking I got after the exercise-yard business. But Harry's right. They're out of the picture for now. Only one problem. The Other Two.

'The fucking Krays will want to move in.'

'Eventually. We could muscle in for a while though.'

Chicka, chicka, chicka. I give him a big lairy grin. Fuck the Twins.

'Look,' says Harry, reading my wicked mind. 'All I want to do is make a bit of easy gelt then fuck off out of it. I don't want to mess with the Twins if I can help it.'

'Those freaks don't bother me.'

'Jack, for fuck's sake, take it easy. Don't get involved in anything that's not necessary. All we got to do is put the frighteners on some bent car-park attendants and baggage handlers for a while, then we're away.'

Sounds reasonable. Harry's known for his powers of persuasion.

'I want some cash to put into legitimate business. The club could do with some capital and all.'

The Stardust is half empty. A band starts up. Some geezer crooning Burt Bacharach over chintzy electric organ. Easy listening. A few bacardis had taken the edge off the black bomber buzz so I can relax into it. No mad chicka, chicka, chicka beat in my head no more. Grab some nosh. Chicken in a basket. Harry's not happy.

'Look at this. This place is fucking dead.'

Shrug. Breadcrumb-coated skin caught in my teeth.

'I need to get some class acts on in here. Get the punters in.'

Suck grease off fingers.

'You could turn it into a strip club.'

Harry wrinkles his nose.

'That's the way Soho's going Harry. Either that or like a mod club or something. If you ask me, a strip club is where the money is. And porn. Real money to be made there.'

Harry looks pained.

'Jack, this is my club. I want it to be a place where I'd like to go. I want it to be a bit classy like.'

'Well, the punters want filth. Especially porn. Ship it in bulk from Scandinavia and sell it at a mad profit. Need to pay off the Dirty Squad of course.'

Harry's ignoring me so I drop it. No point saying wake up, this is fucking Soho we're on about. He's off on some showbusiness dream.

'I need to get some proper cabaret on here. Big-name draws.'

Nod. Yeah Harry, sure.

'I was thinking Dorothy Squires. She's got a residency up at The Tempo on Highbury Corner. You know it? Freddie Bird's club.'

Know it? I'm fucking barred from it. Got into a row. They were using Geordies as doormen. Fucking northerners coming down here doing what they please. I was pissed of course. And pilled.

'I was thinking of going over and checking her out tomorrow night. Fancy coming?'

'Yeah, sure,' I says.

No one bars Jack the Hat.

Few more drinks. The bacardi takes the edge off it all. The club closes. One or two faces left sitting around the table. Couple of tarts. Catch up on the chat. Tony the Greek's fucked off back to Finsbury Park. Bought a restaurant. Gone straight. Big Jock McCluskey's away on a two stretch. Receiving. Jimmy Murphy's disappeared. Common knowledge he had Harry over on a long firm. Diplomatic shrugs all round. Maybe he's propping up the brand-new Westway flyover. No body, no case, though. And nobody sure where the body is. Where the nobody is. Like Ginger Marks. Shot in Cheshire Street then bundled into a motor and spirited away. Only a few spots of blood, his glasses and a couple of cartridge cases left on the street. No body. Should have used a revolver, though. Automatics leave too much forensic.

Harry's making a fuss over some pretty blond boy. Mouthing off showbiz gossip. Friends in high places. Stroking his leg under the table. Feel randy myself. One of the tarts is still working so I leave with her.

Back at her seedy little flat. On with the gas fire. Thump. Give her a bit of a feel standing up as she takes off her clothes. Pushes me away and gets into bed. I get my clothes off and come around the other side. Fucking freezing.

'You going to wear that in bed?' Her screechy voice.

Still got the hat on. Take it off and spin it chairwards. Hits the floor. Bald head showing. Supposed to be a sign of virility. No such luck. All the pills and the booze. Can't get it up. Can't.

Suddenly feel awful. Need to hold on to her. Jaw all clenched. Sobbing gently. Face in her tits. There, there. Touches my neck. Been there before. Another useless punter. Poor Jack. There, there. No hair to stroke so she pats my bald head. No Jack the Lad tonight. No chicka boom a chicka. Can't get it up. Can't. Oh God. Hold on to this tart. Think of Madge. How I pushed her away. How I pushed her out of the car door.

Can't sleep. Tart rolls over and starts to snore. Long lonely night. Cold grey morning. Get up, get dressed. Check the hat in the mirror. Straighten tie. Top pocket wad. Thirty notes. Beardsley. What's that toe-rag want a gun for? Take out five and put them on the bedside table next to an old packet of Durex.

Get out and retrieve the motor. Drive around a bit. Buy a paper. Find a caff. Fry-up breakfast. Place full of workers stoking up for the daily grind. Splat ketchup over snotty egg. Then use sauce bottle to prop up *Daily Mirror*. Headline: CUT-UP BODY FOUND DUMPED IN 2 SUITCASES. *Yard men in hunt for boy's killer. The naked torso of a youth was found in a battered suitcase yesterday. Nearby was another suitcase, containing the limbs*. Eat as much as I can stomach. Speed comedown. Misery.

Drive home. Vodka mouthwash. Collapse into bed. Wake up and it's already starting to get dark again. Four o'clock. Feel like death.

Take a couple of bombers and pick up a bit. Yeah. Have a bath. Shave. Watch a bit of telly. Find a half-clean shirt and give it an iron. No clean underwear so I put on a pair of swimming trunks instead. Dab the suit down a bit. Get ready. *Chicka, chicka, chicka*. Get suited and booted.

Phone Harry. Arrange to meet him in The Mildmay Tavern on Ball's Pond Road. Have a few before going on to The Tempo. Barred? What a joke. Ready to go. Down a couple more bombers just to be on the safe side.

Get to the pub about eight thirty. Harry's there. And Jimmy Briggs and Patsy Murphy. And one of the Lambrianou brothers. Tony.

'Tony's just got out of the boob,' Patsy says.

Been in Bristol Prison. Slip him a few notes. The done thing.

'Anything I can do for you?' I say.

Harry's keeping shtum about the Airport which is just as well because the Lambrianous are getting well in with the Twins. Word is they're being courted by the Other Two. I fanny on about helping Charlie Wilson escape from Winson Green.

Get to The Tempo mob-handed and a bit tanked up. Bother on the door. Some fucking Geordies in monkey suits don't want to let me in. Freddie comes out.

'Look,' he says all reasonable and shit. 'We don't want any trouble from Jack.'

Harry intervenes. One club owner to another like.

'It's all right, Freddie. He's with me. I'll look after him.'

Freddie lets me in grinning nervously. You know he's thinking about his fixtures and fittings. I put up with this shit and stroll in, unimpressed. Feel a bit wound up, to tell you the truth. Down a couple more bombers, chase them with a bacardi and Coke. That's better. Stay out of trouble, Jack. *Chicka, chicka, chicka*. Fuck them. The Tempo is all red walls and chairs sprayed gold. Trying to be classy, I suppose. All fur coat and no knickers if you ask me. At least the teenagers I push pills to know how to enjoy themselves. All this poncing about in dinner jackets. Don't impress me.

Me and Harry grab another drink and a table. Dorothy Squires has started her act. Short blond hair. Looks a bit washed out to tell the truth. Hoarse voice singing some sad song. She's past her best but she can still belt it out good and proper. Harry loves it. But then queers always seem to go for this sort of thing. Some washed-out old bint wailing on about what a mess they've got themselves into. Like old Judy Garland. Harry's a sucker for her and all.

Dorothy's taking swigs from a bottle between numbers. Pretending it's water, I suppose. It's obviously booze. Looks like she's had a few already. Harry looks a bit concerned. Unprofessional, he'd call it.

'She's pissed Jack,' he says a bit affronted.

'Maybe The Saint ain't giving it to her enough,' I reply.

You see Dot's married to Roger Moore who plays The Saint on the telly. Harry doesn't see the joke and goes to take a piss. Dorothy's beginning to slur her words. I feel the speed and the booze surge up inside me. Feel great. Poor old Dot looks fucked, and the crowd's getting a bit restless.

'Where's The Saint?' I shout.

Laughter. Then lots of shushing. Dorothy looks out blearily across the crowd, rotten drunk. *Chicka, chicka, chicka.* I can't stop myself.

'What's he like in bed then?' I shout over. 'The old Saint?'

Get a few laughs. A bit more shushing. Dorothy loses her rag.

'You mind your own business!' she yells, her voice thick with Welsh. 'He's a lot better'n you!'

Laughter. No more shushing. I'm part of the floorshow now.

'Come down here, darling!' I call back. 'We'll soon see!'

'I'll come down and have a fight with you!' she screams, her accent getting Welsher all the time.

More laughter. Everyone turns around to look at me. I stand up. The whole club does a bit of a spin around me. Faces everywhere. Looking at Jack. Jack the Hat.

'Come on then, darling!' I shout out.

I move forward. Knock over a chair and kick it out the way. A couple of doormen are coming over.

'All right, Geordie boy!' I call out to the biggest one. 'Me and Dorothy are just working on our double act.'

This thick northerner's grunting something in a stupid accent but no one can hear a thing because Dorothy's giving the whole place a mouthful.

'Fuck the lot of you!' she's screeching as she leaves the stage.

Game girl. I give her a clap and a cheer. The doormen are moving in but people are getting up and walking out. Lots of pushing and shoving. A ruck starts and the thick Geordie boys go off to deal with it. Booing and whistling from the back of the hall. Some prat of a compère in a crap shiny tuxedo announces the next act over the row. An exotic dancer. I move towards the stage. The row's been settled. The doormen are dragging someone out.

The dancer's music starts. Some mad Turkish racket. Drums going like crazy. *Boom ba di boom ba di boom ba di boom*. And this bird's on stage in a gold bikini shaking it all about. I'm jerking about to this wog rhythm going *chick, chick, chick* on the offbeat as I get nearer the front. Tits shaking along to the beat on stage. Hypnotic.

'Yeaaah!' I call out, showing my appreciation. 'Get them off, darling!'

The bird on stage ignores me. 'Sit down!' someone shouts and I ignore them. Everything's coming up in a mad rush. *Boom ba di boom ba di boom ba di boom. Chick, chick, chick, chick, chick*. I'm climbing onto the stage. What the fuck am I doing? I'm climbing on the fucking stage, that's what I'm fucking doing.

I'm moving about with her. Shaking it all about.

'Come on, darling,' I say to her.

'Fuck off!' she hisses back at me.

Charming.

Suddenly she stops shaking her tits about and walks off. Booing and whistling from the audience. People shouting for me to get off. Throwing things. A glass smashes on the stage. Look down at the sea of faces. Cunts. I'm not scared of you. I'd fucking take the lot of you on. The music's still going so I start dancing in front of all these nasty cunts. Take off the jacket and duck an ashtray. Have to do better than that. Loosen the tie, slip it off and whirl it about my head like a stripper's feather boa. Throw it into the crowd and start unbuttoning my shirt. I'll show this lot I've got bottle. I'll show you.

Take off my jacket and shirt in one go and people stop chucking things. Big cheer as I drop my trousers. I'm entertaining these bastards. A lot of laughter when they see the swimming trunks. Keep the hat on, of course, and dance about a bit to the music.

The Geordies are on stage with me now. One each side, moving in. Take a swing at one of them and down he goes, crashing into a table near the front of the stage. I turn and catch a punch from the other fucker on the side of my face. Stagger back. Manage to chin him with a hook as he comes forward. Follow with a cross and he's down too. Just about to kick the fucker when someone's got me from behind. Both my arms are pinned to my sides and I'm being dragged back.

'Jack! For fuck's sake!'

Harry.

He drags me backstage. Bundles me past the dressing rooms with his coat over my shoulders. The bird in the gold bikini is screeching filthy words at me. Dorothy's taking another swig from the bottle, tired, seen-it-all-before look on her face. Harry pushes me out through the stage door into the freezing night air.

'Come on you stupid cunt!' he says, holding on to my arm.

'Get your hands off me, you fucking poof!'

WHACK. Had that one coming, I guess. Get it right on the hooter and go down. I'm on my hands and knees in this filthy dog-piss back alley with Harry's steamy breath in front of me.

'Want me to leave you here?'

Wipe my nose with the back of my hand. Blood. It's fucking freezing out here and I'm bollock naked but for the overcoat and the swimming trunks. And the hat. Get up and brush myself down a bit. Straighten the trilby.

'I'm sorry, Harry.'

'Yeah, sure. Come on then.'

The stage door bangs open behind us. Shouting. Freddie Bird and the Geordies.

'You're fucking barred, Jack!'

He throws the rest of my clothes out after me. I gather them up.

'Don't fucking come back here!'

One of the Geordies mouths something unintelligible. And another voice, not northern, a London voice, not Freddie, don't know who it is, a whisper hisses in the piss-stained alley: 'You've got it coming to you, Jack the Hat.'

I snarl back.

'Leave it, Jack,' Harry whispers and off we go.

Harry's Jag is parked just around the corner so we go in that. I'm in no fit state to drive. I'll pick up the Zodiac tomorrow. We motor down Upper Street towards the Angel. Streetlights throbbing in my head. Feel like shit. Suddenly need to spew so I wind down the window and lean out. It all comes out. Try to aim at the gutter away from Harry's well-waxed paintwork.

The wind hits my face. Blow-drying the puke around my mouth. It hits me. I'm hanging out the window and it hits me. Madge. The moment I pushed her out of the car. Just gave her a shove. Didn't mean to push her out of the fucking motor. She was yacking on at me. Yacking on and on. Told her to shut up. To fuck off out of it if she felt like that. Gave her a push. I didn't know the door wasn't closed properly. I just meant to give her a shove. But I pushed her clean out of the car.

Remember the sound as she flew out and hit the tarmac. The wind rushing past. The thump of her body against the Great North Road. I didn't mean it. Honest. She's in the hospital. Broken spine. Going to be crippled. Worst thing is no one blames me. I know she won't grass. And nobody else will. No blame. An accident. Everyone agrees. Though everyone thinks I've done it deliberate. Little comments I hear behind my back. 'He chucked his last bird. Gave her the shove.' Big joke. Ha ha ha. No one says anything directly. No one blames me for it so I can never say that I didn't do it on purpose. Even though that's what they think, they never blame me for it. No one does. Except me.

I'm hanging out of Harry's motor. Streetlights screaming past my head. I think. Why not? Go on. Push yourself out. Get it over with, you useless slag. All the pills and the booze. Going bald, can't get it up any more. You're not a face, you're a fucking head case. Go on, get it over with. If you've got any bottle left at all, you'll do it.

I push the door handle down. The door swings open.

'What the fuck!' Harry shouts.

I'm holding on to the door for dear life. Can't let go. Haven't got the bottle. Car brakes screech and as it comes to a halt I get catapulted out backwards. Land on my arse in the gutter.

'What the fuck happened there?'

Harry's leaning through the passenger side to look down at me grabbing hold of the kerb.

'The door just opened, Harry.'

Harry shakes his head at me. Must look a state. Bloodied nose, dried puke round me chops, bruise swelling up where that Geordie thumped me, knuckles skinned where I decked them. There I am sitting on the kerb in swimming trunks and Harry's velvet-collared crombie. Fuck. The hat. Where's the fucking hat? I'm as bald as a cunt. Retrieve the trilby from the gutter, give it a bit of a brush and put it on.

'Come on, get in.'

Yellow streetlight blur. King's Cross. West End. Then Harry's flash Chelsea drum. Intercom buzzer then up in a poxy little lift, just a cage really. Door opened by blond boy Harry was feeling up in The Stardust the other night. Trevor. Harry's new houseboy? Looks at me a bit disgusted like. Get used to it, nancy boy.

Harry chucks me in the shower. Tosses me a poncey silk dressing gown. Trevor makes some coffee. Tie the robe and come through. Probably look a right woofter in this thing. Catch the mirror. Hammer horror. Bela Lugosi eyes, Uncle Fester hair.

Sit down on the sofa. Silk rides up on buttoned leather. Pull the gown down to cover my knees. Talk. Harry: What's it all about, Jack? Me: Madge. It all comes out. Spills out like puke. Tumbles out like Madge rolling out onto the Great North Road. And I really lose it. Boo hoo hoo. Blubbering away like a brat. Harry puts his hand on me shoulder.

'It's all right, Jack. Like you said, it was an accident.'

Sobbing nearly done. Sniffing up salt tears and tobacco phlegm.

'Come on,' he whispers, little pat on the arm. 'You can pull it together.'

Then Harry gives me this stare.

'We all done bad things, Jack,' he says coldly.

A chill shudder brings me out of it. Someone walking on my grave. *You've got it coming to you, Jack the Hat*. Harry's dead eyes. Nothing behind them. Look into them and think: he's topped people. He's seen it and it doesn't bother him. He can hurt without feeling. Use the fear without fearing it himself. He could kill you and the last thing you'd see is those dead eyes, staring at you, feeling nothing about it.

Then he snaps out of this look and grins.

I smile back. Harry's still got faith in me. And I need that faith. Someone who knows I've still got it. Somewhere.

'Sorry I called you a poof, Harry.'

Trevor looks over. Eyebrow arched. Harry laughs.

'Don't worry,' he says, shooting a grin at Trev. 'I ain't as touchy as Fat Ron. Now, get some kip. We got work tomorrow. You remember? The Airport.'

Wake up midday. Wash and shave in Harry's huge bathroom. Load of pills in the cabinet. Check a bottle. Stematol. Never heard of it. Wonder what Harry's on?

Trevor sorts me out a fry-up. He's sponged down the suit and given it a press. Harry's onto a good thing. Better than any bird. Borrow a shirt from Harry's triple-figure collection. Check myself out in the full-length mirror. Get the hat. A bit crumpled so I knock some shape into it. Harry comes in. He's wearing a sports jacket, open-necked shirt.

'You ready?' he asks.

I pull a bit of trilby brim down.

'Yeah.'

Harry in the mirror frowning.

'No one wears hats any more, Jack.'

'Well, that's because no one's got no style no more.'

And I ain't got no hair no more.

'You look like a fucking movie gangster.'

'Well.' Cagney shrug, catch my stupid grin in the mirror.

'Well, come on. We're only going for a shufti.'

Lift cage down to the entrance hall.

'Now look, Jack.' Harry's voice all soft and serious. 'You've got to cut down on the booze. And all those fucking pills.'

'I can handle them. I just got a bit lairy last night, that's all.'

Harry's not buying it.

'Oh, come on Jack.'

'Yeah. Well. What about you? What are all those things in your bathroom then?'

'What things?'

'You know, all them pills of yours.'

Harry's face suddenly goes fierce. Eyes narrow, nostrils widen.

'They're anti-depressants, Jack.'

Deep voice angry but not at me. Matter of fact.

'I need them.'

Harry's famous black moods and crazy outbursts. Not just called Mad Harry because of his reckless skill at violence. Winchester Jail crack-up in '59. Screws think he's working a cushy number to do his time in. Even his own mum thought he was playing up for a change of scene when she visits. Prison shrink tells it different. It's for real. Harry certified. Long Grove Mental Hospital, strait-jacket, the lot. Terror of madness and the authorities denying a definite release date. If you're a loony they can lock you up for good. He gets better and gets out but madness still haunts him.

Lift gate swishes open. Brass trellis shh like relief. Out into the street. Grey afternoon. We get into Harry's gleaming black Jag. Trevor's obviously waxed off the puke from last night. Tan leather upholstery. Lovely motor. Purrs into life.

Go west. Acton, Chiswick, get on to the Great West Road. A VC10 screams overhead, tail lights blinking through the gloom. Coming in to land.

'Thiefrow,' Harry announces as the Airport's control tower comes into sight.

And so it was. There were two main rackets. The car park, where the attendants were helping themselves to a considerable percentage of the takings. Given the amount of motors in and out of that place it was quite a wad. Then there were the crooked baggage handlers. Theft of valuables in transit. The best thing about this was that valuable items of cargo were specially tagged. For security reasons! Might as well slap on a label saying PLEASE STEAL ME. And who were the guardians of law and order amidst all the arrivals and departures? The British Airports Authority Police. Second-rate plod if ever there was. Might as well have had the Royal Botanical Constabulary at Kew Gardens minding it. Didn't even have to pay them off they were that stupid.

Now Harry wasn't planning to do any of the thieving himself. Oh no. He worked in what he would describe as a 'managerial capacity'. A thieves' ponce, more bluntly put. He would rob the robbers. Take his share of the rackets in return for protection and security. A certain amount of persuasion might be needed in negotiating this arrangement. The mugs hard at work nicking might not want to cough up at first. But this was where a villain like Harry came into his own. His well-known powers of persuasion could be brought to bear. Apply a bit of pressure. Be brutal if necessary. Scare the fuckers. Use the fear. And Harry had a real talent in putting the frighteners on. It was all 'psychological', he insisted. I don't know about that. It's diabolical, that's for sure. Harry definitely has a diabolical mind.

So we're wandering about the airport, having a general shufti, clocking faces, checking out how things run. We walk up to the big Departures and Arrivals board. Foreign names clattering into place like some mechanical card sharp shuffling a deck and dealing a hand. PARIS, MILAN, CAIRO. And Harry's looking up at it all wide eyed.

'Amazing, how it does that,' I say, trying to break him out the trance.

'Yeah,' he replies all vague like.

Then I realise it's all those far-off places that are mesmerising Harry. Like he's thinking of doing a bunk or something.

'Imagine,' he starts saying, 'you've made enough of a wad to just step on a plane and fuck off for ever. Disappear.'

I give him a shrug.

'I don't know. Don't know if I fancy that train-robber lifestyle. I'd miss getting a good cup of tea.'

Harry winces and heaves a big sigh.

'Oh, Jack.'

As we walk back to the car park Harry starts talking up our plan of action.

'We need to get another body. No one who's connected to any firm. No one who's being courted by any firm. Preferably no one that's known at all. Any ideas?'

'Well you know me, Harry. I'm a freelancer. But everyone knows me.'

'Yeah, but I don't want anyone to get to hear about what we're doing.'

I grin at him.

'Especially you-know-who.'

'Yeah, especially them.'

Fuck the Twins, I think, but I don't want to rile Harry.

'So,' he says. 'Give it some thought, eh?'

'Yeah, I'll give it some thought.'

We get in the motor and drive up to the kiosk. Harry winds the window down and, as a hand comes down to take the ticket, Harry very deliberately crumples it up and tosses it at the attendant.

'Tell Mr Charles we're going to pay him a visit,' he says, staring hard at this berk.

The berk looks worried. He knows.

'All right?' Harry sing-song with menacing grin.

Berk nodding furiously. Harry nods at the barrier.

'Now, put that fucking thing up,' he commands and we screech off.

Harry drives me up to Highbury Corner to pick up the Zodiac. Says to come around the club later if I fancy it. Walk past the puke and piss-stained back alley of The Tempo club. Half memories of last night's lairyness. Retrieve the motor and head east along the Ball's Pond Road. Another body, I think. Someone unconnected. The Lambrianou brothers are being seriously courted by the Other Two. Who else? Get back home. My drum's a fucking filthy mess. Try and tidy up a bit but just end up throwing a few things into heaps. Need a bird to look after me. Someone like Madge. I can't stop myself fucking thinking about it. Take a slug of what's remained of the vodka bottle. Take a look at the *Evening News*.

SUITCASE MURDER: HOMOSEXUAL LINK. *Detectives investigating the body-in-the-suitcase murder now believe that there might have been a sexual motive behind the killing. The victim, who has been identified as 17-year-old Bernard Oliver from Muswell Hill, North London, was a prostitute who frequented various haunts in Soho used by known sexual offenders. Police are now following up leads in a thorough investigation that will turn a searchlight on the twilight world of homosexuals . . .*

Put the paper down. Think about something else. Someone who's not known. Suddenly think of Beardsley. Snotty-nosed, think-I'm-a-bit-tasty, get-me-a-shooter-Jack, Beardsley. Nah. Then I think, why not? He's a bit wet about the ears but he'd be a right little thug in his own way. Nothing special but he can handle himself. And he's not a known face except to all his mod mates. Bit of borstal form, no doubt. Could train him up. He could be my, like, apprentice.

Get something to eat. Fray Bentos meat pie, instant mash and tinned peas. Feel a bit sluggish after, so I take a few bombers. Think about it. Yeah. Beardsley, my little hooligan. Frightened of me though he tries hard not to let it show. Could be handy having someone else. My own little firm. Pace about. Bombers starting to work. Maybe he's down The Flamingo. Could go and suss him out. No time like the present.

Get in the Zodiac and bomb down to Soho. Tip the doorman at The Flamingo a note and go in. Wailing guitar music and funny-coloured inkblot lighting projected on the walls. Clothes seem even more lairy, hair even longer. Bastards. Like they're taking the piss out of old Jack. No Beardsley. See a likely looking mod type with his hair all brushed down over his face, nehru suit and granny-framed sunglasses. No lapels to grab hold of on his paki jacket so I take hold of the front of the coat and pull him towards me.

'Where's Beardsley?'

'He don't come down here no more.'

'So where is he? La Discotheque?'

'Nah. He ain't into this scene no more. He'll be down the Ram Jam.'

'Where the fuck's that?'

'Brixton.'

I get an address and get back to the motor. South London. Never like going over the water. Injun country, the East London firm always call it. And Brixton? Well, that's fucking jungle land. Take a couple more bombers and head way down south.

The Ram Jam is in a crumbling dancehall on Coldharbour Lane. Spade doormen look me up and down as I go in. Give them my best Jack the Lad grin and hand over a ten-bob note. Inside and it's that mad chicka chicka chicka music echoing around the peeling decor. Full of black kids jerking around to that funny old beat. A few whiteys too but they're all gathered in one corner like. It ain't exactly racial harmony but there are one or two white girls showing out to the better looking coons on the dancefloor.

I make my way over to the white corner. A new song starts. *Changa changa changa* it goes and I sort of slope along to it. WALKING DOWN THE ROAD WITH A PISTOL AT YOUR WAIST, JOHNNY YOU'RE TOO BAD – WHOA OH. Catch sight of Beardsley in the thick of it, checking out the floor, swaying along to the beat. *Changa changa changa*. Beardsley catches sight of me. Surprised grin then a nod in my direction. ONE OF THESE DAYS YOU'RE GONNA HEAR THEIR VOICES CALL, WHERE YOU GONNA RUN TO? – WHOA OH.

'Doctor Livingstone, I presume?' I shout in his ear and he frowns, not hearing or not getting the joke or both.

'What you doing down here, Jack?'

'What you think? Missionary work? I came down to see you, you berk. We need to talk.'

Beardsley nods. He's booted but not suited. A pair of steel toe caps, tight jeans held up with braces, button-down shirt with no tie, crombie coat and on top of it all, would you believe, a fucking hat. A stingy-brim trilby, no less. *No one wears hats any more, Jack.* Well this fucker does. It's either the new height of fashion or else old Beardsley is taking a leaf out of Jack's book, stylewise. I nod towards the exit and he follows me out.

Out on the street, I look him up and down. He looks like a Jamaican pimp.

'So what's up?' I ask. 'You turning black or something?'

He grins and shakes his head.

'Nah. All that mod stuff, they're turning into hairy fairies. At least the spades have got style.'

'And what's this?'

I make a grab at his pork-pie hat. It's in my hand leaving him bareheaded. Bareheaded's the word, because there's his shaved bonce beneath. Boneheaded like old Jack.

'Are you taking the piss out me?'

Beardsley chuckles. Dedicated follower of fashion. Looking like a rude boy with his cropped hair and long coat. Wanting a gun to go in the waistband to complete the look. Question is: would he be any good for real?

'So,' I start.

'The shooter? You got me the shooter?'

'That depends. First you got to prove you could handle it. If you think you're tough enough, I've got a proposition for you.'

'What sort of proposition?'

'Need a little extra muscle on a job.'

Beardsley grins. Evil little youth.

'Thing is,' I go on, 'I don't know if you're hard enough, do I? This ain't just a bank holiday beach fight.'

He gives me his best sneer. Then this big black fellah comes over.

'What you want? Weed? Speed? Black hash?'

I try to wave him away. He sucks at his teeth.

'Wh'appen, man? You don't want buy nothing? Then move. This is *my* pitch.'

Then it comes to me. Beardsley can prove himself right now. I smile at the black geezer and step back. I shove Beardsley in front of me.

'See him off, son,' I say.

Beardsley stumbles a bit from the push then shapes up in front of this guy, hard eyes, the lot. I'm not sure that he'll be able to deal with this loud-mouth coon but it's worth a try. I can always step in if he bottles out.

They move around each other on the kerb. Fierce eyeballing.

'Ras clat,' the black guy fannies.

But Beardsley's fast. Lively. He don't waste no words. A hand comes out of his overcoat pocket and lashes out. A Stanley knife comes from nowhere and slashes the black face with an upward backhand.

Nasty.

The black man's on his knees in the gutter clutching a bleeding cheek. Claret dripping all over the kerb. Beardsley follows through with his boots. Steel toe caps making contact with the bloke's rib cage. He's squealing away and the doormen of the Ram Jam hear the commotion and start to leg it over. I pull Beardsley back by his coat.

'That's enough, son,' I say. I've seen enough.

We make a dash for it, followed by a whole gang of spades. The Zodiac's parked on the corner of Electric Avenue and Atlantic Road. We jump in and tear away.

Drive back north. Over Albert Bridge. All lit up with fairy lights. Pretty. Nice to be back over the right side of the water. Out of Injun country. Up through Victoria, into the West End.

Get to The Stardust and we can't find Harry. He did say he'd be here. See Trevor sitting at a corner table. Waiting for H obviously. Get a couple of drinks and go over.

'Where's the guvnor?'

'He's upstairs in the office.'

'Right. I'll go up.'

Wink at Trev.

'You can keep each other amused,' I say, patting Beardsley on the back.

I go out to the foyer and start going up the steps. One of the doormen cocks a chin at me.

'All right?' he says, all cautious like.

'I'm going up to see Harry. He's expecting me.'

'Careful.'

His eyeballs roll upward.

'There's Old Bill up there.'

'Oh yeah?' I say, coming down a couple of steps to cock an ear. 'Anyone I know?'

'Mooney.'

That filth. Detective Inspector George Mooney. Remember him back in the fifities when he was just a Detective Constable in the Flying Squad. Liked to think he was tasty. Ex-Met light-heavyweight champion with a reputation for heavying into villains. Arresting officer for an armed blag I got pinched for. Tried to get me to name names. Do a trade. I told him to fuck off. Got a kicking in the cells and a three stretch for my trouble.

Then he made his name as a DS working out of West End Central. Number one fit-up merchant. Planting evidence and beating statements out of minor-league villains who haven't been keeping their payments up. Broke a Maltese racket back in 1962. Now he's OPS. Obscene Publications Squad. The Dirty Squad. Aptly named. Skimming off all the porn in Soho. Taking a percentage on all those smudges, yellow backs and rollers being touted down Old Compton Street. 'Licence fees' they called it.

Get to the landing and the office door is half open so I can hear the chat.

'So what's all this got to do with you, George? You're not Murder Squad.'

Harry.

'Yeah, but they reckon there's some sort of sexual angle. This lad, Oliver, he was a rent boy. So I've been seconded to their inquiries.'

'Your specialised knowledge?'

'Something like that.'

'So you're checking on all the homos?'

Mooney coughs. Embarrassed.

'Well, I can be very discreet in your case.'

'Don't bother. I ain't ashamed of nothing.'

'Yeah, well, they're checking on known homosexual offenders. And they asked me and the Dirty Squad to sniff around a few known haunts. Murder Squad are concentrating on a period of eleven days unaccounted for. Where and who this kid was with in that time.'

'So, what's this got to do with me?'

'Come on, Harry. Bernie Oliver was one of your boys. He's been known to attend some of your, er, parties.'

A pause. Harry coughs.

'So. I don't know nothing about what happened to him.'

'I don't care what you do or don't know. This is just a warning. Cover your tracks. You don't want to be implicated in any of this. It's bad for business. Speaking of which . . .'

'Yeah?'

'Well, I was wondering whether you'd be interested in expanding in the bookshop trade.'

'Depends on the competition. What about the Maltese?'

'Don't worry about them. They're still mostly running old-fashioned vice. You know, clip joints, prostitute flats. To be frank, I don't much like dealing with the spicks. The thing is, though, the porn racket's growing. But it's not organised. I'm having to deal with every Tom, Dick or Harry down Old Compton Street. It would be easier to have someone running the whole thing. Easier to regulate. To keep the lid on things.'

'And easier to collect off.'

'Yes. But you need to keep your nose clean. Cover your tracks on this Suitcase business. Make sure everyone connected to you keeps their head down. There's a big "searchlight on vice" operation going on to keep the papers happy. It'll soon blow over. Murder Squad aren't going to waste too much time on this one.'

'Unless they find the sick fucker what did it.'

Mooney coughs.

'Quite. So, think about it. Once this has all died down maybe we can do business.'

Sounds of Mooney getting up out of his chair. He comes out of the office. Nearly walks into me.

'Well, well,' he says, beady little eyes twitching at me. 'If it isn't Jack the Hat.'

I sort of grunt. Don't want to appear too rude. Not if Harry's planning to do business with him.

'Keeping out of trouble, Jack?'

'Yeah, yeah.' Give him a big cheesy grin. 'I'm a reformed character.'

Mooney laughs and shakes his head. Makes his way down the stairs. Cunt. I wander over and rap on the open door.

'Yeah?' Harry's voice weary.

I go in.

'Jack,' he sighs. 'You hear any of that?'

'Some of it, yeah. You thinking about moving into porn then?'

'Yeah. Maybe. I don't mean that. I mean this.'

He taps the *Evening News* lying on his desk. SUITCASE MURDER headline. I nod. Seen something about it myself somewhere.

'Yeah. I heard some of that.'

'Well keep it to yourself.'

Harry rubs at his face. Tired.

'Thing is, I did know the kid. Bernie. Poor little fucker. He was only seventeen, Jack.'

Only seventeen and cut up and turned into luggage. Sick. I frown. Think: Harry's not involved in all this, is he?

'So, Jack.' Harry stretches, yawns. 'What do you want?'

'It's what we want, Harry. And I got it.'

'Yeah, yeah, get to the point. I'm knackered.'

'Well, you know you said we needed another body for the Airport job?'

'Yeah.'

'Well, I've got someone. He's downstairs.'

'Good. I better come down then.'

I lead Harry over to where Beardsley and Trevor are sitting. They seem to be getting along. Beardsley's taken his hat off and let Trevor touch the fuzzy little pelt of his barnet. Trev's all wide eyed and giggling but he straightens up and looks serious as soon as he clocks Harry and me.

'There he is,' I mutter to Harry.

Harry frowns and talks though the side of his mouth to me.

'But he's just a kid, Jack.'

Bareheaded Beardsley does look younger than ever. Innocent even. I try to reassure Harry.

'He's all right. Honest. Got a right nasty streak in him. Can handle himself too.'

'You sure, Jack?'

'Yeah. Of course.'

'Well, I'm holding you responsible if anything goes wrong.'

Then we go over to the table. Introductions. Harry, Beardsley. Beardsley, Harry. Harry has this stern demeanour. This kind of quiet fierceness he puts on when he meets people. His I-mean-business look. Beardsley's impressed, tries to mirror it a bit himself.

'The crop looks great, doesn't it Harry?' Trevor pipes up.

'Yeah,' mutters Harry. 'Look Trevor, we've got some business to discuss so make yourself scarce.'

Trev wanders off in a bit of a huff and we get down to it. Plan to meet up next day and pay a visit to a certain car-park supervisor.

Next day. We take the Daimler over to an address in Brentford. I'm in the front, driving. Harry likes to be chauffeured on jobs like this. I don't mind. Lovely motor, handles beautifully. Harry's in the back with Beardsley explaining the scam, of how the car-park staff have been on the fiddle, manipulating the time clock mechanism of the ticket machines. Also, detailing how we're going to persuade them to hand over a percentage.

'Remember,' he says finally. 'I do the talking.'

We arrive in the middle of suburbia. Nice little semi-detached houses with well-trimmed hedges around them. Follow Harry up the garden path of one of them. Neatly mown front lawn. A gang of gnomes hanging around a stupid little fish pond.

Harry presses the bell. Ding dong. Avon calling. Sound of footsteps. Door opens a crack and Harry gives it an almighty shove just in case the bloke has second thoughts, and we pile into the hallway.

'Hello Charlie,' Harry announces with a big frightening grin.

Charlie's on his hands and knees. I close the front door behind us. Harry points at the door to the front room.

'Come on, Charlie,' he says. 'Show us through.'

He gives Charlie a kick up the arse and he crawls through into the lounge.

'What do you want?' Charlie sobs up at us.

'Now, that ain't very friendly, is it? Not very hospitable. You should say, "Make yourselves at home."'

'What?'

'I said,' Harry goes on very deliberate like, 'you should say, "Make yourselves at home."'

'Make yourselves at home,' Charlie whimpers.

'Well thanks, Charlie. We will and all.'

Harry gives us a nod and we grab the settee. Beardsley plonks his steel-toe-capped boots on the smoked-glass-topped coffee table.

Harry goes over to the bay window and peeps out through the net curtains.

'Nice neighbourhood, Charlie,' he says. 'What's a nasty little thief like you doing in a place like this?'

He starts to draw the chintzy curtains.

'Don't want to upset the neighbours, do we?'

The room darkens. A few shafts of daylight spread out across the wall-to-wall carpet. Harry turns around and looks down at Charlie crouched on the floor.

'Time to talk business, Charlie. A new business arrangement.'

'What do you mean?'

'You know what I mean. Our cut of all the money you've been filching from National Car Parks Limited.'

'That's all finished with.'

'What, because a certain firm's been banged up?'

'Yeah, that's right.'

Harry sighs and shakes his head.

'It ain't finished, Charlie. Why don't you show us around the house?'

We go upstairs. Charlie's a gibbering wreck. Harry sniffs about, looking in the bedroom, the bathroom.

'What's in there?' He nods at another door.

'Spare room.'

Harry grabs the door handle, rattles it about. The door stays put.

'It's locked, Charlie.'

Charlie stutters something. Harry nods over at Beardsley who gives it a good kicking. The frame splits and it swings open.

'Well, what do we have here?'

The room was a sort of office with a little desk and a chair. On the desk were piles of papers. Harry sorts through them, tossing about account statements and flipping through bank books.

'Look at all this.'

He opens a drawer and takes out a handful of bank notes. He waves them in front of Charlie's face and then lets them sail to the floor. He spots a tea chest in the corner and goes over. He looks in and starts to laugh. He puts a hand in and scoops up a handful of silver coins. He lets them slip out through his fingers and clatter into the chest in a pantomime of richness. He tries to lift the tea chest but it doesn't budge. He grunts.

'Give us a hand with this, Jack,' he says.

I go over and we grab it each side. It still won't give so we tip it over. All the silver comes sushing out all over the floor.

'I think we hit the jackpot,' Harry declares.

Charlie starts to yack.

'I, I wanted to stop, I really wanted to, but we couldn't, you see.'

'Shut it,' Harry orders. 'Come over here and sit down.'

Harry grabs the chair and turns it round. Standing behind it he draws it back a little, like a waiter in a posh restaurant.

'Take a seat, Charles.'

Charlie reluctantly comes over and sits down. Harry walks around him and fishes out a few lengths of rope from his pocket, handing them to me and Beardsley.

'Make him comfortable,' he tells us.

I go around the back and start to tie his wrists together. Charlie starts to protest.

'Don't say a fucking word!' Harry orders sharply.

'You'll have time to have your say,' he continues in a softer tone. 'I just need to say a few things. Beardsley, tie his ankles together. You haven't been looking after your accounts very well, have you? You need somebody to help you in putting your finances in order, don't you? Take his shoes and socks off.'

Beardsley does as he says. Charlie starts to giggle as his bare feet are handled.

'Shut him up, Jack,' says Harry.

I grab the socks from off the floor and shove them in Charlie's mouth.

'Hold his feet up.'

Beardsley lifts up the pair of yellowy plates of meat. There's a corn plaster on the right little toe. Harry crouches down in front of Charlie, looking at him with that mad stare of his.

'Naughty of you, lying to us like that. Don't want that to happen again, do we? We want to establish an amicable business arrangement. Don't we?'

Charlie nods frantically, straining to speak through the woollen gag. Harry tuts and shakes his head.

'Don't talk with your mouth full, Charlie. It ain't polite.'

He brings out a cigarette lighter from his pocket. Gold-plated Ronson, very flash.

'Hold him steady,' he says.

He flicks open the top and sparks it up. Charlie strains against us as he sees the flame. Harry lets it lick against the sole of each foot. Muffled shrieks from the car-park supervisor.

After a few seconds Harry clicks it shut. Charlie goes limp on us, heaving heavily through his nostrils.

'See, it's quite simple really. We can do business together. Everything sorted out nice and proper. You just need to know who the guvnor is.'

Harry flicks the lighter on and warms up the feet again. Charlie tenses up. Chewing at the smelly socks in his gob. A choked scream tearing at the back of his throat. Sounds distant.

'This is just a taste. Just a little taste of what will happen if you fuck around with us. If you lie to us. Grass us up. If you do *anything* out of line.'

He stops again. Looks straight into Charlie's eyes.

'All you've got to do is hand over our cut. That's all.'

Charlie's nodding, tears streaming down his face.

'Good.' Harry pats him on the head. 'Good boy. Now, just one more go for good measure, eh?'

Harry burns him again. I catch a whiff of toasted foot. Horrible cheesy stench. Then we're finished. We let go of Charlie and Harry pulls the socks out of his mouth. He's quivering away, wheezing and sobbing. He starts to gibber. Harry nods.

'Yeah, yeah,' he says. 'Tell us all about it.'

'We wanted to stop it,' Charlie blubbers. 'Really we did. Thing is, we couldn't. If we stopped fiddling the machines there'd be such a leap in the takings that head office would have got suspicious.'

'So you just carried on.'

'Yeah, we'd got into a routine. Everyone was getting their whack. It kept everyone happy.'

'Except with certain people away, the main whack wasn't going anywhere, was it?'

Charlie nodded.

'You just didn't know what to do with all this money, did you Charles?'

Charlie shook his head.

'Well, your troubles are over. We'll take care of that now. Let's get down to business. Beardsley, why don't you make us all a nice cup of tea?'

'Uh?' replied Beardsley.

'Put the kettle on son. Jack, untie Mr Charles. I'll bet he's gasping for a cuppa.'

'Right,' says Beardsley, a bit bewildered, and wanders off downstairs.

'And don't forget to warm the pot,' Harry calls after him.

We drive back east. Drop Beardsley off at Shepherd's Bush. Harry slips him a wad by way of a sub. He can afford to be generous. He's set to take a grand a week off the car-park fiddle. Easy money. Get onto the Westway Flyover and bomb down into the City. The Westway. Think about the rumour about Jimmy.

'All right, Jack?' asks Harry.

'Yeah.'

Feel like asking: It true that Jimmy Murphy's helping to hold this thing up? Think better of it.

'Fancy a drink?' Harry offers.

'Yeah, why not?'

Get off the Flyover at Paddington. Go to one of the seedy little drinking clubs in Praed Street that Harry's protecting. A handful of second-rate Lisson Grove faces trying not to gawk. Everyone nervous and polite. Drinks on the house. Respect, that's what it's all about.

'Well, your boy seemed all right,' says Harry as we grab a second bacardi.

'Beardsley? Yeah, he'll be fine.'

'Thing is, it's not going to be so easy when we go up against the baggage handlers. Some of them are proper villains. There's more at stake and they might not be so eager to hand over the swag.'

'Yeah, well, we'll see, eh?'

Beam a big nutty grin over at Harry.

'Silly cunts think they can fence all that stuff themselves,' he says. 'Jewellery, industrial diamonds. You need proper organisation to offload gear like that.'

'Yeah, well, we'll just have to point out the error of their ways, won't we?'

Laughter. We have another drink. Then Harry goes all quiet. Thoughtful.

'There was another thing I wanted to chat about, Jack.'

'Oh yeah?'

'It's a matter of some delicacy,' he says softly, looking around the room.

I frown. What the fuck's he on about?

'The other night at the club. What Mooney was going on about.'

'Dirty Squad business? You thinking of heavying into the Maltese?'

'No, no. Well, not at the moment, anyway. No, the other matter.'

I suddenly get it.

'Oh, the Suitcase Murder,' I blurt out, a little too loud for Harry's comfort.

He winces and puts a finger up to his mouth.

'That kid who got sliced up?' I whisper. 'What about it?'

'Well, as I said,' he goes on, 'it's a matter of some delicacy. I need a hand.'

Hang on a minute, I think to myself. What's all this about? I don't want to get involved in any of this. Maybe he did have a hand in it and wants to cover his tracks. Never know what these queers are into. I don't want to know. And I know what Harry's capable of. This afternoon, that was just kid's play. He's done nasty things, worse things than that. Jimmy Murphy propping up the Westway Flyover. We've all done horrible things. Madge. I crippled her. Poor cow, she didn't deserve that.

'Jack?'

'I don't know, Harry. I don't want to get involved in that.'

'What's the matter?'

'Well . . .'

'Come on. I just want to make a few inquiries of my own. And I need a hand.'

Shrug.

'I don't know, Harry.'

And I don't. I can't fathom this homo business. Nothing against them, mind, long as they keep it all to themselves.

'Come on, Jack.'

He gets up. I heave a sigh and go along with it. Agree to drive him down to Piccadilly. Feel a bit sluggish so I pop a couple of black bombers on the sly.

It's dark by the time we get to the Dilly. Bright lights swirling patterns on advertisement hoardings, extra sharp as the speed rush comes up. *Chicka, chicka, chicka.* Bright lights luring naughty boys away from Mum and Dad and into all kinds of nasty vices. Groups of long hairs sitting around the statue of Eros. Junkies strung out by the entrance of Boots 24-hour chemists, hoping to score a bent script. We cruise by the Meat Rack and one of the Dilly boys comes out to the motor. Harry gives him a nod and he gets in the back of the limo and I pull away.

'What do you want?' asks the renter, all cocky like.

'I want to talk,' replies Harry.

'Oh yeah? Dirty talk?'

'No, nothing like that. I want to talk about the kid who got killed.'

I check the rear view mirror. The kid is looking scared.

'Bernie,' Harry goes on. 'You knew him?'

The kid nods, frightened.

'So did I,' says Harry.

'I don't know anything,' the kid says, terrified, all cockiness gone now. He pleads in a whisper, 'I won't say anything.'

'Look, son . . .'

Harry goes to grab his arm but the kid makes for the door. Trying to get out as we're cruising down the Haymarket. Madge, I think, flinching. I hit the brakes. Tyre squeal, hooter blaring from the motor behind us. Harry and the boy are thrown forward.

'Jack!' Harry shouts.

The boy gets up, hysterical. Harry slaps him.

'Jack!' he shouts again. 'For fuck's sake move us on.'

And I pull away. The boy's sobbing quietly in the back now and Harry's talking softly, trying to reassure him.

'Look, I won't hurt you. Just tell me what you know,' he says, handing him a handkerchief.

The kid calms down a bit. Blows his nose. Then starts the spiel.

'Yeah, I knew Bernie. Not very well. Just that he was on the game like me. Nice kid. Quiet, a bit dreamy. Haven't seen him round the Dilly recently. Last time I saw him he said he wasn't doing trade no more. Said he was going to be a pop star. Found some rich homo record producer he was going to cut a record with. Just like Bernie. Always dreaming. Only thing he'd ever starred in was some tacky porn smudges he'd done with some bloke in Old Compton Street.

Even then he was going around saying that he was going to be a famous model one day. But I don't know anything about what happened. Honest.'

'Right,' says Harry. 'Take us back around, Jack. Look, son, what's your name?'

'Phil.'

'Look, Phil. If anyone asks any questions, keep shtum. But ask around on the quiet if anyone knows anything. If you find out anything then let me know.'

Harry hands him a business card and a few notes as we come around Piccadilly Circus again. As we pull up to the Meat Rack, Harry pats Phil on the shoulder.

'Don't forget, anything you hear, let me know.'

Phil shoves the money and the card into his pocket and gets out of the Daimler. Harry squeezes his arm as he goes.

'Take care of yourself,' he says.

'Where to now?' I ask, hoping that we can go for a drink somewhere.

'Take us up Shaftesbury Avenue. I think we should have a shufti around Old Compton Street.'

Yeah, well the kid was involved in porn so maybe that's a lead. Another reason why Moody's been dragged into the investigation. Detective work. I can see why it's so appealing. But I don't want to get caught up in all this. What's Harry up to? Maybe he's – nah, I don't want to think about it.

We get into Soho. Go up Wardour Street, past The Flamingo. Hang a right into Old Compton Street.

'Pull up here,' says Harry.

I park by a seedy-looking shopfront. ADULT BOOKSHOP, it says in big white letters. We go in. Soft porn in the front part of the shop. Musclemen posing against Greek columns, that sort of thing. Bead-curtained doorway into the back where the heavier stuff is, no doubt. Weedy-looking queen hunched over a book by the till. Looks up and sees Harry.

'Harry!' he whines in a sing-song simper.

Harry nods, grunts.

'Jeff.'

'And what can I do you for?'

'I want a word,' he replies all serious.

The queen blinks and pushes his specs back into the ridge of his nose.

'Better come through here then,' he says.

The curtain makes a little clattering noise as we go through into the back room. Stacks of hard-core books and magazines shrink-wrapped. A pile of rollers in the corner, Super 8 films with titles like *Dark Desires* and *Forbidden Love*.

'What's all this about?' asks Jeff.

'Has a certain OPS officer been around asking questions about this Suitcase Murder?'

'George Mooney? Yeah, he's been in.'

'And what did you tell him?'

'Not a lot. He was more interested in upping his normal licence fee to keep me out of the investigation.'

'And anyone else been around asking questions?'

'No.'

'Good. Right. Well, tell us what you know.'

'Well, Mooney was in and out of here quick as a ten bob wank. In such a hurry to get his money he didn't give me a chance to show him this.'

He rummages about in a pile of glossies and comes up with a handful.

'I don't do much of my own stuff any more. A lot of the stuff is from the States or Scans, you know, Scandinavian. But I meet this kid and he's into it, so I do a session with him. Pretty kid, not really butch enough to tell you the truth, still he looks a lot younger than he is so I figure it would work for the juve market.'

He holds up one of the smudges. Skinny kid looking shyly at the camera. Mop of blond hair, one hand on hip, the other holding on to a hard cock. I look away. Harry grabs the photo and examines it closely.

'It's Bernie,' he says.

'That's right. Poor old Bernie. Or, rather, poor young Bernie.'

Harry looking at the smudge. Frowns all funny like. Looks up at Jeff.

'You weren't involved in anything heavier than this with him, were you?'

'Look, I do a bit of bondage, a bit of fladge, that's it. All harmless fun. I only did the session with Bernie because I ain't going to use real juves. Sure, I get some right weirdos in here. Get offered some pretty heavy stuff as well. But that's all import.'

'So you don't know anything else?'

'On my life.'

'Yeah,' Harry gives him this nutty grin. 'Well, let's hope it doesn't come to that.'

We walk through into the front of the shop.

'Any trouble off the Maltese, Jeff?' Harry asks.

'No, they only deal with the straight stuff. Tight-arsed catholicism, I reckon. Can't say the same thing for the Dirty Squad, though. They're very broadminded. So long as they get their licence fee.'

'I'm thinking of expanding my operations, Jeff,' Harry announces.

'Well, I'm a bit specialised here,' Jeff lisps. 'Not a big market, really.'

'No, I mean the straight stuff.'

Jeff wrinkles his nose.

'I see.'

'I want to start arranging leases on a chain of bookshops sometime soon. Might need a hand in setting up front men.'

'Of course, darling.'

We go to the door and Jeff sees us out. All eyes and teeth. Gives me a big wink as I go out.

'I'll keep hold of this picture, if you don't mind,' Harry says, holding up the glossy. 'And if anyone comes asking about this suitcase thing, let me know.'

We drive back to Harry's flat in Chelsea. Harry's in the front, brooding. I try to snap him out of it.

'So, you are moving into the porn racket,' I say.

'Yeah,' he mutters all faraway. 'I guess.'

'Means having to deal with that cunt Mooney, though.'

'Let's sort out the Airport first. And this.'

He taps the picture of Bernie propped up on the glove compartment. Shy little teenage face peeking out under a blond fringe, staring out at oblivion.

We get to Harry's place. He peels off a few notes. My share plus a little extra.

'Thanks for all your help, Jack. I'll get in touch regarding the baggage handlers. You can get hold of Beardsley when we need him?'

I nod.

'Right then.' Weary sigh. 'I'll see you, then.'

A hard day's work and home to Trevor. What time is it? Just gone eleven. The night is still young and I've still got a bit of a buzz. *Chicka, chicka, chicka*. Time for an after-hours' nightcap. Need a drink, all this queer business leaves a bad taste in my mouth. Nothing against Harry, mind, but you know what I mean. Pick up the Zodiac and head north.

Stoke Newington. The Regency. Big sign says, 'North London's Smartest Rendezvous'. My arse. Three floors of tacky nightclub, more like. Favoured meeting place for many well-respected faces, though. Gets a bit lively on Saturday night when it fills up with young hooligans trying to act tough to impress the birds. But it's Tuesday night so it's bound to be quiet. Yeah. Take it easy, Jack. Just a couple of drinks then fuck off home.

It's half empty in the downstairs after-hours' drinker. A few of the Kray firm are about, lording it over. Nods, grins, all right Jack and all that pony but I can tell they're a bit wary. Yeah, I'm all right. Don't trust any of this lot. No sign of the Other Two, thank Christ. Shouldn't have come here. Harry's right, I should steer clear of all their firm. But fuck it, I ain't afraid of them. The Lambrianou brothers come over. Tony and Chris. Obviously well in with the Twins now. Chris is friendly enough, gentle sort of a bloke really. Tony's a bit more sly. Suddenly feel all alone, eyes darting at me, people whispering: *Jack the Hat, he's a troublemaker, he's got it coming to him*. I'm on my own and I ain't even tooled up. Finish the drink and get out of there.

Get home to my flat. The place is in a right state. A shithole. Can't sleep. Feel uneasy. Maybe it's the pills. Maybe it's something else. Get up and reach up into the chimney breast. Pull out my shooter all wrapped in cloth. Give it a clean. Long-nosed Colt 45. Spin the cylinder slowly. *Click, click, click*. Feel a lot better for giving it a good oiling. Then put it back in its hidey hole. Feel safe it being there. That and the sawn-off under the floor boards. Eventually I drift off. Half sleep. Mad dreams. Luggage going around the Airport carousel. Two suitcases come around, like the ones that kid was cut up and put into. But when I go to pick them up I see that it's my name on the tags.

Get up late the next day. Try and sort out the flat a bit. Take a bag of smelly old clothes down to the laundrette, drop a couple of suits off at the cleaners. Have something to eat in a nearby caff then spend most of the afternoon picking losers out in the bookies. Do a bit of shopping on the way home. Crack open a new bottle of vodka and watch a bit of telly. Stare at the fuzzy old screen until it's all over. National anthem, then that sharp tone to wake up the dozy fuckers who've fallen asleep in front of the box. An empty signal buzzing in my head. Closedown. Drink to stave off nightmares. Go to bed alone.

Lunchtime, Harry calls up to arrange the meet at the Airport. Get a full tank in the Zodiac and drive out west. Get hold of Beardsley and he says to pick him up at a pub just south of Dalston junction. He's outside when I pull up. Looking right flash. New crombie, Ben Sherman shirt, tightly tailored with buttoned-down collar, Sta-Press trousers with razor-sharp creases, a bit short in the leg to show off the lethal-looking ox-blood polished boots. Well, he's been spending some of his newly earned gelt on this get up. No hat this time but he wears his brand-new number-one crop with a well-studied glare. Obviously been practising the look. Learning off the grown-up gangsters. Other little touches too. A silk handkerchief in the top pocket of the crombie held there with a tie pin. And a steel comb poking out from there as well. No doubt its rat-tail end sharpened up just in case there's no time to get his Stanley blade out. Every detail of style spelt violence.

And there's this gang of kids hanging around him. All trying to look like him, act like him. They ain't as flash, of course. Donkey jackets, monkey boots, that sort of thing. But they've all got the regulation crop. It must be a new craze, I suppose. But I ain't seen nothing about it in the papers or on the telly. They're all fannying on about long hair and swinging London. Kind of reassuring to bald Jack that you don't have to have much of a barnet to be fashionable.

So, anyway, Beardsley hops in and I ask him about it.

'So, what? Ain't you a mod no more?'

'Nah, I told you, it's all over now. All that lot down The Flamingo have gone all hairy. Beads and flowers. Peace and Love. Fuck that.'

'So what are you lot called?'

'We ain't got a name yet. We're into aggro.'

'Aggro?'

'Yeah, you know, aggression, aggravation. Aggro.'

'Oh yeah,' I give a little chuckle. 'Aggro.'

We go across town, get onto the Great West Road at Hammersmith.

'So what about the shooter, Jack?' asks Beardsley, a bit too cocky for his own good.

'I told you son,' I reply. 'You got to do your apprenticeship first.'

He goes into a bit of a huff about this.

'Look Beardsley, don't worry. You'll have plenty of opportunity to prove yourself. You're into the, er, ag, what do you call it?'

'Aggro.'

'Yeah, aggro. Well, there'll be plenty of that this afternoon.'

I give him a wide grin and he smiles back. I feel a bit queasy though, to tell you the truth.

Harry's got Mr Charles, the car-park supervisor, to set up a meeting with the main baggage handler. It's a set up of course. We're in the basement level of the multi-storey car park waiting for this mug who fancies himself as boss of all the thieving. Charlie's closed this level to the public so we've got it all for ourselves. We're waiting in the shadows, half hidden by concrete pillars, back lit by sickly yellow sodium lights. Harry likes to stage manage the fear.

Beardsley's a bit twitchy, raring to go. I crack each set of knuckles and give him a wink. Harry's calm as ever, leaning against the Daimler all nonchalant.

Echoed footsteps coming down the ramp. We're on.

'Charlie!' this voice booms around the concrete.

'Over here!' Harry hisses, stage whisper.

This geezer walks into a pool of yellow light. Overalls, loading hook slung over one shoulder. Harry reaches into his motor and turns on the headlights full beam. The baggage handler shields his eyes.

'Charlie? What the fuck's going on?'

'Mr Charles couldn't make it,' Harry announces softly.

Me and Beardsley fan out each side of the baggage handler.

'Who the fuck are you?' the man demands looking each way as we circle around him.

'I'm your new guvnor, Derek,' says Harry.

Derek grabs his hook and blindly makes a swing with it in a

wide arc. Harry steps back from it. I come around the back and kick Derek's legs from under him. He's down on his knees and Beardsley follows in. Putting the boot in. I step on the hand still holding the hook and it lets go. Kick the thing across the floor of the car park. Harry nods at Beardsley to stop kicking. He walks up and stands over Derek who's now curled up in a ball snivelling. Looks down his nose at him.

'We've got to discuss our new business arrangement,' he says, gently prodding Derek with his toe cap.

We tie his hands behind his back and tape up his gob. Harry gets a big sack from the Daimler and chucks it over at me.

'Put him in this.'

Me and Beardsley bundle him into the sack and secure it with some twine. Derek's making muffled noises. Harry kicks the bag and tells him to shut up.

'Right,' says Harry. 'Put him in the boot of the Daimler.'

Then we're off. Beardsley goes with Harry in the Daimler and I follow on in my Zodiac. End up at a disused warehouse in Bermondsey. Unload Derek like he's dry goods. Upstairs, a long dusty space with cast-iron pillars. Empty, except for a table with a few things on it and some chairs. One of the chairs is right in the middle of the room. All on its own. It's been nailed down there.

We get Derek out of the bag and tie him to this chair. Still gagged. Then Harry brings out the black box. It's got a little handle on the top of it and wires coming out with little crocodile clips on the end. The Black Box. I've heard about it. Never sure it was true. The Crank Up, I'd heard it called. Rumours. Not from anyone who ever had it done to him, mind. I mean, that was the whole point, wasn't it? Funny really, you get the idea, like in all them war films and that, that torture's used to make people talk. But Harry uses it for the opposite reason. The whole point's they don't talk, ain't it? Don't grass.

'Take his overalls and his pants down,' Harry says to Beardsley.

Derek tries to protest through the tape gag but he doesn't struggle.

'You want to do the honours, Jack?' Harry asks.

He holds up the wires by the clips, moving their hinged ends so that they snap like two little pairs of jaws. I try not to flinch. Big grin to hide any lack of bottle.

'Why don't we let the young apprentice have a go?' I suggest.

Harry nods.

'Beardsley,' he says, holding up the clips for him to see. 'Attach these to our friend here.'

Beardsley frowns as he takes the wires off Harry.

'Uh – Where do I put them?'

Harry smiles.

'Where do you think?'

And so they get on with it. Harry delivers this long lecture about business, stopping every so often to nod at Beardsley to give Derek a crank up. Derek goes into this sort of short fit every time he's given the electric. The rest of the time he's nodding or shaking his head frantically at what Harry is saying. Desperately trying to agree with him, except he can't because his mouth's taped up. At one point there's some talk of dousing Derek with water or something to increase the conductivity but he's already pissed himself so it wouldn't make much difference. I watch and try not to think about it too much. It will all be over soon. There's a bottle of Johnny Walker on the table and I pour myself one. Take a few sips as Harry delivers his spiel. All this psychology makes me feel a bit sick.

When they finish, Beardsley rips off the tape from Derek's mouth and he's gasping and blubbering away. We untie his hands and chuck him a cloth to wipe up the piss off his legs. We get him to clean up the chair and the floor around it as well. Then we let him get back into his overalls and give him a drink. Let him have about two fifths of the Johnny Walker. He's like a zombie now. He nods, wide eyed, as Harry explains how things are to be organised.

Later, me and Harry have a drink at The Stardust. A sort of celebration, like. H proposes a toast, holding up a tall glass of bacardi and Coke.

'To Thiefrow,' he says.

'Thiefrow,' I repeat.

Clink.

'And to the theft of valuables in transit,' says Harry.

Yeah, looks like that racket's all sewn up for a while. Harry reckons Beardsley's all right for the pick up. I say I'll keep an eye on him. The Stardust's dead as ever. This place must be losing Harry money. It's quiet as fuck and Harry's just sitting there. Thinking about something. Brooding. I hope he's not having one of his black moods. Heard horror stories about him 'going into one'. I get up.

'Just going to put something on the jukebox,' I say.

'Uh?' says Harry, only half out of his trance.

'Just going to put a record on.'

'Yeah.' Harry nodding, all thoughtful. 'Wait a minute.'

He grabs my arm.

'What's up Harry?'

'Remember what that kid said down in the Dilly the other night.'

He's off on *that* business again.

'What?'

'He said Bernie had talked about a "rich homo record producer".'

'So?'

'Well, that could be a lead.'

'So, who do you fancy for this "rich homo record producer"?' I ask.

Must be plenty to choose from, I think.

'Meek,' replies Harry. 'Joe Meek. You know him don't you Jack?'

'Yeah. Sold him pills a while back.'

Big amphetamine customer. Practically bought in bulk.

'Well, it could be him, couldn't it?'

'What?'

Harry sighs, impatient.

'The "rich homo record producer", of course.'

I shrug. So what?

'We should go and see him.'

'We?'

'Come on, Jack. I need a hand with this.'

So I get talked into all this palaver once again. I don't like it. Something wrong about the whole thing. Anyway, before you know it, we're off up the Holloway Road to Joe's flat cum studio. Pokey little place above a leather goods shop. Intercom on the door. Harry buzzes.

'What do you want?'

Joe's yokel voice crackles on the little speaker.

'It's Harry. Harry Starks.'

'Go away.'

'Come on, Joe. Open the door.'

'Leave me alone.'

Harry slips the lock and shoulders it open. Up the stairs. Strange electronic music echoing about the flat. Broken crockery, smashed records and odd bits of recording equipment strewn everywhere. Promotional pictures of Heinz, blond pop star in silver suit, scattered about the floor. Face crossed out with angry black lines. Music's weird, like a soundtrack for a science-fiction film.

'Joe?' Harry calls out.

Suddenly he's there at a doorway. Dressed all in black. Shiny black shirt open at the neck. Face as white as a ghost. Eyes popping out of his head. He's holding a single-barrelled shotgun at waist level.

I look over at Harry. Nod. I'm ready to rush Joe. Harry holds up a hand. Easy. Madness, he understands it.

'It's all right, Joe,' he says softly. 'We just want to talk.'

'It ain't safe to talk,' Joe says in his west country drawl. 'They're listening in.'

'Who are, Joe?' asks Harry, humouring him.

'The police,' replies Joe. 'And EMI.'

Harry slowly moves towards Joe.

'It's all right,' he says, soothingly. 'It's all right.'

He comes right up to him with his hands out.

'Give us the gun, Joe.'

Joe shrugs and zombie-like hands it over.

'You can have it,' he says. 'It isn't mine anyway. It belongs to Heinz.'

Joe starts to sob quietly. Harry hands the shotgun back to me and pats Joe on the back.

'There, there,' he whispers.

'Ungrateful bastard. After all I did for him,' says Joe.

'Come on Joe, he ain't worth it.'

Harry leads Joe to the settee. Chucks some of the junk piled on it off onto the floor and gets him to sit down. I stash the shotgun behind it. Harry sits next to him.

'We need to talk,' says Harry.

'I told you, it ain't safe to talk. They've got this place bugged.'

'Well, we'll whisper then. They ain't going to hear us above this racket.'

The air is still full of this electronic din.

'It ain't a racket. It's my space symphony. It's called "I Hear A New World". I did it back in 1960. Nobody liked it. The rotten pigs.'

'Well I think it's very, er, interesting. And if we talk quietly they won't be able to hear us above it.'

'I hear voices all the time,' says Joe, getting agitated again. 'They're trying to steal my sound. Steal it out of my head.'

'Shh,' shushes Harry. 'It's all right. We're friends, aren't we?'

He pats Joe on the leg and Joe smiles.

'So what do you want to talk about, Harry?'

'Bernie. Bernie Oliver.'

Joe stiffens up, lurches forward. Harry holds on to him.

'Poor little Bernie,' says Joe. 'Chopped up and put in a couple of suitcases.'

'That's right, Joe. And we want to find whoever did that to him.'

'They've got stuff on me. I'm a known sexual offender, Harry.'

'Who's got stuff on you?'

'The police. Highgate nick are in on the investigation, Bernie was from round here, you see?'

'What have they got on you, Joe?'

'They nicked me. Back in '64.'

'What for?'

'"Persistently importuning for an immoral purpose".'

Harry laughs.

'What, at that cottage on Holloway Road?'

'Yeah. But I wasn't being persistent, I can tell you. He was nothing to write home about.'

And they're both giggling like girls on the settee.

'Thing is,' Joe goes on, 'I met Bernie there one night. So I'm a suspect. They want me to go in and make a statement.'

'Who, Highgate nick?'

'Yeah. But then this other copper turns up. Plain clothes.'

'Not out of Highgate nick?'

'Didn't say.'

'Murder Squad?'

'Yeah, maybe. I don't know. Told me I was eliminated from their inquiries.'

'Did he ask any questions?'

'No. He just told me to keep quiet about the whole thing. If I knew what was good for me.'

Harry frowned. Joe went on.

'Maybe he was one of *them*.'

'What?'

'You know, maybe he was trying to steal my sound.'

'Yeah, yeah. So did you make a statement at Highgate?'

'No, no. I'm frightened of leaving the flat, Harry. I'm scared.'

'Well Joe,' says Harry, patting him on the back again all reassuring like. 'Why don't you give me your statement?'

Joe shrugs. OK.

'I meet Bernie at the cottage. You know, the one up the road. He comes home with me. When he finds out who I am he wants me to record him singing. He's a lovely kid, lovely long blond hair. But he can't sing. I play back the tapes for him and we have a good laugh. He says if I play around with the recording enough, put plenty of echo and compression on and that, it'll sound OK. I humour him. I like the kid and he shows a bit of appreciation. Not like some of these selfish bastards who've made a career out of me. So I tell him to come back next week and we'll try again. That was the last I saw of him.'

'Any idea of where he went after that?'

'He said he was going to this party in a big house out in the country. Rich people.'

'Where?'

'I don't know . . . strange name . . . nightmare . . . just a . . . just a . . . heart . . . well . . . just a mare . . . just a . . . nightmare.'

Joe's gabbling. Speed talk. Madness. Harry waits for him to finish.

'And that's the last you saw of him?' he asks.

'Yeah, honest. Next thing I know he's in the papers. Just a, just a nightmare. Do you think they got him, Harry?'

'Who?'

'You know, *them*.'

Harry gets up and looks down at Joe.

'I don't know, Joe. We're going to try and find them, though.'

Harry gives me a look. Time to go.

'I know who might know,' says Joe.

Harry's ears prick up.

'Who?'

'Buddy Holly,' Joe gets up off the settee and starts to move around the room. 'I need to get in touch with Buddy,' he says, suddenly urgent again. 'He'll know.'

Harry nods over at me. We make our way out of there, leaving Joe to mutter away to himself as all this space music is floating around the place.

'Just a, just a—' stutters Joe as we leave. 'Nightmare.'

We go downstairs and get into the motor.

'He's sick, Jack,' Harry says in the motor as if he needs to explain it to me. 'We need to talk to him again when he's not in such a state. He needs help. I know a shrink. Maybe . . .'

Harry's voice drifts off into brooding.

Maybe he could do with some of those loony pills of yours, I think. The ones I saw in your bathroom cabinet. Don't say anything, though. Harry's a bit touchy. But maybe Joe could do with some pills like that. Something to bring him down a bit. All that speed isn't good for you. Sends you loopy.

A week later and I'm driving Beardsley out to the Airport in the Zodiac. Making sure the pick up runs sweet. Beardsley's sporting a holiday look as cover. The bovver boy look might raise a few too many eyebrows. Probably scare the shit out of the British Airports Authority Police but we don't want to upset anyone, do we? So he's wearing a straw pork-pie hat and wraparound shades. Sta-Press but with loafers instead of boots. Bottle-green Fred Perry shirt and a windcheater jacket. Little holdall bag looking like hand luggage for the loot.

Beardsley makes the pick up in a gift shop in the Arrivals area. Derek goes in and leaves a package hidden between the rows of little dolls dressed in national costume all lined up in see-through plastic cylinders. Beardsley follows in and stuffs the package in his holdall on the sly. Picks up a doll to avoid suspicion and pays for it at the counter. Easy. We make our way out to the car park as the Arrivals board clatters away behind us. Beardsley's swinging this little doll by its string tassle.

'You going to chuck that?' I ask him.

Beardsley holds it up and looks at it. It's all dressed up like a Dutch girl. He grins.

'Nah. I'll give it to me kid sister.'

Then the car park. At the barrier we hand in our ticket and the bloke in the booth slips us a big fat envelope. Then we're away. Nothing simpler.

We drop off the stuff with Harry and take our cut. Everything's running sweet but Harry's brooding away. Preoccupied with this other business, no doubt. I worry about him 'going into one'. Don't want things to fuck up now when everything should be just ticking over fine and earning us easy money. Still, there's nothing to be done so we leave him to it. I agree to give Beardsley a lift.

Driving back across town Beardsley talks about our own little racket. Drugs. Pills and that. Might as well keep that scam going in case this one falls apart. Had a little trouble on the supply side, though. Certain people wanting their share of everything. The Other Two. Greedy bastards. Kind of fucks things up. Still, me and Beardsley are on a roll, feel a bit cocky. So we decide to pay a visit to Marty the dealer.

'Need to pick something up from my gaff first,' I tell Beardsley.

Get to my drum and have to wade through all the junk I haven't got around to clearing up yet.

'Christ, Jack,' Beardsley gasps. 'Your place is in a bit of a state, ain't it?'

'Never mind that,' I tell him. 'I've got something to show you.'

I lead him through into the bedroom and reach up into the chimney flue. Pull out the shooter. Unwrap it and hold it up to his face. He gives this little noise of excitement in the back of his throat.

'There you are son. Colt 45.'

Give the cylinder a little spin. *Click, click, click.*

'That's a real fucking shooter. You could blow someone's face off with that.'

Beardsley's all wide eyed like a little kid. I load it up with shells and hand it to him.

'Go on,' I tell him. 'Have a pop. I can tell you're dying to.'

Beardsley feels the weight of the thing in his hands.

'Go on. Fire it into the chimney breast.'

Beardsley's gripping the revolver, squinting and gritting his teeth.

'Keep your arm straight. Squeeze the trigger, don't pull it too sharp.'

Bang. A big flat bang fills the room. Little clouds of blue smoke and plaster dust. The recoil's knocked Beardsley back a couple of footsteps. He's giving a mad little giggle.

'Quite a kick hasn't it, son?'

I take it off him and slip the safety on. Shove it in my waistband and do up my jacket.

'Right,' I say. 'Let's go and pay a little visit to Marty.'

I can tell Marty ain't pleased to see me when he opens up but he puts on this stupid smile to try and fool me otherwise.

'Jack,' he tries to say all friendly but it sticks in his throat. 'How you been?'

'Busy. That's why I ain't been around much, Marty. But me and the kid here want to resume our little arrangement.'

'Want a drink?'

'Let's get down to business.'

'Thing is, Jack,' Marty starts up, trying to be diplomatic. 'Thing is, things are difficult.'

'Oh yeah? Like what?'

'The Twins. I had to pay them off last time I dealt with you.'

'So? That's your business.'

'Well I thought it was sorted out with you.'

'What?'

'That's why I dealt with you. You said it was sorted with them. You were sticking their name up. I dealt to you because I thought it was sorted with them.'

'I don't understand.'

'Well, I've had to pay them off, haven't I? They said you weren't on their firm no more and I have to deal through them in future.'

'So what are you saying, Marty?'

'I'm saying that I can't afford to fuck around, Jack. I don't want to mess with the Twins.'

'You saying you ain't going to deal to me?'

'Jack, this puts me in a difficult position.'

'Well let me make it easy for you, Marty.'

I pull out the shooter and press its long barrel against his nut. Beardsley gives a mean little laugh.

'Let's stop fannying around and do business, shall we?'

'All right, all right,' stutters Marty, shitting himself. 'Point that thing somewhere else, can't you.'

Marty goes off to get some stuff, shaking his head and sighing.

'This could bring a lot of trouble, Jack,' he says as he comes back.

'Don't you worry about the Krays,' I tell him, tucking the shooter back in my waistband. 'They're on their way out. They don't bother me.'

Bravado. Still, I'm not afraid of them am I? Am I?

'Well,' Marty goes on, sighing like he's resigned to his fate. 'Since I ain't got much choice you might as well have something a bit special.'

Marty's beady little eyes light up as he takes out a sheaf of brightly coloured paper. I take one off him. It's blotting paper, marked off in little squares.

'What the fuck's this?' I ask him.

'LSD, Jack. It's the new thing. A couple of chemistry students are knocking up this stuff in a makeshift lab in Canning Town. All the Beautiful People are mad for it.'

'Beautiful People,' Beardsley snorts.

'I'm telling you Jack, it's the height of fashion. Cut them up into little squares and sell them to longhairs for ten bob or a quid a piece.'

'What is it, speed?'

'Nah. It makes you see things brighter. Colours and that. Gets you into all of this peace and love shit. Lasts for hours and all. You only need a tiny bit. Just a drop of it on the blotting paper, that's all.'

What the hell. Have to keep up with the times. We buy a load of it even though Beardsley doesn't look too keen. Get some black bombers and all. Largely for personal use. Though I'm going to cut down. Don't want to end up like Joe Meek.

'Great,' says Beardsley in a huff as we drive off. 'This means we've got to deal with the fucking hairies.'

'Don't worry about it, son,' I tell him. 'Business is business.'

A couple of days later Harry calls me up.

'I've got a meet fixed with Mooney,' he says. 'Want to sit in?'

So Harry's serious about moving into the porn racket. Wants me in on that as well. I'm flattered but also wary. Not sure if I want to be on his firm permanent. Prefer being freelance, me. Still, it's worth sussing out so I say: 'Yeah, sure.'

And I bomb over to The Stardust in the Zodiac. Harry's on the top table all laid out dead flash. Champagne in an ice bucket.

'Kid worked out on the drop all right?' he asks.

'Yeah, no bother.'

Beardsley's working out fine. Don't mention our little drug enterprise though. Never sure if Harry might be greedy and want his cut like the Other Two.

'Seen the papers?' he asks me all agitated.

Shrug.

'Just looked at the racing page.'

'Well take a load of this,' he says handing over tonight's *Evening Standard*.

TOP OF THE POPS COMPOSER AND A WIFE SHOT DEAD, reads the headline. *Joe Meek in double tragedy at recording studio*, in a line above it. I read on: *Joe Meek, 36-year-old composer of the Top Ten hit Telstar and promoter of three pop groups, was found dead today at the Holloway, London, recording studios he always called The Bathroom.*

Beside him on the landing of his flat was a 12-bore shotgun. Down the stairs nearby, dying from shotgun wounds in the back, was Mrs Violet Shenton aged about 52 . . .

I put the paper down.

'Well, Harry,' I say. 'He finally flipped.'

'Yeah, poor old Joe. Thing is, I'm sure he knew something. He was trying to tell us something. Just something. That's what he kept saying. "Just a just a . . ." I don't know what it all means.'

'You think he had anything to do with it?'

'Joe? Nah, I don't think so.'

'It'd explain him topping himself like that.'

Harry shakes his head. Mooney arrives. Strolls in with this superior copper look on his face like he's above it all. He ain't fooling nobody. I hate dealing with filth like him. I know Harry ain't keen himself but he can fake it better than me.

Harry's all gracious charm, pouring out the expensive bubbly for this bent DI. A few pleasantries exchanged then we're down to business.

'Well, if I can speak freely,' announces Mooney, looking around him then looking at me.

'Of course,' says Harry. 'You know Jack, don't you? He's in on this.'

Mooney nods in my direction, grudgingly. Gives a little sniff as if I'm dogshit on his well-polished PC plod shoes. I feel like giving him a slap but hold back. Easy, I think. Have to deal with scum like him. Take a sip of this posh fizzy stuff. Don't know what all the fuss is about. Tastes like Tizer.

'So,' Mooney says. 'The good news is that the Suitcase Inquiry is being wound up. We can all breathe easily now.'

'They didn't find anything?'

'No. The Suitcase is closed.'

A little smile plays across Mooney's lips. Harry frowns. He don't get the joke.

'What about Joe Meek?'

'Yes, I heard about that. An unfortunate business. But he was eliminated as a suspect, I believe.'

'So they didn't turn anything up?'

Harry looks incredulous.

'Well,' says Mooney, all reasonable and shit. 'As I've said, the Murder Squad are winding down their investigation. They haven't managed to find any more tangible leads. There's a considerable concentration of manpower required in maintaining a murder inquiry.'

'And a seventeen-year-old rent boy isn't really worth bothering about,' mutters Harry.

'I'm sure the Murder Squad have their priorities,' Mooney replies softly. 'The thing is, with this messy business out of the way the spotlight is off Soho for a while. We can get on with the main business in hand.'

'Porn,' says Harry bluntly.

Mooney coughs.

'Quite. This permissive society that everyone's talking about means that business is booming. The squad's scale of operations has increased considerably.'

'So have the kickbacks I bet,' I chip in.

Mooney gives me a dull stare.

'I prefer to see it as a work incentive for keeping the lid on things. We can't afford to let things get out of hand. There are dirty bookshops springing up all over Soho and nobody's controlling it properly from your side. The Maltese are so busy with clip joints and prostitution they don't seem to realise what a growing market there is for pornography.'

'So you want someone to take over the porn rackets?'

'It would be a lot easier all round if we just had to deal with one firm.'

'And what if some of these bookshops needed leaning on?'

'That's your business. I'm sure you could persuade them to come into line.'

Mooney's green light on putting the frighteners on.

'And what if the Maltese get riled that someone is taking over their pitch?' asks Harry.

'As I've said, that's your business. You do your job and I'll do mine. Your methods don't concern me. The OPS wants to deal with an organisation that can control all of this. I'm sure, as a businessman, you understand the need for a balance of free trade and protection. Particularly protection.'

Harry grins and fills another glass of champers for Mooney. The bottle's empty and he waves at a waiter for another bottle.

'Well, I'm sure we can work something out,' says Harry, giving me a nod. I grin back. Mooney catches the look and sighs.

'I want all of this done quietly. I can't afford to have some sort of gang warfare on my pitch. As I said, my job is to keep the lid on things.'

'Don't worry, George,' says Harry with a grin. 'We'll be real subtle.'

'Hm. Well make sure that you are. Then we can negotiate our percentage. Remember, if you work with us you'll not only be immune from official prosecution, you'll be immune from narks as well. Any grassing that comes our way can come straight back to you. It's a bloody good deal and we'll expect a reasonable share from it.'

Mooney slurps down his bubbly and gets up.

'I really must be getting off,' he announces. 'We'll talk figures once you've got your side of this arrangement sorted.'

'Yeah,' Harry agrees.

Then we all stand up together, handshakes all round and Mooney's off. Harry slumps back down in his chair. A bit mad about the eyes. Picks up the champagne bottle.

'Fancy another Jack?' he asks.

'Nah. Let's have a proper drink,' I reply.

Next few weeks me and Beardsley are putting the frighteners on a few porno bookshops. Offering them new terms and conditions, reminding them of their fire regulations, that sort of thing. Sticking up the Starks trademark helps but some of these filth pedlars aren't playing. Fannying on about already having protection. So we firebomb a couple of them. Harry's not pleased. We didn't consult with him first. Doesn't want things to get too lairy. I don't know what he's complaining about.

In the meantime me and Beardsley are dealing the funny drugs to the Beautiful People. Those chemistry students in Canning Town are knocking up this stuff on overtime since these hairies can't get enough of it. Acid trips. Looking all lairy in their beads and kaftans and crochet knit dresses. It's all Wow and Flower Power and Peace, Man. Which is fine by me. We don't get anything unnecessary off these fuckers. No aggro, as Beardsley would put it. The weather's getting warmer and everyone's talking about the Summer of Love. Beardsley can barely disguise his contempt but business is business, I remind him.

'I hate the Beautiful People,' he says.

But we're having our own Summer of Love. What with the drugs money and the Airport rackets earning us an easy life and the porn trade about to take off. It's dodgy but it's swinging. Can't seem to do anything with all this bad money though. It all goes on the horses or on the dogs at Hackney or White City. And if I'm still ahead I usually find myself pissing it away in a casino. Get into a spot of bother at the 211 in Balham one night and pull a knife on a croupier. Silly really. Brown Bread Fred gets right narked. He's in with the Twins so it's bound to get back to the Other Two. I need to calm down.

Still, everything's swinging in the West End so I don't have to worry about the East End for a while. Harry should be happy too but he's still brooding about this dead kid. One time I go around to his place I see Trevor's sporting a black eye. Harry's black moods. Been taking it out on Trev no doubt. No fucking good. Just makes him moodier and full of guilt. Trevor's looking sullen.

A sad, fuck-the-rest-of-the-world look on his bruised face. Same as the look on Madge's face when I knocked her about.

Then Beardsley hears something from the Airport. The word from Derek the baggage handler is that a huge consignment of industrial diamonds is due in in a couple of days. A massive haul. Something we could all retire on.

Harry arranges a meet. Derek's nervous, no doubt keen memories of the Crank Up. He goes through all the arrangements in great detail and we start to make plans. This is the big one. No discreet pilfering this time. We're going to take the lot.

Me and Beardsley are in cargo loader overalls as Derek leads us out onto the runway. He's straightened a couple of security passes with the British Airports Authority Police. We get into this little truck with a trailer on it and drive out to this big fat jet plane. It's like a huge bus with stubby little wings on it. Don't know how they get these things off the ground.

The truck's got an electric motor, like a milk float, and it hums away and I hum along to it. A few nerves but nothing to worry about. It's all been planned. We've been through it several times. Harry's worked it out down to the last detail. Not that he's had much experience at this sort of villainy. As I said, more used to just taking a percentage out of thieving. That and fraud and protection rackets is more his style. Still, this one's too big to let pass, so Harry's been playing the big criminal genius. Meetings at his place going over the MO. Maps, little Dinky toys, the lot.

Not that H is with us on the big day, of course. It's just me, Beardsley, Derek and a couple of baggage handlers Derek can trust. They're waiting for us in the cargo hold of the plane. I'm humming along to this electric motor. Look over at Beardsley. He's got a manic grin on his face. Jaw clenched with nerves and maybe the black bombers we've downed this morning. Well, you need a bit of speed for a caper like this. Keeps you sharp.

It's all worked out. We get into the hold and then this conveyer-belt truck pulls up and starts loading the loot. We get it passed through sharpish and drop it out onto the trailer on the back of our truck. Then we tie up Derek and the other cargo loaders. Give them a bit of cosh to make it look like we've overpowered them. Then we're away with a truckload of industrial diamonds over to the maintenance vehicle yard where there's a driver waiting for us in a transit van. We should be halfway down the Great West Road before the alarm's sounded. Need to put the cosh about a bit lively to make it look convincing. Still, the cargo boys won't mind a few lumps for the percentage they'll be getting. We're talking about hundreds of thousands for the haul if it's fenced right. Maybe a million. But best not to think about that. The Train Robbers started to lose it a bit when they realised that they'd got a lot more than they'd been counting on. It went to their heads and they got a bit sloppy. Best not to think about it at all. Just get the job done and then wait. Then wait some more until the fuss has died down.

So we get into the hold with the loading crew. The conveyor-belt thing comes up and is connected into place. It starts moving and the first of the packages come up on it. It's pass-the-parcel time all the way to the back of the plane and dropped out through a hatch onto the trailer. They're a bit lighter than I expected and I suddenly feel something's wrong. Like there's nothing in them or something. I try not to worry about it. How should I know how much these things weigh? Everyone's concentrating on getting it all loaded and unloaded as quickly as possible. Eyes down at the matter in hand. I happen to look up at the loading hatch for a second. I see a head appear at the top of the conveyor belt. Then a body. Somebody crouching on the moving belt. Somebody loading themselves into the cargo hold. I try to call out but the body beats me to it.

'Police!' he shouts.

He tumbles out into the plane, landing on the first baggage handler. He's got a truncheon out and he's trying to get a swing on the overalled body beneath him but he's all tangled up. Then another copper follows him in and there's a pile up. Shouting and bodies rolling around in the hold. One of the coppers is on his feet whilst the other is holding down a cargo loader. They're plainclothes. They ain't British Airports Authority, that's for sure. Flying Squad or something. The whole thing's a fucking set up. The one standing is whacking the next cargo loader with his truncheon as a couple more of this serious filth are pouring in from the conveyor belt. Beardsley's nearest the exit hatch so I give him a shove towards it.

'Out! Out! Out!' I scream at him.

He squeezes himself through the little doorway and drops down onto the trailer below. Derek's coming down along the plane trying to get to the escape hatch followed by all the filth in single file with their truncheons out.

'Got you, you bastard!' the leading one shouts as he grabs Derek by the scruff of his overalls and gives him a knock about the side of the head. Derek balls up and the copper nearly topples over him. I get my cosh out and clock the hunched-over copper right in the gob. He groans as he goes down, spitting teeth and blood as the filth behind him pile up, Keystone style, over him and Derek. I make it to the hatch and swing down onto the trailer. Beardsley's at the wheel of the truck in front.

'Come on son!' I shout. 'Get us out of here.'

He drives off as one of the Old Bill on the tarmac gives chase on foot. He manages to get to the back of the trailer and tries to jump on. I give him a whack with the cosh and he falls rolling onto the runway. (Madge falling onto the Great North Road, for fuck sake, Jack, don't think about that now.) I climb back to the front. Get onto the truck. Sit in the little seat next to Beardsley. I'm facing backwards and I can see a little group of filth about fifty yards back.

'Can't you get this milk float to go any faster?' I ask.

'Jack,' replies Beardsley nervously.

We're starting to slow down. Plod are beginning to gain on us.

'Come on son! For fuck's sake, put your foot down!'

'Jack,' Beardsley repeats. 'Look!'

'What the fuck's the matter with you?' I shout as I turn around.

Then I see what the matter is. A huge VC10 is taxiing out on the runway in front of us. We're heading straight for its front undercarriage. Behind us a load of filth are running after us.

'Fuck!' I say and grab the wheel off Beardsley. I stamp my foot on his and onto the accelerator. He screams, more from fear than pain as we go straight towards the big wheels of the landing gear ahead.

I slam the wheel over hard so we just miss the front undercarriage and then I zig zag around the two even heavier sets of landing gear behind. I'm laughing hysterical now, like a kid on the dodgems and we come out around the back of the jet. Its tail engines are screaming as it brings itself to a halt. We've lost the coppers for a while as all sorts of palaver breaks out behind us. We make for one of the loading bays, dump the truck and leg it back into the Airport buildings.

We slow down a bit and walk down one of the corridors. Try to act nonchalant. Give the old leer to a couple of stewardesses that pass. Somehow manage to find our way out to Arrivals. Go into the gents and get out of our overalls. Normal clothes underneath as planned which is just as well. The place is swarming with filth, though. Uniforms at all the exits, plainclothes snooping around. Just as well the place is really crowded. Don't know how we're going to get out, though.

Just then we hear all this screaming. Sounds like some sort of a riot. High-pitched voices wailing by one of the Arrival gates. Decide to go with the commotion. Might give us some cover. Find a whole mob of teenage girls screaming at a pop group just arrived home from a European tour. Flashbulbs popping, placards saying WELCOME HOME THE STONES, MICK WE LOVE YOU. Me and Beardsley try and blend in.

'Fucking hairies!' Beardsley mutters.

But the police are lost in the crush and we manage to get out to the main exit amidst this gaggle of teenage tarts, screaming and calling out the names of their idols. I join in for the hell of it.

'Aren't you a bit old for this sort of thing?' asks this girl in a mini skirt.

'Nah, I've always been a fan of the boys.'

The uniformed coppers at the foyer are mostly crowd control now, so we manage to slip out unnoticed and grab a cab back to London.

'We were fucking set up, Harry!'

I'm shouting. I'm bloody livid to tell the truth.

'Somebody grassed! Or set the whole fucking thing up with the Old Bill!'

Harry's trying to calm me down. Pours me and Beardsley another brandy. Waits for us to calm down a bit. He shrugs.

'You reckon Derek stitched us?'

'I don't know. I don't think so.'

'So what you reckon happened?'

'Well, I heard something,' he says.

'What?'

'Bit of inside information from a friend on the force. Change of security arrangements at Heathrow. Airports Authority Police are out. It's CID Number Two Area's patch now. I think people were beginning to notice how much stuff was going missing.'

'Well, it couldn't last for ever I suppose. And would your bent copper happen to know who it was that stitched us, Harry?'

'Leave it, Jack. A caper gone wrong. It's no big story. Let's just wipe our mouth and get on with it. Best thing is to lie low for a while as far as the Airport's concerned. Chances are they'll be pulling in the car-park mob and all. We just need to make sure no one can finger us for anything.'

'Yeah, I guess so. Well that's the end of Thiefrow then.'

'Yeah. It was good while it lasted.'

'And now we've got other rackets to attend to.'

'Yeah,' says Harry. 'And I want you to take it easy. No more petrol bombing bookshops without my go ahead.'

Porn. And me and Beardsley's little drugs operation. With the Airport gone at least there'll be money coming in from them. Maybe we should cut Harry into the acid racket. Could do with some wholesale protection if we come up against any opposition. Not that we have any bother with the hairy Peace and Love types we deal to.

Beardsley gets off and we arrange to meet up later. I stay for another drink. I can tell Harry wants to talk. He pours me another brandy and then goes out and comes back with a map. More big-time criminal plans, I think. I hope not, if the Airport fiasco is anything to go by.

'I want to show you something, Jack,' says Harry.

'Oh yeah? What?'

Harry smooths out the unfolded map on the coffee table. Chubby finger points at a bit of green.

'Here's where they found Bernie. That kid in the suitcase.'

'Oh yeah?'

That again.

'Tattingstone,' he says, pointing to a little dot of a village. 'And just along from it, here,' he goes on, tracing a fat finger to a slightly larger dot next to a whole lot of blue, 'is Hartwell-juxta-Mare.'

'Hartwell.'

'Juxta-Mare. It's Latin for by the sea. Remember Joe Meek kept saying "just a, just a" after he told us that Bernie was going to a party in a big house out in the country. Maybe he was trying to tell us something.'

'It's a bit of a long shot, Harry.'

Harry Starks as Sherlock Holmes. I think not.

'No it ain't, Jack. I know of a big country house there where they have just the kind of party Bernie might have gone to. And whose house it is. We're going to pay him a little visit.'

Trevor drives us over in the Daimler but we could of walked. It's only a couple of streets away. Eaton Square. Dead flash. Park the motor and Harry leads us up to the front door of one of these big houses. Trevor comes with us. Harry leans on the bell and after a while someone comes to the door. I'm half expecting a butler or a footman or something but instead there's this flabby-faced fellow in a bow tie, grey hair swept back. He gives a little start when he sees us but you'd hardly notice as he quickly goes into genial mode.

'Harry!' he announces in a posh jolly voice. Sounds a bit ginned up. 'This is a pleasure. Do come in.'

He leads us into a small hallway and I realise that it's just a flat, not the whole house, that he lives in. Harry does the introductions. 'Lord Thursby,' he says. 'Call me Teddy,' insists the jolly little man, beaming a greedy grin at young Trevor.

'Can I take your hat, Jack?' he asks as he shows us through into his drawing room.

'Er, no. I'll keep it on if you don't mind.'

I feel clumsy and awkward. Should really take my hat off. The done thing in posh society, I suppose. I half expect a ticking off. Instead Teddy gives me another of his grins.

'Of course,' he says.

This civil manner, all cultivated to put people at ease, makes me feel uneasy. I ain't used to all this politeness. It's intimidating. Teddy seems so relaxed and unflappable. I do notice his hand shakes a little as he pushes the door open for us, though.

We go through and Harry and Trevor settle down on a settee next to a big marble fireplace. I grab an armchair. Sort of perch on it uneasily. Its rich upholstery making me feel uncomfortable and out of place. Teddy gets us all a drink. Gin and tonics all round. He settles in the chair across from mine with a self-satisfied sigh.

'Cheers,' says Teddy all jovial, lifting his cut-glass tumbler.

We all repeat it like zombies. Like he's got the upper hand.

'So,' he says in this rich voice of his. 'To what do I owe the pleasure of your company, Harry? And of your charming friends of course.'

'Well, it ain't a social call, Teddy.'

'No,' Teddy says with a hint of regret in his voice. 'I somehow thought it wouldn't be.'

Harry takes a sip of gin and plonks his glass on the coffee table.

'Let's stop fucking about and come to the point, Teddy,' he says impatiently.

'Oh dear.' Teddy flinches a little but keeps up his polite front. 'I do hope this isn't going to be unpleasant. I do detest any unpleasantness.'

'That's precisely what it's about. It's very unpleasant.'

Teddy's nervousness is beginning to show. He looks into his gin.

'Then you better tell me what this is about,' he says quietly.

'Bernard Oliver,' says Harry looking for a reaction.

Teddy shrugs.

'Seventeen-year-old rent boy. Found cut up and in two suitcases in a field not more than five miles away from your country seat.'

Teddy traces a finger around the lip of his glass. Looks up slowly.

'Oh,' he says.

'Yes. Oh. He was at one of your parties, wasn't he Teddy?'

Teddy doesn't look so jolly now.

'Well he might have been.'

'What do you mean "might have been"?'

'Well, you can't expect me to remember all these boys' names. But Scotland Yard seem to think he might have been.'

'Scotland Yard? You mean to say they've been to see you?'

'Oh yes. A very high-level investigation, needless to say. The Murder Squad was kept out of it. There were some very high-ranking people at that party. The important thing was to avoid any sort of scandal. Everyone was very keen to avoid that.'

'The murderer could have been one of the guests.'

'It's a possibility. Look, nothing happened at Hartwell Lodge. Nothing like that, anyway. But when the connection was made between this, well, regrettable incident and a party attended by ministers of Church and State, it was decided that the investigation would be wound down.'

'So there was a cover up?'

'Harry, you make it sound like there's some sort of conspiracy. Of course there isn't. There never is. Nobody knows what happened to this unfortunate boy. And everyone wants to keep it that way.'

'And protect some sick bastard who might be well connected.'

'Harry, I'd hardly expect you to get squeamish over another unsolved murder.'

Harry tenses up, eyebrows furrowing with fury, hands clenched. He's about to say something but then he just seethes through gritted teeth. A hand unclenches to pick up his glass. Takes a big slug of gin.

'It's a terrible thing to have happened,' Teddy goes on calmly. 'But there's nothing we can do about it now. And there are other things at stake. There's a Bill for homosexual law reform going through the Lower House at the moment. A scandal like this involving important public figures could do untold damage to it.'

'You're involved in that?'

'I'm championing it in the Lords,' says Teddy a bit smug.

'Doesn't that rather blow your cover, Teddy?'

'Well,' Teddy gives a little chuckle, 'I always insist on my disinterest in these matters. My amateur status as it were. I always declare myself as a non-playing captain.'

'Very fucking funny, Teddy.'

'Now Harry, don't be tiresome. You know that discretion is the better part of valour. And it's an important change in the law.'

'What, consenting adults over twenty-one? Doesn't make me and Trevor legal. Or little Bernie for that matter.'

'But it's a start, isn't it? If we remain discreet and behave ourselves, the law will leave us alone.'

Harry grunts dismissively then gives Thursby his coldest stare.

'Look at me, Teddy,' he says. 'You say no one knows who murdered Bernie. You sure about that?'

Teddy looks him in the eyes and nods.

'Yes.'

Harry gets up and grabs Teddy by the throat. Eyes bulge and flabby face goes all red.

'You better not be lying, Teddy.'

'Please, Harry.' Thursby's deep rich voice gone all high pitched. 'I'm telling the truth.'

Harry lets go of him and sits back down. Teddy sighs and brushes himself down. Trying to regain his composure. His bow tie's come undone. He takes out a matching handkerchief from his top pocket and mops at his sweaty brow.

'Any ideas?' Harry continues.

Thursby shrugs.

'Well, it was odd that the body was so carefully cut up and packed into these cases and then left in the middle of a ploughed field,' he says a bit wheezy. 'As if whoever left it there wanted it to be found. Could be blackmail of some kind. Double blackmail even. But really, Harry, I don't know anything. It's best left well alone.'

Harry stands up to go. Me and Trevor follow suit.

'One more thing,' says Harry. 'Who supplied the boys to the party?'

Teddy's stood up now too. He roars with laughter.

'Don't you remember? It was you, Harry.'

Harry looks shocked. Sways a little like a stunned bull. Trevor's gone pale.

'I don't remember,' mutters Harry frowning.

Trevor looks like he's going to be sick. Instead he suddenly says: 'He's right. I organised it. We'd just met. I was still on the game then. You gave me two hundred quid to gather together some boys for this party. I was going to go down myself. You gave me another fifty to stay with you instead.'

'You see?' Teddy declares a little triumphantly. 'You're implicated in this as well, Harry.'

Harry starts asking Trevor questions as soon as we get back to his flat.

'Why didn't you tell me before?'

'Tell you what? I'd forgotten all about it. I never thought it had anything to do with Bernie's murder.'

'You should have thought.'

This is becoming like an interrogation. Trevor looks pale.

'I was thinking of going down,' he says quietly, full of fear for what might have been. 'Could have been me what got cut up.'

Harry ignores the comment. Carries on the questioning. Time for me to go. Got to meet Beardsley in Tottenham.

'Tell me all the names of the other boys that went down,' Harry demands, hardly noticing me make my excuses.

'I don't remember, Harry.'

'Then start remembering.'

We're in this pub with a little dancehall attached to it just off Tottenham High Road. Full of Beardsley types. Cropped hair, boots and braces, Crombies and Sta-Press trousers. A few sporting little pork-pie hats like junior versions of old Jack. Baldheads, I decide to call them. Mad *chicka-chicka-chicka* music on the jukebox. Baldheads stomping along to it in formation boot dance.

Me and Beardsley recounting the Airport fuck up with post-job bravado. We can laugh about it now. Beardsley's got no idea who might have grassed. We both make filthy oaths of nasty revenge even though it's unlikely we'll ever get our hands on the nark.

Then on to the main item of business. Beardsley's made contact with a couple of big acid customers. A hippy party in Hampstead in the next couple of nights and a fellah over in Ladbroke Grove. I just got to get the gear off Marty and we'll meet up the day after tomorrow in the Mildmay Tavern.

Go for a piss. Fresh graffiti above the urinal. PAKIS OUT. Hear a ruckus in the car park as I come out of the bogs. A small gang of greasers is shaping up. Baldheads pouring out of the boozer. The greebos are game enough, swinging motorbike chains and putting it about a bit lively. But they're outnumbered. Beardsley leads the charge and they go down for a right good kicking.

Get into the Zodiac and head east. Stop off at the Regency for a late one. Take it easy. Don't want to ruffle any feathers there. One of the Kray firm lets it drop that there's a job going. The Twins want somebody doing. A hint that it could be a ticket to being back on their firm. I say I'll think about it.

Next day and Harry wants me to drive out with him to Suffolk to where this kid's body was found. I ain't keen.

'Come on, Harry,' I say. 'You know what that toff friend of yours said. It's best left alone.'

'I promise, Jack,' he says. 'This is the last time. I just want to see for myself.'

See what? Maybe he just needs to put it all to rest somehow.

So off we go for a drive in the country. Up through Essex. Past Colchester and into East Anglia. The land flattens out and the sky gets bigger. Big bright clouds hang above the long horizon, gloomy fields of sugar beet stretch out below. We reach Hartwell-juxta-Mare. Pretty little seaside village. Cliffside road takes us up to Hartwell Lodge. Big mansion with a good view of the North Sea.

'Right,' says Harry, taking the next turn. 'This is the road to Tattingstone. The killing could have happened somewhere along here. So keep your eyes peeled.'

'What are we looking for?'

'I don't know,' Harry mutters. 'I don't know.'

We drive along to the actual field where the kid was found. Harry's got map references and everything. But we don't spot nothing. We get out of the motor and Harry snoops about the hedgerow gloomily.

Well, that's it then, I think. We can go home and forget about it. Get on with some serious business. But Harry wants to drive back along the route just to make sure.

About three miles up the road from Tattingstone, Harry notices a little track leading off into a patch of woodland. Didn't notice it on the way over. Harry stops the car, reverses back and turns up into it.

'Let's have a little shufti up here,' he says.

The bumpy old track winds up into a little clearing among a few weatherbeaten trees. There's a battered old caravan sitting there. Harry looks at me, eyes bulging a bit with tension as we pull up. Harry reaches down to in front of the driver's seat and pulls out a shooter he's got tucked away by the pedals. Tucks it into his waistband and winks over at me.

'Let's see if anyone's at home.'

We get out and walk slowly up to the caravan. Filthy curtains drawn on all its windows. Harry raps on the door.

'Hello?' he calls, one hand fingering at the gun butt poking out of his trousers.

I nearly laugh. All this suspense and it's probably just some gyppo's doss hole. Harry knocks again.

'Anybody there?'

No reply. Nothing.

Harry tries the door, rattling the little handle. Locked. Starts to make to force it with his shoulder then thinks again. Fishes in his pocket and pulls out the car keys. Hands them to me.

'There's a crowbar in the boot,' he says.

I fetch it and jemmy open the little metal door. We go in. Nasty butcher's-shop pong. Harry clicks on a gloomy little lightbulb. A chamber of horrors. Pages of homo porn mags torn out and sellotaped all over blood-smeared walls and windows. Hacksaw and set of butcher's knives on a little table in the middle of the room. A coil of rope and a pair of handcuffs on the floor. A couple of blood-caked scalpels rusting in a tiny wash basin. Kilner jars with things floating in them. Human organs. Suitcase Murder newspaper clippings scattered everywhere. Anatomy textbook lying open on a chair.

I nearly puke. Harry's got this mad gleam in his eye.

'We've got the bastard,' he hisses.

'How did the Murder Squad miss all of this?' I ask.

'Well, they weren't looking, were they? They were put off the scent once the Hartwell Lodge party was covered up. It'll be no use going to them now.'

Harry goes over and touches the kettle on the stove.

'So what are we going to do?' I ask.

'Feel that.'

I put my hand to the kettle. There's an ever so faint warmth to it.

'Someone's been here recently. That means they might be coming back.'

'So we're going to wait for them?'

'Yeah. But first I've got to hide the motor. We give the game away if they see that.'

He walks to the door.

'Wait a minute,' I say. 'You leaving me here?'

'What's the matter? You scared?'

Harry's grinning. Goading me.

'Course not.'

Harry laughs and pulls out the gun.

'Here, take this,' he says, handing it to me. 'You might need it if anyone turns up. Don't kill them. I want them alive.'

And he goes. I pick up the anatomy book and sit down in the chair. Try to make myself comfortable. The gun's a .38 revolver. The weight of it in my hand is reassuring. I pull the broken door to and settle back down again. Watching the door. Listening out.

It's starting to get dark. Strange hooting country noises in the air. Otherwise it's quiet. Dead quiet. I start to feel tired. Search my pocket for black bombers but just come up with lint and old betting slips. I'm knackered. Haven't had a proper night's sleep in a donkey's age. Stretch and yawn. Put the revolver down on the table near to where I can get it and lean back a bit. Fingers lace behind my neck, cradling it. Pull some hat-brim down and give my eyes a bit of a rest from the bare lightbulb. Harry's taking his time. Drift off a bit.

Feel someone prod my arm and give a bit of a start like you do sometimes when you're just nodding off.

'Harry?' I mutter, pushing back the hat from my brow.

I blink and see the barrel of the gun pointing at my face.

'Don't fuck about, Harry,' I say, a bit tetchy.

I blink again and see that it ain't Harry holding the gun. It's a little weasel-faced bloke grinning down at me.

'What the fuck?' I gasp.

'Expecting someone else, were we? And who would that be?'

He clicks the hammer back for emphasis.

'No . . . n . . . no one,' I stammer. 'My dog. Harry's the name of my dog. I was just taking it for a walk. It ran off and I was looking for it when I got tired, and I just thought I'd have a little rest until it came back.'

'And what was this for?' he asks, waving the pistol at me. 'Pigeon shooting?'

'Yeah,' I reply with a nervous laugh. 'That's right.'

Weasel Face presses the barrel of the shooter against my forehead.

'Shut it,' he says.

He picks up the handcuffs and clicks one manacle around my left wrist. Still keeping the gun against my head, he takes the bracelets around the back of the chair.

'Put your other hand in here,' he orders and both hands are now secured behind me and against the backrest.

He backs off, aiming the gun at my head. He picks up a blood-stained rag from the floor and pushes it into my gob.

'There,' he says. 'Let's wait for your little doggie now, shall we?'

Footsteps outside. Weasel Face goes to the side of the door to be behind it when Harry comes in. I try to make a noise but gag against the filthy cloth. Taste stale blood in the back of my throat and feel like retching.

Door opens. Harry frowns at me. I nod like a loony at him. He swings around to see Weasel Face and the gun.

'Put your hands up!' he snaps.

Harry slowly lifts his big paws.

'So who are you?' Weasel asks. 'Old Bill? You don't look like Old Bill. Did they send you?'

Harry frowns, then plays along.

'That's right. They sent us.'

Weasel laughs in his face.

'And who would they be?'

Harry shrugs. Weasel laughs again.

'You don't know anything about this, do you? Do you?'

Weasel sniggers.

'Why don't you tell us about it?' Harry asks softly, managing to stay calm.

'Oh yeah. Tell you about it. Tell you all about it.'

More sniggering.

'I didn't kill the kid, you know. They did it. Left me with this boy's body to get rid of. I know how, you see. Know how to butcher. Let the butcher take care of it, they says. He likes that. Give me some money and the body and think I'll be happy with that. Butcher boy. Delivery boy. Chop, chop. Get the job done. But I'm not happy, see. Don't want to get rid of it all. Want to keep some for myself. Want to show people what a good job I've done. So I pack him up in a suitcase. All cut up perfect into choice cuts. Everyone can see what a good job I made of it. Then they're not happy. Say butcher should have got rid of it properly. Say butcher's greedy, keeping choice cuts for himself. And butcher *is* a greedy boy. Wants more money otherwise he'll tell. They say it doesn't matter. They got powerful friends and don't need to worry about Old Bill.'

'Who are they?' asks Harry.

'Shh. Show you something. Kept the best bits for myself.'

Weasel creeps over and picks up one of the Kilner jars. He holds it up against the lightbulb. The gun's pointing away from us now and I look over at Harry. He holds his breath. Wait.

'See.' Weasel sniggers, distracted by his trophy. 'It's his heart.'

The purple and grey lump bobs in the murky fluid. A tiny stream of bubbles glows silver in the light. Harry nods at me and I throw myself at Weasel. The jar smashes on the floor releasing a sharp tang of embalming fluid. Weasel staggers back waving the revolver about madly. Harry's made a grab for one of the knives on the table. Comes up with it slashing Weasel across the throat. He clutches at his neck, wide eyed with shock, tries to work a finger into the trigger guard. Harry knocks the shooter out of his hand. Weasel falls to the floor, blood spurting out, splattering onto glossy pictures of naked men. Harry crouches down next to him, trying to avoid the blood spurts as he holds Weasel's throat.

'Who are they?' he demands, shouting. 'Who are they?'

But Weasel just gurgles and chokes, the blood bubbling out of his mouth and out of the gaping wound. His vocal cords slashed. He'll never tell now.

He takes a long time to die. Nearly half an hour before all his blood pumps out of him. His breath slows into a rasping wheeze. Then one last sigh and it's over.

Then we set to work silently. Harry finds the keys to the cuffs and I rub at my wrists where the ratchets have cut into them. I try to spit out the clotted blood from my mouth but I feel that the taste of it will be with me for a long time. Even when I've taken a mouthful of petrol and spat it out when I'm siphoning some out of the tank in Harry's motor, it's still there. We spread it all over the caravan and pour the remainder down Weasel's throat, hoping he'll burn really well and there won't be any forensic.

Then we torch the trailer. A gypsy funeral. We watch it go up in a fireball. I feel the heat of it against my face and hope that it burns away all of the evidence. Pray that it burns away the horror that we've witnessed. Then we get in the motor and drive as fast as we can back to the Smoke. Harry's brooding face looking ghostly in the dashboard lights. Cheated. He'll never know now.

We get back to Harry's place at about two in the morning. Trevor's waiting up, looking sullen. Harry undresses in the hallway and goes through to take a shower.

'Get rid of them,' he tells Trevor, nodding at the pile of bloodstained clothes.

Wish I could get rid of the bloodstained taste in my mouth.

Harry comes through into the drawing room in a dressing gown and Trevor gets us drinks. Nobody says much. We just concentrate on drinking enough to blot it all out.

'I've remembered some more names of the boys who went to that party, Harry,' says Trevor.

Harry shrugs.

'That's finished with now,' he says.

'It could have been me,' Trev continues. 'I nearly went to that party. It could have been me what got cut up.'

'Don't talk about it,' Harry orders gruffly. 'It's done with now.'

It takes us a long while to get drunk enough to think about turning in.

'You can kip here if you like, Jack,' says Harry. 'You know where the spare room is.'

Can't sleep. Weasel-faced horrors keep jolting me awake just as I'm about to nod off.

Morning. Breakfast with Harry and Trev. Newspaper headline: DETROIT BURNING *Dead Toll Mounts As Race Riots Sweep US*. Harry gets a phone call. Anxious looks as he speaks down the blower.

'Come on, Jack,' he says as he slams down the receiver. 'We got to get over to Soho. We've had some trouble.'

The homo porn bookshop Harry's been nipping off has been burned down. Gutted. Blackened photos of musclemen, their glossiness charred away, scattered everywhere. Petrol bomb, no doubt about it. Maltese revenge.

'This was personal. It would have made more sense to attack the new shops I've got leaseholds on. But they know that I'm queer so they're trying to wind me up.'

'What we going to do about it, Harry?'

'Nothing. Not yet anyway.'

'But we can't let the Maltesers get away with this. We got to do something.'

'Look, Jack. I told you not to get lairy with this racket. You start chucking petrol bombs and this is what happens. Mooney ain't going to like this.'

'Mooney.' Repeat that filth's name with contempt.

'Yeah, Mooney. That's who we've got to deal with on this.'

Hide a sneer. Harry cosying up to Old Bill.

'So what do you want me to do?'

'I don't want you to do anything. Leave all of this alone, Jack.'

Tempted to question Harry's bottle but I keep my thoughts to myself. This porn racket's taking longer than I thought to build up, and with the Airport gone, I'm running short of cash. Just as well I've got the drugs business going with Beardsley. Can't really afford to cut Harry into that yet, though. And then there is that Kray job someone mentioned the other night in the Regency.

Go home and try to get some proper kip. Wake up around five. Sluggish. Have a bath and get something to eat. Still feel lousy. Take a couple of bombers. There we go. *Chicka, chicka, chicka.*

Get the gear and meet Beardsley in the Mildmay Tavern. This party want a hundred quid's worth. The fellah over in Ladbroke Grove is down for two hundred and fifty. Paying Marty a ton for the gear that's two hundred and fifty quid profit. Half a monkey split two ways. Not bad for a night's work.

We drive to this place in Hampstead. Huge house up by the Heath. Weird music blaring out. Beardsley gives the name of his contact at the door and we're led in. Some bird with her face painted and her tits hanging out hands me a flower. Put it in my buttonhole. Beardsley drops his on the floor and stubs it out with his boot.

We pass through a crowd of hairies. Kaftans and crochet-knit mini dresses, headscarves and flowers. Bleeding flowers everywhere. Spacey music echoing through these big, high-ceilinged rooms. Inkblot light show projected on the walls. Diabolical.

We find a quiet room and Beardsley's contact turns up. He peels off a wad and gives it to Beardsley. I hand over the goods.

'Wow,' he says. 'Thanks, man.'

Beardsley sneers and makes to leave.

'Stay for a bit, if you like,' this geezer offers.

Yeah, why not? I think.

'Nah,' says Beardsley. 'We've got to get off.'

'We could stay for a drink though,' I say.

'Nah. I don't fancy it.'

'Come on, Beardsley. Just a drink.'

I could do with some recreation. Especially after last night's horrors. And this place is mob-handed with half-naked birds.

'We've got business to attend to, Jack. Remember?'

'Yeah, yeah. Relax. We ain't meeting this geezer until midnight. We've got time to enjoy ourselves a bit.'

'I ain't hanging around here.'

'Well, I'm staying for a drink.'

'I'll meet you there later then. You know where it is?'

Plan to meet this bloke in an all-night caff on Ladbroke Grove.

'Yeah, I'll find it.'

Beardsley shrugs and I hand him over the rest of the gear.

'I'll see you later then, Jack,' he says, rolling his eyes in disapproval. 'Behave yourself.'

Then Beardsley's off, shoving his way through the hairy crowd.

'I can see that this isn't your friend's scene,' says this bloke we've just sold the drugs to. 'He seems a bit uptight. But you're welcome here, man. We're all free here. You can turn on with us.'

I'm not quite sure what this geezer is fannying on about but I think I get his drift. He shows me through and gets me a drink. Someone passes me a joint and I take a couple of puffs of it.

Some bird with flowers in her hair starts chatting to me.

'Love the outfit, man,' she says pointing at the suit and hat. 'You look like some sort of gangster.'

'Yeah, well, you could say that.'

'Wow.'

Everyone fannying on with *wow* and *yeah* and *out of sight*. All on the happy drugs that we've been peddling, no doubt.

'Are you tripping?' asks this bird.

'What?'

'Are you turned on?'

'I'm not with you.'

'You know,' she says. 'Acid. It's psychedelic.'

'Nah. I ain't into that.'

'Why don't you try?'

Before I know it she's got a tab of LSD on her finger pointing up at my face.

'Go on,' she says. 'Turn on with me.'

I look down at her smiling face. At her young tits, braless and peeking out of her chiffon blouse. Why not? Everybody seems so happy. I have some of that myself. I put my tongue out and she dabs this little blotter on it like a communion wafer.

'Yeah,' she says.

I chew it up and swallow it. Nothing happens for about half an hour and then, *whoosh!* Suddenly all these lairy colours come to life.

Swirling patterns all around me. Dots before my eyes exploding like flowers blooming. Weird music throbbing around in my skull.

Suddenly I'm dancing with this bird. Joining in with this funny old moving around everyone's doing. Waving hands and fingers about like music-hall conjurers. Like we've all got some sort of magic power. And it feels like we have. Of course, it makes sense now. Wow, I'm thinking. It's all right. Everything is all right.

I start taking my clothes off. Don't need them any more. I'm free. Free of the badness. Naked and free. The bird grins at me as I get my kit off.

'Yeah,' she says. 'Let it all hang out.'

I kiss her on the lips. Feel so happy.

'What's your name?' I ask her.

'Samantha.'

'I love you, Samantha,' I say and kiss her again.

'Yeah,' she says. 'Love, love, love.'

And I really do love her. It's not just randiness. Not dirty old Jack the Lad. I want to be with her. To love her always. Love. It's all suddenly clear to me now.

'Let's go upstairs,' I suggest.

Samantha giggles. I take her hand.

'Come on,' I say.

We find an empty bedroom. Samantha looks wide eyed at me as I help her take off her clothes. Then we just stand there looking at each other. Starkers. Like Adam and Eve. Would you Adam and Eve it? Slowly tracing hands around the shapes of our bodies. Fingers meeting and parting. I put a hand on her breast. Squeeze it gently. She stares at me. Chews at her lower lip. Then grins.

'You still got your hat on,' she says with a giggle.

I take it off. Throw the hat across the room. No more Jack the Hat. No more. Jack's head is bare. He's bareheaded, baldheaded, boneheaded. His head is free of The Hat. My mind is fannying on and I can't stop it. The Hat lies on the floor. No more Jack the Hat. *You've got it coming to you*. Suddenly feel scared. No hat, no head. No face. *You're not a face, you're a fucking head case*. No head, no face. No body, no case. A nobody. Cut up and packed in a suitcase. Nobody. I'm a nobody.

'Hey,' says Samantha. 'You OK?'

I look up at her. Her face is all blurred. I try to focus on it. Then it turns into something else. It becomes Madge's face. Oh God no. It's Madge looking at me. Yacking on at me.

You destroyed me, Jack the Hat. You destroyed my mind and then you destroyed my body. All those times I stuck by you when you got into trouble. You thought it was bad for you. Going inside. Well, what about me, left behind to face it all? The Law always coming around. Looking everywhere. Questions. Dates, times, everything. It made me a nervous wreck. You just walked away from it. I tried to explain but you said I was just nagging you. Yacking on at you. You couldn't see that it was destroying my mind. So you pushed me out of the car and destroyed my body as well. You've got it coming to you, Jack the Hat.

'I didn't mean it,' I say. 'It was an accident.'

'It's all right,' says the face, suddenly turning back into Samantha again.

I back into a corner. I'm frightened. Worried that this bird will turn back into Madge again. Scared that something horrible might happen.

'I'm sorry. I'm sorry,' I sob, curling up in the corner of the room.

'Shh,' says Samantha, leaning over me. 'It's OK. It's just a bad trip, that's all.'

Her naked body looks huge, towering over me. Tits dangling over my bald head. I figure that if I can press myself into this corner I'll be safe.

'You want to stay here for a while?'

Nod nod nod.

'I'll get you a blanket.'

She pulls one off the bed and brings it over. I wrap it around me. Rocking backwards and forwards. Trying to keep the horrors at bay.

'You want anything else?'

Nod nod. Point at The Hat. She passes it over and I put it back on.

Try to calm my head down. Horrors come and go. Torture. The Crank Up. Electric shocks of fear running riot through my shivering body. *We all done bad things, Jack.* Bottle gone. All the fear come back to haunt me. Kilner jars with internal organs bobbing about in them. My organs cut out and floating in fluid. My body cut up and got rid of. No body, no case. Nobody. *You've got it coming to you, Jack the Hat.* Hold on to The Hat and try and keep it all in.

Curled up and rocking backwards and forwards in the corner. Mind yacking on at me. Red demons out to get me. Diabolical liberty. Crippled Madge points the finger. *Chicka, chicka, chicka.* Nonsense horror driving me mad. Jack the Hat is in Hell.

Hours of jabbering terror. Seems like years. Then it eases off a bit. Still flashes of fear and horror. Mad bright colours. Bobbing and weaving. Lairy patterns coming at me at odd moments but I feel I'm coming out of it.

The bloke what we sold the drugs to comes up with my clothes and a cup of tea. I get dressed.

'Bad trip, eh man?' he says. 'Well, it happens.'

'What time is it?' I ask, taking a shaky glug of tea.

'I don't know, man. It's nearly dawn.'

Fuck. Beardsley.

I get the rest of my gear on and run down the stairs. Push my way through what's left of the party. Painted faces. Shadows dancing huge against the oily lightshow. A naked threesome writhe about on the floor.

Get into the Zodiac and drive down the Finchley Road towards West London. Mind still flaky but I hold it together. Streetlamps melting, dripping yellow pools of sorrow. Traffic signs leaping out at me like dreadful warnings. Ignore it all. Concentrate on driving.

Get to the caff and the owner is sweeping up debris. Broken crockery and splintered furniture. Blood on the lino floor.

'What the fuck happened here?' I ask him.

'Fucking greasers causing trouble again. Hell's Angels. Jumped a skinhead guy sat here on his own.'

Fuck. Beardsley.

'Was he badly hurt?'

Guilt. Fear. Panic. Got to hold it together.

'He got a right good beating. Ambulance job.'

Get the name of the hospital and get back to the motor. Gloomy purple dawn coming up over Portobello Road as market traders set up their stalls.

Beardsley's a right mess. Head bandaged, face stitched up. Broken nose, broken ribs, broken jaw, broken teeth. Sat up in a hospital bed, glaring at me. It was my fault. Should have run this racket properly. Should have known it was too easy to be true. Should have cut Harry in and made sure that we were properly protected. And I should have been there, for fucksakes.

'What happened to you?' I ask Beardsley.

'More to the point, Jack,' he mumbles through wrecked jaw and teeth. 'What happened to you?'

He's right. I should have been there.

'It was a fucking set up, Jack. They were saying that it was their racket. They took the money and the acid and beat the shit out of me.'

Fuck. Money gone. Acid gone. We end up owing Marty a hundred nicker with nothing to show for it.

'We've got to get those bastards, Jack.'

Beardsley mouthing vehement through the pain.

'Yeah,' I humour him. 'Sure.'

But I'm thinking: this racket's over. Cut our losses. Acid is bad news. Don't want to deal with that diabolical stuff no more.

'Get me a shooter, Jack. I'll fucking straighten them.'

'Take it easy, son. You just worry about getting yourself mended.'

Beardsley's eyes burning fierce through the bandages. His mind full of revenge.

'Just get me a shooter, Jack.'

On me own again. No more rackets. Airport gone, drugs gone. Harry stitching something up with the Dirty Squad about the porn. Probably doesn't need to cut me in. The Summer of Love is over, leaving poor old Jack skint. Weather's turning colder and I'm damn near boracic. The word keeps coming. A job for the Other Two. Someone needs doing. And I'm up for it. I could get back on their firm. I know I've bad mouthed them but this could straighten things out. Maybe get me back on a pension. Whatever, I need the money.

Arrange a meet. Get ready. New shirt bought for the occasion. Strap on a shoulder holster over it. Put on my best suit and hat. Get out the long-nosed Colt .45 from the chimney flue. Unwrap it and slip it in under the suit jacket. Practise a couple of draws in front of the mirror. Down a few bombers. *Chicka, chicka, chicka*. Pull a bit of hat-brim down. I'm ready.

The meet is at the Grave Maurice in Whitechapel. The Twins are there with some of the firm. Predictable show of strength. Never subtle when it comes to front. Try to stay calm but I'm pilled so I'm flapping about like crazy. Talking too much. Mr Payne, their business front, wants topping. The geezer who runs their long firms is looking dodgy. The Twins are worried that he's going to grass so they want him snuffed out. The Man with The Suitcase has got to go. I get handed a package. £250 up front and then there's another £250 when the job's done. There's something heavy in there. A shooter no doubt.

Billy Exley's doing the driving. We've got an address in Dulwich, so we set off over the water. Billy was a good middleweight in his day but he's past it now. Looks ill.

'It's my heart, Jack,' he says, as if explaining his state to me. 'I got a bad heart.'

I unwrap the package and pocket the money. Pull out the shooter. It's a poxy little automatic. A .32 or something.

'These things are no good,' I tell Billy. 'Automatics are always jamming. And they leave too much forensic. Cartridge cases all over the place.'

I slip the little automatic into my pocket

'This is more like it.'

I pull out the .45 and cock the hammer. Billy gives a start and nearly swerves off the road. He pulls over to the kerb and starts fishing about in his pockets.

'Oh my God,' he mutters, red faced. 'I don't think my heart can take it. For fucksakes Jack, put that thing away.'

He gets out a bottle of pills and downs a couple. I offer him a black bomber but he shakes his head.

'Come on, Jack, let's not fuck about. Let's get this done quickly and quietly.'

We head off again, through Camberwell. I hope old Billy doesn't have a heart attack on me. Some hit squad we turned out to be. Truth is, I've never shot anyone. Still, it should be straightforward enough. I go through it in my mind. Knock, knock. Who's there? Door opens. Bang, bang. And we're away. What could be simpler? Just need to keep my bottle. This will prove I've still got it.

We get to Dulwich and find the address. A nice big house for a nice big businessman. Billy parks up. I go through the routine with him.

Get the motor started when you hear the shots. Stay calm, that's the main thing. I'll walk, not run, back to the car. Then we're away.

I get out and go up to the house. Heart pounding away like fuck. Wrought iron gate squeaks open. Gravel drive crunching away underfoot. Slip my hand into my jacket. Ready. Get to the door. Hit the doorbell. Bing bong. Avon calling.

Hear footsteps in the hallway. See distorted outline of person through mottled-glass panel. Ready to pull out the shooter. Wait. Wait till I see them proper. Then I shoot them. Bang, bang, you're dead. *We all done bad things, Jack*. Never killed anyone before. But I got to do this. Got to. Get your bottle together, Jack.

Door swings open.

'Yes?'

It's a woman. It's a fucking woman standing in the doorway.

'Can I help you?' she asks.

'Er, is Mr Payne in?'

What am I going to do? She's seen my face. I'll have to kill them both.

'He's not here,' she says.

Fuck. Fuck. Fuck.

'Do you know when he'll be back?'

'He won't be back all evening, I'm afraid.'

'Oh, right. Well, sorry to trouble you.'

'Who shall I say called?' she asks but I'm already legging it down the gravel driveway.

'What happened?' asks Billy when I get back in the motor.

'He wasn't in.'

'What?'

'I said, "He wasn't in." Now let's get the fuck out of here.'

What a fuck up. Why does it always happen to me? Still, I've still got the £250 advance. I can keep that and go back and finish the job some other time.

'What are we going to tell The Twins?' asks Bad Heart Billy as we motor back up north.

'You mean, what are *you* going to tell them, Billy?'

'Jack, you can't do this to me.'

'Look, they said he'd be there tonight. I kept my part of the bargain. Tell them to set it up again properly. And tell them to get their information right. Then I'll finish the job.'

'They ain't going to like this, Jack.'

'Well that ain't my problem, is it Billy?'

Poor Billy's shaking his head and rubbing his chest.

'I don't think my heart can take much more of this.'

Beardsley's out of hospital. Meet him in the Mildmay Tavern. His stitches are out but he still looks a right state. Broken nose gives him a new look. He looks proper tough now. Sad really, to see his youthful looks all gone. Even his expression looks old. Bitter and full of hateful brooding. He's done his apprenticeship. He's earned what I'm going to give him.

A few faces in the boozer. Kray hangers-on. Giving me moody little smiles. Not sure whether I'm in on the firm or not. Fuck them.

Me and Beardsley have a bit of a chat about setting something up together. He's got a fix on getting his own back on those greasers. I go along with it but think: some quiet little racket, that's what we want to be looking for.

'I got you something,' I tell him.

'What?'

'Something you've always wanted.' I tap myself under the armpit. Poxy little automatic's almost too small for the shoulder holster.

Beardsley smiles for the first time this evening. His nasty little face beaming. Evil eyes lighting up with joy.

'Let's have a look, Jack,' he says.

I look around the taproom, at all the second-rate faces, all the little Kray spies.

'Not here son. Later. Outside.'

'Fancy another one?' I ask Beardsley.

'They just called Time.'

'Don't worry about that, son.'

I go to the bar.

'Same again.'

'Sorry Jack, we're closed.'

'Come on, don't fuck about. I want a drink.'

'I said, "We're closed."'

'You've done afters before.'

'Yeah, well not tonight. If you want a late one you can go up the Regency.'

'I don't want to go up the fucking Regency. I want a fucking drink.'

'There's no need for that, Jack,' someone says.

Muttering in the bar. *Troublemaker*, a voice says. Cunts. You want trouble? I pull out the shooter. Point it at the barman.

'Just get me a fucking drink.'

He starts pouring out the bacardi sharpish. Everyone's gawking. Turn the shooter on them.

'And you lot,' I say, grinning like a maniac. 'Drop 'em. Go on, you stupid cunts. Drop your trousers.'

And they fucking do and all. Pass a glass over to Beardsley and pick up mine.

'Cheers,' I say, raising my drink and waving the shooter about.

Beardsley's laughing away like a drain. We drink up.

'Come on Jack,' he says. 'Let's get out of here.'

I hold up the pistol. Haven't cleaned it or checked it since it was handed over to me in the Grave Maurice. Common knowledge: Kray firearms notoriously unreliable.

'Poxy little thing probably doesn't even work. Probably jammed or something.'

I aim it at the optics and pull the trigger. BANG. A whole row of bottles explode. Everyone ducks except me and Beardsley.

'Fuck,' I say. 'I didn't expect that to happen.'

'You fucking nutter, Jack,' says Beardsley. 'Come on, let's go.'

Beardsley examines his new toy as I'm driving down the Ball's Pond Road. Pulls out the clip, shoves it back in again. Clicks on and off the safety. He's happy.

'Thanks, Jack.'

'Well, you be careful with that.'

Winston Churchill on the gramophone when I go around to see Harry. Bad sign. Empty bottles of Stematol and Napoleon brandy lying around. Anti-depressants with cognac chasers, a desperate attempt to stave off his gloomy madness. I figure all that grief has come to the surface with this Suitcase thing. And he never really found out what happened in the end.

Trevor's gone. Harry feels he's driven him away. The horror of it all frightened him off.

'He kept saying, "It could have been me that got cut up like poor little Bernie,"' says Harry. 'And after a while I felt he was accusing me. Like he was saying, "It could have been you that did something as terrible as that."'

Trevor's gone and Harry's going into one. Not the best of times to bring up the subject of work. I want Harry to cut me into his porn racket. Figure it would be an easy little number. Keep me out of trouble.

'Thing is, Jack. Word gets around. You've been acting lairy a few too many times. I can't afford for things to get out of hand just as I'm getting started on this. I've got to keep a respectable front.'

'I'll behave myself, Harry. Promise.'

'Jack, you've been winding up the Twins. I told you I didn't want to get into any of that. I can do without another enemy in Soho. I've got enough on my hands with the Maltese.'

Here we go again. The Other Two. Fucking everything up for me again.

'And, well,' Harry goes on awkward like, 'well a certain somebody isn't too happy with you being involved in all of this.'

'Mooney.'

Harry shrugs.

'Yeah. Look. I need someone who the OPS fancy. Someone who can keep his head down. And someone who knows the trade. I'm using Wally Peters.'

Fat Wally. Rumour has it he was running a blue-film racket with George Cornell just before George had the top of his head taken off by a luger in Whitechapel.

'Harry—'

'Times are changing, Jack. It's the Dirty Squad what are calling the shots with this one. Being polite to the Old Bill isn't exactly your style, is it?'

'Yeah, well.'

What he means is: Jack the Hat is bad news. Trouble. A bringer of bad luck. A Jonah.

Shrug.

'So this is it, then, eh?'

Harry sighs.

'Jack, look, sort yourself out. Deal with it. Straighten things with the Twins. There'll be other jobs in the future.'

'Right then,' I say and make a move to get going.

No point in making a fuss. Wipe your face and move on. That's the thing.

'Business is business, Jack.'

What he means is: times change. You're a dinosaur. And he's right and all.

Double handshake at the door. Folded wad slipped into my palm. Rude, and downright stupid, to refuse.

'Be lucky, Jack,' he says.

And I'm off.

Page four headline in the *Evening Standard* a few days later:

MAN HELD IN ARCADE SHOOTING.

Two men were seriously wounded yesterday when an assailant walked into The Golden Goose amusement arcade in London's West End and fired a pistol at them as they were playing on a pinball table. Gunfire caused panic in the crowded arcade. Witnesses say that the victims were both members of a motorcycle gang. Both men are in a critical condition. Police have arrested Simon Beardsley in connection with the incident and he is being held for questioning . . .

Silly cunt. He's gone and done it now. All my fault. Should never have given him that shooter. Well, I'm well and truly on my own now. Doesn't matter. I can look after myself. Feel uneasy, though. Bad thoughts. It's dangerous to be alone.

Can't sleep at night. Can't stay awake during the day without the black bombers. Keep taking the pills. They fuck me up but I can't do without them.

Word gets around. Jack the Hat. Jack the Troublemaker. Had the Twins over one time too many. Making trouble in pubs and clubs they're giving protection to. Still owe them for the bungled hit. Not my fucking fault he wasn't there.

Staying in. Watching telly. Spending what cash I've got left on the horses and bottles of bacardi to help me sleep. Got to get out. Worried about getting into bother. Need some sort of job. Ready for anything. Need to be seen. Need to let it be known I'm still a face.

Fuck it, I'll go to the Regency. *They* might be there, so I need to watch my back. It's dangerous to be alone. Take a load of bombers to shore up my bottle. *Chicka, chicka, chicka*. I ain't afraid of nobody. Nobody. Pull up the floorboards and get the sawn off out. Shell in both barrels. Shove it in the shoulder holster. Doesn't fit quite right but it'll have to do.

JACK THE HAT'S GUNS DON'T ARGUE!

Chicka, chicka, chicka.

Drive up to Stoke Newington. The Regency. *North London's Smartest Rendezvous.* Walk up to the upstairs bar. If any of the firm are here they'll be in the private bar in the basement. Mind throbbing with pills and bacardi. Shotgun butt poking out of suit jacket. People looking at me with fear. Backing away. Giving me a wide berth. Get a drink and stand at the bar, looking around. *Chicka, chicka, chicka.* One of the Barrys comes over. Moody grin. All polite with nervousness.

'All right, Jack?'

'Yeah, yeah.'

'Anything the matter?'

'Should anything be?'

Look around. Shotgun hanging out between the lapels. People backing away. Drifting out of the bar.

'Any of the firm here?' I ask him.

Palms out, big smile. Black and White Minstrel gesture.

'I'll go see,' he says and walks off.

Faces peeping out from behind upholstered booths. Read their minds. *What's he going to do?* I lean back against the bar and sip at my bacardi and Coke. Room swirling around me. I'm on my own now. Pill madness buzzing in my head. People looking at me. Clocking the fact I still exist. I'm still here. I'm Jack the Hat.

Barry comes back.

'There's no one here, Jack,' he says.

'None of the firm?'

'Yeah, that's right. None of the firm.'

'Oh.'

'Why don't you get off home, Jack? You're in a bit of a state.'

'Yeah, right.'

Yeah, right. He's right. What the fuck am I doing? Push myself off the bar. Nearly tumble over onto the floor. Stumble out. People edging out the way like I got the plague or something. Get into the Zodiac and weave my way home.

Hungover. Broke. Find myself driving up West in the afternoon. Looking for a clue. No ideas. Piccadilly. Junkies and tourists gathered around the statue of Eros. Rent boys lined up along the meatrack. Boarded-up window on Golden Goose arcade. Head up into Soho. There's got to be something for me up here. Something to keep me away from the East End and the Other Two.

Old Compton Street. Pull up outside Fat Wally's bookshop. You never know. He might know something. Wally's all smiles and pleased to see me. A little nervous. Knows that I'm bad luck to have around.

Have a chat. Nothing doing.

'I'll let you know if I hear anything Jack, but . . .'

Plastic strip-curtain flutters. Someone coming in.

'Heads up,' Wally mutters softly.

It's DCI Mooney. Doing his milk round no doubt. I hate that fucker.

'Hello Wally,' he announces all casual.

Then he sees me.

'Jack.' He frowns. 'What are you doing here?'

'It's a free fucking country.'

Wally hands over an envelope.

'I don't know where you get that idea,' says Mooney.

He wanders out to the back of the shop. Where all the hard-core stuff is. I follow him through. He starts picking up shrink-wrapped mags. *Schoolgirl Lust*, *Animal Farm*.

'Did you tell Harry Starks you didn't want me on this racket?' I ask him.

'This is my patch, Jack. I think I can have my say about who I deal with.'

'And you told him you didn't want to deal with me?'

'I said that you were unsuitable, yes. That you have a problem with authority.'

He turns to face me. A bundle of smut in his arms.

'You cunt,' I hiss at him.

'You're a hooligan, Jack the Hat. You're just a second-rate thug.'

I lunge forward. Wally grabs hold of me.

'Easy, Jack,' he says. 'Not in here, eh?'

I shrug him off. No, not in here. I make for the door.

'I'm confiscating this material.' Mooney talking to Wally behind me. 'It's far too strong.'

Out on the street. Walking back to the Zodiac. Rage in my eyes. I'll get that cunt. Wait for him to come out. Brown paper bag under one arm. Dirty fucker. Taking his work home with him no doubt. Doesn't see me. Goes to his car parked across the road. Pulls off. I follow him.

It's starting to get dark. Mooney's heading west. Through Victoria. Chelsea. Maybe he's going to see Harry. Wait a minute. He's pulled into a little square. Parks up in front of this big house. I recognise it. Where from? Mooney's going to the front door. Grey-haired man with puffy face opens up. Bow tie askew. It's that posh fucker me and Harry and Trev went to see that night. Lord something or other. One of Harry's friends in high places. Thursby, that's it. What's going on?

Curious. I wait for them to go inside. See a light go on in the front room. Go up to the house myself. Ease the front gate so it doesn't squeak. Tiptoe up to the front door. Slip the Yale lock and creep slowly inside. Easy does it.

I'm in the hallway. Dark. Little wedge of light fanning out from under the door to the front room. Voices. Sidle up to the crack and listen in.

'We haven't heard from our friend the butcher in a while.' Mooney's dull, flat voice.

'Yes, well, that *was* rather unfortunate.' Thursby's rich, fruity tone. 'I thought that the body was being disposed of properly.'

'I didn't know that he was going to get awkward. Anyway, he seems to have disappeared himself. And the inquiry's over. So all that remains is our little arrangement.'

'Yes. I've got the money here.'

'I don't just mean the money.' Mooney's voice whining, hateful. 'I've had to deal with you and your friends' disgusting little vices. I've had to clean up the mess. That boy was still breathing when you called me over. I had to strangle the little fairy myself.'

Thursby sobbing quietly.

'Please . . .'

'I have your filthy sin on my hands. I have to find my own redemption for that. All around me is filth and degradation. I've done your dirty work. So, you and your friends owe me. Not just in money but in influence. In patronage, if you like.'

Thursby blows his nose. Sniffs.

'What do you mean?'

'I don't mean anything just now. But a time might come when I'll be calling up favours. Remember that.'

'Of course.'

'So, it's over for now. You'll have to live with your conscience, Teddy. My sins are those of expedience. I'm surrounded by foul obscenity and the corruption it causes. My job is to contain it. I'll be going. You'll be hearing from me.'

Sounds of Mooney getting up to go. I back off. Make for the door through to the kitchen. Get behind it. They come through into the hall.

'Just one thing, George.' Thursby.

'Yes?'

'Harry Starks was around here. About a week or so ago. Asking questions. I thought we were keeping him out of this.'

'Ah, well, I got Harry to check on a few people. Make sure they were keeping quiet about the whole thing. He got a little over zealous. That's all.'

Thursby sees him to the door. Coldly polite goodbyes. Thursby wanders back through into the front room. Hear the soda siphon shh. Think. Mooney in on the Suitcase Murder. First thought: tell Harry. Gloomy bulb throws light on grubby kitchen. Dirty plates stacked in sink. Empty whisky bottles and box of Complan on the kitchen table. Tell Harry. He'll want to know. But Harry's gone into one. Black mood. No sense from him for a few weeks. Maybe never on this one. Yeah, Harry will want to know. But he won't thank me for telling him. He's in with Mooney for fucksakes. Think: I got something on this cunt Mooney. But that's dangerous for me. He wouldn't hesitate in having me done. Lined up with some powerful fuckers now. He's right, I'm just a second-rate thug. Think: I'll have to think about it.

Thursby's out in the hall. Wandering about. Pissed. Getting ready to hit the pit. Turning off lights. Hand reaches around kitchen door. Click. Darkness.

Think: let's have a shufti in his front room. Wait till Thursby's upstairs then tiptoe through. Turn the light on. Pick up a few bits of silver. Use a tablecloth to gather it up in. The drunken lord's forgotten to double lock the front door so I ease the Yale open quietly and fuck off back to the Zodiac.

* * *

Too many pills. Dope myself with booze but feel like I'm sleeping with my eyes open. Like the speed's given me X-ray vision. See through my own eyelids. Nightmares coming anyway. Madge yacking at me just before I pushed her. Weasel Face choking blood all over the caravan floor. Little Jack, age six, holding up jam jar full of tadpoles turning into bits of body. Mooney strangling a blond-haired boy.

Sleep through the day. Wake up, it's the night again. Time all to cock. Like it's running backwards or something. Lose track. Sometimes not sure whether it's dusk or dawn. Dull greyness in the window. Is it getting lighter or darker?

Think about Mooney. Feel frightened by it all, somehow. Imagine myself getting done and chopped up. No body, no case. Stick to the East End. Want to avoid the Twins though.

Start going to boozers where I'm not known. Dodging anything connected to *them*. Still manage to bump into the odd face. My bottle's going. Fear of the Other Two. Don't want to show it so I mug them off in front of people they know. 'I'm not afraid of the Twins,' and even: 'I'll fucking kill them.' Bravado. Makes me feel better at the time. Feeds the fear later.

Going mad. Start to have nightmares about *them*. Can't stand it. Got to face them. Straighten it all out somehow. Go back to the Regency. Chinese restaurant on the middle floor. Some of the firm sitting at a long table like that picture of the Last Supper. Waiting for Jesus to arrive. Or Judas. Sit in the corner a bit away from them. A few nods in my direction. Moody grins. Wary.

Then suddenly it's heads up, someone's arrived. Everyone's sitting up straight. One of the Twins has just walked in. Difficult to say which one it is at first.

'All right, Reg?' says one of the firm.

He nods and, seeing me, comes over. Glad it's not Fat Ron. At least with Reg you've got some chance of talking things through. Hold on to the table so that he doesn't see me tremble. Smile. Try to act relaxed. Fuck, this is it.

'I want a word with you, Jack,' he says.

Chicken Chow Mein. Weird fucking nosh. Noodles, bean sprouts, bamboo shoots looking like fucking entrails. Strips of meat like bits of gut. Bring back horrible thoughts. Don't care because most of all right now I feel relief. Reggie's gone through it all. All the lairyness and me being out of order in places they've got a part of. All the mugging them off and not giving enough respect. All the drug deals and other scams I never cut them into. The Payne hit not mentioned directly but the gist is, we all keep well shtum about that. And I've sat there and nodded and said, 'Yeah, I've been out of order. I've not been well, my nerves are shot to pieces. But I'm going to change. I'm going to behave myself from now on.' I've said I'm sorry and I feel a lot better for it. Reggie's handed me fifty quid. Two weeks' pension. Back on the firm. I belong to them now.

Feel better already. I *am* going to change. Sort myself out. The Twins aren't bad lads after all. Reg even paid for this chinky meal. No more lairyness, Jack.

Finish the grub and get off home. It's all going to be all right now, I feel sure of it. Have a shit and this chow mein's floating in the pan. Entrails. Gone straight through me. Try not to think what my insides are like. But I'm going to get healthy again. I've been fucking myself up. Going to cut down on the booze and get off the pills. Suddenly feel tired. First time I've felt properly sleepy in weeks. Yawn. Sleep waiting for me like an old friend. No bad dreams this time. No. Everything's going to be all right.

Wake up mid morning well rested. Saturday. Tidy the flat up a bit and get myself some dinner. Money in my pocket so I have a bit of a flutter on the horses. Watch the racing on the telly. Manage to pick a couple of winners. Things are looking up. Collect my winnings and watch *Dr Who*.

Saturday night. I can go out and have a good time now. Put on my my best check suit. Brown trilby with brown hat band. Look sharp, feel sharp. Jack the Hat's back. Get into the Zodiac and zoom off up to the Regency.

The Regency's packed. Full of mouthy hooligans showing off, trying to impress the birds. Wankers. Still, I'm in a good mood. As long as none of them spills beer on my suit. *Behave yourself Jack.* Stay away from trouble. Look around to see who's around. See the Lambrianou brothers. Chris grins. Tony looks a bit shifty. Go over and say hello.

'What are you having, Jack?' Chris offers.

'Lager,' I say. Keep off the heavy booze early on, that's the idea.

He brings me a pint over and introduces me to a couple of chaps from Notting Hill. Tony's sloped off somewhere. Acting a bit suspicious. Something's up. I can feel it.

'I don't trust your brother, Chris,' a whisper to Chrissy.

He looks at me all shocked.

'Come on, Jack. He's as right as rain.'

Shake my head.

'I don't know, Chris. I don't trust him.'

Chrissy smiles.

'I've lived with him an awful long time, Jack. He's all right. Believe me.'

Yeah. Just the old bottle playing up again. Don't need to worry any more. It's all been straightened. I'm on the firm. The Lambrianous are on the firm. Nothing to worry about.

Tony's back. Been for a piss or something.

'There's a party at Blonde Carol's,' he says. 'Plenty of birds and the rest of it. Let's go there.'

'Party?' I say. 'What party? Come on, let's all go.'

So we push our way through the mob and out onto the street. Chrissy suggests we go in his motor but it's blocked in.

'Come on,' I say. 'We'll go in mine.'

So we all pile into the Zodiac. Me and Chris in the front and Tony and the Notting Hill lads in the back.

'You know where we're going, Jack?' asks Tony.

'Yeah. I know where Blonde Carol's is.' I laugh. 'Me and her go back.'

Blonde Carol. Had a thing with her a couple of years back. She knows how to throw a party. Suddenly feel frisky. Feel sure I'm in for a good time. Never know, might get lucky. Might be able to get it up. It's been a long time.

We're there already. It's only around the corner anyway. We pile out. Me taking the lead.

'Come on lads!' I call out.

Up the steps to the front door and in. Soul music coming up from the basement. Go downstairs. *Chicka, chicka, chicka.*

'Where's the party?' I say. 'Jack's here. Where's all the booze? Where are all the birds?'

Go into the basement room. No birds. No booze. Just a couple of boys dancing together. Fat Ron sitting on a sofa watching them.

Leering. Toad-like eyes blink over at me. Reg is behind me. Pulls a gun. Cold metal against my head. Fuck.

Then a click. The gun just goes click. Poxy Kray automatic gone and jammed again. Click. Like a joke gun. Half expect a little flag with BANG on it to come out of the barrel. It's just a joke. That's what it is. Just meant to scare me. Any minute now everyone's going to laugh. We had you there, Jack. I look to Ron. He ain't smiling. Heavy-lidded eyes glaring at me. The boys have stopped dancing. People standing around stock still, like time has stopped. Soul music blaring on. *Chicka, chicka, chicka*. Chrissy sitting on the stairs, starting to weep. No joke. Look at Fat Ron. Ugly lips flatten out like he's about to say something.

Fuck. What have I done? I'm sorry. Whatever it is, I'm sorry. I didn't mean it. *You've got it coming to you, Jack the Hat*. Sorry.

'Do him!' Ron hisses.

4

The Rank Charm School

Oh, we shall allow them even sin, they are weak and helpless, and they will love us like children, because we allow them to sin. We shall tell them that every sin will be expiated, if it is done with our permission . . .

Dostoevsky, *The Grand Inquisitor*

It was then that I realised I'd never be Britain's Blonde Bombshell.

Spring 1962, and I'm in the Kentucky Club on the Mile End Road. The Krays are hosting a party for the premiere of *Sparrers Can't Sing*. Joan Littlewood's sentimental Cockney comedy. Flashbulbs popping as the Twins line up with Barbara Windsor. And I think, well there it goes. Spend all this time waiting for Diana Dors to get past it and now someone's got there before me. Ronnie Kray's cooing around a gang of minor celebrities, trying to herd as many of them as he can into the frame.

'Fancy being in this one, Ruby?' someone calls over.

Shake my head. No thank you. Don't fancy it. Don't fancy being a false smile in the background. Don't need reminding that my career's going nowhere. Why did I bother coming? I hate going to these sort of parties on my own. My agent, bullying on the phone, 'contacts dear, contacts'.

Interesting mix of people, I suppose. The Joan Littlewood Theatre Workshop crowd slumming it prole style. East End villainy dressed up to the nines. The Krays crowing. Their big night. Even if Princess Margaret only came for the premiere and not to the party. Heavy-looking faces in dark suits congregating in little groups accorded by a protocol of respect. Gangsters on their best behaviour, struggling to make small talk with starlets and comedians.

And I'm swanning around, trying to keep the smile going. Trying not to look like my career's up the swannee. Poise, deportment, all that Charm School crap. I need a drink. Push my way through to the bar. Pass by someone I vaguely recognise from somewhere. Slicked-back hair and slightly battered features. Piercing eyes that click with mine as I go by him. Where do I know him from? Then it drops. Oh fuck, I think, *him*. Another bloody reminder. Glance back carefully. He's with a young man, not much more than a boy really. Well, that makes sense. He's watching. A shiver of fear, I try to suppress it. Concentrate on getting to the bar.

'Gin and tonic, please.'

'Let me get this.'

A hand waves a note over the counter. I look around. Him.

He's not with the boy any more but with one of the faces that I've spoken with earlier. Jimmy something.

'Ruby,' says Jimmy. 'Let me introduce . . .'

'Oh, it's all right,' I cut in. 'We've already met. Harry, isn't it? Harry Starks.'

Grinning at recognition brings out a thin scar line in his cheek. He's more thick set than he was back then. It makes him look all the more impressive.

'Yeah,' I say, with a sneer. 'We go back. Don't we Mr Starks?'

Go back. Three years earlier.

Peter must have sent him. I don't know whether he'd followed me or just been lying in wait somewhere. I'd come back to the flat and he walked up as I was unlocking the front door. I tried to get in and lock the door behind me but his hand was on the frame blocking me. He leant against the jamb and muttered to me softly.

'We need to talk, Miss Ryder.'

It would have been stupid to offer any resistance. He was a lot bigger than me. He could have simply pushed me inside and followed me in without much fuss.

'You better come in then,' I said.

We went in through the hallway. I slumped into an armchair as he padded around the room.

'Why don't you make us both a drink?' I said, thinking: act friendly, charm him off.

As he poured two large scotches his eye caught a publicity photo on top of the cocktail cabinet. Me with blonde beehive and Diana Dors décolletage. The one I'd used for the quarter page in the young actresses section of *Spotlight 1958*. He picked it up and wagged it at me.

'You an actress then?'

He seemed impressed as he passed over the drink.

'Yeah, I suppose so,' I shrugged. 'Just walk-ons mostly.'

'Walk-ons?'

'Yeah, you know, background work. You walk on, say a few lines, walk off again. A bit like what you do I suppose.'

He frowned and then let a mirthless grin spread across his face.

'Yeah,' he nodded and sat down in the chair opposite. 'That's a good one.'

He held up the photo and studied it with a shrug.

'Well you got the looks for it,' he said. 'You want to take care of them.'

A cheap line. I sneered. He shrugged.

'I mean it. You could go places.'

'Yeah,' I said. 'That's a good one.'

Not the most illustrious of acting careers. At eighteen I'd been spotted by one of J. Arthur Rank's talent scouts at a Butlin's beauty contest. I got a year's contract with the Rank Organisation's Company of Youth. £20 a week. We were sent to this studio in Highbury to learn elocution and deportment. How to be stars. The Rank Charm School they called it. But after a year of walking about with books on our heads we found there wasn't much work to be had. I had a few walk-ons. Did a Lux soap commercial. I got a small speaking part in *Violent Playground* in 1957 but it wasn't the big break that I had imagined.

When the castings and the cash started to dry up I took a job in the Cabaret Club in Paddington. Dancing on stage. The low lighting hid the peeling decor and the tattiness of the sequined costumes. When you weren't dancing you could sit out in the audience and get an extra £5 hostess fee. You weren't supposed to make any other arrangements with the customers but most of the girls did. If you were discreet the management didn't seem to mind. I was reluctant at first but the money was so easy. You didn't always have to sleep with them anyway. One punter had me whip him with a leather belt while he masturbated. I learnt a few tricks that weren't taught at the Rank Charm School.

The man leant forward in his chair a little and gave me a stare that was piercing and yet seemed to require little effort from him. His nostrils dilated slightly and a frown furrowed a line where his eyebrows met. He wasn't grinning any more.

'You know what all this is about, don't you?'

'Yeah,' I sighed. 'Peter.'

Rachman. I met him at a party in the Latin Quarter Club in Soho. He set me up in the flat. Made me give up the club. 'It'll wear you out,' he said. 'In a few years you'll have nothing to show for it but a lined face, and then what'll you do?' He gave me enough money so that I could start going to castings and auditions again. He even got me a little MG sportscar. He didn't ask for much in return. He would come around every so often and without much ceremony lead me into the bedroom. He was short, fat and bald and had an odd squeaky Polish accent. He always had me sitting on top of him facing the other way so I didn't see his face when we had sex. He'd been in a concentration camp during the war and had never really got over the experience. He was stinking rich but he still hoarded crusts of bread under his bed out of habit. His eyes never lost their cold glittering hardness. I'd heard about his methods as a landlord. Setting thugs with alsatians on tenants that wouldn't pay. He shrugged as if he didn't realise what all the fuss was about. 'Business is business, Ruby,' he'd say. 'If someone agrees to pay ten pounds a week then I am entitled to make sure payment is made. I have my overheads, you know.'

For a while our arrangement worked well for me. I had the time and money to try again with my acting career. Peter had lots of contacts. Usually the wrong ones. And I had become his possession. I lost any sense of pursuing things for myself. I no longer felt that I had any control over my life. Being kept made me lazy.

He had other mistresses but he was insistent that I was not to see other men. He was suspicious of the most innocent circumstances. He could not imagine men taking any kind of interest in women unless it was sexual.

After a while it got too much for me. At first I made excuses to avoid seeing him, to put off his little visits to the flat. But when these ran out I just missed appointments that had been made, knowing that he would be infuriated turning up to an empty apartment. I'd been expecting a visit from one of his heavies for a while now.

'Mr Rachman wants to know where the hell you've been.'

The well-tailored thug spoke softly. He had more style than Peter's usual muscle.

'You don't look like one of Rachman's usual rent collectors,' I said.

The man shrugged and took a sip of whisky.

'I'm not,' he said. 'I'm freelance.'

'So Peter's hiring extras, is he? What's the matter? He in trouble?'

'Yeah, well, your boyfriend is having a spot of bother, actually. Not just from you. Some people are wanting a share in the profits. It doesn't pay to let a racket get too well known. People are liable to muscle in. I think he wants me on his firm.'

'For protection?'

'Something like that. But I ain't getting involved. It's bad business.'

'But you don't mind coming around here and scaring me for him?'

'Hell, he's paying me enough.'

'I still don't get it. Why's he gone to the bother of having you follow me? He could of sent one of his own men.'

'Well he wants this matter sorted with a bit of delicacy. And because . . .'

The man gave a little cough.

'He can trust me with you.'

'Really?' I said smiling. 'Immune to my charms, are you?'

'Yeah, something like that,' he replied rather tetchily.

I'd hit a nerve. For a second his gaze lost some of its toughness and became petulant. He pulled his head back a touch as if to regain his poise. His face tightened with menace as if to compensate for being caught off guard.

'He wants you to start behaving yourself.'

'Or else?'

The man suddenly slammed his glass on the coffee table and I gave a little jump.

'Look, darling. You've got a flat, a car, regular money from him. You know what Rachman's like. He expects you to keep your part of the bargain. It's not a good idea to fuck him around like this. He's liable to turn nasty.'

'Or to get someone to turn nasty for him.'

'Well I ain't here for my own good health.'

He picked up his glass, drained the rest of his scotch and put it back on the table.

'So, what's supposed to happen now?'

'You come with me and we go and see him.'

'And if I say no?'

'That wouldn't be a good idea,' he said flatly.

He looked around the room for a while and then stared back at me.

'So what's it going to be?' he demanded.

I suddenly found myself starting to sob. Real fear mostly but some of the tears were Charm School technique, like I was detached from it, acting it out. Just like he was. He sighed heavily and went over to the cabinet and poured another round of drinks. He handed me a glass and pulled the handkerchief out of the top pocket of his suit for me to blow my nose on.

'You've got yourself into a right fucking mess, Miss Ryder.'

'Ruby,' my voice quavered. 'Call me Ruby. What am I going to do?'

He sighed and shook his head. Then he sat down again and waited for me to catch his stare once more.

'We go and see him. Yeah? Come clean about finishing with him. Give him the car keys and the keys to the flat.'

I wiped my face and stared back.

'But he'll be angry. He'll want to hurt me.'

'Well, you should expect a couple of slaps for the way you've been carrying on. But that will probably be it.'

I nodded slowly as if trying to steady my head.

'OK,' I said. 'OK.'

He got up and patted my shoulder.

'Finish your drink and get ready. We'll go in my car.'

I looked up at him and chewed at my lower lip nervously. He grinned down at me.

'Don't worry about it. It'll soon be over.'

'Yeah, all right. Thanks, er . . .'

'Harry,' he said. 'Harry Starks.'

Harry drove us to an address in North Kensington. It was a crumbling Victorian terrace that smelt of damp. One of Peter's properties. Rachman pulled me by the arm and dragged me into the front room. He slapped me hard about the face while still holding me by the elbow and then pushed me onto a battered sofa.

'You stupid bloody bitch!' he shouted at me.

Harry had come into the room. Rachman turned away from me and walked over to him, peeling off notes from a bankroll he took from his back pocket.

'Thank you, Mr Starks,' he said, suddenly genial as he handed over a wad of money. 'A job well done. I only wish that I could employ you on a more permanent basis.'

'Rent collecting?'

'I was thinking more of using your, um, organisational skills.'

'This wouldn't have to do with a take-over bid from Bethnal Green, would it?'

'Tch, those twins. What am I going to do with them? They were always looking for twins in the camps, you know,' he remarked rather wistfully. 'Experiments.'

'If you want my advice, give them something to play with. Something to distract them.'

'Money?'

'No. They'll spend it quick and come back for more when it's used up. Give them something solid. A racket or something.'

'A property?'

'Yeah, something like that.'

Harry made a move to go. Rachman shook his hand.

'If you ever reconsider my offer, you know where I am.'

Harry looked over at me just before he turned to leave. He gave me a quick nod and then he was gone.

'So, have you come to your senses?' Rachman hissed at me.

'You could say that,' I replied and picked my handbag off the floor.

'Are you going to behave yourself?'

I took the keys to the car and the flat and handed them to him. He weighed them in his hand and narrowed his eyes at me.

'I see,' he said.

He pocketed the car keys and then, holding the flat keys by the fob, made to swing at me with them. Flinching, I curled up into the sofa, then uncoiled as I realised he was faking. He started laughing.

'You little bastard!' he hissed, tossing the keys in my lap.

'I can keep the flat?'

'Yes, you can keep it. But you start paying rent.'

Queenie Watts was belting out a song on the stage of the Kentucky. There was a glass in my hand. I took a gulp of gin without thinking. Reflex action.

'What do you want?' I asked.

What did he want? From what I'd gathered the obvious seemed out of the question. Uneasy thoughts. Blackmail. Was that it? Always edgy about my past. I worked so hard to cover it up. And here he was now like the ghost at the feast.

'I just wanted . . .'

A shrug and a grin. Putting on the friendly act.

'To buy you a drink.'

'And talk over old times? No thank you.'

'Look, I'm sorry. About what happened. It was just . . .'

Another shrug.

'Business.'

'And this is just sociable?'

'Yeah.'

I laughed.

'Go on then. Surprise me. Be sociable.'

'You were good in *Woman in the Shadows*.'

'You saw that?'

After Peter I got a film part. I'd played a tragic whore in a Gaumont feature in 1961. Cruel gossip was that I hadn't had to act very hard. Rumours dogged my attempts at a legitimate career. The film hadn't done much business anyway.

'Yeah, I saw it. You were good.'

'The tart with a heart. Well, as you know, I can play that one from memory.'

'I thought you didn't want to talk about old times.'

'Why not? We know each other's secrets. Where's your young friend, by the way?'

Harry lost his smile for a second. He coughed and looked across the room to where his boyfriend was talking animatedly to Victor Spinetti.

'He can look after himself,' he said gruffly.

'Yeah, you want to watch him.'

'So,' said Harry turning back to me. 'What are you working on at the moment?'

'Darling, I've had fuck all work for months. I think I'm getting past it.'

'Don't say that.'

'It's true. Anyway, never mind my so-called career. What about you? Who are you threatening these days?'

Harry laughed.

'I've come on a bit since then.'

'Not doing walk-on work any more then?'

'I've got my own interests now. I'm a businessman.'

'Of course.'

'No, really. I've got my own club now.'

'Really?'

'Yeah,' said Harry proudly. He did a quick scan of the Kentucky, flaring his nostrils slightly. 'In the West End.'

'Oh yeah.'

'Yeah. You should come down. I'm having a big do there next week. A charity night.'

'Well, I don't know about that.'

'Go on, Rube. It'll be a chance for me to make it up to you for, you know, that Rachman business. There's quite a lot of people in your line of business that come down. You could make some useful contacts.'

'I've heard that one before.'

The Stardust Club. It wasn't exactly part of the fashionable scene. But then it was a relief not to be surrounded by wafer-thin models and slumming public schoolboys. Charity night and Harry packed his club with 'personalities'. Politicians, showbiz types, all sorts of potential friends in high places that he could be photographed with. I realised then what Harry wanted. He had collected me. He wanted me as part of the group of minor celebrities that he liked to gather around him for a bit of social clout and cheap glamour.

There were others there too. People with improbable names up to all kinds of business. Thieves, touts, con men, dog dopers. Harry would introduce me to them, often with a whispered aside as to their status. 'A hoister,' he'd say, indicating a short, well-dressed woman, 'and a good one at that.' He was as proud of the form of the villains that frequented his premises as he was of the fame of his celebrities. And it seemed an active meeting place for criminals. All sorts of people would drop by to gather information. To 'get a clue', as they'd put it.

There was a sort of fairground or circus feel to the place. I have to admit that it was me that nicknamed it the Sawdust. I got to quite like the atmosphere there. I got treated with a lot more respect there than in the trendier places in London. There I was just a tarty actress with a shady past. In the Sawdust I felt legitimate.

And I got to know Harry. He was always charming in that slightly menacing way of his. I remained wary of him. He frightened me a bit – I heard all sorts of rumours about him. And I always had this nagging feeling that he had something on me.

I understood the value of the sort of power people like Harry wielded. I'd lived a precarious life and in the back of my mind I thought there might come a time when I'd need to call on it. I only worried about what it might cost me.

In November of that year Harry phoned me.

'Come for a drink, Ruby,' he insisted, bluntly.

'Harry?'

'Come over Rube,' he went on. 'We should celebrate.'

'Why?'

'You not seen the evening paper?'

'What's all this about, Harry?'

'Rachman. He's dead.'

'No.'

Harry laughed.

'Yeah, the old bastard's dead. Heart attack.'

'I didn't think he had one.'

So I got a cab over to the Sawdust and we held a bit of a wake for Peter. I felt relief that he was dead, that that part of my life was finally over. But I was shocked too. Someone so viciously dedicated to his own survival could suddenly drop dead without warning. I'd almost envied his ruthlessness. After a few gins I had this strange image of all the stale crusts of bread that he hoarded under his bed, blue with mould, being heaped like packing for him into his coffin.

'I can hardly believe that the old bugger's dead,' I said as Harry and I raised a glass together.

'Well,' said Harry. 'At least he brought us together, Rube.'

With Rachman dead, few people knew about me being a whore. Except Harry of course. Now me and Harry had a past. We went back. From then on we started to become close. From time to time we went out together. There were many social occasions where he liked to be seen with a woman. He liked to put on a straight front sometimes. And I was the ideal companion, I was in on the act and my Rank Charm School training came in handy after all. And Harry played his part too. He acted the real gentleman. It was nice to be taken out and fussed over, so it worked out for both of us. Neither of us felt that we were doing each other any favours.

We became friends. As well as wanting an escort now and then Harry liked to have someone to talk to. To confide in. To be able to talk about the boys that he'd fell for or fallen out with. It wasn't something he could discuss with his other friends. And I would confide in him as well. We seemed equally unlucky with men but we could rely on each other to some extent. Harry was prone to depression and at times, during one of his black moods, I'd have his heavy battered face sobbing gently into my shoulder.

In 1964 I was in a film called *A Bird in the Hand*. It was a trashy, very British sort of comedy. Full of innuendo and double entendre. I'd traded in my starlet persona for the blowsy dolly-bird act. I was the oversexed housewife opposite Gerald Wilman who played a travelling salesman selling sex hormones door to door. Gerald was famous for his part in the radio comedy *How's Your Father?* A complete queen but terribly repressed about it. It all got channelled into his performance. Hyperactively furtive, neurotically camp, it seemed to sum up the British fear of sex. And I was the dolly bird gone to seed, playing frustration as comedy.

When he wasn't having a tantrum Gerald could be great fun on set. He could make the most harmless comment or situation seem loaded. His manic behaviour implied a lustful potential that existed everywhere. Except in the act itself. I don't think Gerald ever had sex. Except with himself. He often mentioned masturbation. The 'J. Arthur', he called it, in a rhyming joke against my former employer, the methodist, ever so stainless, Mr Rank. I once said that Gerald should run the Wank Charm School, a joke that he found so funny that he later claimed it for himself.

I introduced him to Harry who was keen to meet him and they got on like a house on fire. Harry tried to get Gerald to come to one of his 'parties' but Gerald would have none of it. He still lived with his mother. He was a bit of a sad case really.

Apart from *A Bird in the Hand*, I did a bit of telly work, but work was a bit thin on the ground. I thought about leaving the business for good but what would I do? Harry always looked after me, insisted that I took a bit of cash from him from time to time to tide me over.

* * *

In 1965 I met Eddie Doyle at The Stardust. Harry introduced us. Eddie would regularly call in at the club. It was a good place to meet other faces and exchange information about jobs. Maybe get a clue.

Eddie was a jewel thief. A climber. He'd made a fortune out of shinning up and down the plumbing of some of the best houses in London and the Home Counties. And it wasn't just drainpipes he was climbing. Eddie was from Deptford but he wore Savile Row suits and shirts by Washington Tremlett so that he could effect an entrance to the classier places in the city and mingle with his potential victims. He regularly read *Tatler* or *Harper's*, scanning features on social engagements, photographs of rich socialites and their splendid homes, sizing up future jobs.

His first interest in me was probably in the possibility of meeting the rich and famous. Even when we started dating, I always suspected that his attention would at any moment stray to a professional interest in any fur or costume jewellery on display in the restaurant or nightclub we were in.

I could tell that Harry became a little jealous when me and Eddie started seeing each other. I still escorted Harry sometimes on social functions when he wanted to be seen with a woman but these occasions became rarer as I got more involved with Eddie. I realised that Harry had become quite possessive of me. But also I felt that Harry worried that he didn't have as much style as Eddie. Eddie was a thief, not a heavy, and consequently his style was sharp where Harry's was blunt. When they met they would talk in an almost competitive way about what to wear, what to drive, even what wine to order. Behind it all Harry always would have the upper hand, even if Eddie could point out that Cartier was not as sophisticated as Ulysses Jardin. Harry wielded real power and Eddie was always careful to defer to that. It was important for him to stay on good terms with people like Harry. Getting rid of stolen gear was often as risky as actual theft and Harry had more control over that end of the business. Gangsters would often prey on thieves if they got wind of a big haul. If Eddie made a lot of money from a particular job he'd often give some to Harry in exchange for protection.

Eddie never begrudged this. He had no interest whatsoever in getting involved in the heavy end of the business. He didn't want his looks spoiled. But he did get off on the risks that he took in burglary. I think he got an almost sexual thrill from a successful job. All that adrenalin. He always kept me slightly in the dark about his activities but I could usually tell if he'd pulled off a big one, a *coup* as he'd call it, because afterwards he'd be a bit lacklustre in bed.

Not that I had any complaints for the rest of the time. I had a very good time with Eddie. He made me feel special. I felt good about myself again. I lost weight, dressed well, felt attractive. I had a much more glamorous time then than I'd ever had with the other 'business'. I didn't worry any more about being a has-been actress.

I did have nagging doubts in the back of my mind that all of this was going to mean trouble in the long term but I paid them little heed.

We drove down to the South of France together in an Aston Martin. We headed for Nice first and stayed at the Hotel Westminster on the Promenade des Anglais. We both loved the open expanse of the boulevards, the palm trees swaying in an offshore breeze from the warm blue Mediterranean. We spent days lying in the sun, evenings happily struggling with the intricacies of *haute cuisine*. We mocked each other's phrasebook French but revelled in the life of acting so fucking sophisticated. Then we moved on to Cannes. Driving along the Croisette, past all the best hotels, the Majestic, the Carlton, the Martinez, Eddie turned to me.

'When I've pulled off the really big one,' he declared, 'me and you could retire down here.'

'It's a nice thought,' I replied lazily. Eddie would always talk of pulling off the really big one.

'I'm serious.'

'Of course,' I humoured him.

'No, I really mean it, Ruby. Me and you.'

'What do you mean?'

'I mean, I'm asking you to marry me.'

I said yes, in the end, after a bit of coaxing and joking that the ring he finally produced was probably a snide (a fake). I'd never imagined that Eddie was that serious about me. Perhaps that he thought it was all a bit of a laugh. I was good company and a useful companion at the social gatherings that he preyed on. I'd got used to being used. I always thought of myself as more of an accomplice than a girlfriend. And I did worry about getting married to a professional thief. He wasn't exactly going to make an honest woman of me, was he?

It was like a romantic dream. Maybe breathing in the clean air of the Côte d'Azur went to my head. But I felt relaxed and free for the first time in my life. It was almost like happiness. I convinced myself that me and Eddie could love each other.

So we went back to London and made the arrangements. Me and Eddie got married in the spring of 1966. It was Harry that gave me away in the church. My mother was in the front pew as we made our vows but Dad had died a few years back. I think that Mum was happy for me that day. She seemed glad that I'd finally found someone. And it was hard not to like Eddie.

'Make sure you look after her, young man,' she said to him at the reception at The Stardust Club.

And for a while, he did. We had a honeymoon in Tenerife. Then we moved into this lovely house in Greenwich that looked over the river. Eddie started an antiques business which was a good cover for his other activities and actually made us money too. And I got a bit of work here and there. A nice part in a television play.

Me and Harry didn't see so much of each other. And when I did see him then it would be with Eddie. Occasionally, after a few drinks, Harry would want to confide in me about something or someone. He was happy for me in my new life but I think he missed our old friendship.

In the summer Eddie and me went back to the South of France. We rented a villa in Haut de Cagnes. 'More sophisticated than St Paul de Vence,' Eddie assured me, 'more arty.' It was a beautiful place, built into the terraced hillside with a wonderful view of the Alpes Maritimes. Intoxicated with the scent of wild thyme and bougainvillea we went into a kind of dream. Eddie was the rich successful man with cosmopolitan tastes and I was his wonderful glamorous wife. But, of course, we'd need a *coup* to make it real. Eddie would have to pull off the really big one.

Back in London everything seemed so grey. It was good living near the river. The way that it curled around the Isle of Dogs out towards the sea gave us a sense of escape. We held on to our dream as the reality of living together became more strained. I never knew where Eddie was or what he was up to. And yet I was expected to provide some sort of security amidst his dangerous lifestyle, to keep house and cover for him. We never seemed to have a regular income. We'd either be flat broke or Eddie would be waving about a big wad of cash, proceeds of God knows what. Our relationship wasn't based on anything settled. The dream kept us going but it burned at us.

A year later we were finally and brutally woken up from that dream. And quite literally woken up. Six o'clock in the morning the Flying Squad raided our house and dragged Eddie out in handcuffs. They had a warrant to search the premises and they pulled everything apart from top to bottom. Eddie had been involved in an armed robbery. It wasn't his usual style but the dream had driven him to desperate measures. The job had all gone wrong and a cashier had been shot and wounded. It was all a horrible mess.

They found a wad of cash from the robbery in my handbag so they held me as an accessory after the fact. This was a way of getting at Eddie. He did a deal in return for all the charges to be dropped against me. He signed a statement admitting to the robbery and asked for eleven other offences to be taken into account, and I was released the same day. I should have been grateful in a way. I didn't fancy a stretch in Holloway, that's for sure. But I felt angry at him none the less. Angry at him for getting involved in something heavy. Someone had been hurt and that gave me a bad feeling. And most of all angry at him for being caught.

His case came to trial three months later. He pleaded guilty and his brief tried to make a strong case for mitigation. But he hadn't named anyone else in the robbery and not all of the loot had been recovered. His previous form went strongly against him as well. He was sentenced to seven years.

The press had a field day. Pictures of me leaving the courtroom in tears. Headlines: RUBY AND THE ROBBER. *Blonde Star Breaks Down As Husband Is Sentenced.* Since when was I a star? It was so humiliating. And just the sort of publicity that I did not need. There goes my so-called career, I thought for the umpteenth time.

I was on my own again. No work and no money. The antique business went into liquidation. The *Sunday People* offered to buy my story. Ruby tells all, that sort of thing. I was almost tempted but they were only offering £500, the cheapskates.

Eddie got sent to Wandsworth Prison. A horrible place. The cons nicknamed it the Hate Factory and for good reason. At least it was close for visits. Our dream of the South of France now seemed so stupid. It was all used up. Reality was like a bad hangover. I'd become a jailbird's wife. Eddie had become what they called in the East End an away. There were regular collections in pubs in that area, where villains congregated, for the aways. So every so often a couple of faces would turn up on my doorstep and hand over twenty-five quid or whatever to 'help out'. They always came in pairs in case a visit to an away's wife was misconstrued. They would never even cross the threshold. The implication was that with Eddie in nick I couldn't be seen with another man. I was supposed to lead a chaste life now, just waiting for the next visiting order. It wasn't as if I had any other prospects but I resented this sort of enforced abstinence. It was like fucking purdah or something. I took the money for a while though and tried to look grateful. I needed the cash.

So I got back in touch with Harry. I could be seen out and about with him. Him being queer meant that no one could point the finger. Also, he was well respected and well feared so I didn't have to worry about taking shit from anybody. I'd lost the house in Greenwich to the receiver so Harry found me a flat in Chelsea. He insisted on paying the rent. At least for as long as it took for me to get back on my feet. I didn't really know what I was going to do, though. There was no work coming in and I didn't even have an agent any more. I was off the books as soon as Eddie went down.

I worried about being in debt to Harry. Of owing favours. And I'd kind of promised myself after Eddie's trial that I'd try and keep away from villains. But I didn't really have any choice.

Harry was still pursuing his dream of being an impresario with The Stardust Club. I think that was one of the reasons he liked having me around. I was a link, however tenuous, with legitimate show business. But Harry's dreams of the big time on that score were about as ridiculous as mine had ever been.

His latest venture was booking Johnnie Ray for a two-week residency at the club. Poor old Johnnie Ray. His career was on the skids and his voice was going. He was off the booze but his liver was wrecked. Cirrhosis had nearly killed him. And he was still hooked on huge quantities of heavy-duty tranquillisers. He'd come to England to escape a pile of back taxes owed to the US Inland Revenue. And here, at least, he could get regular work. Even if it did mean doing the working men's club circuit up North. Harry thought he was lucky to book him. He somehow imagined that Johnnie was still a big-time performer. But he hadn't had a hit since the fifties. With his strange melodramatic gestures and wailing voice he was, at best, merely a novelty act.

On opening night Harry tried to scare up an impressive guest list. As it happened it was the usual mix of ex-boxers, minor celebrities and major-league villains. There was, however, a representative of a social group that had not been regular attenders at The Sawdust before. The police. I knew that Harry paid off policemen from time to time but I'd never expected to meet one in his club. This was how things were changing.

As I sat down at his table, Harry introduced me to a thick-set sullen-faced man in a cheap suit. He had eyes that seemed too small for his face.

'This is Detective Chief Inspector George Mooney,' Harry said.

Harry gave me a sly wink as Mooney took hold of my hand. His palm felt limp and clammy. I gave the Detective Chief Inspector my best Charm School smile. Eyes and teeth.

'Pleased to meet you, Miss Ryder,' he said.

His expression was impassive but there was something sly about how he looked around the room. He seemed to be watching everything but his little eyes gave nothing away. They were like peepholes.

'I've seen some of your films, Miss Ryder,' he said.

'Not exactly cinema classics.'

'No, but *you* had class. It's like you know they're trash and you're acting above it all.'

'Yes, well, that attitude always got me into trouble with directors. One reason my career never went anywhere. Being married to a convicted criminal didn't help either.'

'Yes,' said Mooney, coldly. 'That was unfortunate.'

His attention was distracted for a moment and I started to make a move to another seat, away from him, but I felt Harry's hand on my arm.

'Be nice to him,' he hissed in my ear.

So I sat back down in my seat. Mooney smiled at me and was about to say something but just then the band finished their overture to polite applause, and the compère came to the microphone.

'Thank you, ladies and gentlemen. Now, here he is, the man

you've all been waiting for. The Cry Guy, The Prince of Wails, Mr Emotion himself. A warm welcome please, put your hands together and let's loudly laud the legendary Lachrymose Lochinvar, The Nabob of Sob, Mr Johnnie Ray!'

Johnnie skipped onto The Stardust stage, nearly tripping over the microphone lead, and launched into a song. His performances were always bound to be dramatic. With his degree of deafness he could never afford to be tentative or subtle about how he pitched his voice. He just had to throw it out there with all the conviction he could muster, hoping that he'd hit the right notes as his voice quavered around recklessly. His body flailed about as if it was following his vocal struggle. It was desperate. He became a parody of himself. In the middle of the second number the microphone picked up feedback from his hearing aid and the whole of the club was drowned out by a piercing shriek. He had to stop and start over again. Somehow he managed to get through his set and Harry led a loud and appreciative applause, which seemed more of an expression of relief that it was over than anything else. Except, perhaps, sympathy.

'Well, what did you think of tonight's show, Miss Ryder?' asked Mooney.

I shrugged.

'Johnnie had a bad night.'

'Are you a friend of Mr Ray's?'

I shook my head. I'd never actually met Johnnie. I knew him and Harry went back to a certain extent. Harry had set him up with boys when Johnnie had been in London in the past and Johnnie had been at some of Harry's infamous 'parties'.

'I much prefer Tony Bennett. These over-emotional performances aren't really to my taste.'

Mooney got up to go and talk to Harry. He gave me another limp, damp handshake.

'It's been a pleasure,' he said. 'I do hope we meet again.'

The Johnnie Ray residency was not a great success. Harry had managed to fill the club on the opening night but that was about it. After that nobody came. The Sawdust never did great trade anyway. It was in the wrong end of Soho and it had never managed to build enough of a reputation to draw a crowd. And Johnnie Ray wasn't a big enough attraction to reverse the trend despite Harry's desperate faith in him. When it came to show business he was just far too sentimental. He had some dewy-eyed notion of some magical world of entertainment. To be honest, I don't think Harry ever realised how ruthless you had to be to be a successful booker or an agent. Consequently he made silly and unprofitable decisions. Like booking Johnnie Ray. The thing was he actually *liked* performers, which goes against rule number one in show-business management. And he tended to book the acts that he liked, and that usually meant the ones that were woefully out of fashion.

So anyway, after a week of empty houses for Johnnie, Harry cancelled the residency and paid him off. It was all done very amicably and Johnnie actually appreciated having a bit of a break after all the gruelling trudge around the northern club circuit. Harry shut the Sawdust and put a sign on it: CLOSED FOR REFURBISHMENT. He had plans for it, he informed me.

The Stardust reopened after a few weeks as The Stardust Erotic Revue. Harry tried to appear enthusiastic about it but you could see his disappointment. His dream of legitimate show business had finally evaporated and there to replace it was a strip club.

He showed me around as they were getting ready for the reopening. It looked flash. All black and chrome with a completely rewired lighting system. It seemed cold and sterile now. It wasn't the Sawdust any more. A group of bored-looking girls were rehearsing their routines and out of curiosity I sat in. It was a bit of a shambles, really. Some of the girls could move quite well, obviously trained dancers down on their luck. But some of the others just didn't have any idea. It was all a bit slapdash and when I told Harry what I thought he grinned at me.

'Well Rube,' he said, 'why don't you take it in hand?'

And I thought, why not? I'd learnt enough back in my Cabaret Club days of what worked with the punters, even though we had kept more of our clothes on back then. So I started to knock it all into some sort of shape. Harry was impressed.

'You could be our choreographer,' he suggested.

It was a bit of a grand title for organising a tits-and-arse show. But I set about it with as much professionalism as I'd put into any other job. I used all sorts of things that I'd learnt from the business and parodied them. Routines and costumes that were like a joke version of sex and performance but would work for the punters. Artistic direction based on a simple premise: men are suckers. They'd think that it was all very tastefully done.

And the girls that didn't move so well I put through their paces. Basic things like posture and deportment that I'd been taught when I was under contract with the Rank Organisation all those years ago. Yeah, I even had some of these girls going up and down the catwalk with books on their heads. I couldn't help laughing when I thought about it: The Ruby Ryder Charm School.

I also sorted out the terms of employment of the girls with Harry. It only seemed right to treat them properly. Despite everything else that was going on in Soho those days, The Stardust was run on very orthodox business lines. The club paid the girls' National Insurance stamps and they had Equity contracts. Harry liked the idea that the strippers in his club would be able to go on and do legitimate theatre work.

So although they had to bare all to the dirty-raincoat brigade twice nightly, the girls were well treated, and for the most part didn't mind working for us. They knew they wouldn't get any hassle from Harry. The sight of naked female flesh did nothing for him after all. His detachment made the girls feel at ease and meant that he could be very business-like about the running of the club, unlike the old days when he'd been booking the has-beens of the cabaret circuit.

And I was on a wage. I could pay my own rent now. I felt a lot better about not being beholden to Harry even though I was a bit wary of becoming involved in his world. But it was a job. It wasn't exactly how I'd imagined my career to turn out but, hell, that's show business.

On the night we opened we had a full house. Things looked good. The Stardust could start making real money for Harry Starks at last. As the punters sneaked out, I noticed a cropped-haired man who remained seated at the back of the club. It was Detective Chief Inspector Mooney.

'Inspector Mooney,' I announced, all mock polite.

'George, please.'

'Is this business or pleasure?'

His little eyes twitched. He made a tutting sound and shook his head slightly.

'Now, Ruby,' he said chidingly. 'It's business of course.'

'Really?'

'Oh yes. All official and above board. I have to obtain authorisation from the Commissioner himself to attend theatrical performances that might be of an obscene nature.'

'And how was tonight's show?'

'You've got nothing to worry about. It was all very tastefully done. My report will recommend no further investigation.'

Harry had come over.

'George,' he said, deftly handing him a brown envelope.

'Harry. Congratulations on a successful new enterprise.'

Harry sat down on a chair next to George. I could see that they wanted to talk so I left them to it and went backstage to see the girls.

Harry called me up to the office later. He was sitting at his desk, brooding. For the first time The Stardust was making real money for Harry. Stacks of it. It was bringing the punters in, which it had never done before. But they were flocking in to see filth. It wasn't the club that he'd wanted it to be. There were no more opportunities for being photographed with celebrities or society types at charity evenings. Those pictures lined the walls of the office. He was staring at them wistfully as I went in.

'You wanted to see me,' I said.

He came out of his gloomy reverie and looked at me.

'Ruby,' he said and smiled.

He handed over a wad of notes.

'What's this?'

'It's a bonus, Rube.'

'Harry, you don't need to.'

'Go on, take it.'

So I took it.

'How would you like to earn a lot more money, Ruby?'

I didn't like the sound of this.

'What do you mean?'

'I mean, becoming involved in some of my other business ventures.'

I'd never really pried into Harry's affairs. He'd told me that he'd 'gone into publishing'. I knew that this meant pornography.

'I don't think so, Harry.'

'Now wait a minute, Rube. Hear me out.'

Harry explained how he was paying off the Obscene Publications

Squad in return for a free hand in running his porn racket. He needed a go-between.

'Why?'

'Well Rube,' Harry said with a sigh, 'I can't afford to be seen to be too close to Old Bill. Smacks of being a grass, see? Something goes down and people might point the finger. Word gets around that maybe I've been handing up bodies.'

'So why me?'

'Well . . .'

'What?'

'Well, old George Mooney's taken a bit of a shine to you.'

'Oh, great.'

Harry chuckled.

'Thing is Rube,' he said, 'Mooney's playing hard to get with me. And I've come up against more opposition than I'd bargained for. I thought that this was going to be an easy little racket. Something to retire on. It still can be, but I've just got to get tight with the Dirty Squad, that's all.'

'So you want me to get tight with Mooney?'

'Look, see it as a public relations exercise. Lay on a bit of charm. You're good at that.'

'And what if the Detective Chief Inspector wants a bit more than that?'

'You can look after yourself. See if you can find out what he's into. If we can get something on him then we can use it against him. I've tried setting him up with tarts but he doesn't want to know.'

'Is he queer?'

Harry laughed.

'No. I don't think so anyway. Rumour has it that he's, you know, into watching. He's a, what do you call it? A voyager.'

'A voyeur?'

'That's it. All this porn stuff. I suppose after all this time it's got to him.'

'Dirty old man.'

'Harmless though, I reckon.'

'So what does he see in an old dolly bird like me?'

Harry gave me this shocked look. He could be quite camp when he was laying on the charm.

'Rube,' he protested. 'You've got charisma, darling.'

'He knows about Eddie.'

'Of course. But I think that could be a winner and all. Being a villain's wife. He's bound to be drawn to that.'

'What makes you think that?'

'Just a hunch.'

'You should do a psychology degree.'

Harry smiled.

'So what do you say?' he asked.

'I don't know, Harry.'

'A favour, Rube,' he said softly.

I looked back at his face, caught that stare of his. I realised that 'favour' wasn't a request, it was a reminder. A reminder of all the favours he'd done me. I'd always known that this time might come. Time to pay back.

'I'll cut you in. As I've said, there's a lot of money in it. Plenty to go around. Honest Rube, we're looking at money to retire on.'

'I've heard that one before,' I said, bitterly.

Harry shrugged and nodded.

'Yeah, but we won't be taking any silly risks on this one.'

I realised then the difference between Harry and Eddie. Eddie's crime was driven by a doomed romanticism. Harry did business, coldly and ruthlessly.

'Just take him out and entertain him,' he said. 'Find out what his weaknesses are. And find out where I stand.'

I couldn't really refuse. I was in debt and scraping around for money. No career, no prospects except The Stardust. I relied on Harry. And his ruthlessness at least had a certainty to it. He was on to a sure thing. It didn't seem that I'd have to do very much. But I felt myself being drawn into something. A gravity that governed me. As if I'd always really belonged to seediness and the bad side of things.

Me and George Mooney dined at Kettner's. I chatted him up with showbiz gossip. Secrets of the stars I've worked with, all that crap. He lapped it up. George offered up some gossip of his own. The Krays. The Twins had been arrested back in May and committal proceedings had just been concluded. Nipper Read had stepped up police protection of witnesses. Some of their own firm were ready to go QE.

'No honour among thieves, Ruby,' he droned.

I thought about Eddie. But I didn't say anything. I was supposed to be being charming, after all. I hoped to God my husband didn't find out about me entertaining a bent copper.

'And what about your work, George?'

I tried to sound interested. I wanted to lead the conversation on to the business in hand.

'Well, it's not exactly as glamorous as the Flying Squad. But it does have its compensations.'

'Surely there can't be need for law enforcement in that area. Not now things have got more, well, permissive.'

'Permissive,' Mooney hissed the word back at me with relish. 'Yes, we live, as they say, in a permissive age. But, you see, as laws become more liberal they have to become more tightly regulated. The whole point of permissiveness is permission. We have to be careful what is permitted.'

'I see,' I said, nodding along with him.

'Filth, depravity, we can only allow so much. We can't stamp it out, we can only contain it. Control it. The courts are practically useless in defining what obscenity is. So it's up to the police to decide what's permitted.'

'So, this means you'll be granting permission to certain people.'

Mooney looked up and smiled. His little eyes gleamed at me across the table.

'Ruby,' he said, 'I know that you're here on behalf of Mr Starks. It pains me to think that the premise of our little tête à tête is this sordid business.'

'Now, George,' I purred at him. 'Don't be like that.'

'I'd like to think,' he went on, haltingly, 'that you could enjoy my company. Just a little bit.'

'Of course,' I replied, giving my best Charm School smile.

'Then we can be friends?'

His hand slithered across the tablecloth to rest limply on mine. I tried not to shudder. His palm was warm and clammy.

'Yes,' I agreed through a clenched grin.

'Then I will deal with you, Ruby, as a friend.'

I slipped my hand out from under his as casually as possible and folded my arms. I tilted my head engagingly to one side.

'So?' I asked softly.

Mooney's eyes darted to and fro as if he was checking the room.

'Permissiveness requires a necessary permit charge. It's big business we're dealing with here. "Licensing" we like to call it. Harry Starks knows all about it.'

'So, are you, well, granting him a licence?'

'Yes, to a certain extent. But we're not giving him free rein just yet.'

'Why not?'

'Certain reservations, shall we say.'

'Such as?'

'Well,' said Mooney, 'Mr Starks is a formidable operator, someone who can control the Soho rackets, someone we could definitely do business with on a large scale. This sort of thing needs a firm hand and Harry has a very good pedigree where that's concerned. But we don't want the boat rocked. We can't afford to be seen to be presiding over some sort of unseemly power struggle. This business with the Maltese. It needs to be sorted out.'

'And what do you suggest that he does?'

Mooney shrugged.

'Well, unless he can eliminate the opposition, swiftly and efficiently, I'd suggest some sort of accommodation. If both parties can be clear about who operates what, then we can be sure about who we're dealing with and settle our percentage accordingly. But, however, it needs to be done quickly and cleanly. We certainly can't sanction a messy gang war. That would definitely be bad for business. With the Twins banged up and awaiting trial, West End Central are under pressure to come down heavily on anything that looks like a power struggle. So I suggest that Mr Starks operate with some discretion.'

Mooney insisted on paying for the meal, even though Harry had given me plenty of cash to cover it. He showed me to my cab and I allowed him to peck me on the cheek.

'I look forward to our next date, Ruby,' he said as I got into the back.

I reported back to Harry and he set up a meet with the Maltese. I got back in touch with Mooney so that he could sit in on the negotiations. Harry cut me in as promised and he went through the sort of money he planned to make from this racket. There was a huge amount to be made and I would be on a percentage. It all started to make sense. All I would have to do was play at being nice to that creep Mooney. Hell, I'd done a lot worse for less cash. Now I could get together some capital of my own. I could set myself up with it and I wouldn't have to rely on anyone. I thought about Eddie again. I didn't love him any more. I didn't want to have to worry about him rotting away in the Hate Factory. I wanted to be free of all that.

The big meet took place at the Criterion Restaurant. Harry attended with two of his firm, Big Jock McCluskey and Manny Gould. Three of the Maltese firm were there and George Mooney turned up with a couple of junior officers from the Dirty Squad. And like some diplomatic summit, they carved it all up.

It was agreed that the Maltese would stick to their familiar territory, clip joints and prostitute flats. But they would only have a limited interest in pornographic bookshops. Harry would make few incursions into prostitution and clipping, mostly confined to running rent boys, which in any case the Maltese had no interest in. In return, he would take the biggest share in the pornography trade.

It was a shrewd deal on Harry's part. He knew that the porn trade was booming and was easy to run, and carried with it the minimum risk. Initially the Dirty Squad was to be paid, via Mooney, £5,000 – £3,000 from Harry and £2,000 from the Maltese, and then a continuing percentage from the shops and clubs.

To secure the deal and to make sure that there was less chance of rivalry in the future an arrangement was worked out giving both parties, the Maltese and Harry's firm, joint interest in some of each other's clubs. This meant that if any of the premises run by either group were attacked, the other operator would suffer by it as well. So the incentive for any further trouble was removed.

Everyone went away happy. The racketeers could continue to make a fortune out of vice with the minimum of harassment. The police would get their cut and be able to claim that they were keeping the lid on Soho. Anything that might too easily offend public morality, over-enthusiastic touting by a clip joint, shop-window displays that were too lairy, these could easily be curbed by having a quiet word. It made sense for the Dirty Squad to deal with organised crime, with crime that they themselves had helped to organise. It meant that their patch wouldn't get fucked up by irresponsible and unruly elements. The gangsters could do the majority of the policing for them, and the really dirty stuff at that.

At first I had worried about Eddie. Then I stopped worrying about him and just worried about not worrying. As the months went by with him inside, I felt a sort of emptiness towards him. My visits had already become much more important to him than they were for me. I felt guilty about that, which just made things worse, and I began to go and see him less and less. I started to think about getting a divorce.

By now I had money in the bank. A couple of years of this, I figured, and I could look after myself. The porn business was booming. I got to know how it all worked. How the shops were laid out. Soft core in the front, hard core out the back. And the real money was to be made in the shops. In retail. Especially the hard stuff. The wholesale racket was vulnerable, with risks at both ends, production and distribution. Harry could pressurise the people producing this filth into disposing of their stock at low prices whilst the punters were willing to buy it at any price. Buy cheap and sell dear, the classic profit formula. And there was much less risk involved as well. Harry didn't even own the shops that he ran, he leased them from what was known in the trade as 'the superior landlord'. Managers or wholesalers could be charged with 'possession for gain' but 'possession' or 'gain' could not be proved against Harry. And with the Dirty Squad paid off, Harry was laughing. It was hard not to admire his cunning in all of this. He was offering 'protection' and yet he was the most protected.

I got involved with it far more than I'd really wanted. I got to know the ludicrous nicknames – nobody used their real name if they could help it. And I got to know the slang for all the aspects of the business. Photographs were 'smudges', Super 8 films were 'rollers' and dirty books were 'yellow backs'. Most of the hard-core stuff at that time was imported from Scandinavia. 'Scans', they were called. Some stuff came from America but this was done by people going over to New York, buying up the heaviest porn they could find and smuggling back individual magazines which could be copied 'dot for dot' in some dingy printworks in London. Scans were shipped in in bulk, right under the noses of Customs and Excise. There were careful methods of importation. Smudges and yellow backs would come in in bales of wastepaper that were then being imported from

Scandinavia. Rollers would often be hidden in refrigerator trucks carrying bacon. Flesh with 'Danish' written all over it.

Thankfully, I rarely had to handle this filth. Whenever I saw any of it, well, I felt a sort of sadness. It all seemed pathetic. It was hard not to pity the sad old raincoat brigade who lapped all of this stuff up. The really obscene thing was the huge piles of cash we were making. And most of all, I pitied the people these distorted bodies belonged to. I didn't imagine they were paid much or treated well.

I tried not to think about them or feel guilty in any way, and instead to concentrate on the thought that with enough capital I could set myself up somehow. I could divorce Eddie and, I don't know, maybe even start my own business. Something utterly legal and boring. I didn't have any idea of what, though. The money kept coming in, some of it in my name simply to protect Harry, but a fair percentage would be mine in the long term. Or so I hoped.

I wanted to talk to Harry about Eddie. But I couldn't get much sense out of him. He was in love again. He was stupid over this kid Tommy. I couldn't say I blamed him. Tommy was fucking gorgeous, that's for sure. Blond with pale blue eyes. A tight, muscled little figure. There was something very flirtatious in his manner. He had a slight squint, a lazy eye full of mischief.

Harry had met him a few years back in one of the boys' clubs that he'd donated a boxing trophy to. Harry had got him to give up boxing. 'It'll spoil your looks,' he'd told him. He'd been in trouble and done a bit of borstal. When he was out he came and found Harry.

He wanted to be an actor though I don't think he had any idea of how to go about it. He'd done some modelling and some extra work, that was all. He seemed very taken with me. I guess he thought, rather naively, that I could further his career. I told him straight out that I wasn't exactly a shining example of success when it came to show business but I promised that I'd do anything I could to help. I couldn't tell whether he had any real talent in that direction. He kind of performed with people, sort of craving their attention. He knew he was attractive all right, but he gave off a sort of nervousness, as if he was struggling with something.

Tommy had had a hard time. In and out of care most of his life. You'd often catch a hurt look about him that spoke of God knows what. And I suppose I worried about him. Harry's boyfriends could often have a rough deal.

I introduced Tommy to Gerald Wilman who agreed to help him out with his voice. Gerald had an incredible vocal range and was famous on the radio for his funny voices. He'd done legitimate theatre work as well so he knew all about proper technique. Gerald was very taken with Tommy's boyish good looks and Tommy played all of that up to the hilt. They made an arrangement to do a voice class every week. I warned Tommy of Gerald's notorious short temper.

I took Tommy out from time to time to the theatre or to see a movie. He was quite starstruck. He watched in the darkness with wonder, sometimes grabbing my hand as his eyes gazed upwards to the screen or the stage. It was nice to have the company of such a beautiful young man. It took my mind off worrying about Eddie and wondering how to act friendly with George Mooney. He had a great energy and enthusiasm about him, a curiosity about things. And he was very affectionate. It was as if he was making up for lost time.

At other times me, Harry and Tommy went out together as a threesome. One night we went around to Johnnie Ray's mews house in Chelsea for drinks. Johnnie and his boyfriend manager, Bill, had become quite settled there, even though Johnnie was about to do another god-forsaken tour of working men's clubs. Tommy was very impressed by Johnnie, even though he was hardly a big star any more. Even in small social gatherings Johnnie would go into a sort of scripted dialogue. With his deafness it was always hard to know how much he kept up with the conversation and I think he went into a repetitious patter as a kind of defence mechanism.

'You know,' he announced, for the umpteenth time, 'Sophie Tucker once said to me "Johnnie, you and I have paid our dues but these kids today, they all come up so fast."'

Tommy lapped it up. He nodded enthusiastically. It was as if in his own mad dreams of stardom he actually thought Johnnie was talking about him.

'How's the club?' asked Bill, unaware of the recent changes.

Harry explained rather sheepishly about the 'Stardust Erotic Revue'. Johnnie smiled.

'I used to go out with this high-class stripper back in the fifties,' he said. 'Tempest Storm. You may have heard of her.'

'That was when you were trying to bolster your straight image, wasn't it dear?' quipped Bill, and everyone laughed.

They all seemed happy enough. Harry loved Tommy. Johnnie loved Bill. And I felt like a double gooseberry all evening.

Mooney didn't bother checking the money that I handed over to him in the Celebrity Club off Bond Street. He let a sly smile play across his lips and his peephole eyes darted to and fro as he slipped the fat envelope in his inside jacket pocket.

'Please pass on my thanks to Mr Starks,' he said. 'But also, some of our concerns regarding some of his more, er, flamboyant window displays. There's a few we don't like the look of.'

He handed me a list of shops.

'Get them to tone it down a bit. We need to keep the lid on all of this. Then everybody's happy.'

He poured the champagne.

'And warn him that the *Sunday People* is doing an exposé of the porn trade in Soho. There's nothing that titillates the tabloid reader more than a moral crusade against filth. There's a bloke calling himself Fahmi, claims he's a rich Arab wanting to buy blue films in bulk. He's really a freelance journalist.'

'I'll tell him.'

Mooney smiled.

'It really is a pleasure doing business with you, Ruby.'

I forced a smile back.

'There is something else,' he said softly. 'Something I'd like to keep just between the two of us for the time being.'

He patted my hand.

'What?'

'Well, one of Mr Starks's former cohorts, a certain Tony Stavrakakis. He's in Brixton Prison and itching for an early release date. So he's started talking. Making statements about some of Harry's past activities. Looks like a case is being put together.'

'What sort of case?'

'Once this Kray business is dealt with, the word is that the Yard is going to be coming down heavily on any other organised crime. Don't want anyone filling the vacuum, if you see what I mean.'

He slurped at his champagne.

'We need to be careful, Ruby.'

'We?'

'Yes. You and me. If Harry Starks goes down we need to be as far away from it all as possible. Don't want to get sucked under, do we?'

'Er, no,' I replied cautiously.

'Don't worry. I've started to make contingency plans. I've developed a fondness towards you, Ruby. I wouldn't want you to be implicated in anything nasty.'

1968 was nearly over. I had my last visit to Eddie of that year. Christmas was four days away so it didn't seem right telling him anything of what I thought of us splitting up. I think he knew that something was up, though. I found it hard to look him in the eye. I didn't mention what I was doing, other than to say that I'd got some work in stage management, which was near enough the truth.

Harry went back to Hoxton for Christmas and took Tommy with him. A sure sign that he was serious about the kid. He invited me as well but I stayed in Chelsea and had my mother over for a couple of days.

After Christmas we all went around to Johnnie's and Bill's for drinks. Johnnie had just finished a tour of the northern club circuit and didn't have any engagements until next year so they could relax and see in the new year together.

'How are you going to celebrate it?' Harry asked.

'Well,' replied Johnnie with a grin. 'Judy's in town.'

'Judy Garland?'

'Yeah. She's doing a residency at the Talk of the Town. We thought we'd go and give the old girl some support. She sure as hell needs it. It'll be like old times.'

'You know Judy?'

'Sure. Well, I know her daughter Liza better. But me and Judy go back. I met her when I was working on Sunset Strip. She said to me, "Johnnie, you and I have paid our dues, but these kids today, they all come up so fast."'

'You a fan, Harry?' asked Bill.

'Are you kidding?' Tommy interjected. 'Harry loves Judy. Don't you Harry?'

'Yeah, well,' replied Harry, slightly guarded. 'She's a great talent.'

'Well, we could introduce you,' suggested Johnnie with a smile.

'Could you?' Harry piped up, his voice suddenly full of child-like enthusiasm.

Harry couldn't help coming over all eager. Johnnie and Bill laughed at the expression on his face. He looked like a big kid.

'Well, lookee here,' Johnnie drawled in a Midwest twang, 'Harry's a real friend of Dorothy's, aren't you, Harry?'

Harry went all bashful. But you could tell he quite enjoyed being made fun of. In carefully controlled circumstances, of course. He could relax for a bit, laugh at himself.

Everyone was in a good mood. But I suddenly had this odd sense of foreboding about Judy. She seemed so doom laden. There were awful press stories about her. Breakdowns, disastrous marriages, pills and booze and suicide attempts. Her tax bill made what Johnnie owed in back taxes seem like milk money. The queens still loved her, but maybe all that drama and tragedy was part of the attraction. I was beginning to long for the quiet life myself. And I somehow felt that her coming was a bad omen.

New Year's Eve I went out with the strippers from the club. We went drinking in the West End. They were a good crew of girls to get drunk with. We staggered down Charing Cross Road arm in arm to join the crowds in Trafalgar Square just as Big Ben was pealing midnight.

'What's your New Year's resolution?' asked one.

'I'm going to get a proper West End show. A nice musical.'

'Fuck that! I'm going to marry a rich punter!'

Laughter.

Then one of the girls turned to me and asked me softly: 'What about you, Rube? You got a resolution?'

'Yeah,' I replied. 'I'm going to make me enough money out of this filthy game and then retire. Do something normal.'

I meant it too. But I couldn't help having these uneasy thoughts. I had a bad feeling about 1969.

On the night that Harry and Tommy had planned to go and see Judy at the Talk of the Town, Harry was called away on business. It must have been important to keep him from seeing Judy Garland. He called me up on the telephone.

'You take the kid,' he said. 'Tommy's been dying to see Judy. Wouldn't want to disappoint him.'

He sounded like he was under pressure.

'Is anything wrong?' I asked him.

'Nah,' he replied, distractedly. 'Nothing I can't handle. I'll get Tommy to pick you up.'

And so me and Tommy went to the Talk of the Town together. Harry didn't like Tommy going out on his own. He was jealous and possessive just as Rachman had been with me.

'I hope you don't mind going out with me,' I said to Tommy.

'Course not, Ruby.' He grinned at me with an off-centre stare. 'I can be your boyfriend for the evening.'

We had a good table, near the stage. There was a floorshow on first. Some silly revue with showgirls in feathery costumes. High-class bump and grind. Like The Stardust but they kept their clothes on.

Judy was due on at eleven. She was late. No surprise there. It gave me and Tommy a chance to chat. Tommy's career. It had started well enough. He'd got an agent. One of Harry's connections. And he'd had some nice new publicity photos done. But he'd had no luck with any castings. He'd come to my flat from an audition one afternoon virtually in tears. He obviously wanted reassurance. 'That director was a right bitch,' he'd said. I'd hugged him and said, 'Yeah, I know darling.' Deep down I suspected that he hadn't been any good. And Gerald Wilman had given up on the vocal training. He'd lost patience with Tommy's inability to form consonants, and ended up shouting at him. Tommy had fled, upset.

I tried to sound encouraging but deep down I wanted to warn him off. He didn't really have much going for himself apart from his looks. Someone needed to break it to him gently that he didn't really have any talent as an actor. I decided that I'd talk to Harry about it. I just felt that Tommy was setting himself up for a lot of humiliation and disappointment.

Judy finally made it onto the stage just past midnight and by now the crowd had become more than restless. The spotlight hit her spindly, quivering form as it tottered out in a red trouser suit. She didn't seem to be aware of where she was. The mob became ugly and started to bay. Someone threw an empty cigarette packet. A few bread rolls followed. Booing and catcalls.

Judy just stood there trembling.

'Oh dear,' she managed to squeak. 'Oh dear.'

It was obscene. Like some sort of awful ritual sacrifice. A man got up on stage and grabbed the microphone.

'If you can't turn up on time,' he bawled, 'why turn up at all?'

Judy rushed off the stage in tears. I was glad Harry wasn't there to see this. He'd have probably started a fight with the hecklers. Tommy was in a state of shock.

'Come on,' I said. 'Let's get out of here.'

We drove slowly back to Chelsea in silence. Tommy dropped me off and I invited him up for a nightcap. The poor kid could do with a drink after tonight's fiasco, I thought.

'Well, that was a bit of a disaster,' I said as Tommy poured us both a brandy.

'It was awful,' said Tommy, still wide eyed from it all. 'Those people were so horrible to Judy.'

'Well that's show business,' I said flatly. I felt a cruel satisfaction in his disillusionment.

'But Ruby . . .'

'But nothing. That's what it's like. You don't come up with the goods, and they'll tear you apart. You should remember that.'

Tommy looked hurt. He took a gulp of brandy and squinted at me.

'You don't think I'd be any good as an actor, do you?'

I sighed.

'I don't know, Tommy. Maybe you shouldn't set your heart on it too much. It's a tough business, believe me.'

'But I want to be somebody.'

I smiled at him.

'You are somebody, Tommy.'

He went to the window.

'No I'm not,' said Tommy. 'I'm a nobody. I don't even know who my parents were. I want to make something of my life. That's why I took up boxing. I thought that could be something.'

I turned around to look at him. Head down, eyes up looking at me in a dewy squint. I went over and touched his face.

'I'm glad Harry made you give up boxing. You are very handsome.'

Tommy pulled away.

'Harry,' he said resentfully. 'He'd make me give up everything. Give up myself. For him.'

'He cares about you,' I said.

'Does he?' Tommy's voice was suddenly cold. 'He doesn't even know me. I don't even know me. I've never—'

He stopped abruptly, turning away to look out of the window. A hollow reflection of his face in the darkened pane.

I put a hand on his shoulder. He turned back and looked at me. I was mesmerised by his squint. His pale-blue eyes. He was so pretty. I kissed him gently on the mouth. He kissed me back and before I knew it we were at it. Arms snaking around each other. Mouths greedy. We tore at each other's clothes and staggered into the bedroom.

This is crazy, I thought as we climbed onto the bed together. I think we both got carried away with the sheer recklessness of it. A passionate sense of danger. *Harry would kill us for this.* Tommy raked his fingers over me clumsily, sucking at my tits in a kind of blind hunger. I stroked his taut body, tracing the little ripples of muscle, and arched myself up against him as I guided him into me.

Afterwards we lay on the bed in silence for quite a while.

'Tommy?' I said finally. 'Are you all right?'

There was a strange low laugh in the darkness. I rolled over onto one side and tried to look at him.

'This is a very bad idea,' I said.

'It's all right,' Tommy whispered, stroking my hair.

'What's all this about, anyway?' I asked.

'What do you mean?'

'I mean, I thought you were, you know . . .'

'Queer?'

'Well, yeah.'

'I told you. I don't know what I am.'

I sighed heavily and rolled onto my back.

'Don't worry,' Tommy insisted. 'It'll all be all right. I promise it will, Ruby.'

I didn't know what on earth he meant by this. But I felt too exhausted to ask. All I knew was this could fuck everything up really badly. And all I could think was: Harry mustn't know.

Harry phoned me the next day sounding flustered and I had a sudden fear that he'd found out. He said that he needed to talk to me.

'What's the matter?' I asked.

'We've had a spot of bother.'

I felt a wave of relief. He was talking business.

'Meet me at the club,' said Harry, and I made my way over there.

I got to The Stardust and went up to the office. Harry was sitting at the desk glancing at the *Daily Mirror* and smoking a cigarette. KRAYS AT THE OLD BAILEY, read the headline. I could see the tension in his jaw.

'Shocking,' Harry said, tapping the paper. 'All these guys the prosecution's calling. All these faces going QE. It's a bad omen.'

He shook his head slowly and looked up at me.

'Glad you could come, Rube,' he said, agitatedly stubbing out the fag.

'What's happened, Harry?'

'We've been fucked over. That's what's happened.'

'What?'

'A whole shipment of Scans. Busted at Felixstowe. Customs and Excise. Somebody grassed. They had a tip off, that's for sure. Three lorries' worth, pinched. Worth fifty grand retail. I need to know what the fuck's going on.'

'What do you want me to do?'

'I want you to have a meet with Mooney, pronto. I want to know who grassed. I want to know where it's safe for me to bring this stuff in to.'

'Right.' I nodded.

'And I need to know what he's up to,' said Harry.

'What do you mean?'

'Something's up. I'm paying him off for the whole squad but I've heard a rumour that the Chief Super isn't getting his fair whack. Money we're giving him isn't going upstairs. If he's keeping it all for himself then I'm soon going to have his guvnor breathing down my neck. It's all a fucking mess.'

Harry was completely wound up. It wasn't like him.

'Is this what last night was all about?' I asked him.

Harry sighed.

'Nah,' he said, darkly. 'That's something else.'

He lit another cigarette.

'What is it, Harry?'

Harry sighed out a stream of smoke.

'Nothing you need to know about,' he muttered. 'Look, just get a meet with Mooney and find out what's going on.'

I didn't have any time to do anything about it that day, though. I had to go over to Wandsworth. I had a VO to see Eddie in the Hate Factory. Eddie looked well enough physically. A fine example of how jail keeps young men lean and fit, mean and ready for more crime once they're out again. Scores of plans for scams and really big ones trod out on the inner circle of the exercise yard.

The conversation began to flag once it went past the how are you, how's it going stage. Then we hit silence. After about a minute, I came right out and said it: 'I want a divorce, Eddie.'

He sighed. More silence.

'Ruby,'

'I'm sorry.'

He sighed again.

'Look,' he said, 'don't do it now. Not yet.'

'Eddie . . .'

'Think how it would look to the parole board. They might well think if they let me out, I'll be after you with a grudge. Give it a bit more time, eh?'

Eddie looked over at me desperately.

'Ruby, there's two ways you can do your time, you know? With love or with hate. Either one will keep you going. Don't make me hate you. At least let me pretend for a while.'

And we left it at that.

I met Mooney in a pub on Brewer Street. He gave a little show of surprise at me coming empty handed.

'What, no envelope?'

'No George. No envelope. As a matter of fact, Harry wants to know where all the money's been going. You've been keeping it all for yourself, haven't you?'

He smiled coyly.

'I've been a naughty boy, Ruby.'

'Cut it out, George. Some of that cash needs to go upstairs. That was the deal.'

Mooney shrugged, noncommittal.

'And a whole shipment from Scandinavia's been seized. What's going on?'

'I'm afraid Customs and Excise is a little out of my patch.'

'So who tipped them off?'

He shrugged again.

'Look,' I said. 'I thought the deal was that you'd be able to hand up grasses.'

'I can. If it's in my jurisdiction.'

'Can't you ask Customs for a name?'

Mooney laughed.

'I'm afraid that the Excise men don't really trust the Dirty Squad. They have this nasty notion that stuff we impound simply turns up on the market again with just an extra mark-up price.'

'Well, Harry needs to know where he can bring the stuff in safely.'

'He'll think of something.'

'And the money you owe your Chief Super?'

'Well, that's another matter. Mr Starks might just have to make another payment.'

'Harry won't like that.'

'No, I don't suppose he will. But then I would have thought that he has more pressing matters on his mind at the moment.'

'What do you mean?'

'Harry's headed for a fall. Tony Stavrakakis is now officially an RI.'

'RI?'

'Resident Informer. Doesn't fancy such a long stretch, so he's dictating his memoirs to the Serious Crime Squad.'

'Harry needs to know about this.'

'Oh, well, I've got the feeling he already does. Not much he can do, though. Not with Stavrakakis in a nice secure cell with a colour telly and all. Once this Kray trial is over and they're put away for good, Harry's next in the firing line. There's a lot of pressure from up top to make sure no one fills the vacuum. So maybe Mr Starks won't be with us for very much longer. We need to think how we might go about business without him.'

'You can't be serious.'

'Why not? We just need to find somebody who can take over. This racket won't last for ever. *The Sunday People* are snooping around, trying to stir up an anti-filth crusade. And some of the top rank of the Met are beginning to get suspicious about the Dirty Squad. It's good for a couple of years, I reckon. Plenty of time to make plenty of money, Ruby. Harry or no Harry.'

'And then what?'

'I'm thinking of taking early retirement. With all of this cash I should be able to find somewhere warm and quiet to live out my days. Southern Spain, I was thinking. Somewhere on the Costa del Sol.'

He gazed off, looking wistful. Then his eyes narrowed on me.

'It would be nice to have a companion, Ruby.'

'What?'

'I mean it, Ruby. Starks has run out of luck. I could offer you a safe haven. Protection. You never know, you might need it. I wouldn't ask much in return.'

'George . . .'

'Think about it, Ruby.'

I phoned Harry the next day.

'Harry, we need to talk.'

'Ruby!' He sounded excited. 'Come over. We're going for drinks with Johnnie. Guess where we're going?'

'Harry, this is important.'

He didn't seem to hear me.

'We're going around to see Judy.'

'Harry . . .'

'*Judy*, Ruby. Judy Garland. Can you believe that? Come and join us.'

Judy Garland was staying in a mews house just around the corner from Sloane Square with her new fiancé, Mickey Deans. Judy was wearing a psychedelic paisley trouser suit, her deathly pallid face framed by a shock of dyed-black hair. Mickey had carefully tousled shoulder-length hair and sideburns. He wore a polo-neck sweater under a mohair suit. He had a washed-out look about his face that made him look older than he was. He still looked a lot younger than Judy. But then everybody did.

Harry, of course, insisted on photographs. Finally completing his showbiz gallery with the long-sought-after prize of his collection. Harry with Judy Garland. The gangster looking stern but benevolent, Judy's death mask suddenly coming to life with instinctive eyes and teeth animation by the miraculous light of the flashbulb. Everybody took turns at lining up as if we were all old friends at a reunion.

Tommy was camera shy, which wasn't like him. It may have been because he was sporting a bit of a black eye but there was something else as well. He'd become kind of sullen in the past couple of days. He'd given up all his dreams of acting. Instead he'd started getting involved in Harry's businesses. He'd become serious. He seemed to be viewing the whole occasion with a newly found disdain. He sidled up to me and nodded towards Judy.

'Look at her,' he muttered conspiratorially. 'She's falling apart right in front of us.'

'Tommy,' I chided him softly.

'Well,' he said with a casual cruelty, 'who needs a healthy Judy Garland?'

Meanwhile Harry talked up his charity work to Judy.

'Boys' clubs, deprived kids, that sort of thing.'

'That sounds nn, very rewarding,' slurred Judy.

'In fact, I often organise special events. Charity evenings. If you could be a guest at one of them . . .'

'You mean nn, sing?'

'No, not sing. Well, you could if you wanted to. But I mean if you could make an appearance. The boys would really appreciate that.'

Judy smiled and nodded blankly.

'An appearance,' she repeated.

'At my club.'

'You run a club?' Judy asked. 'My fiancé runs a club in New York. Don't you, Mickey?'

Mickey nodded. Harry looked over and they sized each other up for a second, and then smiled. The talk was all Judy and Mickey getting married once the divorce had come through, Judy and Johnnie Ray working together. They'd done an impromptu duet one night at the Talk of the Town and brought the house down. No one mentioned what terrible shape she was obviously in or how she'd barely made it through her last residency. Everyone colluded in the Judy Garland Lazarus act.

I finally cornered Harry in the kitchen as he was preparing the next round of martinis. I told him about Mooney keeping the money.

'Bastard,' he hissed. 'Well there's not much we can do for now.

I'll just have to pay his superiors direct. He thinks he can have me over. We'll find some way of dealing with Mooney. In the meantime, we need to get our hard-core stuff into the country. We need to know where we're safe bringing it in. Does he know anything?'

'He said it was out of his jurisdiction.'

'Well, we'll have to think of something otherwise no one's getting any gelt. Look, let's talk about this tomorrow.'

We went back into the drawing room. Johnnie and Judy were at the piano going through a rather shaky version of 'Am I Blue?' Harry talked with Mickey in a quiet, business-like intimacy. They talked up clubs and possible joint-business ventures.

I took a drink over to Tommy. I couldn't help staring at the yellow-edged bruise under his right eye.

'What happened to you?'

He frowned.

'Your face.'

'When he's in a bad mood he takes it out on me,' he replied flatly.

I felt a sudden stab of anger towards Harry. He could be a real bastard. I gently stroked Tommy's face, then quickly took my hand away, looking around guiltily.

Johnnie's and Judy's harmonies grated. Bill looked on, forcing encouragements. Harry and Mickey talked of a European tour. They're still big stars there.

'Can I walk you home after this?' asked Tommy. 'I want to talk to you.'

I nodded. Piano chords plodded like a funeral march. Harry mentioned Scandinavia. Judy squawked off key. Mickey winced.

'You'll have to do better than that!' he hollered. The music stopped.

'Now, Mickey that's not nn, very nice,' Judy muttered softly.

Then it all started to get ugly. Brandy, their alsatian dog, started to bark along to the row like he knew the routine. Johnnie and Bill looked on helpless. Me, Harry and Tommy made our excuses and left.

'What a bloody farce,' Tommy commented as he walked with me back to my flat.

'Tommy,' I said to him. 'We need to talk.'

'I know, Ruby,' he replied, almost indignantly. 'I know.'

'What happened the other night, well, it was a mistake. It's best if Harry doesn't know about it, though. It's best if we just forget it.'

'Ruby . . .'

'Please, Tommy. Let's be sensible about this.'

Tommy chuckled softly.

'You worry too much.'

'Yeah, and with good reason.'

'It'll all be all right, Ruby. I promise.'

We reached the door to my flat.

'I've got plans,' he said rather grandly. 'It'll all be fine.'

I didn't like the sound of this.

'Goodnight, Tommy,' I said and went to kiss him on the cheek.

He grabbed me and held me in an embrace, pressing his mouth into mine. I gave in to it. *Stupid cow*, I thought to myself. But I couldn't help it. My resolve just melted inside me. He drew his head back and looked at me. His eyes looked grey and determined.

'We'll be all right,' he said, and then he was gone.

I was going through a new routine with the girls at The Stardust. We spent most of the morning working on how to get tit tassels to rotate properly. Harry arrived about lunchtime. He looked terrible. His face was pallid, eyes all puffy from booze and anti-depressants.

'Very nice,' he commented wearily, looking up at the stage.

'OK girls,' I called out. 'Let's break for lunch.'

I followed him up to the office. He had a bundle of daily papers under one arm. He dropped them on the desk. All the headlines screamed out about the Krays. END OF A REIGN OF TERROR, THE FIRM THAT RULED THE EAST END BY FEAR, THE NEAREST WE CAME TO AL CAPONE.

'Thirty years for the Twins,' Harry muttered. 'They're really crowing over this one, Rube.'

'An end of an era.'

Harry gave a hollow laugh.

'Yeah. And no love lost there. But it means I'm vulnerable. I've got a feeling that I'm next in line.'

'Really?' I acted surprise.

'Yeah. Somebody's grassing. And I can't get to them. There's a case being built up against me. I need to start pulling a few strings myself. I want you to talk to Mooney about it.'

I nodded.

'See if he can't bring some influence to bear on the Serious Crime Squad,' he went on. 'Slow it all down a bit, at least. Buy me a bit of time.'

'I'll try.'

'In the meantime I need to sort out our wholesalers. We need to keep our supplies coming in, whatever else is happening. I might have to go abroad for a few days soon.'

He lit up a fag. I stood up.

'I'll talk to Mooney,' I said.

'Thanks. There is one other thing.'

'Yeah?'

'Tommy.'

I froze.

'I'm worried about the kid,' he said. 'Something's bothering him. I know he's disappointed about this acting business not working out. He's got involved with the firm but he's acting all lairy. Throwing his weight about like he owns the racket. I don't know what's got into him.'

Harry took a drag and sighed the smoke out.

'I know I'm not easy to get on with. But it's like he's winding me up.'

'How?'

'I don't know, Rube. Little things. I don't know what he's talking about half the time. Could you have a word? I know you're close. And he talks to you.'

'Yeah, Harry,' I said. 'Sure.'

'Thanks, Rube.' He stared at me. 'I love that boy.'

Mickey Deans became Judy Garland's fifth husband at Chelsea Register Office at noon on March 15. They both looked slightly bewildered as the registrar droned out their real names. Will you, Michael De Vinko, take you, Frances Ethel Gumm? Judy slurred her words so that when she tried to repeat the line: 'I know of no lawful impediment why I cannot marry this man,' it came out as 'I know of no, nn *awful* impediment . . .'. One of the journalists sniggered and quickly scrawled something in shorthand.

Judy wore a chiffon mini dress festooned with ostrich feathers. Thick eye liner darkened sockets in a ghostly white face. She looked like some strange bird. Exotic and near extinction. She clung on desperately to Mickey with claw-like hands. He sported a plum-coloured suit with a regency-style collar and a cravat. Johnnie Ray was best man.

The reception was at Quaglino's. There was an impressive guest list, including many American stars who were currently working in Britain. Bette Davis, Veronica Lake, Ginger Rogers, Eva Gabor, as well as John Gielgud, James Mason, Peter Finch and Lawrence Harvey were all invited. None of them turned up. There was Glyn Jones and Bumbles Dawson, Johnnie Ray, Bill, me, Harry and Tommy. The small crowd of journalists and photographers present were unable to make the occasion look well attended. The only other guest was a crippled fan who believed that listening to Judy sing could make her walk. She was treated to a croaky rendition of 'You'll Never Walk Alone' but she remained in her chair throughout the reception.

The cake arrived, courtesy of the Talk of the Town, but it hadn't been defrosted. It was frozen solid and could not be cut. Judy got horribly drunk. Harry talked intently with Mickey Deans.

Judy and Mickey then left to fly off to Paris for a honeymoon. Four concert dates in Scandinavia with Johnnie Ray had been booked by Mickey, and they were all going to meet up in Stockholm for the beginning of the short tour.

After the party Harry broke it to us that he was going to go over to Sweden for a few days too. He'd been involved in the bookings in some way and he had some business lined up as well. No doubt sorting out a way of getting Scans into the country safely.

We saw him off at the airport a few days later. He and Tommy said their goodbyes awkwardly. Harry patting Tommy on the shoulder, wary of showing affection in public. Tommy nodding solemnly as Harry said a few words. Then Harry quickly leaned over and kissed me on the cheek.

'Keep an eye on the kid,' he whispered and turned to walk through to his Departure gate.

But I kept away from Tommy. Harry being away was a great temptation. I tried not to think about it. It was all too dangerous.

Instead I concentrated on business matters. I met Mooney in a hotel bar in South Kensington. Kray talk was still in the air.

'Nipper Read held this big party in a hotel in King's Cross. I wasn't invited. Once the celebrating's over, Harry will be definitely in the firing line.'

'Harry wants to know if there isn't anything you can do about that.'

'I doubt it. The squad is notoriously incorruptible. They're not even based at the Yard. They're running everything across the river at Tintagel House. Can't be got at. No, I think our mutual friend's days are numbered. He's out of the country, I believe.'

I nodded.

'Well, it's probably good for him to be out of the way for a while. And it's a good time to think about how we can work things out without him.'

'Come on, George.'

'I'm serious, Ruby. I've already talked to someone on his own firm who's ready to take over once he goes down.'

'And what if I tell Harry that you're planning to stitch him up?'

'Oh, you wouldn't do that, Ruby.'

'Wouldn't I, now?'

'No, I don't think so. You see, it might force me to let slip a certain bit of information.'

'Like what?'

'Like about you and this young lad, Tommy.'

Mooney gave an evil little smile. I sat staring with my mouth open. *How did he know?*

'He wouldn't like that, now. Would he?'

'How . . .'

'How do I know? Oh, you'd be surprised what I know about people. I can't say that I approve, Ruby. But I'm willing to keep quiet about it. For now. But maybe you'll consider my offer more seriously.'

'What do you mean?'

Mooney fished about in an inside pocket and pulled out a photograph. He handed it over to me. It was a picture of a whitewashed villa.

'Llanos de Nagueles,' he announced. 'It's near Marbella. My little place in the sun. A couple more years of making money out of filth and then I'll have somewhere to retire to. The day might come when you'll need somewhere to escape to.'

'I don't think so, George.'

'Oh, I can understand your reluctance. But you'll come around. I can fix things, Ruby. I can fix things so that you come out of all of this all right. Or, I could fix things so that—'

He shrugged. His little eyes blinked.

'Let's put it this way, you wouldn't want me as your enemy.'

I spent the next few days just trying to carry on and trying to figure out what the hell to do. Everything was out of control. A husband in prison I didn't love any more. Harry out of the country using the Judy Garland/Johnnie Ray Scandinavian tour as a cover for hard-core porn smuggling. The Serious Crime Squad all ready to nick him for a list of past misdemeanours as long as your arm. Detective Chief Inspector Mooney virtually trying to blackmail me into becoming his 'companion'. I tried to think it all through. And I kept coming back to Tommy.

How did Mooney know? Who else knew? Whatever happens, I thought, we need to get our story straight. At first, when there was no word from him, I felt relieved, as if I could put the whole thing out of my mind. Then I started to worry. Then I had a thought as disturbing as any of the others. I missed him.

Finally he phoned.

'Why are you avoiding me, Ruby?' he asked.

'Why do you think?'

'Harry's not back for a couple of days.'

'Yeah, I know.'

'Come over, Ruby. We need to talk.'

He was right about that, so I agreed. I went over to Harry's flat with all the best intentions. I promised myself that I'd be sensible. When I got there, Tommy got us some drinks and we made small talk for a while. I found myself talking nervously about trivial things. I hadn't realised how tense I was. I had a few more drinks to relax. We sat on the sofa together. Tommy looked more handsome than ever. He seemed strangely cool and collected. He talked softly as if trying to calm me down. I wanted all the mad thoughts in my head to go away and leave me alone. I let him put his arm around me. We started kissing.

I remember thinking, as we went through into the bedroom, that this would be the last time. That this would be a way to finish it. And I felt a kind of sadness about that.

'Tommy,' I said afterwards. 'We've got to stop.'

'You don't mean that.'

'Yes I do. When Harry gets back . . .'

'Don't worry about Harry. He's finished. Old Bill are on to him. He'll be going away for a long time. Then it'll just be you and me.'

'Tommy,' I said sternly. 'Think about this for a second, will you? Harry could find out about us. Somebody already knows.'

'Yeah?'

'Yes. Mooney knows. We're in trouble.'

'Yeah, well, don't worry about Mooney.'

'What do you mean, "Don't worry about Mooney"?'

'I know he knows.'

'How do you know?'

'Because I told him.'

'You did what?' I nearly shouted at him.

'Calm down, Ruby. It's all under control. I told you I'd make things all right, didn't I? I talked to Mooney. I knew he was looking for somebody to take over the porn racket once Harry's put away. So I kind of put myself forward. He wants you in on it as well. So I told him about you and me.'

'You stupid fucker.'

'Don't get angry, Ruby. I did all this for us. Once Harry is inside, it can just be you and me running things.'

'And George Mooney.'

'Yeah.'

'And any number of faces lining up to move in. Tommy, this isn't a game you know. There are a lot of heavy people out there.'

'I can look after myself,' he said, petulantly.

'And what if Harry finds out about all of this while he's still at large?'

Tommy paused as if he was thinking something through.

'Then I'll kill him,' he said suddenly.

'What?'

'I mean it, Ruby. Look.' He reached under the bed and came up with a small automatic pistol. 'See?'

'Tommy, please—'

'He thinks he owns me. Thinks he can order me about. Knock me about. I'll show him.'

'Tommy, put that thing away.'

Then I heard a sharp click from the hallway.

'What was that?'

'What?' asked Tommy.

'That sound.'

Another click. A key was being turned in the door.

'Harry!' Tommy whispered. 'But he's not due back until the day after tomorrow.'

There was the sound of the door being opened and heavy bags dropped in the hallway.

'Tommy!' Harry called out. 'Come and give us a hand with these bags!'

I tried to gather the bedclothes around us. There was no time to do anything. We looked at each other, horrified. Harry was walking through the flat.

'Tommy! Where the fuck are you? Judy cancelled Göteborg, so I came back early.'

He was at the bedroom door.

'The flat's in a fucking mess. What you been doing while I've been away, eh?'

He came in and looked down at us naked in bed together.

'What?' he asked, bewildered. 'What?'

He just stood there staring. His face all creased up with disbelief. I got out of the bed and went up to him.

'Harry . . .' I started to speak.

Dull eyes registered me. His nostrils flared slightly. He slapped me hard across the cheek and I spun off away from him.

'Come here you,' he said softly to Tommy.

Tommy pulled the gun from out of the bedclothes. He pointed it at Harry. Harry snorted.

'Now, I've seen everything. Go on, shoot me you little fucker.'

He started to advance on Tommy. Tommy used both hands to keep the gun steady.

'Don't come any closer,' he said. 'I'll shoot.'

'You haven't got the fucking bottle. Come on,' he said, holding out his hand. 'Give me that fucking shooter.'

The gun went off, clipping Harry on the shoulder and sending him spinning. The recoil threw Tommy back as well and he fell back against the head of the bed. Harry was on the floor clutching at his upper arm, grunting in pain and anger. Tommy knelt up on the bed and took aim again, pointing the gun down towards Harry. Harry frowned at the blood on his hand and then looked fiercely up at Tommy.

'You bastard!' he hissed. 'Go on then, kill me!'

Tommy gritted his teeth and pulled his face back, away from the gun. His finger tightened on the trigger.

'No!' I shouted and dived onto the bed towards Tommy, grabbing for the gun.

It went off in his face. I don't remember hearing the shot, I must have sort of blacked out. But when I opened my eyes I was on top of Tommy's naked body on the bed. There was blood everywhere, splattered against the headboard and the walls. Half his face was blown off. His hand was still curled around the pistol. There were flecks of red all over the top half of my body.

'Tommy? Tommy?' I started to whimper, pressing my fingers against his body.

I don't remember much else. Harry had to pull me off and sit me down in a chair. I just sat there shaking and trembling in shock. Harry had taken off his jacket and put it over Tommy. There was a huge red stain all down one side of his white shirt. He took that off too and started to feel around the wound.

'You, you . . .' I stammered.

'I'm all right. It's gone through. Just a flesh wound.'

He tore off the clean arm of the shirt with his teeth and bound it around his wounded shoulder. He went out into the drawing room and came back with a bottle of brandy and a glass. He handed me the glass and filled it. My hand was shaking wildly and some of the booze sloshed onto the floor. He took a big swig from the bottle. He closed his eyes and tried to slow down his breathing.

'Fuck,' he said softly.

I drained the brandy in the glass in one gulp. Harry refilled it. I drank that down too.

'Right,' he said. 'Go and have a shower.'

I wandered numbly into the bathroom. I turned on the water and stood under it, shivering and gulping for breath. I lost track of time. When I came out into the drawing room Harry was on the telephone, talking calmly. My clothes were on the sofa, neatly folded.

'Yeah,' said Harry into the phone. 'Bring one of them up to the flat. Leave it in the hallway. Yes, right away.'

He replaced the receiver and looked over at me.

'You better get dressed.'

'What are we going to do?'

'It's all being dealt with. Put your clothes on.'

As I dried myself down and dressed, Harry got a first aid box. He unwound the sleeve from his shoulder and started to dress his own wound. He mopped at a small dark red hole with a cotton pad soaked in iodine, hissing with pain through clenched teeth. He taped a bit of gauze over it and then bandaged it. Blood seeped through at first so he wound it tighter. When he'd finished, we had another drink and sat for a long time in silence.

'He was going to kill me,' Harry said, finally.

'Harry, about—'

'I don't want to talk about it,' he cut in. 'This never happened. You understand?'

There was a knock on the door. Harry went out into the hallway. There were voices, instructions. Something heavy was lifted in and placed on the floor. The men who brought it left. Harry came through again.

'Right,' he said. 'You're going to have to help me.'

'What are we going to do?'

Harry sighed.

'We've got to get rid of the body.'

'But . . .'

'But nothing. We don't have any choice. Come on.'

He grabbed me firmly by the hand and led me into the hall.

'You've got to help me with this,' he said. 'No one else can know. I can't trust anybody else.'

There was a large steamer trunk by the front door. Harry opened it up. Inside were stacks of shrink-wrapped magazines. Hard-core porn. Scandinavian. Smuggled in as part of Judy Garland's luggage. Harry started to fish out the glossies with his good arm, handing them to me.

'Take them through into the drawing room,' he ordered.

It took us about a quarter of an hour to empty the trunk and stack all the magazines in a row of piles behind the sofa.

'Right. You need to help me again,' he said, and led me towards the bedroom.

I froze.

'I can't go in there, Harry.'

'Come on, I can't lift it by myself. I've only got one arm.'

'I can't.'

'Come on. We don't have any choice.'

We went into the bedroom. Harry had already rolled Tommy up in the bedclothes and cleaned some of the blood off the walls. We slid the body around on the mattress. I took the head end, lifting under the shoulders, Harry put his good arm under the knees and we shuffled it out to the trunk.

He closed the lid and locked it.

'Right. Someone's going to come and take this away. Only you and me know about this. We keep it like that, OK? This never happened. Tommy never had any family so no one's going to report him missing. If anyone asks, you don't know where he is.'

'Harry . . .'

'We don't talk about this. Not even to each other. I've got to finish clearing up. You go home now.'

Home. I had a dinner date that evening with Gerald Wilman. I had to go, I told myself. Mustn't let anyone know that anything's wrong. Pretend that everything's all right.

I went to the bedroom and sat down at the dressing table. A ghost face stared at me from out of the mirror. I pulled my hair back and slapped on a mask of foundation. Stuck on false eyelashes, drew eye liner across the top lids. Blue eye shadow, some eyebrow pencil. I concentrated on the process, tried not to think. I spat into a dried-up cake of mascara and was nearly sick. I swallowed hard and worked the mascara brush into the pigment and spittle, and painted it thickly on. A bit of rouge. Some powder. Deep-red Chanel lipstick.

The hair was a straggly mess. The roots needed doing. With plenty of backcombing and lacquer, I worked it all into some sort of shape.

Got out my favourite dress. A Belville Sassoon evening number in pink beaded organdie. I could still get into it. I looked OK. A little dab of Shalimar and I was ready. I went out.

* * *

The next few days passed in a blur. Alcohol numbness interspersed with anxiety and horror. I started having nightmares. I still have them from time to time. I got some yellow pills from the doctor to help me sleep.

And waited. I kept away from Soho. I didn't go into The Stardust. I kept away from Harry and from Detective Chief Inspector George Mooney. But nothing happened. I didn't know what was going on. I didn't want to know, but not knowing drove me even more crazy.

All sorts of horrible visions came to me. I kept seeing Tommy covered in blood, his face blown off. I imagined awful things that Harry might do to me.

So finally I went around to see him. He came to the door, his eyes all bloodshot and bleary.

'Ruby?' he croaked, as if he hardly recognised me.

He showed me through to the drawing room. 'Get Happy' was on the gramophone.

'You heard about Judy?'

I hadn't but I immediately knew what he meant. The only shocking thing about Judy Garland's death was that there was no shock. You just wondered how she'd lasted so long.

'She had an overdose. Mickey found her dead on the toilet.'

'Harry, about what happened . . .'

'I told you, Rube. I don't want to talk about it.'

'But . . .'

'But nothing. It's all over, Rube. The Dirty Squad have started raiding my bookshops. Mooney's incommunicado. Most of the firm's scarpered. I'm finished.'

'Isn't there something that can be done?'

'Nah.'

'But you could implicate the police. Accuse them of corruption.'

'Nah, the Dirty Squad have got nothing to do with the case they're building on me. It's all the long firms I did way back. Besides, it's no good screaming on about bent coppers. Doing that only means that you're not going to be able to deal with them in the future. You're a wrong 'un and they'll never do business with you again. One look at your file and then it's over, that's for fucking sure. No, you don't want to go at the Old Bill. You want them to fancy you for the next time. Sometimes you have to go down. You have to wipe your mouth, do your time, and the next time – and there will be a next time, Rube – you can start off again.'

'So what do you think will happen?'

'I don't know,' Harry sniffed. 'A seven stretch, maybe even ten if the beak's feeling brutal. I need to get my affairs in order.'

He smiled thinly at me. Garland croaked jauntily on the gramophone. *Forget your troubles c'mon get happy*. We never mentioned Tommy. Harry tapped his fingers in time to the record on the arm of his chair. *We're headed for the judgement day*.

'Poor Judy,' he said, as if it summed everything up. 'Poor, poor Judy.'

Harry was arrested the next day. One count of GBH, another of making an unwarranted menace. These were holding charges. Once he was away they could get more witnesses to come forward. By the time of the committal proceedings there were fourteen counts of Grievous Bodily Harm against him and several charges of fraud and uttering menaces.

It went to the Old Bailey, and the press had a field day. Reporting with relish all the testimony of the beatings, the pliers that pulled teeth, the black box that was used to give electric shocks. *The Daily Mirror* dubbed Harry THE TORTURE GANG BOSS.

As the trial continued it looked like Harry's own sentence prediction was a little on the optimistic side. But there was no mention of Harry's pornography racket. Mooney would have seen to that. And nothing was ever heard of Tommy again. There was no investigation. I don't think he was even reported as a missing person. Harry was right. He had no family, no permanent contacts. No one who missed him. Except Harry. And me.

So I sort of picked myself up and tried to start all over again. I managed to keep out of the way of George Mooney. And I got a casting. A part in a comedy filming out of Pinewood. Same old stuff but I really needed the work. I think Gerald Wilman put in a good word for me.

The last time I saw Harry was on the day of the verdict. I managed to get a seat in the packed public gallery of Old Bailey's Number One Court. The jury found him guilty. The judge passed sentence.

'Harold Starks,' he said. 'Over a period of years you led a disciplined and well-organised gang for the purpose of your own material interests and criminal desires. You terrorised those who crossed your path in a vicious and sadistic way. That you set yourself up as judge, jury and executioner in heinous attacks on innocent citizens is particularly odious and a disgrace to civilisation. Your punishment must be severe because it is the only way in which our society can show its repudiation of your crimes. I won't waste any more words with you. In my view society has earned a rest from your criminal activities. You will go to prison for twenty years.'

If the sentence was a shock to Harry he didn't show it. He casually scanned the court, nodding to the jury and gazing up at the gallery. As if two decades were just a shit and a shave.

'Thank you very much,' he said, like it was the end of a performance.

'Take him down,' boomed the judge.

5

Open University

After two hours the felt stub is removed, for the man no longer has the strength to scream. Here in this electrically heated bowl we put warm rice porridge, of which the man can, if he feels inclined, take as much as his tongue can reach. Not one of them misses the opportunity. I am aware of none, and my experience is considerable.

Franz Kafka, *In the Penal Colony*

THE TIMES FRIDAY NOVEMBER 30 1979

Harry Starks writes to The Times

Why I have escaped from prison

This extraordinary letter arrived at The Times yesterday from Harry Starks, the gang leader who broke out of Brixton Prison earlier this week. We publish it as it stands, as a unique contribution to the debate on the rehabilitation of offenders.

Sir, I am writing to provide an explanation as to why I escaped from HMP Brixton and to put into context the charges for which I was sentenced to 20 years' imprisonment. I hope to counter the image society has of me from the gutter press with their prurient and overstated reports of my alleged activities in an attempt, desperate as it may seem, to counter-balance the biased opinion of my case and bring attention to the unfair treatment which I have received in my application for a conditional release on parole.

Firstly, I would like to address the nature of the offences of assault for which I was convicted. It is important to bear in mind the environment in which I was socialised. A subculture in which conflicts were resolved without recourse to authoritative norms or judicial agencies. A harsh world maybe, but one whose logic can only fully be understood within the terms of differential association. I must stress that the individuals upon whom such assaults took place were themselves part of a system of closure, not unknowing members of normal society. I do not wish to excuse my behaviour but to point out that I was operating in accordance with, and necessarily guided by, the perspective of a value system that I, myself, was part of and ruled by. I was found guilty of assault, not murder, on men who themselves were far from blameless and yet I have served more time than many criminals who have murdered or raped innocent people.

Given the nature of my transgressions, I feel that the price I have already paid (ten years) is far more than my debt to society.

These years of incarceration have certainly taken their toll, mentally as well as physically. In particular, the effects of sensory deprivation, the lack of stimulus, the sheer weight of mental confinement can be too much for many men to bear. Scandinavian studies on institutional environments have concluded that after seven years in such conditions a subject will suffer severe psychological deterioration.

I have managed to stave off mental atrophy through study. In the course of my sentence I have taken up education, culminating in an Open University degree. Through this process, I believe, I have rehabilitated myself, though at times it seemed the only way in which I could keep mind and spirit alive. The prospect of another ten years inside has driven me to despair and ultimately to take the desperate course of escape.

I do assert, however, that my attempts at rehabilitation have been genuine. In studying psychology, sociology and political philosophy I have learnt new perspectives and concepts that have challenged my hitherto negative and parochial mores. I am a changed man. I now accept that no man can be a law unto himself no matter what social category of deviance he is subject to. I was convicted for offences that arose through disputes within my entrepreneurial enterprises. As I have had time to reflect and adopt more positive attitudes and values I know now that my methods in resolving such disputes were entirely wrong and the process of self awareness that I have been subjected to means that the possibility of being involved in such situations again is negligible.

I realise that any freedom granted to me in the future will have necessary limitations. Given the attention paid by the popular press to me in the past, my own supposed notoriety in itself would secure a good deal of scrutiny and surveillance. I accept that my pariah status has formed part of my punishment, albeit somewhat excessive in its severity. I wish to put all of that behind me now. My only desire is to fulfil a useful role in society that could be afforded by a conditional release on licence.

In the final analysis, it's my assessment that this worthwhile opportunity to humanely rehabilitate effectively enough, now is nigh. Enough over-zealous legal deterrence. Continuation of my punishment thus only negates society's tentative reforms, exceeding equitable treatment.

Yours faithfully

Harry Starks

Of course I'd heard about Harry's escape. It was all over the papers. TORTURE GANG BOSS IN DRAMATIC BREAK-OUT. STARKS ESCAPE: BRIXTON SECURITY PROBE ORDERED. Police-file photographs in dot matrix reproduction. Blurred front and profile shots, hardly much use for identification as they were a decade old, but sending a little shiver of recognition up my spine none the less. The tabloids ran other pictures. Sixties highlife and lowlife grinning for the cameras. Nightclub line-ups, Harry phalanxed by 'personalities'. Stories ran all week. Grave-robbed scandal and nostalgic gossip made good copy for page six or seven. *Ruby Ryder Speaks Out On Escaped Gangster: Exclusive interview with busty blonde star of ITV's Beggar My Neighbour*. A graffiti campaign started up all over the East End: STARKS – 10 YEARS LONG ENOUGH.

All this coverage helped to quell my unease at the thought of Harry being out there somewhere. All the details of his criminal career, his public-enemy status, reassured me that I was a very small part in the story. Then came the letter to *The Times*. Suddenly I was involved again. I couldn't avoid it. It was a message.

I hadn't thought about Harry for a long time. We'd lost touch after his last parole knock-back. To be honest, I thought he'd had a serious breakdown. Something that he'd always dreaded. The fear of it had at least been partly the reason for taking up education. He had a desperate will to keep that phenomenal brain of his together through the long years of incarceration. And it was this that had brought us together in the first place. Though to say 'brought us together', well, we were never exactly together at any time over those years. Letters, prison visits, even the sociology classes I did at Long Marsh where we'd first met, in every instance we'd occupied a very different reality.

And my interest had always tended to the academic. 'Your

little experiment,' was how Karen described it. But then I'm a criminologist. It would hardly seem natural for someone like me not to be fascinated by someone like Harry. It was something that Karen and I argued about. 'Ethnographic work based on participant observation,' is how I justified my methodology. She called it 'zookeeping'.

I'd actually believed that the relationship that Harry and I formed had a sort of dialectic energy to it, that something essential could be learned from a discourse between a criminal and a criminologist. I was wrong of course.

I remember someone using a quote by Chekhov to explain our duty as radical sociologists: 'We must take the part of the guilty men.' That's what I'd tried to do with Harry. But it was I who had the problem with guilt. The Catholic upbringing, I suppose. I think it was this that attracted me to criminology in the first place. It offered me a way out from guilt.

Harry, as the letter confirmed, always seemed less troubled by his conscience. Consequently the general response to it was cynical. Harry was using sophisticated terminology to excuse his crimes. He wasn't showing adequate remorse for his wrongdoings. The press was mocking. One columnist joked about Harry's new vocabulary, contrasting it with the vernacular more commonly used to describe his activities. 'Sociology is a cruel and unnecessary punishment in Britain's prisons,' he concluded. 'It should be abolished forthwith.'

But they didn't see the real joke. The letter had its purposes, as a stunt to bring attention to his case, as a way that Harry could prove he was educated and 'reformed' and not just some mindless thug. But it was a wind up as well. He was taking the piss. The terms he used mocked my own lost faith in a theoretical system. A faith that he himself had shattered.

And there was a real meaning to what he wrote. In the final analysis. A message hidden in the text. Something that addressed itself to me. A semiology of sorts. Signs, signifiers, the lot. In the final analysis, that was the key phrase that unlocked it. *In the final analysis*.

Long Marsh Prison's maximum-security-section wing was known as the Submarine. After going through three sets of gates to get into the main prison, I was led down to a metal door. A small shutter in the door slid open to reveal a peephole. It scrutinised me and the two officers who formed my escort. The double-locked door was opened from the inside and we entered an antechamber. I waited as more routine signals were exchanged by officers on both sides of another double-locking door beyond. There was a row of closed-circuit television screens in the antechamber. A couple of bored-looking screws sat watching them. The blue light from the tubes flickered as the screens gave the occasional horizontal-hold blink. Then the next door was opened and we went down into the maximum-security section itself.

E Wing. The Submarine. A tunnel-like building about fifty yards long and twenty yards wide. An underground bunker that entombed twelve Category Double-A prisoners. Hiding some of the State's most dangerous criminals from the light of day. There was no natural light let in to any part of the wing. Instead, harsh artificial fluorescence flooded the grey mausoleum. The lighting had to be kept at a high level of brightness in order for the closed-circuit surveillance to work. All these famous villains were well lit for the cameras.

There was no natural air either. No windows that opened to the outside. A ventilation system throbbed incessantly throughout the concrete and steel vault. An unfathomable stench pervaded the whole wing. A sickly sweet smell.

I was led to the end of the wing. The workshop. In the corner were bags of kapok, of fake fur and shredded foam rubber. Making soft toys was one of the few activities the inmates of the wing were offered.

There had been a riot earlier that year. An inquiry had recommended some changes in security and also a 'liberalisation programme'. As well as stuffing furry animals, sociology classes were suggested as part of that programme and I had been employed by my University's Extra-Mural Department for this purpose. On my appointment, the Governor was nervously insistent that I should follow the rules and guidelines laid down for prison teachers. Prisoners were not allowed to keep notebooks, for instance. I wasn't to discuss anything connected to their personal lives.

I'd nodded solemnly in his office and tried to conceal my enthusiasm as a criminologist to have privileged access to such an elite group of criminals. It had come just at the right time. It was an exciting period for criminology. Radical ideas were everywhere. The National Deviancy Conference in 1968 had really shaken things up.

We didn't talk any more of criminology per se but of the sociology of deviance. We had made a clean break from positivism and with siding with the agents of state control. We spoke of attempting to create a society where the facts of human diversity would not be subject to the power to criminalise. *We must take the part of the guilty men*. Going into a maximum-security prison to teach sociology seemed to epitomise this approach. I thought, in a quietly determined way, that I could be at the sharp end of a whole movement.

I turned from the bags of fur and stuffing in the corner of the workshop and met the combined gaze of seven heavy-looking and strangely familiar guys, all with expressions of bored malevolence. The Guilty Men. I swallowed and gave a little cough. I nodded to the prison officer who had come in with me and who was about to sit down in a chair by the door.

'Thank you,' I croaked.

He frowned up at me from a half-crouching position over the seat. I smiled and shrugged at him. He stood up straight again.

'I should really sit in, sir,' he said.

'I really don't think that's necessary.'

'Hm.'

'Please,' I implored.

'Very well,' he replied wearily.

He picked up the chair and scanned the room. Stares of hardened boredom came back at him. He slowly made his way out of the workshop.

'I'll be outside the door,' he insisted.

As he left I raised my eyebrows mischievously. A few smirks appeared briefly on the faces in front of me. I'd hoped I'd broken the ice a little but the cold expressions returned as they turned their gaze from the departing screw back onto me. *Who the fuck's this hippy?* I could almost hear them thinking.

I coughed again and sat down in front of this class. I tried to make my body language as relaxed as possible. I thought I recognised some of the assembled. Faces that matched blurred newspaper photographs. Tabloid headlines involuntarily flashed up in my mind. I tried to ignore these strange images and got on with the matter in hand.

I introduced myself and, in a tentative and casual way, outlined what we would be looking at in the course. I tried to get them to ask questions but very few were forthcoming. Well, I reasoned, incarceration in maximum security was hardly a conducive atmosphere for open discussion. They eyed me suspiciously and made guarded comments, cautious of giving anything away, wary of ridicule from fellow inmates.

The most vocal member of the group was a thick-set man with streaks of grey in his slicked-back hair. Heavy-lidded eyes that stared intently beneath thick eyebrows joined in the middle. He seemed to be the dominant member of the group. Others deferred to him, glancing carefully at his reactions if they spoke. But there was an engaging quality to him as well. He smiled a lot even though his grinning often seemed a reminder that teeth had other uses.

I finished the lesson by saying that although I had my own ideas about what we would study, I'd welcome any suggestions from the group as to areas of interest.

'Well, Lenny,' this man announced with his trademark smile. 'If you can prove that it's society what's to blame for me being in here, then it would be worth my while, wouldn't it?'

There was laughter at this. I joined in, trying not to force it too much. I didn't mind a joke at my expense. Indeed, I naively thought then that this comment wasn't too far removed from what I intended myself. I felt relieved that the first session was over and it had gone, yeah, it had gone OK. Now we could get started.

'Thank you, gentlemen,' I announced, standing up. 'See you all next week I hope.'

On my way home my mind was racing. All sorts of ideas and theories swarmed around me. About symbolic interactionism and the labelling perspective. About the nature of imprisonment and the potential for real-live exponents of social deviancy to define themselves. But all these buzzing thoughts were swatted by something else. I couldn't help but dwell on the uniqueness of the men I had encountered. Rather than putting them in the context of social norms, I found it impossible not to be fascinated by their very criminality and its individual characteristics. Many of them were famous, after all. Their faces had become matrix dot icons, their identities bound up in thick block headlines. *The Train Robber*, *The Panther*, *The Shepherd's Bush Cop Killer*, and the man who smiled so much, *The Torture Gang Boss*. I tried to avoid thinking like this.

It ran so contrary to my theoretical standpoint. Rather than being objective about labelling theory, I was doing the labelling myself. I was regressing into crime as pathology. As mythology even. I tried to ignore these thoughts and concentrated on my methodology. Then the faces of the Guilty Men came back to me. Their terrible and audacious crimes. Did they *feel* guilty? I knew that this was the wrong way to think about them but it was all part of the experience, after all. There was something exciting about it.

I stopped off at a pub near the University. I needed a drink. I needed to wind down. Cool out a bit. The pub was full of students. I stood at the bar with a pint, staring out into the middle distance. I found my face hardening into a gaze of the type that the men in the Submarine wore. A sort of numbed alertness. The bleak expression that spoke of the empty years of confinement. The *what-the-fuck-do-you-want?* look.

'Lenny?'

A girl's voice behind me. I turned around.

'What?' I said, somewhat sharply.

'Are you all right?'

It was one of the first-year sociology students. Janine. She had long blonde hair, wide green eyes and a big pouty mouth. I smiled.

'Yeah,' I replied. 'Sorry.'

'You look like you've seen a ghost, Lenny.'

I laughed flatly.

'Yeah, well, I've just been in a room full of them.'

I told her about my evening in E Wing.

'Wow,' she remarked.

She was impressed. I was the youngest lecturer in the faculty. The students liked me, trusted me. I could relate to them and they appreciated my radical credentials.

'Do you want to come over and join us?' she asked.

I was tempted but I declined.

'I'd love to,' I said. 'But I've really got to get back.'

'We're having a party at my house. Saturday week. You will come, won't you?'

There was a flirtatious lilt in her voice. I grinned and nodded.

'Sure.'

'See you then, Lenny.'

'Yeah, see you.'

I finished my pint. I really did have to get back home. Back to Karen.

Karen and I had met at the London School of Economics in 1966. We were both Sociology undergraduates. Heady days. Full of fervour and activity. Even the Chess Society defined itself as Marxist Leninist back then. We occupied the LSE in 1967. We went to Paris in May '68. We actually participated. SOYEZ RAISONNABLE, DEMANDEZ L'IMPOSSIBLE! And when we got back to London, Hornsey College was occupied, a 'state of anarchy' declared. We joined the International Socialists. There was something in the air. Revolution. And we were going to make it happen. Herbert Marcuse had said that the workers had become stupefied by the products of their own labour and so revolution must come from those outside the system. It was up to us: students, hippies, freaks.

The second demo at Grosvenor Square, in October, was to be the climax of the year. Officially an anti-Vietnam War protest outside the American Embassy, it was intended as a catalyst. We would take revolution to the streets of London. As it happened, after a brief battle, the police kept control. And at the end of the day we trudged home to lick our wounds.

Then the National Deviancy Conference happened. That was when we saw the potential for putting radical ideas into academic work. When the next LSE occupation, in January 1969, ended in failure, we resolved to concentrate on our studies.

I got a first and applied for a post-graduate post in Criminology at Leeds. Karen got a 2:1 and started a Diploma in Social Work. And so we headed North. That in itself seemed a political decision. We moved into a big communal house in Chapeltown with some members of the Agit Prop Theatre Group who had come up from London at about the same time.

The sixties came to an end. It was a bit of an anti-climax. A time of reaction. The Tories got into power again. It was necessary to regroup. Karen concentrated on radical social work and began to define herself as a feminist. I focused on the sociology of deviance and theories of resistance to oppressive social norms. But it didn't seem so exciting any more. Until the Long Marsh project came up. Now this was something that I could really get my teeth into.

* * *

Karen was in the kitchen when I came in.

'You're late,' she commented.

'I stopped off at the pub on my way home. It was quite a heavy evening. I needed a drink.'

'Uh huh. Well there's some food left. It's in the oven.'

I got myself a plate and retrieved what was left of the evening meal. I started to tell Karen about the high-security wing, about the famous villains I'd met. She nodded blankly for a while and then rubbed at her face.

'Look, Lenny,' she said wearily. 'I'm tired. I've had a hard day myself, you know.'

I shrugged.

'I'm sorry. I thought that you'd be, like, interested.'

'Yeah. Well, you don't take much interest in my work.'

'I do.'

'No you don't. You just nod for a bit then try to change the subject. You always think that your work is more important than mine.'

'No I don't.'

'Well, more glamorous then. It's like these criminals are exotic specimens or something. I have to deal with ordinary people struggling to survive day in and day out. Maybe that just seems boring to you.'

'I don't think that,' I protested. 'Of course your work's important. But mine is too. I just wanted to share it with you. It's very exciting.'

Karen sighed. She put both her elbows on the kitchen table and slumped over them.

'Yeah, well, maybe I don't get a great deal of excitement in what I do.'

I reached over and put a hand on her shoulder.

'I want to get involved in something,' she said.

'Of course,' I said, stroking her back. 'Once I've got this project rolling we can both get involved. Together.'

She straightened up and brushed my arm away.

'Yeah, well, I want to get involved in something that doesn't involve you.'

I didn't follow.

'What do you mean, "something that doesn't involve me"? You mean an affair?'

'Oh, Christ, Lenny.'

'Babe, it's all right,' I said soothingly. 'I won't be jealous. We're supposed to be an open relationship, after all.'

'Is that all you ever think about? Do you think that's all women are for?'

'It's just that you said "something that doesn't involve me". I thought . . .'

'Yeah, you thought. I meant political involvement. You think politics is all about men. Well it's not.'

'I didn't say that.'

'Yeah, but you thought it. Well, anyway, I'm not putting up with all that any more. I'm starting a women's group. And that won't involve you.'

I smiled and said I thought that it sounded like a good idea. She chided me for being 'patronising'. But I did think that it was a good idea. I was glad for her to get involved in something. I did feel a bit disconcerted, though. I mean, what was she getting so angry at me for?

At the next class at Long Marsh E Wing I went through some of the fundamental ideas of sociology. I talked about Max Weber, the Protestant Work Ethic and the rise of capitalism. I wasn't sure at what level to pitch the classes but I was determined not to have any kind of patronising approach to these men. I treated the sessions as if they were like any other class at a further education institute. Some of the group had dropped out but those who remained proved to be very sharp. They were all experts in one area of criminology, after all.

The Torture Gang Boss, Harry Starks, seemed particularly intelligent and lively in discussion, if a bit domineering, as I'd noticed before. He told me that he was determined to keep his mind alert amidst the stupefying effects of high-security imprisonment. He was worried that his long sentence might turn him into a zombie.

'A lot of old lags, they get into exercise, body building, you know,' he said. 'They get obsessed by it. Some of them, I reckon, would prefer an extra inch on their biceps rather than a year off their sentence. Thing is, they neglect that very important muscle that lies gasping for exercise in their skull.'

The rest of the group agreed. One of the biggest fears of long-term imprisonment was mental deterioration. Education could be of some use, simply as a resistance to the mind-numbing effects of incarceration in the Submarine. I wanted it to be more than that.

I introduced Durkheim and the development of the concept of anomie that came with the growth of industrialisation. I mentioned the Chicago School and their studies of urban environments and social disorganisation. It was all leading somewhere. I wanted to guide the group into an understanding of deviancy theory. Then I could really take the part of the guilty men, or rather let them take their own part, in a discourse that would put their crimes in the context of a political struggle. That all forms of deviant behaviour were in some way a challenge to the normalised repression of the state.

But when I brought up the word deviant, there was a reaction in the group I hadn't foreseen.

'You mean we're not criminals but deviants?' someone asked.

'That could be a way of looking at it,' I replied.

'What do you mean, deviants?' Harry Starks demanded fiercely. 'Like fucking nonces or something?'

The group bristled with barely suppressed fury. I felt that it could get ugly.

'Are you saying we're weirdos or perverts or something?' someone called out. 'Is that it?'

'No,' I tried to placate them. 'That's not what I mean.'

I waited for the room to calm down. It gave me time to think.

'What I mean is,' I went on, 'all social groups make rules and find ways to enforce them. They decide what is normal for the group and what is deviant. Howard Becker talks about this in *Outsiders*. And when someone breaks a rule it's not only the action that is seen as being outside the law, the person is as well. That's what I mean by deviant. That someone is labelled as an outsider.'

The group chewed this over for a moment. Some looked towards Harry to see what he would say. He smiled.

'Our problem isn't that we're outsiders, Lenny,' he said, looking around the walls of the windowless workshop. 'It's that we're insiders.'

And the room broke into much-needed laughter.

'Right,' I said when it had all died down. 'Any other questions before we finish?'

'Yeah,' someone piped up from the back. 'Why are you such a scruff, Lenny?'

'What?'

'Yeah,' someone else chipped in. 'You must be on a fair whack but you come in here looking like a tramp.'

I realised that appearance was everything to these men. A raw atmosphere demanded that one looked sharp. Even in drab prison-regulation gear they made an effort. To appear in control. My hippy aesthetic didn't impress them at all. It didn't look confrontational, it merely looked sloppy.

So I resolved to take their advice and smarten up. I felt that it might empower the group to show that I respected their value systems. And I might gain a bit more of their respect myself. I got rid of my old army-surplus jacket and bought a fingertip-length black leather coat. I dug out an old pair of chelsea boots and wore them instead of the tattered desert boots I habitually wore. I trimmed my beard into a sharp Van Dyke style and gathered my long hair into a ponytail so that it resembled the swept-back look that Harry Starks sported.

But Karen was not impressed.

'You look like a pimp,' was her dismissive judgement.

I managed to meet with her disapproval at almost every turn these days. It was like she was laying all of this resentment onto me.

'The problem with all of this deviancy theory,' she ranted on, 'is that it's all so male dominated. And it's always male environments that you study. Skinheads, football hooligans, bank robbers. I think you get off on all this machismo.'

'I think you can take this feminist critique a little bit too far,' I countered.

'Really? Well what about rapists?' she demanded. 'I suppose there's rapists in that place you go to.'

I hadn't thought about that. Were there rapists amongst the men that I taught? Again, ugly images of the Guilty Men and the bad things they had done flashed up in my mind.

'So where do they fit into your theory of deviancy?' Karen went on. 'Eh?'

'Well,' I tried to reason. 'Of course some things are, well, unacceptable. But maybe they're better treated by something other than simple long-term imprisonment.'

'Oh, I agree,' she said with a gleam in her eye. 'We think that they should be castrated.'

I didn't ask Karen if she wanted to come to the party at Janine's house. I didn't think that she'd enjoy it and I figured, the way thing's were, we needed a bit of space.

'You look great, Lenny,' Janine enthused as I came into the party clutching a bottle of wine.

At least she approved. She was wearing a tight flowery T-shirt and blue velvet hipster jeans.

'So do you,' I told her.

And I felt good about my new image. It gave me an edge. Some of the arrogance of the E Wing inmates had rubbed off.

A rather loud second-year cornered me in the kitchen.

'The thing is, about your theoretical base,' he droned, 'is it's all American. The Chicago School, Goffman, Becker. All Yanks. It's like cultural imperialism.'

'So,' I shrugged casually. 'It's like Rock and Roll. We're taking American ideas and doing it better. That's all.'

That shut him up. Someone passed over a joint and I took a long toke, smiling at my own cleverness. I couldn't help feeling pleased with myself. Sociology was by far the most fashionable, the hippest subject in academia of the time. And here I was, young, cool and at the heart of it.

Janine was trying to open a big Party Seven can of bitter.

'Let me do that,' I said. 'You have some of this.'

I offered her the joint. She took it with a smile that showed a row of perfect white teeth. Someone put on 'Street Fighting Man' by the Stones.

'Come on,' I said to Janine. 'Let's have a dance.'

We strutted our stuff together in the tiny living room. Janine's eyes half closed, her mouth half open, as she wiggled about in front of me. Her breasts bobbed up and down in time to Keith Richards's power chords.

Later, we met on the stairs as I came out of the bathroom. She smiled up at me. I sat down on the top step so that our faces were level. I couldn't think quite what to say.

'Great party,' I declared.

'Yeah. Glad you came.'

'So am I.'

I moved my face closer to hers. She blinked and pouted slightly. I kissed her on the mouth and ran a hand gently against a velvet-encased thigh. She pulled back and blinked again.

'Not here,' she whispered.

She continued up the stairs past me and, taking my hand, helped me to my feet.

'Come on,' she said, and led me through the door next to the bathroom. She clicked on a light. There was a poster of Che Guevara over the bed.

'This is my room,' she announced.

It all happened very quickly. Janine giggled as we took all our clothes off together. She giggled as she lay on the bed and let me put myself slowly inside her. Then she pushed at my chest.

'Let me see,' she demanded. 'Let me see it going in and out.'

And when I had granted her request she giggled some more.

Afterwards we lay on the bed for a while and shared a cigarette. I tried to relax but I kept thinking that I had to get back. After a while I got up.

'I've got to go,' I said.

'Don't you want to do it again?'

I smiled thinly.

'I've really got to go.'

Janine frowned.

'Have you got a girlfriend, then?'

I nearly laughed. *Girlfriend*. Karen would love that.

'No,' I replied. 'Well I mean, not a girlfriend. I'm in a relationship. An open relationship.'

'So, they wouldn't mind?'

'No,' I lied. 'They'll be cool about it. But I really should be getting back.'

I travelled home in a taxi in a state of elated drowsiness. But as we pulled up in front of the house I found myself anxiously checking the windows to see if any lights were on. I felt something strange in the pit of my stomach as I paid the driver. The garden gate squeaked, delivering a verdict. Guilty.

There was much laughter at my next entrance to the workshop in the Submarine. Catcalls and wolf whistles greeted my sartorial transformation. But I felt a rough sort of camaraderie in it all.

'You look like a Maltese ponce,' commented Harry. 'Still, it's an improvement.'

I felt that I was beginning to gain their trust and that I was starting to get results from my work with them. Most of the class had already used some sort of reading or study or even writing in order to deal with the mental punishment of confinement. Now sociology gave them a structure within which they could understand their situation and a vocabulary with which they could resist it.

Power was at the heart of it, of course. Despite a constant assertion of authority over them, the men on E Wing always tried to display a superior attitude to the screws. They considered themselves both intellectually and culturally distinct. Being mostly from London, they endowed themselves with a metropolitan, or even cosmopolitan, smartness with which they looked down upon the dull, provincial mentality of their captors. They sometimes revelled in being pariahs since it gave them an elite status and even celebrity. Harry Starks once commented that: 'These poor screws, spending all their waking hours on the wing, watching me, then when they get home and jump into bed with the missus, all she wants to know is: "Darling, did you speak to Harry today?"'

And as they studied their own predicament they could use a theoretical language in any verbal confrontation with prison staff or governors. A new-found articulacy could be a weapon for their embattled position in a power struggle that formed the very centre of gravity of prison life. Not as direct or as cathartic as the physical force they had used in the riot all those months ago, but a resistance of sorts none the less.

Sometimes its form would merely be humour.

'So, this screw, you know, the stupid Geordie, he asks me at the end of last week's class: "So Jeff, what did you learn tonight?" And I tell him, all straight-faced like, that we'd been discussing a report that gave conclusive evidence that prison officers are predominantly authoritarian psychopaths. And the silly cunt just smiles at me and says: "Very good."'

We'd spend a good deal of time in the classes discussing words. Sometimes to be clear about defining terms but sometimes just for the pleasure that some of the men had for understanding their meaning. For their own sake. They would enjoy having new definitions which they could apply to their own condition. They would use these words to spar with each other. Harry was particularly obsessed with expanding his vocabulary and applying new terms to his own experience or the environment around him. *Recidivist* became a particular favourite of his, I suspect partly because he found it so hard to pronounce at first. Once he had mastered it, it became something that he threw around with great regularity, often using it as a mild put-down to other cons. 'That's just what a recidivist would say,' he'd retort to someone's comment or: 'Typical recidivist thinking.'

During one session he launched into an anecdote that he felt epitomised the definition of his new pet word.

'When I was in Durham I came across this bloke, right, who must have held the British record for recidivism. He's on the security wing and word gets around that he's in under the Sexual Offences Act. He ain't on Rule 43 with all the nonces, but if someone's Category A, and it's sexual, it's bound to be something heavy. So, some of the chaps take a bit of an interest in this bloke, Frank was his name. He keeps himself to himself, but soon enough a couple of fellahs corner him on the landing. Looks nasty, like they're going to do him with a razor or something but first they want to know what heinous crime he's in for. They've got him up against the railings, he's pleading and shit, then suddenly, they let him go and come down into association, pissing themselves laughing.

'Turns out Frank wasn't into little boys or little girls. He was into pigs.'

There was some laughter at this. Harry looked about the room with a mischievous gleam in his eye.

'Yeah, old Frank had been making bacon in a big way,' he went on. 'Thing is, he couldn't stop himself. His first offence dated years back to when he was a young impressionable lad, working on a farm. The head pig man catches him at it, shops him, and he does a couple of months. But what do you think is going through his mind at night in his cell as he's doing the old five-knuckle shuffle? Yeah, his little curly-tailed friends. So as soon as he gets out he finds himself another job on another pig farm, and he's at it again. He keeps getting caught, keeps going back to it. Over the years he notches up over fifteen separate convictions for bestiality and a fair few for breaking and entering pig farms. The sentences pile up and he ends up Category A.

'He got a bit of stick on the wing, but it was mostly verbal. Mind you, I did give him a slap myself once. One day, just out of curiosity, I turned to him and asked, "Frank, tell me, all those pigs you fucked, were they male or female?" And he looks at me, all affronted, and says, "They were sows, Harry. What do you think I am, queer or something?"'

There was more laughter which quickly petered out as Harry glared at the group.

'So I decked the bastard. He said *that* to the wrong person, that's for sure.

'Anyway, the point I'm making is how fucked up this system is. I mean, it creates that sort of recidivism. Think about how much it costs society to keep Frank banged up every time he gets the urge. Then there's the court costs, legal aid, police time. It's a fucking fortune over the years. And it's not as if Frank's a menace to society. A menace to those little piggies maybe, though he always said they never complained. So wouldn't it make more sense, in the long run, for the Home Office to buy Frank a couple of porkers and a little sty somewhere and let him get on with it?'

Harry had not only defined recidivism but had also outlined a fine example of deviancy theory. But the absurdity of the story seemed to undermine the very thesis that it proved. The sociology of deviance was already under attack from critics as a 'misfit paradigm' which deflected from any real attack on the power of the State. Anthony Platt accused us of 'trivia and politically irresponsible hipsterism'. Whilst Alexander Liazos condemned an apparent preoccupation with 'nuts, sluts, and perverts', as he put it. In this context, Harry's impromptu case study was vaguely disconcerting. And I couldn't help thinking that he'd made up the whole thing to wind me up.

But it was the first time Harry made any reference to his sexuality. I felt there was an opportunity for some sort of symbolic inter-actionism there. I was to be disappointed. I brought up Gay

Liberation at the next class and after a bit of sniggering someone asked: 'What do you think of that then, Harry?'

Harry's nostrils widened slightly, his mouth flattened into an impassive sneer.

'I'm not *gay*,' he said sternly. 'I'm homosexual but I'm not *gay*.'

Oo, get madam, someone muttered behind him and his head swivelled sharply around. I pondered on his use of a pathological term in preference to a subcultural one, but I let it pass.

'Yeah, well,' he went on. 'At least I'm open about it. I know what goes on inside. I tell you, Lenny, I ain't queer in prison. It's normal in here. Just because I'm like this naturally some people think it gives them the edge over me. They actually imagine that in any kind of normal setting I'd fancy them. As if I could get any real hard on for the old lags in here.'

'So what do you think about Gay Liberation?' I asked.

'Nah,' he replied dismissively. 'They're all too poofy and scruffy. I'm not into long hair neither. I like a boy to be well turned out.'

'Yeah, but what about their ideas?' someone asked.

Harry chuckled darkly.

'Well,' he said with a gleam in his eye. 'Someone once called Ronnie Kray a fat poof. Ronnie took the top of his head off with a Luger. That's my sort of Gay Liberation. Though, to be honest, I think it was the fat part what got to him. Ron's, well, touchy about his weight.'

But I couldn't help but be fascinated by the concept of a homosexual gangster. I talked about it to Janine when we were in bed together one afternoon.

'Doesn't it surprise you?'

'No, not really. I mean, we're all a bit gay aren't we?'

'Not me,' I replied hastily.

'Well, I am.'

'Really?'

I smiled. The thought of it rather excited me.

'But surely, this guy's sexuality isn't that important. He's a man, and a very violent one at that. It just proves that all men are predisposed to violence. Gay or not.'

'So where have you been picking up these ideas?'

'Don't patronise me, Lenny. I've been learning a lot recently.

Things that I never really thought about before but sort of knew all along. "Consciousness raising" we call it in the women's group.'

'In the what?'

I sat upright in the bed.

'Oh,' Janine sighed. 'Didn't I tell you? I've been going to Karen's women's group.'

I stared at her, open mouthed.

'You haven't,' I stuttered. 'You haven't told her, have you? About us?'

'No. I thought you might have. You did say it was an open relationship.'

'You're not going to tell her, are you?'

'Of course I'm going to tell her,' Janine replied, indignantly. 'It would be very unsisterly not to. Karen's a wonderful woman. I've learnt so much from her. The group's really changed my life.'

I felt suddenly sick. I got out of bed and started pulling on my jeans.

'What's the matter, Lenny?'

'What?' I choked. 'Oh Jesus!'

'You really do look silly, Lenny. Karen's right, you know. She always says men are like children.'

There was a power cut on the night of Karen's next women's group. I went about the house putting nightlights on saucers in strategic places for illumination. The smell of wax smoke conjured unwelcome altar-boy memories. I felt horribly guilty. I knew that I should have told Karen before Janine had had a chance to. But I didn't dare. The front door slammed. A group of little flames flickered on the kitchen table. Like votive candles lit for atonement. Karen walked in, her shadow dancing across the ceiling.

'What's going on?' she asked.

'It's the power workers. The unions are really starting to get militant. A few more months of this . . .'

'Yeah,' she cut in flatly.

'Karen, look . . .'

'You bastard,' she hissed at me in the half darkness.

'I'm sorry.'

'Oh, you're sorry, are you? Well, that's great. Men. You're all the fucking same.'

'Now look, don't make a political point out of this. It was just an affair.'

'The personal is political, Lenny.'

'It's not a serious thing . . .'

'I wonder what you do take seriously, Lenny.'

'Well, this never used to be an issue.'

'Oh right. Back in the swinging sixties. Some great sexual revolution that turned out to be. We lost out, you know, Lenny. Women lost out. It was only men who gained any freedom. We were supposed to just lie back and pretend we were enjoying it. Men get to do all the fucking. Women just get to do the faking.'

'Karen, look . . .'

'You're pathetic, you know that? You think you're some kind of stud in your leather jacket and ponytail. You're just using, or rather abusing, your power on impressionable young women.'

'Now, wait a minute . . .'

'You are, Lenny. Like all men. You use your power to try to dominate women. You're an oppressor, don't you forget that, because I won't.'

And with that she stormed out and slammed the door.

Directly as I came in from the main gate of Long Marsh, I was escorted for a short distance along by the perimeter wall, past the main wings of the prison, on the way to the maximum-security section. As we passed each block there came a now familiar humming sound. Hundreds of indistinguishable voices hovered up from every cell, landing and wing. Like the buzzing of insects in a hive, strangely soothing. Then we went down into the Submarine.

I had begun to get worried about group dynamics in the classes. Jeff, a mild-mannered triple murderer, dropped out. He told me in the corridor at the end of a session that he didn't feel he was getting any proper attention. He felt Harry always took over the class.

'He always dominates everything,' he said, looking around to make sure no one was listening. 'It's like in the TV room. We'll have a vote, like, about which programme we're going to watch and then he'll come in and say, "What, we having the film on then?" and change it over. And nobody says anything because they know he could have a right row about it. I thought it'd be different, doing this class, like, but it's the same, him taking over as usual. It's like he's running the sessions, not you.'

'You think I let him dominate the group?'

'You know you fucking do, Lenny.'

'Well, I'll try not to let it happen so much.'

Jeff laughed flatly at this.

'You think you control him any better than we could? You're as intimidated by him as we are.'

'Well, I could try. I wouldn't want you to stop coming to the classes just because of this.'

'Nah,' Jeff replied with a shrug. 'I ain't that bothered, to tell you the truth. At least now there'll be one night a week that we can watch whatever channel we want.'

'Well, I'm sorry you feel that way.'

'Don't worry about it, Lenny. I mean, Harry, he's like your star pupil, isn't he?'

I was a bit disturbed by this observation. It was hard to deny that I could be intimidated by Harry Starks. The Torture Gang Boss had a fearsome reputation. I soon found out that in the nomenclature of villainy he was known as Mad Harry. His violence could be explosive and unexpected. I also found out that this referred to an actual history of mental illness. Again it was hard for me not to be intrigued by the potential application of deviancy theory to this. I brought up R.D. Laing's work in one of the sessions. We discussed conformity and how creative potential is often seen as madness. The social construct of mental health and the labelling perspective of mental illness. Harry was his usual critical self.

'Yeah, that's all very well,' he commented. 'But without my pills I go off the fucking rails.'

In fact, Harry had his own version of anti-psychiatry: if you go mad they can lock you up for good. He had a deep fear of ending up in Broadmoor with no fixed release date. And this fear was at the heart of his obsession with exercising his mental capacities. Education was a way of keeping on top of things.

And he had a very sharp mind. I suppose that Jeff was right, I didn't manage to do anything that effectively pulled him back from dominating the group. But he was so relentless in his questioning, so consistently full of ideas. This was as intimidating as his physical presence. He never let me off the hook nor let me assume any kind of expertise in what was, after all, as much his field as it was my subject. 'You've really crow-barred that idea, Lenny,' he'd complain if I ever appeared clumsy in my analysis. He kept me on my toes. As with other areas of his life, he demanded rigour.

And whilst many of the other inmates readily took to deviancy theory, sometimes as a way to explain their crimes, Harry was reluctant to go along with this. It was as if it represented an excuse for failure. For some of the group, a bank robber for instance, their actions could easily be seen, somewhat romantically perhaps, in the context of an attack on advanced capitalism and conformity. In Harry's case his career rather held up a mirror to it.

'I wasn't a gangster,' he insisted, with no conscious irony. 'I was a businessman.'

Despite this, I laboured through theory with the group. Harry went along with it, elusive and obscure as ever. And though he displayed a natural resistance to my central thesis, he remained fascinated by self-analysis. 'I've always been interested in psychology,' he said. And I felt that I'd planted a seed. He wanted to learn and I felt that his self-examination would bear fruit. I was sure that he actually embodied the argument I was advocating. There was something tantalising about the ambiguity of Harry's criminality. It seemed to go to the heart of the whole academic enterprise that I was engaged in. With all his contradictions, he was a living discourse on the sociology of deviance.

About this time I published a paper: *Gangsterism: The Deviancy of Capitalism*. I started by examining the roots of deviancy theory itself. It seemed no coincidence that its formation took place in the Chicago School of the '20s and '30s. A time and place of widespread racketeering and mob activity. Amidst a post-war boom, furious demographic changes and the chaos of commercial deregulation, moral uncertainties emerged. Al Capone could be seen in this light as the Godfather of the sociology of deviance. His criminal corporatism had so thoroughly confused images of normality with spectres of abnormality that there was an inevitable change in attitudes to social norms.

And so, the gangster provides a realignment of these norms. Placed at the edge of modern values, he reassures it, gently mocking it in his mimicry of the trappings of big business, the well-tailored suit, the fast car, etc. The gangster's very extremism co-operates with the everyday world of the free market. 'Their alienation from our reality frees them to be subtly induced into realising our moral fantasies' (Goffman, 1972:267). Furthermore, they can project a dynamic of character in order to reify the adventure of capitalism.

At this point enter, stage right, the Hollywood gangster. In his seminal essay of 1948, *The Gangster as Tragic Hero*, Robert Warshow asserts the startling idea of the gangster as fundamentally an aesthetic as much as a physical threat. 'The gangster, though there are real gangsters, is also, and primarily, a creature of the imagination' (ibid.).

I then used my inside knowledge of Harry to examine gangsters of our own time and culture and how they epitomised the contradictions of our own age. In a sense, Harry Starks, the Kray Twins, *et al.*, were already following in a tradition. In the context of a post-austerity boom, they represented a dark undercurrent beneath the so-called 'swinging sixties'. A brooding presence that undermined the notion of this era being one of liberation and permissiveness. Liminal behaviour kept the lid on a potential social revolution with superficial charm. The glamour, the style, the friends in high places and showbiz personalities were all shot through with a deep sense of menace. 'Extreme seductiveness is at the boundary of horror' (Bataille, 1932:17).

Presuming the authority of working-class culture, the gangster actually upholds the binary systems of late-stage capitalism. Charity work goes hand in hand with protection rackets. In seemingly opposing operations of extortion and philanthropy, he becomes both malevolent folk devil and benevolent folk hero. Furthermore, he resolves the dichotomy of the individual and the collective. Despite semantically implying adherence to a gang, the gangster instead becomes a distillation of mass culture into an individual pathology. Like Robert Musil's criminal Moosbrugger in *The Man without Qualities*, the gang boss inhabits a psychological as well as a social underworld. 'If mankind could dream collectively, it would dream Moosbrugger.'

Thus he provides catharsis. In acting out the deep fears and potentially dangerous ambitions of the individual in the market economy, the very deviancy of the gangster allows capitalism to exorcise itself and reassert its moral normalcy.

* * *

The course came to the end of its allotted span and there was no indication from the Prison Education Department that it would be renewed as an activities option for the inmates of the Submarine. All I heard were rumours that the Governor and the Assistant Governor had decided that the project had a dangerous whiff of subversiveness to it. Officers had been complaining that the prisoners taking the course had become even more gobby than usual. They'd gained a further articulacy in asserting their rights. Stuffing soft toys was clearly a better way of encouraging rehabilitation.

Many of the men I got to know on E Wing said that they wanted to continue some sort of study. I was always encouraging, even though I thought at times I was merely being humoured. Harry was particularly enthusiastic about the idea. As usual, he had his reasons.

'You know those Scandinavian studies you talked about?' he said to me on the last day. 'You know, the psychological effects of long-term incarceration. Sensory deprivation and all that. Well, they reckon, what? Five years, seven years at best before you start to crack up. Seven years, that's all I've got. Seven years bad luck. But bad luck is better than no luck. You know what I mean?'

'I'm not sure that I do, Harry.'

'Listen,' he hissed, drawing my face closer to his with a casual beckoning gesture. His eyes narrowed on mine. 'I mean, I looked at you and thought the only thought that makes any kind of sense in here. I thought: are you my way out of here? Seven years, then I'm up for my first parole board. Eat your porridge every day, do your time the easy way. So what's this? I'm thinking: is this the easy way? You know, this education racket. O levels, A levels, Open University, open sesame. Know what I mean? If I educate myself, it's like I'm reforming, ain't it? It's bound to go down well with the board, isn't it?'

He smiled at me. There was an enacted confidence in his manner. He sounded desperate. I dreaded being the one responsible for getting his hopes up.

'Yeah,' I said cautiously. 'I guess.'

Harry sniffed doubt. His eyebrows knitted as he frowned piercingly at me.

'Yeah,' he insisted. 'But what do you think?'

'I think,' I replied quickly, wary of any tension that a pause might produce, 'I think that you want to do it anyway. You want to learn. You want to study, don't you?'

Harry grinned, for once sheepish rather than lupine.

'Yeah, I do,' he grudgingly admitted.

I promised to put in a good word with the Education Officer, for what it was worth. Harry suggested that we stay in touch. I said that it sounded like a good idea. After all, it seemed a logical thing, for a criminologist to get to know a criminal. And I felt sure that I could maintain a certain professionalism in our acquaintance.

So Harry started his O levels. I only managed one visit after the course had finished before he was moved to Leicester. This was part of the dispersal system whereby Category A prisoners were moved around to different maximum-security wings. It was a policy implemented to try to avoid the problems of the long-term concentration of groups of dangerous cons, and little warning was given before a prisoner was moved. It became known as The Ghost Train. Or, as Harry more grandly put it, The National Tour.

We started to write to each other. Over the next few years I was able to visit Harry only occasionally, but we kept up a fairly constant correspondence. The letters would often have a purely practical focus, he might want to discuss an essay he was writing on differential association for his sociology A level, for example. Otherwise he might simply want to let off steam, complain about conditions or conflicts with screws or other cons. All letters were subject to censorship, Category A correspondence being particularly closely vetted, so he had to be careful not to be too explicit in his criticisms or descriptions of prison life or references to criminal activity, anything, in fact, that the censor could deem 'objectionable' under Standing Orders.

So Harry developed a code. If he used the phrase 'in the final analysis', it meant that a message was contained in the initial letters of the words that followed. Usually it wasn't terribly subversive stuff but it provided Harry with another way of undermining the system that dominated him. A little game, a little system of his own.

The thing about writing to someone in prison is you don't really remember very well what you've said to them because your life is changing all the time. But theirs isn't. Harry would refer meticulously to some point or other of a previous letter which I would have completely forgotten. And so he became a marker, a sort of fixed point which I could remind myself by.

Things were changing. On the outside at least. As the seventies wore on I felt a growing confusion about ideas that had seemed so certain. My academic career was going well. I had papers published, articles in *New Society*, even a little broadcasting work. I was getting a few ideas together for a book. Everything seemed to be going so well and yet I felt insecure. All the excitement that had come out of the National Deviancy Conference had seemed to peter out. There were scarcely any meetings any more. All these great radical ideas had gone a bit stale. Notions that had once seemed controversial now began to look threadbare and otiose. A smell of revisionism hung in the air and academics now turned on each other. That sense of a collective enterprise had all but vanished.

And in the meantime Karen was more confident. More assertive. She'd been writing for *Case Con*, the radical social work journal. She talked of the need for consciousness raising and the important input of new ideas from the Women's Movement for social change. She wrote of the implications that a feminist understanding of aspects of the family and child rearing could have for political understanding of social work. Feminist ideas were now in the ascendant and could no longer be ignored as a critical framework.

I couldn't help but feel somewhat undermined. I can't say that I took too kindly to my newly supposed status as oppressor. It bothered me, this 'all men are bastards' analysis. It was too familiar. A doctrine of original sin, where all men are profoundly bad.

So our relationship became frosty, to say the least. We had separate rooms in the house now. We still had sex but it would always have to be Karen who instigated it. A 're-alignment of the economy of sexual relations', she called it. The personal is political, she kept reminding me.

Though it struck me that rather, our politics had become personal. She always insisted she was involved in something positive, something that would 'make a difference', as she put it, whilst I was merely obsessed with the more exotic aspects of the male psyche. And it was at this time that she first started using the 'zookeeping' jibe against deviancy theory. She was particularly dismissive of my continued contact with Mr Starks. 'So, how's your pet experiment?' she asked me once when I'd finished intently reading a letter from him. And another time she declared: 'You wouldn't want him to be released, would you? That would spoil everything. He's like your little rat in a maze.'

And the awful thing was, she was right. I was fascinated by his predicament. It was hard to resist seeing him as a long-term project. As a subject. But what bothered me wasn't any desire for him to be incarcerated but rather an odd little fear at the back of my mind at the thought of him being given his freedom. The notion of Harry Starks at large scared me a little.

Then one evening Janine came to the house. I hadn't seen much of her since the affair. She was a second-year now so she wasn't at any of my lectures. To be honest I'd been avoiding her.

She'd cut her hair short which accentuated her wide eyes and full mouth and made her look quite gamine. She blinked mischievously as she stood on the doorstep.

'Janine,' I announced as cheerily as possible, hoping that she detected no nervousness in my tone. 'Good to see you.'

'Hi, Lenny,' she drawled as she walked past me into the hallway.

'Come in,' I said, stupidly, and closed the door.

She looked up at the walls and ceiling and gave a little sigh.

'What a lovely house,' she said.

'I wasn't expecting you,' I said, a little more frantically than I'd wanted. 'Can I get you a drink? Go through into the living room.'

She turned to me suddenly. Her eyes and mouth formed Os on her face.

'Oh,' she said. 'I haven't come to see *you*, Lenny.'

I frowned, and at that moment Karen came thundering down the stairs.

'Janine!' she called out.

Janine looked up and smiled. Karen virtually landed on her, planting a big wet kiss on her mouth.

'I'm so glad you've come,' said Karen breathily, not even acknowledging my presence. 'Come on. Let's go upstairs.'

Later that night as I lay in bed I could hear strange noises coming from Karen's room above mine. Tremulous moans, urgent cooing and deep-throated laughter. Distant night sounds murmuring through floorboards and plaster. I tried to ignore it all and get some sleep but I couldn't help myself straining to listen.

* * *

Harry had started a BSc in Sociology with the Open University in 1973. He wrote and told me he thought that the course 'would be a piece of piss. The work you did with us back at Long Marsh has really come in handy.' He seemed to have settled at Leicester, for the time being, so I could arrange visits with some sort of reliability.

'You look a bit fraught, Lenny,' he told me. 'Still having trouble with your bird?'

I'd written to him about my problems with Karen. He was easy to confide in. He was so blunt and oblivious to the intricacies of sexual politics.

'I think she might be becoming a lesbian.'

Harry gave me an open-mouthed stare, then burst into laughter.

'Sorry, Len,' he said, trying to straighten his face.

'I don't know what to do, Harry.'

He shrugged.

'Search me. I never had much truck with dykes, to tell you the truth. The Twins used to run a lesbian bar. In the basement of Esmeralda's. Right old dive, it was.'

'Well, anyway, how are you?'

'I dunno,' he said with a sigh. 'Doing my time, I suppose. Thing is, it's not my time I'm doing. I've had my time taken away from me. I'm doing their time. It's turning me into a zombie.'

'I don't know, Harry. You seem pretty sharp.'

'Oh yeah. Abstract thinking. I can do that, no bother. But if I start to think about anything real in my life, I feel I could crack up. I've seen it happen enough times. Remember Jeff? Little Jeff from the Submarine?'

I nodded. The mild-mannered murderer.

'He's flipped. He's only gone and found God, hasn't he? I suppose he thinks he's found some sort of reality. He said to me, "I have decided to live inside my head." I told him, "Well, I'm sure there's enough room inside there, Jeff old son."'

Harry laughed flatly.

'Thing is,' he went on, 'Jeff reckons he can escape from it all by going inside. Well I couldn't do that.'

'Yeah, but in a way, you're using the inside of your head as a refuge. By studying.'

'Nah, Lenny. You're missing the point. What's inside is neither here nor there. It's not what's inside of me that'll make a damn bit of difference. It's what I'm inside. That's the reality.'

Then, a few months later, when I turned up at Leicester with a Visiting Order to see Harry, I was told that the visit was cancelled. Harry had had all privileges suspended for twenty-eight days. For offences against 'Good Order and Discipline', was all I was told. I had no idea what had happened. I wrote to him but got no reply. At first I worried about losing contact with him. But as the weeks went by I found myself forgetting him.

Yet unexpectedly, like a particularly vivid dream, strange images of Harry would begin to haunt me. If I concentrated on him, I figured that maybe he had, as he'd always feared, gone mad. It was a disturbing thought but there was nothing I could do about it, I reasoned.

Then, about three months later, I received a letter from Durham. Harry had been moved back there on the Ghost Train. I got a Visiting Order and went to see him. I dreaded what state he might be in. But as he was led out to meet me, he seemed in good enough spirits. His hair had got longer and he didn't seem to be making so much fuss about his appearance. But he looked almost relaxed with an indifferent air about him that I recognised from all my time at universities. He looked like an academic.

The suspension of privileges and a spell in solitary had come about, it turned out, from a fight with a fellow prisoner.

'What the hell happened?' I demanded, almost chidingly.

Harry shrugged.

'This bloke on the wing at Leicester. Poisoner. He's doing a post-grad Open University course and he reckons he knows it all. He was always winding me up. Kept going on that sociology was a soft option. How what I was studying wasn't rigorous enough. That I was just doing a mickey-mouse degree. Got right on my wick. So I did him. Gave him rigorous. Right in the goolies.'

'Harry . . .'

'I know, I know,' he protested. 'It was stupid. But he was driving me crazy. Going on about how social sciences didn't have the right to be called sciences. Acting all superior.'

'So, what's he studying?'

'Chemistry.'

I laughed.

'I know. A fucking poisoner studying chemistry. Show's you how stupid the Prison Service is. That cunt ought to be in Broadmoor. Still, it was a stupid thing to do. I've really got to stay out of trouble.'

'That wouldn't be a bad idea, Harry.'

'I don't mind punishment. I can take that. It's losing remission that bothers me. I don't want to add another second to my time in here. Thing is, Lenny, back in the fifties I'd probably have got the birch or the cat and that would have been that.'

I winced and Harry chuckled softly at my response. Of course, as a criminologist, I knew that corporal punishment hadn't been abolished in British prisons until the early sixties, but the thought of it still shocked me.

'Nah, it would have been better,' Harry went on. 'Because with corporal punishment you didn't lose any remission or have to do any other punishment. It hurt like fuck at the time, and of course it was humiliating.'

'It was barbaric.'

'Yeah, yeah, but then it was over with. To be honest Lenny, a lot of these reforms, they don't necessarily make it any easier for those condemned. It's more for the benefit of liberal fuckers like you, so you can sleep easily thinking that you're living in a civilised society. I mean, a few strokes over someone's bare arse, that's barbaric, but locking up some poor fucker for years, pretending that you're rehabilitating him, that's OK. It's all nicely hidden away and forgotten about. I mean, look at what I did. If someone owed me money and couldn't pay up in time, I'd smack them around a bit. Oh yeah, that's terrible. But look at what happens in normal society when someone's in debt. Their house gets repossessed or the bailiffs call around to take everything that's not bolted down. Which would you rather have?'

I shrugged, preferring to leave it as a rhetorical question.

'Yeah, anyway. I've lost a bit of remission which is a bit of a piss off. But I'm going to be a good boy from now on. Concentrate on my studies.'

He gave me a shark-like grin. I smiled back.

'Well, it's bound to go down well with the parole board, isn't it? And when you come to think of it, it does kind of let me off the hook and all. I mean, this sociology of deviance. I could tell them that my actions were consistent with the value system of the subculture within which I was socialised. Couldn't I?'

He looked at me intently. I didn't know what to say. He suddenly burst out laughing.

'Don't worry, Lenny. I ain't that stupid. Your face. No, I know that won't wash with any kind of board. Harry Starks, they'll think, still a criminal but now he knows why he does it. No, don't you worry, I'll be all remorseful and shit.'

'You've got to play along with the system.'

'Yeah, I know Lenny, I know. Thing is, I always have, in a way. But yeah, keep my head down. No more kicking the shit out of chemistry graduates. But to tell you the truth Lenny, it did get to me. What he said.'

'What do you mean?'

'I mean, maybe he's right, in a way. Maybe sociology isn't rigorous enough.'

'Do you think that?'

'Well, I don't know. Some things. Like deviancy theory. I wasn't doing all that to rebel, you know. I wanted to be legitimate. I was just a bit, you know, heavy handed.'

He looked down at his heavy hands.

'I just think,' he went on, 'you know, there's something missing in a lot of these theories.'

'Well, that's a good thing, surely,' I replied. 'It means you're developing a critical approach.'

Harry certainly developed a keen intellectual insight into sociological theory as time went on. I found myself wanting to run things by him now, as a way of checking my ideas. His comments were always direct and often quite ruthless but he came to represent a test to sloppy thinking, particularly on criminology. And I felt I needed that now more than ever.

For my part, I could still guide him to key texts and references that might be relevant to the rough ideas he started to formulate. He exhibited a strong tendency towards structuralism. It seemed almost instinctive and maybe, after all, he scarcely had any choice in this way of thinking. He'd spent years of experiencing movement through rigid structures in both time and space. This, for him, was where meaning resided. So I pointed him towards Levi-Strauss and some other French thinkers I thought might be useful to him.

We developed a strange kind of discourse through letters and occasional visits. I never envied his predicament but I was sometimes jealous of his ability to concentrate, with few distractions, on study. This was, of course, all bound up with the act of will he was exerting in order to get through his sentence without going mad.

He was constantly surprising me. I was astonished that he was able to articulate political as well as intellectual criticisms on deviancy theory.

'You're a Marxist, ain't you, Lenny?' he asked on one of my visits.

'Yeah,' I replied, somewhat hesitantly. 'Not an orthodox Marxist, but, yeah.'

'Well, it strikes me that old Karl wouldn't have much truck with the sociology of deviance. I mean, criminals, misfits, deviants. Now, my old man would have called them *lumpenproletariat*.'

'Your father was a communist?'

'Yeah. And an orthodox one at that. Party member. It was big in the East End back then.'

'So he was at Cable Street?'

Harry laughed.

'Christ yes. He was always bloody reliving it. "We turned them back." Yeah, it was like Stalingrad to him. Thing is, a lot of people credit Jack Spot and his gang for beating the blackshirts, but my old man always maintains it was the Communist Youth League.'

'Who was Jack Spot?'

'Jewish gangster. He ran the spielers and protection in the East End before the war.'

'So you were never tempted to join the Party?'

'Nah. The old man wanted me to, of course. I could never see the point myself. I mean, communism, it's a cheap racket. They've got nothing and they want to share it with you. Sorry to disappoint you, Len.'

'So you joined Jack Spot's gang instead.'

'Nah, I never liked Spotty. The Twins worked for him for a while. That was before they got this idea that they were going to take over the world. Nah, I worked for Billy Hill at first. Before I got set up on my own. Billy and Jack didn't exactly see eye to eye. Anyway, going back to my original point. How can you square Marxism with deviancy theory?'

'That's a good point.'

Harry cackled, knowing that he'd got me on this one.

'Strikes me,' he went on, 'that it lets too many people off the hook. Now I know you've got some sort of romantic notion about crime. Yeah, you have Lenny, don't try and deny it. I bet you wish that I was a bank robber, something glamorous like that. At the heavy like some sort of modern-day Robin Hood. But it wasn't like that. You see, crime, well what I did, it was just business with the gloves off.'

'Yes, but it's still labelled deviant if it breaks social norms . . .'

'Yeah, yeah,' Harry went on, impatiently. 'But what's important is what you can get away with.'

At the end of 1975 I started work on my book, *Doing Time: Social Control and Subcultural Resistance*. I used some of the observations I'd made of the men on Long Marsh's E Wing and made comparisons with ethnographic studies of other deviant groups. *The Subculture of the Submarine*, I titled this section (rather snappily, I thought). But I began to feel that it was the system itself that needed analysing, not just those groups of people who found themselves in opposition to it. I found myself using Harry's impromptu critique of Becker; *our problem isn't that we're outsiders, Lenny, it's that we're insiders.* I found that so many of Harry's opinions were informing my approach to my subject. The rat in the maze had yielded results. But his thoughts always seemed to challenge rather than confirm my theories.

Karen left and went to live in a women-only household. She now defined herself as a lesbian separatist. I felt quite empty about the whole thing. Inadequate. I tried therapy. Some Reichian nonsense which didn't get me very far. I even went along to a men's group meeting. Sat in a circle with a lot of other sad blokes. Talking about getting in touch with our feelings. It was embarrassing.

In 1976 Harry graduated from the Open University with a 2:1. No gown or graduation ceremony of course but Harry looked pleased with himself when I got a VO and went to congratulate him.

'Letters after my name,' Harry mused. 'That ought to impress them.'

I guessed that he meant the parole board. I smiled weakly, trying to hide my discomfort. There was that spasm of anxiety again. The thought of Harry getting released.

'So what will you do with your qualifications? Once you're on the, er . . .' I coughed, 'outside.'

'Dunno.' Harry shrugged then grinned. 'Maybe move in on your racket. You know, academia.'

'Really?'

Harry burst out laughing.

'Only joking, Len. Christ your face. Nah, don't you worry, old son. I was thinking of something more practical, you know.'

'What like?'

'Well, I was thinking, with the combination of my experience and my studies I could work in an advisory capacity. Management consultancy, something like that. I don't know what you think's so funny, Lenny. A lot of people would give their right arm to know what I know about business.'

Doing Time got published in 1977 and I sent Harry a copy. It had had mixed reviews but it was Harry's opinion that I was most interested in.

'So?' I asked him. 'What do you think?'

'Well,' Harry shrugged. 'It was interesting. Yeah, it was all right.'

He sounded noncommittal. Polite. So unlike Harry.

'Come on,' I urged him. 'Tell me what you really think. Be brutal.'

Harry sighed. His eyebrows knitted.

'To be perfectly frank, Lenny,' he said, 'it's a bit old hat.'

'Yeah?'

'And a lot of your arguments are confused. They don't seem to go nowhere.'

'Yeah, well . . .'

'Look, you wanted my opinion. Face it, Lenny. The bubble's burst. Deviancy theory is dead in the water. It's all over, bar the shouting. Maybe that's all it was anyway. It wants to be radicalism but it's just liberalism with a loud mouth. Sorry, Len.'

'Well I said "be brutal".'

'Yeah,' he grinned. 'Well I have got a bit of a reputation. I liked some of it. That bit about the institutionalisation of power and that. I tell you what, though—' He leaned forward, eyes darting to and fro – 'I've been reading something else. Something very tasty.'

His sudden enthusiasm for another writer compounded his excoriation of my own work. I felt a bit sick.

'Who?' I asked, swallowing.

He uttered something I couldn't recognise. *Foe cult*, it sounded like. I had strange images of oppositional subcultures.

'Oh, come on Lenny,' he protested as I squinted at him. 'You know I can never pronounce these names. French geezer. *Discipline and Punish*.'

'Foucault, you mean.'

'Yeah.'

He muttered *foo co*, *foo co*, under his breath a few times, making sure that he'd got it, then looked up at me.

'You seen it?' he demanded.

I had. I'd even tried to read it but had not got very far. It seemed deliberately obscure, the long description in the first section of an eighteenth-century judicial torture rebarbative and brutal. Designed to shock perhaps but all a bit *grand guignol*.

'It's a bit heavy going,' I said.

'Yeah, well,' Harry chuckled. 'It ain't for the squeamish.'

The irony of the Torture Gang Boss reading all of this suddenly hit me and I laughed. His knowledge of brutality gave him insight, perhaps. And, as I remembered, straight after the torture account in the book came a description of prison routine of some seventy years later. Something that he also had first-hand experience of. Foucault was setting out two very distinct penal styles, one shocking and one familiarly modern, and inviting the reader to reflect on how, in less than a century, such huge changes had taken place. This much I understood and that any notion of 'humanisation' was to be avoided in the subsequent analysis, but that's about as far as I'd got. Harry was very keen to explain it all to me.

'It's all about the economy of power, Lenny. The modern penal system can present itself as being more just, more rational, but in effect it can exercise far greater power over people. Everything is controlled much more efficiently as with all other forms of industrial institutions. Remember what I said about the cat and the birch. Losing remission is a far worse punishment but it's seen as being less brutal. In fact punishment isn't seen any more but instead becomes the most hidden part of the process. So you abolish corporal punishment, you know, punishment on the body. Instead you punish the soul.'

'The soul?'

'Yeah, you know, the psyche, the consciousness, whatever. When you're banged up you're allowed exercise, you can study and pretend you're not turning into a zombie. But all along your personality, that delicate sense of freedom and integrity, is constantly being exercised and disciplined in time and space. That's the soul. The effect and instrument of a political anatomy. They imprison it, it imprisons you. The soul is the prison of the body.'

I tried to take all of this in as Harry went on. He was determined to use the rest of the visiting time to conduct a brief lecture outlining the whole thing. He talked of Bentham and the Panopticon, his design for an ideal prison where each inmate could be clearly seen by a central observer.

'You saw what it was like in the Submarine. We were hidden away, our punishment was hidden away from civilised society, literally submerged, if you like. Yet at the same time we're under constant surveillance. Constantly aware of our visibility to the system. Constantly isolated, with the only real intimacy being our relationship with the power exercised over us. Now, of course, this system produces delinquents, recidivists, deviants. This is prison's vengeance on justice. So what do you do, in a scientific age? Come up with another science to keep a check on this new species. Criminology. Sociology. Study the deviants then you can extend the surveillance. That's where you fit in to all this, Lenny. All this radical posturing. You just help to maintain the system. Make it appear more liberal, more civilised, but ultimately make it work better.'

'That's pretty damning, Harry.'

'Yeah, I'm afraid it is. But it's all there. You really should read it. You see, the problem with deviancy theory is that it never really analyses the structures we're supposed to be deviating from. Oh, you love the subjects. So strange and exotic. Like going to the zoo. You love all of these wild creatures because they're behind bars and can't hurt you. You want to like us but deep down you're shit scared of us.'

'Yeah, maybe.'

'Sorry, Lenny. I'm being a bit hard on you. Fact is, I'm in a good mood.'

'Yeah?'

'Yeah. Well, I've got my first parole board coming up in a couple of months' time.'

'So, you're optimistic?'

'Well, Lenny, you know, you've got to be careful how you think about these things. You can't afford to be hopeful about your situation. That makes you vulnerable, and the fuckers can grind you down easily. But you can't afford to be hopeless, neither. Because then they've really got you beat. It's like Antonio Gramsci said: "Pessimism of the intellect, optimism of the will".'

I smiled.

'You've been reading Gramsci?'

'Yeah. Now don't get a hard on just 'cos I'm quoting a commie, Lenny. I didn't buy all of that hegemony stuff. But anyone who's done that much time and held it all together deserves some respect.'

My mind was reeling as I came away from that visit. It was as if our roles had been reversed. I had become a student to Harry's teacher. He had acquired such clarity in his analysis of things whereas I had become more and more confused. My whole theoretical base was challenged. I had to start again.

I struggled with Foucault. I was jealous of Harry's clear grasp of it. And I felt guilty because deep down I didn't really want him to get parole. In a strange way I wanted him kept where he was so that I could have occasional access to his understanding. I didn't want him on the outside, roaming free. The thought of that always left me with a twinge of fear.

I didn't have to worry. Harry got the knockback. Later that year, six weeks after his board had met, he received a letter. 'The Secretary of State has fully and sympathetically considered your case for release under licence, but has regretfully concluded not to authorise it on this occasion.'

I managed to get a visit with him near the end of 1977. He looked terribly depressed. Puffy eyes stared at me gloomily.

It was an awkward visit. There wasn't much I could say about his being turned down.

'Well, you can carry on with your studying,' I suggested, hoping that we could talk academically. There were things I wanted to discuss with him. But Harry wasn't in the mood.

'It's all been a waste of fucking time.'

He gave a hollow laugh.

'Not that there's anything to do in here but waste time. But you've loved it, haven't you? I bet it's really been interesting for you.'

'Harry,' I murmured.

'Do your own time, Lenny. I've fucking had enough of it all.'

There was silence for about a minute. I cleared my throat.

'They're bound to lessen your category, at least,' I ventured. 'You'll probably get moved to an open prison.'

Harry's nostrils widened and he glowered at me.

'Open fucking prison. Open fucking university. Yeah, everything's fucking open, isn't it? You know what the worst thing is? Cunts like you looking in on me thinking everything's going to be all right because of their fucking bleeding hearts.'

Harry was becoming quite agitated. A screw came over.

'Now, now, Starks. Turn it in. Otherwise visiting time's over.'

'Fuck you,' he said to the guard. 'Fuck the lot of you. I don't need visiting time, anyway. It's a waste of fucking time.'

A couple more screws came over and they started to manhandle Harry.

'Get your fucking hands off me!' he shouted as they dragged him away.

I lost touch with Harry after that. He had got into trouble again over Good Order and Discipline. The last I heard of him was that he had been moved to Brixton. I reasoned that he might have finally cracked up as he had feared he would. Thoughts of him troubled me from time to time. But after a while it all receded in my mind. And that peculiar fear I had of him in the back of my mind nearly disappeared altogether.

I was left with the legacy of what I had learnt from him. The seed that I'd planted bore bitter fruit. I lost faith with my ideas, my once treasured theories. He had proved them wrong. I tried to keep up with new bodies of thought, new paradigms. Harry was certainly right about Foucault. His influence was tremendous. And all these other French guys. Post-structuralism, post-modernism, everything became fractured. The very consensus that deviancy theory envisaged (and indeed relied upon) was falling apart, so deviancy theory itself petered out very quickly. I carried on lecturing, without much enthusiasm. I was going through the motions.

Punk arrived and suddenly I became old fashioned. Students started criticising me for being an 'old hippy' or even a 'boring old fart'.

Funnily enough, punk regurgitated all that situationalist stuff from the late sixties. All that King Mob anarchism. The self-proclaimed deviants seemed ready to be digested as the new folk-devil pariah elite. I started to write an article for *New Society* but it just turned out turgid and flat. Stan Cohen had already done all that years ago with the Mods anyhow. I was bored, but not like these kids with their blank generation aesthetic. I was bored because I had become boring.

The Tories got in again in 1979. That seemed to epitomise the lost opportunities of that decade. Some people on the Left said it was a good thing. That it would give the people something tangible to rebel against. I wasn't so sure. Consensus was dead and our radicalism seemed burned out. In fact it looked like the very idea of radicalism belonged to the Right now.

Then, that same year, Harry hit the headlines. TORTURE GANG BOSS IN DRAMATIC ESCAPE, read one headline. STARKS ESCAPE: BRIXTON SECURITY PROBE ORDERED. I felt a familiar shiver of fear up my spine. It gave me quite a thrill.

It had been a meticulously planned escape. At Brixton, Harry had noticed that the external wall at the end of his wing connected to a flat roof. By bribing a couple of key warders, Harry had engineered a change in allocation that got him the cell at the end of the block. He wanted a better view, he assured them. Then, with the patience of an archaeologist he set to work. He started to cut into the mortar around a whole patch of brickwork. He used drill bits, fragments of hacksaw blades, anything that could be smuggled in or bartered for with other prisoners. He worked slowly and carefully and at night. He stole sugar from the canteen and sprinkled it on the floor of the corridor in front of his door so that he could hear the crunch of the rubber-soled boots of an approaching screw. That way he could time the lengths of the landing patrols and know when it was safe to work.

At dawn he would carefully sweep up the brick dust and mortar rubble from the night's labours and dump it in his chamber pot. In the morning he would slop it all out undetected. He hid the growing hole by pushing a wooden locker up against the wall.

It took him nearly three months to chisel out around fifteen bricks that were to provide him his exit. But he knew that any haste might lead to mistakes or clumsiness. He had time on his side, after all.

On the night of his escape he gently pushed out the loosened brickwork and crawled through the hole onto the flat roof. He had attached a short rope to the back of the locker so that he could pull it up against the wall and cover his exit. On his bed was a dummy, prison clothes stuffed with newspapers to fool the night-duty warders inspecting the cells. His disappearance would not be detected till much later that morning.

He made his way across the roof, over the security fence. He then simply hailed a cab on Brixton Hill and he was away.

I followed all the news stories about Harry that week. When the letter to *The Times* was published it took me a while to suss it out. Then it glared right out at me. Our letter code. It had been such a long time since it had been used. *In the final analysis*, that was the trigger phrase. *In the final analysis, it's my assessment that this worthwhile opportunity to humanely rehabilitate effectively enough now, is nigh. Enough over-zealous legal deterrence. Continuation of my punishment thus only negates society's tentative reforms, exceeding equitable treatment.* I decoded it. Spelt it out.

IMATTWOTHREENINEOLDCOMPTONSTREET. *I'm at Two-Three-Nine Old Compton Street.* Soho. Harry was hiding out in the West End of London. And he wanted me to meet him there.

An invitation. A summons more like. For a moment I felt indignation at Harry's presumption that I was going to drop everything and go and meet him. Then I felt fear knowing that I couldn't resist the adventure of it. A sense of excitement I hadn't felt for years.

I made some oblique excuses to the faculty. Family crisis, affairs to be sorted, arrangements to be made. I could be gone for a few days, I warned them. I threw a few things into my car and drove down to London.

PRIVATE SHOP was the sign above the storefront that was 239 Old Compton Street. I parted the coloured strips of plastic forming a curtain at its doorway and went in. There were racks of shrink-wrapped magazines. *Danish Blue*, *Swedish Hardcore*. A man in an anorak was surreptitiously examining the covers. There was a glass case in front of the counter which displayed strange pink objects like holy relics. Behind the counter a very fat man with lank greasy hair and froggy eyes was reading *Exchange & Mart*. On the shelves above him were displayed Super 8 films. *Fanny Get Your Gun*, *Ranch of the Nymphomaniac Cowgirls*.

The anorak man wandered out. I sidled up to the counter. The fat man was absently picking his nose. I coughed. Froggy eyes looked up from the auto-spares section and he wiped a finger on his sleeve.

'There's more hard-core stuff out the back,' he said, thumbing at the doorway behind him.

I drew in close to the fat man.

'I'm Lenny,' I whispered, conspiratorially.

'Nice to meet you, Lenny,' he whispered back with a knowing smile. 'What is it, S&M? Animals? Whatever you want, Lenny. I'm sure I can find it for you.'

'No,' I sighed. 'I've come to see Harry.'

His heavy-lidded eyes flashed for half a second and then looked down, pretending to find something interesting amongst the small ads.

'Don't know what you're talking about,' the fat man said flatly.

'Tell Harry Lenny's here.'

He looked me up and down and chewed at his lower lip.

'Right,' he said finally, coming out from behind the counter. 'Mind the shop for me will yer?'

Harry paced up and down in a tight pattern in the flat above the shop. Still measuring cell dimensions. He looked lean and mean, his greying hair slicked back tight against his skull. He had evidently gone through a rigorous exercise regime in the run up to his escape. He grinned at me. His eyes had a wild and hunted gleam in them. His stare was as piercing as ever.

'Glad you could come, Lenny,' he said. 'I knew you would. I knew I could trust you.'

I didn't know quite what he meant by this. I had no idea what he wanted from me.

'Good to see you, Harry,' was all that I could think of to say.

'Yeah. Likewise. Look, I was hoping that you could help me with this campaign of mine. Get it noticed. You know, like that George Davis thing.'

'"Harry Starks is Innocent, OK"?'

Harry laughed darkly.

'Nah, I don't think that would stick. A few friends have been doing this graffiti: "Free Harry Starks", "Ten Years is Long Enough". That sort of thing. It just needs a bit of a boost.'

'Well I don't know what I could do.'

'I dunno, get a petition together, hold a public meeting, I don't fucking know. You know more about these things than I do.'

'I don't know . . .'

'Come on Lenny. I ain't asking much. It's a human rights issue. I need all the help I can get. And it'd be good for you and all. You might learn something.'

'Well . . .'

'Go on,' he urged, his eyes narrowing into mine.

'I'll see what I can do,' I replied, timidly.

'Thanks, Lenny,' he said, patting me on the shoulder. 'I appreciate it.'

That evening, making sure the coast was clear, we went to The Stardust. Wally, the fat man in the sex shop, provided cover as we moved quickly through the dark streets. The Stardust had been Harry's club in the sixties, and Wally was running it for him.

'There've been some changes,' Wally explained as we walked around to the club. He seemed a bit nervous.

'We ain't just doing the Erotic Revue any more. We've sort of, er, branched out.'

'You mean like proper cabaret?' Harry asked, his eyes lighting up.

'Yeah,' replied Wally, hesitantly. 'Sort of.'

The Comedy Club, the sign on the door announced as we arrived. We went in and stood at the back near the bar. Drinks were brought over. On stage was a tubby, crop-haired man in a tight-fitting suit and a pork-pie hat, jerking about in front of the microphone stand.

'Thing is,' Wally went on, almost apologetically, 'your tasteful striptease revue just ain't making money any more. Peepshows, that's the business these days. Smaller premises, fewer staff, faster turnover. And no choreography or nothing. Just some tart rubbing away at herself.'

Of course, you lot don't go down the pub, do yer? The man on stage had a thick scouse accent. *Oh no. It's down the wine bar, like. That's the new thing. Got them all over Hampstead.* Harry frowned.

'So this bloke, right,' Wally went on, 'he's seen this thing in the States. Comedy clubs. Really get the punters in.'

You know why they call them wine bars, don't yer? It refers to the conversation, like.

'What the fuck is this?' Harry demanded.

Whine, whine, whine. Laughter.

Wally looked uncomfortable.

'I think they're calling it "alternative comedy",' I suggested.

'Yeah,' Wally agreed, eagerly. 'That's it.'

'What, you mean alternative to funny?'

We didn't stay at The Stardust for very long. Harry had some business to attend to and suggested that I come along too. We walked through Soho and across Oxford Street into Charlotte Street. Harry turned into a doorway with a brass nameplate which announced: *G. J. Hurst, Chiropodists.* He buzzed the door and muttered something incomprehensible into the intercom. The door opened to let us in.

'A spieler,' Harry told me, as we mounted the staircase. 'Be good research for you to see what one of them looks like. Just don't start fannying on about "subcultures". Keep your head down and your gob shut.'

The spieler was on the third floor. The room stank of cigar smoke. In the corner there was a table with a card game in full swing. There were six men playing and maybe about ten others looking on. It was a hard game to follow. Cards were taken and discarded at high speed. There was a pile of ten- and twenty-pound notes in the centre of the table.

'Kalooki,' Harry explained. 'Jewish game. The old man ran a spieler when I was a kid. He used to say to me, "Look at that son, that's the death agony of capitalism."'

Hundreds of pounds changed hands in flurries. The well-dressed men at the table handled their playing cards with intense concentration and their money with absolute nonchalance.

Eyes darted about. People talked out of the side of their mouths in a language I didn't understand. This was the world I'd spent all these years studying. I felt out of place. Conspicuous. I'd only seen criminals in captivity before.

Everyone in the club was clearly aware of Harry's presence but the little greetings that were made were carefully understated. A firm but brief touch on the shoulder as someone passed. A whispered: 'Well done, Harry, good to see you.' One of the card players, a small man with round spectacles who sipped thoughtfully at a glass of milk by his side, looked up and winked. There was a hiatus in the game and he drained the milk in one. Throwing in his hand and picking up a pile of notes, he stood up and came over.

'Hersh,' he announced with a shrug.

'Manny,' replied Harry.

The two men hugged each other, Harry stooping to slap the little man on the back.

'Manny,' Harry said, 'this is Lenny. A friend. It's all right, he's kosher. He's running the "Free Harry Starks" campaign.'

Manny's magnified eyes blinked at me for a second. He nodded.

'Come,' he said, cocking his head towards a door behind the card table. 'Let's go out the back.'

'Yeah, right,' said Harry. 'Come on, Lenny.'

In the back room were a few leather-covered armchairs. Copies of *Sporting Life* and *The Financial Times* lay folded on a coffee table. Manny produced a bottle of Remy Martin and some glasses and poured us all a drink.

'Mazeltov,' he murmured, jerking up his glass.

'So?' Harry asked.

Manny took a sip of spirit and sharply exhaled. He gave a little shrug.

'So,' he replied. 'Your business affairs are in good order, Hersh. Fat Wally has been skimming the profits of the porn shops and the peepshows and sending it all down to Spain. Jock McCluskey's down there dealing with it all.'

'Wally's been behaving himself?'

'Yes, yes,' Manny nodded. 'If anything, it's the Scotsman I'm worried about.'

'What, Big Jock?'

'I know, I know, he's usually so reliable. Some of the figures don't seem to completely add up. He's said that he's had to pay some people off but even so. You know, sometimes I get, what you say, a gut feeling.'

'I know, Manny. That's what makes you indispensable. But it's all safe down there, isn't it?'

'Yes, yes. The extradition treaty between Britain and Spain fell apart last year and it doesn't look like it's going to be patched up for quite a while. It's a safe bolt hole. A lot of faces are already relocating to Andalusia.'

Harry sighed.

'It'll be heaving with East and South London recidivists in no time,' he lamented.

'Well, they're already calling it the "Costa Del Crime".'

'Hm.'

'Don't worry, Marbella has, I gather, largely escaped the worst excesses of the tourist industry. It's well situated for business as well. Big Jock's procured a lovely big villa. Swimming pool and everything.'

'You must come and visit, Manny.'

'I'm sorting out all the paperwork for your travel arrangements. I'll need a passport photo.'

'Of course.' Harry stood up. 'Look, we better be getting back.'

As we walked through the main part of the spieler, a short stocky man came up to Harry.

'We've had a whip,' he said, handing over a considerable wedge of notes.

'Thanks,' said Harry, taking the cash and patting him on the shoulder.

'Be lucky,' said the man.

We walked back to Soho.

'So, you're planning to skip the country?' I asked.

'Yeah, well it's not a bad idea, don't you think?'

'What about the "Free Harry Starks" campaign?'

Harry chuckled.

'Well, it's not a bad smokescreen. I mean, if I can persuade people that my escape is some sort of publicity stunt to bring attention to my case, that I might be ready to turn myself in after a few days, then the Old Bill aren't going to be wasting too much manpower in looking for me are they?'

'I guess not.'

'Besides, I'm making a point. I don't expect much from the British justice system but I'm making my fucking point, ain't I?'

As we came into Old Compton Street, Harry slowed down. He led me into a shop doorway.

'What's the matter?' I asked.

Harry peered out of the alcove and cocked his head towards Wally's shop.

'Something's up,' he said. 'There's a couple of moody-looking cars parked up there.'

I peeped out myself. Two saloon cars were pulled up on the kerb outside the shop. A man was standing by one of the cars looking down the street in our direction. Suddenly there was a commotion at the doorway of the shop. It was easy to make out the considerable figure of Fat Wally, surrounded by smaller figures who were awkwardly bundling him into the back of one of the cars. It drove off quickly. A siren started up and it wailed off into the night. The other car pulled off the kerb and parked itself opposite the shop.

'Fuck,' Harry muttered. 'Where's your motor?'

I'd parked it at the other end of Old Compton Street.

'It's up the other end, Harry.'

'Well, go and get it and bring it back here.'

I walked up the street and passed the car parked across the road from Fat Wally's shop. I felt my legs almost buckling with nerves. I could barely stop myself from looking in at the men waiting in the car. I felt them watch me pass.

I drove back and picked Harry up. Harry laughed as he got into the passenger seat of my Citroën 2CV.

'Classy motor, Lenny,' he said.

'Yeah. Sorry about that.'

'No, this is perfect. No one's going to suspect Britain's most wanted gang boss being driven around in this jalopy.'

He told me to drive north, to Tottenham.

'I thought you said that the police weren't going to do a big manhunt for you,' I said.

'Hm, that weren't no fucking manhunt. They aren't that fucking clever. Somebody grassed, that's for sure.'

We reached Tottenham High Road and Harry checked in my *London A – Z* and gave directions.

'Thing is,' he spoke softly, as if to himself, 'only Wally, Manny, and Jock knew where I was.'

He looked up from the map book and stared at the road ahead.

'And you of course,' he said, bluntly.

We reached our destination. It was a row of large Victorian terraced houses. I parked up in front of them.

'Right,' said Harry briskly. 'Come on.'

'Wait a minute, Harry. Look, I think I've got more involved in all this than I planned to, Harry. Maybe it's best if I leave you here and I get off. All right?'

Harry frowned and slowly turned his head towards me.

'What the fuck are you talking about?' he demanded.

'I just thought, you know . . .'

'You just thought. You just thought. What? Drop me off here and go and make a little phone call. Is that it?'

'No, Harry. Of course not.'

'I trusted you, Lenny. If I ever found out that you betrayed that trust,' he whispered gravely, his face now close to mine.

'Honestly, Harry, I never . . .' I found myself pleading.

Harry suddenly grinned and tapped me on the side of my face.

'Good,' he said and drew back. 'Now come on.'

We went up the stone steps of one of the houses. Harry rapped on the door. It was opened by a cropped-haired man in a Lacoste cardigan.

'Yeah?' he said vaguely, then peered more closely. 'Harry? Fuck me, Harry Starks.'

'Hello Beardsley,' Harry said with a smile. 'How's it going?'

'Fucking hell, Harry. Come in, for fuck's sake.'

He ushered us into the hallway, and checked out the street as he closed the door. We went through to his living room. Beardsley produced a bottle of scotch and he and Harry caught up on old times for a while.

'Anything I can do, H?' Beardsley said.

'Well, we were wondering if you could put us up. Just for a couple of days.'

Beardsley drew in a breath and looked fraught for a second. Then he nodded.

'Yeah, fucking hell, of course you can. It's just the missus, you see. I've gone straight, as far as she's concerned. As long as she doesn't know nothing.'

'And have you? I mean, gone straight?' Harry asked.

'Yeah, well, mostly. I'm in the music business now. I'm managing this band called Earthquake. They're doing all this ska stuff. You know, all that skinhead music I used to be into. It's all the rage again. I'll tell her you're a couple of session musicians. You can share the spare bedroom. But keep your heads down. I don't want her kicking off at me again.'

The next morning I went out and bought all of the papers. Some of the dailies ran a small piece on Wally's arrest. The headline on page 5 of *The Sun:* STARKS SLIPS NET IN SOHO SEX SHOP SWOOP. *Police acting on a tip-off raided the premises of a pornographic bookshop in London's West End last night, believing it to be the hide-out of escaped gangster Harry Starks. But the notorious Torture Gang Boss evaded capture. The proprietor, Walter Peters, is helping police with their inquiries.*

'Right, let's get a press release together today, Lenny. Let them think I'm going to turn myself in.'

Beardsley brought up a meal for each of us on a tray.

'The wife's getting suspicious,' he said. 'There's all this stuff in the papers and she knows I used to run around with you.'

'Just a couple of days, Beardsley. Then I'm fucking off out of this poxy country.'

'Spain is it?'

'How do you know?'

'I don't. I just figured. You know, this extradition thing.'

'Yeah, well, you might as well know. Got a villa in Marbella all lined up.'

'Lovely. Weather's fucking lovely down there. My cousin runs an English Bar down that way. Fuengirola. It's great. Full English Breakfast, Sunday Roast, English beer and a proper cup of tea when you get homesick.'

'Right,' Harry said, giving me a sideways glance.

'"Pete's English Bar" it's called. You should check it out.'

'Yeah, sure. Look, thanks for putting us up B.'

Harry fished out a bundle of notes and offered them to Beardsley.

'Look, Harry,' said Beardsley, putting up his hands. 'There's no need. Old times and all that.'

'Go on, take it. Buy the missus something nice. Keep her sweet.'

We worked on Harry's press release through the day. Harry spent most of the time coaxing and cajoling ideas from me that he would then proceed to attack vociferously. There was heated debate over lines of argument, ordering of points and the choice of words. The habitual and mind-numbing questioning of every assertion and every subsequent criticism. It was just like old times.

Finally we hammered something out and we went through it together. Harry shrugged and pursed his lips.

'Yeah,' he admitted. 'It'll do.'

'You sure you don't want to change that last bit? You said you thought it sounded a bit weak.'

'Nah, it's fine. The main thing is that they should think that I'm going to come quietly.'

'Who do we send it to?'

'*The Times*, I guess. They ran my letter, after all.'

'Yeah,' I agreed.

We sat in silence for a while enjoying, for a moment at least, the calm blankness of having finished something. Finished business, I thought wistfully. I could go now. I looked up at Harry. Our eyes met.

'Right,' I said. 'Well . . .'

'Come to Spain,' said Harry.

'What?'

'Look, I'll level with you. I need something bringing back.'

'You've got to be joking.'

'It's nothing. Just some, you know, paperwork.'

'Paperwork?'

'Stuff for Manny. Look, the less you know the better.'

'Harry, I don't want to know about this at all.'

'Come on,' he implored. 'Come to Spain. Just for a few days. It'll be a bit of a holiday.'

'I've got to get back. The University.'

'Listen to you. The University. Fuck me. I thought I was becoming institutionalised.'

'Harry . . .'

'You need a bit of extra-mural activity, Len. Think of the research value. You're a criminologist for fuck's sake. Here's a chance to really know your subject. Extend your methodology a bit. Fieldwork, if you like. What do you call it? Ethnographic study based on participant observation.'

'This is a wind up.'

'Well, granted, it's bullshit if it's just intellectual analysis. This is a chance to really experience something. Admit it, you're tempted.'

'I don't think so.'

'Come on. You're drawn to the excitement of it. That's what got you interested in the first place.'

'Maybe. But I can't just drop everything and go to Spain.'

'Why not? Christ Lenny, you've spent all these years studying deviant behaviour and yet you've always acted according to social norms. You're supposed to be a fucking radical. When did you ever do anything radical in your life?'

'Harry . . .'

'Nah, it's true, isn't it? You're scared of doing anything that might constitute an adventure, anything that might upset that safe little life of yours.'

I sighed. Harry grinned that grin of his.

'Well, anyway,' I retorted. 'I can't leave the country. I haven't got my passport with me.'

Harry laughed.

'Don't worry, old son. We can get you one.'

My stomach sank as we dropped in altitude. Not air sickness. Ground sickness. Coming down to earth. I suddenly thought: *what the fuck am I doing?* Gone was the heady sense of escapism I'd felt when I'd first agreed to go along with Harry. I'd somehow found myself in a dilemma. My freedom had seemed as much at stake as Harry's. I'd felt a fatalistic tranquillity in recklessness. I'd calmly phoned the faculty again, answering frantic inquiries with obscure reasons for my absence. I needed time to think. Things had got on top of me. Compassionate leave was extended. They probably imagined that I was having some sort of nervous breakdown. They wouldn't be far off the mark there.

But it was as we were making our final descent on Malaga Airport that I felt the gravity of it all. Coming in to land. *Please fasten your seatbelts and extinguish all cigarettes.* Landing is the most dangerous part of flying. *What the fuck am I doing?* In a foreign country with a fake passport, accompanying a fugitive of British justice. Harry sensed my rediscovered nerves.

'Keep calm, Lenny.' His voice hoarse and soft. 'For fuck's sake.'

We were only carrying hand luggage so we could go straight through to customs. We cleared it quickly and without incident. A driver was waiting for us.

The drive to Marbella took about an hour. We caught occasional glimpses of the dull-blue Mediterranean usually accompanied by huge white concrete developments.

'The Costa Del Sol is a bit trashy,' Harry commented. 'But we could go inland for a couple of days. Go to Granada, have a look at the Alhambra.'

I nodded and closed my eyes, seeing a red glow.

We finally arrived at the villa. Marble steps led up to a series of whitewashed blocks. There was a cylindrical turret inlaid with coloured glass. By the wrought-iron gates at the top of the stairs we were met by a short balding muscular man. The sun had par-boiled his battered face. An open Hawaiian shirt revealed a greying hairy chest and a pot belly that hung over elasticated shorts.

'Harry,' he growled.

'Jock,' replied Harry, hugging the burly man. 'How the fuck are you? This is Lenny. He's in charge of public relations.'

'Pleased to meet you Lenny. Come on in.'

He led us through the gates, we passed through a tiny courtyard with a font heavy with dark-green foliage, then through panelled and studded doors. Portuguese pink marble floors, textured-plaster wall with a dado of ornamental tiles and clusters of more coloured glass inlay. A stone fireplace with a driftwood sculpture above it. Huge urns at each corner of the room. Moroccan wall hangings. A smoked-glass and tubular-steel coffee table surrounded by a massive sofa and armchairs in white leather. There were sliding french windows at the far end. Beyond, a turquoise swimming pool shimmered in a blue-tiled patio.

'Very nice,' said Harry, scanning it all. 'Yeah. It's all been very tastefully done.'

Jock produced a bottle of Krug and some glasses. He popped the cork and filled a glass full of foam. His hands were shaking as he guided the neck of the bottle. He picked up a glass, his hand a bit more steady now.

'Well, here's to crime,' he proposed, and we all drank the toast.

A roll call passed between them. A litany of names, of faces, of those 'away'. When it seemed exhausted, Harry sighed.

'So, let's get down to business,' he said. 'I want to go through everything I've got down here.'

'Yeah, sure, Harry,' Jock replied. 'But you'll want to relax a bit first, eh? It's been a long journey.'

'Yeah, well, let's get it all sorted and then I can relax.'

Jock cleared his throat.

'Yeah,' he said, nodding, rubbing his fat hands on the front of his shorts. 'Of course.'

Just then there was a shout from the patio. *¡Señor Yock! ¡Señor Yock!* Jock grumbled and rubbed his face.

'The pool boy,' he explained. 'There's something wrong with the filter.'

He stood up.

'I just need to see to this. I won't be long.'

And he went out through the sliding french windows.

Harry stared straight ahead and sipped at his champagne.

'Something's up,' he muttered. 'Jock's in a fucking funny mood.'

Agitated voices out on the patio. Two sharp cracks like heavy branches breaking and then a loud splash.

Harry was on his feet and racing to the glass doors. I followed him. We came out onto the patio. Someone was vaulting over the high stone wall.

'Oi!' Harry shouted.

There was the sound of undergrowth breaking. A motorcycle starting up and screaming off into the hot afternoon. Jock was face down in the swimming pool. Dark clouds of blood diffused in the water.

'Fuck!' said Harry, looking down at the floating body.

There was an automatic pistol lying on the poolside. Harry picked it up and looked at it. He sniffed.

'Fuck!' he whispered harshly.

He pocketed the gun and started to move quickly, back to the house.

'Shouldn't we get him out of the water?' I asked.

He beckoned to me.

'Come on,' he insisted.

I gazed at the bobbing body. I frowned.

'Something wrong with the filter,' I muttered.

'Come on!' Harry repeated.

He went into the house and pulled at the white fur rug in front of the fireplace. He lifted up a small section of marble to reveal a floor safe, worked the combination and opened it. Reaching down, he scooped his hand around it. It was empty.

'Fuck! We've been cleaned out.'

He stood up and adjusted the gun in his pocket. The sound of police sirens came from not too far off.

'Come on,' he ordered and made for the front door. 'We've been set up.'

We ran down the steps and down the street. Behind us cars were screeching to a halt in front of the villa. Another police car came racing from the direction we were headed. Harry pulled me in by a hedge and we watched it pass. We found ourselves in a small square. There was a taxi at the corner. We jumped in.

'¡Vamos!' Harry demanded.

'¿Adonde?' the driver inquired.

Harry pointed ahead.

'That way,' he said.

The driver pulled away and started down the road ahead.

'You English?' he asked.

'Si, yes,' Harry replied. 'English, yes.'

'Where you want go, English?'

'Oh, I don't fucking know,' he complained, rubbing his face with his hand.

Suddenly his hand stopped in front of his mouth. His eyes lit up.

'Fuengirola,' he gasped with a look of inspiration.

'Sure,' replied the driver. 'Fuengirola is 800 pesetas.'

'Take us there. Take us to Pete's English Bar, Fuengirola.'

FULL ENGLISH BREAKFAST, promised Pete's English Bar. FISH 'N' CHIPS 200 PSTS. SUNDAY ROAST SERVED DAILY. FULL RANGE OF ENGLISH BEERS. The interior was half-timbered white plaster. Horse brasses, a Union Jack and a portrait of Her Majesty framed by an alcove. A formal photograph of two ranks of a football team, one standing, one squatting. A maroon scarf tacked above with the legend VIVA EL FULHAM. Framed pictures of Henry Cooper and Winston Churchill. 'Una Paloma Blanca' was blaring out of the jukebox. A ruddily tanned man with a bleached-blond perm was wiping the bar. He looked up and smiled wearily at us.

'What can I get you, gents?' he offered.

'Are you Pete?' Harry asked.

He stopped wiping and squinted at us.

'Who wants to know?'

'A friend of Beardsley's.'

He smiled.

'Right. How is the old cunt? Keeping out of trouble I hope. Wait a minute . . .'

Pete craned forward and studied Harry's face.

'You're . . .' Pete began.

'Yes,' said Harry, holding a finger up to the side of his nose. 'I'm.'

Pete looked about shiftily then cocked his head backwards.

'Come out the back,' he said.

We went through the kitchen. It reeked of bacon and chip fat.

'We need somewhere to lie low for a bit,' said Harry, handing him a wad of notes.

'Sure,' said Pete, pocketing the money. 'I've got a room upstairs.'

Harry took off his jacket as Pete showed us the room. The pistol fell clattering onto the floor. Pete jumped back.

'Fucking hell,' he gasped.

'Don't worry,' said Harry. 'We won't be staying long. I need to get across the water to Morocco. You know anyone who can take me? Someone who won't ask too many questions.'

Pete nodded.

'Yeah. I know someone.'

* * *

Someone arrived three hours later.

'Hi, I'm Giles,' he announced in a lazy public school drawl. 'Mind if I skin up?'

'Be my guest,' Harry said.

'I understand you want to hitch a lift across the Straits of Gibraltar.'

'Yeah, that's right. You got a boat?'

'Yah,' Giles affirmed licking a rizla. 'Absolutely. Moored down at Puerto Banus. Planning to set off dawn tomorrow, actually.'

'So you could take me?'

'Oh, yah. For a price of course.'

'And nobody else needs to know about this?'

'Absolutely. There's my crew of course, but Juanalito's terribly loyal. I can trust him.'

'And can I trust you?'

Giles flicked open a brass zippo and lit the joint. He took a sharp pull. A smile emerged from a wreath of hash smoke.

'Don't worry, man. I'm terribly discreet. I have to be.'

'And why's that?' Harry demanded, with a slight edge to his voice.

'Because I'm picking up half a ton of resin from the Rif mountains next week and bringing it back over here. If you're planning to relocate to Morocco, perhaps we could do business sometime.'

He handed the joint to Harry.

'Yeah,' Harry toked thoughtfully. 'Maybe. Look, Giles, you know who I am, don't you?'

'Not necessarily.'

'Yeah, but just supposing that you do. What's being said?'

'That you shot Jock McCluskey by his swimming pool.'

'Right. Well I didn't. OK?'

'I'm very glad to hear it.'

Harry passed me the joint. I took a drag and held the smoke in my lungs.

'You knew Jock?' Harry asked Giles.

'Knew of him. And that weird guy he was doing business with.'

'What guy?'

'Calls himself the Major. Supposed to be ex-army. Looks more like ex-Old Bill to me.' Giles gave a stoned little giggle. *'El Viejo Guillermo.'*

'What sort of business were they doing?'

I exhaled and felt the hashish rush into my bloodstream, a prickly warmth rising up from my legs.

'Well, this Major guy, he's supposed to be well connected, knows all the bent *policia* down here. He's been approaching all the villains who are moving down here and offering protection. You know, acting as liaison with the authorities.'

'And Jock was dealing with him?'

'That's what I heard.'

'And where might one find this Major chap?'

'He's got a place up in Llanos de Nagueles. I could find the address if you want.'

'Yeah, you do that.'

At nightfall we drove up to a moresque villa overlooking the sea. It seemed dark and empty. We got out of the car. Cicadas chirped in an expectant rhythm. There was a firework display down by the beach.

Harry went up to the front door and rapped on it. He peered up at the windows. Nobody stirred. He came back out.

'Nobody home,' he said. 'Let's have a look at the back.'

He told the driver to wait and we walked around the premises. A burst of green cinders blossomed against the skyline and a gentle patter of thunder rolled up from the seafront. There was a low pillared balcony at the back of the house.

'Right then,' he muttered. 'Let's have a little look, shall we?'

'You're going to break in?'

'*We're* going to break in.'

'Harry, look . . .'

'Shut up and listen. A bit of practical work for you. Now concentrate. I'm going to explain breaking in. Here's the *modus operandi*. A team of three. Right?' Harry held up three fingers. 'Driver, minder, goer.' He counted off. 'The driver's obviously Pepe over there, I'm going in, so that leaves you to mind. Keep watch and keep your wits about you. If anything turns up, give me a shout. And then make sure the motor's ready to go when I come out. OK? Remember, rule number one, no one gets left behind.'

'I'm really not sure about this.'

'Don't worry. You're nervous, that's natural. Use your nerves to keep you on your toes. Oh,' he added, 'and you get to hold on to this.'

He slipped something into my hand. I felt cold heavy metal. It was the gun.

'Oh, fuck,' I groaned.

'Don't worry. I put the safety catch on.'

He padded across to the balcony and started to scale it. A rocket whooped up into the night. A bright orange star shell dropped slowly behind a row of palm trees. I could hear Harry rattling the shutters, forcing an entry.

Cars passing. A group of revellers in the distance breaking into a terrace chant. Syncopated pyrotechnic clattering. An engine sighed to a halt in front of the house. The sound of a car door clumping.

I walked briskly around to the front, clutching the pistol in my pocket. Someone was at the front door. Keys jingled, slotted, ratcheted. I ran back to the balcony.

'Harry!' I whispered harshly.

No response. A light went on.

'Harry!' I repeated, a little louder.

Still nothing. I started to climb up the balcony myself. The light went on in the room beyond. I crawled to the french windows and crouched behind the shutter Harry had forced open.

Harry was stooped over an open suitcase on the bed. It was full of money. There was a stocky man with close-cropped grey hair and piercing little eyes standing by the door. He had a gun in his hand.

'Hello, Harry,' he said. 'Long time no see.'

Harry gave a little start. He looked up.

'Mooney,' he moaned. 'Fuck.'

'I see you've found your legacy.'

Harry picked up a sheaf of notes and let it drop back into the suitcase.

'You had Jock killed, didn't you?' he asked.

Mooney sighed.

'Jock,' he said, shaking his head. 'Yes, that was unfortunate. I tried to work things out with him but he could so easily have fucked things up. And after I'd done so much for him. When he first came down here he really stuck out like a sore prick. It was easy to track him down. I've been here for quite a while, you know, established some very useful friends in the *guardia civil*. I could have had him thrown out on his ear. Instead I suggested a more co-operative approach. I helped him get set up. So much gelt coming in from Soho. Some of it owing to me now, let's face it. Plenty to go around. Then you break out of Brixton and Jock gets all flustered. Like an old woman. I say it's simple, let me know where you are and I'll just make a little call to some old pals at West End Central. And he's whining on about not wanting to grass you up. Dreary petty-criminal morality. When he does finally squeal, it's too late, you've already moved on. Then Jock gets near enough hysterical. You're on your way, what are we going to do. Like it's always up to me to sort all the shit out. I could have had you arrested at Malaga. But then I think, why not get rid of you both? Jock's becoming far too unreliable. I get him to hand over the loot to me for safe keeping. Tell him not to worry, I'll deal with you.'

'And then you have him bumped off?'

'Yes.' Mooney smiled. 'It seemed such a perfect solution. To do it while you're at the house. You're the most obvious suspect, after all. And it has been pinned on you, you know. There's a very good set of fingerprints on a glass found in the villa. Scotland Yard have already confirmed that they belong to you.

'But once again you have evaded capture. You've become quite a desperado, Harry. Now I can bring you in myself. A bit of glory. Retired detective collars the Torture Gang Boss. It'll do my reputation no end of good. You know, there's still some nasty rumours about my past, my time in the force. This will shut all of that up for good. And it'll impress my friends in the *policia*. A minor gang war cleared up. Just the sort of thing that they're dreading with this extradition difficulty. I can persuade them to let me have a free rein. Keep in line all the old lags that'll be coming down here to lie about like lizards in the sun. It'll be quite like old times, really. Familiar faces, just a bit of suntan. And bigger and better deals. It'll be my duty to properly police the expatriate criminal community. And it'll make me very rich. Now, put your hands up where I can see them.'

'Isn't there something that can be done?' Harry asked.

'Ah! That ancient phrase. It quite takes me back, it really does. You're of the old school, Harry, I'll give you that. I'd really like to be able to say yes, just for old times' sake. But I'm afraid, I'm going to have to hand you over. A little offering, as it were. Don't try anything. I've got a licence for this thing and using it to shoot a dangerous intruder would suit me just as well.'

Keeping his pistol trained on Harry, Mooney picked up the receiver of the telephone on the bedside table. He clutched it, then used the forefinger of the same hand to start to dial a number. I pulled out the pistol Harry had given me and edged forward. Suddenly the window shutter that obscured me swung inwards noisily. Mooney looked across, his little eyes narrowing in on me. I raised my gun and pointed it at him.

'Go on,' Harry urged gruffly. 'Shoot the fucker.'

I pulled at the trigger but it wouldn't budge. I tried again. Mooney swung his pistol around in my direction and fired.

Glass exploded next to my face. I staggered back out onto the balcony.

'The safety catch, you stupid cunt!' Harry called out.

Mooney followed me out, bearing down on me, both hands holding his gun, steadying its aim on me. My arms dangled at my sides uselessly. I still felt the weight of my pistol at the end of one of them.

Mooney pointed his gun at my face. I stared at the little hole at the end of it. Mooney grinned at me. I gasped a breath. My brain screamed with fear.

Then, with a thud, he fell forward, collapsed into a sprawling heap in front of me. Harry had hurled the suitcase against his back. Its hinged shells now gaped open, spilling out bundles of money onto the tiled floor and all over the back of the ex-policeman. Mooney stirred, coughing. He looked up over his shoulder at me. I only needed to lift my weighted arm a few degrees to bring the barrel of the gun in line with his view. I clicked off the safety catch.

Mooney curled up foetal. His beady eyes gleamed in panic. He made little palsied spasms of terror.

'Please,' he squealed.

All my fear turn into disgust. I felt a surge of animal loathing for weakness. Aerial maroons exploded in the sky behind me. My shoulder spastic with recoil. Cordite stinging the back of my throat. The gun was hot in my hand. I don't know how many bullets I put into Mooney. Harry got hold of me.

'That's enough, Lenny,' he shouted in my ear, pulling the gun arm gently down. 'That's enough.'

He carefully prised the pistol from my tense grip. Unthreading the forefinger from out of the trigger guard, unclawing the rest from the butt. There were neat little wounds in Mooney's face. The back of his head was a red and pink pulp. Blood grouted the tilework floor of the balcony.

I started to hyperventilate. Harry pulled me away from the body and slapped me across the face a couple of times.

'Come on. Breathe out slowly. That's it,' he spoke softly, soothingly. 'Let it go.'

I grabbed the window frame to steady myself and retched a couple of times. Not much came up. I drooled a few drops of bile over Mooney's well-polished shoes. Warm, sickly sweet odours wafted up from the voided body beneath me. My head throbbed with knowledge. I had killed. I had killed without mercy.

'Right,' said Harry, crouching down to repack the suitcase. 'We're going out the front door. Nice and calm now.'

Puerto Banus Marina. It was nearly dawn. Giles was loading his yacht. He nodded at Harry's suitcase.

'Is that all you're taking?' he asked.

'It's all I'll need,' Harry replied.

I was still shaking a bit. I chain smoked bitter Spanish cigarettes and paced up and down the quayside. Harry came over. He was carrying a holdall that he had been using for hand luggage.

'The bullets in Mooney will match the ones in Jock. Same forensic. They've already pinned McCluskey on me, so I'll be in the frame for Mooney and all.'

I nodded blankly, then suddenly thought about what Harry was saying. He was going to take the blame. My blame. He handed me the holdall.

'There's stuff in there for Manny,' he said. 'And something for you.'

I unzipped the bag and peered inside. There was a sheaf of papers and a few bundles of cash.

'Your cut,' Harry explained. 'Be careful taking that back home.'

'Where will you go?' I asked him.

He shrugged.

'Tangiers, I guess. Still got a few contacts there. Some of Billy Hill's old mob.'

The sky was getting lighter in degrees of purple. The morning star burned low in the sky. My mind was calm. Horrible clarity. I was a murderer. I would go back to England and carry on with my unremarkable life. Happy enough as a boring academic. No one would suspect a thing. The dreadful knowledge of it would sometimes haunt me amidst empty theorising about social taboos and individual transgressions. A hidden pathological self. A guilty secret. I was one of the Guilty Men now. But Harry would take the blame. I would become the type of criminal that criminologists never study. The ones that get away with it.

Harry jumped down onto the deck of the boat. Giles started up the outboard.

'See you,' Harry called as they chugged slowly out of the mooring. 'Be lucky.'

I stood and watched them sail out into the bay. There was a faint phosphorescence in the wake of the yacht. Like a silvery snail trail. A trace. Soon the water washed over it leaving only a homeopathic mark: the trace of a trace. But unlike me, Harry would leave some sort of imprint on the world. Most of us will vanish, leaving no real signs that we ever really existed. A fugitive leaves behind some clues. They disappear from view but leave evidence of their flight. A desired trail. They are wanted men.

A red blob of sun strained against the horizon. I lost sight of the boat. That was the last I ever saw or heard of Harry directly. But in time a whole series of rumours and stories emerged. He was an unsolved mystery. A regular feature in 'true crime' books or articles about the 'underworld'. He was in Morocco, running a huge drugs cartel. He was seen in the Congo, organising a treasure hunt for millions of dollars of gold buried by mercenaries in the jungle south of Brazzaville. He was running mercenaries himself for UNITA in Angola. He was running guns from Libya to Southern Ireland. He was the real brains behind the Brinks Mat robbery. I somehow knew that he was the source for at least some of these stories, not just to confuse the scent but also because he loved their smell.

JAKE ARNOTT

He Kills Coppers

SCEPTRE

'For I ain't, you must know,' said Betty, 'much of a hand at reading writing-hand, though I can read my Bible and most print. And I do love a newspaper. You mightn't think it, but Sloppy is a beautiful reader of a newspaper. He do the Police in different voices.'

Charles Dickens, *Our Mutual Friend*

1956

Immediate Action Drill

I

Billy's hand rested against the trunk of a tree.

The tree was damp.

He felt along the ridges of bark.

Damp. Warm.

He sniffed his fingers. They smelt of piss.

Human piss.

He looked down. At the base of the tree wet moss bubbled.

He turned to the men behind him. A four-man Reconnaissance Patrol. Tony Wardell, Ronnie Allen, Chin Ho, their SEP tracker, and himself. Billy Porter, Service Number 32265587. Acting Corporal, Section Leader. Lance Jack. Not bad for a conscript. Drafted into National Service straight from Youth Detention. 1st Battalion of the Queen's Own Royal West Kent Regiment. Basic Training at Mill Hill and Canterbury. He found the discipline easy compared to borstal.

He caught the eyes of the rest of the patrol. Everybody froze.

He sniffed again. The sharp tang of urine cut through the funk of jungle humidity and he caught something else in his nostrils. A whiff of exhaled smoke. The unmistakable smell of Chinese cigarettes.

After Basic Training they were shipped out. Malaya. The Emergency. Anti-terrorist operations. Jungle bashing. Stationed at Kuala Kubu Bharu. Taken up-country in Whirlwind helicopters. Fighting Patrols secured rubber plantations and cut into the jungle to set up ambushes against Communist Terrorists. CT. The Charlie Toms. Bandits. Seek out and destroy. They were on a four-day op in the Selangor valley. The Assault Group had sent out Reconnaissance Patrols to track down a CT camp in the area, fanning out into the jungle like the fingers of a hand. A Recce Patrol was supposed to avoid contact with the enemy, seek information and report back to the main patrol. But they had to be ready for anything. Billy was

Patrol Leader. He had to decide what to do.

He leaned up against the piss-stained tree and gently pulled a vine to one side to look beyond. Three bandits were sat in a clearing, sharing a cigarette. Their rifles in their laps, they talked in singsong voices. He turned to the rest of the patrol and gave hand signals. A thumbs-down sign meant CT. He then held up three fingers.

If they withdrew now their movement might alert the bandits. They were so bloody close. If they started firing they could disclose the presence of the whole Assault Force. He only had seconds to decide what to do.

He gave the sign for Immediate Ambush. A hand placed over his face.

Immediate Ambush. This drill is designed to deal with an ideal situation, when there is no problem in gaining the initiative but rather one of making the best use of such an initiative. It is a drill which depends on a very high standard of discipline and training – and the ideal circumstances. Given these factors the killing potential is extremely high.

He pointed to where the bandits were. Tony and Ronnie moved slowly and silently into position. Tony crouched low and brought his .303 up to his shoulder. The clearing where the bandits were resting gave them a good killing ground. Ronnie found a standing position, his Owen gun held against his hip. Billy unslung his Sten and slowly and quietly cocked it.

This method demands high standards of jungle craft and self-reliance which can only be achieved and maintained by training and rehearsal.

It was Chin Ho, the SEP, he was most worried about. He had stayed crouched behind the rest of the group, staring ahead. SEP meant Surrendered Enemy Personnel. Chin Ho had spent nearly fifteen years in the jungle and it had taken its toll. He'd fought the Japanese with the MPAJA until '45, then the British with the Min Yuen until '55, when he had taken amnesty and had been used to hunt down his former comrades. He was a broken man. SEPs often reacted badly during an encounter. There were even cases of them leading troops into ambushes.

An Immediate Ambush should be sited only on one side of the CT line of advance to avoid confusion.

Billy motioned for Chin Ho to lie flat and got into position himself.

The automatic and split-second reaction to a chance encounter must continually be practised again and again under different conditions of terrain and varying circumstances.

All three of them had acquired targets and were ready for Billy's signal.

The Ambush should have depth.

They fired in concentrated bursts, spraying the whole clearing. The CT fell back in spasms as the bullets tore into them. Basic Jungle Warfare Course. Weapons Training. Classification Course Instructional. Shooting on the Classification Range, the Malayan Range, the Jungle Lane Range.

Good instruction and practice – the constant need for shooting practice cannot be overemphasised. If properly taught and coached on the Classification Range, a man will have learned to align quickly and to release the trigger steadily without dwelling on the aim.

They ceased firing. Gunshots echoed down the valley towards the Selangor river. The jungle clattered into startled life above them. They moved forward to check the bodies.

Brass everywhere. All the Patrol officers. The bodies were being searched. Identified. Recovered weapons and equipment lined up on display like a hunting bag. Chin Ho was jabbering away with the JCLO interpreter trying to keep up with him. Not sure if he could actually recognise any of the dead CT. Lots of pointing and crying hysterically. Jungle happy. A Special Branch Liaison Officer was supervising the identification of the dead CT. Everything would need to be collated for police records. The army, after all, were only assisting the civil authorities in their fight against insurgency. The ambush had occurred too far away from a landing zone for it to be feasible to evacuate the bodies by helicopter. So fingerprint kits were issued and an army photographer was on hand. Soldiers were detailed to clean the hands of the dead for fingerprinting. Others washed the faces of the bodies and brushed back their hair so that clear shots could be taken.

The rest stood about in groups talking. The officers in a huddle, assessing the situation. The commanders of the Assault Group and the Support Group in deep conversation. Billy stood near by. He'd already given the brass a short account of the engagement. He could hear the officers chattering away.

'They really should have reported back, sir. I mean, this action's rather given away our whole presence and position to the enemy.'

'That is if there are any other bandits in the area.'

'Well, we won't know that now, will we, sir? They'll be miles away by now.'

'Look . . .' It was the Company commander speaking. 'We can't afford to be dogmatic about operational conduct. We rely on junior leaders to make snap decisions. It's what they're trained for, for Christ's sake. It's what this whole bloody campaign depends on.'

'I'm just concerned about discipline, sir.'

'Well, morale is as important as discipline. They've bagged three bandits, for goodness' sake. We don't want the men to think that they've done something wrong, do we?'

The officers moved on. The Company commander patted Billy gently on the shoulder as he passed by.

'Good hunting, Corporal,' he said. 'We'll have a proper debriefing when we're back at base.'

The whole unit was buzzing with the dull euphoria that comes after a kill. Billy stood on his own, looking up at the canopy of the rainforest. The jungle too chattered away. Throbbing with life. Every living thing fighting for the light above. He lit a cigarette. His hand was shaking but his head was calm. Wonderfully calm.

1966

Breaking the Queen's Peace

EVENING STANDARD, FRIDAY, JULY 1 1966

Before the soccer thousands arrive . . .

'CLEAN UP' FOR WORLD CUP

Drive on London 'clip joints'

An intensive police 'clean-up' is being made of London's West End ready for the thousands of World Cup visitors who will begin pouring in this month.

A special 12-strong squad of detectives working at night with their own radio cars has been visiting 'clip joints' and coffee bars in Soho and Mayfair for the past two weeks.

Scotland Yard CID chiefs have approved the plan of Det.-Supt Ferguson Walker, West End CID chief, to organise a drive against confidence tricksters waiting to fleece the thousands of foreigners looking for a good time in the West End between World Cup matches.

Fruit juice

The 12 detectives, led by Detective Chief Inspector Leonard Read, one of the West End's two deputy CID chiefs, are to be reinforced as visitors begin to arrive for the first World Cup match between England and Uruguay at Wembley on 11 July.

The squad, operating between 9 p.m. and the early hours of the morning, has visited more than 20 one-room 'clip joints' where visitors are lured in – sometimes to one drink, usually a harmless concoction or a glass of fruit juice – and then asked for money on the false promise that they will be introduced to a girl.

The detectives have taken lists of names and addresses of girls working in these one-room 'clubs' and made inquiries to establish their ownership. At least one has closed following police inquiries, but detectives have learned of others planning to open.

Powerless

Frequent complaints from people who have paid sums of money, usually £5 to £20, or handed over 'tips' on the promise that the girls will meet them after the club closes, have generally left detectives at West End Central police station powerless to prosecute for obtaining money with false pretences.

The complainant usually is not prepared to lay a formal complaint or give evidence in court, and many of those who have gone to the police for help after handing over money are usually leaving London within a short time and cannot stay to give evidence.

2

A verbal.

It's always good to start with a verbal.

When giving evidence in court, that is.

A verbal isn't just subtly incriminating. It primes the jury. Sets the scene. Lets those twelve people know that there's been a wrongdoing. It sets the scene, all right. The scene of the crime.

A verbal is just a little bit of dialogue that you put in the mouth of the accused. Something he was heard to say just before, or just after, he was cautioned. Something tasty.

Who grassed this time? That's a good one. Read that out of your notebook in court and it places your man for them. It's about language, see? That's why it's called a verbal. The right words, well, they can place someone. You know what I mean? *Yeah, I done it but you'll never prove it.* Hasn't that one got a ring to it? You see, you're not allowed to mention previous during the trial so the jury isn't to know that the defendant is a villain. That would be prejudicial. But how else are they supposed to know that he's been at it in the past? Do a verbal and it puts them straight. Gives a bit of atmosphere to the proceedings.

It's not as hookey as planting actual evidence on a suspect. You ain't fiddling with the forensics as such. You're just planting the odd word or two.

That's a verbal.

So if this was evidence I was reading out and you wanted a good verbal, how about: 'On the evening of the second of July, Detective Sergeant Frank Taylor was heard to say to Detective Constable Dave Thomas: *Here comes trouble.*'

There. That sets the scene for you. Except it doesn't really count. Not as a verbal, I mean. You see, I actually did say it. I just didn't have any idea how fucking true it would turn out to be. But let's start at the beginning, shall we? Or at least the start of that day.

West End Central, Savile Row. C Division. Crowded Crime Room briefing. Nipper Read out front giving the spiel. Clampdown on vice in Soho. Reinforcements drafted in to swamp the patch. Subtle hints: West End Central needs a bit of a clean-out itself. The area has a reputation – nasty rumours abound about officers on the take. Newly appointed DCI Nipper wants to change all that, apparently. Wants to make his mark. Well known as an absolutely straight-down-the-line copper. Well liked by those who work under him. Short he may be, but tough and tenacious. A fighter. Lightweight boxing champion for the Met in 1950. Story has it that he did stretching exercises to beat the height regulations to get into the force. Transferred from the East End, still smarting after having his case against the Kray twins thrown out of court in the spring.

I'm there as part of the extra officers drafted in from all over the Met, crowded together at the back of the Crime Room. I'd just come out of the one-year Special Course at Bramshill College, waiting to go up to the Flying Squad. Part of the new Rapid Promotion Scheme. Eyed with suspicion by old-school coppers who'd been around longer and hadn't got as far. Not that I gave a fuck what they thought. Time-servers, most of them. I was a bloody good thief-taker. And I was ambitious. I knew where I was going and I didn't mind cutting a few corners to get there. I thought I was fucking clever, I really did.

Right next to me at the briefing was Dave Thomas. We went back. We were aides to CID together back in '62. F Division, Shepherd's Bush factory. Just out of uniform, temporary secondment to plain clothes. He was my partner. My buck. No closer bond, really, than the person you're teamed up with when you're trying to prove yourself to CID. It's a trial period when you're an aide. If you fuck up in that period you can be back plodding the beat in no time. So who you're partnered with, who your buck is, is dead important. We looked after each other. Watched each other's back. There was a shit-nasty DI in charge of us on Division back then. Three pairs of aides went back to uniform in one month. You had to get results. And we got them. Dave had the makings of a good detective, better than me, I reckoned. But he'd always play it dead straight. He'd never do a verbal or scriptwrite a statement.

I was more, shall we say, flexible. Not bent. Well, not bent for myself anyway. Bent for the job? Well, just a bit. Only when you know that they've been at it. When you know they've been at it a little too much and it's their time to go away for a bit. You know they're guilty but you might have to fit things up a bit to take them off the pavement. No harm in that. After all, they might have some smartarse brief who could get them off on a technicality. But Dave never saw it that way. Always wanted to do it all to rights. Impossible to get around him if it was a job we were working on together. And if he noticed anything the slightest bit hookey that I might be doing he'd have a go. 'What are you?' I used to say. 'My bloody conscience?' But he insisted that it wasn't the morality so much as that he didn't want to get into bad habits. Besides, he'd argue, if they're at it there'll always be another time to nick them properly.

And I'd never be bent in a bad way. I'd never take bribes or anything. Do deals for information or bodies, for sure. But never the bung. If you can turn a villain into a snout, well, that's the crucial part of being a good thief-taker. Knowledge, that's what you need.

And as things turned out, me and Dave made a good team. A good double act. Good cop, bad cop, a tried and tested formula. And we both made it on to CID permanent. But it was me that went up for Rapid Promotion. I was the ambitious one, you see. Dave just loved being a detective and wanted to concentrate on getting the experience. And the Bush was a good patch for that. Busy. But I wanted to get on. Did my Sergeant's and got on to the one-year Special Course at Bramshill. Came out made up to DS and just waiting for appointment to Flying Squad while Dave was still stuck in Divisional CID as a detective constable.

I gave him a nod at the end of the briefing. He smiled back and gave me a wink. He was still my buck – you don't break a bond like that. Nipper Read was dividing Soho up into nine different areas, two detectives to each patrol.

'Let's make sure we're working the same relief,' I suggested.

'Yeah,' he replied, still smiling. 'As long as you promise to behave yourself.'

Morale was good on Nipper Read's Clean-Up Squad. For those of us seconded for a fortnight or so there was a chance of a better arrest and clear-up rate than you'd ever get out on Division. Bound to look good on your record. And definite chances of commendations for those who excelled at nicking. But I was itching to get to the Flying Squad. Always a big ambition to work for the Heavy Mob. An élite team. But as temporary secondments go this wasn't at all bad. A bit of fun maybe. And it gave me a chance to work with Dave again.

The regular West End Central officers had already gone around the clubs and clip joints and given the 'warning formula'. Taking names down and letting the dodgy Soho operators know, in no uncertain terms, that their freedom to fleece the suckers was over. Showing the flag to all those Maltese ponces. But a lot of places clearly didn't get the message. Or else they felt the temptation was far too great. World Cup fever. Tourist season gone mad. The chance to make easy gelt from all the gullible fans that would crowd into the West End. And a lot of the foreigners weren't exactly innocent themselves. The draw of the Jules Rimet Trophy brought in con artists and tricksters from all over the globe. An international event. Fraudsters from Mexico and Venezuela, dipsters from Italy, drug-pushers from Holland and second-storey hotel thieves from America. And as they preyed upon the crowd, so we preyed upon them. Me and Dave pulled a whole team of pavement artists doing the three-card trick on Tottenham Court Road. Nicked a pair of Argentinian pick-pockets on the whizz, Latin style, with their own particularly nimble little stall-and-hook routine on the tourists that poured out of Oxford Circus Tube. But it was the home crowd that was really at it. Clipping crazy. Just as one near-beer joint would be closed down through pressure from us, another would set itself up for business. And we'd be ready to play at being the punters, the suckers, the mugs.

'Here comes trouble,' I joked to Dave when this clip girl sauntered over to us.

That's when I said it. The verbal, if you like. We were on the corner of Brewer Street, just acting dumb, like we'd just drifted into Soho looking for a good time like all the rest of the tourists. If only I'd known then what trouble that girl would bring. We knew what she was, or at least what she was up to. But she was different. Not your usual dolly-bird type. She had mousey blond hair cut short, Vidal Sassoon style. She wore a low-cut top and miniskirt, but there was something altogether relaxed about her demeanour, something casual about her dress and the way she held herself. With most tarts it's all superficial. I mean, that's the whole point, isn't it? But with her, well, it was like you might not have noticed with your first look.

But then the second glance. That was the killer. Yeah, then you'd see how beautiful she was and it was like you'd discovered her. It was *you* who'd seen how good she really looked.

'Looking for a good time, boys?' she drawled.

She had these huge mottled green eyes that looked us up and down. It wasn't hard to appear enthralled by them. And there was such a playful way she had of pretending. It made you enjoy the sense of being taken in. Acting innocent. Dave was always better at this than me, of course. And he was a handsome bastard, with his dark Welsh looks. He gave this bird a bashful smile and they just sort of clicked.

'I know this great club,' she went on. 'You could buy me a drink.'

Me and Dave sort of shrugged at each other, like we didn't know the score, and I said:

'Yeah, all right, darling,' with a lecherous tone to my voice. 'Why don't you take us there.'

Let me explain clipping. It has many variations. Sometimes it ain't exactly subtle. The most common variety is the Corner Game. Promise a punter sex but ask for money up front and arrange to meet them later. Then this silly cunt who's already parted with his cash is left hanging around at this supposed rendezvous with no fucking bird. Sometimes the mug is told to wait 'around the corner' (hence the name of the game) and that the money is a deposit on a hotel room, or whatever. Other times the arrangements are more complicated. Under the clock at Victoria Station is a well-worn favourite. Marble Arch, by Big Ben, outside the Ritz – at any number of tourist sites you'll find a clipped punter waiting in vain for a tom who's stitched him up. Nipper Read, in his briefing, said his favourite was Morden, right on the end of the Northern Line, where a poor Dutch seaman was waiting for a girl. He'd paid her £100 and still seemed completely bemused: 'Well, this is where she tells me she is living,' he had said. And although the clip girls don't have sex with punters, they can still be prosecuted under the 1959 Act, if you can prove that they are loitering for the purpose of selling sex. Soliciting. If they are working the Corner Game it is, of course, bloody hard to track them down. But if they are taking you to a club, a clip joint, well, then you can nick them there and then. And then turn over the club itself. They would've had their warning by now, after all. And anyone we didn't actually nick would be logged and cautioned, for the next time. Nipper was dead serious about closing these places down if they didn't get the message. So there we were with what we thought would be a simple job. Put the pressure on, maybe get a few tasty little arrests. Simple? It bloody wasn't simple.

Her name, she assured us, was Jeannie. And the place she was taking us to was described with as much playful confidence as 'a right kinky scene'. But the Pussycat Bar was a depressing place. A couple of bored-looking heavies on the door, obviously employed to stop people leaving too early rather than to prevent anyone entering its plastic bead curtain entrance. The low lighting in the dive couldn't quite hide the peeling flock wallpaper. Six chipboard tables, all empty, were covered with thin paper tablecloths. On a raised area, supported by what looked like beer crates, two tarts who'd long since seen better days did a listless bump-and-grind routine to chintzy organ music piped out on a crackling sound system.

Jeannie showed us to our table and a waitress sauntered over with the near-beer drinks list. I gave it a quick scan and winked at Dave.

'Let's push the boat out,' I declared, tossing the menu on to the stained table-top. 'Champagne!'

'Oh!' Jeannie gave this mock giggle. 'You certainly know how to have a good time.'

'We certainly do,' I agreed, and we waited, expectantly, for a couple of wineglasses filled to the brim with Tizer or fizzy grape juice.

I picked up the drinks list again and squinted in the gloom at the microscopic small print. 'All drinks are de-alcoholised by law,' read one line. And below it: 'Seated covers with a hostess warrants a hostess fee of £10. Acceptance to buy a drink for the hostess is done with the understanding that the customer is going to pay.'

The waitress returned with our drinks on an aluminium tray. All eyes in the dingy club were now looking sidelong at our table. A thickset little Maltese guy in a cheap suit and slicked-backed hair had come behind the bar to eye up his latest victims.

I picked up one of the dirty glasses of fizzy pop and proposed a toast.

'To Jeannie,' I said. 'Our hostess with the mostest.'

Jeannie half smiled, half frowned as she lifted her glass. I stared at her.

'Well, that's what you are, isn't it? Our hostess. That's what it says here.' I picked up the menu and flapped it at her.

If she was at all fazed by this she was bloody good at hiding it. She just smiled. Lovely teeth. Yes, she was good, all right. Too good for this cheap racket.

'Yeah,' she replied. 'I guess. Let's have another drink.'

'Yeah.' I downed the glass in one. Tizer. 'More champagne!' I demanded, clicking my fingers at the bored-looking waitress lighting a fag.

'The thing is, Jeannie,' I went on, 'my friend Dave here is looking for a good time. Aren't you, Dave?'

Dave gave his best nervous nod and grinned.

'Yeah,' he said, all wide-eyed innocent.

'And do you think, Jeannie, as our hostess for the evening, you could arrange something?'

Jeannie leaned across the table and ruffled Dave's thick black hair with another false giggle, her green eyes all wide and limpid. Dave squirmed, part act, part obviously affected by the seediness of the whole charade. I saw his deep brown eyes catch hers for a second. Like he was actually looking into her for something. For a moment it was fucking sad. The whole thing. But it worked. It looked like he was gullible. The waitress, fag in mouth, returned with a fresh tray of Tizer.

'So . . .' I pursued my line of questioning. 'Could you sort something out?'

Jeannie straightened up and coughed, taking her hand from Dave's ruffled locks. She shrugged.

'Well,' she said, breezily, 'let's see.'

The Malteser was starting to hover around our table, making eyes at the boys on the door. Jeannie looked up at him and with a nod he came over.

'Well, can you, I mean, arrange something for me and my friend here?'

But Jeannie was looking up at the man with the slicked-back hair, who was by now standing at our table.

'Gentlemen,' he said tersely, 'it's time you settled your bill.'

We both looked up. I grinned. Dave folded his arms and gave a hard stare.

'Really?'

'Yes,' replied the Maltese. 'Concha,' he barked at the waitress. 'Bring these gentlemen their bill.'

The door heavies moved across to our table. Concha appeared with a hastily scribbled addition. It was placed on a saucer in front of me. *Champagne: £10/Hostess Fee: £10/Cover Charge: £5/Service Charge: £5/Total: £30.*

I picked up the bill and laughed. I handed it to Dave.

'You expect us to settle *this*?' I demanded.

The doormen were now on either side of us, looking menacing. The Malt laughed back at us and nodded slowly.

'Oh yes,' he replied. 'We most certainly do.'

I laughed again, and everybody joined in, even the door gorillas. But not Dave. He was looking at Jeannie with a frown.

'OK,' I said with a shrug. 'Let's settle this.'

I pulled out my warrant card.

'We're police officers. And you are fucking nicked.'

The Maltese blanched and backed off a little. I heard one of the doormen mutter *oh fuck* under his breath. Jeannie looked puzzled.

'Now, gentlemen,' said the Malt guy, suddenly all friendly and shit. 'Let's not be too hasty. Maybe you'd like a real drink. You do drink, don't you?'

Drink. Well, we all know what that means. A nice little enveloped bribe. I could see this was winding Dave up. I'd have been willing to say: *Sorry, son, not this time, we're on our best behaviour*. But Dave wouldn't have seen it like that. Then Jeannie really let the cat out of the bag.

'But,' she said, looking towards her boss, 'I thought we'd already paid.'

Dave's ears pricked up at this.

'What?' he barked.

The Maltese glowered at Jeannie. A slight shake of the head, an open-palmed gesture. Showing out to her to keep shtum.

'What?' Dave continued. 'What do you mean you've already paid?'

Dave was staring at Jeannie. The Malt leaned across to block his view.

'She don't mean nothing, Officer. Do you, Jeannie?'

'No. I mean, I meant, you, you know, have already paid.' She was thinking fast, this one.

'No we haven't,' Dave came back.

'Haven't you?' Jeannie's eyes lit up, all innocent. 'I thought you had.'

Dave frowned at her for a second and then stood up.

'You're nicked, darling.'

'What? What for?'

'Soliciting. Come over here.'

He led her away from the table. The Maltese followed. Dave turned on him and pointed a finger at his chest.

'You, you fucking stay where you are.'

Dave started to read Jeannie her rights. I went over.

'Dave,' I muttered sharply out of the side of my mouth. 'I don't want to start pulling rank here but do you mind telling me what the fuck is going on.'

'You hear what she said?'

'Yeah, I heard. So what?'

'I'm sorry, Frank. But I ain't standing for this.'

This was trouble we could do without.

'Come on, Dave. Leave it, for fuck's sake.'

'But you heard what she said. "We've already paid." You know what that means, don't you?'

'Well, I ain't stupid.'

'So?'

'So what?'

'So, what are we going to do about it?'

'I'll tell you what we're going to do. We're going to take their names, caution them, close down this filthy little joint and then call it a day. That's what we're going to fucking do.'

'But if we can get her to make a statement . . .'

'Saying what? The club bungs a bit of cash towards the Old Bill once in a while. So what, Dave? It happens all the time.'

'Yeah, well, I ain't standing for it.'

'And you want to start making a case against fellow officers?'

'Yeah,' he cut in. 'I know, Frank. I know. Turn a blind eye. Don't make any waves, it ain't good for your career.'

That stung.

'That ain't fair, Dave. You know I'm not bent.'

'Yeah, Frank, I know. And I also know you want to get on in the department. But listen. Any other time we'd have no fucking chance clearing up something like this. We'd be back directing traffic within a week. But we've got special circumstances. This operation is supposed to be cleaning up Soho. Top to bottom. If we can't catch these hookey coppers at it now we never can.'

I sighed.

'So what are you suggesting?'

'Take this bird in. Get a statement out of her and follow it up from there. Take it up to Nipper if need be. We know he's clean and wants this sort of thing dealt with.'

Nobody wants to deal with this sort of thing, I thought. But I didn't say anything. I just sighed again and shook my head. Trouble. Any luck it wouldn't lead anywhere.

'All right,' I agreed. 'You take her in and I'll clean up here. I'll see you back at the factory.'

So Dave radioed the area car and I went about taking names and issuing cautions. The Maltese guy gave a moody name. Arthur Springer. Malt ponces would often stick up English-sounding names as cover. I made a mental note to check with CRO for anyone using that alias.

I got back to West End Central and checked with the custody sergeant. Dave was just finishing questioning Jeannie in an interview room.

'So?' I asked him as he came out into the corridor.

He shrugged and fished in his pocket for a fag.

'She hasn't said much.'

'You charging her?'

'Not yet.'

'You going to?'

Dave sighed and frowned. He took it all so fucking seriously sometimes.

'I don't know, Frank,' he said. 'I was thinking of using her as an informant.'

'For fuck's sake, Dave. A tart as a snout. That ain't a very good idea, you know.'

There's an old copper's rule. The three Ps. Prisoners, Property and

Prostitutes. Any one of them spells trouble. You have to be bloody careful. Standard procedure and common fucking sense. Deal with any of these things in the wrong way and it's you that can be made to look hookey. Especially a tart. She can make all kinds of accusations as to how you've behaved with them.

'I know, Frank,' Dave went on. 'We've got to tread carefully. But we're on to something here. Maybe we should take this upstairs. Like I said, talk to Nipper about it.'

I had to stall all of this. The last thing I wanted was to be caught up in a full-scale investigation against other officers. That sort of shit sticks to you for good.

'Wait a minute, Dave,' I said, thinking on my feet. 'There's no point going anywhere with this without a statement from her. I mean, we haven't got much so far, have we?'

Dave took a drag of his fag and nodded.

'Yeah, you're right.'

'You want me to have a go?'

'Yeah,' he replied hesistantly. 'All right. But go easy.'

I grinned at him. Just like old times. Nice cop, nasty cop. Good cop, bad cop. Except back at the Bush it was me that would go first. Heavy into them. Shake them up, wear them down. Then Dave would appear with a nice cup of tea and a fag and a *tell me all about it before that nasty bastard comes back*. Best way to get them to cough something up. And here we were working it the wrong way around. Arse about front. And I thought, well, maybe this ain't such a bad idea since I don't want her to talk. I want her to keep shtum. *Go easy*, yeah, sure, I'll go easy. I'll scare the stupid bitch into staying quiet about all of this nonsense.

I walked in and slammed the door behind me. She looked up. I'd made her jump a little but she soon regained her composure. I strolled in, slowly, staring down at her. She managed to hold my glare for a moment with those terrific green eyes of hers. Kind of flecked, they were. Like flint.

Then she looked away and chewed her lip. Crossed her legs slowly. Uneasy at first but adjusting into a more upright posture. Shaping up the front.

'How long you going to keep me here?' she asked.

'You ain't bad-looking, you know,' I said as I sat down. 'For a tart. Not been on the game for long, have you, love?'

'I'm not on the game.'

'You know what a tom looks like after a few years. The face starts to go first. It ain't a pretty sight.'

'I told you, I'm not a prostitute.'

'That right? Just clipping, is it?'

No response.

'Just a bit of fun, is it? Conning the punters. Bit of a laugh? Thing is, darling, all the clip joints are being closed down. The fun's over. And your boss might have other ideas for you.'

'What are you talking about?'

'He might want to set you up in a nice little flat. Get you working properly. Would you like that? Nice little flat in the cheap end of Mayfair, new punter every quarter of an hour.'

She tapped a finger against the side of her mouth. Nail varnish chipped on incisor enamel. I leaned over the table a little.

'Would you like that?' I said, a little louder.

'Look,' she snapped. 'I'm not a whore. You can't get me on that.'

I leaned back in my chair and gave a little chuckle. I was enjoying this.

'Oh,' I singsonged. 'Know your rights, do you?'

'I don't have to say anything.'

''Course you don't. I could verbal the statement for you. Look, darling, West End Central is coming down hard on vice. There's a permanent queue of tarts and ponces outside Marlborough Street magistrates'. One girl last week, she knew her rights. Decided to go to Inner London Sessions instead. She got three months. Fancy a stretch in Holloway, do you?'

'No, I don't.'

'Then start co-operating.'

'What do you want?'

'That's better. Your boss's name.'

'Arthur Springer.'

'And I'm the Queen of Romania. His real name.'

She shrugged.

'Attilio something. I don't know his second name.'

'And this business about him bribing policemen.'

Jeannie looked up at me. Flinty eyes wide. She looked worried.

'Look, please, I don't know anything about this.'

I nodded slowly at her.

'Good. We'll keep it that way, shall we? What did you tell my friend about that?'

'I didn't say anything.'

'That's right. You see, my friend has got it into his pretty little head that there's been some naughtiness beyond the usual going on. Now you don't know anything about this, do you?'

She shook her head slowly.

'That's good.' I grinned. 'You liked my friend, didn't you?'

She gave a flat little smile.

'He's a lot more nice than you are.'

Nice. For a moment her face was soft. Childlike. Just for that second she looked so serene. Beautiful. A horrible hunger deep inside. Desire. I thought about how much she must hate me. It made me feel empty.

'Maybe you'd give him one for free,' I said with a sneer.

Her face tensed with disgust.

'You're a sick fucker,' she muttered quietly, contemptuously.

I suddenly felt an unaccountable pang of jealousy. Couldn't place it. Then I thought: maybe Dave's fallen for this tart. Maybe this is what this is all about. I wouldn't blame him. I decided to wrap things up as quickly as possible.

'Well, Jeannie,' I announced. 'It's your lucky day. We're just going to caution you.'

I stood up and my chair scraped against the floor. Jeannie looked up at me, frowning.

'Come on, darling. We're letting you go.'

She walked around the table to the door. I blocked her path.

'You're right to keep quiet about your boss. Those fucking Maltese can be brutal. You know, I once saw a tart whose face had been striped with a razor. Right across. She obviously hadn't been behaving herself. Wouldn't testify against her ponce, though. Silly cow was terrified out of her wits.'

And then I let her pass.

'You want to get out of that business, Jeannie,' I called softly after her. 'It ain't healthy.'

Outside I had a quick chat with Dave.

'She ain't saying nothing,' I told him. 'I'm letting her go. That all right with you?'

'Yeah, sure,' he agreed, a little too readily.

I let Dave process her out. They walked down the corridor, chatting to each other. I felt jealous, sure, but also uneasy, there was a nagging feeling in the back of my mind. Something wasn't right or something was about to go wrong.

Sid Franks always liked there to be a nice story somewhere. Sid was the news editor on the *Sunday Illustrated*. Human interest. Well, that's what it was all about. And amidst all the exposé and gossip you needed something reassuring, something sentimental. A feature that would make the female readership emit a collective sigh of delight. The 'womb trembler', he called it. 'Get me a nice picture of a baby, Eric,' he said one week to the picture editor. 'I'll find a way of putting it in.'

Elsewhere was titillation and scandal – morality through the keyhole. Some big exposé of contemporary importance (THE GREAT SHRINKING BANGER MYSTERY had been the most recent example of the paper's major investigative journalism). And the nasty stories. Something sordid – sex or crime or, hopefully, sex and crime.

'There you are, Tony,' Sid would say, handing me the TORSO MURDER or whatever. 'You'll like that.'

Sid maintained that I had a nose for a nasty story, and he was right. I have a morbid fascination for such things. There's something primal about them that I find reassuring. An infantile pleasure. It could be said that the whole of the *Sunday Illustrated* was an exercise in infantilism, but it was in this, I always thought, that the nasty stories were crucial. Horror is the most infantile feeling of all. A return to childhood when all stories are dark and sinister.

And maybe that's where it all began for me, right at the beginning. I'd had a traumatic birth. My mother never ceased reminding me what a difficult delivery it had been. When she wasn't saying *I've brought a monster into the world*, that is. But it was her fault. She'd nearly strangled me at birth. I'd nearly died, the umbilical cord tangled about my head as I emerged, a noose around my neck as I was pushed through the trapdoor. My birth a hanging, the long drop. Well, nearly. I got a last-minute reprieve, a stay of execution. A diligent midwife managed to unknot me before I choked. Otherwise my whole existence might have been dispatched there and then without too much fuss. Instead it was commuted to Life.

And maybe that's why I turned out the way I did. Difficult

birth, difficult child. My poor stupid mother clinging on to me, always suspecting something sickly about me, something gruesome. I liked to collect things in jam jars. My specimens, I called them. Creepy-crawlies. I found a dead cat and brought it home. I wasn't sure what I was going to do with it – some infantile notion of taxidermy. Of course, Mother wouldn't let me keep it so I buried it in the garden. With full ritual, of course.

I suppose I'd always wanted to write. Ever since I can remember I was making things up, telling tales, nasty stories. But this creativity was never nurtured when I was a child, never understood. *You're a dirty little liar*. My own mother's words. Can you imagine the effect of such an accusation on a young mind? I did well at school but I got into trouble, an unpleasant business that meant that I left earlier than I might have done. I wasn't expelled but the headmaster asked me to leave. Mother was very upset but she never saw my side of the story.

I worked as a clerk in a pickle factory for two years. I did shorthand at night school and got a job as a junior reporter on the *Reading Mercury*. Not terribly exciting, I must say, but at least I was writing. I stuck that for a year or so but as soon as I'd saved enough money I came up to London and got away from Mother, at last. I had some mad idea that it was here that I would become a great writer. I got a cheap bed-sit in West London. Just a few meagre possessions – a Remington typewriter, a battered chest of drawers that I improvised as a desk. I was a loner. I'd always felt different, apart from people, like Colin Wilson's Outsider. I was an existentialist, I decided. As with Barbusse's hero that Wilson refers to, the Man Outside. I had come to the capital with 'no genius, no mission to fulfil, no remarkable feelings to bestow, I have nothing and I deserve nothing. Yet in spite of it, I desire some recompense.' I was meant to be a writer, I felt. This could be my revenge, my way of getting back at them all, my way of articulating my painful solitude. The problem was what to write about? I waited in vain for inspiration. I managed a half-finished first draft of a novel – derivative stuff, purple prose and descriptions of emotions I'd never felt. I couldn't bear to look at it. I kept it in a shoe box under my bed, collecting dust. I had this received notion that a novel should be somehow autobiographical, that fiction should be personal. But the very thought made me feel sick. I didn't want to write about myself, I had no desire to express my inner feelings. On the contrary. I wanted to use ink the way an octopus does, to hide.

The money ran out and I started doing bits of freelance journalism. I had the basic skills for it, after all. The gutter press was teeming with life, with stories. I found what I was looking for, a peephole to look through. I particularly liked crime stories, the more brutal the better.

I worked as a casual on the *Sunday Illustrated*, one of the 'Saturday Men'. On the Saturday shift at the *Illustrated* the newsroom was crowded with casuals, extra staff brought in to get the paper to bed. The inside pages had already gone, so most of the permanent staff didn't have to be in. Sid Franks would pace up and down with a fag in his mouth, browbeaten. He always seemed to wear the same brown suit.

For the Saturday Men there was the day shift for ten guineas or you could work until three in the morning to make it twenty. A lot of the casuals worked on local rags during the week or freelanced for other nationals. I sold the odd story here and there but I hadn't had much luck lately and the Saturday shift had become my main source of income. I needed the money, and I also needed some sort of proof that I could write. And I still harboured literary aspirations. Here, perhaps, I could plumb the depths. I had this little thought in the back of my mind: if only I could find a story, a really big one, something that could get me out of Grub Street for good. Truman Capote had just published *In Cold Blood* that spring, the story of an actual murder done in full. The whole case in beautiful detail with no subs to hack it to death. True Crime executed as High Art. It was hailed as a new form – the 'non-fiction novel', they were calling it. Ken Tynan criticised Capote in *The Times* for waiting for the boys to go to the scaffold before finishing the book, but that was the genius of it. The story needed an ending. It was all done so objectively, as ruthless as the murder itself.

The *Sunday Illustrated* suited my purposes, but what I really wanted was a staff job. It was still nominally a Labour paper back then, but it was no secret that its new proprietor, who Sid Franks always referred to, half in derision, half in fear, as 'The Boss', wanted to make it more racy. Ted Howard was kept on as editor-in-chief to maintain a semblance of continuity and Sid Franks was made up as deputy to lower the tone. The old 'mission to educate' values dropped in favour of a more populist approach. But I'd never been interested in politics, just stories.

I'd been working in Soho that day, getting a bit of colour for the 'Clampdown on Vice' feature we were running that week. Alf Isaacs, the *Illustrated*'s 'snatch man', a photographer whose speciality was catching on film *in flagrante* those who were up to no good, had got a nice shot of a clip joint being raided by some of Nipper Read's Clean-Up Squad. A lovely picture of a clip girl being led out of a near-beer joint into a waiting area car. The circulation manager was a happy man – the northern working-class readership always lapped up vice. The Evils of the Capital, the decadent fleshpots of London – they loved that sort of thing.

I managed to catch Sid in his office. He hardly ever used it except for highly confidential meetings or to bawl out one of his minions. The staff always referred to it as the 'bollocking room'. Sid had started as a casual on the Saturday shift himself back when he'd worked on *Tribune* during the week. He'd once been a leftie, CP member and everything, but after '56 he'd torn up his card and had been moving increasingly to the right ever since. Now he constantly railed against the print unions and loved any excuse to do an exposé on 'pinkos, liberals, do-gooders'.

He'd just come from the Saturday conference. The Big Table, they called it. All the editors would hammer out that Sunday's edition with Ted Howard, still nominally editor-in-chief, with his Thermos flask and greaseproof paper packet of sandwiches next to him, nodding silently at the head of the table.

Sid closed the frosted-glass panelled door, sat down behind his desk and stubbed out his cigarette. He gestured at the seat beside me. He picked up a finished page on his desk and gave a pained expression. He sighed and waved it absently at me.

SUMMER SCORCHER, was the headline. *Crowds clamour for the coast as temperatures soar*. There was a picture of a girl in a bikini, caught in midair jumping for a beach ball with her chest thrust out.

'Look at that,' he muttered. 'Another of Franklin's titless wonders.'

Harry Franklin was the paper's main portrait photographer, specialising in the obligatory glamour tit pics. He was good at getting a photo of some near-naked bird in a salacious pose next to a flimsy excuse for a story, but for some reason he always managed to pick flat-chested girls.

'We're never going to get our circulation figures up unless he can get birds with bigger tits. I mean, what do you think of that?'

He thrust the picture in my face. I recoiled slightly. I never quite knew what to say about girls.

Sid shrugged and dropped the sheet on to his desk. There was a white crust around the corners of his mouth. He took sodium bicarbonate to combat nervous indigestion and his lips were regularly flaked with it. He squinted at me across the desk. I handed over my copy and Alf Isaacs' snatch of the clip girl being arrested.

'That's more like it,' he said, picking up the glossy. 'Now she's really got something. Good work, son.'

'Sid . . .' I began.

He looked up at me with a suspicious frown.

'What do you want?'

'Well, I was wondering if there was any chance of a staff job.'

He sighed and rolled his eyes.

'I'm a good reporter. You said so yourself.'

'Yeah, yeah. Well, you've got a nose for it, I'll give you that.'

'So?'

'Well, I thought being casual suited you. Gave you time to work on your masterpiece.'

When word got around the paper that I'd been trying to write a book it had become a running joke. I gave a thin smile.

'Look, son,' he went on, 'I'm running a tight ship here. I can't really afford to give out too many permanent contracts.'

He was right. It made better sense to employ a lot of casuals for the Saturday shift than to take people on a weekly basis.

'I think I'm worth it, Sid.'

'Oh, you do, do you?'

'Yeah, I do.'

'Well, if something comes up, I'll bear you in mind.'

'You'll think about it?'

'Look, if you come up with something really tasty' – he licked his powdery lips – 'if you can prove you're worth it, well, you never know.'

A mystery. That's what they called them. A girl come down South to escape God knows what drudgery. A runaway. No past, no history.

A mystery. Looking for somewhere to stay. Easy to pick up. Easy to impress.

Billy noticed her first. He was sitting in a booth of the Ace all-night café on Goldhawk Road with Jimmy and Stan. They'd done a job that day and were flush with cash and still buzzing from the excitement of it all. She was at the back peering gloomily over a long-nursed cappuccino. Froth turned to scum on the glazed rim of the cup. Duffle bag on the seat next to her and a worn-out look on her young face. Telltale signs.

A couple of mod kids were showing off at the pinball table. Thrusting away with their hips as they tickled the flippers, like they were giving it one. Stealing glances over at the mystery girl to see if she was watching. She ignored them and lit another cigarette.

'We want to do something proper next time.' Jimmy was talking animatedly in a low voice. 'A bank. We want to do a bank. Need to nick a good motor for the getaway.'

Jimmy was always talking big. Stupid Glaswegian thinks he's hard, thought Billy. Thinks he's the leader because he's the oldest. Hair scraped over his stupid balding head like Bobby Charlton. Billy had met Jimmy in the Scrubs. Always talking big plans in association or as they plodded around the exercise yard. They'd met up again earlier in the year and Jimmy had introduced him to Stan one night in the Hop Garden Poker Club in Notting Dale, and they'd all kind of teamed up.

Stan just sat there nodding. Docile. Some fucking gang, thought Billy. He was bored already. Sure, they'd screwed a bookie's that very afternoon. And he'd been the one waving the shooter around. He was the one that knew how to handle guns. Jimmy and Stan were hardly more than gas-meter bandits.

'Uh,' croaked Jimmy, nodding towards Billy. 'What you reckon, Bill?'

Jimmy sounded nervous. He was a bit scared of Billy but anxious not to sound like he was deferring to him too much.

'Yeah, sure,' replied Billy, looking over at the mystery girl.

They hadn't got much from the bookie's. Just over three hundred quid. Not many in the shop. Everyone watching the football. The England–Mexico game. Not many punters about, which made it easy, but also meant that there wasn't much in the way of takings. Bit of a thrill, holding the place up. Stocking masks, American Tan. Made the face look yellow and flat. Like a bloody Chinese. Bandits. Weird feeling, the head squashed into something that should be around a bird's thigh. The mesh wet about the mouth and nostrils. A bit kinky. The mystery girl was stubbing out the cigarette, picking up the packet of Park Drive. Empty. She let the hollow cardboard drop on to the Formica.

Billy got up to go over, picking up his fags from the table. The mod boys had their backs to him, in a huddle over the pinball machine. Bill saw a bag of purple hearts on the glass surface.

'This face I know works for Roche out at Welwyn Garden City. He's nicking 'em and selling 'em six quid a thousand down Wardour Street.'

The mod doing the talking was wearing a fishtail parka. *The Who* stencilled on the back. *Maximum R&B*. The Who? Who the fuck are the Who? thought Billy. An arrow coming out of the O. No fucking sense. The parka like a uniform. Jungle green. Army surplus. Like Billy. Surplus to requirements. They didn't want him. Tried to get into the SAS after National Service. He had a good record. Corporal stripes and plenty of commendations. He'd seen a lot of action. But his borstal form counted against him. He was offered a place in Two Para in the Territorial Army Regiment at White City. Territorials. Fuck that for a game of toy soldiers, he'd thought.

'Excuse me, boys.'

The parka mod scooped up the pills and turned around. Speed-nervous, jaw chewing away. Billy gave them a grin that brought out the scar below his right eye. Intimidate the little hooligans. The cold stare that says *I've killed people, you cunts*. They moved back. Gave Billy a wide berth. The mystery girl looked up.

She saw Billy, suddenly woken from her runaway reverie to clock his arrogant swagger. A hard man with a boyish face. Late twenties, she reckoned.

'You seem to be out of cigarettes,' he said.

'I was trying to give up anyway.'

He offered her one from his packet. She shrugged.

'Oh, go on, then,' she said with a tired smile. She pulled the cigarette out of the packet. Grubby fingers. Chipped nail polish, bitten cuticle.

'Mind if I join you?' he asked.

'Suit yourself.'

He sat down and lit her fag, lit one for himself. Tried to place her accent. Northern.

'Where you from, darling?'

'What's it to you?'

She was acting all tough. Like a kitten that puffs itself up for protection.

'Only asking,' he said.

'Leeds.'

'So, what, you've run away?'

'You're full of questions, aren't you?'

Billy smiled and took a drag from his cigarette.

'Give us another cup of tea, mate!' he called out over his shoulder. 'And what do you want?'

'Cappuccino.'

He grinned.

'Yeah. And one of those frothy coffees for my friend here. What's your name, love?'

'Persistent, aren't you?'

'Yeah, that's right.'

He knew all he had to do was keep chatting. Chatting her up. She was all alone in the big city. Nowhere to stay. In the end she wouldn't really have any choice but to come home with him. The café owner came over and put two steaming cups down on the Formica table between them. She stirred her cup thoughtfully and looked up at him.

'Sandra,' she said. 'My name's Sandra.'

'Pleased to meet you, Sandra. I'm Billy.'

She scooped a spoonful of froth into her mouth. A dab of foam stuck to her upper lip.

Billy watched her sleeping. Sandra was curled up with her thumb in her gob like a little kid. She'd hitch-hiked down from Leeds the day before. A lorry driver had dropped her off on Shepherd's Bush Green. 'What you come down to London for?' he'd asked her, and she'd just shrugged. He'd lit the gas fire and they'd undressed under the gloomy forty-watt bulb that hung unshaded from the ceiling of the bed-sit. She'd gone through it all without any fuss. Like she knew what was expected of her. A blank look on her face like that Chinese whore in KL. Afterwards they lay together on the bed for a bit. She traced the tiger tattoo on his right shoulder.

'That's nice,' she'd said. 'Never seen one like that before.'

'Had it done in Malaya,' said Billy.

Sunlight streaming through the dirty cutains. Picking out motes of dust in the air. He lit a fag. It was Sunday morning. He'd have to get going soon. He gave her a nudge.

'I got to go out.'

'Where you going?'

'Going to see me mum.'

'Oh.'

He didn't have time to get rid of her. Couldn't really take her to see Mum. Couldn't just kick her out.

'You can stay here if you want.'

'Can I?'

'Yeah. Just don't touch anything.'

Billy would always try to visit his mother on Sunday. It took him back to when it had just been the two of them. Little Billy. Mummy's little soldier. Mummy's little man.

He'd been born in the Red Lion Hotel in Wanstead. Just a big pub, really. Mum always wanted things to be better. She was always trying to make it work as a hotel. Dad just drank away the profits, bringing in all sorts of dodgy clientèle. Making it just a big pub again. Dad was supposed to be the manager. All he could manage was to get drunk by lunch-time. All sorts of things went on in the public bar. Dad used to fence stuff.

Rows, shouting matches. Little Billy at the top of the stairs listening.

Then Dad left. Came into Billy's room to say goodbye.

'I tell you what your mother is, son,' he muttered boozily. 'She's a whore.'

Billy didn't even know what a whore was. When he found out, he wanted to kill his father for saying it.

Business picked up a bit after Dad left. Mum had never realised how much of the takings he was drinking or spending on horses. Or dogs. Or tarts. But the brewery said that they couldn't stay.

They moved to Paddington. Mum got a job in a restaurant. Manageress. Put enough money aside to send Billy to a private school in South London. But he didn't fit in. The other kids laughed at his accent. They called him 'Southend Sid'.

He started getting into trouble. At fifteen he was on probation for receiving. Two years later he was done for assault with intent to rob. Eighteen months' borstal. Gaign's Hall, Huntingdonshire. A strict regime. Plenty of exercise and hard labour. He went straight from there into National Service.

After demob he got a job driving a van in North London. It bored him shitless. He got the sack when he was caught nicking from the warehouse. He met this girl who worked as a stripper in the Cabaret Club in Praed Street. Trixie. She had strung him along, let him spend his money on her. He'd drifted back into trouble again. House-breaking. He did a tie-up one night in a house on the Burma Road and the stupid old fucker wouldn't tell where he'd stashed away his savings. Billy had cracked a cut-glass decanter over his head. The old bugger had nearly croaked. Trixie got picked up on a soliciting charge and she'd grassed him up, the rotten bitch. He ended up in the Old Bailey. Robbery with violence. He got seven years. Wormwood Scrubs. He served four years eight months.

Sunday roast. Billy bought a bottle of Mackeson's for her and a large bottle of light ale for himself. Best linen tablecloth laid out. Napkins in silver rings he'd nicked in a house-breaking and given to her as a present. He'd carve.

'How's business?' she'd ask.

She'd saved up a grand while he'd been inside. Given it to him to start a business. He'd learned a trade in the Scrubs. Bricklaying. He'd also done art classes. This bloke had come in once a week to teach painting. Billy had loved that. The teacher had said that he had a 'real feel for it'. This had brought sniggers from the other cons and sneers from the screws. Billy didn't care. He found himself absorbed by it. Form and colour. The classes had lasted only a couple of months, though. Prison was all right. Eat your porridge every day, do your time the easy way. Discipline. He was used to that in the army. Coming out, he was supposed to just go straight. Mum was always worried about him. Gave him the hard-earned money to set up a little building firm. And he'd gone along with it. But it bored him rigid. He hated laying bricks. He hated walls.

He'd started to lose jobs and end up in all the pubs and clubs he'd frequented before he'd gone inside. He'd bumped into Jimmy in the

Cabinate Club in Gerrard Street, and before he knew it he was at it again.

'Going through a lean patch, Ma. Bloody Harold Wilson's bad for trade.'

'Billy,' she said chidingly. 'You staying out of trouble?'

'Oh, don't go on, Ma.'

He got back to the flat at about four in the afternoon. She'd found the gun. Silly cow had found the .38 revolver. Billy had left it under the bed. The bloody thing was still loaded. He'd lost all his training discipline, he thought. Post-operational procedure. Zero your weapons. Armourer's inspection. He'd become fucking sloppy.

'Put it down.'

She held it up in front of him.

'Is this real?' she said, with a stupid grin on her face.

'Put that fucking thing down!' he barked at her.

She let it drop on to the dresser.

'How was your mother?' she asked.

He picked the gun off the chest of drawers and pulled out the cylinder. Bullets clattered over the floor.

'You ever shot anyone?'

He sighed.

'No,' he replied. 'Not as a civilian.'

A civilian. That was a joke. Demobbed and chucked out on to the street. Borstal training. National Service. Prison. He'd had no time to be a civilian. He felt the weight of the gun in his hand. It was reassuring. He could trust it. He couldn't trust Jimmy or Stan with their stupid plans for blags and capers. And he couldn't trust this northern girl.

He slapped her across the face and she fell on to the bed.

'I thought I told you not to touch anything,' he said coldly.

She started crying into the pillow like a child. He felt a bit bad about that. After a while he sat on the edge of the bed and stroked her shoulder. He put the revolver down carefully on the bedside table. He'd get another one soon. Maybe an automatic. Sandra was still sobbing. He ran his fingers through her hair.

'There, there,' he murmured.

The sobbing subsided. She was just a little kid, really.

'Shh,' he shushed, soothing his own mind with the white noise of it as he stroked her hair. 'Shh.'

3

I didn't have this Maltese ponce Attilio's second name so I couldn't request a file search from CRO. I had to go down myself. Scotland Yard. Central Office. Coco, we always called it. Looking for a body with only a first name to go on. I thought of going through the Method Index but I didn't have any particular MO for my man. Then I figured on cross-checking alphabetically. A lot of the Maltese would use English-sounding moody names but keep their first initials. For example, Alfredo Messina called himself Alfred Martin. Not exactly subtle. But then most detective work is looking for the bleeding obvious. You'd think that they'd be a bit more clever. Maybe they've got bad memories or they're scared of losing their identity or something.

So I went through foreign-sounding names starting with S. It took a bit of time but there he was: Attilio Spiteri, known to use the alias Arthur Springer. Checked the file. Blurred photo of him. On the form: convicted of Living Off Immoral Earnings in 1962. Malicious Wounding in 1956. Known associate of the Messina gang. Suspected of being active in prostitution rackets in Soho and Mayfair.

On my way out I nearly bumped into Vic Sayles. Flying Squad DI. Tall, dark-haired, charismatic man in a well-tailored suit. A reputation for cultivating snouts. Known as the best-informed police officer in the Met. My future Guvnor, I hoped. We'd worked together when I was in F Division and his team were plotting up an armed blag on our patch. It was him that recommended me for the Flying Squad.

'Sir,' I said, giving him a nod.

A squint, then a smile. Recognition.

'It's Frank Taylor, isn't it?'

'Yes, sir.'

'I thought you were coming to join us. There's a gap in my team. My best DS has just got promotion, the bastard.'

'Yes, well, sir, I've kind of been drafted into West End Central. They needed extra officers.'

'Nipper Read's Clean-Up Squad, is it?'

'Yeah. It's just for a couple of weeks. I'd much rather be on your squad, sir.'

'Well, I'll see if I can't hurry things along. Been at Bramshill, haven't you?'

'Yes, sir.'

'Could do with a college boy. Hope you're good at paperwork. I need a good scriptwriter. If you know what I mean.'

He gave me a sly wink. I smiled back.

'Thank you, sir.'

'Well, I'll be seeing you.'

He started to walk off. I had a sudden hunch. Sayles's encyclopedic knowledge of villains.

'Sir?'

He stopped and turned.

'What is it, son?'

'You don't know anything about a certain Attilio Spiteri, do you?'

'Spiteri. Let me think. Yeah. One of the Messinas' old gang, ain't he?'

'Yes.'

'Well, look, son, vice ain't exactly my manor. But I tell you what. You want to ask George Mooney. He's the expert. He knows all the Maltese.'

Tracking down George Mooney wasn't difficult. The Premier Club on Little Compton Street. Known for its mixed clientèle on both sides of the law. A bit seedy. A good place to get information, though. George Mooney, new DI at OPS. Obscene Publications, the Dirty Squad. West End Central used to be his patch. Known for heavying into the Maltese. Commendation for breaking the Ricardo Pedrini racket back in '61. A bit of a reputation for over-the-top fit-up tactics here and there. Rumours of him planting bricks in leftie demonstrators' pockets. A bit of bother with the National Council for Civil Liberties but nothing proved. A stocky man with cropped hair and beady little eyes. I introduced myself and bought him a drink.

'You at West End Central?' he asked.

'Well, temporary secondment. I just finished the Special Course at Bramshill.'

His little eyes lit up.

'Ah!' he exhaled. 'On the Rapid Promotion Scheme, are we?'

'Yeah, and I was going to Flying Squad but they needed extra officers on this West End operation.'

He nodded and pursed his lips.

'Nipper Read's Clean-Up Squad,' he announced with contempt.

'Yeah.'

'Shortarse Read. The new broom sweeps clean.' He grinned. 'But the old broom knows all the corners.'

Mooney tapped his nose.

'I used to work West End Central,' he said.

'Well, it was that I wanted to talk to you about,' I began.

'I tell you what you need to do,' he cut in. 'You have to contain it. Filth, vice, lustfulness. The sins of the world. You can't clean them all away. That's what that little cunt Read fails to understand. Nick them and they just start to fester again. You need to keep a lid on it. You have to deal with the temptations of the outside world but remain above them. One has to look within.'

'Sorry?'

He was starting to lose me.

'To keep oneself clean. There's none more pure than the purified.'

He sipped his Scotch thoughtfully.

'Anyway, it was your knowledge I was after,' I said.

'Really?' He smiled. 'What do you want to know?'

'I wanted some information on a certain Soho face.'

'Who?'

'Attilio Spiteri.'

Mooney's little eyes flickered for a moment but otherwise he remained impassive. He put his drink down.

'Oh yeah?' he murmured. There was a soft caution in his voice.

'You know him?'

'Yeah,' he replied. 'He was an informant of mine. What's the matter? Has he been at it?'

'Well . . .'

'Can't trust the spicks,' he spat with sudden venom. 'What's the little Maltese toerag been up to? Maybe it's time he went away for a bit.'

'Well, it's a delicate matter.'

'Really?' he asked with a prurient smile. 'What?'

'I've heard a little rumour that he's on the bung.'

Mooney picked up his glass and held it in front of his face.

'He tell you that, did he?' he asked flatly.

'No. Not exactly.'

'Because they do, you know. Always trying to implicate others in their sordid little ways. What did he say?'

His beady eyes narrowed into a piercing stare.

'Well, it wasn't him so much, just this tart we picked up who clips for him.'

Mooney looked thoughtful. He took a sip of Scotch. He swallowed and let out a sharp sigh.

'A woman?' he declared disdainfully. 'Well, you can't trust them, can you? Irrational creatures. She's probably lying.'

'You think so?'

'Second nature to them. Look, people are always trying to implicate police officers. It's an old trick.'

'So you wouldn't know about anything like this?'

'Certainly not.'

Mooney held up his empty glass. I bought him another drink. As I sat down next to him his little eyes darted around the room then settled on mine. He leaned closer.

'Are you on the level?' he whispered.

'Sorry?' I retorted, a bit indignant.

'I mean' – he smiled – 'are you on the square?'

Then I twigged. This was freemason talk. One of their codes.

'Er,' I replied hesistantly, 'no.'

'You know, West End Central, Vine Street, Bow Street, all of C Division. The Manor of St James, if you like. It's a forcing house, that's what it is, son, a forcing house. A hotbed of vice, wealth, deviousness of all kinds. A fetid place. It's so easy for a young officer to go astray. Temptation. You know what I mean, don't you? I mean the spirit is willing but the flesh . . .'

Mooney sniffed and gave a little shrug. I started to say something but he held up a hand and went on.

'You know what they say, don't you, son? If you're off the track, get on the square. You know?'

I nodded indulgently.

'You know what profane means, don't you?'

I frowned.

'Well, um, swearing and that, isn't it?'

'Blasphemy, yes, son, certainly. But it literally means "outside the temple". You get my meaning?'

'Well . . .'

'The profane world can drag you down. Through the Mysteries of the Craft you can keep yourself clean. The All-Seeing Eye of the Great Architect. *Lux e tenebris*.'

'Sorry?'

'Light through darkness. That's your actual Latin.'

'Really?'

'Ancient arcane knowledge. Oh, yes. There is a world within the world. And it can bring much comfort. I mean, the work that I do – all the filth, the sinful and beastly degradation I have to be witness to. I couldn't do that without my lodge. It's a purifying thing. A column of mutual aid and support. Think about it.'

I nodded.

'A young officer like you amidst the fleshpots exposed to desires and temptations. You need guidance. Society has given up on moral standards. You know what I had to do this week? Investigate a so-called art exhibition. Pure filth. A group of dirty long-haired hippies have filled a gallery full of obscenities and called it art. Full-frontal nudity. We take them to court and they make a joke out of the whole thing. *Regina versus Vagina* one of these hippy rags call it. Charming. The thing is some of the so-called respectable papers take their side. Standards are falling. No respect for authority. Society has lost its way. One has to give up any arbitrary social notion of morality. The Craft teaches you to look to the restraining standards of morality that reside in one's own soul.'

'Really?'

'Oh, yes. You know what I do?'

'No.'

'I ask inside. This is the Path of Honesty.'

'Yeah, well . . .' I started, trying to change the subject, but he went on.

'More than you'll ever learn from college, you know. And it offers its own promotion scheme, if you know what I mean.' Mooney emitted a dark little chuckle. 'The Winding Stair. Believe me, if you really want to get on, get on the square.'

'I'm sure you're right,' I agreed. 'But about Attilio Spiteri.'

'What?' Mooney frowned. 'Oh yeah, that little slag. Want me to have a word?'

'Um . . .' I hadn't really thought. 'Yeah, all right,' I agreed.

'I'll find out what he's been up to. Now, listen.' Mooney leaned close to me, bad breath sweetened with Scotch. 'You could join my lodge if you wanted to. I could propose you as an Entered Apprentice. A rough ashlar. The stone that must be hewn and shaped. What do you say?'

His tiny eyes twinkled. I coughed.

'Well,' I replied hesitantly, 'I'll certainly give it some thought.'

'Good lad. Now, let me buy *you* a drink.'

'When they got rid of hanging it was an end of an era in crime reporting,' Sid Franks once told me. 'You just don't get the sense of drama any more. The place of execution. The wait for the last-minute reprieve which hopefully never comes. The long drop. There was this one freelancer I knew, Harry Tibbs. Bit of a con man really. He used to get in to see the condemned. Not as hard as it sounds. He'd usually pose as a clergyman. I used to see him wearing a dog-collar in the Feathers on Tudor Street. He'd get all these letters off people waiting to hang and sell them to us and other papers. Good stuff, it was. Funny thing was he was an abolitionist. "I'm against it in principle," he said, "but when they get rid of it it's the end of my profession."'

The sense of completed narrative was all gone. A conclusion, that's what gives it all some sort of shape, makes it a story. Can't have a story without an ending. The climax, if you like (speaking of which, Sid also told me that he'd heard that a certain High Court judge would have an orgasm when he passed the death sentence. The Clerk of the Court would be instructed to have a spare pair of trousers ready whenever he was to put on the black cap, but that's beside the point), the End, that's the point. Life, well, it just doesn't have the same ring to it. That's why Truman Capote had to wait for the boys to swing and did nothing to help save them.

With particularly brutal murders the *Illustrated* would often call for a return to capital punishment. 'Bring Back the Rope' was one of Sid's routine editorial comments. And if not then Life should mean Life. A life sentence, it should mean something. Life should mean Life.

And he was calling for the noose that spring. The Moors Murderers were rich pickings, dark tales unfolding in what Jack Appleyard, the *Illustrated*'s northern correspondent, described as the 'sunless assize court of Chester'.

I got a week's freelance work with the paper. We were trying to buy up witnesses or family members connected to the killings, knocking on doors and leaving calling cards with a fiver tucked underneath. The *News of the World* beat us to it with David Smith, the main prosecution witness, who'd actually been there when Edward Evans was hacked to death by Brady. Promised him £1,000, after the trial, if the terrible two were convicted. So we ran a spoiler instead, denouncing these deplorable journalistic practices, discrediting witnesses and so on. An inside source said the police had found a diary of Smith's with the entry *people are like maggots, small, blind & worthless*. I liked that.

I managed to get a couple of days in the press gallery during the trial but it was Jack Appleyard's story. His style was flat and sombre. He did nothing with the extraordinary forensic evidence, the dog hairs found on Evans's anus, the photographs and the tape recordings. This was all rather played down. Instead he seemed obsessed with Myra Hindley's hair. 'Blue-rinsed and ash-blond, piled up in a sort of semi-bouffant' at the beginning of the trial and 'fresh-yellowed in a peroxide perm' at the end. The copy in double-page half-columns on pages ten and eleven squeezed between the advertisements for underwear and constipation cures.

Nylon Corselet at pre-Budget prices! A delightful corselet in Nylon Taffeta. Absolute comfort is assured with full length Elastic side panels.

In the dock they 'showed no emotion' as the sentence was passed.

RUPTURED But 'On-Top-of-The-World' Thanks to the NEW *'Autocrat'* AIRMATIC RUPTURE APPLIANCE.

Life should mean Life.

I wanted to write something about the motivation behind the killings. I saw a twisted romantic angle, a classic *folie à deux*.

'*Folie à deux?*' Sid Franks had retorted. 'What the fuck's that, some French dance act with birds with their tits hanging out?'

'No, Sid,' I replied patiently. 'It's madness shared by two people. An obsessional relationship that leads to crime.'

'Well, we ain't having none of that. No explanations please. No "A Doctor Writes" with these two bastards. They're evil, pure and simple,' he declared, licking his crusted lips.

Pure and simple. Given the nature of my entrance into the world it seemed hardly surprising that I became obsessed with strangulation. My own nostalgia for the noose, my own lonely call to bring back the rope. I experimented from an early age with asphyxiation, on myself and on others. Just childhood playfulness at first, making each other faint on the playing fields, stuff like that. But with the onset of puberty I found that the pleasure of masturbation could be greatly enhanced with something tight around my neck, and with the thought of myself strangling somebody else. The mass murderer Carl Panzram enjoyed pain so much that he imagined that he was endowing it on his own victims, that he was bringing them joy as he killed them. The fact that I had similar thoughts frightened me. I began to want desperately to repress them, but I couldn't – there were too many things that gave rise to lustful visions in my mind.

Then one day, in the school library, leafing through Roget's Thesaurus looking for long words to show off with, I came across 'Punishment': *bodily chastisement, smacking, trouncing, hiding, dusting, beating, thrashing, t. of a lifetime, kicking, caning; whipping, flogging, birching; scourging, flagellation, running the gauntlet; ducking, keel-hauling; slap, smack, rap, rap over the knuckles, box on the ear; drubbing, blow, buffet, cuff, clout, stroke, stripe; third degree, torture, peine forte et dure, racking, strapado, breaking on the wheel, death by a thousand cuts*. And so it went on: *rack, thumbscrew, pilliwinks, Iron Maiden, triangle, wheel, treadmill, torture chamber, scaffold, block, gallows, gibbet, Tyburn tree, cross, stake, Tarpeian rock, hemlock*. I became more and more excited as I read all these awful things. The very words themselves caused a dreadful tumescence. But, I reasoned, if words could stimulate such feelings in me, then might not I be able to use their own power to articulate and control my desires? I suppose it was then that I felt the lonely impulse to be a writer. It could be a salvation of sorts –

I could write out my awful wishes, create word-hoards of my secret longings.

So if my imagination could be given a free rein in artifice I might be spared its degradation in reality. My nickname at school was 'weirdo'. Not a particularly cruel example of playground nomenclature. Being perceived as strange was a fairly good defence policy. I had crushes on other boys but I resolved to resist enacting any of my urges. But I gave in to what I thought might be a harmless fascination and it proved my downfall.

In a locked wooden cabinet in the biology lab was a stillborn baby in a jar, curled up in a cylindrical womb of fluid. I was transfixed by it. It reminded me of the 'specimens' I'd collected as a child and I wanted it. It seemed to glow from within when held against the light, wreathed in silvery bubbles, glistening with augury. Translucent skin, tiny hands clutching at the broken cord that was wrapped around it like a fouled anchor, lizard lidded eyes bulging with sleep. It looked so peaceful, so perfect. I felt a kind of jealousy of one dispatched at birth as I should have been. Can there be any worse fate than to be sentenced to Life? Existence is a cruel trick. Life should mean Life. The dead baby looked so calm, so much at peace, not like me, tormented and cursed. So I stole it.

The headmaster made a big fuss when they found out it was missing. It was a terrible crime, he announced in assembly the next morning. The culprit would be punished severely, he promised. Somebody blabbed and I was accused of it. But I denied it. The head said if I'd only admit to it, there and then, they could deal with the problem. Something was wrong with me to do something as sick as that. If only I'd come clean. Then I could be sent to the school psychiatrist or whatever, they could straighten me out. But I wasn't admitting to anything. They couldn't prove it, you see. They'd never find the baby. I'd buried it by the edge of a field, in the damp warm earth beneath an electricity pylon that hummed with power.

So I was asked to leave the school and it broke my poor mother's heart.

Another Saturday shift. The rest of the newsroom was buzzing with the World Cup game. Bloody football everywhere. England v. Argentina. It was a dirty game, though, that was some consolation at least. Argentina's captain sent off, police on the pitch as he'd refused to leave, the referee exiting the field with a uniformed escort at the end of the match.

'Dirty fucking dagos,' was Sid Franks' unofficial leader comment.

Alf Ramsey, the England manager, was himself outspoken about the game. The splash-sub led on the front page with: *'ANIMALS!' says Alf. Foul Play as Latin Lunacy plunges game into chaos.* A nice touch, we all agreed. But otherwise it was a slow news day and Sid only needed me for the one shift so I knocked off at ten. I arranged to meet Julian after work. The *Illustrated* was on Shoe Lane. I wandered down through Holborn into the West End.

Julian was another Saturday Man, though less of a regular than me. His real speciality was gossip. He'd wasted his youth by being kept by various rich queens, one of whom had said to him, 'Jules, what will you do for money once your looks start inevitably to fade?' And so he'd decided to write. He'd become quite well connected. He'd feed tidbits of scandal to Sid Franks and any other editor who was keen. What he really wanted was his own column, but he was too lazy and prone to drunkenness to get ahead. Always a slothful eye on the lookout for the easy way.

We usually met in the Casbah Lounge coffee bar but it had been closed down for the duration. The big Clean-Up had taken hold of Soho. Most of the clip joints and tacky dives closed up, hardly any girls on the streets. Or boys. We ended up meeting in a dingy drinking club in Piccadilly.

I'd first got to know Julian when I went back to his bed-sit on Portobello Road after we'd both done a second shift. We drank Nescafé and I talked earnestly about existentialism while he sat nodding at me languidly. In the early hours, his patience gone, he leaned over and patted me on the knee. I tried not to flinch. The sudden contact made me feel a bit sick.

'So tell me,' he'd said. 'Are you so?'

'So?'

'Yes.' He'd rubbed my leg. 'You know.'

I'd pulled back. So?

'I . . .' I coughed. 'I don't think so.'

'Then' – he'd smiled mischievously – 'are you TBH?'

'TBH?'

'You know. To Be Had.'

To Be Had. Was I to be had? I felt an awful tightening around my throat as we fumbled about on the sofa. Bad thoughts in my head. Horrible urges. Julian grabbed at my crotch. I was hard. I suddenly stood up.

'What's the matter?' he'd asked softly.

In proper crime journalist style I made my excuses and left.

I remained friends with Julian, though. He could be horribly bitchy and scathing, but when he wasn't too drunk he was quite entertaining.

That evening the talk was about Teddy Thursby, who'd just started to do an opinion column for the *Illustrated*. I told Julian how he'd made a pass at me. I'd been helping him get his copy filed and I'd noticed his intent, knowing gaze. 'You shouldn't be on a paper like this,' he said to me furtively. 'Let me take you to the south of France to meet Somerset Maugham. If he places his hand on your knee, do not recoil as you do with me.'

'Mmm, I know a thing or two about that one,' said Julian.

He noticed a man earwigging our conversation.

'*Vada the homi marconi*,' he hissed.

Julian still used this archaic homo slang. *Look at the man listening in*, he meant. *Marconi* being used to indicate a gesture of eavesdropping, hands to the ears like radio headphones. He glared over at the man, who shuffled away sheepishly.

Later on he chatted up a swarthy-looking man with lank greasy hair. They planned to go to a party somewhere.

'Want to come?' he asked. 'We might find somebody for you.'

'No thanks,' I replied.

'Go on,' he tried to insist. 'Live a little.'

Live a little. Life should mean Life. I walked out into the night. Piccadilly very quiet, the Meat Rack nearly empty. A few sad junkies huddled around Eros, loitering outside Boot's 24-hour chemist's, keeping their heads down. Tourists drifting in happy groups up through theatreland. Above, the flashing advertising hoardings, coloured lights pulsing, constellations spiralling over my head. My temples throbbed in drunken melancholia.

A young man in a denim jacket leaned by the doorway to an amusement arcade, a mop of blond hair, blue eyes that clicked with mine as I walked past. Pinprick pupils, voice hoarse and languid.

'Got a light?'

I struck a match. The boy's face underlit with phosphor flare, his pinched little face marvellously demonic. He was trying to look tough, a rough-trade act that might work on a timid old queen. The 'I'm-not-bent-I'm-rent' demeanour. Murderous thoughts in my head as he sucked at the damp pith of the filter tip and glared at me, his throat pulsing as he inhaled.

I hurried off to find a cab to take me home. Life should mean Life.

Billy had heard about this Greek guy who was selling. He arranged to meet him. The Dionysus Restaurant. Finsbury Park. Run by this big guy Tony. Rumoured to be part of Harry Starks's firm. A private room out the back. A bottle of Metaxas on the table. Costas, the seller, sat with a small glass in front of him. He stared at Billy intently. He nodded at the chair opposite. Billy sat down.

'Costas,' he announced, and offered his hand.

Billy took it and shook it.

'Billy,' he replied.

Costas poured Billy a drink.

'Tony says you are looking for something.'

He spoke slowly, with a heavy Cypriot accent.

'Yeah, that's right.'

'Well, I got something.'

'You got it here?'

'Yeah.'

'Well, let's have a look, then.'

Costas reached under the table into a toolbag on the floor. He brought out something heavy wrapped in a grease stained cloth. He rolled it out on the table. A pistol. Billy picked it up. The angled butt fitted into his palm pleasingly. He slid the magazine out and clicked it back in again. He worked the action on it. Brought it up to his eye to look along the barrel.

'Luger,' Billy named it. 'Nine-millimetre. Very nice.'

He weighed it in his palm. Held it up in front of Costas.

'Now, this wouldn't be the gun that shot George Cornell, would it?' he asked with a smile.

Costas grinned back. He had a blackened front tooth.

'No,' he said, shaking his head. 'No. It has been in my family for years. My uncle took it off a German officer before the partisans hanged him from an olive tree.'

Costas grinned again. Billy put the gun back down on the rolled-out cloth on the table. Costas looked down at it, then up at Billy.

'You know how to use a thing like that?' he asked.

'Sure,' replied Billy. 'I was in the army.'

Costas leaned back in his chair. He frowned across the table.

'Where you serve?' he demanded.

'Malaya.'

Costas leaned forward and picked up the gun.

'I was in EOKA,' he said, quietly. 'If you had served in Cyprus, I might have shot you.' He held up the gun. 'With this.'

'Yeah,' Billy agreed, smiling. 'And I might have shot you and all.'

They both laughed. Billy picked up his glass and held it up. Costas took his and knocked it against Billy's. They drank.

'So,' Billy went on, 'how much you want for it?'

4

Late relief with Dave. We had a fairly dull evening of it. All quiet on the patch. I didn't mention my little meeting with DI Mooney. I hoped he'd forgotten all about that girl. I couldn't quite get her out of my mind, though. Dave seemed quiet, pensive. But that's the way he is.

This German fan comes into the station with a complaint. Seems he's picked up this tart on Old Compton Street. They've gone back to his hotel room and she's whizzed his wallet. Familiar story.

'I do not understand,' he said. 'She seemed such a nice girl. And so good is the sex we were having.'

He gave us a description. She wasn't hard to find. There she was plying her trade in the same place. She was Indian or half-caste or something. Petite with delicate features. Very pretty. She didn't make any fuss when we nicked her.

But there was something odd about her. Something I couldn't quite put my finger on. She had this mannered way of talking. Exaggerated gestures. Play-acting flirtatious. There was no sign of the wallet. Dave was doing the reasonable approach and I was supplying a bit of threat as per usual.

'You're very sweet,' she said to Dave. 'But I like your friend better. He's *so* tough.'

She was taking the piss.

'Look,' I cut in, with an edge to my voice. 'This is getting us nowhere. Let's go and get a WPC to search her.'

Well, she just rolled those big brown eyes of hers.

'I think you better do that yourself, big boy,' she drawled, her voice just a little bit too husky.

Then I twigged. I started to laugh.

'What's up?' Dave asked.

'Well, for a start,' I said, 'we're going to have to charge our friend here with importuning, not soliciting.'

'You mean . . .' Dave was wide-eyed. Slow on the uptake, but he'd been a bit vague all evening.

'That's right honey.' She-who-was-really-a-he fluttered his eyelashes. 'I'm a talented girl.'

The German tourist was shocked when we told him.

'This, this cannot be so,' he spluttered. 'I am not believing this.'

I did a quick frisk which gave the little tranny an excuse for more camp nonsense. But we didn't find the wallet. Understandably, our foreign visitor didn't want to press any charges. So we just did the fairy for importuning for an immoral purpose.

'You're very convincing,' I told him. 'On the face of it.'

'So are you, darling,' he replied with a wink. 'So are you.'

We came off duty at about three in the morning. I asked Dave if he wanted to go somewhere for a drink.

'Nah,' he replied. 'I'm going to get off.'

I wanted to have a bit of a chat. We hadn't really talked much that relief. That business with Jeannie kind of hung in the air between us. Unfinished. I found myself brooding about the situation. About her. I wanted her off my mind. And I relied on Dave. I could trust him. I could trust his judgment. Usually. But with this thing, well, I wasn't so sure. I wanted to tell what I'd found out about the ponce, Spiteri. That maybe we should go up against him. He was the real villain, after all.

'Come on, Dave,' I pressed him. 'Come for a quick one. We could do with it.'

'Not tonight, Frank,' he replied wearily. 'I'll see you tomorrow night.'

I don't know what it was that made me follow him that night. Dave kept himself to himself, for sure, but we were pretty sociable with each other. I just felt there was something edgy about him. It made me worried. And suspicious.

I watched him leave the station. He walked in the opposite direction from where he'd parked his car that evening. Something was up and I was on his tail.

Now, it ain't easy tailing somebody on foot at the best of times. It makes me laugh when you see it done in films or on the telly when they are, what, fifteen yards behind the person they are following.

I mean, that's a fucking joke. And with an experienced detective like Dave was, I had to be bloody careful. But the West End is a maze of little streets so I let Dave get to the end of the road he was on and hoped that I could judge which way he was turning, catch up and watch him again from the next corner. I felt like a fucking rubber-heeler. Checking up on him like that. A fellow officer. A friend.

He went along Clifford Street and crossed over Bond Street into Mayfair. Curzon Street. Shepherd Market. A row of prostitute flats. Dave rang the buzzer of one of them. I saw him talk into the intercom. Another buzz and Dave pushed the door open. He went in. I watched all of this with incredulity. Dave was the straightest copper I ever knew. What the fuck was going on?

A light went on in a third-storey window. I could make her out. The short-cropped hair. Jeannie. It was her. She had ended up just where I said she would. She was opening the door of the room for Dave. For a minute I could see the both of them in profile. I felt sick. Dave gone over the side with this tart. Good cop gone bad. That's what this was all about. And I was jealous. I wanted her. I wanted her even more seeing her with him.

Jeannie went to the window and pulled down the blind. I'd seen enough anyway. I had a horrible sinking feeling. Like I wasn't sure of the ground beneath my feet. I mean, Dave, for Christ's sake. Mooney was right, I thought, the West End had a bad atmosphere about it. Vice duty could drag you down. Take you over the side.

I went up to the flats. A row of buttons by the door. Third floor was marked NEW YOUNG MODEL. I pressed second floor: FRENCH LESSONS. The door buzzed to let me in.

I flashed my warrant card at the tart on the second floor and ushered her back into her flat.

'Close the door and keep your mouth shut,' I told her.

I crept up to the next landing. Ear to the door. I could hear them.

'There's nothing much I can do unless you make a statement.'

'But I'm scared. Your friend's right. Attilio's a real nasty bastard.'

'How did you get involved with someone like him?'

'I was working as a go-go dancer in this club in Paddington. He took me out. We had a really good time together. Then he got me clipping. It was a laugh, at first, then, when the clip joint got closed down, he made me work here.'

'Made you?'

'He beats me. Threatens me with worse if I don't do what he says.'

'Look, Jeannie, you've got to get away from all of this.'

'Help me,' she pleaded.

'I will. But you've got to be prepared to testify against him. Look, think about it. Keep in touch. You know how to get hold of me.'

I could hear Dave walking towards the door.

'Stay for a while.'

Her voice soft, plaintive. Touching him, holding him.

'No, Jeannie.' Dave's voice clear, definite. 'That ain't what I'm here for.'

'Please.'

Dave at the door. I crept up the next flight of stairs and flattened myself against the wall. The door opened.

'Don't go yet,' she said. 'I'm frightened.'

He patted her shoulder tenderly. Gentle, innocent.

'Look, Jeannie, we can work this one out. Call me.'

And he was gone. I waited until I heard the front door slam and then went down and rapped on her door. She opened it. She was wearing a silk red kimono thing.

'Hello, darling,' I said.

A gasp of shock. Flinty eyes flashed. Pinprick pupils. Probably doped.

'You,' she said. 'But Dave said . . .'

'Dave doesn't know I'm here. I followed him. I thought he was up to something.'

'What do you want?'

'Aren't you going to let me in?'

She stared at me with a slight sneer. Then a little smile opened up on her mouth.

'Yeah,' she drawled. 'Sure.'

We went inside. The room was bare-bulb bright. A cheap Formica sideboard with a bottle of Johnny Walker's on it. A mirror screwed to the wall by the bed.

'So, what did Dave say?' I asked.

'What?'

'You were about to say. "Dave said", you said.'

'Oh yeah.' She sounded vague. Acting dumb or just stoned. Or both.

'Well?'

'He tracked me down. Wanted to ask me some questions. I said what about that bastard partner of yours and he said it didn't involve you.'

So Dave didn't trust me on this one.

'Want a drink?' asked Jeannie, picking up the bottle.

'Yeah,' I replied. 'Why not? He tracked you down?'

She gave a bitter little laugh.

'Yeah. It wasn't difficult. You said yourself that this is where I was headed. He wants to help me get out of here. Isn't that sweet?'

I stared at her. A head full of ugly thoughts. She handed me a glass.

'But you,' she went on, 'you're not like that, are you?'

She pulled at her gown, showing a shoulder and part of a breast. Creamy white skin brought out by a purple bruise on the top of her arm. 'You want this. Don't you?' she taunted. 'You want a free one.'

She smiled, her mouth slashed with lipstick. I drank down the Scotch in one.

'Come here,' she said. 'You'll do just as well. Better.'

'What are you playing at?'

'Come.'

She grabbed my lapel and pulled me over to the bed.

'Look.'

She nodded at the mirror, loosening the sash of her gown. The kimono thing came open, exposing her naked figure. I watched her and me staring out from the glass.

'Me, you, me, you.' She pointed and chanted like a child doing dibs. 'All four of us. Quite a party.'

'Whatever you're on, darling, you ought to go easy.'

'Oh yeah. I go easy. Come.'

She pulled me down on the bed and ran a hand down my front to the fly of my trousers. Unzipping me with an ugly little laugh. I was hard.

'C'mon, honey,' she whispered, huskily. 'I'm supposed to be nice to you.'

I tried to kiss her on the mouth and she pushed me away.

'Uh, uh.' She grabbed my head and turned it to the mirror. 'Keep watching the show.'

I knelt over her as she scissored her legs around me. She arched her back and, lifting her hips, guided me into her.

'This is what you want, isn't it?' she taunted.

She went through the motions. Talking dirty to make me come quickly. Coarse oaths, pretend ecstasy. Easily learned. Me panting and thrusting blindly. Full of need. Part of my brain hating it all. Hating her. Hating me. The rest of my head sick with desire. Hungry. Eating up all of the hatred, lustily. I looked down at her. She pushed my face towards the mirror again.

'Keep watching,' she said.

I saw my face in the glass. All clenched up. Blood thumped around my head in a steady rhythm. Beating it into blackness. Calm oblivion for a second then a sharp dawn of the senses. Red haze then white light, bare-bulb sharp.

All over. I felt all choked up. She sighed and pulled away from me. Lit a cigarette. I stood and did up my trousers.

'Well,' she said, mouth wreathed with smoke. 'That was easy enough. Got what you wanted?'

I raised a hand to slap her then let it drop and ran it across my face. My mind dull. Her face tightened then straightened out to stare back at me. Flint eyes. Cold, hateful.

I got out of there. As I went I noticed a silver-grey Ford Consul parked up with somebody in it. Someone else was plotted up. Watching.

Dawn. Birdsong in Soho Square. The sun coming up over the grimy city. I got a Sunday paper and found an all-night caff open in Tottenham Court Road. Breakfast. I barely had the stomach for it. Match report from the England–Argentina match on the front page. A dirty game.

Julian became my only confidant and a pretty unreliable one at that. He wasn't exactly known for his discretion. I tried to explain to him that I was more than just queer. But he didn't really understand. I'd allude to my actual proclivities and he'd just giggle and make some fatuous remark. He thought I was just 'kinky', as he'd put it. But at least there was some fellow feeling between us, a kind of *esprit de corps* against normal people. 'The norms,' Julian would call them dismissively. 'Look at them all, norming about.'

The *Illustrated* ran a feature, HOW TO SPOT A HOMO, a while back. There'd been another spy scandal and a lot of talk about the danger of queers in security-sensitive postitions. The article had expert advice from a 'psychiatrist' who was actually Dr Kenneth Forbes, the *Illustrated*'s resident drunken quack, who'd narrowly avoided being struck off by the BMA back in the fifties and was usually responsible for the 'A Doctor Writes' column in the paper. Various 'types' were identified and all sorts of clues offered as to how to 'pinpoint a pervert'.

THE MIDDLE-AGED MAN, unmarried, who has an unnaturally strong affection for his mother. THE CRAWLER. THE TOUCHER. The man who has a consuming interest in youth and is ready to give ALL his spare time to working and talking with boys or youths. THE FUSSY DRESSER. THE OVER-CLEAN MAN. The man who is ADORED BY OLDER WOMEN. The man in the bar WHO DRINKS ALONE and is forever looking at other customers over the top of his glass.

Julian found the whole thing hilarious and sent it up terribly. He could somehow get away with being camp and flamboyant. I think the rest of the shift were a bit scared of him. And Sid Franks tolerated him because he always felt he could verify scandal and gossip. 'Say what you like about these poofters,' he once confided to me after a few drinks in the Three Feathers, 'when you're checking those kinds of facts they're rarely wrong.'

'Anybody with a grain of sense can *smell* the homos among these men,' the booze-ridden Forbes assured the readership. But I made sure nobody sniffed me out. I could not have chosen a profession in which being queer was more of a handicap than it was in Fleet Street. Its morality was that of the saloon bar. Every sexual excess was spoken of and usually bragged about just as long as it was 'normal'. I managed to passably imitate this demeanour. It wasn't difficult, going along with the comments about 'crumpet', the jokes about queers and pansies. They wouldn't find me out – I was to be nobody's 'type', nobody's specimen.

She began to notice how badly he slept some nights. Twisting about in the bed. He'd tense up and mutter hoarse oaths. His face clenched up in fear and aggression. He was back in the jungle. She knew that much about him now. He'd said something about it once when he'd woken up in a cold sweat, screaming. But he didn't like to talk about it much.

It wasn't easy living with him. The bed-sit was small and only half furnished. But it was better than the back-to-back in Hunslet where she'd come from. Her bedridden father drunk half the time. Invalided from an industrial injury in a cardboard box factory in Kirkstall. Sickness benefit didn't go far. Dad crippled and full of hate. Banging his stick on the floor of the bedroom when he wanted something. Swearing at Mum, leering at her. Finding any excuse to touch her. Calling her his *little princess*. She hated him and she hated Mum for putting up with it all. But Mum couldn't help it, poor cow. Trapped, she was. I'll never be trapped like that, she promised herself. She got a job on the broken biscuits counter in Woolworths in the town centre. She'd go out with her girlfriends on a Saturday night. Get chatted up by lads who might splash out on a brandy and Babycham and try to impress her with some tired old patter in the hope of a knee-trembler in one of the shop doorways on Briggate. There's got to be more to life than this, she thought. She dreamed of escape.

And one morning she simply upped and left with just a holdall and the little bit of money she'd saved. She had no idea of what she would do, of what would happen when she got to London. But at least her life had some sort of story to it.

Billy had called her a 'mystery'. She got to know that this was what guys in London called runaways. Strays. No past. Easy to prey on. Easy to get rid of. Cheap. But she liked the word. It was romantic to her.

Billy wasn't easy to live with. Moody. Always liable to fly off the handle. She learned quickly not to ask too many questions, not to touch any of his stuff. Especially his guns. He'd regularly take them out, strip them down and oil them lovingly. She knew that she should have been more frightened of all of that than she actually was. She understood it somehow. How he loved these little mechanisms of power. The way their parts clicked together was so satisfying, so reassuring. And Billy would show her their differing principles. Automatic. Revolver. Spring-loaded magazine. Rotating cylinder. An automatic was faster, Billy explained, but if it jammed your whole magazine was fucked. A revolver was slower but more reliable. And it left less forensic. No cartridge cases all over the place. But it took longer to reload. Have one of each, Billy insisted, and you're sweet. She was determined not to be scared by all of this. Billy had been in trouble before and would probably be in trouble again. She didn't care. In fact, for the moment, she found it all quite exciting.

It was a hot summer. She had thought about looking for work but Billy always insisted that they wouldn't have to worry about money. She'd get a job when the weather turned colder, she decided. In the meantime she could enjoy the sunshine. She felt carefree for the first time in her life. She knew that it couldn't last. She'd spend whole days with Billy. Going into the West End. The city was full of people showing off the latest fashions. She got Billy to take her to Carnaby Street. He bought her a multicoloured minidress. They spent the afternoon lazing about by the Serpentine Lido. Watching people in the hazy sunlight. She liked the childish sense of freedom in the air. The Swinging City. The Beautiful People. Of course, Billy had no truck with these types. 'They ought to bring back National Service,' he'd mutter resentfully. But Sandra felt that he was a lot more exotic than any of these so-called rebels. On the inside, at least.

In the evening they went to Shepherd's Bush Odeon to see *The Glass Bottom Boat* with Doris Day and Rod Taylor. In the cool darkness Billy held on to her hand. A stupid Hollywood film. Technicolor. People don't fall in love like that, she thought. Love isn't like that. Love is – she squeezed Billy's hand as she thought this – desperate. She felt cleverer than the brightly coloured images up on the screen. And more romantic.

5

I went to see Nipper the next day. I thought hard about what I was going to say to him. I didn't want to drop Dave in the shit, just get him away from the West End. I figured Nipper would simply want it nipped in the bud and just transfer him back to Division, sharpish. I wanted a transfer of my own, too. I wanted to get to Flying Squad sooner rather than later. And I wanted to get out of West End Central. Away from her. Jeannie kept nagging at my mind. It was me that had gone over the side. And someone had been watching that night. Someone plotted up in a motor.

'I'd like a word, sir.'

I towered over him. He smiled and nodded at a chair.

'Well, sit down, son.'

Nipper sat on the edge of his desk.

'So, what's this about?' he asked.

'Well, it's the DC I'm working with, sir. He's kind of got a bit friendly with one of the girls.'

It was an easy lie. Nipper sighed and shook his head.

'Oh dear,' he said.

'He's a good officer, sir. And a good detective. It isn't like him. It's just . . .'

'He's given in to temptation. Well, it happens.'

'I don't think there should be a disciplinary or anything, sir.'

Nipper nodded slowly then looked straight at me.

'So, what do you think I should do?'

'Send him back to his own factory.'

'Out of harm's way?'

'Yes, sir.'

'Right. Well, that's probably the best course of action. Thanks for bringing this to me swiftly, son. I can't afford to jeopardise the operation. I'll deal with it.'

He stood up.

'Another thing, sir.'

'Yes, son.'

'I wondered if I might be taken off this particular duty too, sir.'

Nipper frowned at me.

'Why's that, son?'

'Well, with respect, sir, the operation hardly needs so many officers any more. Soho's never been so clean.'

'Yeah,' Nipper nodded, thoughtfully. 'But for how long? I guess I could spare you too. Where are you?'

'Well, I was about to go to Flying Squad when I was seconded to you.'

'Oh, yeah. You're the Bramshill boy, aren't you?'

'That's right, sir.'

'Keen to get on?'

'Yes, sir.'

'Ambitious?'

'Well, I guess so, sir.'

'Not too ambitious, I hope.'

'I love the job, sir.'

'Well, that's the main thing.'

Late relief. Orders had come through transferring us from the operation. We went for a drink. Now Dave did want to talk.

'I don't understand it,' he said as I brought a couple of pints over to our table. 'What the fuck's going on?'

I sat down and took a sip of beer. I let out a sigh.

'Well,' I said, 'they don't need so many bodies on this job any more. It's all quiet on the West End front.'

I smiled. Dave didn't see the joke. He supped away, brooding.

'Look, it's nearly all over. It's the final on Saturday. Most of the tourists are on their way home. The whole of West One is as clean as a whistle. We ain't needed. I'm glad to be out of it, if you ask me. If anything they'll need extra Old Bill to protect the referee, if that Argentina game's anything to go by.'

'But they haven't transferred any other officers. Just me and you.'

'Well, Nipper's probably reducing the squad gradually, you know? Anyway, if we beat Portugal Tuesday we'll be in the final. Do you reckon Ramsey will play Greavesie?'

Dave frowned at me.

'I didn't come for a drink to talk about the football, Frank.'

'Right,' I said flatly.

I traced a finger around a circle of liquid that my pint glass had made on the table.

'So,' I went on, 'what's on your mind, Dave?'

'Did you know about this?'

'About what?'

'About us getting transferred.'

'Look, Dave, if you must know, I had a word with Nipper.'

'You did what?'

'Certain things were getting out of hand.'

'You can say that again.'

'Look, mate, I know you've been to see that tart Jeannie.'

Dave stared at me. Fierce.

'I told you I wanted to find out what was going on with that clip joint,' he said.

'And you didn't think to tell me that you were actually going to do anything about it?'

'No.'

'You didn't trust me?'

'No. To be honest, Frank, I didn't.'

'Thanks a lot, mate.'

'Well, let's face it, you weren't exactly keen to do anything about this, were you?'

'Do anything? Do anything? What the fuck have you been doing? Visiting whores off duty? You're well over the side on this one.'

'What do you mean?'

'Well, it just looks like you've got a thing for this bird. The way you've been going at it. It looks well dodgy.'

Dave looked at me pityingly.

'You really think I'm like that?'

'It don't matter what I think, Dave. If anyone else found out what you'd been doing, what would they think, eh?'

Dave shook his head.

'You're such a cunt, Frank.'

'Look, even supposing anything was up, do you think anyone's going to believe the word of some cheap tart? Allegations against serving officers? Do me a favour.'

'So it was you, wasn't it?'

'What?'

'That asked for this transfer.'

'I was protecting you, Dave.'

'You were what?'

'How do you know that this girl wasn't trying to set you up? She's a clever bitch, that Jeannie.'

'You bastard,' said Dave quietly, and stood up.

'Look, Dave, stay and have another drink. I didn't mean it to turn out like this. But it's for the best, mate. Really it is.'

He started to walk out.

'Dave!' I called out after him.

'Goodbye, Frank,' he said, without looking around.

The 'rich and rare' is another of Sid Franks' favourites. Strange but true, believe it or not stuff that was always a staple of the *Illustrated* which the splash-sub would have fun with. LAWN ORDER – a man sells his house but takes all the turf from his garden when he moves; THUGS BUNNY – a public house's pet rabbit, brought up with dogs and imagining itself to be one, savages an after-hours intruder. Sid would often think that the particular eccentricity of some of these stories was wasted on the great unwashed. 'This story is too good for our readers,' he'd say. 'They just won't appreciate its rich and rare quality.'

And summer, of course, was traditionally the silly season. It was also, that World Cup summer, when people started talking about 'Swinging London'. There had been that *Time* magazine article in the spring and suddenly even the yellow press had terms like 'groovy' and 'with-it' turning up in its copy. Julian was allowed the occasional fashion spread for the *Illustrated*. He decided to investigate the 'Beautiful People'.

Of course, with the West End Clean-Up clampdown, Soho wasn't actually that swinging. So he ended up dragging me along to the homo haunts on the King's Road instead – Le Gigolo coffee bar and the Hustler, with that ridiculous motorbike hanging from its ceiling.

And our own area had become fashionable now. I was living in a crumbling rooming house in Walmer Street. West Eleven, the Bed-Sit Jungle. Half the street had been demolished to make way for the new Westway flyover. To the west was Notting Dale, a white working-class enclave; White City, dog track and dodgy council estate. To the east was the black ghetto between the Groves, Westbourne and Ladbroke, West Indians everywhere. The Polish woman in the flat below complained that things had gone bad ever since *Rachman got the schwartzes on the de-stat.* White long-hairs into jazz and bluebeat; hippies, attempting to look cool as they nervously hung out in the shebeens and record stalls around the Grove and the Gate, trying furtively to score a 'quid deal' of grass. Squats and communes sprouted up here and there, multicoloured graffiti on the crumbling stucco of the half-derelict mansions along Elgin Avenue. Protest, that's what they were all talking about. And Letting It All Hang Out. I didn't like the sound of that. Keeping It All In, that was my slogan. I lived there because it was cheap. Julian loved the atmosphere. I think he hoped that these long-haired bell-bottomed types might be TBH.

There were other expeditions. We went to the El Rio on Westbourne Grove. We sat awkwardly amidst the lively atmosphere of the place, West Indians grouped noisily around tables eating chicken with rice and peas, drinking Cockspur rum they'd brought in themselves. There was the sound of dominoes being noisily slammed on a table at the back. We were the only white men in the place. A peroxide blonde and a ginger-haired girl were being chatted up enthusiastically in the corner. We were eyed up suspiciously. Julian began to put on his coquettish act. I kicked him under the table.

We were harassed by this young dealer and ended up purchasing a quid deal. Julian was very keen to try it. We went back to his flat and he clumsily assembled a joint.

'Come on,' he said with a smile, 'let's "turn on".'

I wasn't so sure. I didn't want to mess about with my mind. But we both ended up smoking this horrible, reeking stuff, coughing and spluttering.

Nothing seemed to happen at first.

'Think I'd prefer a pink gin,' Jules declared, and then collapsed into a fit of giggles.

I just felt a bit nauseous and a nasty paranoid state descended upon me. Julian talked of a new magazine he was getting involved with, an 'underground' publication. He was their token queen, it seemed. In his heightened state he was burbling on about colours, offset litho printing. Why didn't I get involved? he was asking. They needed writers, they were having a meeting next week. Why didn't I come along? There was a party afterwards. A Happening.

The room went into a lurching spin. I went out to the bathroom and retched into the sink. My head throbbed with horrible demons.

He took her to see Mum. Sunday dinner. Billy seemed more nervous about it than Sandra was. He made such a fuss. He wanted her to look as smart as possible. It was a special occasion. He bought wine and put on his best suit.

'Has Billy been behaving himself?' Billy's mum asked Sandra.

'Oh, Ma, please,' Billy interjected.

'Well, he's fallen in with a bad lot in the past. He needs someone to look after him. Someone to keep him on the straight and narrow.'

'I can take care of him, Mrs Porter,' said Sandra.

Billy's mother smiled.

'Call me Lily, dear,' she said. 'Everybody does.'

Lily asked Sandra all sorts of questions. She lied about her age and the fact that she'd run away from home. Lily asked Billy how the business was going.

'It's looking up, Ma,' he said with a smile. 'We got a big job coming up.'

After the meal Billy took a cup of tea over to the armchair in the corner and read the Sunday paper. Sandra went to help Lily wash up in the kitchen.

'He's a good boy really,' Billy's mum explained. 'It nearly broke my heart when he went inside. He's always been up to something, has that one. I tried to do right by him. Sent him to a good school but he got thrown out of there. He treating you right, dear?'

'Yeah.'

'All I ever wanted was for him to do well for himself. To better himself. I never had the chance. I just wanted him . . .'

Lily's voice broke into a sob. Sandra saw that she was crying. Her hands were covered in suds and so she was dabbing at her eyes with her wrists. Sandra went up to her and, wiping her hands on the dishcloth, patted her on the back.

'It's all right, Mrs Porter,' she said softly.

'Lily, please.' Lily snorted up tear phlegm. 'I'm just a silly old woman.'

'No you're not, Lily,' Sandra lied.

'Come on,' Billy's mum announced, pulling herself together. 'I got something to show you.'

She led Sandra into the front room. Billy was slouched in the chair reading the sports page. He glanced up. His eyes were dull, cold.

'Been having a natter, have we?' he asked, and slurped at his tea.

'Look,' said Lily, taking a photograph album down from the shelf. 'You can see what he was like when he was a kid.'

'Oh, Ma,' Billy complained. 'For Pete's sake.'

The two women sat on the settee, poring over the pages, cooing at the images of infant Billy. Billy sighed and looked sheepish. Sandra thought about how his mother had spoiled him. Doted on him. *Silly old woman*. It hadn't done him any good. One of the pictures showed Billy, aged six, dressed up in a little army uniform.

'Look at that,' said Lily. 'Mummy's little soldier.'

A hot, muggy night. It brought the jungle back. Tangled up in other memories. Playing in the woods when he was a kid. The tension of being on patrol merged with the dark excitement of childhood games. Insurgency, counter-insurgency. Hide and Seek. Seek Out and Destroy. *If you go down to the woods today, you're in for a big surprise*. Count to a hundred. Moving slowly and silently through dense rainforest. Always alert. Always ready. *Remember Track Discipline. DO NOT signpost the route with litter, such as cigarette packets, sweet papers, cigarette ends and waste food. All these should be kept and burned. DO NOT while away the time by plucking leaves and breaking twigs – this blazes a trail.* Boys playing at war in the forest. *If you go down to the woods today you'd better go in disguise*. Count to ten. Identification of Dead CT. The bodies of the dead bandits they had killed being prepared for photographing and fingerprinting. *It must be borne in mind by Security Forces at all times that while the killing of individual CT is in itself a worthwhile object, the identification of the body may be of even greater value*. 'Smile, please,' somebody joked. The bodies being searched. Sometimes men took some sort of trophy off a dead enemy when the officers weren't looking. For good luck. *Picnic time for teddy bears*.

Landing Zone. A Whirlwind helicopter clattering above like a huge insect. Rapid Eye Movement. Flickering into life. Billy was semiconscious. Coming to the surface. Trying to debrief his thoughts. After the ambush in the Selangor valley he'd given a full report to his CO. All the details of the engagement. Then on to the range. Whenever troops had fired their weapons in contact with the enemy, they were sent out on to the range when they were back at base. It was an opportunity to correct any mistakes made in an ambush. There was a tendency to aim high, at the light face of a bandit, rather than at the body. A tendency for each member of the patrol to select the same target. There were misfires and stoppages through failure to clean, inspect and test weapons and magazines. It was never said, but Billy suspected, that being ordered on to the Jungle Range after a kill was a way of depersonalising the whole process of killing. Making it routine and systematic again.

The sun streamed in through the dirty curtains. Billy blinked at the light. Sandra snored softly beside him. He rubbed his face; his mind felt drained from his dreaming. Everything was so vivid there, so alive. Intense. Malaya was still more real than the dull grey city that he awoke to.

6

Last day at West End Central. Paperwork to finish off. I tried to find Dave but he wasn't about. Or else he was avoiding me. Instead there was a message for me from George Mooney. He wanted to meet me in the Connaught Rooms in Great Queen Street. I suddenly remembered the business about Attilio Spiteri. I'd forgotten about him. Maybe Mooney had found something out. He said he was going to have a word.

At first I figured, well, that's all done with now. But then I thought about that greasy little ponce and all of my anger and frustration kind of got fixed on to him. It was all his fault. This whole business had soured things between me and Dave. It had got out of hand and I was fuming about it. Someone, as sure as fuck, was going to pay for all this aggravation. Too late to nick him since I was no longer on the patch. Officially, that is. But I wanted to get him. It had all started with him. And her, of course.

Jeannie. I couldn't stop thinking about her. The purple bruise on her china-white skin. He'd done that. Spiteri. His hands on her flesh. Anger mixed with the sickening feeling of lust I had for her. And something else. An empty feeling. The look of contempt on her face as I did up my trousers. Humiliation. A sad longing that I couldn't throw off.

She gave me so much grief.

Horrible confusion. I'm not a complicated person. I'm a policeman, for fuck's sake. College didn't prepare me for anything like this. All I wanted to do was get the bloody job done. To get on. But everything seemed skewed. I couldn't fathom it. Dave was the one person who I could talk to about shit like this and I'd gone and blown it with him. He'd always been so solid for me. Kept me on the straight and narrow. Well, tried to, anyway.

I was glad to be getting out of the West End detail. Flying Squad would make sense after this, I thought. Going after the heavy villains, not dealing with ponces and tarts. But this was unfinished business. I wanted to get that bastard.

I cleared out my locker and chucked all my stuff in the boot of my motor. I went off for this meet with Mooney.

Covent Garden. Found a parking space on Drury Lane and walked down. The huge, dirty-white Masonic Temple looming over Great Queen Street. Of course. Mooney had been fannying on all the time about me joining his lodge. My first thought was: we'll soon put him straight there. Then I chewed it over in my mind.

As I walked down the street the Temple got bigger. The great ugly power of it bearing down on me. And I thought: why not? I wanted to get on and no copper had ever done his career any harm by being on the square. Far from it. And maybe there was something to all that mumbo-jumbo after all. Maybe I needed something that could make sense of things.

I got to the Connaught Rooms and ordered a double Scotch. A group of business types were filing through the hall, all carrying little briefcases. Mooney was at a corner table. He gave me the nod and I went over.

'Good news,' he declared. 'I've got a seconder.'

'Sorry?'

'A seconder. To initiate an Entered Apprentice to the lodge you need a proposer and a seconder. Well, I've put your name forward and got somebody to second the proposal. They're always keen to have serving police officers among the Brotherhood.'

'Look, sir . . .' I began.

His little eyes blinked intently.

'You said you'd think about it.'

'Yeah, but . . .'

'I've arranged it all. I'm a Worshipful Master of the lodge, so I've been able to make it all really simple. We can do it today. What do you say?'

'Well . . .'

'You given it some thought?'

'Yes.'

'So what do you say?'

'I'm not so sure.'

'I'm disappointed, son. I thought you were a bright lad. Think what you could gain by learning the mysteries of the Craft. Think what you could lose by missing this opportunity.'

'What do you mean?'

'Well, you're off to Flying Squad soon. You want to get on, don't you? Want to make sure that you make the right friends? There are lots of brothers in the old Sweeney Todd, you know. Half the Squad's on the square.'

He leaned across the table.

'You're lost, son,' he whispered intensely. 'I can tell. You need guidance. A true path.'

'I just need time to think, sir.'

'Well, I rather think it's time you made up your mind, son.'

There was a gentle hint of threat to his voice.

'What do you mean?'

'This Spiteri business. There's been a rather disturbing development.'

I didn't like the sound of this. Mooney pulled out a large bluff envelope. He handed it to me.

'Have a look at that, son.'

I reached in and felt a glossy surface. A photograph. I suddenly felt queasy.

'Go on,' he insisted. 'Take it out.'

It was a black-and-white print. A man and a woman having sex. Bodies. Faces. My face clenched with need staring into the mirror. Staring out of the photograph.

'Oh, fuck,' I blurted out.

'You really are off the track, aren't you, son?' Mooney muttered furtively. 'You need to be cleansed of these iniquities.'

A two-way mirror. I thought these things only existed in cheap thrillers and scandal sheets.

'I was set up.'

'Indeed you were. Spiteri and his whore were trying to entrap your colleague. It seems they got you instead.'

'What does he want?'

'Well, he wants you and your jumped-up little DC to leave a few things alone. Luckily he approached me. It would be terrible for something like this to fall into the wrong hands.'

Mooney glared implicatingly. I felt sick. I tried to reason my way out.

'It's all sorted. I got me and Dave transferred off Nipper's squad.'

'That's all straightened, then. And I'm sure that I can persuade our Maltese friend to see sense. Of course, as a serving officer in the Obscene Publications Squad, I should really be holding on to this as evidence.'

His thin lips twisted into a nasty smile.

'You wouldn't . . .' I began.

'Wouldn't what? It certainly counts as material that would tend to corrupt or deprave persons exposed to it. I have to do my duty.'

'What do you want?'

'Want? What do I want, son? I want to help you. And you are in sore need of help. A lost soul. I see it as my duty to help my brother officers that have fallen by the wayside. You need the purification offered by the sanctity of the lodge. Say you'll join and I'll have no more said about this filthy business.'

Mooney stared right into me. Beady eyes, hypnotic. Offering me a way out. A way in.

'You've got promise, son. I can see that. Ambition. The Craft will nurture that. You'll go farther than me in the job, I know that. One day you might even be my guvnor. But I'll always be a higher degree in the Craft.'

Mooney's implication was clear: I'd always owe him for getting me out of this mess.

'So what do you say?'

'OK.'

'Good lad.'

'Just one condition.'

He frowned.

'Name it.'

'I want the negative.'

Mooney nodded thoughtfully.

'Yes, well, we should be able to get that from Spiteri. Let's go and see him now. Then we can be back in time for the ceremony.'

We took Mooney's car and drove over to Soho. Spiteri's flat was on Greek Street. Arthur Springer on the name-plate. Mooney buzzed and gave his name. We were let in and we went upstairs.

Spiteri looked edgy. Wary of looking me in the eye.

'Hello, son.' Mooney's voice all fat-copper jovial, nodding over at me. 'I believe you've already met Detective Sergeant Taylor.'

Spiteri grunted an affirmative. I stared him down.

'Well, my colleague has agreed to deal with this business off the record. He's had that DC that was snooping around transferred off the patch.'

'That's good,' said Spiteri, managing a weak smile in my direction. 'No hard feelings, eh?'

I glowered at him.

'The thing is,' Mooney went on, 'my friend here wants the negative.'

'Hang on a bloody minute,' Spiteri replied. 'That wasn't part of the deal.'

'What do you mean?' I demanded.

'I keep the bloody negative. It's my insurance.'

'Now that's not very friendly,' said Mooney. 'Don't you trust us?'

'I don't understand, Mr Mooney. This wasn't part of the plan.'

Mooney suddenly punched him hard in the stomach. Spiteri doubled over, wheezing.

'You have the right to remain silent,' Mooney intoned softly. He nodded over at me. 'Go on, son,' he implored.

I kicked Spiteri's legs from under him and he collapsed into a sprawling heap on the floor.

'Please, no,' he groaned.

'Don't get above yourself, son,' Mooney told him. 'You're my informant. I run you. You understand?'

'That's not true,' Spiteri sobbed.

'Oh yes, my little darling. Oh yes. A nasty little grass. Uncle Georgie's snout. Wouldn't be very nice for you if that got around, would it?'

Mooney turned to me, his face glowing.

'Discipline,' he hissed. 'That's what these people need. Discipline.'

He pulled out his truncheon. He bent over and prodded at the prone figure beneath him.

'Maybe Mr Wood wants a word, eh?'

He swung the club against both sides of Spiteri's lower back. Aiming at the kidneys. There were nasty retching sounds.

'And you can tell your bosses,' Mooney panted, a little out of breath from his exertions, 'they're finished. The Messinas are finished. Understand? I might have moved to OPS but this is still my patch. I say what goes. You got me?'

Spiteri whimpered in compliance. He vomited. I caught a whiff of bile. Mooney wrinkled his face in disgust.

'Fucking spicks,' he muttered. 'Only way to deal with them. Now, the negative.'

Spiteri crawled across the floor and pulled himself up on the arm of the chair. He pulled open a drawer and took out an envelope. I snatched it off him. A small brown negative was inside. Mine and Jeannie's ghostly figures just visible as the afternoon light caught it. I fumbled in my pocket for my cigarette lighter. I touched the flame against the edge of the film and it soon caught. I dropped it and it zigzagged down to the floor, smouldering. We left Spiteri groaning and muttering in the chair with a smell of sick and burned celluloid in the air.

Out on the street Mooney seemed in a good mood. Whistling merrily as he got his car keys out. I got into his silver-grey Ford Consul and we drove back to the Connaught Rooms.

I wasn't feeling quite so jolly. I felt a bit jittery from the violence. Adrenaline. *Well, that's what you wanted, wasn't it?* I said to myself. But it just made me feel anxious. I thought about betrayal. Myself betrayed by Jeannie. No, that wasn't right. It wasn't as if there was anything between us except my own obsession with her. No, I had betrayed. I'd betrayed Dave and my own instincts as a copper. We'd never found out who Spiteri had been paying off. Not that any of that mattered any more.

And I wasn't looking forward to this ceremony thing. My mind started to race. Mooney was jabbering away as we sped along Shaftesbury Avenue.

'Some lead, others grovel,' he was saying. 'You'll learn that in the lodge. The Brotherhood respects all social distinctions. Some must rule, others must obey and cheerfully accept their inferior positions. You're ambitious. You know what it takes to get on. Not like that goody-two-shoes DC of yours. He ain't going nowhere.'

There was a connecting passage from the Connaught Rooms to the Grand Temple. We went down this corridor into a little vestibule. There was a bloke in full regalia waiting for us.

'This is the Tyler,' Mooney told me. 'He will prepare you.'

I was told to take off my jacket and tie and my right shoe. Mooney unbuttoned my shirt while the other man rolled up my left trouser leg and my right sleeve. Some sort of slipper was put on my left foot. Mooney slipped a noose over my head and pulled the knot snugly at the back of my neck. I shuddered.

'Don't worry,' he whispered. 'It's the cord of life. New life. New birth. Now the hoodwink.'

I was blindfolded.

'I must go and prepare myself,' he added.

Darkness. I was being led. *This wasn't part of the plan*, Spiteri had said. What did that mean? Mooney had laid into him after he'd said that.

The man who led me knocked on a door in front of us. I could hear muffled voices in the room beyond. The door finally opened.

'Whom have you there?' a voice droned.

'Mr Frank Taylor,' another voice responded. 'A poor Candidate in a state of darkness who has been well and worthily recommended, regularly proposed and approved in open lodge, and now comes of his own free will and accord, properly prepared, humbly soliciting to be admitted to the mysteries and privileges of freemasonry.'

There was a murmuring of voices throughout the room. Someone put the point of a blade against my chest, just above the heart. Cold metal against bare flesh. I took a sharp gulp of air.

'Do you feel anything?' someone asked.

'Yes,' I replied.

The blade was taken away and I was led by my right hand until my knees touched a chair or a stool.

'Mr Frank Taylor, as no person can be made a mason unless he is free and of a mature age, I demand of you, are you a free man and of the full age of twenty-one years?'

It was Mooney's voice.

'I am,' I replied.

'Thus assured,' he went on, 'I will thank you to kneel, while the blessing of Heaven is invoked on our proceedings.'

I knelt on the seat in front of me. I could hear shuffling around me, feel myself being surrounded by the people in the room.

'Vouchsafe Thine aid, Almighty Father and Supreme Governor of the Universe . . .' Mooney droned, chanting a litany of words.

My mind drifted again. Spiteri denying that he was Mooney's grass. Mooney wanting him to keep quiet. Going on about the West End still being his patch.

'. . . and grant that this Candidate for freemasonry may so dedicate and devote his life to Thy service . . .'

Mooney standing over Attilio Spiteri, his face beaming. Whistling a little tune and jangling his car keys after we'd kicked a man half senseless.

'. . . by the secrets of our masonic art, he may be better enabled to unfold the beauties of true godliness, to the honour and glory of Thy holy name.'

'So mote it be,' came another voice.

The car. Fuck, the car. The silver-grey Ford Consul. The one I'd seen that night I'd followed Dave. It hadn't been Spiteri's. It had been *his*. Mooney's.

'Mr Taylor.' Mooney spoke directly to me. 'In all cases of difficulty and danger, in whom do you put your trust?'

It had been him. Of course. How could I have been so stupid? He was the copper that the Maltese were paying off. He must have set the whole thing up. The photograph, everything. He'd even beaten up his own man to cover his tracks and fool me. Set me up with Jeannie. They'd wanted Dave to fall for it but they got me instead. *I'm supposed to be nice to you*, she had said in that awful drugged-up voice. I had been such a mug.

I pulled the blindfold off and stood up. Mooney was standing in front of me in full masonic fancy dress.

'It was you,' I said to him. 'You set me up.'

'Put your blindfold back on at once!' Mooney ordered.

'Fuck you,' I muttered.

A hand grabbed my arm. I wrenched myself free. I pushed my way through the crowd of weirdos around me. There were gasps of outrage and muttered comments. Mooney called out after me.

'You have violated the sanctity of the Temple! The wrath of the Great Architect will come down upon you!'

I had too much time on my hands, time to kill. I couldn't seem to concentrate on work. I didn't have enough of a routine. I found the days drifting by and my mind wandering, dwelling on my own story rather than seeking out others. Bad brooding thoughts again. If I had a staff job I'd have something to distract me from distraction, I reasoned, a calm occupation.

I spoke to Sid Franks about doing a big exposé on organised crime in London. The Richardson gang had all been arrested and were due in court at the end of the week. *Sub judice* rumours of torture and beatings that piqued my interest, a reign of terror. There were hints that the Krays might be arrested for the Blind Beggar shooting in March. I talked up the story as a call to SMASH THE GANGS, to come down heavily on the racketeers and mobsters. Sid liked the idea but I couldn't seem to get down to it.

I found myself lurking in the underground public toilets off the Portobello Road, the afternoon sunlight streaming through the glass tiles above. Cool shadows, a low hiss of plumbing punctuated by a rhythmic, echoed dripping, like submarine sonar, created a tranquil ambience. Even the smell of piss and disinfectant was somehow reassuring. I stood, balanced on the tiled ridge in front of the cracked and stained porcelain, and waited.

The wall was covered with inscriptions. Hastily sketched figures and crude outlines of penises illuminated the text here and there. Childish scrawl described innocent depravity. Dates were given, chronicled entries. 4/3/66 I'M 35 SLIM 7″ – WANT FUCKING BY 3 COCKS ONE AFTER THE OTHER, 5/6/66 SLAVE SEEKS MASTER MAKE DATE. Often GENUINE, or even 100% GENUINE, were added, as if to insist upon the authenticity of the records. MAKE DATE, many implored, and indeed there was some haphazard correspondence, entries in an endless logbook of want. The wall was cleaned intermittently but one could make out traces of older writings, a palimpsest of desire.

Like splash subheadlines, self-declared scandals. There were also subtitles of invective. I HATE QUEERS and I WOULD LIKE TO HANG A POOF UNTIL I HEAR HIS NECK SNAP. Little haikus of hatred, articulating the lonely impulse of murderous longings. Words – I'd always tried to use words to give vent to my frustrations, but here the words were calling out to me, leading me astray. The poetry of psychopaths. The mass murderer William Hierens had left a message on the wall by one of his victims, written in her lipstick:

FOR HEAVENS
SAKE CATCH ME
BEFORE I KILL MORE
I CANNOT CONTROL MYSELF

I knew this feeling so well: self-loathing, fear of what I am. And yet here I was, waiting. I hardly dared think what for, hardly remembered what brought me to these lower depths.

There were echoing footfalls on the stairs and I was suddenly alert. A middle-aged businessman, on his lunch break no doubt. He caught my eye with a horribly implicating gaze. *He knows*, I thought. He came closer, opening his mouth to say something. I couldn't bear to hear what nasty accusation might pass his ugly thin lips. I was in a sudden rage, grabbing at his throat.

'No,' he squealed. 'Oh God, no.'

His voice was small and choked, real terror in his eyes. He didn't even try to struggle he was so paralysed with fear. He knew that he was guilty, that he deserved this. I felt my hand tighten around his cheap school tie.

Then I regained control, and pushed him against one of the lock-ups. The door banged against the tiled wall and I ran up the stairs out of there.

Back at my bed-sit I tried to calm myself down. I attempted masturbation but felt the hateful thoughts flood through me. I collapsed on to my unmade bed sobbing.

Against my better judgment I went in the evening to this meeting that Julian had spoken of. It was in the basement of a bookshop on Kensington Park Road. A motley crew assembled – beards, beads, multicoloured clothes, peace sign badges. Everyone talking about Utopia, Peace, Liberation, Revolution, Love. God, did they go on about Love. Julian and I both stood out as being the only people in the room with short hair and ordinary clothes. I guessed they must have thought us real squares. Normal. But when I saw the way that one of the women talked, looking in our direction, trying to include us as she rambled on about 'sexual liberation', I figured that the beatniks were trying to include us. Julian suppressed giggles as this silly cow wittered on. This bunch of well-spoken hippies liked to call themselves 'freaks', as if it were something glamorous and bohemian. As if they had any idea what horror it was to be a real freak.

Somebody talked about offset litho printing and the magazine having really bright groovy colours. He showed the group some of his designs – art nouveau lettering, strange fluorescent figures and rainbow skies. There was a discussion as to whether this was affordable yet. Then a long, inconclusive debate about the title. Nobody was sure what to call it.

We went for a drink afterwards. Henekey's on Portobello Road. It was full of 'freaks'.

'Not very beautiful, are they,' I commented. 'The Beautiful People.'

'No.' Julian sniffed. 'They're all unwashed and hairy too. Not my favourite combination. What is it about the English character that is so averse to soap and water? You really notice it in the summer. That tang. And look at that dolly bird with no bra on. Shocking.'

Julian sniffed again.

'And you smell that?'

A pungent scent hung in the air. I recognised it from the other night. Cannabis. A joint was being passed around in the beer garden, a couple of West Indians, obviously dealing. Julian wanted to know if I was interested in the magazine. My mind was elsewhere. I suddenly realised the potential for a story. An exposé – long-haired decadence, the drugs angle. Sid Franks would love it. And I hated this hippie crowd with their Free Love, thinking themselves so exotic and wild. I could have some revenge. There was muck here to be raked.

We went along to this party later. A Happening, they called it. It was in a disused warehouse in Camden Town. Naked figures on a stage doing some sort of performance art, a light show, oily blotches projected on to a whitewashed wall. Music, a heavily amplified electric dirge, a tray of sugar lumps passed around, supposedly laced with hallucinogens. I demurred, but Julian grabbed one like a greedy child. Surprisingly, I quite enjoyed the atmosphere. But although it was all supposed to be so beautiful, in fact the scene was quite grotesque and ugly. Like a Hieronymus Bosch vision of Hell. A Garden of Earthly Delights. Julian pointed out one of the Rolling Stones lurking in a corner, smoking a joint. I thought about what a great scoop it would be, a snatch shot of a pop star taking drugs.

They met at Stan's flat in a tower block off Ladbroke Grove. Stan's missus made no attempt to conceal her disapproval of Jimmy and Billy. Their talk of big money, easy money, made her sick. She knew what they were. Petty villains acting tough. She worried that they would lead her Stanley astray. He had held down a job for over a year now. She wanted him to keep going straight. She wanted him to be respectable.

She frowned at Stan as his friends shuffled into the flat and made themselves comfortable on the settee. They had come around to watch the football. England–Portugal. But they were up to something, she could tell.

'I'm off to bingo,' she announced, grabbing her handbag and going to the door.

Stan followed her out.

'See you later, love,' he said, leaning towards her to kiss her cheek.

She pulled her face away.

'Just you make sure those two are gone before I come back!' she hissed.

'Don't be like that, love,' he muttered quietly. 'They're my friends.'

She slammed the door. As Stan came back through to the living room, Jimmy and Billy were laughing.

'Fuck me,' said Billy. 'Your old lady's in a bad mood.'

Stan grinned uneasily. He turned on the telly. *World Cup Grandstand* had just started.

'She still think you're working?' asked Jimmy.

'Yeah.' Stan nodded sheepishly.

Jimmy and Billy erupted into laughter again. Stan hadn't worked for over a month. But he hadn't told his wife. So every weekday morning he got up at eight and kissed her goodbye. She thought he was off to an engineering works in Northolt. He'd drive off in his blue Standard Vanguard to a café to have breakfast and study the day's racing form. He might be meeting up with Billy and Jimmy during the day. Otherwise it would be the pub at lunch-time and the betting shop in the afternoon. He'd get back to the flat at about half past five. The wife suspected nothing. So he hoped.

'You're fucking henpecked, that's what you are,' said Billy.

Jimmy got a bottle of Scotch out of a carrier bag. Stan got them some glasses.

'Right,' Jimmy announced when they'd settled down. 'The thing is, we need to get a proper motor.'

'Yeah, well, that old banger of Stan's not much cop, is it?'

Stan smiled. Jimmy cleared his throat.

'Yes, well, as I've said, we need a proper getaway vehicle. I've got an idea.'

'Oh yeah?' Billy remarked with a grin. 'What's that, then?'

'There's a blue Ford Executive parked on my road. We get some plates made up the same as this motor and nick one the same. Then if we get spotted the Old Bill will track down this other car. It'll put them on a wild-goose chase.'

Billy nodded slowly. Stan frowned. He didn't understand why they should do something so complicated. Why not just nick the original Ford? He didn't say anything.

'Yeah,' Billy said, continuing to nod. 'That's a good plan. We just need to sort out where we're going to hit.'

'We should do a jug,' Jimmy declared.

Billy laughed.

'A jug?'

'Yeah,' Jimmy went on. 'You know, a bank.'

'I know what a fucking jug is.'

'Well, what's so funny?'

'You're talking like you've been at the heavy all your life. "We should do a jug." What do you fucking know about it?'

'Listen, son . . .' started Jimmy.

'Fellahs, please!' Stan came in. 'Take it easy. Let's all have a drink, eh?'

He poured out the whisky. The TV flickered. The teams were lined up on the pitch. The Royal Marines Band playing the Portuguese national anthem.

'If we want to do a bank,' said Billy, 'we need to be properly tooled.'

Billy reached into the holdall by his feet. He pulled out the Luger and held it up in front of the group.

'I've got us another shooter. Here you are, Jimmy,' he said, handing it to him.

Jimmy examined the pistol with pretend expertise. Stan smiled nervously and chewed at a hangnail.

'Want me to get you one?' Billy asked him.

'Nah,' he said. 'I'm the driver, ain't I. I don't need no gun.'

7

It was the day of the final when it all came tumbling down. The end of my first week with the Flying Squad. C8. I'd got where I wanted to be. The new boy on Vic Sayles' team.

The squad's plainclothes style was a bit more flash than Divisional. Tailor-made suits rather than off-the-peg Burtons. Leather or sheepskin topcoats so that you could dress down to be less conspicuous when you were plotted up somewhere on surveillance. The job of the squad was to go after the top villains. It was expected that you'd get close to them. Dress like them. Think like them.

I was wary of my fellow officers' attitude to me. One of the Bramshill lot. A Special Course college boy. Very careful to act humble, not say anything that might sound know-it-all. I was also worried about the freemason business. Mooney's comment about Brothers in the the Flying Squad. Word must have got around about what had happened at the Temple. I just thought I'd keep my head down. Get on with the job. Get on with my career.

I felt all right about what had happened with Dave. I kidded myself that I had done him a favour. Got him out of the West End. Out of danger. He'd be better off back at the Bush. I figured he'd thank me for it in the long run.

I'd spent the first day getting used to procedure. I was worried that I'd be kicking my heels all week. I was keen to get my teeth into something after all that palaver at West End Central. It had left a bad taste in my mouth. Well, vice is a dirty job. You're bound to get tainted by it sooner or later. Here I'd be up against serious villainy. I wanted to prove myself. Then the second day Vic Sayles came up to me.

'Frank,' he said.

'Yes, guvnor?'

'Fancy a job, son?'

Stupid question. Stupid grin on my face.

'You busy?' he asked.

'Nothing special, guvnor.'

'Right. Get an operational unit together. Something's come in off a snout of mine. A whole lorry-load of phosphor bronze was had away last week. Expensive stuff. Use it to make aeroplanes and that. He reckons he knows where it's being slaughtered. I got the address. A scrapyard in Harlesden. Get a brief and go and check it out.'

So I got the brief – the search warrant, that is. Got together a couple of DCs and three drivers. One for each car and an extra one to drive the truck if we got a result. Turns out that this phosphor bronze is very valuable. The lorry-load was meant to be worth a hundred grand.

The scrapyard looked deserted when we arrived. Just a fat little geezer on his tod in a trailer that was used as an office. He was just sitting there picking his nose and reading an *Exchange & Mart*. When I flashed my warrant card and the brief he looked up and rolled his eyes.

'Fuck,' he said. 'Someone must have grassed.'

Now I nearly laughed out loud at this. That was a verbal if I ever heard one. Straight out of the notebook. I'd never actually heard a villain utter anything so pat. I should have been suspicious, but I just figured that this little toerag had been watching too much *Dixon of Dock Green* or he was taking the piss.

We found the lorry and nicked the bloke for receiving. A good day's work. Lovely little job. First week in the squad and I'd got a result. But I had a nagging little feeling that it had all been too easy.

World Cup Final day. A bit of a buzz about that in Coco. That and events in South London very early that morning. Charlie Richardson had been nicked in a dawn raid. Now we had the whole gang in the frame.

I was finishing off the paperwork for the recovered lorry-load in Harlesden and the receiving charge against the bloke in the scrapyard. We'd been working on a tip-off so the informant would be entitled to payment from the Information Fund. If the stuff had been properly covered the insurers could pay ten per cent of the recovered value into the fund. A tidy little sum. But it was Vic

Sayles' informant and he would have to authorise the application to the fund anyway, so I went to see him about it.

'Nice little job, Frank,' he said.

I mentioned the Information Fund and he nodded slowly and lit a cigarette.

'Sit down, son.'

'What is it, guvnor?'

'You're new to my team and I want you to get to know how things are done here. That's why I gave you that job.'

'I don't understand.'

'Yes, well, it ain't exactly covered in the one-year Special Course. Information, that's what it's all about, isn't it? I mean, without that we can't be expected to solve crime, can we?'

'Of course not, guvnor.'

'That's why I put so much emphasis in the way I work on cultivating informants. And they do need cultivating. It's give and take. Sometimes you need to keep your boot on their neck, other times you need to sweeten them up. Do you get me?'

'I'm not sure, guvnor.'

I didn't like the way this was going.

'This little job, for instance. Your initiation into my team, if you like. Talking of initiation, I heard about that fiasco at George Mooney's lodge, but don't worry, you won't have to roll your trousers up to be part of my firm. No, you just have to remember that things get divvied up properly.'

'Guvnor?'

'The insurance reward. Ten per cent of the recovered value. Tidy little sum. Well, some of it will go to the team that blagged it. With the understanding we'll want bodies handed up from time to time in the future. The bloke you nicked for receiving, well, he'll have his share. He's some mug with no form and he'll be happy to do six months' bird. And the rest of it goes to us. Some of it goes upstairs, the rest is divvied up among ourselves. I'm giving you your share in advance.'

He pulled out a brown envelope and tossed it on to the desk in front of me.

'There you are, son. Welcome to the firm.'

I felt such a fucking mug. That's why it had been so easy. I should have spotted that. Dave would have noticed something like that. I was always in such a fucking hurry. Now what was I going to do?

'Look, sir . . .'

'Pick it up, Taylor. Don't be a cunt. Nobody got hurt. Everything weighed off nicely with a little sweetener. It'll buy us information for the next time, you mark my words.'

I stared at the envelope.

'Go on. Pick it up. You know how long it took me to get to DI? No fucking Rapid Promotion Scheme, I can tell you. It was a fucking hard slog. Look, college boy, we keep the peace. Take a few heavy villains off the pavement now and then. We get to know where everybody is so that when it's their turn to go away for a while, by Christ we make sure that they do. The great British public sleeps soundly in its beds and lets us get on with it. We deserve a little extra every now and then for that, don't we?'

I looked up at Sayles. He caught my stare without flinching.

'Pick it up, son.'

I lifted the envelope and put it in my pocket. That was that. Either that or transfer back to Division. I walked out of his office, bad money in my pocket. I had to get out. Think about what to do. A voice says:

'We're setting up a telly in the briefing room, Frank. To watch the match.'

The final. I'd been looking forward to it up until now. Didn't have the stomach for it any more.

'Got to go out,' I replied. 'Got a job.'

Out. Need to think. Talk. Dave. I need to talk to Dave about this. He was right all along. Need to talk to him. Ask him: *What the fuck do I do now?*

Motor over to West London. Shepherd's Bush factory. Desk Sergeant Reg Wilson with a big smile as I come in. He was skipper when I first started here.

'Hello, stranger,' he said.

Radio on in the background. The match.

'The Krauts have just equalised. I hear you're on the Flying Squad now. A bit more glamorous than Division, I'll bet.'

'Yeah.' I nodded vaguely. 'Dave Thomas about, skip?'

'He's out on Q-car duty.'

Q-car – an unmarked CID car on constant patrol. So named

after the Q-ships which hunted U-boats disguised as merchant vessels.

'Right.'

'I could radio him for you.'

'Nah. It's all right.'

Leave the station. Walk along Shepherd's Bush Green. Feel in my pocket. Thick wad of notes in the envelope. Think: What am I going to do with this bent cash? See a bookie's and go in. I decide to punt the whole lot on a horse. Hardly anyone in the place. A big West Indian with yellowy teeth scribbling out a Yankee. Turns to me and asks:

'How's your luck, man?'

Put the whole lot on Horned Moon in the 3.30 at Thirsk. The fucking nag comes in at 5–1. Collect my winnings. Four hundred-odd quid. Try to put the whole lot on again but they won't take the bet. It's too much and they haven't got time to lay it off.

Manage to lose three races in a row. But I put forty quid on King's Bounty in the four o'clock at Newmarket and it fucking wins.

No use. Walk out of the bookie's. Yellow betting slips all over the floor like trampled party decorations.

Get out of there and walk over to the White Horse. Crowded with punters watching the game. England are winning, 2–1 up. A lot of shouting and cheering. I stand at the bar. A double Scotch. Then another. It's nearly full time and we're still ahead. Everyone in the pub rared up, shouting at the little figures on the screen.

I feel sick of all this. Stupid national pride. Queen and Country. Showing the Flag. Can't believe in any of that any more. Can't believe in the job.

From the telly I can just hear the strains of 'Rule Britannia' coming from the terraces. *Come on, England!* somebody shouts in the bar. *Never, never, never shall be slaves*, groans the crowd from the terraces. I feel suddenly traitorous. I want them to lose. Want us to lose.

Four minutes left, comes the commentary. *The clouds have parted, the sun is now streaming down on Wembley.*

People are already celebrating. Then two minutes to go and Jack Charlton gives away a foul. Groans from the pub. Nobby Stiles arguing with the referee. Free kick outside England's penalty area.

The wall lines up. The ref gets them to move back. Pacing out the ten yards.

The pub is almost hushed. Just a few votive mutterings. One minute to go. And I want the Krauts to score. The free kick is taken. It beats the wall. It's free in the penalty area. Everyone in the pub is shouting. Urging it clear. Goalmouth scramble. The commentator is flustered. Unable to make out the confusion.

And it's . . . he splutters. *Oh yes, they must. They have done.*

It's in the net. Mournful keening all over the saloon bar. They've equalised.

'Yes!' I hiss to myself through gritted teeth.

England have just enough time to kick off when the referee blows his whistle.

Full time. Wander about the Bush. Find another pub without a telly and drink my way through five doubles. It's quiet and I try to think things through. Bad money in my pocket. Have to find a way of getting rid of it. I'm part of a bent team. I'm the sort of copper that Dave despises.

Extra time. Crowded around the telly in Stan's flat. Jimmy, Billy and Sandra round to watch the football. Even Stan's missus going along with the spirit of the thing. Putting on a spread. A few sandwiches, cocktail sausages, slices of veal-and-ham pie. Beer. Jimmy joking that he's supporting the Krauts because he's Scottish. Extra time and Billy's feeling bored by the whole spectacle. The whole nation going crazy over a poxy game of football.

A clock comes up on the screen. Ten minutes of extra time gone.

Just twenty minutes of the match left, intones Kenneth Wolstenholme calmly. Of the old school. His commentary avuncular, unintrusive.

Nobby Stiles in possession in the centre circle. Alan Ball finds an opening on the right wing. Stiles passes quickly, scarcely looking up. An instinctive long ball. Thirty yards through the air, dropping, let's say, five yards in front of its intended receiver. Ball races towards it on tired legs, Schnellinger chasing. For a second Ball thinks he's finished. All run out. Extra time has taken its toll. Socks rolled down to his ankles, calves aching with the onset of cramp. Then, maybe in desperation itself, he finds energy, acceleration. Schnellinger beaten, he has space.

Here's Ball, running himself daft.

Wolstenholme enunciates *daft* with a shortened vowel sound. Northern rather than BBC. The excitement betraying a long-tamed native accent.

First touch. Ball hooks a low curling cross square. Geoff Hurst in the penalty area. Just outside the six-yard box. He traps the pass with his right foot and turns. Tilkowski, the German goalkeeper, stays on his line, crouching down, ready for a low shot.

Now here's Hurst. Can he do it?

But Hurst is not over the ball as he swivels to make the shot. He's leaning away from it, falling back as he drives. So it goes high. Right over the keeper. It hits the crossbar. The net shudders slightly as if anticipating a catch. A deafening exhalation from the crowd as its line of flight skims the surface of the goalmouth. The ball cannons down on to the goal line. The noise echoing around the stadium into a crescendo. A heightened sigh of relief. Then an in-breath of doubt as the ball bounces back out. The triangular path of the ball. The rectangle of the goal. The two shapes join but do they bisect? The odds of a shot hitting either solid line of woodwork or painted line on turf are long enough. To hit both, in close sequence, in the same trajectory, is a miraculous trigonometry. The ball flies back into play. Weber heads it away. Roger Hunt turns and appeals. Did the ball cross the line? The crowd roar comes again, more in belief than in certainty. Consumed by the sacred geometry of the moment.

Yes, yes, Wolstenholme enthuses. Then suddenly: *No. No. The linesman says no.*

Again, emphatic:

The linesman says no.

The players make signals of appeal. The Germans waving arms or shaking hands. Dismissive gestures. The English indicate certainty by holding their upper limbs aloft, rigid.

The referee is running up to meet the linesman. Close-up of Hurst on the screen. He has dropped his hands to his knees. For a moment despondent. Then he leans forward, looking intently towards the meeting of officials. Eyes plaintive.

The crowd roar subsides into a low ululation. Then the whistling starts up. Demanding judgment rather than mere arbitration. Meaning triangulated. Hurst's shot, the impact on the crossbar, the ball finding the limit of the playing area. Surely this is enough?

But there are other meanings beyond these tangents. The referee, Gottfried Dienst, is Swiss. Supposedly neutral. The linesman, Tofik Bahkramov, is Russian. Much is made, in the recounting of this incident, of the fact that Bahkramov had served in the Red Army in the Great Patriotic War against the Third Reich. There are reports that there were shouts of *Remember Stalingrad!* that came provocatively from the terraces as they conferred.

But the fact was, at any angle, it was a hard one to call. Within the rules of Association Football, for a goal to be allowed, the whole of the ball must be over the line; if any part of it does not cross it must be disallowed. No one, least of all Bahkramov, was in a position to accurately judge the physics of it.

The officials had no shared language. Bahkramov could, as Wolstenholme had already commented, *only speak Russian or Turkish*. Only the English can be so dismissive of bilingualism. But the semantics of the situation are simple. Binary. Yes or no.

The officials are face to face now. Bahkramov nods his grey head. Dienst turns and blows his whistle. He starts walking back down the pitch, pointing at the centre spot.

It's a goal. It's a goal. Wolstenholme deadpan. The crowd ecstatic.

The German players continue to protest. The English are jubilant. Martin Peters runs up to his West Ham team-mate Hurst, arms outstretched. He hugs him about the waist, lifts him off the ground.

The action replay comes up on the screen, silently. No commentary as there had been with the other goals. Slow motion reveals how dubious the decision was.

Stan has risen from the settee, a beer bottle held aloft, cheering.

'That was never in,' Jimmy mutters.

'It does look a bit dodgy,' agrees Billy.

'Yeah, but it doesn't matter now, does it?' Stan with a stupid grin on his face. 'The ref's given it, hasn't he?'

Suddenly there's noise out on the street. The match is over. People are singing and chanting. I go outside.

We won the Cup, we won the Cup, ee-ay-addio, we won the Cup!

Cars driving past hooting their horns, some with Union Jacks fluttering from them. People dancing, actually dancing with each other on the street. Strangers hugging each other. Calling up to people hanging out of their windows. Flags flying everywhere. It's like fucking VJ day.

Find myself in a crowded pub propping up the bar. Some bloke looks at me and frowns.

'What's the matter, mate? We won, didn't we?'

I turn away. We won. Everyone fucking won. I won. Got a result the bad way. Got what I wanted.

I stagger out of the pub. The street party in full swing.

We won the Cup, we won the Cup, ee-ay-addio, we won the Cup!

I want to lose. Lose all of this bad cash in my pocket. Think about throwing it in the air around me. But that would add to the party atmosphere. And I hate all these happy bastards. Lose it, that's what I need to do. Gamble it. Tried that on the horses. I'll have to go to the dogs. I head over to White City.

Final whistle in Stan's flat. Everybody getting carried away. Shouting and cheering. Except Billy. He watches the screen morosely.

Bobby Moore goes up to the Royal Box to collect the trophy. Bobby Charlton is weeping openly.

'Look at that silly cunt,' Billy mutters to himself.

And they want Alf Ramsey, Wolstenholme announces. *And Alf Ramsey doesn't want to come.*

Why don't they leave the poor fucker alone, thinks Billy.

The Band of the Royal Marines strikes up 'God Save the Queen'. The crowd sing along, dirgelike. Stan is on his feet.

'Send 'er victorious,' he chants.

'Leave it out, Stan,' snaps Billy.

The band breaks into 'When the Saints Go Marching In'. A lap of honour. Moore hands the trophy to Nobby Stiles. Stiles does a funny little victory dance. A pixilated hornpipe, gapped teeth showing in his demented grin. Jimmy laughs.

'Will yer look at the mad wee fellow,' he says.

And throughout it all, comes the commentary, *Alf Ramsey walks quietly off the pitch.*

'Right, then,' says Stan, switching off the telly. 'Let's get down the pub. It'll be heaving.'

They all go out on to the street. It's crowded with people.

Flags everywhere. Clapping, chanting, spontaneous choruses of 'Rule Britannia'. Victory. Billy felt so fucking lonely. He couldn't understand it. He couldn't join in. Didn't feel any part of it. He'd fought for this fucking country. Killed for it. No fucking thanks at all. Demobbed and forgotten about. No fucking parade.

We won the Cup, we won the Cup, ee-ay-addio, we won the Cup!

'Let's go home,' he said to Sandra.

'But we've won, Billy. We ought to celebrate.'

'Why?' he asked, flatly.

Sandra put her arm around him.

'What's the matter, love?'

'Nothing,' he replied. 'I just don't like crowds. Let's go home.'

She looked at him. He seemed distant. Alone. She'd never quite understand him. A car raced by blaring its horn, a Union Jack fluttering from the back window. She kissed him on the cheek.

'All right,' she whispered in his ear. 'Let's go home.'

The noise on the streets went on all night. *They think it's all over*, thought Billy, lying on his back in bed. He tried to sleep. He'd drift off for a while but the sounds outside disturbed him. And the memories inside. Back in the jungle. Always alive with something. Crickets, cicadas, tree frogs. A bloody racket. They'd build temporary shelters with groundsheets and ponchos. *Bashas*, they call them. Make a frame with branches to support a hammock. British Nylon Pattern. Spare set of clothes for sleeping dry. Then in the morning it's back in your filthy half-sodden combat fatigues.

One night there was a firefight in the darkness. Tracer bullets lighting up the forest like Guy Fawkes Night. One of the officers grabbed a Very pistol. A flare gun, used to signal or dislodge air-drop canisters from high trees by burning off the parachute canopy. They held fire as this beautiful orange light fell slowly through the trees. Picking out shadows. But there was nobody there. The CT must have slipped away into the night. Maybe they'd never been there at all and they'd been firing at ghosts.

He woke up in a cold sweat. Sandra was snoring next to him. He got up and went to the window. Lit a cigarette. *Everybody's happy*, he thought. *What's the matter with me?* Victory celebrations. *They think it's all over*. The intermittent sounds reminded him of a street riot one night in Kuala Lumpur. Anger and joy indistinguishable.

Stupid bastards, he whispered to himself with strange and vague thoughts of revenge. *They think it's all over*. It ain't over.

The Saturday shift was as hectic as ever. It was a 'World Cup Final Special', of course, so more pages than usual had to be kept back until we knew the result. Even Teddy Thursby came in to finish his copy, saying that his comments depended on whether England won or lost. Not that he seemed particularly impressed by the event.

'Bread and circuses, dear boy,' he muttered to me. 'A post-Empire consolation prize. It's all downhill from now on.'

Sid Franks' ears pricked up.

'Don't worry, Sidney,' Thursby continued. 'I won't be sharing these gloomy thoughts with our esteemed readership.'

Extra time played havoc with the deadlines. Sid was pacing up and down with a glass of bicarb in one hand and a fag in the other, looking like he was going to have a coronary any moment. Loudly cursing the print unions.

'Those cunts want extra for working on World Cup Final day.'

Jubilation when the final result came in. A mad rush to get all the match reports and photos composed. Then Sid got any spare staff men and casuals to go over to the big reception for the team at the Royal Garden Hotel, Kensington. The main brief was to get a comment from Alf Ramsey. Apart from the rather choice declaration after the Argentina game, Ramsey had been far from loquacious with the gentlemen of the press. 'Tight-lipped,' was how the *Illustrated* had described his reticence earlier in the tournament.

'Tight-arsed, more like,' Sid had said. 'Get that cunt on the record with something, for fuck's sake.'

So a load of us went over to the Royal Garden. A stag do, no wives or girlfriends present. Jimmy Greaves, left out of the team for the last three crucial games, was also conspicuous by his absence. Jack Charlton, in preparation for the heavy drinking ahead, wrote on a card: 'This body is to be returned to room 508, Royal Garden Hotel,' and put it in his top pocket.

Outside, a huge crowd had assembled, singing 'You'll Never Walk Alone'. And the familiar chant striking up at any opportunity.

We won the Cup, we won the Cup, ee-ay-addio, we won the Cup!

Players took turns to walk out on to the balcony to receive the ovation. Calls for Ramsey to appear, and he wandered out briefly, looking reserved, slightly bemused by the whole thing.

Harold Wilson was swanning about, making the most of the happy occasion. There were gloomy forecasts for the economy, a wages freeze announced to deal with the crisis, the boom time officially over. A couple of members of his cabinet there, Jim Callaghan with a big friendly grin on his face, George Brown staggering around, already three sheets to the wind.

No comment from Ramsey. One prominent sportswriter went up to him, offering congratulations and thanking him, on behalf of all the press, for his co-operation. Ramsey frowned, beetle-browed and disbelieving, and said:

'Are you taking the piss?'

I phoned in what I had to Sid and he ordered me over to the West End to cover the crowd celebrations there.

'Get out there and get a bit of colour,' he said. 'You know, the people of England celebrate. It's a fucking national womb-trembler, son.'

The West End was afire, motor horns blaring, flags fluttering amidst passing traffic. World Cup Willie mascots hanging from car aerials, Trafalgar Square packed with people. A circle of girls was doing a knees-up in one of the fountains.

Piccadilly teeming with revellers, a mad charivari. A young man on top of Eros waved the red, white and blue. The mob struck up 'Rule Britannia'. I had to push my way through the crowd. The horrible squirming intimacy of all these bodies made me quite sick. Back at the *Illustrated* we had plenty of copy. Everyone was half pissed as the paper was put to bed in high spirits.

White City Stadium. Putting as much as I can on trap number three. Think about how easy it is to fix the dogs. Jumbo Edwards, a trainer who ran ringers and did the odd bit of doping, used to phone up the Bush with tips for the night's racing. All a bit of fun. It's all fucking fixed. Geoff Hurst's shot never crossed the bloody line.

Punt away a load of cash but I've still got some left at the end of the meeting. Feel I've got to keep gambling. Gamblers are losers. Loners. No loyalty. No side. Only odds. The longer the better. Got to get rid of the bad money.

The Hop Garden Poker Club in Notting Dale. One of the hundreds of little casinos that sprang up after the '59 Betting and Gaming Act. Roulette table in the front. A real mug's game. *Faîtes vos jeux*, says some tatty-looking croupier with a Black Country accent. I buy a load of chips and start making silly bets. Big piles on single numbers. Lose a lot then one of the bastards comes up. Big gasps around the table as a whole load of chips gets shovelled back at me. More than I fucking started with.

The wankers running the place think something's up and come over.

'Everything all right here?' asks some cunt in a monkey suit.

I push the chips back on the same number.

'Excuse me, sir,' he continues. 'I don't think the house can cover that bet.'

'You don't understand. I want to fucking lose.'

'Maybe you've had enough, sir.'

Go up West. Piccadilly Circus heaving with bodies. Someone's climbed on top of the statue of Eros and is waving a flag. *You'll never walk alone*, sings the crowd. Want to bet? I think to myself. Want to bet? Waste of fucking time. The money should go to its rightful owner. Whoever the fuck that is. I'm living off immoral earnings. We're all living off immoral earnings.

Suddenly think: Jeannie. Yeah, why not? I'm just another sucker in the West End ready to waste all my money on a whore. Immoral earnings, ought to share them about. And I want her. I don't care if she's been involved in blackmailing me. How much she despises me. I don't care if I have to pay. I want her. I push my way through the crowd. Head up towards Shepherd Market.

Get to the flat and press her buzzer. No reply. Kick the door in and stumble inside. Shrieks come from the ground-floor flat. Geezer buttoning himself up hurriedly. Looking frightened, trying to avoid my mad-eyed stare.

'It's all right, son,' I tell him. 'We won, didn't we?'

'What the fuck do you think you're doing?' the ground-floor-flat tart screeches. 'Get out of here before I call the police.'

'I am the fucking police, darling.'

I pull out a load of notes and hand them over to her.

'What do you want?' she demands, her voice a little less harsh.

'I want to see Jeannie.'

'Well, she's not here.'

I stumble up to the first-floor landing. Knock on the door. Another tart opens up. Not Jeannie.

'Where is she?' I demand.

'It's all right, Joan.'

Jeannie. Her voice coming from the landing.

'What do *you* want?' she demands.

'I've got something for you.'

I start up the stairs. Jeannie has a bottle in her hand. She's holding it by the neck.

'It's all right,' I croak. 'I don't want to hurt you. I got something for you.'

'What?'

I pull all the cash out of my pocket and hold it up for her to see.

'It's dirty money, Jeannie.'

I sniff at the pile of cash. Used banknotes have a horrible smell. Of all the sweaty palms they've rubbed by. All the filthy palms they've greased.

'I want you to have it,' I mutter, pushing all the notes at her. She starts laughing.

Everything starts to spin. I stagger on to the landing.

'I got to lie down. Let me lie down for a bit.'

'Oh, Christ,' she groans. 'In here.'

She leads me into a room.

'We won the Cup,' I start singing.

'Yeah, yeah.' She guides me across to the bed.

Everything spinning, falling.

'Ee-ay-addio.'

Falling. Mattress springs squeaking. Blacking out.

8

I woke up, fully clothed, laid out on top of the bed. Didn't know where the fuck I was at first. Hung over, my mouth dry, my head throbbing in dull agony as it struggled to think. Then it all fell painfully into place. Jeannie was gone. So was the money. All the bad money.

I staggered into the bathroom and splashed some cold water on my face. The sound of an argument out on the stairs. A man and a woman. Voices high and low like some bloody duet. Female protestations making shrill stabs at my bleary mind. I dried my face on a threadbare towel and went to the door.

I pushed it open and looked down. Attilio Spiteri and one of the tarts framed by the stairwell.

'I told you,' the girl was saying, 'I don't know where she went.'

Spiteri caught sight of me.

'All right,' he muttered to her sharply. 'Go on. Get downstairs.'

Spiteri mounted the stairs, eyeing me warily. He moved awkwardly, probably still smarting from the beating he'd taken the other day.

'Well,' he said with a flat grin, 'the little bird has flown.'

'Don't you . . .' I blurted out, grabbing the front of his jacket.

He winced painfully.

'Take it easy, for fuck's sake,' he protested. 'I ain't going to do nothing. She's more trouble than she's worth. I'm surprised that you care after what she put you through.'

I let go of him.

'Mooney set the whole thing up, didn't he?' I asked.

'Yeah,' he replied, leaning forward to whisper, as if we could be overheard. 'You want to be careful of him.'

I pushed past Spiteri and went down the stairs and out into the street. The bright morning hurt my eyes. I looked a mess but then the whole of London seemed to be recovering from the hangover of last night's victory celebrations. I crossed the street and a car pulled out and kerb-crawled me. It was a silver-grey Ford Consul. Mooney.

'Get in, son,' he called out, and I tried to ignore him.

'Well, well,' he continued, chidingly. 'You can't keep away, can you? You really are off the track, brother.'

'What do you want?'

I stopped and he put on the brake. He opened the passenger door and I climbed in reluctantly.

'Just to get a few things straight,' he said. 'That girl of yours has gone missing. Oh yes, Uncle George sees everything.' His peephole eyes twinkled with pride. 'The All-Seeing Eye of the Great Architect guides me. And a few very good connections. You know the motto of the Temple? *Aude, vide, tace*. Hear, see and be silent. Now we want to be sure that certain people remain silent, don't we? If that little tart has run off to that DC friend of yours there could be trouble all round.'

'So?'

'So, I want you to warn him off. And her.'

'You set me up.'

'Yeah, well.' He sniffed. 'That was meant for your friend. It wasn't my fault that he wouldn't play ball and you were all too keen. Look, Taylor, it's best for all concerned if you make sure that this little unpleasantness goes no farther. And I'm prepared to overlook the disrespect that you have shown towards the Brotherhood. You have shunned the protection of the Temple, that is your lookout. I am taught to view the errors of the profane with compassion and show the superior excellence of my faith by the purity of my conduct. Now fuck off.'

I got out of the car.

'My regards to Vic,' he called out after me. 'Remember, both me and him have your best interests at heart.'

I felt completely burned out. Everything had moved so fast. I'd known so much and understood so little. That's the problem with rapid promotion. There's so much to learn in the job. It takes time. There's no substitute for that. So easy to get into bad habits. To get led astray.

And I was tainted now. On the bung, like the rest of Vic Sayles' team. Not just bent for the job. Bent for myself. And the thing was, I really liked Vic. He was a good guvnor in so many ways. He got results and he treated those that worked for him well. He was just very, very hookey. I started to see how easy it was to go along with it all. A close-knit team, good morale and plenty of perks. Pretty soon it would all become second nature. I felt like I was falling into it. But deep down I knew that it was just all wrong. And that ate away at me.

Booze helped, or rather helped to numb all the doubts I had. For a while anyway. Then a maudlin sense of self-loathing would come to the surface. I tried to think about what I could do. I could always ask for a transfer, but that wouldn't do my precious career any good at all. I had no one to turn to. To talk to. Except Dave. And I'd really fucked up there. But I did need to talk to him. I needed to warn him. Mooney was diabolical, he seemed capable of anything. If Jeannie had gone to him and spilled the beans he'd have to be very careful. Being right wouldn't be enough. He'd have to be devious about it. Maybe I could help him out there. And maybe with Dave I could muster enough courage to do the right thing. He was my conscience, my better half. But I was on my own now. Lost.

I tried getting in touch with him but he was hard to track down. He was on Q-car duty so he was hardly ever at the Bush. I left messages but he never got back to me. To be honest there was something else I wanted. Jeannie. I wanted to see her again. It was a sad, stupid obsession. Another reason to hit the bottle.

I finally managed to get through to Dave after a skinful one night.

'Detective Constable Thomas,' came his voice down the blower.

'Dave?'

A pause then a weary sigh.

'What do you want, Frank?'

'I've been trying to call you.'

'Yeah. I know. What is it?'

'I'm sorry, Dave.'

'Bit late for that now, Frank.'

'Look, can't we talk? Go for a drink or something. For old times' sake.'

'Oh, please.'

'Everything's turned to shit, Dave.' My voice broke, almost sobbing with booze melancholia. 'I need you, mate.'

'Take it easy, Frank. For fuck's sake.'

'I mean it, Dave. I need to talk to you. There's things I need to tell you.'

Another pause. Another sigh.

'Yeah, all right,' he agreed, not nearly as grudging as he should have been. 'Look, I'm off Q-car duty next week. Why don't you come around then?'

On the Monday after the final, in Austin, Texas, Charles Joseph Whitman, an ex-Marine, climbed a tower in the campus of the University of Texas and shot fourteen people dead with a high-powered rifle. He had already killed his wife. And his mother. 'I didn't want,' he explained, 'her to be embarrassed by this.' A noble enough sentiment, I thought.

Later that week Julian said that he could arrange a meeting with the Kray twins. I was still trying to shape up this story on London gangs for the *Illustrated*. Julian knew one of Ronnie's ex-boyfriends. He took us to a small pub in Bethnal Green. The place was crowded; a celebration was in progress. Ronnie had been in another identity parade for the Cornell shooting that day at Commercial Street police station. The Flying Squad had once again failed to get anybody to finger him and he'd been released that afternoon.

We sat in the corner as the ex-boyfriend gingerly approached Ronnie Kray. Ronnie patted him on the shoulder gently and squinted his heavy-lidded eyes in our direction. The saloon bar was filled with all kinds of characters – heavy-looking men, tarty-looking women and some curious types. A huge African with a shiny bald head called Cha-Cha seemed to be some sort of master of ceremonies, referring to Ronnie Kray loudly as 'Mr Ronald'. A pair of dwarfs play-acted fighting moves with the largest of the heavies present, to much laughter. There was a strange circus-like atmosphere in the pub.

Ronnie finally came over and offered us both a drink. We stood up as he approached, but he motioned for us to be seated and joined us at the table.

'So, you're journalists, are you?' he demanded. His voice was soft and slightly sibilant.

'Yes, Mr Kray,' I replied.

'Well, there's been loads of rubbish written about me and my brother by you lot.'

'Maybe it's time you told your side of the story,' I suggested.

'Yeah,' he agreed. 'That would be a good idea. It'd be a good story, you know? I've met loads of famous people. I've got loads of – what d'you call them? – antidotes.'

'Anecdotes?' I corrected him stupidly.

He glared at me with those toadlike eyes.

'Yeah,' he declared. 'That's what I said.'

'Maybe you need a biographer.'

'A what?'

'Someone to write your life story, you know, like Truman Capote did with *In Cold Blood*.'

Suddenly the idea of writing a book came back to me.

'Who's he?' Ronnie asked brusquely.

'You know, *Breakfast at Tiffany's*?'

'Oo!' Kray announced. 'I liked that. Saw the film with Audrey Hepburn. Lovely. You reckon you could get him to do it?'

'Well, I didn't mean him actually. I was just using him as an example.'

'What do you mean? You think we're not good enough for him or something?'

'No, I didn't mean . . .'

'Because we want a proper writer to do our story. Not some twopenny-halfpenny hack.'

'Of course.'

'Well, you get on to this Truman geezer. I'm sure he'd be interested.'

'Er, right,' I agreed, not quite knowing what to say.

'Well, if you'll excuse me.'

He stood up and was gone. So that was that. We left the pub empty-handed. At least I did have a story for Sid Franks that week. I'd set up a drugs bust at Henekey's on Saturday afternoon with a police contact I had at Notting Hill nick.

9

Fucking gas-meter bandits, thought Billy. Some fucking gang. I'm stuck with a couple of gas-meter bandits.

Stan and his nagging missus. His non-existent job that he's never late for. He's never knocking off early from. Clocks in and out of this gap in the middle of the day to keep the missus happy. Makes her think he's on the straight. Evil little looks from her every time him and Jimmy go around to Stan's poxy flat. Mean little expression trying to warn them off. Too fucking late.

So's there's Stanley with what must be the best work attendance record in West London and she goes and says that he needs to take Friday morning off to take her to St Mary's Hospital. An appointment at out-patients. The very morning that they were planning to do the blag.

'I'm sorry, chaps,' he says, all sheepish. 'She's got to see this doctor.'

'Nothing trivial, I hope,' Billy replies.

Stan is all red-faced. Embarrassed.

'It's, you know, women's trouble.'

Yeah, yeah, thinks Billy. Women's trouble. That's Stan for you.

'Well, we'll have to do it next week.'

'Bugger next week,' says Billy. 'I'm fucking skint. We'll do it tomorrow.'

'Tomorrow?'

'Yeah.'

'But tomorrow's a Saturday.'

'I know tomorrow's a fucking Saturday.'

'Well, Billy, the banks don't open on Saturday.'

'I fucking know! We'll do a bookie's again. We've got to do fucking something. I'm sick of all this wanking about.'

Jimmy flustered. Trying to look calm. Act calm. In control.

'Aye,' he agrees, nodding sagely. 'We'll do it tomorrow.'

Jimmy. Thinks he's so fucking clever. At least Stan knows he's useless. Jimmy thinks he's some sort of tasty villain. Big plans. Big talk. *Right, well here's the MO* and all that pony. Big talk in the exercise yard in the Scrubs. He acted like a criminal genius in association. Outside he's just another gas-meter bandit.

His big plan. The moody number plates, duplicate of a Ford Executive parked in the area. Nick one like that and if we're clocked they'll trace it back to that motor. Complicated. It always has to be complicated with Jimmy. He doesn't know how useless he is. Thinks he's the brains behind it all.

So, on Saturday morning they were driving around in Stan's beaten-up old Standard Vanguard van looking for a particular motor to steal. They drove up to Regent's Park and cruised around the Outer Circle, because a lot of commuters parked there all day and there'd usually be plenty of motors to choose from. But they'd forgotten that on a Saturday there weren't many cars around.

They ended up motoring out of London. Up north towards Harrow. There were more people about, it being the weekend, so it was more risky. They finally found a blue Ford Executive parked in a side street by Park Royal Tube station.

Billy and Jimmy got out of the van and sidled up to the motor. Jimmy crouched down and pushed a small piece of wire into the lock on the driver's side. He jiggled it about as Billy kept watch. The wire broke in the lock.

'Fuck!' Jimmy hissed.

'What's the matter?' Billy asked, impatiently.

'It's broke.'

'What?'

'It's broke. The fucking wire's broke.'

'Oh, for fuck's sake!' Billy snapped, and stomped back to the van.

They drove down through Northolt, along Western Avenue. They found a pub and parked the van. Billy was still fuming. Impatient. They had some lunch and a pint and Billy calmed down a bit. He even had a game of darts with Stan.

'Shall we have another?' suggested Jimmy.

'Nah,' replied Billy. 'Let's get back to work.'

They headed back down towards the Bush. There was some talk about doing the bookie's anyway, nicked getaway car or no nicked getaway car. Coming down Scrubs Lane the prison came into view. Bad memories. *Wormwood Scrubs*, thought Billy. The devil himself couldn't have come up with a more evil-sounding name.

Stan noticed a car behind them in his rear-view mirror. A Triumph 2000.

'I tell you what we could do,' Jimmy said. 'We could do the rent collector.'

'You what?' said Billy.

'The rent collector. The bloke from the council who comes around to collect rent.'

'I know what a fucking rent collector is.'

'Hang on a minute,' said Stan.

'You see, I've watched him. I know the route he takes. We could jump him.'

'Hold up,' said Stan.

'So when does he do his rounds?' asked Billy.

'Look at that car behind us,' said Stan.

Billy turned around.

'Friday,' said Jimmy.

'Great,' muttered Billy.

'Looks like it's following us. What do you reckon, Bill?' Stan asked.

'Nah. Slow down. Let it pass.'

Stan did what he said. The car accelerated and overtook the van. A hand came out of the passenger side and flagged them down.

'Oh, fuck,' said Jimmy. 'The Old Bill. That's all we need.'

Stan pulled the van up by the kerb. Two men got out of the car and walked slowly towards them.

'Just stay calm,' muttered Billy.

'But we've got the fucking guns with us!' Jimmy hissed.

'I know we've got the fucking guns,' replied Billy.

On the back seat of the van was a shopping bag with a pair of overalls in it. Underneath the overalls were the revolver and the Luger. One of the men was tapping on the window. Plainclothes. CID. Billy grabbed the bag. Stan wound the window down.

'We're police officers,' the man by the window announced.

'Really?' Stan all fake cheery. 'What seems to be the trouble, Officer?'

'Mind telling me what you're all doing, running about three-handed this time of day?'

The copper nodded at Billy and Jimmy.

'We just been to the pub. For a game of darts.'

The copper laughed and said to his partner:

'We've got a darts team here, Dave.'

The other copper smiled knowingly and peered into the van.

'Yeah, well, they're some kind of team. That's for sure.'

'This your vehicle, is it, sir?'

Stan nodded.

'Yeah.'

'Your tax disc is out of date.'

'Yeah, well, I've applied for a new one. It's in the post.'

'Let's see your driving licence and insurance.'

One copper asking all these questions, the other snooping around the van, looking in at them. Billy felt the shape of the pistols in the shopping bag. Staring gloomily out of the passenger window, careful not to meet the eyes of the coppers, he caught sight of the walls and parapets beyond. Wormwood Scrubs. The prison loomed down at him.

'Your insurance is out of date too.'

'Give us a break, guv,' Stan pleaded.

'Let's have a look inside.'

One of the coppers looked in at Billy.

'What's in the bag, sir?'

Billy pulled out the overalls and held them out.

'Yeah, and the rest.'

Billy reached in again. He found the butt of the Luger. He clicked off the safety. This was it. This was the drill. Immediate Action Drill.

'Come on, you cunt. Empty the fucking bag.'

Billy pulled out the gun and shot the copper by Stan's window in the face. The other office froze for a second and then started to run back to the car. Billy got out of the van. He fired at the back of the fleeing man. The first shot missed.

The third policeman put the car in reverse. Jimmy grabbed the revolver and was in the road shooting at the police car. Billy fired again at the running man, who was now level with the car. He got him this time and the copper collapsed on to the tarmac, in front of the Triumph.

Kids playing on a patch of grass across the road. They hear the dry crack of gunfire. The delay of the sound of the shots from the movement makes it all look surreal. 'It's the telly,' one of them says. BBC down the road at White City. Often using local streets for filming exteriors. The man on the ground is twitching, one foot fluttering. Sudden knowledge. Horror. There are no cameras. This is really happening.

Jimmy was shooting out the windows of the police car. The driver, in a blind panic, crunched the gearbox into first and the Triumph shot forward, its front wheels running right over the body before it, jamming it beneath its chassis. Jimmy shot the driver through the windscreen. He slumped against the steering column. His weight was still on the accelerator but the body wedged under the car had lifted the back wheels a fraction off the ground. They spun wildy, free of any traction.

Billy and Jimmy ran back to the van. Stan was wide-eyed, muttering:

'Fuck, fuck, fuck.'

'Right, get us out of here,' ordered Billy as they got back in.

'What the fuck have you done?' whined Stan.

'Just fucking drive!'

All Flying Squad units are to telephone in immediately.

It came over the radio. Something big, I thought. Maybe I had a funny feeling around then. I don't know. Looking back it's hard to tell.

I was with an operational unit plotted up by a breaker's yard in Harlesden. Two cars. Me, DC Micky Parkes and a driver in one. C11 surveillance boys in the other. We had some information about a team at the jump-up. Lorry hijacking. This breaker's yard was supposed to be their slaughter. Maybe another of Vic Sayles' set-ups. I wasn't sure. I'd begun to lose track of what was to rights and what was hookey. Micky went to use the phone.

He came running back to the car.

'What is it?' I asked.

There was a puzzled look on his face.

'A Q-car's been ambushed in Shepherd's Bush.'

A Q-car in F Division. Dave.

'What do you mean, ambushed?'

'There's been a shooting.'

'A Q-car from the Bush?'

'Yeah.'

Foxtrot Eleven. Dave.

'What should we do?' Micky was asking. 'Hang on here?'

Dave Dave Dave Dave.

'Let's go!' I shouted at the driver.

Everything mobile was going west. The air alive with alarm bells. We got to Scrubs Lane. The whole street heaving with Old Bill. Uniform, plainclothes, motorbike coppers wandering about with their helmets still on, dog handler vans. Chaos. Officers trying to seal off the area as more bodies and vehicles came and went. Facts coming through the blur. Shocking stories running around. A shooting incident. Rumours of policemen dead.

The crime scene. Q-car with its windows shot out in the middle of the street. Foxtrot Eleven. A body lying in the gutter being covered with a bit of tarp by two officers. Blood on the tarmac. A figure in the driver's seat slumped over the wheel. Under the car a horribly twisted corpse. I wander up, flashing my warrant card at nobody in particular. Dazed, like everybody else on the scene. I crouch down and peer at the mangled body beneath the chassis.

Dave. It's Dave. I can see his face, twisted in shock and agony. Still recognisable. Dave. I'm on my hands and knees crawling towards him. Someone's pulling me back. I want to pull him out of there. I can't believe he's dead.

'Take it easy, Frank,' someone says, leading me away.

Sirens wailing in lamentation. Two-note keening into the summer sky. Dropping in pitch as they pass. Doppler shift. A semitone more mournful.

The sun in my eyes. Blinking at tears, red blotches swimming across my pupils. My mind racing. I'd done Dave a favour. Got him out of the West End. Out of danger. Back to the Bush. To this.

Guilt and anger. Guilt that it had been me that had put Dave here. Anger at Dave. Hard to account for. I just felt: *You stupid bastard, what did you want to go and get yourself killed for?*

Disbelief. He can't be dead. Dave, you can't be dead. I need to talk to you.

I was in Henekey's on Portobello Road with Alf Isaacs when it happened. I was there for the drugs bust I'd set up. I'd pitched the story to Sid and he let me have Alf for a couple of hours to supply the pictures for a nice little story. THE MENACE OF THE DRUGS RACKETS, that sort of thing. I was wearing a big canvas money-bag full of pennies in case I had to call into the news desk. Chances were, on this story, I wouldn't have to phone anything in. We'd have time to get back to the *Illustrated*. But, I thought, you never know.

Alf Isaacs told me that there was this American press photographer who got the nickname Weegee, from Ouija board, because it was like he had a sixth sense. He'd always be first on the scene of the crime, sometimes even before the police had got there. Now Alf's a good snatch man, meaning that his speciality is getting a photo of someone who'd rather not have their face splashed all over the papers. Scandal, exposé, someone seen coming out of a club they shouldn't have been at with someone they shouldn't have been with. A con man or racketeer's likeness revealed to the public he'd cheated. He had good instincts but hardly the clairvoyance of this Yank. But this time, well, we were charmed.

It was a hot afternoon and Henekey's beer garden was full of long-hairs, their dirgelike music blaring out of the juke-box. A couple of West Indian guys, who'd clearly been dealing, now looking worried by the presence of a pair of rather obvious plainclothes who were trying to mingle with the crowd. Alf kept his camera hidden but we didn't exactly blend in with the surroundings. The black guys knew the game was up and were trying to ditch their gear. The Drugs Squad boys made their move and Alf got ready for the snatch. Then a whole squad of uniformed officers came trooping in. There were half-hearted protests from the freaks; some hippy girl tried to give a flower to an inspector. Sniffer dogs were panting in the heat. A couple of arrests were made, the rest of the crowd were searched. Alf Isaacs snapped away merrily.

Then suddenly there was a strange lull in the police activity. One of the uniforms spoke intently to his inspector. Something was up, I could tell; so could Alf. He lowered his camera and we glanced at each other in anticipation. Then the inspector started barking orders. The operation was aborted and they all started trooping out of the pub. The two black guys were laughing with relief. Something was happening, something serious was up. I looked at Alf and he frowned back.

'Come on,' I said. 'Let's go.'

We followed the convoy of police vehicles as it crossed Ladbroke Grove, going westwards towards Wormword Scrubs. The air was filled with bells ringing. It seemed that the whole of the Met was racing towards something on Scrubs Lane. Wormwood Scrubs loomed before us.

'Maybe there's been a jail-break,' Alf suggested.

We got there before the scene of crime had been cordoned off. We were the first press there – we even beat the BBC television crews who were just around the corner at White City. Alf got some extraordinary snatches before the whole area was sealed off, some that we'd never be able to use. The dead policeman slumped at the wheel, looking like he was just having a nap, a grotesquely mangled body beneath the car. The third policeman lay sprawled in the gutter. It was a bloody massacre.

I felt quite exhilarated, thrilled to be amid such slaughter. It was hard not to smile at all the shocked faces. I had a sense of being complicit in the brutality. This was my story. Soon the whole scene was screened off.

'Move back now,' a traffic cop commanded gruffly.

Kids had been playing in the street when it had happened. I got quotes from them. One of the killers looked like Bobby Charlton, they said. Somebody else was driving past when it happened. They got the number plate of the killer's car. I made a note of it as it was being taken down by a police officer. It was all happening so quickly I hardly realised how big it was.

I found a phone box and called Sid, piles of pennies laid out in front of me.

'I've got a big one, Sid,' I told him. 'Front-page stuff.'

'What is it, Tony?'

'Well,' I said, thinking that now was the time to bargain, 'you know you said if I got a real corker of a story there'd be a staff job for me?'

'Stop fucking about. What's going on?'

'I could go somewhere else with this. Just being a casual.'

They'd have Alf's pictures, of course. But I'd got lucky and I knew that I could push it a bit.

'You cunt,' he hissed down the phone. 'You better not be having me on.'

'On my life, Sid,' I said. 'Something really big is just breaking.'

'Well, tell me what it is.'

'And I'll get the job?'

Sid Franks sighed heavily.

'Yeah, yeah, whatever. This better be good.'

So I told him. He sent down all the Saturday Men he had spare and a staff man to co-ordinate it all. I ended up running it all, though. I knew more of what was going on than anyone else. The word was out and all the other Sundays were soon scrambling over it. But we had the drop on them. We got the story out in time for the first trains for the provincial editions while the enemies were struggling to meet the late deadlines. MASSACRED IN THE LINE OF DUTY was how the splash sub told it. Alf had got the best pictures, shocking images that emerged from the darkroom. The lead story had 'The *Sunday Illustrated*'s Crime Team' as its byline but I had my own piece on page three: 'First Man on the Scene, Tony Meehan'.

Sid himself grandstanded the whole edition with a Page Two Opinion: *TOUGH ACTION MUST BE TAKEN: In a quiet West London street where children played in the August sunshine an answer was given, a final sickening answer to the theorists, to the namby-pambies, to the misguided do-gooders. To those who have given crime and brutality a far too easy run in this country; who have removed the fear of death from even the most callous murderers.* And so on. Sid started the *Illustrated*'s campaign to bring back hanging. He wheeled out Lord Thursby, for a bit of punditry. A 'Why We Should Bring Back the Rope' column.

We put the paper to bed very happy men. The circulation manager was delirious, wandering about with bottles of champagne, declaring: 'It's a coup, gentlemen, it's a fucking coup.'

10

They headed south. Over Hammersmith Bridge and east towards Vauxhall. Stan had a lock-up there. On Battersea Bridge roundabout the van's engine started to pink and they slowed down.

'What the fuck's the matter now?' groaned Billy.

'The tank's empty,' muttered Stan. He slapped the steering wheel in frustration. 'Jesus Christ, we're out of petrol.'

He kept his finger on the starter motor button and the van lurched along the road.

'There's a garage up ahead,' Jimmy observed.

They made it to the petrol station and pulled up behind a Morris Minor. A little old lady in a tweed suit was having the full works and there was only one attendant.

'Could you check my oil?' she was saying.

Police bells ringing in the distance. Panic in the city. Stan drummed his fingers on the wheel nervously. Jimmy looked wild-eyed. Billy's head was numb, calm. Just as it was after a jungle killing.

At last they got some petrol and sped off through Nine Elms to Vauxhall. The lock-up was in a railway arch by the river. Stan crunched a wing of the van as he backed it in. They walked down to the Embankment. The tide was low. A pram skeleton washed up on the muddy banks of the river.

'What the fuck are we going to do?' Stan asked nobody in particular.

'We got to get some money,' Billy answered. 'We'll have to screw somewhere.'

'Leave it out,' said Stan. 'Fuck this. I'm off.'

And he ran off down the road. Billy and Jimmy watched him disappear. Jimmy was very edgy now, sweating like a pig. Never killed anyone before, thought Billy. They saw a bus coming and they ran for it. A number 68. They travelled on it to Euston, went into the station café and had a cup of tea. Jimmy's cup rattling against the saucer as he picked it up with a shaking hand.

'You look as white as a sheet,' Billy told him. 'What's the matter?'

'What do you fucking think?'

'You ain't going to lose your bottle, are you?'

'For Christ's sake, Billy.'

'So what's the plan this time, eh? What's the SP? What's the MO?' he needled Jimmy.

Billy had a mad grin on his face. Shock. Jimmy sucked noisily at the hot tea.

'I'm getting out,' said Jimmy.

'Oh yeah? Where you going to go?'

'Back to Glasgow. Lie low until all of this calms down.'

Billy laughed contemptuously.

'This ain't never going to calm down. Never.'

They split up after that. Billy felt safer on his own. The other two, well, they were a fucking liability. He still had the guns.

He went back to the bed-sit. A smell of fried fish in the hallway. Sandra came out of the kitchen to greet him.

'What's the matter, love?' she asked. 'You look terrible.'

'I feel terrible.'

'I got a nice bit of rock salmon for tea.'

'I'm not hungry. I feel sick.'

He pointed at his throat.

'Sick up to here.'

'Did you hear the news?' she asked. 'About the policemen being shot?'

He stared at her.

'Oh no, Billy.'

'Shut up!' he snapped. 'Keep quiet about it.'

I badly wanted to be in on the investigation. Things were moving very fast. Detective Superintendent Tommy Fairburn had been appointed to take charge of the case. He was 'in the frame'. Quite literally. There was a wooden frame in Coco listing three senior officers on call to take on major murder investigations. It was Tommy's turn. He'd only just got back from Gloucester assizes, where he'd been giving evidence in a murder trial. DCI Jack Walker was his second-in-command and DI Ernie Franklin had been chosen from the Flying Squad. They were putting the operational team together. I managed to get to see Ernie.

'I really want a transfer on to the operation, sir.'

'Yeah, well, a lot of people are keen to get involved. It's understandable.'

'But I know the manor, sir. I've still got informants on the patch.'

'You worked F Division?'

'Yeah. I mean yes, sir. At the Bush.'

'So you know the men who were killed.'

'Dave Thomas, sir. We were bucks together.'

A sharp intake of breath.

'That's tough, son. Look, maybe you're too close to it. Anyway, it ain't up to me who's on the team. You're new on the Flying Squad, aren't you, son?'

'Yes, sir.'

'Well, look, the Heavy Mob is going to have an important role in this operation. We need to put the pressure on the other side to hand up the bastards that did this. Who's your guvnor?'

'Vic Sayles.'

'Well, don't worry, he'll keep you busy.'

And busy we were. Firearms were issued and the squad spent the night tearing about all over the place. Along with the newly formed Special Patrol Group, the Flying Squad's brief was to check on every possible hiding place in the city. Every dodgy pub, club, spieler or lock-up. Every known team of villains, anybody who had form for being at the heavy. They were all going to get a visit that night. The whole of gangland was going to get the shakedown.

Vic Sayles' role was obvious. He knew all the major-league faces. He'd done deals with all of them in his time, cut them enough slack in order to maintain his who's who knowledge of the underworld. Favours were owed. Now it was payback time.

'We want to start with the big guys,' he told me as we motored over to the West End. 'Well, we can forget about the Krays. The twins aren't going to be much use. They don't stray very far from the East End and they just don't play ball. The Richardsons are all wiped up. That leaves Freddie Foreman and Harry Starks. Frank Williams knows Freddie well so he's going after him. So we're going to have a word with Mr Starks.'

We got to Soho. Harry Starks' nightclub. The Stardust. Starks was a good place to start. He had West London connections. He'd worked for Rachman before he'd set up on his own. And though he wasn't known for being involved with armed blagging himself, he was known to offer protection to those getting their hands dirty. And his club was a regular meeting place for any number of London faces.

At the entrance to the club I whipped out my warrant card but one of the doormen was already nodding in recognition at Vic.

'Evening, Mr Sayles,' he muttered with gruff deference.

'Want a word with your guvnor,' Vic announced.

'Yeah.' The bouncer nodded again. 'Right. You'd better come in, then.'

He led us into the club. On stage some tart in a sequinned evening gown was bawling out 'You'll Never Walk Alone' in front of a mangy backing band. A lot of eyeballing from tables here and there. Dodgy-looking customers shuffling uneasily. Knowing who we were and wondering whether this was a raid, no doubt.

Harry Starks was at the head of a big table in the corner. A young blond kid next to him. A couple of business types being entertained with plenty of booze and a brace of busty tarts. A doorman went ahead and whispered in Starks' ear. Harry looked up at us as we came to the table. He stood up, smiling.

'Vic,' he said, all affable. 'To what do I owe the pleasure?'

'This ain't a social call, Harry,' Sayles replied.

'What's up?'

'I think you know why we're here.'

Starks frowned. Heavy eyebrows knitted.

'There's been a massacre, Harry. A bloody massacre.'

Starks sighed heavily.

'Terrible business,' he said, shaking his head. 'Terrible. Look, gentlemen . . .' He turned to his guests. 'You must excuse me.' Back to us. 'We better go upstairs.'

In his office Harry Starks poured us all a large brandy and we got down to business.

'Surely, Vic,' he said, 'you don't imagine I had anything to do with this, do you?'

'Yeah, but you might know who did.'

'I ain't heard nothing. Honest.'

'Don't fuck me around, Harry. Most of London's villainy come through this gaff at one time or another.'

'Straight up. Don't you think that I want this sorted out as much as you do? It's completely out of order. It fucks everything up. If I knew anything, you'd be the first to know.'

'I'm glad you see it that way, Harry. It's bad enough when you lot are killing each other. But this is something else. Our side is angry, fucking angry, and we want blood. My DS here' – he nodded at me – 'lost a best friend this afternoon.'

I felt an odd kind of shock as Vic said that. It still hadn't sunk in yet, I suppose. Dave dead. Dead. My face darkened as I stared at Starks. He looked a bit shaken.

'I'm sorry, son,' he muttered. 'I'm . . .'

'This is fucking grief, Harry. We want a result soon. A lot of us have played the game with you lot. Straightened things, done deals to keep the peace. Well, we're on the fucking warpath now. If anybody's hiding these bastards they better hand them up now otherwise there'll be hell to pay.'

'Look, Vic . . .' Starks all soft-voiced, reasonable. 'As I said, we all want this business dealt with.'

'Just let everybody know. Every firm, every team. Every fucking villain in every fucking manor. Anyone who so much as gives these cunts the time of day will have their cards marked. And I suggest you don't wait around for the duration. I suggest you lot find the killers and turn them in, pronto. 'Cos in the meantime there's going to be the biggest fucking clampdown you ever did see.'

'Yeah.' Starks nodded, thoughtfully. 'Point taken. I'll see what I can do.'

'Any information, no matter how small, let me or my DS here know. OK?'

We stood up to leave. Starks came around the desk to the door.

'Don't worry,' said Vic. 'We can find our own way out.'

Sunday and the story was everywhere. My story. Thanks to me the *Illustrated* had scooped most of it. A nation in shock, Union Jacks half-masted everywhere. There were constant bulletins on the television and the radio, endless angry comment. The bring-back-the-noose brigade was in full throat. That would keep Sid happy, I thought.

The Home Secretary visited Shepherd's Bush police station. Television cameras were there and a large mob, baying for blood. As he was being interviewed, hecklers in the crowd were shouting out to bring back hanging.

'I can well understand the strength of feeling at the present time, of, quite rightly, outrage at this heinous crime, but it would be quite wrong for me to make a major policy decision in the shadow of one event, however horrible that event may be.'

The mayor of Hammersmith launched an appeal for a fund for the dead policemen's dependants, and all across the country citizens were emptying their piggy-banks to make a donation.

Then came all the theories. What on earth had been the cause of the massacre? Two main notional motives were firming up. It had been a planned jail-break from Wormwood Scrubs or an underworld power struggle. The Q-car had come across two rival gangs and had been caught up in the crossfire of a shoot-out.

I was summoned to lunch at the proprietor's that day. I went with Sid Franks to his huge penthouse on Park Lane.

'You lucky cunt,' Sid muttered to me. 'The Boss hardly ever invites me, let alone a fucking reporter.'

It meant that my staff job was secure and I'd been noticed. I felt pretty pleased with myself.

'Just don't speak unless you're spoken to,' Sid was briefing me as we went up in the lift. 'And if he offers you a drink, decline. The old bastard's teetotal.'

We were ushered in by a butler with bulging eyes and a fishlike mouth.

'How is he, Francis?' Sid asked.

Francis gave a hollow chuckle.

'Oh, you know, tetchy. Very, very tetchy.'

The Boss was pacing up and down his cavernous apartment. He had a small shrewlike secretary who sat in the corner and would occasionally make shorthand notes on her pad when he wanted a comment recorded. Ted Howard, the washed-out-looking editor-in-chief, was already there, perched on the edge of an enormous black leather sofa.

Lunch was extraordinarily bland. Boiled fish in a tasteless parsley sauce, potatoes, carrots and peas, also boiled. Ted Howard had a plate of sandwiches instead and sat there munching at them, looking ghostlike. Francis, the butler, came around with a chilled bottle of Pouilly Fumé and a mischievous look on his face, knowing that we'd all settle for iced water, like the Boss. He fired questions at Sid and Ted and nodded at their answers, occasionally turning to comment to his secretary. The conversation moved on to stories the paper could run.

'I think we could do an investigation into psychic phenomena,' Ted suggested in his slow, gloomy voice.

I caught a glimpse of Sid barely concealing his impatience with this. Ted Howard had increasingly become obsessed with the paranormal; he appeared to have already joined the other side. Sid could often be found fuming in the newsroom, muttering, 'Ted wants another fucking table-tapping article.' There was some discussion that Sid steered back to general aims. They talked of the 'enemies', the *News of the World* and the *People*. Sid offered an obvious opinion.

'We've got to give the readership what it wants,' he declared.

'No, no, Sidney,' the Boss retorted. 'You've got it the wrong way around. We've got to get the readership to want what we give it.'

Eventually the big story of the day came up.

'Terrible business,' said the Boss. 'Terrible. But a great issue. Circulation figures were tremendous.'

He turned to me for the first time.

'And you're the young man that broke it.'

'Yes.'

'How did you manage that?'

'I don't know. I mean, I was in the right place at the right time, I suppose.'

'That's what the paper needs, gentlemen!' the Boss exclaimed. 'People in the right place at the right time. You'll see to that, won't you, Sidney?'

11

They hardly slept at all. They held on to each other in the darkness. When dawn came Billy turned the radio on to listen to the news. The police had the registration number of the van. They'd soon be on to Stan. He'll grass us all up in no time, thought Billy.

And the van. Fuck, the van. There was forensic all over it. They should have burned it. Too late for that now.

Billy started packing a small case. Sandra watched him wandering about the bed-sit like he was in a trance.

'I've got to get away,' he explained.

'I want to come too,' she said.

He stared at her, wondering how far he could trust her. He remembered Trixie, grassing him when she was picked up by the Tom Squad. You couldn't trust a woman. Sandra looked back at him, imploringly.

'Please,' she said, softly.

He smiled.

'Yeah,' he replied, nodding slowly. 'OK.'

So she packed her little duffle bag. The same one she'd packed when she'd run away from home. She was running away again. But anything was better than going back there.

'Where are we going to go?' she asked.

'I don't know yet. But I'll tell you what we'll do first.'

'What?'

'We'll go and see Mum.'

Sandra laughed. She couldn't help herself.

'What's so fucking funny?' Billy demanded.

It was just like the usual Sunday lunch-time ritual except this time they went first to Paddington Station to leave their bags in the left luggage. Lily was full of the news of the shooting.

'I don't know what the world's coming to,' she declared.

Sandra checked Billy's response, and his eyes darted to hers. But they both remained impassive. Giving nothing away, except perhaps in being so subdued. She felt that maybe they should join in the outrage, comment on how terrible things had become, but she knew that neither of them had the stomach for that.

They ate in near-silence. After they had finished eating Billy coughed and looked towards his mother.

'So, Ma,' he began. 'I need to ask a favour.'

'What is it, Billy?'

He sighed.

'It's the business.'

She frowned.

'I thought you said the business was going well.'

'It is, Ma, it is. The thing is, I've got a bit of a cash flow problem.'

'What do you mean? I thought you said you had a big job coming up.'

'Well, that's just it, Ma. I need to invest in some new plant to get this contract done. As I said, it's just a cash flow problem.'

'Cash flow?'

'Yeah, I need a bit to tide me over.'

Lily stared at her son. Sandra saw an awful look of knowing.

'Are you in trouble, son?' she asked.

Billy laughed nervously.

'Of course not, Ma. It's just . . .'

Billy's mother turned to Sandra with a piercing gaze. Sandra dropped her spoon and it clattered on to her plate.

'Oh, Billy.'

His mother's voice was a soft, mournful wail.

'It's all right, Ma,' he tried to placate her. 'Honest.'

But she had already got up from the table and gone over to the tea caddy on the mantelpiece. She knows, thought Sandra. She watched as the older woman stoically counted out the notes. It looked as though there was actual physical effort in her holding herself up. She was pretending not to know. Only this was bearable. Giving in to the knowledge of it would send her crashing to the floor. She sniffed and lifted her head as she closed the lid of the box. As she came back to the table with the money her eyes were glistening. She handed the little bundle to Billy.

'You better go, son,' she said.

'Well,' he said, 'we don't have to go yet, Ma. We can stay a little while longer.'

'No,' she said deliberately, coldly. 'You'd better be off.'

As Billy kissed her on the cheek, Lily's eyes shut tight and a tear squeezed out from each one. As they closed the front door behind them they could just hear a muffled sobbing from inside.

They got their bags and found a hotel near the station. They signed in as Mr and Mrs Crosby. A young married couple on holiday, thought Sandra, almost believing it herself for a moment.

In bed Billy smoked incessantly, staring at the ceiling. She moved up close to him. He put an arm around her and held her against his chest. Suddenly she wanted him. She slid her leg slowly over his groin and moaned softly. He sighed sharply and pushed her away.

'Leave it out,' he hissed. 'For Christ's sake.'

She rolled over and curled up into a ball. She put her thumb in her mouth and rocked gently on the bed. She soon found sleep. There was nowhere else to go. Billy lit another cigarette and stroked her back. His hand was shaking. She was a liability. Sooner or later he'd have to leave her behind.

Monday morning and the van's owner had been traced via a car dealer in Kilburn. We had a name, Stanley Mullins, and an address in West Eleven. A whole load of us were issued with arms and sent to surround a block of flats off Ladbroke Grove. The Special Patrol Group was there in force too. Their first big operation, so they wanted to make a good show of it. Two of their guys in position with tear gas pistols. There was a strange feeling on the raid with us all being so tooled up. An expectancy of something we didn't quite know yet. We weren't ready for this. It was like we were playing with new toys. And a kind of rivalry was emerging between the SPG and the Flying Squad. It had been plainclothes officers who had been killed so we wanted to get the bastards before anyone else. And I suppose both teams considered themselves to be the élite of their type. The SPG for uniform branch, Flying Squad for the Department.

So there was a whole mob of us waiting, dogs and dog handlers at the ready. When we knew we had all the angles covered, Ernie Franklin kicked the door in and stormed in with a couple of lads, Webleys at the ready. I clocked this bloke they hauled out but it wasn't anyone I recognised. His wife was bawling away on the access balcony. The estate forecourt was filling up with onlookers; the SPG went into crowd control as he was bundled into a black Maria. I started thinking, maybe he was just small fry. All these theories about a planned jail-break or a gang shoot-out, well, they didn't really add up. Maybe it was just a minor-league team. Time to look farther down the food chain. Maybe I could get a lead from my local informants. I got in touch with Golly, who'd been a snout of mine when I'd been at the Bush.

I figured that maybe I could get the drop on the investigation. Ernie Franklin would already be hard at work on this Mullins bloke, but if I could come up with some other names I'd be ahead of the game. Golly always liked to meet at the cinema. He was paranoid about being seen in daylight. I arranged to meet him at our usual place for a matinée at Shepherd's Bush Odeon. I got there for the second show. One for the circle. A bored usherette tore my ticket and handed me the stub. Upstairs. The place was nearly empty. Just a couple in the back. Boy and girl. Furtive teenage movements. Truant fumbling. I could make out Golly easily enough from his trademark shock of frizzy hair. There he was in his usual place at the front, rattling a little box of chocolate-covered peanuts.

The Pearl & Dean advertising fanfare started to blare out as I sidled along the row to sit next to Golly. Giggles from the back row. *Probably think we're a couple of queers*, I thought.

'You know what this is about, don't you?' I whispered.

Golly rolled a nut around his rotten molars, mashing it thoughtfully.

'Mmm.' He sucked at his teeth and probed cavities with his tongue. 'Long time no see, Mr Taylor. Or should I say Detective Sergeant Taylor.'

'Yeah, yeah.'

'In the Flying Squad now, aren't we?'

'Golly . . .'

'We have come up in the world. I suppose it's kind of a promotion for both of us, isn't it?'

'What the fuck are you on about?'

'Well, now you're a DS. In the Heavy Mob. That makes me . . .'

'Makes you what? You're a grass, Golly. Don't get above yourself.'

'Yeah, but a Flying Squad grass.'

'Look, stop fucking me about, Golly. I need some info.'

'All I'm saying . . .' Golly smacked his lips.

'Golly . . .'

'Congratulations, that's all.'

'Right. Now, you know what this is, don't you?'

'The shooting.'

'Yeah, that.'

'Terrible business. Let me take the opportunity to offer my condolences to . . .'

'Golly, for fuck's sake, let's just get on with it, shall we?'

Golly rattled another nut from his box and popped it into his mouth.

'Stanley Mullins,' I said to him. 'Mean anything to you?'

'Mm.' Golly worked the nut around his mouth. 'Stan, mm, yes.'

'You know him?'

'Mm, yeah. Petty thief. Small-time. Wouldn't expect him to be involved in this.'

'What about associates?'

'Yeah, well, he was knocking around with a couple of geezers.'

'Who?'

'Jimmy something. Scotch. And this bloke Billy. They were kind of teamed up. Nothing big, though.'

'Right. What about second names?'

Golly made a fluid sniff.

'Sorry. Dunno.'

'Well, that'll do for now. See what you can find out and I'll be in touch.'

I got up to leave. Golly grabbed my arm.

'Mr Taylor?'

'Yes?'

'I expect there'll be quite a reward for information leading and so on.'

'I expect so, yes.'

'Well, I was wondering if I couldn't have a bit of a sub, like.'

'You're a fucking parasite,' I told him, and handed him a fiver.

I rushed over to the Bush where Mullins was being held. I got someone to haul Ernie Franklin out of the interrogation. He sighed heavily when he saw me.

'Taylor,' he said impatiently when he saw it was me. 'I thought I told you there's no room for you on this investigation.'

'I know, sir, but I've got something.'

'What is it?'

'Something off a local snout, sir. Known associates of this man you're holding. Ask him about two blokes he knocks about with. Jimmy and Billy.'

'I'm still in the process of checking his alibi, son.'

'Yeah, but just ask him.'

'Listen, son, let's not jump the gun. We've got to be methodical about this.'

'But, sir . . .'

'But nothing. Listen, Taylor, you've got your orders on this operation and I suggest you stick to them. We can't afford to have every officer in the Met conducting his own private investigation.'

'I'm sorry, sir, it's just . . .'

'Yeah, yeah. Look, thanks for the information. And if you'll excuse me I've got an interview to attend to.'

My first day as a staff reporter on the *Illustrated* and I was put in charge of the paper's 'Crime Team' covering the Shepherd's Bush shooting. When I asked who else was on the team Sid said:

'You're it, son. We'll use other staff men and casuals whenever we get any breaks. Your job, for the moment, is to stay on top of it. And let me know as soon as anything happens.'

So I put together all we had on the case so far. I called it the Shepherd's Bush Shooting Crime Dossier.

'Yeah, I like that,' said Sid. 'Sounds dead professional.'

He, in the meantime, was working on the public outrage angle. His latest idea was a 'Readers' Poll: Should We Bring Back the Rope?' Some Tory MP had already brought this up in the House. Sid was sure that this aspect of the case would be a winner, no matter what happened before the Saturday deadline.

'And we'll need a bloody good womb-trembler,' he announced to the whole newsroom. 'All this doom and gloom is going to be too much otherwise.'

I felt a sudden sense of confidence in myself. Something had gone right for once in my life, a dream of a story. Sid drew up a contract for me to sign. And there was something about the crime itself that made me feel bold. It had been so ruthless. Someone had taken their revenge – it was reassuring in some way.

Then news came through that a man had been arrested and taken to the Bush. I rushed over there with Alf Isaacs. He got a good snatch of the man being bundled into the nick under a blanket, but there was only a brief comment to the press about a man 'helping with their inquiries'. No name yet. So we decamped, with the rest of the press, to the White Horse.

I realised then that there would be a hell of a lot of waiting around. And a lot of drinking. I'd known that that was part of the routine but I'd never really got into it when I was a Saturday Man. But there just wasn't much else to do. All the press men in huddles, swapping stories and theories, an endless buzz of information and opinion and gossip. We had to be on call around the clock, and that would usually mean holing up somewhere where you could get a drink and maybe a sandwich.

I met up with Julian after work. I bought him dinner at the Gay Hussar.

'Congratulations,' he said. 'Legitimate at last.'

'If you can call the *Illustrated* legitimate.'

'Don't knock it, darling. It's a job. Now if only I could get a gossip column somewhere.'

Julian told me that he was cultivating Teddy Thursby.

'He's a great source. And, you know . . .'

He shrugged and gave this queeny smile. He was up to his old tricks of latching on to an older and richer homo.

We went on to Le Gigolo on the King's Road. I can't really remember very much about the evening as I got very drunk. Woke up fully clothed on my bed with no idea of how I'd got home.

12

Billy lay in the grass in Hyde Park. A sunny day. A red glow on the backs of his eyelids. Killing time. *Here I am*, he thought. *I'm the one you're looking for*. His mind was reeling. Ever present. An animal paranoia. Of being hunted. He couldn't relax for a second. When he was a kid he thought if he closed his eyes and everything disappeared he would disappear too. He would become invisible. But now he felt himself being watched all the time.

He sat up. A group of hippies in a circle near by. Having a picnic. Passing around a joint. He had to wait until five. Then he'd go to see Sam. He'd phoned him that day and made an appointment.

Sam was a forger he'd met in the Scrubs. Maybe he'd be able to get him a bent passport. Then he'd be off. To Ireland, he reckoned. Sandra was wearing the minidress he'd bought her. She sat beside him, eyeing him nervously. They'd run out of things to say to each other. He'd have to get rid of her.

She went and got an *Evening Standard*. They'd found the van in the lock-up. His dabs were all over it. What a fucking mess, he thought. He sent Sandra back to the hotel and got a bus to Camden Town.

Sam had a second-hand bookshop on Chalk Farm Road. A musty smell of old paper in the place. Sam closed the shop and led him out to the back. He lit a fag.

'What can I do you for, Billy?'

'I want a passport.'

Sam took a drag and smiled.

'What's the matter? Petty France closed, is it?'

'You know what I mean.'

'Yeah, sure.'

'So?'

'Well, I'll need a photograph. Should be able to sort something out by tomorrow.'

'How much?'

'A ton.'

'You're joking, ain't you?'

'Take it or leave it, Billy.'

Tuesday. Vic Sayles called me into his office.

'Got a message from our friend, Mr Starks. Says he might have something for us.'

'That's great, guvnor.'

'Yeah. Thing is, Frank, I've got to go to a senior officers' briefing. Seems like this bloke they've pulled has coughed. Can you go over and check it out?'

I went over to the Stardust and met Starks in his office.

'Well,' he said, 'I've been checking on all the faces I know who are known to use shooters. Nothing. But then a business associate of mine knows somebody who's been dealing them quite recently.'

'A business associate?'

Starks grinned.

'Yeah. Bubble,' he said. 'He reckons he knows something.'

Tony Stavrakakis, he meant.

'I thought the big Greek had gone straight.'

Starks shrugged.

'Well, he keeps his hand in, you know? Turns out one of his fellow countrymen was looking to sell a Luger. Could be a lead. Anyway, Tony's got a restaurant up in Finsbury Park. I'll give you the address.'

He wrote something on a scrap of paper.

'We want these bastards caught, you know. This whole thing has been a pain in the arse. Your lot breathing down our neck all week.'

He handed me the address.

'Be lucky, son. If you don't get them' – he grinned – 'we will.'

I got up to go. At the door he slipped a wad of notes into my hand.

'Wait a minute,' I said. 'What the fuck is this?'

'No, no,' he said, pushing the money into my palm. 'Don't get me wrong. It's for that benevolent fund thing.'

The Dionysus restaurant, Finsbury Park. Stavrakakis was in the kitchen watching the chef putting these chunks of meat on big skewers. I flashed my warrant card and he nodded. He'd been expecting me.

'Listen,' he said, 'if I tell you what I know, that's it, innit?'

'That depends on what you've got.'

'No, you listen here. Harry said I just tell you what I know and there ain't no trouble for me.'

'OK.'

'It's a deal?'

'Yeah, sure. It's a deal.'

He smiled and shook my hand with a big meaty paw.

'OK. Look, this man Costas. He's political. A troublemaker. He sell a gun to this man.'

'Where? Here?'

'Look, I told you. I tell you what I know and that's it. I no involved in anything else. OK?'

'OK.'

'Well then, I tell you where you can find this man Costas.'

I got my notebook out.

There was a press conference at Scotland Yard on Tuesday morning. I went along, bleary-eyed and hung over. The man who had been helping the police with their inquiries was named as Stanley Mullins. He had now been remanded in custody. Two other men suspected of being involved in the killings were named as Jimmy Drummond and Billy Porter. Descriptions were given. Distinguishing marks: Drummond, tall with balding hair, the man the kids at the scene had remarked 'looked like Bobby Charlton'; Billy Porter, thick brown hair, a tattoo of a tiger on his right shoulder.

The public were warned not to approach these men, they were dangerous, possibly armed. All of this would make the late editions of the evening papers and the six o'clock news bulletins. My deadline seemed miles away. I had a long boozy lunch.

Sid called me into his office in the afternoon, the 'bollocking room'. I knew I'd done something wrong. He waved a handful of pink expense forms at me dismissively.

'This is no good,' he said. 'No bloody good at all. It really won't do.'

'I'm sorry, Sid,' I said. 'I didn't realise it was too much.'

'Too much?' he retorted. 'Too bloody much? It's not too much, you silly cunt. It's too little.'

I frowned and he sighed and sat me down, patted me on the back and whispered in my ear.

'Listen, son. If accounts start noticing that one of our reporters is claiming less than half everybody else is they might start adding a few things together. And we don't want that, do we?'

I felt exhausted so I went home and had a long soak in a hot bath. Julian came around to my flat later. He had a mischievous look on his face.

'Well,' he declared as I let him in, 'didn't we have a good time last night.'

'What are you talking about?'

'You, darling. You were quite on form.'

I couldn't remember a thing. I had an awful sinking sensation. I had made a fool of myself, no doubt.

'Oh, Christ,' I murmured.

'Yes, dear,' Julian continued with an evil smile. 'You were quite the entertainment for the evening.'

'What did I do?'

'Well, you went into this extraordinary . . .' Julian paused to conjure a word. '. . . routine. It was quite wild.'

I felt sick. The thought of making an exhibition of myself was nauseating. But I worried more about losing control.

13

Billy and Sandra went to Paddington Station to the photo-booth there to get a picture for Billy's passport.

'Where are we going to go, Billy?'

'I don't know, love. Over the water somewhere. Dublin, probably.'

He suddenly thought that he was stupid telling her anything. As soon as he'd ditched her she'd blab everything. But he needed to keep her sweet for just a bit longer.

As he was putting the money in the machine she suddenly had a thought.

'Billy?' she said.

'Yeah?'

'You only need one picture, don't you?'

'Yeah.'

'Well, once you've got that, I could come into the booth with you.'

'What?'

'So we could have our picture taken together.'

'Are you fucking mad?'

'I just thought . . .'

'What if somebody found that on you? That would look good, wouldn't it?'

'I just haven't got a picture of us together.'

'A nice little souvenir, is that what you want?'

She started to cry.

'I'm sorry, Billy.'

She looked pale and pathetic. She was just a kid, after all. She could crack up at any time. He had to be careful with her no matter how stupid she could be. He put his arm around her.

'Don't worry, love. We'll get our picture done. One day.'

She went back to the hotel and he went up to Camden for his appointment with Sam. He passed a newspaper stall. YARD NAME TWO 'ARMED MEN' was the headline. Stan had cracked. It was all closing in on him. He hoped to God that Sam hadn't seen the evening paper.

Sam closed up the shop again and they went out the back. Billy handed over the passport photo. Sam took it and sat down at his desk. He had a passport there that had its photograph removed. Sam placed Billy's picture over the original photo, turned them over and picked up a pencil. His hand was trembling. He began to move the pencil to and fro across the back of the photographs.

'Piece of piss, really,' he explained as he worked. 'You see, there's an embossed stamp that goes over the corner of the photo and on to the front page, see?'

He showed Billy the round seal on the front page of the passport, a quarter-circle missing in the box where the photograph had been.

'It's like brass-rubbing. All you've got to do is transfer that impression from one photograph to another.'

He continued to scrawl away with the pencil. He seemed agitated.

'There,' he declared, turning both pictures over again. There was now an impression of the stamp on Billy's likeness. 'Instant new identity.'

He placed the photo on the passport.

'All I got to do now is trim it so it fits flush. And bingo.'

He gave a big nervous smile.

'Bet you're wondering why I need a moody passport, aren't you, Sam?'

'Oh, no, Billy. You know me. No questions asked.'

Billy saw Sam sneak a look at his watch.

'Running late, are they?'

'What do you mean?'

'The people you're expecting. The people you've told I'm going to be here.'

'I haven't told anybody.'

'You fucking liar.'

Billy pulled out the Luger, pointed it at Sam's head.

'You've grassed me up, haven't you?'

Sam was shaking.

'No I ain't, Billy. Honest.'

Billy pressed the gun against his head.

'Tell the truth, Sam.'

'Honest. I haven't. I ain't said a word to the Old Bill.'

There was a rapping against the glass in the door of the shop.

'Then who's that, then?'

'It ain't the Old Bill.'

'What?'

'It's the other side. They want to hand you up, Billy. What you did has caused so much aggravation. No firm's going to get any peace until it's cleared up. Everyone knows I do bent passports so they figured that you might be paying me a visit.'

The rapping came again. Louder, more insistent.

'I wouldn't grass to the Old Bill. But I'm hardly going to say no to that lot, am I?'

Billy shut the door of the back room and pushed the desk against it.

'Where's the back way out of here?'

'You'll have to go through the window.'

'Right. Turn around. I better give you a lump. Don't want to get into trouble with that lot, do yer?'

'No need for that, Billy.'

'Turn around, you silly cunt.'

Billy whacked Sam around the back of the head with the butt of the pistol. He could hear the sound of glass breaking as the shop door was kicked in. He put the gun back into his waistband and opened the window. He turned back to the desk for a second and looked at the passport. That would be no use now. He pocketed his photograph and climbed out.

Ernie Franklin called me into his office.

'I just want to thank you, Frank. Those names your snout gave you, well, they jogged a few memories.'

'I didn't want you to think that I was jumping the gun, sir.'

'No, of course not. It's just that everybody's so bloody keen to be in on the sharp end on this one. I just have to make sure that we're allocating resources properly. We don't want officers duplicating each other's investigations.'

'I've got another lead, sir.'

'Christ, you've been busy. What is it?'

'I think I might have found the bloke that supplied the guns to the gang. Greek Cypriot. Ex-EOKA apparently.'

'What have you got?'

'A name and an address. Finsbury Park.'

I jotted it all down for him. Ernie sat there for a while looking at this scrap of paper. Then he peered over it at me.

'Look, Taylor. Since you've been so busy and all maybe you'd like to be in on it when we pull this Greek bloke.'

I grinned.

'Not half. I mean, yes, sir.'

'Well, I'll have a word with Vic Sayles.'

So early the next morning we got an operational team together and plotted up plenty-handed outside the address Tony Stavrakakis had given me. A dawn raid. We sledgehammered his door down and went in, guns drawn. This Costas guy was in bed with a blonde tart. We dragged him out half naked and bundled him into the back of a black Maria. We found a small arsenal of guns and ammunition under the floorboards of his dingy little flat.

After five hours of questioning Costas admitted to selling a Luger to a man fitting the description of Billy Porter but denied knowing of his whereabouts. This didn't get us very far but Ernie was pleased with the result.

'Well, at least it's something,' he said.

'Yeah, but it doesn't get us anywhere closer to Porter, does it, guv?'

'Maybe not. But at least we're seen as doing something. That's good for morale. Look, Frank . . .'

'Yes, sir?'

'I'm going to recommend a commendation for this.'

'Thank you, sir.'

'You've been busy. But more importantly you've been lucky. And that's what we need right now. A bit of luck. So how would you like to be drafted in as part of the main investigation team?'

'I think you know the answer to that one, guvnor.'

'Right. Well, you're in.'

The front page of the *Illustrated* that week was a blown-up photo the police had issued. MANHUNT FOR BILLY PORTER, splashed the headline. *Yard warn public: 'He is armed and dangerous, do not approach him.'* Sid Franks was drumming up the lynch mob with his Readers' Poll on Capital Punishment: 'Let The Powers That Be Know What *You* Think'. There were reported sightings of Porter everywhere. My byline was on the 'Profile of a Killer' feature on page five. I collated the sparse details: borstal as a teenager, National Service, a GBH charge in the late fifties. He was shaping up as Public Enemy Number One. Attention was drawn to the intense gaze in the police photograph. Dark, hooded eyes, thick arched eyebrows. 'The Eyes of a Killer,' I wrote, 'the ruthless stare of evil.'

I found myself studying the face. It seemed to be looking out at me, quizzical, goading, the eyebrows joined. That was supposed to mean something, wasn't it? Born to hang. That's what they said. Maybe Porter was as cursed as I was. Everyone was still trying to work out what the motive for the killings was. Maybe this was it.

Physiognomy, the knowledge of outward signs. Stigmata. *It's written all over your face*, my mother used to accuse me when I'd done something wrong and was refusing to admit to it. And could not physiognomy be used as divination as well? Just like the reading of a palm, you could tell by the face the fate of its wearer. I wondered what my own features betrayed. I looked at Porter and thought I recognised a fellow monster.

All of these mad thoughts seemed to possess me, as if they were driving me on to something. Porter's mouth, slightly open as if he were about to say something, to tell me what to do. I was drinking too much. Too many long boozy lunches were taking their toll on my mind and I felt that if I wasn't careful, I'd lose it. I almost yearned for such a release.

Walking back to the office from lunch one day, I caught my reflection in a shop window. Through a glass darkly. It hovered over a display, transparent and ghostly, a hunted, frightened expression. And something else. The eyes of a killer.

14

He sent Sandra out in the morning to get a paper. Jimmy had been picked up in Glasgow. The stupid bastard had been staying at his father's house. Two down, one to go. Now he was on his own. Well, almost. He'd already decided what to do.

They checked out of the hotel. Billy tried to look relaxed as the manager added up their bill. Every glance, every delay could be significant. The police photo was everywhere. He wasn't safe in the city.

They got a bus over to King's Cross. Billy held hands with Sandra. This would make him look less suspicious, he thought. Part of a young couple. She could give him cover for a while. But it couldn't last.

He led her to a shop on Pentonville Road. CAMPING AND ARMY SURPLUS, it said above the door. He bought a groundsheet, a sleeping bag, a Primus stove, some mess tins, a combat jacket, combat boots, some thick white socks and check shirts, a small radio and a rucksack to put it all in.

Special Operations, he thought. They want a hunt. I'll give them a fucking hunt. He stopped off at a grocer's and got some provisions. A loaf of bread, three tins of beans, Oxo cubes, a packet of tea, dried milk. Rations. He bought a couple of tins of Old Holborn tobacco and some green Rizla papers. They got the 720 Greenline bus to Epping Forest. They got off at a stop at the edge of the forest.

Billy changed into his new boots, lacing them up slowly.

'Are we going to hide in the woods?' asked Sandra.

'I'm going to hide. It's time for me to go it alone.'

Sandra started to cry.

'But I can help you,' she sniffed. 'Please let me come with you.'

'You can't. I got to do this on my own, now.'

'But,' she sobbed, 'I've got nowhere else to go.'

'Get the bus back into town,' said Billy. 'Maybe you should go back home, you know.'

'I ain't going back there,' she replied.

And she meant it. She wouldn't go back. Never.

Billy held her and kissed her hard on the mouth. He pulled away.

'I got to go,' he announced.

He turned and walked away into the forest, without looking back. He started making ground. He had a long way to go but knew where he was headed. Epping Forest was too obvious. And he couldn't be sure that Sandra wouldn't go to the police. Thorley Woods by Bishop's Stortford. That's where he would go. Where he had played as a boy. His mother had taken him there. The thought that she might know where he was was vaguely comforting. *If you go down to the woods today, you'd better go in disguise.* He knew the lie of the land. He would find a hiding place. Some of the bandits he had hunted in Malaya had lived in the jungle for years. He was the bandit now.

The bus took Sandra back through North London. On her own once more. Left behind. She'd have to start all over. Like none of it had ever happened. She was a mystery girl again. And she would keep the mystery. Keep the secret. She knew that she could. She would never tell and that would give her strength. She would never betray him. He was a stupid bastard for what he had done. But she knew why he had done it. It didn't excuse it, didn't even explain it. But she knew she would never speak of it to anyone. Because she knew. He'd never talked about it but she had felt him moving and muttering at night, twisting and turning next to her in bed. The horror he had been through. She knew that.

Vic Sayles had organised a stag night for his team. 'Time for some shore leave,' he announced. We had been busy, after all. He hired out a club in Paddington. It was all laid on. A buffet dinner, a couple of strippers and all the booze you could drink. A regular part of his team's 'work hard play hard' ethic. All paid for by DI Sayles' own version of the Police Benevolent Fund. And we did need a morale boost, after all. We'd got some results. Two down, one to go. But the pressure was on. It seemed that this Porter bloke was the real killer – the rest had just gone along with it. If we couldn't catch this bastard there'd be hell to pay. I mean, if the police couldn't protect their own, how the fuck was the general public supposed to feel safe?

And it wasn't just police. It was detectives that had been killed. Plainclothes. Our lot. It almost seemed a point of honour that someone from the Department should bring him in. The unhealthy competition between the Flying Squad and the SPG continued. And with different command structures it could cause confusion when there was a sighting and two different groups of officers would arrive on the scene. Of course, CID always considered themselves superior to uniform, and the SPG resented this arrogance. They had special training, particularly in large-scale operations. Probably saw us as a bunch of wankers swaggering about in sheepskin coats.

For me, of course, it was a lot more personal. Dave. I couldn't get his mangled body under the Q-car out of my mind. His murder had been so senseless. A routine check on a dodgy motor. I mean, you expect to take risks in this job, that's part of the glamour of it, but something as stupid as an out-of-date tax disc. It made you wonder what was the bloody point. And I guess I still felt a little twinge of guilt about it. It was me getting him sent back to Division that put him on Q-car duty that day. I know it's stupid thinking like that but I couldn't help it.

So I sort of concentrated all these thoughts and feelings on to getting this Porter bloke. Now I was with the main investigation team I could really focus on that. I just had to tell Vic that I was being transferred. I hoped he wouldn't take it the wrong way.

I'd already had a skinful when he called me over to a quiet corner in the room.

'I hear you're going over to Ernie's team,' he said.

'Yes, guvnor.'

'You might have told me.'

'I was going to.'

'I suppose you're glad to get away from me.'

'It ain't that. I just want on to the main investigation.'

Vic nodded slowly.

'Yeah, yeah. Makes sense. You're a fucking pushy one, aren't you, Taylor?'

I sighed.

'I need another drink,' I said.

'Ernie does things slightly differently from me, you know?'

'Yeah?'

'Yeah. A bit more, let's say, orthodox. You probably prefer that.'

It was probably the booze but I suddenly had a strange thought. That being on the investigation could get me back on the straight and narrow. That Dave was looking after me even after he was dead. Like some sort of fucking guardian angel. And if we could find his killer then maybe that would be some sort of redemption.

Julian wanted to go to some new club just off Leicester Square and he dragged me along. It was all black leather chairs and gleaming chrome, full of fashionable media types.

'What do you think?' he asked.

'It's a bit pretentious.'

'Not for the gutter press, then,' he said with a supercilious sneer.

'I suppose not.'

'We are all of us stars,' Julian announced with the flourish of one hand, as if to signal he had come up with something clever. 'But some of us are looking at the gutter.'

He thought he was so clever. Probably considered me dull and suburban, which was right. London was becoming 'sophisticated', 'swinging'. I loathed the cheap decadence of it all. Julian talked of his new friendship with Teddy Thursby. 'His Lordship,' he insisted on calling him.

'He isn't as rich as he makes out, though,' he said sniffily.

Of course, I ended up paying for both of us. Julian got into a very elaborate conversation with some awful woman from a fashion magazine. He was obviously angling for work and generally showing off. It annoyed me that he always needed to draw attention to himself. I just sat there and brooded. I drank quite heavily. I felt a sense of disgust rise within me.

'Let's get out of here,' I said to him when the woman had left.

'All right. Where do you want to go?'

'Don't care,' I muttered.

I stood up and the whole room swayed. Julian grabbed my arm.

'Oops-a-daisy,' he said, steadying me. 'Are you all right?'

'I'm fine. Let's go.'

We wandered into Soho. The 'Clean-Up' was over and the streets were busy with tarts again. We got to Piccadilly. The Meat Rack thronged with delinquent rent boys, sad-eyed junkies huddled outside the 24-hour chemist's. *People are like maggots, small, blind and worthless.* The Casbah Lounge had reopened.

'Come on,' Julian said.

'No,' I protested. 'I don't want to go in there.'

But he insisted. I tried to sober up with an espresso. Lights were swirling around my head, the shrill voices of the queens in the place reverberating in my mind. Their faces contorted in laughter, betraying their disgusting physiognomy. They were guilty, all of them. I felt the hatred for them burn inside me, hatred for myself. I had to control it all, I reasoned. I wanted to get out, get some air. I turned to Julian but he was chatting somebody up, giggling inanely. They were going through the sordid ritual.

'I'm going for a walk,' he murmured to me. 'I may be some time.'

'Wait a minute,' I mumbled. 'Wait.'

But he was gone.

'All on your own?'

Somebody sat next to me, taking Julian's vacant stool. He had pale skin and a mop of mousey hair, dark-rimmed eyes, sunken cheeks and a tight little mouth. He wore a short-sleeved shirt open at the neck.

'Don't mind if I join you?'

His eyes made contact with mine, like he was trying to beguile me with his evil intent, tempting me. The neck, the throat, his oesophagus bobbing as he talked. As he swallowed. A fleck of spittle on the side of his mouth. He smiled and I smiled back, knowing. I could tell his fortune by the look on his face, his implicating stare. I had to take control.

I remember going outside, the air cold against my face. His hand stroked my leg, warm. We took a taxi back to his place. Streetlights strafed the cab as we drove through the night. A bed-sit in Earl's Court, Dusty Springfield wailing from the flat below, him spooning Nescafé into two mugs, kettle whistling on the Baby Belling. I sat on the edge of the bed.

'You're a quiet one,' he said as he came over with the coffee.

He put the cups on the floor by the bed and sat next to me.

'Here,' he whispered softly.

His lips brushed against mine, a horrible flick of his tongue against my teeth. He pulled back.

'What's the matter?'

'You know,' I said. He frowned.

My mind darkened then came to. Mouth, lips, neck, throat. Fingers and thumbs, itching. His adam's apple, tempting.

I pushed him onto his back and straddled him. We thrashed about on the bed. So much of a struggle, I thought, it's all so much of a struggle. But in the end he gave in and so did I. My mind darkened again and I gave in to all my pent up desires. I rolled off him and felt such a sense of relief flood through me. I had done it, I thought calmly, I had finally done it. As he lay quietly next to me I stroked my fingers along his body gently, touching his flesh with a marvellous sense of possession. He was all mine. I lay there watching over him until the dawn came and then crept out into the morning.

15

The canopy above glowed with light. The sun burned the edges of the leaves a bright emerald. Welded them to the sky. Camouflage patterns in the bracken about his feet. He had walked for hours. Making tracks gave him a sense of purpose. Distance between him and the city. The damp, earthy smell of the forest floor was ancient, primal. He was going to ground. Returning to a more natural state.

And he knew what to do. All his army training could be put to use. Jungle craft. It was simple. All he had to do was survive. And he knew how to do that.

At sundown he began to flag. He was exhausted and maybe ten or fifteen miles from his destination. And he was parched. He needed to find water. He found a secluded coppice and made a makeshift camp, then set off with a water bottle. In a field he found a cattle trough. There was green scum on the surface. He wiped it away and filled his container with murky water.

He boiled it up on the Primus stove and made tea. It tasted dank and fetid but he was so thirsty it didn't matter. He took off his boots. His feet were covered in blisters. He rested his head on his rucksack and soon fell into a deep sleep.

He woke to a cacophony of birdsong. He rubbed at his face. For a couple of seconds he had no idea where he was. There was a light film of dew on him. He blinked and looked around at the shadowy dawn. His whole body ached. He felt the awful sinking realisation of his predicament. The brief respite of sleep was over. He had to be on the move again. He washed himself with the water left over from the night before. He leaned against a tree and pulled on his boots again. His feet were so sore it was almost unbearable but he had to get going. A few yards of tramping through the woods and the pain subsided. He made his way to the edge of the forest.

He had to travel on the roadside now. This would be more dangerous. He just hoped that people would take him for a holiday hiker. After a few miles' walking a car pulled up beside him.

'Want a lift, mate?' the driver called out.

Billy kept on walking, turning his face slightly so he would not be recognised. He was so tired that the prospect of a lift was almost irresistible. But he couldn't risk it.

'Come on, mate,' the driver continued. 'Where are you headed?'

'No thanks,' Billy muttered, his face still turned away from the road.

'Fuck you, then,' the driver said as he pulled away.

It was getting dark again when he reached Thorley Woods. Childhood memories flooded back to him. He knew the lie of the land, that was a comfort. He would have to find an isolated place. Somewhere ramblers and dog walkers wouldn't stumble upon. But he was overcome with fatigue. He found a little hollow and unrolled his sleeping bag. He would set to work making a proper shelter tomorrow.

Billy found an area of thick undergrowth that was isolated from any beaten track in the woods. He tunnelled through the thicket and found a small clearing. He dug a shallow hole with his hands, which he carpeted with the groundsheet. Then he cut a series of short branches and stuck them into the ground as picketing and using the earth that he had excavated made a kind of breastwork around the whole area. He pitched his tent over this and then camouflaged it with bits of bush and bracken.

He set up his stove, his sleeping bag and the radio inside. He felt safe within. The earthworks gave him the sense that he was in a burrow. That he was hidden beneath the ground. They'd never find him here. He set up a tripwire near his camp attached to a string of bottle tops that would rattle if anyone stood on it. He had enough supplies to keep himself going for a week or so, then he'd have to go out foraging.

The radio was his sole company but he only listened to hourly news bulletins because he needed to save the batteries. He'd hear reports of the hunt for him. It was strange listening to his name being repeated again and again over the airwaves. Curiously reassuring as loneliness began to gnaw at him. He was also comforted by all the false sightings and red herrings that had put them off the scent. Epping Forest had been combed by police, as he thought it would be. There was a quiet satisfaction in outwitting them. *Billy Porter, the police murderer, is still at large*, a voice would announce. *At large*, he thought, a stupid way of putting it, made it seem that he was conspicuous. But instead he was hidden from view. Obscure.

Then, on the third or fourth day (he had already started to lose count), he heard a familiar voice on the wireless. At first he thought he must be dreaming or that he had gone mad. It was his mother speaking. He turned up the volume, his heart pounding in his chest.

'Billy, if you're listening,' the voice wavered in maternal lamentation, 'this is your mum speaking. Give yourself up, son. Please, Billy, before there's any more bloodshed. I'll come with you if you want. We'll go to the police together. Please, Billy. This is your mum. Everything will be all right.'

Billy started to sob. Her voice sounded so sad. She was the only person that ever really cared for him. He felt torn apart. She was betraying him. And yet she sounded so gentle. Gently scolding him as she had when he was a child. *We'll go to the police together*, just as they had when he'd been shoplifting as a kid or whatever.

'Sorry, Mum,' he whispered as he choked on tears.

He left the radio on for a while longer, hoping that he might hear her again. But the news report ended and he switched it off.

The funeral. At a church opposite the Shepherd's Bush factory where me and Dave were bucks together. The Church of St Stephen and St Thomas. The Martyr and the Doubter. Not hard to tell which was which. A long cortège coming around the corner of Uxbridge Road. The streets lined with crowds. A canopy of umbrellas, like scales on a huge beast. It was a wet, miserable day. The first rain since the World Cup Final. Dave in the back of a hearse. His mangled body in a box. They're burying the better half of me today.

The rain steaming off the hot tar of the roads from the long hot summer. A smell of washed asphalt in the air and the sickly scent of hundreds of cellophane-wrapped floral tributes and gaudy wreaths that were piled up by the church gates. Bells tolled as the coffins were brought up the path. Family mourners out front then pews filled with top brass.

The Commissioner read the eulogy and a passage from Revelation. *And there shall be no more death, neither sorrow, nor crying, neither shall there be any more pain.*

I spotted George Mooney sitting a couple of rows in front of me, nodding along to all this nonsense. The Metropolitan Police Choir sang 'Abide with Me'. Uniformed pall-bearers took the coffins out. Weeping relatives followed behind and we all tramped out into the wet graveyard.

The vicar was saying his piece over the boxes as they were each lowered down in turn.

'Hello, Frank,' came a voice by my shoulder.

Mooney.

Man that is born of woman hath but a short time to live, and is full of misery.

'A terrible loss.' His voice was soft, unctuous. 'But then who can judge the Mysteries of the Craft? He was meddling in matters that did not concern him. The Temple protects its own, you know.'

'What do you want?'

'Want, son? Want? I'm just a fellow mourner. Surely it is incumbent upon brother officers to console each other at a time like this. Of course, for you, it's quite a personal loss, isn't it?'

'Leave me alone.'

'A soul in torment? I wouldn't dream of it. A terrible tragedy. Of course, it's been wonderful for our image. There's been an unhealthy tide of criticism of the force lately. But through sacrifice we are cleansed.'

Earth to earth.

Mooney wouldn't stop talking. I wanted to get away from him.

'This shows the public what risks we take in keeping the Queen's peace.'

Ashes to ashes.

'And it brings us all closer together.'

He was up close. I could feel his steamy breath.

'And though you shun the solace of the Brotherhood, we follow the same path, if you get my meaning.'

Dust to dust.

I shook him off and pushed my way through the throng and out of there. A mob of gawping civilians around the gates. A girl in a cheap raincoat near the front. Soaked through. Holding a sad little bunch of sodden pink carnations against her breast. It was Jeannie. She spotted me seconds after I'd clocked her and she turned to walk quickly through the crowd. I followed. She was impeded by all the bodies standing around in the rain, so I was easily able to catch up with her. I caught her arm. She tried to shake it off.

'Jeannie,' I implored. 'Please. I just want to talk to you.'

We walked along the road, away from the crowds, in silence. The rain subsided into a drizzle.

'Come on,' I said. 'Let me buy you a drink.'

She turned to me with those green eyes of hers. Her face was wet. Maybe she'd been crying. Maybe it was just the rain.

'All right,' she replied.

We found a quiet corner in a pub near by. I didn't really know what to say. It was hardly a time for small talk. Her little bunch of bedraggled carnations on the table. She picked them up. Water dripped from the cellophane wrapper. She stared at them.

'I just wanted,' she said quietly, 'to pay my respects.'

'What happened with you and Dave?' I asked.

'Nothing much. He promised he'd help me get away from Spiteri. He found me a flat where they wouldn't reach me.'

'And did you make a statement?'

'Yeah. I told him everything I knew. It wasn't much. He wasn't sure that it would be much use.'

I thought about this for a moment. If I had any kind of bottle I could follow it up, make a case. But I was a coward. And something else was playing on my mind.

'And you and him?' I asked, tentatively.

She stared at me.

'What?'

'You know.'

She looked down.

'Well . . .' she murmured.

'I see.'

'Look, it just happened,' she said, picking at the damp flowers on the table. 'One night. I was scared. He stayed with me. He was very sweet.'

She looked up. Her eyes brimming with tears. I felt sick with jealousy. For the both of them. I fancied her like crazy but I loved Dave. Not in any queer way, you understand. But I felt jealous because she'd been close to him while I'd been far apart. I'd never made it up to him and now he was dead. And buried.

'He liked you, you know? He really did. He was worried that you were getting into bad ways. He was a good person. Not like you. Not like me either.'

'So, how are things, you know, with you?'

'You mean, am I still on the game?'

'I didn't mean . . .'

Jeannie laughed.

'I know what you mean. I understand you better than I did him. We're both of us not very nice people, are we? But no, I'm not on the game any more. I've got a job at a hairdresser's. And that money you gave me. That's tided me over a bit. Thanks for that.'

'It was bad money anyway.'

'Yeah, well. I never want to rely on bad money again. Not ever.'

I looked at her. Her hair was a mess from the rain and make-up streaked down her cheeks. She was still beautiful. I still wanted her.

'Jeannie,' I said, drawing closer to her, 'I'd like to see you again.'

She pulled her face back from mine and frowned.

'I don't think that would be a very good idea.'

'But . . .' I struggled for the words. 'We, you know, understand each other.'

And that's how I felt. This washed-up girl was the only person I could think of that would understand what had happened. All the awful feelings of guilt that I had about Dave. I wanted to talk to her about that. Tell her everything.

She looked at me with a sad smile. Pity in her flint eyes. We ended up getting drunk. It seemed the right thing to do. Our little wake for Dave. There wasn't much to say so we just sat there and knocked back the booze until chucking-out time.

She let me see her home. She had a little flat in Earl's Court.

'I'm sorry about setting you up like that, Frank,' she said at the door. 'I hope you don't hate me for it.'

'No, I . . .' Stumbling over the words, all choked up.

And I started to blubber in the drizzle by her doorstep.

'I'm sorry,' I mumbled, turning away.

'Hey,' she whispered softly, touching my arm. 'Come here.'

She held on to me and I sobbed away. She let me come inside. I wiped at my face with my big stupid hands and she made us a cup of tea. I stayed with her that night. We didn't have sex or anything like that. We just held on to each other through the darkness.

There were constant sightings of Billy Porter once his photo had been issued. They were all false leads but the great British public were seeing his face everywhere. In the crowd at Speaker's Corner. Drinking in a pub in Camden Town. Eating breakfast in a café in Euston. Walking out of a flat in Dolphin Square. There was even a story going around that Porter was masquerading as a woman. A girl in a beauty salon swore that she had dyed the hair of a masculine-looking woman who had a deep-set stare and thick eyebrows just like Porter.

People are so open to suggestion – show them something and they start seeing it everywhere. They're vulnerable on a subliminal level. The masses are conditioned – like those dogs that start salivating when they hear a bell ring.

Porter had become an ogre, a bogeyman. A convenient hate figure upon which all of society's ills could be heaped, an embodiment of evil, something other. A specimen. It reassured them that sin existed outside, not in the depths of their own souls. He was a wanted man. All the time, haunted by his photograph, they dreamed of Billy Porter, a creature of their own imaginings.

And it allowed them to vent their own hatred. Sid Franks crowed over the reaction of the *Illustrated*'s readership. Results of the 'Readers' Poll on Capital Punishment': *89% Say: Bring Back the Rope!* There was another tub-thumping leader comment from Sid calling for 'strong action'.

Since that night in Earl's Court I had been possessed with a warm glow of contentment. But it was a fugitive sense of happiness, something that I could not or would not fully comprehend. I'd felt an extraordinary euphoria and a gentle calm had followed it. But what had happened? I had been so drunk and there had been moments of black-out. Flickering images of savage physicality, disjointed flashes of frenzy and violence. It was hard to tell what was real and what was imagined. There was something, well, only just palpable in the memory, something dark and dreadful and exquisite. I should have taken something, I thought, some sort of souvenir, evidence of some kind. I had a fearful longing for some proof.

Then it came through the crime desk. A news item. *Police seeking the killer of 32-year-old Denis Fowler say that his assailant was most probably known to him as there was no sign of forced entry into his flat in Earl's Court. Fowler was a known homosexual and police believe that there may have been a sexual motive to the murder. They are investigating a number of clubs and coffee bars frequented by homosexuals where Fowler may have met his killer.*

There was a photograph with the piece. It was him all right. I had done it, I had really done it. It all came back at once, his face contorted into a grimace as I had throttled him, his body growing cold and stiff as I lay in the bed next to him. I had done it, it was real, the typewritten copy proved it, the flesh made word. I nearly swooned with the sudden knowledge of it all.

'Are you all right?' said the copy boy who had handed me the piece.

I managed to regain my composure and I felt a smile spread across my face.

'Yes,' I replied. 'I feel fine.'

And I did, I really did. It was as if a terrible weight pressing down on me had been taken away. I felt free. I had done it. It gave me a sense of confidence and power, my body relaxed, my head clear for the first time in my life. A peaceful lucidity, as if I had broken the curse, that I had killed my hateful desire, cleansed myself of it. I had put it to rest.

16

I was put in charge of surveillance on Billy Porter's mother. We ran a rota system of WPCs that would shadow her. One or two detectives but mostly seconded from uniform branch. It was mind-numbing work. Plotted up in a van outside her flat, logging the same routine every day. To the shops, from the shops. To the pub, from the pub. Bingo on Tuesdays and Fridays. But observation had to be kept up. There was always a chance that Porter would make contact with his mother. Like most of these supposedly hard villains, he loved his dear old ma. She had co-operated on the investigation, made that radio broadcast appealing for her son to give himself up. But we couldn't trust her to turn him in if she knew where he was.

Nothing glamorous about being on the plot all day. Boring as fuck. But it felt OK putting the hours in. Routine police work. I was glad of it. It felt normal.

And I started seeing Jeannie. It was all very gentle and proper. We'd go out for a meal or catch a film. I'd see her home and we'd have a chaste little kiss on the doorstep. I didn't try anything on. I didn't want to, to be honest. I wanted us to be able to trust each other and, given our past, this wouldn't necessarily be easy. We were wary of each other. But the caution we showed to each other was sort of romantic. Like we were trying to find something that had been lost. I think we both played at being innocent as if it was something we both needed in our lives. Something we'd both missed out on. It was as if we could somehow redeem each other by going through the motions of a courtship. We wanted to be good people, not the bent copper and the ex-whore. We clung on to the idea of it in hope and desperation that we weren't kidding ourselves.

I'd talk to her about Dave. Keeping his memory alive. Reminding myself of what I should be like. I didn't feel that urgent sense of lust that I'd first had for her. Something else took its place. Affection. Us not having sex made it all the more intense. I guess it was a whole mess of confused feelings and hopeless longings.

As the weeks passed the 'sightings' of Billy Porter continued. So many false alarms and frustrated leads. The longer he was at large the more damage it did to public confidence in the police. And it burned away at the confidence we had in ourselves.

It had gone quiet on the Porter case. After the arrest of a Cypriot gun dealer in connection with the case a new theory had emerged that he was being sheltered by members of EOKA, the Cypriot guerrilla organisation, but that was about it.

So I had time to work on my own story. I got in touch with the detective in charge of the investigation into the murder of Denis Fowler and I took him for a drink. They didn't have much to go on.

'I'm afraid we've sort of run out of leads,' he said.

I felt a tremendous thrill at talking about a murder I myself had committed. I was almost disappointed that they hadn't got anywhere with the case.

'What about the clubs and bars that you visited?' I asked.

'Yes, well, Fowler was known to frequent one of them. The Casbah Lounge in Piccadilly. But that's about as far as we've got.'

Someone might have seen me there with him, seen us leaving together. But I didn't panic. I felt utterly cold-blooded about the whole thing. No one would suspect me, after all.

'I don't suppose we'll turn anything up,' the detective said. 'Unless the killer strikes again.'

I gulped at my drink, nervously, and nodded. I hadn't thought of this.

'Well,' I said, handing him my card, 'let me know if anything comes up.' I got back to the *Illustrated* and typed it all out. I had to control it. Turning it into a story made perfect sense. Words. I'd always been able to channel my impulses with words, and this would be my souvenir, my memento mori.

Sid Franks came by my desk and looked at the copy. He wrinkled up his face.

'Jesus,' he said. 'Some people really are sick.'

'You going to run it?'

He shrugged.

'Well, it's got a nasty little angle. The "Twilight World of the Homosexual", that sort of thing. Yeah, we might fit it in somewhere.'

I became obsessed with whether the story would stand up at the Big Table of the Saturday conference and how it might be subbed. I was horrified at the prospect of it being spiked. A spike through my heart. As it was it ran and was perfect, a small piece at the bottom of page seven. HOMOSEXUAL HOMICIDE. *Man strangled 'knew his killer', say Police.*

Billy would go foraging at night and sometimes risk a journey into town during the day. He found that there was a gypsy caravan farther into the woods from his camp. He figured that this might afford him some cover when he was out in the open. He could avoid suspicion. Town people would take him for a gypsy. And if the gypsies spotted him, they would think he was a townie.

He'd walk down to to the nearest main road and get a bus into town. He still had quite a lot of the cash that his mother had given him but sooner or later he would have to start stealing to buy the provisions he needed. He'd wander around the supermarket, clutching at the wire basket in his hand, trying to look intently at the rows of tins and boxes. His mind would throb as he tried to concentrate on shopping and not let his head dart about too much. He felt a paranoia that was wild, instinctive. Like any animal that is constantly sensitive to being hunted or preyed upon. He kept one of his pistols firmly tucked in his waistband.

Once, in a newsagent's he had entered to buy some tobacco and rolling papers, he found himself standing between the shopkeeper and another customer, caught in the drone of their conversation.

'Well, I'd know him if I saw him,' the customer was saying.

Billy hadn't spoken to anyone for weeks. Except to himself. *Think we need some more wood*, he'd say. *Well, better go and chop some, then.* Little muttered exchanges with his own shadow. The radio provided some sort of company, though he had to ration its use. The Home Service. Calm and soothing. He sometimes wondered forlornly if he'd hear his mother's voice again.

'They reckon you ought not to approach him. Armed and dangerous, they say,' the shopkeeper chipped in.

He realised they were talking about him. His stomach sank and he suddenly felt the hardness of the gun against his gut.

'What do you reckon, mate?' the customer asked.

'What?' Billy muttered.

'About this Porter bloke. Where could he be hiding out?'

'Uh?'

Billy didn't know what to say. He tried to avoid engaging with people in shops at the best of times. Any little pleasantry or comment would be greeted by him with just a grunt or nod of acknowledgment. His heart was racing. He'd grown a beard but surely up close they would recognise something from the police pictures that were everywhere.

'I reckon he's gone abroad. That's what I reckon,' the shopkeeper said, looking at Billy.

Billy flinched a second then looked back.

'I wouldn't know, mate,' he said quickly. 'Can I have an ounce of Old Holborn and some green Rizla papers?'

The shopkeeper looked a bit slighted, as if Billy were cutting him.

'Please?' Billy added, to placate the situation, but in its urgency the word came out terse and demanding.

The shopkeeper shrugged and with a grudging sigh turned and reached for the tobacco and papers on the rack behind him. He rang them up on the till. Billy's hand was shaking as he handed over the money, but the two men had already started chatting about something else and they didn't seem to notice. He picked up the items that the shopkeeper had dropped on the counter and walked briskly through the shop. As the bell on the door chimed someone called after him.

'Oi, mate!'

Billy froze in the doorway. The dull roar of the traffic filled his head. Should he run? Or turn and face them? His hand was in his pocket with the tobacco. He could feel the outline of the gun.

'You forgot your change,' the shopkeeper said.

Billy felt safer not spending too much time outside in the broad daylight. He became intermittently nocturnal. Sleeping securely in his hidden camp during the day and venturing out after dark. Night manoeuvres. He felt a greater sense of freedom in the darkness. At night he was the hunter, not the hunted. He found an allotment within walking distance of his camp. He could supply himself with fresh vegetables from there. There was a poultry farm, though he had to be careful; sometimes the farmer would check the big battery sheds with a torch and a dog. He mapped out his territory. When the money ran out he would have to find places to break into.

He became quite bold. Wandering into the outskirts of the town. There was a small factory that he cased out, finding where the main offices and the safe were. Reconnaissance patrols. He felt a sense of power roaming around fearlessly. He had his guns with him. All those people tucked up in their beds, what would they think if they knew he was so close at hand? He'd climb into the back gardens of houses and peer into the windows. Just for the hell of it. There he was, he thought. Their worst nightmare.

He began to get used to living in the woods and his strange routine. It was like time was turned on its head. It played tricks with him. Upside down – maybe it was going backwards, too. He sometimes lost track completely. He'd forget why he was hiding out. Maybe they had forgotten about him. It made him reckless.

He went out with the intention of house-breaking one night. He was halfway up the back garden path of this place when he suddenly heard a thumping noise. It sounded like somebody running downstairs. He quickly pressed himself against the wall by the back door and waited. The thumping sound came again. Someone was coming quickly out to the back door to check on it. They must have heard something. Billy made his way slowly and quietly back up the garden path, ready to run if the back door opened. More thumping. What the fuck was going on in that house? Maybe the bloke was rushing around, checking each room. Billy kept moving stealthily up the path. He went past a squat little shed. Thumping again. This time much louder. He suddenly realised that the noise was coming from the shed. It was a rabbit hutch. Rabbits, he remembered from somewhere, thump their back legs when they sense danger.

You little fucker, he thought, and opening the lid of the hutch he reached in and pulled the animal out by its long floppy ears. He shoved it in the sack he had brought and took it back with him. He broke its neck, skinned it and cooked it on a spit over the fire.

He had to be more careful, he reasoned. He had been clever so far. Planned things out. He had survived, against all the odds. One false move could be the end of him.

Just then the string of bottle tops rattled. Someone had trodden on the tripwire. Someone was outside his hideout. He grabbed a gun and crawled out. It was very dark and he could only just make out a figure standing there. He didn't know what to do.

'Hello, mister,' came a young voice.

'What do you want?' asked Billy.

'Just passing. Saw the light from your den. Thought I'd say hello.'

Billy hadn't realised that light could leak out of his camp.

'Hello,' he said to the young man.

This is ridiculous, he thought. Then he realised that this must be one of the gypsies from the caravan in the woods. He'd play it carefully. Be friendly and get rid of him. It would probably mean that he'd have to move on the next day. Or he could kill him. But that would complicate things.

'What are you doing this time of night?' he asked, stalling for time.

'Hunting rabbits,' replied the youth.

Billy burst out laughing.

'What's so funny, mister?'

'Well, I just caught one. Want some?'

And Billy invited him into the camp.

The youth looked around at the cramped but neatly organised interior with wide eyes.

'This is a crafty little place,' he said.

Billy brewed some tea. The youth had raven hair and piercing blue eyes, sparse dark hairs on his top lip.

'You a gypsy, then?' Billy asked him.

'Half and half,' the youth replied. 'Diddicoy, that's what Dad calls me. Mum was a gorgio.'

'Gorgio?'

'You know, outsider. Met her when he worked the fairgrounds. She ran off when I was just a little chavo. He blames me, I reckon.'

'So it's just you and him?'

'Yeah. Miserable old bugger.'

'I suppose you're wondering what I'm doing hiding out here.'

'Ask no questions, mush.'

'But maybe you've got to thinking.'

Billy had to make sure what this youth might know or suspect. Only him and his dad. He could kill them both if he had to. The youth shrugged at him.

'What with all that's been in the papers,' Billy went on.

'Don't have no business with them.'

'Don't you read the papers?' asked Billy.

'Can't read. Dad neither. Welfare people came on to a site once and tried to get us sent to school. Didn't bother with that.'

Billy smiled with relief and started to pour out the tea.

'What's your name, son?' he asked.

'Danny,' replied the youth. 'Yours?'

Billy thought for a moment.

'Joe,' he said. 'The name's Joe.'

17

I'd managed to get a Saturday night off and me and Jeannie went up West. It was a warm autumn evening with plenty of people milling about. We couldn't help but feel in a good mood. Holding hands as we walked through the crowds around Cambridge Circus. Jeannie looked great and I felt pretty pleased with myself. I'd got tickets for the second show at the Palladium. As we walked through Soho she went a bit quiet. I didn't think anything of it at the time.

We passed a pub and I said:

'Let's have a drink.'

She nodded and we went in. There was a bit of a crush at the bar and it took me a while to get served. Whisky and soda for me, gin and tonic for her. As I threaded my way back with glasses aloft I caught sight of her in the far corner. Some bloke was talking to her. My first feeling was distrust, right there in my gut. I thought, yeah, there she is, showing out to the first guy that comes along once my back's turned. Then I saw the look on her face. It was frozen with fear and anxiety. She had turned away from the man and was trying to ignore him but he was up close, leering at her.

I pushed my way through quickly and handed over her drink. She smiled thinly at me.

'Come on, Jeannie,' this bloke was saying with a drunken slur to his voice. 'You remember me.'

'Leave me alone,' she said.

'What's your problem, mate?' I demanded, staring straight at him.

He grinned at me.

'Well, look what my little pussycat's dragged in,' he taunted. 'It's all right, son. Me and little Jeannie here are old friends, aren't we?'

'I think you'd better fuck off,' I told him.

Jeannie saw the look on my face.

'Please, Frank.'

'Oh, she's good, you know. Really good.'

I still had the whisky glass in my hand when I smashed him in the face. He knocked over a table as he went down. There was shouting and a commotion. I looked down at him sprawling on the floor. My hand was cut and bleeding. I sucked at a knuckle. Jeannie had grabbed my arm.

'Frank,' she pleaded. 'Come on, let's get out of here.'

And she started to lead me away. The landlord had come out from behind the bar and was confronting us.

'Oi!' he shouted. 'Just you wait a minute. Someone call the police.'

I took out my warrant card and waved it in his face.

'I am the fucking police!' I shouted back at him.

Jeannie was crying when we got outside. I was so stupid. I only had one way of dealing with things. But I'd felt so protective of her. So clumsy.

'Take me home, Frank,' she croaked.

We drove back to her flat in silence. I figured she despised me for making a horrible scene. I'd wrapped a handkerchief around my bleeding hand and it throbbed as I held tightly to the steering wheel.

'I better find a bandage to put on that,' she said at her door.

'It's all right.'

'Come on,' she insisted, and led me inside.

The sting of the Dettol came almost as a relief. It cut through the awful numbness in my mind. At least I could feel something. She put a wad of gauze on the cut and wound a length of sticking plaster around it to hold it in place.

'There,' she said.

'Look, Jeannie,' I began. 'About what happened . . .'

I wanted to apologise for how I'd behaved. For making such a scene. It was because of how I felt about her. But I didn't know how to say it.

'Frank, I know,' she cut in. 'I can pretend that it's all in the past. But there'll always be people to remind me of what I was. What I am.'

'What are you talking about?'

'You know.'

'No, I don't.'

'Yes you do!' she suddenly exclaimed. 'You know all about me. That's why you didn't say a word on the way back here. You know as well as that man in the pub what I am. You just can't bear to talk about it.'

'It's not that.'

'Then why didn't you say something?'

'Because I felt like an idiot. Lashing out like that.'

'I thought . . .'

'No. No, it's not that. I don't think about you like that.'

She looked me in the eye.

'So, what do you think of me?'

'I . . .' I swallowed hard. Feelings that felt like a solid lump in my gullet. 'I love you, Jeannie.'

She frowned at me. Like she couldn't quite understand what I was saying. I realised then that no one had ever said that to her. Not properly. She gave a thin nervous laugh.

'Oh, Christ,' she said.

'It's true.'

'Then why don't you want to touch me?'

'Because . . .' I brushed her cheek with my bandaged hand. 'I want more than that. Than this. I want . . .'

'Oh, for God's sake, Frank,' she sighed. 'Touch me.'

That night we made love. At least, we tried to.

The weather was changing. It was getting colder, wetter. Billy had mended the holes in his tent and made the whole shelter waterproof again. He dug a small drainage trench on the sloping side of the hideout to channel away water during rainstorms. In heavy downpours he'd have to fight against leaks, using cooking utensils to catch the rivulets and cataracts and to bail out the rainwater. But when he had it all under control, he quite liked sitting in his camp in the rain. Its reverberation on the canvas roof was soothing. Like the sound of distant applause. It was then he felt most safe. Safe in his dugout. Beneath his canopy. Buried. Under the ground. It was a sense of being inside. Hidden away. The outside was washed away. It lost any sense of coherence. Sound and vision blurred like interference on the telly. Inside was all that mattered.

The season was changing too. The undergrowth that covered his shelter was losing some of its foliage. The whole area around him was becoming more and more sparse as the leaves began to fall. Billy set to work to recamouflage the camp. Smoke was more visible now, in the damp air, so he had to be careful with fires and did his cooking at night.

There were still news reports about him on the radio, though less and less frequently. He would limit his trips to town as much as possible but he'd always buy a paper. There would be the occasional item about the search for him there too. Lots of mistaken sightings. Red herrings. But interest had started to wane after the initial press hysteria. He knew he couldn't stay where he was indefinitely, but if he could last the winter and into next year, when things might calm down even more, then he might make a move. He would have to find some sort of cover, though.

Danny, the gypsy boy, turned up from time to time. Billy knew that this contact was a weak point. Danny swore that he hadn't told anyone about him, least of all his dad, whom he obviously didn't get on with, but even Danny knowing was a terrible risk. Even if he couldn't read the papers, something about Billy would be bound to turn up one day, and then he might put two and two together. Billy knew that the real weakness of it was that he allowed himself to imagine that, even if Danny knew, he might not betray him. He had become his only human contact and he couldn't help himself wanting to trust him.

He told Danny that he was a deserter from the army. Danny had nodded – it was common enough for those AWOL to end up on the road. The irony was that Billy had done his service. Not some easy billet, either. He'd met plenty of blokes in the Scrubs later who'd never turned up for National Service. For some of them that was their first taste of porridge. It was that that had got them off the straight and narrow in the first place. From then on they'd learned all these bad habits from being inside and never looked back. For Billy the army was part of the process too. It had taught him to kill. How to survive on the run.

Danny would go out working with his dad most days. 'Calling,' they called it. Going door to door, asking for scrap. At other times there might be odd jobs here and there. Picking potatoes or a bit of tarmac work. But when he had time Danny would often come to visit. He felt he'd never quite fit in. Half and half. Diddicoy. Not quite Romany nor gorgio. Billy, despite himself, looked forward to Danny's visits. Of course, they were a liability, but as he began to work out in his head how he might survive on the run in the long term, he realised that Danny might, after all, be invaluable to him. If he were to pass as a traveller, for instance, there were all sorts of codes and customs that would be useful to know. And Danny needed little encouragement to start holding forth. And Billy, in spite of everything else, found his voice and his strange twitching demeanour fascinating. He just had to remember that he was Joe in Danny's presence. Danny told him that he wanted to get away from his dad, that he planned to work as a 'gaff boy', working on the fairgrounds when the season started up again.

Danny also explained gypsy rituals with a clarity and precision that only someone with a certain amount of doubt about their own identity could master. He had a slight distance from it that gave him a lonely understanding that longed for an intimate mystery. Joe had the obvious gorgio ideas about Romanies and Danny tried to provoke him into bringing them up.

'You reckon we're dirty, don't you?' he'd say. 'You seen some gyppo site and there's filth everywhere, ain't there?'

Billy shrugged. He didn't want to seem rude. Danny was making some sort of point, that was clear.

'They see the site, but they never look inside the trailers. Always spotless, they are. Clean on the inside. Gorgio never understand this. They keep everything nice on the outside but inside their houses they're all dirty. They use the same water they'd use to clean themselves and do their business as they would clean their plates and eating irons. Put their own filth in their own mouths. Keep their own rubbish inside.'

Billy could vaguely understand what Danny was saying. He couldn't afford to leave anything outside his hideout that might betray his presence. He had to bury any rubbish. Cover up his own filth. But somehow the idea of keeping oneself clean inside made sense to him. Danny talked a lot about what was clean and what was not. *Moxadi*, he'd often say, meaning dirty, ritually unclean.

'Some animals, right, we reckon are moxadi. Cats, for instance. They clean themselves with their own tongue. Bring their own dirt into themselves. They can lick their own arses. Moxadi, that is. Horses, they're clean, rabbits too. But cleanest of all is the hotchi-witchi.'

'The what?'

'Hedgehog.'

Billy had heard about hedgehogs being a delicacy for gypsies.

'So you eat them, do yer?' he asked.

Danny laughed.

'Not often,' he said. 'But, like I say, they're clean. They can't groom themselves with their mouth, can they? All them spikes. And you look at a hotchi. Full of fleas in its coat. All manner of dirtiness in them spines. But that's on the outside, ain't it? That don't matter. If you're clean on the inside, that's the main thing. Ain't it?'

The real dread of what had happened soon caught up with me. What I had done, the cold truth about myself. The initial euphoria I had felt turned to despondency and depression. And fear, fear of the future. It could happen again if I wasn't careful. I musn't let it become a habit – I'd end up in Broadmoor.

I tried to console myself with stories of murderers more heinous than myself. The Boston Strangler, Albert deSalvo, had throttled thirteen women to death. And then there was the case of a certain Hungarian, Sylvestre Matuscka, who could only achieve full sexual satisfaction by seeing a train crash. He blew up a bridge that was carrying the Budapest–Vienna express in 1931. Such excessiveness put my little misdemeanour into perspective, didn't it? But I realised that I was reading these stories, as usual, for the salacious effect they had on me. And they did nothing to assuage my darker urges. On the contrary, rather like drinking salt water to slake one's thirst, they instead made my mouth dry with anticipation.

I had got away with it, I reasoned, and would more than likely not be detected. *Unless the killer strikes again*, the detective had said. Might he not strike again? Might I not be able to control him?

DeSalvo had been known as the 'Measuring Man' on account of his modus operandi in gaining access to the apartments of young women. He would pose as a representative for a modelling agency, with a tape measure and a clipboard, and persuade his victims to let him check their vital statistics. Initially he would merely sexually assault his prey, but he soon moved on to murder, attacking old and young alike. Given the necessity for opportunity in crime, my own

MO was, by comparison, devastatingly simple. I could so easily pick up a homo somewhere, go back with them and just let myself out after I'd finished. So I really did have to resist temptation.

I resolved to keep busy, to stop drinking altogether and to stay away from those places where homosexuals might congregate.

The Porter story had quietened down considerably. We set to work trying to buy up friends or relatives. The trick was to move quickly as soon as you found anybody who showed even the slightest inclination to sell their story. Then you'd set them up in a hotel, somewhere where the enemies couldn't get to them, and sign them up for an exclusive. Sid Franks was an old hand at this.

'They used to call me the Smash and Grab Kid,' he assured me.

We managed to buy up Trixie O'Rourke, a former stripper who had been Porter's girlfriend before he was convicted on a GBH charge in 1959. She had shopped him, apparently. We ran a good shot of her, performing at the Cabaret Club in Paddington.

I began gathering all kinds of Porter ephemera. Photos of him as a child, details of his army record, anecdotes from all manner of sources. And I began holding some of the good stuff back from the *Illustrated*. I had formed a sort of attachment to Billy. I liked the idea of possessing parts of him. He was my specimen, my subject. If I busied myself with him I could avoid any nasty distractions. And I had another plan. This could be the book I'd always dreamed of. I could do a Truman Capote job on him. It could be a way of getting away from the claustrophobic environment that I felt trapped in. Away from Grub Street, away from London. The city made me mad – the filth, the crowds of ugly humanity. It was an immoral place. Maybe I could go away somewhere quiet and desolate and write it all up.

I approached a publisher on the quiet. They seemed quite keen but were not prepared to give me an advance. Not yet, anyway.

'Of course,' they said, 'once he's been caught and it's gone to trial then we'd be ready to commission it.'

So I waited for the End. Of course, the most satisfying dénouement would be a dramatic shoot-out with the police. A properly dramatic finish to the narrative. But while I longed for a conclusion so that I could have my story, part of me wanted him to escape. For him to be free, to get away with it.

18

Two months later and Jeannie told me the news.

'I'm pregnant, Frank,' she said.

I didn't know what to say. We'd been sort of going steady but we hadn't made any plans, any promises.

'So,' I stuttered, 'um, er . . .'

'Don't look so fucking worried.'

'No. I mean, yeah, well. What are you going to do?'

'I want the baby. But that doesn't mean you . . .'

'Yeah?' I interrupted her. 'That's good. That's really good.'

'But what I mean to say is . . .'

I didn't let her finish. I grabbed hold of her and kissed her.

'So,' I said, 'things need to be sorted out.'

'What are you saying?'

'I'm saying, let's get married.'

She kind of smiled and frowned at the same time.

'What, you're going to make an honest woman of me?'

'Well, yeah. As long as you can make an honest bloke out of me.'

She sighed and shook her head.

'Look, Frank, you don't have to do this, you know.'

'No, really. I mean it. I want it. Let's do it right.'

And I did mean it. I so much wanted to do something right for a change. I tried not to pay any attention to something that nagged at the back of my mind. That it might not have been my kid she was carrying. That it might have been Dave's. I didn't want to think about that.

We had a registry office wedding. We wanted it done quickly so there was no time for a proper ceremony. Things had slowed down in the investigation but as it was I only just about managed to get a few days' leave so we could have some sort of honeymoon in Brighton. The fact was we didn't want a big do. I didn't want too many people in the job to know about it, to be honest. I mean, it wasn't exactly kosher given how me and Jeannie had first met. It could have got me into trouble. I worried about George Mooney finding out. Given his demonic ability in prying into private affairs, I knew that it was only a matter of time. I just wanted to get it done and face the consequences later.

And we were both in a hurry. I think we knew deep down that any hesitation would have killed the whole thing dead. I know that Jeannie had felt vulnerable when I'd proposed to her. She felt scared of her own past. Of what might happen to her if she was on her own. I could offer her protection. And some sort of respectability. So she rushed into it without thinking too much.

It had been a secret affair up until then. Desperate. We just hoped that in time we could emerge from it into some sort of normality. Mr and Mrs Taylor. We just had a couple of witnesses. Jeannie got a girl from the hairdressing salon where she worked. I got Micky Parkes, a DC on the Flying Squad I'd been on the plot with the day Dave got murdered. I'd got to know him fairly well and felt I could trust him to keep quiet about it. Micky was a solid sort of a guy. Didn't say much, which was promising. I liked him. He wasn't my best man, though. Our best man was dead. Though it would be a long time before his ghost was put to rest. Especially with his killer still on the run. Dave was always there. Between us.

The four of us went for a drink after the ceremony. Micky went off to phone in. He was officially still on duty. When he came back there was an alert look on his face. I knew something was up.

'I've got to get off,' he said. 'There's been a sighting.'

He didn't have to explain anything more. It was obvious what that meant. Porter.

'Where?'

'Somewhere in Hertfordshire.'

'What do they reckon?' I asked.

There had been so many false sightings that a wariness had now developed about any information received. So many phone-happy civilians wanting to be national heroes and convinced that any dodgy-looking tramp was public enemy number one. I'd like to have thought that I hoped it was a hoax call and that I could go off on my honeymoon with a clear conscience. The fact was the desire to be there when we got Porter was stronger than anything I felt for Jeannie. Desire for revenge, ambition, and the plain fact that, despite all the witnessed vows I'd gone through less than an hour ago, I was married to the job.

'They're pretty certain this time, Frank,' Micky replied. 'All units are being called in.'

I think Jeannie saw it too when she caught my eye, my reaction to what Micky had said. I had to go. To be there. I tried to explain but there was nothing to say that she didn't already know. She turned away from me and bit her lip. Waking up to what she had got herself into.

'The yokmush,' Danny had said. 'The yokmush are coming.'

Billy was still in his sleeping bag when he heard the signal on the tripwire. He sat up and called softly for Danny to come into the hideout. He rubbed his face. It was a cold morning. Cold and damp.

'What is it?' he asked Danny.

Yokmush was a gypsy word. Yok meant eye, mush man or men. The eye men. The police. Danny explained how the caravan had been raided that morning.

'Been some thieving in the area so of course they blame us, don't they?'

It must have been all of his break-ins, thought Billy.

'So, have they arrested your dad?'

'Well, he's helping them with their inquiries. But thing is, he told them about you.'

'I thought he didn't know.'

'Well, I didn't tell him, Joe, honest. He must have seen you out and about. He told the yokmush about a stranger in the woods. They start getting all interested. Showing him photographs.'

Billy had already started to gather up some things into his rucksack. He would have to get moving again. He looked up at Danny.

'You see the photos they were showing?'

Danny nodded.

'You know who I am?'

Danny shrugged and looked away. He nodded again and turned back to Billy with a nervous smile.

'I always knew,' he said.

'But you said you didn't read the papers.'

'Yeah, but we got a telly, ain't we? I had to say I didn't know first time. But after that, well, you became a pal, like. 'Sides, it would be bad luck to turn you in. You're a hotchi-witchi. I better be going. I'll try and keep them off the scent if I can.'

We assembled on the outskirts of Thorley Woods. About 500 officers in all. Flying Squad and other CID, SPG and ordinary uniform units, dog handlers, the lot. It looked impressive enough at the start, but it soon dawned on us that no one really had any fucking clue what we were doing.

There was a shortage of firearms. What we did have was mostly ex-service weapons, many of which were wholly unsuited for the job. Some of them not even complete or without the correct ammunition. On top of that there was an even greater shortage of officers authorised or trained to carry guns. There were stories of briefings where guvnors were issuing firearms and when they had run out of authorised officers they would ask 'Right then, who's been in the forces?' or even 'Who wants to have a go?'

Some revolvers had holsters, others not. Some were carried in one pocket with the ammunition in the other. I saw more than one CID officer carrying a loaded and cocked pistol casually thrust into their waistband until it was pointed out that they stood a good chance of damaging a particularly delicate part of the anatomy. I'd done some weapons training. Range shooting. I didn't really have any idea of how to use a gun in the field, though. I'd drawn an ancient ex-army Webley that didn't look like it had been fired since the relief of Mafeking.

I heard one guy mutter:

'This is going to be the biggest fucking balls-up since the siege of Sidney Street.'

And so we moved off, forming up the search line, beating our way into the woods.

Billy heard them coming for him. A cacophony of noise. Whistles and calls, the threshing of undergrowth as they hacked away. They had no idea. No track discipline. No jungle craft. No stealth.

But he was ready. He was trained for this.

The automatic and split-second reaction to a chance encounter must continually be practised again and again under different conditions of terrain and varying circumstances.

He checked his guns.

There was confusion in their lines. He could use that against them. He could move quickly and quietly through the woods with frequent halts for observation and listening. He knew the lie of the land. They were getting closer.

Billy went to ground and waited. He would wait until they were right up close. Any distance might give them clarity. If he moved away they might spot him. But if he stayed close, with all those bodies stumbling about, they wouldn't see him. He would wait until they were right upon him, then he would break cover. In the chaos he might just be able to cross their line.

We were bloody lucky not to have an awful accident that day. A game of toy soldiers. Cowboys and Indians. Except there were 500 cowboys and only one bloody Indian and he still managed to get away. There was confusion between the SPG and the Flying Squad. Arguments about who was supposed to be in charge of the bloody operation.

The search line was a mess. Parts of it became disconnected altogether. Some officers found themselves beating through the undergrowth only to flush out other police groups. And as the forest was more overgrown in the centre, the middle of the line moved more slowly than the flanks. This meant that the ends started to curl in. The line turned in on itself. We'd managed to surround ourselves. And one of those untrained and trigger-happy officers could so easily have ended up shooting a fellow policeman.

We found his hideout. That was something. Something to give to the press and hope that they didn't report just how much of a cock-up we'd made of it all.

The fact was we just weren't prepared for something like this. The police had never had to go through something like this before. One thing was sure. Things were going to have to change.

It was all over by the time I got to Thorley Woods. They had found his hideout but Porter had somehow managed to slip the net. His camp had been extraordinarily well constructed and equipped, camouflaged to blend in with its surroundings. Inside they found a home-made stove and a neatly stacked pile of firewood, a sleeping bag, two army blankets, a Primus stove and a bottle of meths, cooking utensils and mess tins, two clean shirts and some handkerchiefs all neatly folded, a store of canned food, fishing tackle, a transistor radio, a bottle of whisky and a pile of newspapers. THE FOXHOLE OF THE FASTIDIOUS FUGITIVE was how one of the enemies subbed it. Any hopes that Porter was unable to survive on the run were dashed. A holster was recovered but no gun.

He had outwitted them. Outmanoeuvred them with animal cunning. He had sown confusion in their ranks and had somehow managed to spirit himself away. The scent had gone cold.

There were all manner of stories flying around about police incompetence. Lack of preparation, lack of equipment and firearms training. Unclear lines of command and a breakdown in communication between the Flying Squad and the Special Patrol Group. Sid Franks made me play all of this down when I wrote up the story. It was assumed that, with such a near-miss, Porter would soon be picked up somewhere in the area. But he'd got clean away.

So my book idea was on hold for a while longer. This was not the End, not yet. I felt an odd sense of being left behind. He was out there somewhere, at large, a killer on the run. My killer was still trapped inside of me.

1971

Supergrass

19

'So, is this fucking swede taking over the inquiry, then, guvnor?' I asked Ernie Franklin as we climbed the stairs to the fourth floor of Coco. Ernie gave me a sour look.

'Frank, Thomas Harrington is Her Majesty's fucking Inspector of Constabulary. I don't want to catch you using the word swede anywhere near him. Understood?'

'Yeah, sure, guvnor. But what, is he running this thing now?'

'Harrington's role is to advise the inquiry.'

'Yeah, but what does that mean?'

'Look, Frank, it says here.' Ernie read from the Home Office statement. '"The Home Secretary, at the request of the Commisioner of Police of the Metropolis, has agreed that in view of the wide public interest someone independent should be associated with the investigation of allegations recently published about the conduct of Metropolitan Police officers."'

'"At the request of the Commisioner"? That doesn't sound right.'

'Well, of course it isn't, Frank. The fucking Home Secretary has set this one up himself, hasn't he? It's political, "public interest" and all that.'

'So, he's brought a swede in to make it all look kosher?'

Ernie sighed.

'Yes, Frank. And we're to give him our full co-operation.'

Ernie didn't look well. A messy divorce and a bit of a drink problem had taken their toll. Not exactly uncommon in the job but something you'd rarely confide to a fellow officer. I suppose because it could be seen as a sign of weakness. And what could I say to Ernie? Just go through all my own failures and bloody well compound the matter. And I think, like me, he'd never quite got over the Shepherd's Bush shootings. He was still officially in charge of the case, though nothing solid had turned up for nearly five years. Mullins and Drummond had been convicted on three life sentences but Billy Porter had never been caught, and that hurt.

'This is all I fucking need, Frank,' he muttered. 'Trust my luck to be in the frame for this one.'

A couple of journalists had wired up a petty thief in South London and recorded incriminating conversations with CID officers. There was evidence of fit-ups and of receiving money in exchange for dropping charges. More damagingly, there were allegations of more widespread corruption. An internal inquiry was set up. Ernie was in the frame for this one and I was brought in to assist. We were to brief the Deputy Assistant Commisioner. It seemed straightforward, if a little messy. Discredit the journalist's evidence. Keep the lid on it. Let the silly fuckers who'd had their hands caught in the till twist in the wind but make sure it didn't spread too far.

Then a week later they brought the swede in. That's Met slang for provincial coppers. The whole thing had caused a lot of grief. A lot of bad press. It had to look like we were going through the proper motions. But Ernie didn't have much stomach for all of this. He'd always been a very straight copper. He couldn't believe that there could be such widespread corruption – it just didn't fit with the way he saw things. He was unswervingly loyal to the Met, to the Yard, to the job. What with his personal problems and now this, you got the feeling that at any moment a wheel might come off of his whole career.

I got made DI in 1969. I was part of a special team that went after Harry Starks. We got a result largely because I was able to get Tony Stavrakakis to go QE against him. I got a commendation for that. But some of the rest of my career wasn't so sweet. At the Flying Squad certain teams were just as hookey as ever. I ended up taking the bung now and then. I'd been tainted, marked by it, so it kind of came my way. I know that makes it sound like someone was just shoving money in my back pocket without me noticing, but that was the awful thing about it. Half the time I was just turning a blind eye to whatever scam might be occurring. Passive. But as bent for it as the rest of them.

It didn't go down too well with Jeannie. I'd kind of promised her that I'd go straight. That was what we both wanted. To put the bad part of our lives behind us. But it was just too tempting to take the money – don't make a fuss, just make sure your own back's covered. So I implicated her too. I put the bad money in her account just in case anyone checked my bank statements. I reasoned that I had responsibilities, a family to support. The baby was born on 12 May 1967. A son. We called him David. Sort of an acknowledgment of something that we never talked about. That he wasn't my flesh and blood. You could tell, especially after a couple of years. The dark hair, the eyes. I recognised them, all right. But I didn't care about that. Or at least I made sure in my mind that it didn't matter. I wanted to do right by him. And the occasional bent money meant that he'd never need for anything, I told myself. And Jeannie came pretty sweet out of it too. She ended up with enough cash to set up a hairdressing salon of her own. She didn't want to become just a copper's wife, a quiet little housewife. She avoided the occasional socialising that went with the job, which suited me fine. She wanted a bit of independence, so having her own business suited her well. But she wasn't happy about where the money for it had all come from. She'd give me this look when I'd come home with a payment. She'd rarely say anything, just this resigned expression on her face and a little shrug. Like all I'd said about getting clean had been a waste of breath and we were still living off immoral earnings.

And I think that's what got to her about it. It reminded her of whoring. Doing something dirty for cash. Being ponced by someone. She wanted to be her own woman. She was happy to have her own business, but where the money had come from still rankled. She doted on the kid. A little bit too much, I thought. I felt this kind of distance from him. I couldn't help it. I tried to be a good father, but Flying Squad hours were long, weekends got fucked up by operationals. So I put in for a transfer. I wanted to go straight. It wasn't scruples so much as the nagging thought that it all might catch up with me. And I wanted to get on. I was going up, I was still sure of that. Still driven by ambition. Ambition that sometimes gave me an awful sick feeling, like vertigo. But it was all right just so long as you didn't look down. Not a fear of falling but a strange urge to jump that would occasionally give me nausea. It wasn't a fear of heights. It was a fear of depths.

So I ended up at C1. Rubber-heeling on a corruption case. That was a joke. Back with Ernie. Good old straight-down-the-line Ernie. The whole investigation had whitewash all over it from the start.

And working with Ernie brought back unfinished business. The Billy Porter case. There had been periodic sightings that all proved to be false alarms. Resources and manpower on the case lessened slowly as time went on. It had been a public relations disaster for the Met, and in the end they all but gave up on it. But I couldn't. I kept my own private file. Every lead, every clue cross-checked. The memory of Dave and how I'd failed him haunted me. One day we'd catch that bastard, and I could put his ghost to rest.

I didn't like the look of Thomas Harrington. Stiff, formal, ramrod straight. A churchgoing teetotaller, by all accounts. Cold eyes behind steel-rimmed glasses. He'd been given an office in C1. All the stuff we'd collated so far on his desk. We exchanged the briefest of pleasantries, then we all sat down and he launched into it.

The allegations of corruption had come from a petty thief from Peckham, one Dennis Woods. His flat had been raided by Detective Sergeant John O'Neill and Detective Constable Ian Campbell. They had found twelve bottles of stolen whisky and on his kitchen table some electrical components and a nine-volt battery. 'A bit of jelly would go nicely with that,' O'Neill had remarked. 'And I know a man who can get some.' The implication was that they were prepared to fit Woods up with a safe-blowing kit. Woods had laughed this off, saying that he was merely repairing a transistor radio. 'We ain't joking, son,' O'Neill had retorted. 'We want some bodies, otherwise you're going away for that.' Woods was told that they wanted the names of receivers to further their investigation into a gang raiding premises in the area using skeleton keys.

Woods was duly charged with dishonestly handling the whisky. While he was in custody, waiting to appear before Tower Bridge magistrates, Detective Constable Campbell had visited him in his cell and said: 'We'll get it over today but the big bloke will want a drink.' Woods had taken this to mean paying off O'Neill and had agreed to hand over £25. This he duly did to Campbell in a pub in Camberwell the next day. He'd asked the detective constable if this was the end of it or would they still be on his back, and Campbell had answered: 'You're in the clear for now. If you get into any more trouble, give me a ring. Don't matter where. Anywhere in London I can get on the blower to someone who talks the same as me. There's a little firm in a firm, you know?' And he had given Woods his extension number at the Yard.

Then five days later Woods had been stopped on Camberwell New Road by O'Neill and a carload of plainclothes officers. 'Let me see your hands,' O'Neill had insisted, and as Woods had held them out O'Neill had pressed a sausage-shaped object in greaseproof paper into the fingers of his right hand with the words: 'There's the jelly I promised you.' Woods was told again that they wanted the names of people handling stolen goods from the duplicate key burglaries. 'Or else,' O'Neill had warned, 'it'll cost you.'

It was at this point that Woods had approached the journalists, and subsequent encounters between himself and police officers had been taped. Woods had been wired up with a radio mike and the pressmen had been plotted up in the carpark with the recording equipment. It seemed that, in lieu of information, Woods could instead pay off O'Neill and Campbell. In the Father Red Cap pub on Camberwell Green, O'Neill was recorded as saying that 'the whole business will cost you a twoer', meaning £200. Woods only had £50 on him, which he handed over, and further meetings to continue the instalments were arranged. These were also taped. Also, pressure had been put on Woods to plant stolen goods at various premises so that their owners could be charged with receiving.

The 'firm in a firm' phrase had really put the cat among the pigeons. It was bad enough what O'Neill, Campbell and various other as yet unnamed officers had been up to. But the spectre of widespread hookeyness hung in the air like a bad smell. So many of us had known what had been going on and had just let it slip. Or even got tangled up in it. A lot of really good detectives had kept themselves clean. I couldn't help thinking about Dave. His straight-down-the-line approach. Ernie Franklin was an innocent, really. Something sad and naïve about him. The poor fucker probably had no idea of half of what went on. Well, he was in for a shock. The rest of us, well, we just accepted that you had to be a little bit bent for the job. It wasn't good when this became being bent for yourself, but when something like this came to the surface the best thing to do was find a few scapegoats lower down the ranks and paper over the rest of it.

But now, with this swede in on the inquiry, it was not going to be so simple. It was easy for the Met to look down on provincial coppers. Like they were a bunch of yokels or something. But Harrington wasn't stupid, that was for sure.

'Gentlemen,' he began. 'I'm aware that I'm a week behind the ball on this one. This has given the officers named in these allegations a chance to destroy evidence and cover their tracks. This means we're going to have to go over the whole background to this case in meticulous detail.'

'With respect, sir,' Ernie broke in, 'the officers involved have all strenuously denied the allegations made.'

'With respect, Detective Superintendent, until such time that the words "except police officers" are written into the statute book, I think that we can assume that they must be dealt with in the same way as other offenders.'

'Sir?'

'It seems to me that the normal conduct of a criminal inquiry – searching suspects' homes, desks and lockers – has so far been totally neglected. Instead the energy of the investigation has so far concentrated on disproving the veracity of the initial complaint.'

'Well, sir,' said Ernie, 'it is a possibility that these allegations have been at best exaggerated. After all, they are based largely on the word of a professional criminal. And the journalists concerned, rather than coming to us with their evidence in the first instance, chose instead to publish them in a deliberately sensationalist manner.'

'Documents have gone missing. Diaries, notebooks, evidence. And what has the inquiry concerned itself with so far? Taking lengthy statements from the journalists. Some of them have been held for questioning for periods of over eight hours. There have been complaints by them of harassment by this inquiry.'

Ernie shrugged.

'Well, they would say that, wouldn't they?'

Harrington sighed and leaned across his desk.

'Gentlemen, I'm acutely aware that I'm seen as an outsider. That I'm perceived as interfering in a delicate situation for the Met. But I trust that we can work together without conflicting loyalties.'

Ernie Franklin nodded cautiously. Harrington looked at us in turn.

'Well?'

'Er, yes, sir,' replied Ernie.

'Sir,' I echoed in assent.

'Right, then. Let's start with the basics. All of the detectives named were involved in an operation against South London-based gangs raiding shops and stores using duplicate keys.' He looked down at a file on his desk. 'Operation Skeleton, it was called, yes?'

He turned to me.

'Well, Detective Inspector, I suggest that is an area you might like to look at. I want you to build a complete dossier on Operation Skeleton and how it pertains to this inquiry.'

Five years on and Porter still evaded capture. All manner of stories as to what had happened to him began to emerge as he slowly became part of modern folk mythology. My book on him remained unwritten but my journalistic career, which had really taken off with his story, continued its strange progress.

He was free. I was trapped. We were both outsiders but at least he had got away. He was a real fugitive. I had avoided justice in a secretive and cowardly way. I hid in the streets and corridors of normality, inside. But I longed for the outside, to smell the fresh air.

And the stench of immorality around me was appalling. The Permissive Society, the Sexual Revolution – everyone was demanding their right to pleasure. Women's Liberation, Gay Liberation, it all made me feel sick. I had not given in to my terrible urges. I remained a stoic amidst all the decadence. No one would guess at the depth of my self-sacrifice.

Of course, the *Illustrated* really capitalised on all this depravity. We'd do vice every week if we could. Either that or uncovering the excesses of the permissive society – nudist colonies, wife-swapping in the suburbs. 'Any excuse for a bit of tit,' was Sid's maxim.

We could now show the whole breast in the paper. Before, Sid had operated what he called his '*National Geographic* nipple policy'. Partial nudity had to have some anthropological meaning. Up until the late sixties this had meant black flesh, a sort of Third World soft porn. But lately this had been extended.

'You know what all this sexual liberation means, don't you?' he once remarked to me. 'It means we can put white tit in the paper.'

So the breast became ubiquitous in the *Illustrated*, giving comfort to the bottle-fed masses. At the same time the paper insisted on its moral stance. There was an emerging backlash against the loose values of the Swinging Sixties, spearheaded by Lord Longford's report on the pornography trade. This was grist to Sid Franks' mill. A chance for morality through the keyhole, loudly tutting away at depravity while providing vicarious titillation to the readership. Longford travelled to Denmark to examine first hand the effects of a more permissive approach to obscenity laws. Sid sent me off to Copenhagen to join the press pack that shadowed him, eager for copy. He'd already become 'Lord Porn', a figure of fun, a bald-pated, bespectacled, music-hall professor in an incredulous examination of the flesh pots. As part of the Danish expedition he'd visited a live sex show but had left after only a few minutes.

LORD PORN REFUSES THE WHIP, was how my copy had been subbed. *Danish débâcle in den of depravity as dirty damsel demands discipline. At sizzling Scandinavian sex show Lord Porn was confronted by a gorgeous pouting blonde who pressed a whip into the prudish peer's palm and invited him to beat her. Naturally his Lordship declined and fled . . .*

'This is fucking great,' Sid had said, looking at my piece and the smudge of a semi-clad girl that went with it. 'You know what we've got to do, don't you? The *Illustrated*'s own investigation. Our own in-depth report on pornography. An exposé on the Soho bookshop trade, something like that.'

'It's a good idea,' I agreed.

'Look,' he said, 'it's yours. I want you to mount an investigation. "We expose the blue film racket", or whatever. See if we can't set up some of the people peddling this filth. And make sure we've got plenty of examples of this depravity.'

'How big?' I asked, meaning how much could I spend on it.

'Well,' Sid replied, 'I'll have to take it to the Big Table. But I'm sure they'll be keen. We can probably throw money at this one.'

Sid came back from Tuesday's conference with a big grin on his face as he walked up to my desk.

'You got *carte blanche*, old son. Start working on it pronto. I want this to be a big one. A real coup.'

So I started to put the investigation together. The previous Christmas a light aircraft had crashed on the Belgian coast. The aeroplane had been carrying more than a thousand blue films all carefully disguised in Yuletide wrapping paper. The makers of the films were a Danish company, Hot Love. It was hard-core stuff –

sadomasochism, bestiality, the lot. And it was all *en route* to Britain. I decided to target this company and try to find out who was bringing the stuff into the country. I had a couple of reporters trawl the Soho bookshops and talk to any contacts they had. But it wasn't the retail end that I was aiming at. I wanted to get to the wholesalers.

I didn't really relish the prospect of all this muck-raking. I would be exposing myself to obscenity, most of which would merely inspire nausea, but it was the S&M stuff that I was worried about. Of course, I felt a grim fascination with it, which, I decided, I would resist. It was a test of my self-control, I reasoned, that I could stay above it all. The investigation was, after all, a chance to get on at the *Illustrated*, and work was really all I had.

The plan slowly formed itself in my head. If we could get someone to pose as a potential customer, someone who was wanting to buy in bulk, then we might be able to make contact with the people running the wholesale end of the racket. Live bait for the big fish. Some gullible businessman that the porn dealers would think they could take for a ride. A con always works best when you can make the people that you're setting up think they're the ones doing the conning. Somebody living it up in the West End and prepared to make a big wholesale order beyond the usual dealings of the small-scale filth peddlers. A convincing enough lure that could secure an introduction to whoever it was that was running the rackets. Then they could set up a business deal, a meeting at which we'd be ready for them. Tape recorders, photographs, the lot. That would be our coup. WE EXPOSE THE SOHO PORN KING or whatever. It was bound to work. But first I had to find our bait.

A fairground sky. The late September build-up on Woodhouse Moor. Back-End Time. The season nearly over. Silvers, pinks, purples in nimbus streaks over Buslingthorpe Ridge. The dying sun scrolling the edge of the clouds in gold. The horizon decorated like the Swirl front he'd done for the Bone Brothers. Not enough light left to get any work done today. He'd need to be up first thing tomorrow and maybe try and find a spare hand. But that gave him a bit of thinking time. The sunsets at this time of the year were always good for inspiration. He got most of his ideas from the sky.

Most of the big machines were up by now. The main rides. The Parachute and the Dive Bomber. The Dodgems and the Octopus.

As Mick walked through the site the Waltzer was being set up. The stacked cars unloaded off their wagon. The ground packed and levelled as the main frame was laid out. Then the plates of painted wood, chrome and alloy were slotted into the skeleton and the whole structure was locked together.

Tomorrow they'd set up the generators. Do the layout and cable connections. Test the lamps, circuits and power systems. The final safety checks on the mechanisms and structures. Then the machines of joy would be ready to fly. The fair would come alive. A city of light. And he'd see his work the way it should be seen. Illuminated. Lit up by thousands of coloured light bulbs.

The sky was darkening now, the light diffusing into a warm red. Years of painting had taught him to see every colour in terms of pigment. There was alizarin crimson there, maybe some indigo. It all bled into the red fire of the Ghost Train. Mick smiled as the firmament brought inspiration once again. *Bang*, he thought. That was it. That's how he'd repaint the ride.

Mick was a fairground artist. He'd always been good at painting and drawing. By rights he should have gone to art school with his talent. But he'd drifted. Found himself working for Lakins before the war. Big firm, did most of the decorating for rides and sideshows. Then he went freelance. He liked the travelling life.

He had thought of settling down once. He'd had this idea of setting up a tattoo parlour. Something steady. He'd seen plenty of them during the war and he reckoned he could do better than most of them himself. When he was in Burma with the Forgotten Army he got to see some real beauties. Out East it was an art form really. The delicate oriental needlework inspired him. He spent idle hours drawing designs on any old bit of paper he could find.

So after demob he got himself a tattoo rig and rented a small shop just off Brighton seafront. But the novelty of it soon wore off. Most customers wanted the standard designs from flash sheets you could find in any parlour in the country. He missed the scope for colour and inventiveness. The sheer scale of decorating a big machine. And the movement. How you could bring flight to a ride in the way it was painted. And how the mechanism of the ride would bring the decoration to life. When you got it right it was beautiful. And he missed another kind of movement. His own.

So he shut up his shop, sold his gear and went on the road again.

There seemed a purpose in travelling. Not that he quite fitted in with the fairground world. Not really a showman. Not in the circle, as it were. But he didn't mind that. It gave him a bit of distance, a perspective on his work.

The evening star had risen and now burned low in the sky. He'd start the maintenance job on the Ghost Train tomorrow. He already knew which colours he'd use. It was just a retouching job but he could do with a hand if he was to get it done in time.

He asked around and someone directed him to a bloke named Joe. This Joe wasn't a showman. He was an outsider. What circus people call a josser. With the fairground lot it's simply in the circle or out. And he certainly wasn't in. Not a showman, not part of any family. Just casual labour for the build-up. This wasn't that usual. Showmen are naturally suspicious of outsiders but Joe had obviously been around a bit. He knew the assembly order for the Waltzer. He was hanging around to see if there was any work going. A bit too old to be running about taking fares on the Dodgems like the other gaff boys, but there might be something going on the joints or the side stuff.

When Mick asked Joe if he wanted to work with him, Joe hardly said anything. He merely nodded his head and grunted something in acknowledgment. For a moment Mick thought that the man might be halfwitted but there was an intense, hunted look in his eyes that told another story.

They started work at first light, and although Joe's labours were confined to the menial it was soon pretty clear that he had a feeling for it. Mick could always tell if somebody had the eye. Joe was good company. He didn't say much but he listened as Mick explained the designs and techniques. The man seemed to come alive as he laid on paint with the enthusiasm of an apprentice. He seemed to know something about painting. In a brief exchange on the subject Joe let slip that he learned a bit when he'd 'been inside', then suddenly drew in on himself again, obviously regretting the admission. In the now embarrassing silence Mick muttered something about not caring about another man's past.

'It's all right,' he remembered saying. 'You've paid your debt, haven't you?'

By the end of the day Mick had let Joe do a couple of the grinning skulls around the hell-mouth while he finished the marbling on the pillars. They worked in virtual silence, just an occasional word or gesture. They understood each other.

The generators started up and the monstrous engines were powered into life. A charivari of pop music echoed across the site, punctuated by the hiss and clatter of the machines. Lamplight constellations outlined the shape and play of the rides and brought out their vibrant hues and markings. An artificial landscape that reeled with mad delight. A baroque mechanism of light, colour, form and motion. Industrial pleasure. An electrified arcadia. The modern engines spinning in pure imitation of ancient ritual. Timeless festival only children can fully understand.

Sparks flew up the poles of the Dodgems to crackle against the wire ceiling above. Mick and Joe walked through the fair in the quiet contentment of a good day's work. Joe had a go on the rifle range. He weighed the .22 air rifle in his hands, cradling it thoughtfully, then broke it at its barrel and lined up his five lead slugs on the counter. Each shot found its target with a dull crack. The man on the stall indicated the prizes. Soft toys of fuzz and kapok. Lurid plastic troll-like dolls with bright hair and idiot eyes. Brittle china dogs and figurines. Joe chose one of those and held it up. Mick smiled and caught that strange stare of his. Close and yet absent at the same time. Joe made a vague gesture with the cheap ornament. It took Mick a while to realise that he was offering it to him.

20

Operation Skeleton had begun in 1968. There had been a series of burglaries of shops and warehouses in London and the Home Counties with no sign of forced entry. The gang responsible had an obvious modus operandi, the use of duplicate or skeleton keys. Information gathered indicated that those responsible for the robberies were a gang of criminals based in South London. So an operation was set up to break the so-called Skeleton Gang working out of C9 Department – the Metropolitan and Provincial Police Crime Branch – based at Coco. O'Neill and Campbell were both part of the squad, and records showed that they had been very active in various investigations. O'Neill had been responsible for over twenty arrests and had received at least ten commendations for catching thieves. However, it appeared that almost all of the charges brought thanks to his activities were for receiving and handling stolen goods from the Skeleton jobs. Only one man was charged and convicted for an actual robbery and he was on record as saying that he had been wrongly arrested, having merely been in the vicinity of a clothes shop that had been turned over. A crime in which none of the stolen property had been recovered.

Also, there seemed to be a strange pattern to the Skeleton gang's activity. There would be a wave of robberies that would subside after a period of about six months. In this time a certain amount of knocked-off goods would be recovered and fences arrested while the actual gang seemed to be taking a well-earned rest. The operation itself would apparently wind down during this period. Then the gang would start busying itself again in a short but concentrated burst, and the detectives involved in the case would also go into action, again raiding a series of premises where a partial quantity of bent property would be recovered and a few minor-league receivers busted.

Dennis Woods, O'Neill and Campbell insisted, was an important informer for Operation Skeleton. Far from paying them off, they alleged, he had instead received money from the Information Fund for squealing on his associates. Having been exposed as a grass, they reasoned, he was covering his tracks and attempting to protect himself from retribution by crying 'foul'.

So far, so bad. The whole thing reeked of hookeyness. I'd come across this sort of thing so many times by now. An operation appearing to get results, taking a few mug villains off the pavement for a bit while it was lining its own pockets. If the inquiry could confine itself to this one operation, hopefully to the officers already named in the journalist's tapes, all well and good. Damage limitation, that was what it was all about. That was what everyone at the Yard was hoping for. With Harrington breathing down our collective neck it wasn't going to be easy, but he was still only involved in an 'advisory capacity' (which could mean fuck-all if we played our cards right). If need be, the whole of Operation Skeleton would have to be sacrificed, cut off at the knees. The important thing was to make sure the swede didn't start prying farther afield. This 'firm in a firm' equation was making everybody jumpy.

Ernie Franklin wasn't having such an easy time. He was having to work closely with Harrington and that was taking its toll. They were going over the press allegations together and interviewing Woods to compile their own statement of what had occurred. He was up close to all the bad stuff and it was doing him in. Ernie was old-school in that he couldn't stomach the sort of behaviour that was being described every day as he went over the evidence with Harrington. But he was also old-school in that he was fiercely loyal to the Met. He was being pulled apart by it. It didn't help that Harrington was a cold fish, to say the least. Ernie felt himself being judged daily by this upright and sober swede. His disintegrating private life and heavy drinking didn't help. We went for a swift one at the end of the first week of the inquiry. I hoped that it could be recreational but he was still absorbed by it all.

'This is diabolical, Frank,' he said to me after his fourth double Scotch.

'I know, guvnor,' I replied, unable to change the subject.

'I just can't believe the stuff I'm hearing. Can you?'

I could, of course, but I couldn't tell him that. His hand started to weave a little as it went for the glass.

'You know, Frank . . .' His voice was beginning to slur. 'It makes me feel . . .' He winced, his face screwing up in front of me. 'Dirty. It really does. I feel . . .'

There was another pause as he struggled for a word.

'Tainted,' he declared finally. 'It does, you know. It makes me feel tainted.'

'Look, guvnor,' I reasoned, 'maybe you should get off home.'

He gave a hollow, pitiful laugh.

'Home?' He laughed again. 'I ain't got a home, son. She chucked me out. You know that? Fucking threw me out on the street. I'm back to kipping in a section house like a fucking woodentop on probation.'

He slurped the dregs of his glass, sucking at the spirit's vapour.

'Fucking diabolical.'

Alan Khalid was a good-looking man in his mid-thirties. Half-caste, with black hair and a hawklike nose. I hadn't really thought of the angle before meeting him but it suddenly made sense: that the 'businessman' looking for hard-core pornography in large quantities should be an Arab. It would be a good cover for setting up a deal, and Alan Khalid would clearly be able to play the part of the gullible Levantine.

Alan was a freelance journalist but he could easily have been an actor. There was something mischievous about his demeanour. Vain and flirtatious, he always smiled a little bit too readily. He was convincingly shifty, perhaps a little too much so. But he was ideal for the part. My only other concern was that he might be just a little bit light skinned.

'Don't worry,' he assured me. 'I'll go on the sunbed.'

When I pitched my idea to him he was very keen and set to work on developing his seedy Arab persona. We decided that he would be from the Lebanon, keen to purchase bulk orders of blue films. He kitted himself out with a Savile Row suit and plenty of gold jewellery. He grew a little goatee and developed the appropriate speech patterns for his dirty Beirut businessman. I was worried that he might be getting a bit carried away. He tried sporting a keffiyeh but I told him that was a bit too much.

We set him up with a very swish apartment in Mayfair and he started doing the rounds of the bookshops in Soho.

Julian had really fallen on his feet with Teddy Thursby. The old lord had successfully sued *Private Eye* in 1970 over allegations that he had been connected with the gangster Harry Starks. He'd come away with £20,000 and Julian had latched himself on to him, ostensibly to help him write his memoirs.

As he sponged off the ancient peer, Julian began to cultivate an awful kind of assumed sophistication that was quite disgusting. He went all High Church, under Teddy's influence, all smells and bells and sanctimonious ritual. I'm sure he hardly believed in any of it. He indulged himself in the sins of the flesh and desired some kind of spiritual redemption. It really was horribly hypocritical. And I felt increasingly that he was looking down his nose at me, the grubby gutter-press journalist.

I had arranged a meeting with Teddy Thursby through Julian. I was keen to get any inside information that Thursby might have about Lord Longford. We met in the French House on Dean Street.

'Frank Longford?' Teddy said when I enquired about him. 'Decent enough chap, a ghastly puritan, though. Socialist and Roman. Awful combination. Why do you want to know?'

'Well, I'm doing this piece about the porn inquiry.'

'Ah, yes, of course. Another moral crusade for the illustrious *Illustrated*.'

Teddy and Julian exchanged a smile. They were laughing at me.

'Well, actually, Teddy,' I said, somewhat indignantly, 'we're doing our own inquiry.'

'Really?' he said, leaning forward. 'What are you going to do?'

I found myself telling him of my plan. I was quite proud of it. Teddy listened intently and gave a deep chuckle when I had gone through the basic details.

'Oh yes,' he muttered. 'An Arab, very good. Well, I can tell you something about Longford. Jules, get us another round of drinks, there's a good fellow.'

Julian stood up and waited.

'Oh, for fuck's sake,' complained Thursby. 'I gave you some money already.'

'I'll get these,' I insisted, and handed a note to Julian.

'Useless fucker,' Teddy muttered. 'He's pocketed half the advances for this book and he still wants more. Hardly seen any work yet either.'

'You were saying . . .'

'What?'

'Longford. Something about Longford.'

'Yes, well.' Teddy lowered his voice and leaned towards me. 'Here's a funny thing. He's visiting Myra Hindley in jail. Can you believe that? Myra fucking Hindley.'

'Really?'

'Yes. He's got her to rejoin the faith apparently. Thinks he can save her soul. He's absolutely mad.'

Sid would love that, I thought. LORD PORN VISITS EVIL MYRA, something like that. Julian returned with the drinks.

'Here he is,' Teddy announced in mock solemnity. 'My faithful amanuensis.'

Julian gave a tight little smile.

'Well,' he said, 'I'm more like his confessor, really. Isn't that right, Teddy?' He turned to me. 'It would make your hair stand up on end, some of the events in our noble lord's life. You see, Teddy's been one for absolute discretion all these years but he's afraid that once he croaks it'll all come out. Aren't you, Teddy?'

'That's quite enough, you little shit.'

'That's why he wants me to help him paper over a few cracks in the old reputation.'

'I said, that's enough,' Thursby insisted, and we changed the subject. Teddy started bitching about Ted Heath.

'There's a bloody war going on. The unions trying to bring the country to its knees. The Blasted Heath's got no stomach for a fight. Well, some of my friends have other plans.'

The end of the season was the busiest time for Mick. All the showmen would be in winter quarters doing repair work. And it was then that he got most of the orders for the repainting of old machines and designing the decoration for any new ones. He rented a disused aircraft hangar in Lincolnshire. The showmen would arrive and lay out the parts of the machine that they wanted retouching. If it was a new job, a ride he'd not worked on before, he'd get them to set it up. He'd have to see how it moved before he could even start. Then he'd go through his designs with the showman. His repertoire, he called it.

He'd always have new ideas to try out as well. They usually trusted his judgment but Mick liked it best if they came to the final choice themselves. Showmen could often be vague about decoration and would say: 'You decide, it's your job,' something like that. Quite often the wife of the owner would have a better idea of how things should look and he'd talk it out with them.

He did his business word of mouth during the season. He'd visit all the main fairs and see what was wanted for the next, as well as doing the odd bit of on-site work. His past jobs were always the advertisement for future contracts. Not that there was ever much paperwork. It was all mostly done on trust. A spit on the palm and a handshake. It was best to be around a build-up when a new or repainted ride was being put together and other showmen would be around to appraise the decoration. 'Who's machine is that?' someone once asked of a Dodgems that Mick had painted with four-foot-high letters spelling the name of the ride's owner on it. Mick was about to point to the name when he suddenly realised that the man obviously couldn't read. Fairly common among the showmen. Many of them couldn't read their own names on the rides they owned.

There was a lot of work over the winter and he sometimes brought in extra help. When things got really busy he'd have to subcontract work out to other painters. But he didn't like doing that. He relished the feeling of being on his own when the boards and the panelling of a ride were laid out on the floor of the hangar ready for fresh paint. He would walk around them figuring out ideas. The designs and the drawings, the colours and illuminations. But as he worked through a job he'd sense an oncoming loneliness. As a ride neared its completion he'd feel an awful sorrow. An emptiness as his work would inevitably cease being his own. His work for which he had no other term than the raw, intimate, painfully embarrassing word: art. His art was dying out just as he would. He had no particular desire to pass on his trade, his craft, but at times there was a silent urge to share the strange feelings that he had about what he did. He'd been on his own far too long. Through the winter months he'd find himself talking in a low, urgent tone as he paced around, laying on paint. Trying to explain it somehow, though the words that came out hardly made sense to him.

When Joe had asked him, after they had finished the Ghost Train job, if there was any more work to be had, Mick had been cautious.

He'd stalled him all the time the fair was on Woodhouse Moor. Joe had got work on the Penny Arcade. Mick had stayed around to see what future jobs there were to be had. Then, when the fair was over and all packed up – pull-out time, as they call it – Mick went over and spoke with Joe. He'd been thinking it over. He was getting on, he'd reasoned to himself, and he needed a hand to get all the work done these days. He hated it when he had to farm out work. Joe had some sort of knack. A bit of an eye for it. And he wasn't too old to be taught a few tricks. He'd give him a month's trial and see how things went.

21

Stamford Bridge. Chelsea v. West Ham. Needle match. The North Stand and the Shed End warming up their voices. Call and response. Tribal. *Zigger! Oi! Zagger! Oi!* A seething echo around the ground. Like a Zeppelin-field *sieg heil. Zigger-zagger-zigger-zagger! Oi! Oi! Oi!* West Ham strikes up with 'I'm Forever Blowing Bubbles'. Substitute *fortune's always hiding* with *Chelsea's always running*. Taunting. The Tannoy crackles into life. 'Blue is the Colour'. Chelsea's FA Cup anthem from last year. The Shed and the North Stand sing along, dirgelike. Slightly embarrassed at such a crap song. Christmas-carol trite. *Blue is the colour! football is the game! we're all together! and Chelsea is our name.* Greeting-card poetry. The Chelsea mob breaks into a guttural chant at the end with relief.

Tannoy crackles again. Bass line throbbing into a double slam. Repeated, then vibrato organ picks up on the offbeat. Chicka-chicka-chicka rhythm guitar riff holds the space between the bass and the melody. Rock steady. Organ grinding into a mad calliope. The Harry J All Stars' 'The Liquidator' fills the stadium. A roar goes up on both sides. The skinheads' overture. Instrumental. Every terrace's soundtrack. A single tremulous note hits the rhythm. One-drop four-four time. The fans on both sides pick up the beat. Four claps and a two-click chant. *Chel-sea!* and *West-Ham!* vie for supremacy. Boot Boy choreography. Ox-blood or cherry-red Astronauts with Dr Martens' patented Air-Cushioned Sole. White Boy Reggae. Carried along by the instinctive blue-beat pulse, the whole of the Shed is moon-stomping. Boneheads, number one clipper shorn, some with the shaved-in parting. Buttoned-down collars. The suedeheads growing out the crop, smoothies in crombies and Sta-Prest. Some with longer hair, feather cut. Blue-and-white scarves tied at the wrist, forming banners with each finger-pointed salute. Tattoos displayed.

Mum & Dad. CFC. Chelsea lion rampant. Scrolled hearts. CUT HERE dotted lines. Borstal spots. On the faces. Tattooed tears.

Everyone's really geared up as the song comes to an end. The teams are coming on to the pitch. Chopper Harris leading the Blues out to a huge roar. Then there's a commotion at the back of the Shed End. A large group of West Ham fans are pouring down the terraces in combat formation, chanting. Chelsea, taken by surprise, are in retreat, scattering. A gap opens up on the Shed in front of the advancing hordes. West Ham baying triumphantly. They are taking the Shed End. Suddenly a lone figure moves into the breach. Tall and distinctive in a white boiler suit and *Clockwork Orange* bowler hat. 'Don't run, Chelsea!' he shouts, rallying his comrades from their rout. Suddenly, emboldened by this reckless rearguard action, Chelsea counter-attacks. Both sides engage, boots and fists flying.

Then the police waded in and everything changed. The tribes came together against a common enemy. Something in the air. Somebody starting a chant. A song of hatred. Something that has been taken up on terraces across the land. No one was sure where it had come from, which ground, which end, but every gang of hooligans knew it by heart. A malevolent anthem sung with mutinous fervour.

It was my idea to go to the football. I just thought it would be good to have a bit of time off with Ernie that didn't involve heavy drinking. Ernie was spending far too much time in 'The Tank', the bar at Coco. Not having a proper home to go to didn't help. But his boozing was beginning to draw comments, which, given the usual intake of your average Met officer, was saying something. As it was he brought a hip flask, but with Ernie's alcohol intake it was probably just as well he had something to stave off the DTs. He studied the programme. A bit of banter about the game. Chelsea on good form, Osgood a bit temperamental, that sort of thing. An inevitable drift in the conversation towards the inquiry. I didn't mind, as long as we could be relaxed about it. I wanted to talk, off the record, away from Harrington, about Operation Skeleton and my thoughts on how we could seal it off there, not let the whole thing spread. And in a gentle way, to get Ernie to be part of the cover-up. He unscrewed his flask, took a glug of Scotch, handed it to me.

'The thing is, Ernie,' I said, 'it all started going wrong when you got these students and hippies arrested for troublemaking at demos or picked up by the Drugs Squad. Then you'd have these middle-class leftie cunts banged up with your career villain. What happens? They start infecting them with all this civil liberties shit. And before long you've got these guys, you've known they've been at it, they know you know, but instead of putting their hands up they're fannying on about their rights.'

'Yeah, well.' Ernie sighed. 'It's a different world, Frank.'

'And now we've got Harrington and the Home Office breathing down our necks.'

'Well,' he said with a shrug, 'the swede ain't all bad, you know.'

'Really?' I replied with a little wince from the neat whisky at the back of my throat.

'Yeah, well, maybe the Met does need to clean up its act a bit.'

'Yeah, but we can do that ourselves, can't we?'

'Can we, Frank? Can we?'

I didn't like the way this was going.

'It would be good for public relations,' Ernie went on. 'A lot of people have lost confidence in the Old Bill, you know.'

'Yeah, a lot of troublemakers stirring things up. Lefties, career criminals, bent briefs. Gutter journalists noseying about for a good story.'

'I ain't so sure, Frank.'

This was not good. Ernie could suddenly become a loose cannon in this whole thing. Wreaking havoc in the Yard. Suddenly there was a big fuss at the Shed End. Fighting had broken out on the terraces. This was the way football was going. Hooligans spoiling it for everyone. A phalanx of woodentops waded in, putting it about a bit lively with their truncheons, cutting a wedge between the ranks of rival fans. A few bodies were grabbed and hauled out. A tall bloke in a white boiler suit and bowler hat was being frogmarched away by a couple of uniforms.

'Look at that silly cunt,' I remarked to Ernie.

Another officer moved in to give him a couple of punches as he put up a struggle. Boos, whistles and catcalls from the crowd. A song started up. I couldn't make out what they were singing at first. Something to the tune of 'London Bridge Is Falling Down'.

Then the chant was repeated through all the parts of the Shed End. It spread quickly, like a drop of ink in water. Both sides were singing together. It united them. The police were unable to keep the fans apart now. They joined together and started to push back the uniforms as one army. The song echoed around the stadium now. A war cry. I could make out what the bastards were singing.

Billy Porter is our friend,
Is our friend, is our friend.
Billy Porter is our friend,
He Kills Coppers!

At the end of each refrain the combined mob broke into cheers and laughter. The woodentops were driven to the back of the Shed now. They brought on dogs to hold the crowd at bay.

I looked at Ernie. Pale faced, taking nervous little sips from the flask.

'You hear what those cunts are singing?' I asked him.

'Yeah, yeah,' he muttered. 'Just a bunch of hooligans.'

'They fucking hate us, Ernie. How come they hate us so much?'

'Take it easy, Frank.'

But I was fuming. I turned to him.

'Look,' I said, 'I've had enough of this. Let's get the fuck out of here.'

So we ended up getting pissed in a local boozer after all. I took Ernie back to the section house. He wasn't in very good shape. And I was late. I'd told Jeannie I'd be home hours ago. We were only supposed to be going to the match, after all.

On the way home that song was haunting me. I mean, you get used to abuse. It's part of the job. Being called the filth and stuff like that. 'All Coppers Are Bastards' and so on. But that song, that was fucking evil. Barbaric. This bloody inquiry was supposed to be 'in the public interest', but what did it matter if the public could hate us so much? What was the point of being to rights if that's what they thought of you anyway? And it was personal. *Billy Porter is our friend*. Dave's killer had become some sort of hero. Nothing made sense any more.

I got back and Jeannie was watching *Come Dancing* on the telly.

'Where the hell have you been?' she demanded.

'Sorry, love,' I told her. 'A bit of business.'

I leaned over to kiss her on the cheek. She sniffed at me and pulled away.

'You've been drinking.'

'Yeah.' I shrugged. 'A couple after we booked off. I'll just go up and see David.'

She sighed.

'Well, don't wake him up. I've just got him to bed.'

I crept into his room like an intruder. I left the door open a little so I could look at him by the light from the landing. His little face was squashed up against the pillow. He looked so calm and innocent lying there. Little David. He looked so much like him. I felt a sad loneliness well up inside of me. Like I didn't belong. I gave him a beery-breathed kiss on his forehead. *Poor little fucker doesn't know what he's in for*, I thought.

I went back downstairs. I felt all these emotions choked up in the back of my throat. I wanted to talk to Jeannie. About how I felt. I just didn't know how.

'Jeannie,' I said as I came back into the lounge. 'Look, I'm sorry.'

'Don't bother,' she replied, walking past me. 'I'm going to bed.'

I went to the sideboard and poured myself another drink and sat brooding at the telly. The judges were holding up numbers. I had another drink. And then another. *Match of the Day* came on. I switched off the set and collapsed on to the settee.

A blond-haired youth opened the door to me when I went around to Alan Khalid's flat. He had milky-blue eyes that rolled back and forth in their sockets. A nervous little snigger. *Heh-heh, heh-heh*.

'Yeah?' he breathed languidly, letting his mouth hang open, the staccato giggle coming again from the back of his throat.

Heh-heh, heh-heh. The deranged laugh seemed to insist upon complicity in its furtiveness. He licked his lips and gave an idiot smile. He looked like a degenerate cherub.

'Where's Alan?' I demanded.

'Alan!' he shouted, swinging slightly on the half-open door.

I pushed past him. The flat was a mess. Clothes and empty bottles on the floor, magazines scattered about with the remains of their shrink-wrapping, little piles of shed skin. Alan came into view, walking out of the kitchen with a glass in his hand. He was wearing a silk dressing gown.

'Tony, effendi,' he declared in his exaggerated Arab accent. 'Have a drink.'

He handed me the glass.

'What the hell is going on?'

'Just getting into character,' he said, reverting to his usual voice.

'I can see that.'

My concerns about Alan Khalid getting carried away with his role as the decadent Arab seemed well founded. There was a dark-haired woman sitting on the leather sofa in the middle of the room. Behind her there was a film projector on a stack of books piled up on a side table. A screen had been set up in front of the sofa. She looked up at me as I walked in. She had eyes as near black as her hair, pupils wide and empty, like pitted olives.

'Who are your friends?' I asked.

'This is Magda,' he replied, gesturing vaguely. 'And this is Ralph.'

He sounded drunk. Ralph gave a coy shrug and a *heh-heh* in acknowledgment.

'And I suppose they're expenses, are they?'

'Well, you want me to be convincing, don't you? I've had to entertain some of my new-found business associates, after all. I want to put on a bit of a show for them.'

'Well, maybe this is going a little bit too far.'

'Oh, don't worry, old boy,' he insisted. 'The *Illustrated* is getting its money's worth. You can be sure of that. You won't believe some of the filth I've managed to get my hands on. Ralph, get one of the films for our friend here.'

Heh-heh.

'Which one?'

'Oh, I don't know,' Khalid mused. 'The one with the animals.'

Ralph busied himself looking through a collection of Super-8 films on the sideboard. I took a sip from the glass in my hand without thinking. It was sickly bittersweet.

'Come and have a look at this,' Alan said, walking around to the sofa. 'Budge up, Magda.'

'Never mind this,' I said, standing above them. 'I need to know what contacts you've made.'

Khalid sank into the soft leather. Both he and the woman looked up at me with a calm impatience that made me feel ill at ease. Ralph threaded a film through the projector.

'Don't worry,' Alan said. 'I've been busy. I'll tell you all about it. But first . . .'

He patted the cushion beside him.

'Sit down. Watch.'

Ralph dimmed the lights and switched on the projector. The machine clattered into life. A white square shifted about on the screen. Credits came up. *Beauty and the Beasts.*

I really didn't want to watch. I gulped down my drink, nervously. Alan refilled it. I shouldn't be drinking, I thought to myself.

'So?' I pressed him.

Alan Khalid sighed.

'Well, I've been around the bookshops and let it be known that I'm a serious customer. I've asked this Danish company you mentioned, Hot Love, if there is a London agent that deals with their stuff, but I've found it doesn't quite work like that.'

On the screen a buxom redhead was lasciviously stroking a German shepherd.

'What do you mean?'

'Well, the way the thing is organised. Wholesale and retail, they seem to be completely different operations. Oh, look at that!'

The woman in the film was crouching obscenely in front of the dog. The animal jumped up on her, tottering on its hind legs like a badly trained circus act. *Heh-heh, heh-heh*, came the hoarse voice behind me.

'Oh, Christ,' groaned Magda. 'Do we have to see this again?'

'What do you mean, different operations?' I asked, trying to ignore the spectacle.

'Well,' Khalid went on, 'the wholesale side has the greater risk. It entails smuggling the stuff in and selling it fairly cheap. But on the retail side the mark-up is phenomenal. It's better organised because there are bigger returns. It's a matter of keeping the shops legit but selling the really hard-core stuff out the back or under the counter. And I've managed to get some really hard-core stuff, as you can see.'

The German shepherd was now humping away with a bewildered look on its lolling face. The woman mimed open-mouthed ecstasy. A sudden jump cut and a new image flickered up. The woman was kissing a pig's snout.

'So,' Khalid went on, 'the really big operators are the guys running the retail end. What we want to do is set up a deal with them.'

'And who are they?'

'Well, they're pretty elusive, as you can imagine. But I think I've tracked down one of the biggest of them.'

The camera pulled out to reveal the two creatures on all fours facing each other. The screen washed out for a second, gorged with grotesque pink flesh. I drained my glass again.

'And who's that?' I asked, catching my breath.

'Fat Wally,' he said, looking down at my empty glass. 'Magda, get us some more drinks, will you, poppet.'

Magda sighed and sullenly heaved herself off the sofa.

'And Ralph, take this tiresome rubbish off. Let's have a look at that other film.'

'Which one?'

'Oh, you know,' Khalid urged softly. 'The nasty one.'

Heh-heh, complied Ralph as he stopped the film and rewound it. Magda came through with two glasses that she handed to us. The celluloid clattered out of the projector and the screen held a white square while he changed the film. I took a sip from the glass. Some horrible cocktail. My head swam a little. Maybe the drink was spiked with something.

'This you must see,' Alan Khalid insisted as the machine whirred and the next film was fed through the gate.

'Who's Fat Wally?' I asked.

'Walter Peters. It seems he runs a whole chain of shops with different frontmen.'

The image on the screen was even more jerky and unclear than in the last feature. Black and white this time rather than gaudy colour. Badly lit with a grainy quality. My temples throbbed as the camera focused on a supplicant figure. A woman – it was only just possible to make out the form – kneeling with her hands behind her back. A man walked into shot. Ralph came around from behind the projector and sat on the floor between us.

'What the hell is this?' I asked.

Heh-heh.

'It's called a snuff movie,' Alan Khalid said. 'It's supposed to be a film of someone being murdered. I'm sure it's all faked. But it's the hard-core stuff you want, isn't it?'

There was a close-up of the woman. Naked breasts heaving with quickened breathing. Eyes looking up, wide with fear.

'So, you've met this Fat Wally, then?' I asked.

'No. He likes to stay in the background. I've talked to one of his frontmen, a bloke called Ian Hesper. I've managed to convince him that I'm a serious customer but that I want to meet the main man.'

The man on the screen looped a thin leather strap around the woman's neck. He twisted it with one hand and groped at her with the other. Squeezing her breast, tugging at the nipple.

'I thought if we got a meeting with Fat Wally, that could be the set-up, couldn't it?'

Both hands were on the ligature now, pulling it tighter and tighter. Her mouth open wide in a silent scream. Eyes bulging, tongue lolling out. Her face darkening, swelling slightly with the blood rush. A sense of constriction in my own throat, a choking feeling as I swallowed. Thoughts rushing through my head – desires, dreams, memories, feelings I worked so hard at repressing. The face on the screen blurring, losing focus, losing definition. Fantasy and reality flickering. His hand on her throat. My hand trembling.

'Tony?'

'*Heh-heh*. He's enjoying this one.'

The camera pans out. The man lets go of one end of the strap and it snakes free of her neck as she slumps to the floor. Close-up of her face, eyes wide, mouth slightly ajar, still. The reel finished, the end of the film fluttering in the projector like a trapped bird. A white square on the screen.

'Well?' Alan asked.

I rubbed my face.

'Yeah, sure,' I agreed. 'That sounds like a good idea. You set up a meeting and we can be waiting for them.'

I stood up. It was time to be going.

'Well, I better be off,' I said.

'Stay and have another drink.'

'Yeah, *heh-heh*. You were just beginning to enjoy yourself.'

I had to get out. My head was spinning. I walked to the door and Alan saw me out.

'I'll be in touch,' I said.

I wandered about Mayfair. I needed some air, needed to calm my head down. I felt sickened by the disgusting films I'd been exposed to, frightened by what the snuff movie had stirred up inside of me. *I'm sure it's all faked*, Alan Khalid had said. What was real? My head was spinning, I was drunk. I needed to sober up, get control. Get a grip.

I found myself in Shepherd Market. There were a couple of sad-looking whores soliciting. It's a nasty, rotten world, I thought, oozing with corruption. All my pent-up feelings screaming for release. The killer inside me taking over, a killer on the loose.

I found myself walking towards one of the tarts. She smiled as she saw me approach, shameless, a fleck of lipstick on her teeth.

'Looking for business, love?' she asked.

In her flat, red light bulb throbbing in my head. She runs through what's on offer, what it costs. The room grainy and out of focus like eight-millimetre celluloid. Yes, that's it, I thought. All faked, just a film, just a dream. None of it real.

I looped my belt around her neck. It's all over soon. Show's over. The film fluttering in the projector like a trapped bird. The End.

It was the tattoo that nagged away in Mick's mind. He'd got used to Joe being elusive or even downright deceptive about his own past. But why did he have to go and lie about a thing like that? It had already started to fade but it was a lovely piece of work. He'd caught sight of it on Joe's upper arm in odd moments. A tiger that curled around his shoulder in yellow and black. Round-eyed with a snarling grin. Like it was ready to strike. One day, when Joe was changing his shirt in his wagon, he caught Mick staring at it. He turned slightly away.

'Nice tattoo,' Mick had said.

'Yeah,' Joe grunted, picking up the clean shirt. 'I guess.'

'Let's have a look at it.'

Joe frowned and quickly displayed it for Mick to see. He started to put his shirt on.

'Hang on,' Mick insisted. 'Let's see it properly.'

Joe sighed and let Mick examine it. His torso tensed as Mick came close. The tiger hunched up a little, as if endowed with a musculature of its own.

'Nice,' said Mick.

Joe glared at him.

'Seen enough, have we?' he demanded with an indignant hint in his voice.

'Yeah,' Mick replied, withdrawing slightly. 'Sure.'

Joe hastily pulled on the shirt and started to button it up.

'I mean,' he went on, 'we don't want to be eyeing each other up too much, do we? Two blokes on their own in the middle of nowhere. People might talk.'

Mick smiled. Joe broke into a nervous laugh.

'Looks like a Jap piece,' said Mick.

'What?'

'The tattoo. Looks Japanese. Or Thai. Where you get it done?'

'Paddington,' Joe replied quickly.

Are you sure? Mick felt like saying, but that would have seemed such a stupid question. But it was an old tattoo and Mick was pretty certain that it hadn't been done in a London parlour back whenever. Even now, there were very few places you'd get work as finely done as that. His mind whirred with possibilities of a hidden narrative Joe might be holding back. That amount of fading would mean it had been done in the fifties some time. Maybe Joe had done National Service in Korea. Got it done on leave to Seoul or Tokyo. Or Hong Kong, maybe. He didn't want to pry and felt a little guilty about trying to expose Joe's past, even though it was all going on in his head. You had to trust a bloke you were working so closely with. But why did he have to go and lie about a thing like that?

Mick tried not to dwell upon it. Everyone has secrets. And there was work to be done. Joe had the knack. He knew that now. He had a good drawing hand and was beginning to learn about colours. Mick found a pleasure in imparting his craft. It was the work that was important. It would live on.

Someone brought in a wagon one day for repainting. They wanted it done just the same. The background was kind of a buff colour. Mick didn't have an exact match so they had to think of what colours to mix to get the right shade. He called Joe over.

'Take a long look at it,' he said. 'The thing is to try to see what colours are in there. What do you reckon?'

Joe frowned.

'Well, it's sort of ochre, ain't it?'

'Yeah, but what's in it?'

'I don't know, Mick. How can you tell?'

'By looking. Long and hard. It takes experience. Have a go. That's how you learn. Have a look.'

Joe gave Mick a puzzled smile.

'Go on,' Mick insisted. 'Have a look.'

Joe turned to look at the wagon. He squinted at it.

'Look, Mick, I don't know,' he said.

'Take your time.'

They stood there for almost half an hour, peering at it. Joe tried to see what was bound up in the surface of the paint. He couldn't really understand what Mick was on about at first, and after what seemed like an age was ready to give up. Then suddenly something happened. He spotted something.

'Yeah,' he said tentatively. 'Well . . .'

'Go on,' Mick encouraged.

'Raw sienna,' he declared with a little chuckle.

Mick nodded.

'Yeah. What else?'

'I don't know. Orange. Maybe . . . oh, I don't know.'

'A lot of it's guesswork, Joe. You're searching for something hidden. You have a look, then you try it out. But you have to be able to see it. You know what I mean?'

Joe looked at Mick then looked back at the wagon. For a second something made sense. He grinned. If he could have given tongue to all that flooded through his head at that moment he would have talked for hours.

'Yeah,' was all he said.

Mick encouraged Joe to work on his own designs. He came up with an idea for the decoration of a shooting range that they did that winter. It was a small job and Mick let him have his head. Wild West motifs, gunslingers and cacti with a huge six-shooter as the central illustration.

Joe could appear absent a lot of the time. He'd mumble to himself. Bits of songs and catches. Nursery rhymes. Like he was pretending to be simple. Sometimes when Mick called his name he wouldn't respond at first and Mick would have to repeat it.

Mick had figured for a long time that Joe was not his real name.

Sometimes, when they had been talking and a pause descended between them, Joe would frown and look at him, opening his mouth slightly as if he were about to utter something. It was then that Mick thought he might tell him his secret. But Joe's mouth would just tremble for a moment and then close into a dead smile. Mick always felt these moments pass with a sense of relief. He really didn't want to know.

Joe had a battered old Bible that he kept in his wagon. 'It's all in here, you know,' he once said, looking up from it. 'Sex, violence, the lot.'

They were clearing up after their last winter job. It was only three weeks off Valentine's Day when the fairground season starts. Mick saw Joe staring at a scrap of newspaper. Folding it up and stashing it in his overalls. Joe looked up but Mick had already turned away deliberately. Joe's secretive nature made him anxious not to appear over-curious. He'd thought of offering Joe some sort of partnership. He wanted him to feel that he could trust him. They had worked so well together. That was the important thing.

22

Monday morning and the Deputy Assistant Commissioner called me into his office.

'Just a quick word, Frank,' he said.

I felt a bit edgy. Maybe something had come up. Something with my name on it. The longer this inquiry went on the more uneasy everybody felt. I mean, everybody who had something to hide, that is. And it was beginning to get to me.

'Take a seat, Frank. I won't take up too much of your time.'

'What's this about, sir?'

'How are things going with the inquiry?'

'Well . . .'

I didn't know what to say.

'We all know what a difficult job it is,' the DAC went on. 'It can put an awful lot of pressure on officers involved.'

'I'm fine, sir.'

'It's not you that we're worried about, Frank.'

'No?'

'No. It's Ernie. I mean, Detective Chief Superintendent Franklin.'

'Sir?'

'Well, he's been under a lot of pressure recently. Marriage breaking up, drinking a little bit too much. You know he's been to see a shrink?'

'Really?'

'Yeah, his nerves are shot to pieces. The thing is, Frank, this is off the record, but keep an eye on him. It's a very delicate situation and we can't afford to let things get out of hand. And Franklin's been acting a bit odd lately. We're worried that he might be backing the wrong horse, if you know what I mean.'

Getting too close to the swede, he meant. I nodded. The DAC smiled.

'Just give us the nod if anything gets too lairy. We can deal with Harrington. He's only on the case in an advisory capacity, after all. But let us know about Ernie. If it all gets too much for him, well, we might have to replace him.'

'What did the DAC want?' Ernie asked me later.

I mumbled something about some paperwork that needed sorting concerning my secondment to the inquiry. Ernie had come up with another lead. Some villain called Tommy Hills had been picked up for a blag on a ladies' outfitters in Dartford. They'd got away with a whole load of schmutter, about £2,000 worth. No sign of a forced entry, so the MO made it a classic Skeleton job. The gang had been disturbed as their van had been loaded up. The van had managed to drive off in time but without one of their number, this face Tommy Hills. He was none too pleased about being left behind and he didn't take much persuading by Kent CID to start naming names. But they'd got more than they'd bargained for when he began coughing about certain arrangements with Met officers. Detective Sergeant O'Neill's name came up, and one of the Kent officers was bright enough (and, presumably, untainted enough) to get in touch with the inquiry. Still in custody, Tommy Hills had been brought up to Wandsworth prison. Ernie and I drove down to the Hate Factory to interview him.

'I'm worried about the security of the inquiry,' he told me on the way down there.

'What do you mean, guvnor?'

'Well, we're right in the middle of the Yard. Any cunt can wander in and have a sneak at the files. Or nosey about the typing pool.'

He was right. Curiosity about how the investigation was going was rampant. Certain faces very jittery about it. One DI from C9 came up to me one morning and said: 'If any of my snouts' names come up, you will let me know, won't you?' And I was happy enough to oblige. Cracks needed papering over, that was for sure. I was on the lookout for anything that might even vaguely implicate me. But Ernie, of course, didn't see it that way.

'And you know the Action Book's gone missing,' he went on.

This was a record where entries were made instructing investigating officers on their next task. It had been mislaid. These things happen.

'I think,' Ernie went on, 'we need to move the whole inquiry.'

'What?'

'Yeah. Get it out of Coco altogether. I've talked to Harrington about it. I reckon over the water to Tintagel House.'

'Aren't you being a bit paranoid, guvnor?' I asked.

Well, this obviously hit a nerve. Maybe this shrink business had got to him.

'No, Frank,' he fumed, 'I am not paranoid! I've been twenty-three years in the job and I never realised what hookeyness goes on. I've been a bloody fool. But I am not fucking paranoid! All right?'

'Yes, guvnor.'

He was right. If anything I was the paranoid one.

This Tommy Hills character was a sly one. Obviously used to doing deals. Knowing when to cough and when to clam up. We went through the statement he'd made to Kent CID and then got to talking about his relationship to DS O'Neill. Ernie did the talking.

'Yeah, well,' Hills began. 'I was working on his patch and he tried to fit me up for receiving.'

'So what happened?' asked Ernie.

'Well, he said to me: "We can do something about this."'

'And what did he mean by that?'

'Well, it was bodies or money, know what I mean? I wasn't so keen on squealing so I opted for payment. A "licence fee", he called it.'

'And how much was this "licence fee"?'

'He wanted two hundred, I knocked him down to a hundred and fifty. He agreed to that, but made it clear that this would be topped up from time to time. It cost me a bluey every time I come across him.'

'A bluey?'

'Yeah, a fiver. Whenever we met he'd pocket that.' Hills gave a mean little smile. 'I reckon he was saving me up for a rainy day.'

'Hills, these are serious allegations. We'll need dates, times, places.'

Hills smiled again.

'Listen, darling, I ain't even started. There's been much more going on than the Old Bill turning a blind eye to villains letting themselves into premises with a bunch of twirls. I could tell you stuff that would really get you sharpening your pencils. But I want certain assurances.'

'What the fuck do you mean, assurances?' I broke in.

Ernie held up his hand.

'Frank,' he chided. 'Let him talk. What assurances?'

'Well, look, I can tell you the whole lot. All the duplicate key jobs and how officers were paid off. But more besides. Stuff that would make your hair curl. But I want something in return.'

'I'm sure the courts will look favourably upon your co-operation,' Ernie assured him.

'Yeah, but I'm putting myself on the line here. If I do this, I ain't just a grass. I'll be a bloody supergrass.'

'As I said,' Ernie went on, 'if what you tell us can be verified, it will certainly mitigate against any charges against you.'

'Yeah, but that ain't good enough. I don't want to end up even doing a couple of months' porridge. I'd be a marked man. On Rule Forty-three with all the nonces. Having to watch my back all the time. Fuck that.'

'So, what do you want?'

'Full immunity.'

I laughed out loud. I turned to Ernie, expecting at least a smile on his face. He looked deadpan.

'Well . . .' he began.

'You can't be serious,' I said.

'I'm dead serious. If you want me to go QE then that's the deal. And I want proper protection and all.'

'Well . . .' Ernie said again. I glared at him but he ignored me. 'I'll have to take this to my superiors, of course.'

Hills nodded. We stood up to go.

'In the meantime,' concluded Ernie, 'I suggest you get yourself a brief.'

On the way out I quizzed Ernie about all of this.

'You aren't going to take that toerag's word for anything, are you, guvnor?'

'Well, it will all have to be properly investigated.'

'But that full immunity bullshit. I mean, he's taking the piss, isn't he?'

'I don't know, Frank. It could turn out to be the key to the whole inquiry. I'm going to talk to Harrington about it.'

'Shouldn't you go to the DAC, guvnor?'

'Not necessarily, Frank. It's all very sensitive. And if we are going to do a deal, well, Harrington can take it straight to the Home Secretary.'

This wasn't good. It wasn't good at all. This whole inquiry was getting out of hand. Ernie just wouldn't see that we had to keep the lid on it. The DAC was not going to like him going over the Yard's head to Harrington. But I had to let certain people know about this little supergrass. Hills' comment that *I could tell you stuff that would really get you sharpening your pencils* was unnerving. Maybe he was just bluffing, pretending to be bigger and better connected than he really was. But I wasn't prepared to take the risk. The firm within the firm would have to know.

Ideally I would have gone to Vic Sayles. But Vic had quit the force in 1969. Medical retirement. He was dying of lung cancer. So I didn't really have any choice. I had to see George Mooney.

I arranged a meet at the Premier Club. He was the best person to see about all this. Basically there're two types of corrupt persons. Your meat-eater and your grass-eater. A meat-eater is active in pursuing opportunities for personal gain, a grass-eater simply accepts the earners that come his way by chance. And by Christ was Mooney a meat-eater. He was bloody carnivorous. The money the Dirty Squad was taking in bungs was astronomical. It kind of created a whole economy of police corruption, sucking in people all over the Met. It was like a bloody feeding frenzy. I was, of course, more of a grass-eater. One of the grazing beasts. Bovine, docile. But I was worried that something somewhere might implicate me. I was concerned for my precious career. I just couldn't afford to let anything get in the way of that. And although I despised Mooney I knew he was the only person who could make sure that this thing wouldn't spread. I knew it was wrong going to him, but I didn't give a fuck any more.

I could see his evil little mind go to work as I walked over to his table. I knew he must already have been busying himself with attempts to undermine the investigation.

'Ah, Frank,' he announced. 'I understand you have some knowledge to impart.'

'Well, you know what it's about.'

'Hm, yes. This *inquiry*.' He pronounced the word with distaste. 'Outsiders snooping around in our affairs. I trust you realise the need to keep certain things secret.'

'Yeah, well.'

'Then we understand each other at last. Darkness is for those without.' He leaned towards me across the table. 'Enlighten me.'

I told him all about Hills' veiled allegations and Ernie Franklin's intention of following them up.

'And you say that he's willing to go straight to the swede on this one? Well, the DAC isn't going to like that.'

'No, I don't think he is. He's already had a word about how he doesn't like the way Ernie's been playing it.'

'Really?'

Mooney's little eyes lit up.

'Yeah, he's said as much, that they have been thinking of bringing someone else in.'

'I see.' He nodded thoughtfully. 'Well, Franklin isn't on the square. But the DAC is.'

I checked up on Walter Peters. Fat Wally. He ran the Stardust Erotic Revue in Soho, one of the more up-market strip clubs, very popular with Japanese tourists. The club was entirely legitimate – its performances carefully avoided showing anything that went beyond what was permissible under the obscenity laws. There was nothing that could directly link Peters with the bookshop trade, but it was rumoured that he controlled a number of premises through various frontmen. In the meantime Fat Wally had cultivated his image as a successful businessman. He had bought a seventeenth-century mansion in Surrey and had a swimming pool built in the grounds. There were stories of lavish parties where Peters entertained local dignitaries who'd often, quite unknowingly, find themselves rubbing shoulders with some of London's most dangerous criminals with whom Fat Wally was also keen to ingratiate himself. He had even joined the local Round Table and had appeared as Santa Claus in their Christmas charity drive.

He was an ideal subject for an exposé. 'The Blue Film Boss', his corpulent form revealed by one of Alf Isaacs' snatch shots. We'd get a picture of his mansion too, maybe an aerial photograph showing the swimming pool so that the punters could see where all the dirty money had been going. Some examples of the filth he was peddling as well. It would be a big spread, a main feature on the centre pages perhaps.

There wasn't much else coming through the crime desk that week. Kevin, my junior reporter, had a story for me. A prostitute had been found strangled in her flat.

'I thought this one might stand up,' he said. 'You know, the sex angle.'

I took the copy off him. I had tried to forget about what I had done, repress it, but here it was in black and white. The memory of it was like a dream, or rather, a horrible nightmare. Print made it real. A story. But it was like someone else's story, someone else who did these terrible things, someone who lived inside of me. Banner headlines throbbed in my head: SEX MURDERER, EVIL BEAST. I felt like screaming. I felt like laughing out loud.

'Tony?'

I was in a trance.

'Yeah?'

'What do you think?'

I had to snap out of it. I felt a drop of sweat go cold on my neck. I musn't panic, I thought, musn't lose control.

'Yeah, sure,' I said, handing the story back to him. 'And see if you can get a picture.'

He turned and started to walk off. It was all right. Everything was all right.

'Oh, and Kevin,' I called after him. 'I need you to check up on Fat Wally.'

'Who?'

I showed him the stuff we had so far.

'Dig the dirt. Check to see if he's got any criminal convictions. Dodgy associates. Stuff like that.'

I then went to meet with Alan Khalid and we went through the set-up.

Alan had contacted Ian Hesper and ordered 4,000 hard-core Scandinavian films for which he was willing to pay £20,000. Hesper was to deliver the merchandise in batches of 500, handed over at a motorway service station on the M4 in return for cash payments of £2,500. Khalid was to inspect a sample of each consignment before delivery. So a meeting was set up at the Mayfair flat. Hesper was to bring one of the films and, more importantly, Walter Peters, who was to confirm the contract in person.

Alan and Magda were in the flat with the projector and screen set up. Khalid was wired up with a microphone so that the conversation could be recorded. The sound man, Alf Isaacs and myself were hidden in the bedroom. At the right moment Alf would go in and get a snatch of Fat Wally. We were hoping that we could get a picture of him while the film was rolling. It would be a good picture, the porn king with blurred images of nakedness and obscenity in the background.

The whole piece was falling into place. It could kick off a campaign that could last for weeks. I'd even got Kenny Forbes, who did the 'A Doctor Writes' column, to do a little piece on the psychological effects of pornography.

The doorbell rang. I closed the bedroom door.

'Are you picking it up?' I asked the sound recordist.

He looked up and nodded. Suddenly there was commotion in the next room, voices raised. The sound man jumped a little and slipped his headphones from his ears. I looked at Alf.

'Come on,' I said, and we went through.

Four men had come into the flat. There was Hesper with a heavy-looking minder standing next to him in the classic hands clasped in front of the bollocks pose. There was a photographer taking pictures, and a little fellow in horn-rimmed spectacles who was loudly introducing himself as 'a solicitor, acting on behalf of Mr Hesper'.

The photographer was taking pictures of all of us in turn. This really threw Alf Isaacs. He was holding his own camera up in front of his face, trying to hide behind it, going 'Oi, cut that out, will you?', his huge frame all hunched up as if in pain. The little solicitor continued his prepared speech.

'My client has good reason to believe that he is being blackmailed by persons in the employ of the *Sunday Illustrated* who have attempted to unlawfully entrap him for the purposes of discrediting his good name with scurrilous allegations that he is dealing in illegally obscene material. We will be issuing a writ to this effect, gentlemen, and we have approached the *News of the World* with our own story on this unwarranted harassment.'

And with that the group of them turned on their heels and walked out. We were stunned, of course. How had we been rumbled? I spent the rest of the evening going through every move that Alan Khalid had made, but we still couldn't work it out.

Sid Franks was furious when I reported back to him the next day.

I spent the whole morning in the 'bollocking room'. Pausing only to take the occasional gulp from the cloudy glass of bicarb on his desk, he berated me.

'You know how much this fucking farce has cost us? What the fuck has this cunt Khalid been up to? He must have fucked up really badly for them to find out what we were doing. How did they know?'

'That's what I've been trying to work out, Sid.'

'Well, it doesn't look like you've been very discreet, does it? What about the Arab? Could it have been him that blew the gaff?'

'I don't know, Sid.'

Could it have been Alan? He'd certainly been extravagant in the way he'd conducted himself. Maybe he had been paid off by Hesper and Peters.

'I'm still going through the expenses that cunt has been claiming. It's outrageous.'

'I'm sorry, Sid. I really don't know what went wrong.'

'Well, that's all very well. I've got to go to the Big Table and explain all of this. Heads are going to fucking roll, that's for sure.'

'So,' I ventured cautiously, 'what do you want me to do with the piece?'

'Do with it? You can shove it up your arse. The whole thing's spiked. It's going to be a complete embarrassment.'

He took a swig of bicarbonate and spluttered.

'And you! You can forget about investigative journalism for a bit, old son. You can make yourself useful with something a little bit more within your capabilities. Madame Kismet's in St Thomas's having her varicose veins done. You can do the fucking horoscope this week. And believe me, whatever your star sign is it ain't looking rosy.'

He shouldn't have gone into Joe's wagon. He should have waited for Joe to get back from his morning stroll. It was a bright frosty morning. Crystals of ice clustered on dry stalks of cow parsley. Jewelled spider's webs were strung amidst the undergrowth like little chandeliers. Joe had borrowed a can of three-in-one oil the day before and Mick needed it. He was packing away his tools and he wanted to make sure that they didn't get rusty in storage.

He wandered into the caravan, careful not to disturb anything. The oilcan was on the side table next to something wrapped in cloth. Something Joe had been oiling. It was when he reached over to the oilcan that he noticed the crumpled slip of newspaper on Joe's unmade bed. He knew that he should just take the can and go but he found himself picking up the paper. He had a premonition of something bad in the smudged letters before he read them. He wished he could just leave it all be. *This will spoil everything*, he found himself thinking, and yet he went on with it despite his better judgment.

FIVE YEARS ON AND COP KILLER STILL AT LARGE, read the headline. There was a police file photograph with the caption: *Billy Porter, the ruthless murderer of three unarmed policemen.* It was Joe. Take away the beard and the straggly hair and it was Joe all right. Or rather, it was not Joe. It never had been.

Mick reached for the wrapped-up object with even greater dread. He unwound the cloth, felt the curved butt of the German automatic in his palm. Freshly lubricated. It was a Luger, he knew that much.

Then everything happened very quickly. Joe was at the door, looking in.

'What you doing in here?' he demanded.

Mick turned, the gun in his hand.

'Give me that,' Joe insisted.

Mick felt horribly betrayed. He hadn't wanted to know. He had thought that they could just get on with it all with no thoughts of the past. He had wanted company, someone to work with. Someone who would really care about the work. Someone to share the tradition of it. Nothing else mattered. He had been prepared to turn a blind eye to all of it. But now Joe had spoiled everything. He had let Mick find out about what he had done. He had implicated him. He'd even kept the gun, for Christ's sake.

'I just came for the oil,' said Mick.

He wanted Joe to know that he hadn't been snooping about. That he was innocent of that. *If only you had covered your tracks better none of this would've happened.* All of his life he had wanted to get away from the evils of the mundane world. That was why he'd travelled. Lived on the outside of things. The childlike pleasure of decorating the machines of joy. Amusement Arcadia. It was kitsch, and cheap, but for him there had been no greater calling in life. He'd sought refuge in innocent pleasure. And yet here and now the badness had entered into it like a serpent in the garden, a mechanism of death held in a trembling hand.

'Give me the gun, Mick,' Joe said flatly, moving towards him.

'You,' Mick spluttered. 'You.'

Joe made a grab for the pistol. There was a struggle, an awful little dance as they both held on to the deadly little thing between them. They wrestled into a kind of embrace, staring at each other. Eyes wide, teeth clenched.

Then the gun went off with a muffled retort. The clinch broke and one of them fell to the floor. It all happened so quickly. A body slumped on the floor of the trailer. A rasping sound in the back of the throat and then stillness. The oilcan had been knocked over in the fracas and as blood seeped out over the floor of the caravan strange rainbow patterns diffused on its surface.

He had killed him. His mind reeled. For a second he forgot who he was. He had to think quickly. Get his story straight and decide what was to be done. It was a stupid bloody accident; it could have been either of them that stopped the bullet. But he had killed him. He threw the gun down and rubbed at his face, trying to make sense of it all. He had killed Joe. Yes, that was it. Joe was dead. And Mick would have to move on. He would have to get away from all of this and find a new life.

He dragged the body out to the field behind the hangar. He got a shovel and buried the corpse deep. He knew what he would do now. He would destroy every trace there was of Joe. No one would miss him, after all. He was an outsider. No one in the circle knew him. He was only familiar through being with Mick. So Mick would have to be careful. Suspicion would fall upon him. It would be best if he distanced himself from the fairground circuit. He had the truck and the other wagon. He would do a repaint job on his vehicles and move away from the work he was known for. The fairground jobs were in decline, after all. Mick had been fooling himself that there was any real future in it.

He gathered together all of Joe's things and put them in the wagon. He emptied a jerrycan of petrol all over the caravan. It washed away some of the brown stain of clotted blood on the floor. He lit a match and watched it blaze for a while like a beacon in the night. Then he drove off with the other wagon hitched to the truck into the darkness. He'd gone nearly fifty miles when he realised he'd made one simple little mistake. He'd left the gun behind.

23

Ernie was in an agitated state when he called me into his office.

'Something's turned up. After all this fucking time,' he told me, almost out of breath.

'What is it, guvnor?' I asked, trying to read the look on his face, wondering if he'd twigged what I was up to. 'Something about the inquiry?'

'No, Frank. This is something else.'

He sat down and caught his breath.

'A couple of days ago in this field in Lincolnshire there's this caravan fire by a disused aircraft hangar. A couple of local bobbies check it out and they find this.'

He picked up a plastic bag on his desk. There was a charred and rusted metal object in it. It was a pistol. A Luger.

'You know what this could mean, don't you?'

Of course I did. Billy Porter. One of the murder weapons, maybe. After all this time: a lead.

'So, what do we do about it?' I asked Ernie.

'Well. Forensics have got to check this with the bullets and the cartridge cases found at the crime scene. But I reckon we should make a little trip to the place they found it.'

'But what about the inquiry, guv?'

'Sod that. This takes precedence. Come on. I'll sort a driver out.'

So we motored up to Lincolnshire. It was a relief to be getting out of London for a bit. Away from the Met and all the badness. I'm not a big fan of the countryside but it felt good to be getting a bit of fresh air. And it felt right to be engaged in proper police work instead of rubber-heeling. There was a buzz inside as we speeded out of London: we were going after Porter again. I felt bad about stitching Ernie up on the inquiry. As we hit the open road I had such a real sense of escape from it all I even toyed with the idea of coming clean. But that wouldn't be a good idea, I reasoned. Not yet. We reached the place that had been marked out on the map. A couple of patrol officers met up with us and took us to the scene.

There wasn't much left of the caravan. A charred shape in the field. A shadow left behind. Me and Ernie circled it a couple of times but there was nothing to see except the burned out shell of the trailer. There was a disused aircraft hangar about fifty yards from it. Ernie nodded towards it.

'Let's have a look in there,' he said.

One of the local officers slid the heavy door open and we went inside. A bird fluttered up towards the light from a hole in the ceiling. The building was empty. There were shapes and coloured patterns stencilled on the cement floor. Splattered paint abruptly framed by blocks of dull concrete. Outlines of large objects that had been laid out on the floor.

'This place was used by a fairground painter,' one of the officers explained.

'What?' Ernie asked.

'You know. Fairground rides. They painted them here.'

'And do we know who this artist is?'

'Well, the farmer who owns the land says it's a bloke called Mick.'

'And where is this Mick now?'

'He doesn't know. Said that he had an arrangement with him every winter. Nothing in writing. He reckons he'll be travelling around on the fairground circuit.'

'Right,' said Ernie. 'Well, that's where we need to look, isn't it?'

As we were walking out of the hangar I noticed something caught beneath the sliding door. It was a crumpled-up piece of paper. I unfolded it carefully. It was a drawing. Coloured pencils described intricate patterns and scrollwork.

'Let's have a word with this farmer, then,' Ernie told one of the local officers.

We got a description of this Mick bloke. It didn't match up to Porter at all.

'Was anyone else with him?' I asked.

'I don't think so,' the farmer replied. 'I didn't see him leave. He did a runner. He left a right bloody mess behind with that trailer. That was a bit bloody strange, wasn't it? Burning that caravan. And he didn't pay me. He was usually so reliable. That's the last bloody time I'm renting out to him.'

'Well, let us know if he's in contact again,' said Ernie, writing down his number at the Yard.

And with that we drove back to London.

'What do you reckon, guvnor?' I asked.

'Well, we've got to wait for the forensics report. If that comes up positive then we're on to something.'

Ernie looked enthusiastic for the first time in weeks.

'We need to check on the fairground world. It ain't going to be straightforward tracking this Mick down. That lot are always on the move.'

It was dark when we got back to the city. A yellow sickly glow above it from the streetlights. Ernie sighed heavily.

'Well,' he said, 'we've still got this bloody inquiry on our hands.'

I nodded grimly but thought: if the lab turns up something definite this could be our way out of it for good.

TAURUS: With Jupiter in conjunction with your ruling planet Mars there are opportunities in the workplace and possibilities of travel . . . Doing the astrological column was a horribly tedious punishment. And the thought that thousands of our halfwitted readership would imagine it to be arcane wisdom wasn't any consolation. I was keeping my head down. 'I want that column done properly, Meehan!' Sid Franks had insisted. I was hoping that when he had calmed down a bit I could approach him with the Lord Longford visiting Myra Hindley story and maybe get back in his good books. But for the time being I was *persona non grata* in the *Illustrated* office.

The threatened writ from Ian Hesper never materialised and I had it on fairly good authority from an acquaintance on the *News of the World* that they weren't planning to run a story about our débâcle. I'd quizzed Alan Khalid thoroughly about what could have gone wrong, but he assured me that he had no idea how we had been exposed. He was quite irate that the *Illustrated* weren't honouring all of his expenses.

I looked up to see Kevin hovering over me.

'What do you want?' I demanded tetchily.

'I found some stuff on Walter Peters,' he replied.

'Well, it's a bit fucking late for that now, isn't it?'

'Well, excuse me for breathing,' he mumbled, and started to walk away.

I was venting my spleen on him simply because he was a junior. All the other staff men had been avoiding me like the plague. I couldn't afford to alienate everybody on the paper the way things were.

'Kevin,' I called after him, as gently as I could muster. 'I'm sorry. I'm just not in the best of moods. What did you find?'

'Well,' he said, turning back, 'criminal convictions: bound over to keep the peace for house-breaking at fifteen. He went to Banstead Approved School a year later for taking away a car without the owner's consent. Then borstal for theft. And then a year in Brixton for receiving a lorry-load of stolen sweets. That was all in the fifties. He's been clean since then but he has been involved in running strip clubs and pornographic bookshops for the last ten years or so. And there are rumoured connections with some major villains. He was running a blue-films racket with one of the Richardson gang, George Cornell – you know, the one that Ronnie Kray shot. And of course there's the Harry Starks connection.'

'Harry Starks?'

'Yeah,' Kevin retorted, as if this was common knowledge. 'Well, you know, the Stardust. That was Starks' club. Wally Peters took it over when Starks was put away.'

'Right,' I said. 'Well, thanks, Kevin. Sorry about losing my rag.'

'Oh,' he added, 'and I got that photo.'

'What photo?'

'The murdered prostitute.'

He handed me a smudge of this tart. A police file photograph, no doubt. A heavily made-up face looking resentfully out at eternity, an accusing stare, so much paint and powder. I should have felt guilt, remorse, but I didn't. I didn't really feel anything at all except a brief shiver of panic when I put the photo down and saw my thumbprint on it. As if that could somehow implicate me. What forensic evidence had I left behind? I really had to be careful.

'Yeah.' I nodded at Kevin. 'That ought to do it. But I'm not exactly running the crime desk this week. You'll have to take it to Sid.'

'Right.'

'Do you read your horoscope, Kevin?' I asked him.

'Nah,' he replied. 'Can't be bothered.'

'Oh well,' I said, looking back at my unfinished column. 'Thanks anyway.'

Pisces, I thought, flicking through a little guide to the zodiac. What does Pisces mean? Harry Starks, I thought. Fat Wally and Mad Harry. What were their star signs, their planetary conjunctions? Starks. Something clicked – THE PEER AND THE GANGSTER *Private Eye* allegations. Lord Thursby linked with Mr Starks, disproved in a court of law. A heavy libel settlement, but the gossip was that Teddy had only just got away with it. Teddy, Harry, Wally. Their orbits aligned. My mind spun for a second with cosmic influences. For a moment I could almost believe in this astrological nonsense. Then my thoughts came back down to earth with a bump. Harry, Teddy, Wally. Wally, Harry, Teddy. No, Teddy in the middle. Teddy, Wally. Wally, Teddy. I'd told Thursby about the investigation at that meeting in the French House.

I got up from my desk and took the jacket off the back of my chair. Sid Franks was walking down past all the newsroom desks.

'Where the fuck do you think you're going, Meehan?' he demanded.

'I've got a story,' I said, pushing past him.

'Now wait a fucking minute!' he called after me.

24

I was doing a bit of homework on fairs and fairground operators when Ernie came in with the ballistics report. He didn't look well pleased.

'Well?' I asked him.

'Well nothing, Frank. The tests on the gun were inconclusive.'

'What do they bloody mean, "inconclusive"?'

'The gun was too badly rusted and damaged by the fire for them to be able to be definite, one way or another. It's the same calibre as the cartridges recovered from the van and from Scrubs Lane but that doesn't exactly narrow things down.'

'So what do we do now?'

'Well, it might have escaped your notice but we do have another job on. It took some explaining to Harrington us just disappearing like that.'

'How did the swede take it?'

'Well, he did have the hump a bit. But I think I've established a good working relationship with him. And he's in a good mood. There's been some movement on our resident informer Tommy Hills.'

'Our little supergrass.'

'Yes indeed. It seems that Harrington has the authority to offer the full immunity he wants. If he can come up with the goods, that is. This could be the breakthrough in the inquiry.'

'Assuming Mr Hills isn't just telling a lot of porkies.'

'Well, obviously his testimony will have to be verified. But we can start the ball rolling. I want you to go over to Wandsworth and get a preliminary statement from him.'

'Don't you want to come, guvnor?'

'No, I can't. I've got the DAC coming to see me this afternoon.'

I knew what this might mean and I felt pretty bad about it. But then, I reasoned, if Ernie was taken off the inquiry he could get to work on the Porter investigation. And I could request a transfer to work alongside him. Everything could turn out for the best after all. It was a bastard that the gun test had turned up inconclusive but if Ernie was keen on following it up anyway and maybe getting the case reopened properly then everyone would be happy. The Skeleton Inquiry would all be nicely sewn up and we could get back to some proper detective work.

I got a driver and went down to Wandsworth. Tommy boy didn't look half as clever as he did on his last appointment at the Hate Factory. He was as white as a sheet. I chucked him a packet of Dunhill fags and he tore at the cellophane clumsily. His hand was shaking as he lit a cigarette.

'So, Tommy,' I said. 'Looks like you're going to get what you want.'

'What?' he muttered, drawing heavily on his fag.

'Your immunity from prosecution, of course.'

'Well, I'm not sure about all of this.'

'What?'

'I want to withdraw my allegations.'

'You what?'

'You heard.'

'I don't believe this. Just the other day you were ready to tell us a nice long story. What's the matter?'

'Well . . .' He sighed out a long stream of smoke. 'Things have changed, haven't they.'

'What's that supposed to mean? You got cold feet or something?'

'Yeah. Something like that.'

'Has someone in here got at you?'

Tommy Hills laughed and shook his head.

'What's so bloody funny?'

'Look, I ain't saying nothing. OK?'

'Are you not happy with the protection you've been offered in here?'

Hills laughed again.

'I ain't worried about anyone in here,' he said. 'It's out there I've got to watch it. From your lot.'

A look of fear on his face. I knew what it meant. Mooney had got to him.

'That's a serious allegation, Hills. Would you be prepared to make a statement to that effect?'

'Look, I don't want my card marked. It's more than I'm worth. Too much fucking grief.'

'You sure?'

'Fucking right I'm sure. I want to go back to my cell.'

So that was that. I got back to Coco sooner than I expected. I went to Ernie's office to give him the bad news. Outside the door I heard raised voices. The Deputy Assistant Commissioner.

'It's a matter of loyalty, Franklin.'

'Loyalty? Loyalty to who exactly, sir?'

'To your superior officers.'

'Well, maybe there's a higher loyalty than that, sir.'

'Don't get clever with me, Franklin. You think you're involved in some sort of moral crusade? You're just bloody incompetent. Going to Harrington to clear some sort of deal with a supposed witness? You should have cleared things like that through your line of command. You should have been briefing me instead of passing everything on to the swede.'

'I'm sorry, sir.'

'Sorry? I should fucking think so too. Do you realise how much damage you've done? Harrington is on the inquiry in an advisory capacity. The responsibility for the investigation rests with the Met.'

'I'm sorry, sir, I just did what I thought was best.'

'Well, you've been playing for the wrong side for too long, Ernie. We're taking you off the inquiry.'

'Sir,' Ernie croaked, barely audible, broken.

'And what's this I hear about you interrupting your work here to go on some wild-goose chase in the countryside?'

'That was pertaining to the Porter case, sir. I'm still nominally in charge of it.'

'But I've heard that this gun they found doesn't even match with the cartridge cases found at the murder scene.'

'The tests were inconclusive, sir.'

'And on the basis of that you go off, taking another officer with you, leaving a major investigation in the lurch? Without consulting me?'

'I'm sorry, sir.'

'Look, to be honest, we haven't been exactly confident of your operational abilities of late. Your personal problems are interfering with your judgment, if you ask me. Ernie, you're just not fit psychologically. I suggest you take some time off. You know, sick leave.'

Julian came to the door when I went around to Teddy's flat in Eaton Square.

'Tony,' he announced with forced bonhomie. 'To what do we owe the pleasure?'

'I want to see Thursby.'

'You'd better come in, then.'

Thursby was reclining on a sofa in the drawing room. He was wearing some sort of kaftan. There were piles of papers all over the room.

'Ah, Tony,' he said as I walked in.

'Teddy and I were just going through Tangiers,' Julian explained.

'Marvellous place. Just after the war. All sorts of types. The International Zone and all that.'

'Shall I get us all a drink?' Julian asked.

'Isn't it a little early?' muttered Thursby. 'What the hell.' He shuffled through some papers on his lap. 'Jules, remind me to find those letters from Brian Howard. They're here somewhere.'

'Gin and tonic all right?' Julian asked me.

'Sure,' I replied.

'So, dear boy. How's Grub Street?'

'Not so good, actually.'

'Oh, I am sorry to hear that. What's wrong?'

'Well, Teddy, I was going to ask you about that.'

Julian came through with the drinks, frowning at me.

'What on earth's the matter, Tony?' he asked, handing me a glass.

'I think you both know what the fucking matter is,' I said tersely.

'Now, dear boy, let's not be tiresome. I'm sorry that I had to spoil your little investigation. I'm sure you had the noblest intentions in your moral crusade.'

He grinned. His liverish mouth parted to reveal discoloured incisors.

'I just couldn't afford for things to get too close to home,' he went on. 'I am sorry if I've got you into trouble. I did give you that tidbit about Frank Longford. I'm sure that I could come up with some other gossip for you if you want.'

'I'm sure what you could tell me about yourself would be far more interesting.'

Thursby sighed.

'But then it wouldn't be gossip, would it?' he said. 'Gossip is about other people, not oneself.'

'I could do an exposé on you, you know.'

He chuckled softly.

'Oh, I don't think so. The boys from Greek Street tried that and it cost them. No, you'll not get me. I've got some very high-placed friends, most of them with something to hide. I know enough about Reggie Maudling to bring the house down. Then there's Lord Goodman. And MI5. No, you wouldn't stand a fucking chance. I shouldn't think that Sid Franks would be too keen to run a story on me. You see I've always maintained a good relationship with the yellow press. It's been very useful. Your little campaign has already cost them enough now, hasn't it? And that Arab boy you used. I mean, oh dear, we've got plenty on him.'

'You're a fucking fraud, Thursby.'

Thursby sighed again.

'What is real and what is phoney? Hm? We've all got something to hide. Julian tells me that you're not all you appear to be.'

I shot a glance at Jules. He shrugged vaguely.

'We really should keep up appearances, you know. Surely you understand that. There's been far too much criticism of the institutions of state. Stupid inquiries into the police force drummed up by subversive troublemakers. Trots running the unions and trying to bring the country to its knees. Now more than ever we need to maintain public morale.'

He stared into his glass.

'Get us another drink, Jules. Tony?'

'No,' I said. 'I'm fine, thanks.'

Julian went out to the kitchen.

'You realise how much that queen is costing me. He's a bloody parasite. Maybe I should employ you to help with the memoirs. I'm sure you're not as extravagant. And more, shall we say, discreet.'

Julian came back and handed Teddy a refilled glass.

'Oh well,' he said, lifting it. 'Cheers.'

So that was that. There wasn't anything that I could do. Not yet, at least.

25

I went for a drink with Ernie at the Tank after that dressing-down he'd got from the DAC. I felt guilty about the way things had turned out. He'd only done what he'd thought was best and he'd been treated like shit. Squeezed between the Yard brass who wanted the whole thing smoothed over and the firm of bent coppers who wanted to cover their tracks. He'd been far too innocent, of course. If he'd known beforehand some of the things that had been going on he might have been forewarned. He would have been able to conduct the inquiry with more caution. As it was the whole thing ruined him. And it was my fault as much as anyone's.

'What are you going to do, guvnor?' I asked him.

I was hoping that he'd try to get back to following up these leads on the Porter case. They were pretty tenuous but it was something to be going on with. We could work on it together. I could get away from all the shit I'd found myself up to the neck in. Maybe it would help Ernie get back to form too.

'I tell you what I'm going to do, Frank. I'm taking early retirement. I've already talked about it with my doctor. I'll get a full pension and everything. Fuck them.'

'You sure?'

I wasn't expecting this. My heart sank.

'Yeah. Twenty-three fucking years' service. For what? Well, I'm better off out of it if this is the way the force is going.'

I wanted to say something. Something about how at least he'd tried to do the right thing. But it would be hypocritical coming from me.

'What about the Porter thing?'

'Oh, Frank,' he sighed. 'I'm tired. I'm tired of it all.'

'But you can't give up on that.'

'Can't I?'

He caught my eye. I was staring at him fiercely.

'Look, Frank, I know you lost a friend. We all lost something from that. But maybe we ain't going to catch the bastard. Even if the gun was the same one, that bloke's description doesn't fit. Five years on and nothing. Maybe Porter's dead. Maybe he topped himself or something. Look, we'll pass it all on to whoever gets assigned the Porter case. I'm out of it.'

There wasn't much else to say. But I didn't want to leave Ernie on his own. So we sat there drinking until the place closed.

Ernie's replacement on the inquiry was, of course, Detective Superintendent George Mooney. Seconded from the Obscene Publications Squad, he'd obviously managed to manoeuvre himself into the job. There was a horribly perverted sense of logic to it all. The Yard brass were happy and the firm within the firm was safe. I didn't particularly relish the prospect of working so closely with Mooney but I had to live with that.

And he played it all very cutely, you had to give him that. Instead of trying to stall the inquiry as you might expect he appeared to be full of zeal and enthusiasm. But the apparent energy he was putting into the investigation generated more heat than light. The swiftness with which he brought forward charges relating to the initial allegations against the two officers involved in Operation Skeleton ensured that there would be no time for suspicions of wider corruption to be properly unearthed. This, in turn, undermined Harrington, whose more careful and methodical approach was made to seem almost incompetent. The swede became increasingly marginalised and Mooney did little to disguise his contempt for the provincial officer. I'll never forget one evening when he and Harrington were walking out to the carpark together. Mooney drove a brand-new Jensen Interceptor, a really flash motor. Harrington had an Austin 1800. Mooney sniffed at the swede's car as he passed it, turned to him and said with a sneer:

'Is that the best you can do?'

Detective Sergeant John O'Neill and Detective Constable Ian Campbell were both charged with perverting the course of justice. Other Operation Skeleton officers faced disciplinaries. Convenient scapegoats had been found and the whole thing seemed nicely sewn up. Or so we thought.

Which is more than can be said for the Porter case. Eventually a senior detective was assigned to it but there seemed to be a general reluctance for anyone to take it up. It had bad luck written all over it. It represented failure. There had been so many false leads and wrong sightings over the years that nobody wanted to act upon anything unless it was definite. Another cock-up would just mean more bad press for the Met on a case that they'd failed to clear up. I knew some officers that were superstitious about even mentioning it, like it was tempting fate or something. For me it was more of a personal curse, like part of me was damned by it. I passed on what me and Ernie had on the gun and the caravan. I hadn't had time to follow any of it up so it didn't amount to much. I kept the drawing I'd found on the hangar floor. I don't know why.

All that was left to do on the Skeleton inquiry was to see through the committal proceedings on O'Neill and Campbell. Mooney had yet again taken the initiative on this. Harrington was hamstrung. His recommendations for reforming the Met were politely acknowledged and completely ignored. Soon he'd be packed up and gone. Few people at the Yard would be sad to see the back of him.

Then one afternoon Mooney came into my office. He looked ashen.

'Frank,' he said, 'I need a word.'

'What is it?'

'Not here,' he muttered, his little eyes darting to and fro. 'Meet me after work. At the Premier.'

'I can't.'

'Why not?'

'I'm baby-sitting tonight.'

Mooney laughed out loud at that.

'Oh, sweet fucking Jesus,' he declared.

But it was true. I'd promised I'd look after David that evening. Jeannie wanted to visit a friend in hospital.

'I'm sorry but that's it.'

'Well, this is important, Taylor,' he hissed. 'A fucking wheel's coming off if we're not careful. The whole lot of us could be going down. Yourself included. If we don't do something sharpish there could be two new lodges on the Isle of Wight.'

He was making reference to the two high-security prisons there: Albany and Parkhurst. I didn't know what he could mean specifically but it sounded bloody serious.

'Look, I've said enough here,' he went on. 'We need to meet somewhere private. Can't you get out of your parental duties?'

I sighed. I didn't want to let Jeannie down.

'It ain't going to be easy,' I said.

Mooney grinned.

'Then why don't I come around to your gaff?' he suggested softly. 'That'll be nice and cosy.'

I really didn't want that bastard in my house but I didn't really have any choice in the matter. David was a bit overexcited that night and it was hard to get him settled and ready for bed. We were watching *The Virginian* together when the doorbell rang. I let Mooney in. He was carrying a holdall.

I fixed him a drink as he sat down in an armchair and beamed at David.

'Here's the little soldier,' he said.

David went all shy. Then he pointed at a Stetsoned figure on the screen.

'Cowboy,' he said.

'Yes,' said Mooney. 'That's right, son. Cowboy.'

I handed him a glass and sat down on the settee.

'So what's all this about, George?'

'It's O'Neill. The cunt.' He coughed, looking sidelong at David. 'Sorry. I mean, he says he won't just duck his nut for the Skeleton thing. Says he isn't going to go away when everyone else is off the hook. He's threatening to name names.'

'Shit. I mean . . .'

David laughed.

'Rude word, Daddy!'

'Yeah, sorry about that,' I said.

'He's agreed to do a runner.'

'Right.'

'But he wants paying off, of course.'

Mooney held up the bag.

'Five grand. He's going to skip the country in the next couple of days.'

'Well, that's sorted, then.'

'Thing is, Taylor, we need someone to carry the bag. He doesn't trust me. Can't think why.'

'Oh, Christ.'

'I'm afraid so. You're going to have to be the goby on this one.'

He handed me a scrap of paper with the time and address of a meet. I heard a key turn in the front door. *Shit,* I thought.

'Mummy!' David called out, and went to meet her in the hall.

'Ah,' Mooney announced jovially, 'the dear lady wife.'

He patted the holdall and muttered:

'There's a little bit extra in here. Your commission.'

Jeannie came through into the lounge with David in her arms. Mooney stood up as she entered. I cleared my throat, nervously. She froze as she saw him. David wriggled free from her and went to sit on the settee.

'Jeannie,' I said, 'this is George. We're working together.'

Mooney's peephole eyes narrowed in on her. She was spooked.

'Oh,' he said softly. 'We've met before, haven't we?'

The past flooded back into her face. Fear in her eyes.

'I'll see myself out,' said Mooney.

And he was gone.

'What the fuck was he doing in our house?'

'Jeannie . . .'

'He's the one that Attilio was paying off. He's the one that . . .'

She flinched from saying any more. Her face creased up at the hateful knowledge of it. Then she caught sight of the bag.

'And what's this?' she demanded, bending down to grab at it.

I made a move for it myself. She pulled at the zip. I'd got hold of one of the handles. Bundles of cash tumbled out on to the carpet.

'You bastard,' she spat at me. 'You lied to me.'

'Jeannie, look . . .'

She picked up a wad of cash and threw it at me.

'Bringing bad money into the house. All this time. Saying that you'd gone straight. You bloody liar.'

'Yeah, well, look around, Jeannie. We've done all right out of all of this. You should remember that.'

'Don't try and justify it like that. Like you were doing it for us. Don't you dare.'

'But it's true. I've provided for you. And more. I've made sure that David has never wanted for anything. Even though . . .'

Jeannie's flintlike eyes went wide at this.

'Yeah?' she taunted. 'Go on.'

I felt a horrible sinking feeling in my stomach.

'Please, Jeannie,' I begged. 'Don't.'

'Don't what? Don't say it, even though we both know it's true?'

'Please.'

'Well, I'll say it, then. He's not yours. And you know what? I'm glad he's not yours. I wouldn't want to raise a kid that might turn out like you.'

There was an awful silence. We just looked at each other. I didn't know what to say. There wasn't anything to be said. David was watching us intently. You'd think with the row going on he'd react in some way. But he just looked on like it was a scene on the telly.

'Right,' I declared finally, and started to pick up the cash and put it back in the bag. I walked out of the lounge. I had a meeting to keep.

Behold, thou hast driven me out this day from the face of the Earth; and from thy face shall I be hid; and I shall be a fugitive and a vagabond in the Earth.

Lines of flight. Juggernauts that thundered along the motorways. The A roads and the B roads. The circle. Turning and returning. He felt he was forever falling. In an orbit of perpetual descent. Never coming to rest. Always moving on.

He had all the money they'd made during the winter and that kept him going for a while. He made sure he avoided the fairground circuit. If the gun was found people would be asking questions among the showmen, so it was best he kept well out of the way of that world. He would miss it, but then he'd never really been part of it. Never really in the Circle.

And it was easy enough to do in practice. It was then that he realised that traditional travellers don't really move. They cling to a fixed pattern. And merely oscillate within it. He could always make sure that he wouldn't run into any of that crowd since their sense of time and place was so fixed and predictable. Dates and locations of every build-up or pull-away predestined and constant. The litany of sites, King's Lynn Mart, St Giles, the Goose Fair, immovable feasts, townships that were forever being built and taken apart, that would always exist at a particular time and place.

In his mind it was harder. He went through a vertiginous delirium. Delineation. He lost track. Once, on Scotch Corner, where the A1 meets the A66, he had to pull up on a lay-by. He didn't know which way he was supposed to be going. He had no memory of how and why he had got there and which road he was supposed to take. He wasn't even quite sure who he was. Was he Mick? Maybe, for safety's sake, he should call himself something else. Become someone else. Was he someone else? It took him a while to clear the confusion in his head. *Maybe we're always on the verge of becoming someone else*, he reasoned against the awful madness of it. Sometimes he imagined that he was already dead. Riding the Ghost Train. It was then that he had to remind himself that it was Mick that had killed Joe. He had to remember that, though the terrible truth of it all would remain hidden.

And he wandered with scarcely any purpose other than being on the run. Without the nomad's sense of territory he drifted. He didn't really belong anywhere. But then he was not a traveller. He was a fugitive. As time passed he felt ludicrously charmed that he had not been caught. But maybe this was his curse.

Whosoever slayeth Cain, vengeance shall be taken on him sevenfold.

The loneliness seemed unbearable. And yet he bore it. He often thought of the other man, of their quiet comradeship. The awful guilt of what he had done. *My punishment is greater than I can bear*. But it had been Joe's fault. He had been so careless. And now Joe no longer existed.

Circumstance. Fate billets you where it wants and demobs you without warning. Orders you around the exercise yard of life. The sky wheeled above his head. The great emptiness of the firmament. The dim cinders of night like waning fireworks, burning out and falling to the ground. A road map of stars, junctions and conurbations. Mighty lonesome. Like an old and echoing country-and-western song. *Yippy-ay-oh, yippy-ay-ay. Ghost Riders in the sky.*

He found bits of painting work here and there. And the truck was good for picking up scrap metal. And he came across the new travellers. They were young and strange. Long-haired with brightly coloured vehicles. He was suspicious of them at first but they were friendly towards him. They thought he was authentic. Gypsy blood and all that. Silly fuckers. They were mostly middle-class drop-outs that hardly knew any better. Most real travellers held them in contempt. But he started to hang around with them. They were good cover and they treated him with respect. They didn't ask too many questions.

1985

Embrace the Base

26

There was trouble every Saturday night on the Hardcastle estate. It would always start in the local pub, the Queen's Head, just before closing time. Fights would break out. The landlord would call the police. Before they could respond, the pub and the flat above it would be set on fire. The affray would then spread to the estate. Six hundred people would gather and build barricades across its main entrances. Armoured vehicles would be sent in to break them down and units of police in riot gear would follow to try to take back the territory.

Sometimes the police would gain control of the situation by midnight. At other times resources would be misallocated or over-stretched and they would be beaten back by the mob. On a good night they would be able to clear the area well enough for fire crews to ensure that there was no significant damage to the estate. On a bad night the whole place would be burning and the police would come under such a concentrated hail of missiles and petrol bombs that they would be lucky to come out of it in one piece.

Every Saturday night it was the same. The Hardcastle estate seemed to have no other purpose than to stage endlessly repeated dramas of public disorder. It was what it was designed for. Its labyrinth of forecourts, low-rise walkways and access balconies, blind alleys of fear and danger. Its high-rise vantage points a silhouette of menace. Its whole architecture was a solid fortress of deprivation, resentment and unrest.

I knew the Hardcastle estate quite well. So did most of the other senior officers that morning. We'd all heard of it, at least. Every force in the country had it as part of their training resources. A table-top map of its layout. A box full of wooden police vans and little wooden crowds with numbers of rioters printed on them. A set of counters with codes indicating units of the local constabulary. Four wooden police dogs, each labelled DOG.

I was part of a training seminar. In a real room with four other real officers. There was a facilitator and next to him a VDU screen that would periodically flash up information as to how events were unfolding. A room full of high-ranking uniforms. I was the only CID officer there. The only one from the Met. And the only one in plain clothes. We were to take turns in being in command of the situation. In the simulation it was early evening on the estate and trouble was brewing. The officer whose turn it was to make decisions, a superintendent from Cambridgeshire Constabulary, had spotted a problem. The eleven to seven o'clock day relief was just about to come off duty. He wanted to keep them working on overtime. The facilitator nodded and said that he was sure that the Assistant Chief Constable would support the decision, given the circumstances.

There were nods around the group as well. Overtime. It was what had kept the woodentops going all through the miners' strike. There had even been some disappointment when the strike finished and the extra hours' cash bonanza was over. The Met lads, the 'white-shirts', hadn't exactly been on their best behaviour on their tours of duty in the pit villages. We'd got a bad reputation for steaming in and asking questions later. No surprise really when you start billeting coppers in TA barracks. And the whole thing had a knock-on effect back home. Battle fatigue. All the community policing approach went up in smoke after a couple of weeks up North. Your average copper was liable to want to go out and crack a few heads on his first normal relief back on his own patch. There was a strange mix of euphoria and disillusionment. We got called 'Thatcher's Boot Boys' so often that we started to believe it ourselves.

And there was an easiness about some of the stuff that went on. Roadblocks stopping people from going into Nottinghamshire. Turning people back merely on suspicion that they might be flying pickets. That was a bit hookey, not exactly legal really. The state going bent for the job. It was political, and a lot of the lads weren't happy about it. But then coppers always seem a bit confused when it comes to things like that. I've never really been able to understand these things myself. I knew one officer who'd always be dropping some change into these collection buckets for miners' support groups that seemed to be on every street corner during the strike. I'm damn sure that although half of him was feeling a bit guilty about what the families had to go through all those months with no money, the other half was wanting to keep the strike going and all that overtime money rolling in.

The computer simulation kept churning out problems for us to solve. Fights had broken out in the Queen's Head. A hardware store on the other side of the estate had been broken into, a large quantity of paraffin had been seized. The next officer who had taken his turn in making decisions had withdrawn all remaining foot patrols so that they could be mobilised into Police Support Units. The Assistant Chief Constable had been requested to contact neighbouring forces to get reinforcements under the agreed system of mutual aid. The pub was now on fire. Barricades were going up on the Hardcastle estate. Mobile units were being issued with riot gear, or rather 'protective equipment'.

Now all the talk was of 'bridgeheads', 'pincer movements' and 'flanking manoeuvres'. I hadn't joined the force for all this. I'd wanted to catch villains. This was more like being in the army. Being plainclothes meant that I'd managed to avoid all of this public order stuff, but it was still depressing. Like we'd become paramilitary.

The PSU units are plotted up in their vans now. They need authorisation to start deploying 'protective equipment'. 'Riot gear' was a phrase that we weren't supposed to use. There's a brief discussion about how the appearance of being, well, 'tooled up' in this way will affect the mood of the crowd. The scene in the simulation is at the stage of 'sporadic disorder'. It's agreed that it's time for the mobile units to respond appropriately to this scenario and the game moves on.

It was my turn now. I had to try and articulate what CID input would be in this situation.

'I'd investigate the burglary of the hardware store,' I began. 'Get some idea of the amount of flammable materials stolen and find out if there had been thefts of milk bottles or other containers in the area.'

There were nods from around the group.

'I'd also have the events of the previous evening reviewed to see if there was a pattern or whether it was just a spontaneous thing. I see CID involvement here as being the gathering of intelligence in order to prevent the situation happening again. I'd set up an incident room to process information and debrief officers so that we can provide a proper system of intelligence for the officer in charge.'

'Anything else?' the facilitator asked.

'Yeah,' I went on. 'I'd make sure that there were a couple of officers in a forward position maintaining surveillance of all that was happening. I'd want a constant stream of information supplied to the command post.'

The rest of the group looked at least a bit impressed.

'Very good, Mr Taylor,' the facilitator commented, and we continued with the exercise.

By now the table-top map was so crowded with wooden vans and yellow incident flashes that it was hard to see the outline of the estate beneath them. In the central forecourt was a single crowd block with the number 600 on it.

The officer now taking his turn in the exercise was a superintendent who'd seen service on Merseyside. A veteran of Toxteth 1981. The year when all the inner cities seemed to go up in flames. District Support Units had arrived by now and he was requesting ACPO approval to use bulldozers to break down the barricades and send in snatch squads of short-shield serials. For all the talk of 'controlled dispersal' and 'containment formations', the scene now had the appearance of medieval siege warfare. Ancient imperial infantry tactics. The legions against the barbarians. He talked of the importance of making sure that the crowd didn't get control of the high ground on the estate.

Police had gained control of the Hardcastle estate by two o'clock on Sunday morning. The crowd was finally dispersed and some of the serials that had been on duty since seven the previous morning could start to stand down. A few District Support Units stayed on the scene to protect fire-fighters, who were damping down the last of the fires from petrol bombs. The facilitator congratulated us and said it was time for lunch. As we filed out he started to clear the wooden counters off the board and put them back into their respective boxes. Ready for the next time.

After the Skeleton Inquiry I went back to Flying Squad for a spell. In 1972 Robert Mark was appointed Commissioner for the Met and all hell broke loose. He actually set about implementing reforms that people had been fannying on about for years. He set up an independent unit, A10, to tackle corruption. CID would no longer be able to get away with investigating itself. Uniform branch finally got the upper hand and the power that the plainclothes department had had over the Yard was broken for good. And A10 didn't fuck about. Heads began to roll in the Drugs Squad, the Flying Squad, the Dirty Squad. I managed to get away with it. With each highly publicised corruption case I was always worried that my number might come up. But it didn't. And I got made up to Detective Chief Inspector in 1975.

George Mooney got away with it too. He took early retirement in 1973. Went to live in Spain in a nice little villa he bought with all that bent money. But he got his comeuppance in the end. He was shot dead by Harry Starks in 1979.

In 1976 Robert Mark inflicted his most humiliating reform on the Department. A new interchange policy that meant that no CID officer could expect much promotion unless they went back to uniform for a spell. Plainclothes really resented that and some said it was the end of the career detective. But I just got on with it. It felt strange being back in the blue serge.

I ended up teaching at Bramshill for a while. All those little Rapid Promotion Scheme and graduate intake faces looking up at me. Clever little bastards. Just like I had been. I was put on a training course myself. Run by the Management Services Department. We were supposed to be looking at the 'distribution of functions and responsibilities within the Metropolitan Police'. Issues of 'man management', stuff like that. We were now supposed to call ourselves the Police Service rather than the Police Force. That stuck in the throat a bit. There was a whole new set of jargon. Recommendations, restructuring. I was bored rigid.

But it paid off. Eventually I got back to the Yard made up to Detective Superintendent. C11. Criminal Intelligence. And five years later a post came up in this new team they were putting together to work with the National Reporting Centre. The Central Intelligence Unit, it was called. It meant promotion up to Detective Chief Super. I got sent on this public order seminar and I was to report the next day.

So everything was going well on the job front. I'd come through the shit smelling of roses. At the highest operational rank for

CID and still only in my early forties. I was a fucking high-flier.

My personal life wasn't so sweet. A cold and loveless marriage with Jeannie. I always hoped that we could work it out somehow. But any feeling that we had had for each other seemed to have been poisoned, corrupted. Oh, it was amicable enough. No rows or anything like that. Just a sort of bitter silence. We lived our own lives. She had the salon and her own set of friends. I had my career, my precious ambition. We only stayed together for David's sake. We played the respectable couple.

We never told him that I wasn't his real father. I always felt deep down that we should have. But I didn't do anything about it. As the years passed he grew more distant from me. I kind of thought Jeannie might tell him but she didn't. I think she was scared that he might find out about her past. She still doted on him. And he was a real mummy's boy. A bit soft. He went into this teenage rebellious phase. Wearing lairy clothes and sulking about in his bedroom. I felt that he began to resent me. Saw me as some kind of authority figure, I guess. Though I never felt that I had any authority where he was concerned. I felt helpless, left out. At least he didn't get into any real trouble. He did well at school. He was doing his A-levels. But he got all of these stupid political ideas in his head. Clearly having a copper for an old man wasn't very cool. Probably called me a 'fascist pig' behind my back. He rarely said anything to my face, though. Just gave me the silent treatment.

And he got to look so much like his real father. It really spooked me sometimes. I'd catch him looking moodily at me and I'd see Dave's eyes staring out at me. My conscience. Just like the old days.

MURDER MONTHLY. Free binder with first issue. Collect and keep to build an extensive dossier of the most horrific homicides in history. Each edition a fascinating study of the ultimate crime. Such was the pinnacle of my journalistic career. To be editor of such an esteemed organ. To be honest, I was lucky to get the job. All my years on the *Sunday Illustrated* had taken their toll, a decline in the ability to write that comes with years of hack work. My meagre talent wrote itself off slowly into virtual aphasia, having endlessly manipulated a familiar set of clichés into incoherence. I continued to have a dim desire to write something substantial one day, but as time went on this became more distant and less probable. I had for a long time occasionally confided to others in the Grub Street racket, usually after a lengthy drinking session when one's sense of self-esteem shrivels just as the tongue loosens, that I was still 'working on a book'. This was forever curtailed one evening in the Three Feathers when a red-faced colleague had turned on me rather bitchily with the riposte 'Yes, neither am I'.

But fate took me out of Fleet Street, just as Fleet Street itself was moving on. The *Illustrated* was moving into new premises in Docklands. Fully computerised and deregulated. The unions were shafted. There was an angry picket line outside the new high-security headquarters, violent clashes with the police and the private-contract lorries going in and out. I took early retirement as there was a fairly good offer on the table. Natural wastage. They were glad to be rid of me as I had long since become merely part of an inventory of unwanted fixtures and fittings. And I was well out of it. I heard from fellow hacks who'd made the transition, complete with computer training and a shiny new job description, that it was pretty soulless. Huddled over their screens like cloistered monks. Hardly ever going out to find a story, scarce opportunities to spend time in the pub. And they felt under siege. The scenes outside the gate could get pretty ugly, and it was hard not to feel the anger of it all. Sid Franks would have loved to have seen all the Fathers of Chapel he'd fought with over the years get it in the neck but he'd died of a heart attack in 1981.

And I was glad to be out of it. My career had never fully recovered from the porn inquiry fiasco. I'd struggled to keep my head above water, to be honest, struggled to stop myself from sinking into the horror. I hadn't given in to my urges since that last time, I'd controlled myself, but it had meant that I'd needed to take things quietly. My mind calmed down as I got older. I entered the Middle Ages with a sense of relief that maybe the Dark Ages were over.

And *Murder Monthly* was an ideal place for me. I had been headhunted for the job – I'd done some freelance work on a similar publication years ago and my name must have come up when they were stealing ideas. It was a pretty failsafe formula for the anorak psychos. Along with the occult, UFOs, conspiracy theory, stuff on the war that had a slight obsessiveness about the

Third Reich, True Crime would always be a consistent draw. Offer a binder and the punters would comfort themselves with thoughts of self-improvement. There was a whole suburban death cult out there hungry for arcane knowledge. Perhaps the publishers of *Murder Monthly* knew that I had a nose for this. I certainly understood their vicarious pleasure in sordid detail, their lonely hunger for evil. As I fought with my own personal Enemy Within I could content myself with voyeuristic pleasures in the slow surcease of my desperate longings.

It was a pretty easy brief even for my now diminished powers. I'd decide on the monthly theme then farm out the work to writers I knew could deliver the goods, some of them quite successful in the field. Some had written books on particularly notorious cases and were only too happy to regurgitate their research for a reasonable fee. A lot of these books were full of psychobabble and 'insights' into the minds of evil men and women. I felt that the genre was in danger of becoming respectable. But maybe this was just resentment on my part. After all, I'd never managed to write a book myself.

But there was still time. Hack work had got in the way, but now there was space to concentrate. *Murder Monthly* wasn't exactly taxing. Coming up with the particular theme for each issue was never that difficult. The gaudier the better, I always thought. Sometimes we would merely concentrate on one particular case: Crippen, Christie, Cannock Chase, Mary Bell, the Moors Murderers – a familiar litany of infamy. Then we'd do more than one case in one issue, something linking them. The two Rippers was an obvious choice. 'The Most Famous Stranglers in Criminal History' was one of my favourites. The weight of infamy somehow balanced the burden of my own guilt. Compared to them my crimes were not so unforgivable.

Billy Porter had appeared twice in the series, with no complaints from the readership. They were themselves recidivists, happy to have the same crimes repeated; they were compulsive, serial killers in their own imagination. Porter had been the main subject of issue 11, 'The Cop Killers', and had appeared in issue 23, 'The Missing Murderers', along with Lord Lucan and Harry Starks. His disappearance had secured his legend. There were all kinds of theories as to what had become of him. Many thought that he must be dead after all this time, as they did with Lucan. But his story was very much alive as part of popular mythology, lacking only an end. And a sexual angle, as this was always a big selling point with the *Murder Monthly* readership. Though one of the more pyschologically inclined writers on the magazine did go as far as to conclude that his crime was essentially Freudian. 'An Oedipal revolt against authority', he called it, which was a bit rich, I thought. Though it did maybe explain why he had become something of an alternative folk hero.

Porter was still my story. I was something of an expert on it. I still had a big file that I periodically updated. One day I'd write it all up in a book, my own great work of True Crime existentialism. But another, altogether different kind of literary opportunity came up when Teddy Thursby phoned to tell me the news.

'Julian's dead,' he announced flatly in that sonorous voice of his.

'Oh,' I responded, not knowing quite what to say.

'Can you come over?'

They marched up a muddy tracked hill towards the USAAF base. A long procession with banners and effigies, drums and chanting.

Double-rotored Chinooks clattered overhead. Huge malignant dragonflies. The airbase came into view. Its perimeter fence snaking through fields of corn.

Embrace the Base. An Easter protest against Cruise Missiles. CND, the Peace Pledge Union, Quakers Against the Bomb. Candlelight vigils at Peace Corner and the Rainbow Village Camp. Songs and prayers. The bank-holiday sky was grey with fine drizzle.

As they encircled the airbase, pennants and flowers were hung on the wire. There were a few arrests as some people attempted to cut the fence with bolt-cutters. The protesters went limp as they were apprehended. This was to be a peaceful demonstration.

Mick was there with the Peace Convoy. These were the new travellers he'd fallen in with. Hippies, drop-outs. They didn't use caravans. They converted trucks, coaches or ambulances into moving homes or lived in teepees or benders. At first he didn't have much to do with them. Weirdos, he thought. But he slowly began to realise that he was safe among them. They were mostly harmless enough. And they seemed to like him, took him for an authentic traveller. He never put them right on that one. He pretended he was from an old showman family, that he had real gypsy blood in him. He could talk the talk. And he found work. Painting their vehicles.

They would ask for all kinds of lairy designs on their lorries and buses.

He'd met Janis at Glastonbury. He'd got a job painting the sets for a travelling theatre group. They were into circus skills and sideshow spectacle. They appreciated his ability to paint traditional showman designs. It made a change from the usual psychedelic stuff that people wanted. Janis was part of the troupe. He was working outdoors on a backdrop when he first saw her. She was practising juggling with a tall, lanky man. They were passing six clubs between them in a rhythmic ellipse. When they took a break she came over to look at his work. *Wow*, she had said, *it's so real*. She was, he guessed, in her early thirties. She had long hennaed hair and a nose-ring. Her face was ruddy and weathered from the travelling life.

She was living in a converted Post Office van. Multicoloured with a window installed in its side.

'I'm bored with how it looks,' she had said. 'Will you paint it for me?'

He had shrugged and nodded. They had shared a chillum of sensimillia that evening. Its sharp tang burned against the back of his throat. He felt the prickling rush of it surge up from his calf muscles into his weary head. She'd encouraged him to talk of the fairground life. The showman routine he'd repeated so often he almost believed it himself.

'Wow,' she had said as she exhaled a stream of blue from deep in her lungs. 'I suppose a showman is like a shaman.'

'Yeah,' he'd replied with a grin, not knowing what the hell she was on about.

They had slept together that night in her creaking van. It had been so long since he had had sex with anyone. He felt the deep warmth of it afterwards flood through his tired body. They curled up together and he trembled slowly into a warm and intimate night.

They ended up travelling together. They got a coach and converted it. He did the painting and the coachwork, she did the mechanics. She didn't ask too many questions, which was good. He didn't do too much talking. He had plenty of tales he had picked up over the years on the road to keep her happy. She spoke a lot more and he'd listen patiently. It was nonsense, mostly. About the Goddess and spirituality. And Peace. She'd always be banging on about Peace.

Luckily it was largely a women's thing. She'd go off to join groups of feminists in peace camps pitched outside missile bases across the country. It would give him time to himself which he needed. He'd become so used to it.

But this time they went on a demo together. He felt a bit edgy as a phalanx of police came into view lined up by the main gate of the base. He'd spent so much time avoiding trouble of any kind.

The staccato of the helicopters above was deafening. Memories hovered over his head. Searching for landing zones in his consciousness. The perimeter fence was littered with banners and flowers, all kinds of mementos entwined into the chain link. Military police stood silently on the other side. The 'modplods', the peace people called them. Beyond were huge concrete bunkers and missile silos.

It's all about identity, someone had once said in some political discussion that he had struggled to keep up with. He offered no opinions but that thought flooded into his dulled mind. Identity. That's what it's all about. If only they knew. But he kept his thoughts to himself. He was an outcast, after all.

And walking past all the half-sodden detritus choking the weld-mesh fencing like colourful weed, he had a sudden and strange thought. Looking at the dull faces of the modplods on patrol he felt something jar inside. Vague memories of when he was a young man. He had more of an affinity with the people on the other side of the fence than those that he marched with.

Peter was with a group of Class War anarchists that had come to the demo intent on causing trouble. IF YOU WANT PEACE, their paper declared, PREPARE FOR WAR! *If you think building chapels, planting seeds, and putting balloons on fences can stop nuclear weapons . . . then you're a fucking idiot. If you want to join in some effective action instead of holding hands, saying prayers, and other middle-class wank-offs then join the Class War mobs.*

Bright red spiky hair crowned his face. Shock-headed Peter with locks like flame. Each filament a spire or minaret calling out for angry justice. The pacifists were the enemy. Class War had already had some success that day. They had pelted Joan Ruddock, the chair of CND, with mud as she had tried to talk to the press. Now, if they could kick off a bit of trouble with the police then trudging all afternoon through the rain would be worth it.

A crowd had gathered near the wire where a couple of women had tried to cut the fence and had been arrested. Police reinforcements arrived and were trying to cordon the area off. Peter and the other Class War anarchists joined the mob that began to line up against the hastily formed police ranks. There were other militant protesters among the throng. Trots, Peter observed with disdain. SWP, RCP, RCG. Leftie wankers, thought Pete, but at least they weren't averse to a bit of a scrap.

Official CND demo stewards tried desperately to keep the peace as the pushing and shoving began. 'Remember, this is a peaceful protest,' one of them said. 'Fuck off!' Peter spat out at him.

'Fucking great,' one officer muttered gloomily to another as their serial filed into position. 'Rent-a-Mob's arrived.'

The part of the march that Mick and Janis were in had reached this point. The mob jostled against the police lines and the main part of the crowd became sucked into its heaving mass. A ululating whoop rose up. Protesters oscillating their palms in front of their mouths like childhood Red Indians. A chant went up. NO CRUISE! NO CRUISE! A few missiles sailed over into the uniformed ranks.

The police retaliated. A snatch squad stormed into the crowd and cleared a path with swinging truncheons. They dragged someone back into their lines.

I've got to get out of here, Mick thought. Janis was shouting something beside him. He tried to get her attention. The crowd was surging forward, pushing him towards the police ranks.

A huge lump of mud struck a policeman in the face. Peter laughed manically. He felt the adrenaline rush through him. He grabbed a placard from someone next to him and hoisted it over the heads in front of him. It fell short, into the mud. A senior police officer was addressing them with a loudhailer, telling them to disperse and continue on the march. More CND stewards had arrived and were trying to move people on. Peter and the rest of the Class War mob started barracking them, but the crowd did start to dissipate a little.

Peter started up a song. This'll wind them up, he thought. He was sick of all these hippy chants and peace-loving dirges he'd heard all day. Hymns, for fuck sake. Embrace the Base. Give the state a big hug and everything will be all right. There's the enemy. The Old Bill. Right in front of us.

'Billy Porter is our friend,' he began, a little haltingly. Self-conscious. If you started shouting something and no one joined in it could be embarrassing. But it was taken up as a group song by other anarchists around him.

Is our friend, is our friend,
Billy Porter is our friend,
He Kills Coppers!

There was laughter and then the refrain began again a little louder. Peter moved forward to the front of the mob.

Mick was walking away from the trouble with Janis when he heard it. At first it didn't register. Then the second time he heard the name. Recognised it. He hadn't heard that name in years. He turned back, transfixed.

Some of the officers in the line bristled at the taunt. They'd heard it first on the terraces; now it had been adopted by the Rent-a-Mob lot at political demos. The 'outside agitators' that had been described by senior officers in briefings. The crowd was thinning out now and the group of chanting anarchists became more visible.

'That's the cunt!' shouted one of the coppers, pointing at Peter, whose shock of hair stood out among the others, many of whom had covered their heads with the hoods of their track-suit tops.

'He's the fucking ringleader!'

A group of police broke ranks and advanced on the anarchists.

Mick stood listening, dumbfounded. Janis tugged at his sleeve but he ignored her. Billy Porter. They were shouting that name at the police. He suddenly felt vunerable. It was calling to him. Calling him back. He should try and stop them, he thought. Try and stop them calling out that name. It could give the game away. In a confused kind of panic, he started to walk towards the spiky-haired man who was leading the song. It was partly fear but also a strange desire to make contact. Billy Porter was their friend. What could that mean?

The Class War mob began to scatter as the police advanced. They no longer had the cover of the rest of the march which was now moving on. Peter lost his footing in the mud. He slipped and fell on to one knee. He managed to pick himself up but the uniformed officers were already upon him.

It was then that a stranger's hand caught hold of his and tried to pull him to safety.

'Mick!' Janis called out.

But he paid her no heed. For a moment he forgot that name and thought only of another's: Billy Porter.

27

I was teamed up with a guy called Derek Barnes at the Central Intelligence Unit. The Unit was set up to work alongside the National Reporting Centre which dealt with organising mutual aid during the miners' strike. Barnes was a smooth type, well spoken. Graduate intake, I guessed.

'What are your theories on public order, Frank?'

I shrugged.

'Well,' I said, 'to tell you the truth I don't really have any.'

Barnes smiled indulgently.

'Gut feelings?'

'I dunno. In my day it was just crowd control. You know, link arms and push.'

He gave a dry little laugh.

'Well,' he said, 'we all know things have changed since then. You don't mind if I give my overview?'

'No, fire away.'

'Well, I was on the original Community Disorder Tactical Options Inter-Force Working Group.'

'Bit of a mouthful,' I retorted quietly.

'Yes, quite. Anyway, it was set up at the end of 1981. All those inner-city riots. We had to do a complete rethink. So we got some experts in from a force off the mainland. Who do you think they might be?'

'The RUC?' I suggested.

'No, actually not. A lot of people would have thought so. No, it was never made public but it was the Royal Hong Kong Police that we got most of our new tactics from.'

'Really?'

'Oh yes. You see, there's a lot to be learned from our colonial forces. A long experience of dealing with the sharp end of public order. The natives are always restless.'

He grinned coldly.

'And the Hong Kong boys,' he went on, 'well, they had the blueprint for keeping the peace when it all gets out of order. It's funny, you know. All that time with the Empire, thinking that we were exporting some sort of civilisation out to the colonies, and in the end we import colonial policing back to the mother country. I guess that's why it was never made public.'

'Yeah,' I agreed, not quite sure what he was getting at. 'Makes you think.'

'But it paid off. You see, we had to have a systematic training blueprint. If one force was to reinforce another we had to make sure that they were working along the same lines. The mutual aid system depends on it.'

'Of course,' I said, not wanting to appear stupid.

'And with the miners' strike, all of this really came into its own. Remember Orgreave?'

A big scrap with a load of miners picketing a coke depot in Rotherham. I'd seen it all on the telly. I nodded.

'That was the first proper unveiling of colonial police tactics on the mainland. A show of force by long-shield officers. Dispersal and incapacitation by short-shield units. The use of horses to create fear among the crowd. It was a set piece designed to show what we could do. From the point of view of strategy and tactics it was damn near perfect. It was almost Napoleonic.'

'Yeah, well,' I said with a shrug, 'but was it policing?'

Barnes broke into a broad smile, like I'd got his point.

'Exactly!' he hissed sharply. 'That's the dilemma. If we keep entering the fray like we're in a state of siege we can so easily give the enemies of the state, the Enemy Within, as the great leader insists, we can give them a sense of justification in stirring up trouble. Can't we?'

'Well,' I said, 'I wouldn't know. I'm just a detective.'

'But that's just the sort of input we need, isn't it?'

'I guess. We need to have the right information.'

Barnes nodded.

'And intelligence. One feeds the other. Information is our raw data. If from that we can identify trends, patterns and tension indicators that affect operational bearing on deployment and resources, then we have not just information, but intelligence. Intelligence, Frank.'

I thought he was having a go now. Bandying about intelligence like I was stupid or something.

'Look,' I said, 'I'm just a detective. As I said.'

'Yes,' he concurred. 'I've seen your record. Very impressive.'

'I'm a thief-taker. Or at least,' I went on, almost apologetic, thinking about some of the hookeyness in the past, 'that's what I like to think I am.'

'But these are transferable skills, are they not?'

'Are they?'

'I think so, yes. During the strike the need to introduce a greater degree of co-ordination between forces in receiving, assessing and disseminating information and intelligence relative to the dispute was recognised. That's why this unit was set up. Officers have been selected with an ability for handling information and for having analytical skills. Experienced officers, like you, who can collate information and pass on the relevant intelligence, processed and disseminated through to force command and control.'

'But the strike's over.'

The miners had gone back in March. Without a deal. Trudging back to the pitheads with brass bands and ancient union banners. Like funeral processions.

'Yes, well, the Unit doesn't exactly have permanent status. It's an *ad hoc* thing like the National Reporting Centre. But our job is to see if we can develop a compatible system of information and intelligence for dealing with all types of disorder.'

'Can't Special Branch do that?'

Barnes pursed his lips.

'Ah, well, Special Branch, bless them. They do tend to be rather busy doing MI5's dirty work for them. And often they report directly to them and keep us in the dark. No, what we are looking at here is an intelligence unit that feeds in directly to operational structures pertaining to mutual aid.'

'A column of mutual aid and support,' I blurted out, remembering how Mooney had described the masons all those years ago.

'Sorry?' asked Barnes with a frown.

'Nothing.'

* * *

Jeannie got me to tell her about the new job that evening. I knew something was up. She never took much of an interest in my work.

'Well, I'm glad it's going well,' she said. 'Look, Frank . . .'

She coughed. I looked her in the face and waited.

'We've got to talk.'

'I thought that's what we were doing,' I said.

'No, I mean . . . This isn't going to be easy.'

'Then you better just say it.'

'All right.'

She coughed again.

'I want a divorce, Frank.'

I sighed.

'Right,' I said.

'I'm sorry, but it's for the best.'

'Yeah?'

'Look, don't pretend it's not.'

'Any particular reason you've sprung this on me?'

'What do you mean?'

'You seeing someone else?'

'No.'

'Then why? I mean, why now?'

'Well, it might have escaped your notice but David will be leaving home soon. Going to university.'

'So?'

'Well, there's really not much point us staying together, is there? We can go our own ways. Start new lives.'

'This is what you want?'

'Yes, it is. If we could wait a bit. I don't want us to be going through this yet with David having his exams coming up.'

'Christ, you really have worked it all out, haven't you?'

'And it would be nice if we could stay on friendly terms.'

'Well, how bloody civilised. A nice friendly divorce.'

'Please, Frank. Don't make a scene.'

'How do you think this makes me feel? After all this time? Eh?'

But there wasn't much else to say without shouting so I went out for a walk and tried to calm down. It was a warm clear evening. Everything looked at peace in our little middle-class suburb. She was right, of course. Poor cow had had to put up with me all this time for the sake of the kid. I wondered if she'd ever had any real feelings for me. I had for her. Still did. I felt so empty and lonely. What was the bloody point? I thought.

Thursby had been going through a long decline. His wife had finally divorced him in 1977 and he'd had to sell his country pile, Hartwell Lodge. 'She wants a settlement before he drinks it all away,' Julian had told me. And Julian had certainly been helping Teddy along in that direction.

Of course, I'd never quite forgiven him for spoiling the porn exposé back in 1971. But I bore my grudge in private. He'd been a useful source for bits of gossip here and there over the years.

I hadn't been very close to Julian for a long time. Once witty and flamboyant, he'd become one of the Soho bores, that pack of would-be writers or artists or hangers-on that drank themselves stupid and imagined that they were being bohemian. And the booze really started to bring the poison out of him. He was always best avoided after six o'clock. It was a bit of a shock to hear that he'd croaked. I had a vague sense of grief, a sort of general unsettling feeling about mortality. A feeling that was only intensified by setting eyes on Thursby.

He looked dreadful as he came to the door. His face had gone from flabby affability to a drawn, gaunt death-mask. His skin was mottled with liver spots and had a jaundiced tinge. He let me in and hobbled around his untidy flat to get us both a gin and tonic.

'Well, the bastard beat me to it,' he said, handing me a glass. 'It's not fair. I feel a bit cheated, to tell you the truth. You know, at seventy-five euthanasia should be voluntary. At eighty-five it should be compulsory.'

'What happened?'

'His fucking liver gave out, of course. All those years drinking himself to death on my account. I mean on my account, quite literally. He always took advantage of our financial arrangement. They took him into the Westminster Hospital but there was nothing they could do. But do you know what he had the audacity to do?'

'What?'

'On the admissions form he had the cheek to put me down as next of kin. That was the last dirty trick he played on me. So when he croaked I had to go and identify the body, didn't I? They pulled back the sheet and there she was with a stupid expression on her face. "Oh yes," I said. "That's him, all right." It's funny, you know. In death he had this funny look on his face. He looked shocked. I thought, "You've got nothing to be surprised about, Jules." And I tell you, that's the first time I saw that queen with her mouth shut.'

Thursby stumbled over to get the gin bottle and refilled our glasses.

'So I supposed he expected that I was going to pick up the bill for him in death as in life. Imagined that I'd pay for some ritual mass in St Margaret's or something. He wanted absolution for all his beastliness, I guess. We all do, I suppose. Wanted a proper send-off, that's for sure.'

'So are you going to arrange it?'

Thursby chuckled hoarsely.

'Heavens, no,' he declared.

He sniffed and the light caught a triumphant glint in his eye.

'We're burning him at Golders Green tomorrow,' he said.

He leaned forward and looked at me imploringly.

'You will come, now, won't you?'

Julian's send-off was a depressing affair. A handful of his drinking friends turned up at the crematorium. A strange-looking creature in a black silk dress and a veiled hat sat at the back. At first it was assumed that she was a transvestite, but it turned out she was a maiden aunt from Eastbourne. Teddy said a few words and managed to sound convincingly moved by the occasion. There was a rich sob to his voice as he intoned some solemn words about one called before his time. Then he pressed the button, the curtains opened and the coffin trundled mechanically into the furnace.

There was a wake in the the French House. Thursby plonked the urn unceremoniously on the bar.

'I don't know what the hell I'm supposed to do with this,' he declared.

Some queen suggested that we should scatter his remains over the parade ground at Chelsea Barracks. Teddy had slumped down in a chair in sudden melancholia.

'Oh, why does death have to be so bloody?' he groaned.

I'd had quite enough of all this. I made my excuses and turned to leave. Thursby tugged at my sleeve.

'Come and see me,' he said, looking up plaintively. 'At my flat. I've got something to show you.'

Mick sat staring at the cell wall. *This is bad*, he thought. In all his time on the run he'd tried to be careful. *Stay out of trouble*, that had been his watchword. At the merest smell of it he'd be off. He'd covered his tracks well over the years. And here he was banged up over a stupid demonstration. He'd only gone on it to please Janis. How could he have been so fucking stupid after all this time? It was that song. That was it.

They'd charged him with obstruction. He'd been fingerprinted and photographed. This could be the end of it now. It could all come out. No more running. All of that had been an illusion of freedom. This was real. The cell. This was now. The past had only existed as a prelude to this. This was where he belonged. This was where he had always been headed. He tried not to give in to an awful sense of relief. A desire to give himself up.

Maybe he should kill himself. That would be a way out. They hadn't taken his belt away. He could hang himself. He looked around the cell to see if there was some way of attaching the belt to something.

Then the door banged open and somebody was pushed inside. It was the spiky-haired kid he had tried to pull away from the police.

'Wait a minute,' he had said as he'd tugged at him. 'Wait.'

Then he'd been grabbed himself by a couple of the uniformed squad and had been dragged off and taken into custody.

Mick came out of his suicidal reverie and looked up at the young man. The cell door banged shut. Peter smiled down at him. *Maybe he can help me*, Mick thought. He didn't know how, he just felt a strange pang of hope.

Peter looked at his cellmate. He had long greying hair and a beard. But this guy wasn't a hippie, he thought. He looked like a real traveller, not like those stupid crusties with their 'alternative' lifestyles. Middle-class drop-outs and lunched-out hash-heads. This bloke looked like he'd really lived it. There was something familiar about his eyes as well, but he couldn't quite place it.

'Thanks for trying to pull me out of there,' he said.

'Yeah.' Mick shrugged. 'Sure.'

'Pete,' said the man, and held out his hand.

They shook hands.

'Mick.'

'Thanks, Mick. I owe you one.'

Peter sat next to him on the bunk. Mick didn't know what to say. A childish tune was going through his head. A nursery rhyme. He turned to Peter. His spiky hair gave his face a startled look, thought Mick, as if he were in a permanent state of shock.

Still the song went through his head. The tune of it. What was the tune? 'Oranges and Lemons'? He hummed to himself. *When will you pay me say the bells of Old Bailey?* Peter frowned at him as he lullabyed softly, trying to murmur out the melody. *Here comes the candle to light you to bed, here comes the chopper to chop off your head.* No, that wasn't it. But something about London. 'London's Burning'? No. 'London Bridge Is Falling Down'. That was it.

'That song,' Mick said.

'What?'

He dah-dahed it quietly. Wary of the naming words. Peter joined in in a whisper.

'. . . is our friend, is our friend. Billy Porter is our friend. He kills coppers!'

Peter hissed the last line and chuckled softly.

'You know who Billy Porter was, don't you?'

Mick shrugged. *I don't know*, he thought. Act like I don't know.

'He killed three of the filth back in 1966. Geoff Hurst wasn't the only one who scored a hat-trick that year.'

'Don't like the Old Bill much, do you?'

'They're the enemy,' Peter replied flatly.

'I thought you lot were into peace and all that.'

'No. Not peace. War.'

'What?'

'The class war.'

'Oh, yeah,' said Mick. 'That.'

Politics again. He'd never understand it. But this bloke was different from the Peace Convoy lot he'd got to know. All that stuff that Janis went on about. About men being to blame for everything and stuff like that. Going back to nature. Dropping out. He'd just felt he'd been falling slowly all of these years. No, this was different. They were angry. The hippies he'd known were anti-police, that was for sure. They called them 'Babylon' and stupid names like that. But this lot, they wanted them dead. Billy Porter was their friend. Maybe he could make sense of that.

Friend. But. Friend. There was grief in the word. He remembered when he had been a fairground painter. He'd had a friend. Then. A friend he had murdered. Now he had been caught. It might all come out and he would have to face the truth. But he didn't understand it. What was the truth, after all? *Billy Porter is our friend*. They seemed so certain of that. They knew something that he didn't. Maybe it could explain what had happened.

The cell door opened and they were taken out to the charge room. He could scarcely make out what the custody officer was saying. He felt a dull, calm sense of one condemned. It was all over. Then the words that the officer was saying began to come together. They were being released with a caution. He was supposed to give an address and Peter suggested that he give them his. He owed him one, as he said.

A couple of friends of Peter's had been waiting for him at the station. Mick felt drained. An empty sense of relief that seemed like disappointment. He wanted it all to end now. He'd had enough of running. Janis was nowhere to be seen. Maybe she didn't know where he was.

'You want a lift, mate?' Peter asked.

He should wait for her, he thought. But he needed to get away.

'Where you going?' he asked.

'London.'

Mick grinned. *London Bridge is falling down*. Yeah, that's where he'd go. That's where he'd settle all of this.

The Class War Transit van dropped them off on an urban clearway just south of Vauxhall Bridge. 'You can crash at our place, if you want,' Peter had said. He meant a squat that he and another occupant of the van, Johnny, were living in near by.

A whole square of houses had been taken over by squatters. The area had been earmarked for demolition in the late seventies to make way for a new school. The existing tenants had been rehoused and the properties were boarded up. But then the plans for the school were postponed indefinitely and the education authority was left with over a hundred empty homes on its hands. Squatters started to move in at the beginning of the eighties and within five years the whole neighbourhood, save for a smattering of the original occupants who had refused to move, had been taken over by them.

They walked through the square. The half-derelict houses had been renovated in a haphazard way. Windows fixed with what was at hand, plumbing improvised, front doors painted garishly in a bricolage of occupation. There were graffiti on the walls: NO CRUISE, MEAT IS MURDER, STOP THE CITY, EAT THE RICH – strange apocalyptic warnings. One graffito announced: BEWARE OF MONSTER No. 15. Mick had heard about the squats in the city. Janis had gone to stay in one a few times. Many of the Peace Convoy seemed to use them as winter quarters. Mick had always declined. He had wanted to avoid the cities up until now. And staying on-site all year round had helped to establish his reputation as a real traveller.

'Here we are,' Peter announced.

They had arrived at a house with a black front door with a huge circled A on it. An old ambulance with a tarpaulin covering it was parked outside. There was someone underneath it. A pair of legs protruded from it and was moving crablike along the tarmac. Peter banged on the side of the vehicle.

'All right Mutt?' he called.

A metal tool clanged to the floor and a figure emerged from beneath the engine. It was short and stocky and wore tattered overalls, tongues sticking out of unlaced and scuffed boots. His hair was cropped short at the front with long, matted dreadlocks hanging down the back. He was covered in oil and grease.

'Uh?' he grunted, looking up at them from the gutter, squinting against the light.

'Meet Muttley,' Peter said with a grin. 'He's our liberated animal.'

Muttley smiled, showing a gap in his front teeth.

'Go to the shops, Johnny,' Peter told his friend. 'I'll get the tea on.'

They went upstairs to the kitchen. They was a huge stack of unwashed utensils in the sink. The table was littered with pamphlets and papers. There was a black flag hanging on the wall. Beneath was a clipping from *Class War*. It was a photograph of a policeman with blood running down his face. HOSPITALISED COPPER, it read. BACK BY POPULAR DEMAND. BRIXTON PC BASIL BASTARD BASHED ON THE BONCE BY A BOULDER IN THE BLOODY BATTLE OF THE BARRIER BLOCK. Next to it was a smudged and long-neglected rota.

Johnny returned with the groceries, cradled to his chest. A box of tea bags, two tins of baked beans and a packet of digestive biscuits. He dropped them on to the table. Peter picked up the tea and broke open the cellophane on the packet. Muttley grabbed the biscuits and groaned.

'What's the matter?' asked Johnny.

Muttley pointed the digestives accusingly at Johnny.

'The ingredients,' he said. 'Read the ingredients.'

Johnny took the packet from him and looked at the tiny writing on its side.

'What?' he said.

'Just read the fucking ingredients.'

'Leave it out, Muttley,' Peter commented as he poured water from the kettle.

'Wheat flour,' Johnny began falteringly. 'Vegetable oil and, um, hydrogenated vegetable oil and . . .'

He stopped for a second.

'Go on,' Muttley insisted.

'Muttley,' Peter groaned.

'Animal fat,' said Johnny finally.

'Yeah, animal fat. I told you digestives were no good.'

'There can't be that much of it in them,' said Peter.

'That ain't the fucking point, is it? I thought we agreed that this was a vegan household. Fucking animal biscuits.'

Johnny put the digestives on the table. Mick stared at them. He was starving, but he thought it best not to make a grab for them as he was tempted to. He would have to go along with all of these strange rules and rituals. He would have to try and fit in. Until he was ready to make his move. Peter handed him a cup of tea. It was made with soya milk. He took a sip. It had a powdery texture to it, like sawdust in his mouth.

Muttley made a veggie stew later. They sat around the kitchen table with a bottle of cider and a couple of spliffs. Peter held forth with exaggerated stories of rebellion and complaints that 'peaceful demos were a waste of fucking time'. He talked of the need for direct action.

'We should do something really spectacular, you know?' he said, looking around the room.

Peter seemed very much the boss of the group. Muttley would argue with some of his comments but Johnny seemed in constant deference. Occasionally Mick would be asked his opinion at various stages of the rambling discussion, and he'd nod or shrug. All he could think about was where he was going to sleep that night. As it got late Peter said that he 'could have Frank's room' and Johnny led him to a chaotically untidy bedroom.

28

I didn't really know what to do after Jeannie asked for the divorce, so I threw myself into work, as per usual. Plenty of overtime to be had. I could half convince myself that it was an important job. It was easy to feel clever at the Central Intelligence Unit. A sense that we were looking on things from some higher ground, getting some sort of view of it all. We had the use of PNC2, the Police National Computer, and we were given privileged access to classified documents. The ACPO Public Order Manual was restricted to Assistant Chief Constable rank and above, but I got to have a peek at it – well, Section Three on intelligence-gathering, that is. It gave my ego a bit of a boost, that I was somehow in the know, that I was trusted by the higher-ups and on my way up there myself. The manual defined three areas of intelligence: 'live' – that of immediate concern to effective planning of operations; 'strategic' – long-range stuff of little immediate operational value; and 'counter-intelligence' – used to respond to or neutralise anti-police propaganda or rumours. All three ingredients would combine to form a 'total intelligence product', like some advertising slogan. A miracle cure.

It was just the sort of jargon that Barnes thrived on. He was always turning practice into theory. He was the new generation of copper. Happiest when he was staring at a computer screen. He was OK to work with, I suppose. He could be a patronising bastard but he was always civil. The first time we went for a drink together and he ordered a Perrier water, well, I knew he'd never be a bundle of laughs.

We would identify trends, patterns affecting operational bearing on deployment and resources, identify individuals engaged in crime who crossed force boundaries. There was much talk of 'tension indicators', of being able to spot flash-points that could lead to unrest and disorder. We were constantly on the lookout for the Enemy Within. The local troublemakers or the outside agitators. But when the inner cities went up again in the autumn, in Handsworth, Brixton and Tottenham, we missed the one factor that had sparked off the riots in all of those areas: police action itself. We had become the Enemy too. Sent into the ghettoes like the occupying force of a foreign power.

But before that, at the beginning of the summer, we just thought that we had all the angles covered. We weren't going to be caught out like back in '81. And the government owed us. We'd won the miners' strike for them, for Christ's sake, and it was up to them to back us up. But it was that summer that something else happened which brought everything back and to a head.

It was the first big job for the Unit post the miners' dispute. This year the annual Stonehenge Festival was to be banned. It was a hippie carnival that coincided with the summer solstice and had always been a bit of a public order nightmare. There were fears of damage to the the ancient site, apparently, and access to the stones was to be dramatically curtailed. English Heritage, who were responsible for the site, and the National Trust, who owned the thousand or so acres that surrounded it, secured 'precautionary injunctions' against certain named persons, forbidding them from trespassing on the property. Wiltshire County Council had closed certain roads around Stonehenge, using the Road Traffic Regulation Act that had been passed only the previous year and allowed such action if there was a 'danger to the public'. On top of this, the Wiltshire Constabulary had been setting up roadblocks on other routes and were warning travellers not to proceed and threatening to arrest them for obstruction if they tried to. As with the flying pickets trying to travel into Nottinghamshire during the miners' strike, they would be in breach of the peace, they claimed. It all looked pretty tight.

Our job was to provide information and intelligence as the travellers, the Peace Convoy as it became known, were crossing force boundaries. A large part of the convoy had come straight from Cambridgeshire, where they had been involved in a large demo against cruise missiles in Molesworth. We had to try and collate all that was known about this ragtag band, in particular to identify the 'certain persons' named in the injunctions. It was hard to build up any clear patterns about their behaviour. Their moving lifestyle didn't help. There were rumours that among this supposed peace-loving gang was a hard core of armed troublemakers. But there was no structured leadership or organisation. There were links with CND and the Peace Camps but nothing official. They didn't really shape up as enemies of the state as far as I was concerned. Barnes went into this whole analysis of the 'counterculture', something he'd picked up from university, no doubt. But there was something about them being travellers which struck a chord with me. I didn't know what it was, but it was as if I were looking for some other sort of evidence. By the end of May the convoy had crossed the border into Wiltshire.

There was all sorts of literature, pamphlets and newsletters, but none of it made any sense. Pure hippy mumbo-jumbo, most of it. There was a simple bright orange flier that merely stated: STONEHENGE *85* FREE FESTIVAL STARTS JUNE 1ST MID-SUMMER EVE 23RD A303 WILTS BE THERE OR BE SQUARE. I started looking for clues elsewhere.

There was a big stack of surveillance photographs of the convoy *en route* that I went through. All these brightly painted vehicles. Trucks and double-decker buses, coaches and vans. There were slogans daubed on the sides of some of them. PEACE CONVOY, FIGHT TRUTH DECAY, MYSTERY TOUR, STONEHENGE – GO FOR IT! And there were all these strange symbols. Rainbows and peace signs, suns and circled As, weird Indian writing. I was looking for patterns, connections. All these hippie designs started to swirl around my head. There was something that I couldn't quite figure out that was in the back of my mind. The answer to something. For a moment I even thought that I was having some kind of fucking mystical experience. Then it hit me. I found it. One of the vehicles, a converted coach, had been more delicately decorated. Older-looking. I looked closely at the photograph. It was a beautifully crafted paint job with a more traditional design than the others. It looked like a fairground wagon. I'd seen it before. I felt a brief shudder inside. Someone walking on my grave. Someone walking on Dave's grave.

I put the photograph in my briefcase. I made some sort of excuse and left work early. When I got home, David was mooching about the house.

'Shouldn't you be at school?'

'I'm revising,' he replied indignantly. 'I've got my second English paper tomorrow. A-levels. Remember?'

I put my hands up.

'OK, OK.'

He gave me his habitually resentful stare. There was something odd about his eyes. Eyeliner, it looked like.

'Are you wearing make-up?'

'Yeah. So?'

'Oh, for Christ's sake.'

He grinned and I immediately regretted reacting in that way. It was just the effect he was after. I went into the spare room. I dug out my Billy Porter file and shuffled through it. There it was, the drawing I'd found on the floor of the disused aircraft hangar all those years ago. I got the photo out of my case and compared them. It was the same bloody design. I stared at it. The pattern. I didn't know what it meant. But it was a clue, a lead. Something else had slipped out of the file. It was a newspaper clipping. Police file photographs of the three officers murdered on Scrubs Lane in 1966. Dave's face staring out from oblivion at me.

I went downstairs and phoned the Yard. I found out that the Peace Convoy was being herded into the Savernake Forest as a containment measure. Harsh music coming from David's bedroom. I called up to him. He came out on to the upstairs landing.

'What?' he called back.

'Can you come down a minute, please.'

He sighed heavily and clumped down the stairs.

'Yeah?'

'Look, I've got to follow up a job. Can you tell your mother I might not be back tonight?'

'Sure.'

He turned to go back up to his room.

'David?'

'What is it now?'

'Look, I know that we don't always get on but I wish . . .' I shrugged, not sure of what I might say next. 'You don't hate me, do you?'

He blushed. Now I was embarrassing him. His face was so full of life. I loved him so much but I could never find the way to show it. Dave was still alive. In him. I was the one that was dead.

'Dad,' he moaned.

'Look, I know we don't talk much but there's something I have to tell you. Something you have a right to know.'

I should be the one to tell him, I thought.

'What are you talking about?'

'I'm not your father,' I blurted out. 'Not your real father.'

'What?'

His face creased with incredulity.

'Let me explain.'

'No!' he exploded. 'I don't want to hear this! I do not want to hear this!'

'David . . .'

'You bastard!' he shouted at my face, and ran up the stairs.

I went out and got into the car. I felt numb. It was done. It was all over. I tried to concentrate on the matter in hand. I was after Dave's killer again. That would keep me going when I wanted to give up altogether. As I pulled out of our close I thought there was rain falling. As I reached across to turn on the windscreen wipers I realised it was tears in my eyes.

Thursby staggered about his flat in a stained dressing gown. The drawing room was cluttered with piles of papers, scattered books, empty bottles and glasses, discarded clothes and crusted plates. Teddy backed into a side table and it crashed to the floor.

'Bugger,' he muttered, and continued to rummage around.

'Ah,' he said finally. 'Here it is. Yes. And this.'

He had gathered up a box file and a bundle of notes tied together. He brought them over, cleared the sofa of its detritus with one sweep of his hand, and we sat down together. He held up what he had recovered and offered it to me.

'I want you to have a look at this.'

'What is it?' I asked, taking it from him rather gingerly.

'It's the book me and Jules were working on,' he replied. 'My memoirs.'

'Why are you giving them to me?'

'I need someone to finish the work. It's nearly all there. It just needs writing up.'

'I'm not so sure, Teddy,' I said.

He patted the back of my hand.

'Have a look. That's all I'm asking,' he implored.

'Why me?'

Teddy coughed.

'Well, I need someone I can trust,' he said. 'To be discreet. You've always understood the importance of discretion, Tony. I admire that. And I know you've always had literary aspirations.'

'Well, I don't know about that.'

'Don't deny it. Here's your chance. I know you've always wanted to write a book. It'll be worth your while. Julian drank all the advance away but I'm sure that we can, you know, renegotiate a contract with the publishers. I only ask . . .'

He looked about the room furtively.

'I only ask that you, you know, put a little gloss on my reputation. That's all I want now. I'll be dead soon. I want to be remembered for the good things. I don't mind a bit of colour, you know, my "flamboyant" lifestyle and all that. But some things are better left unsaid. You know what I mean, don't you?'

I knew exactly what he meant. He feared the truth about his own life as much as the extinction of it. He was terrified of all his indiscretions being made public when he was dead and unable to sue for libel. An authorised biography might preserve his precious reputation. We'll see about that, I thought to myself.

And I was quite flattered to be asked. It was a chance to write a book after all. I took all the papers home with me and spent the night looking through them. There was some sort of manuscript but it was all a bit threadbare. Sparse chapter outlines. Childhood, youth at Lancing College, Oxford in the twenties, the Bright Young Things. Plenty of anecdotes about Evelyn Waugh, Harold Acton and Brian Howard. Stories of wild parties and gossip about sybaritic goings-on all dealt with in a thoroughly discreet manner. Entry into politics: member for Hartwell-juxta-Mare, the rising young star of the Tory Party. Opposition to appeasement and sticking by Churchill during his Wilderness Years highlighted. Marriage to Ruth Cholmondely-Parker in 1935. The childlessness of the union delicately commented upon, the lovelessness of it omitted. Cabinet office and the high point of his political career was rather crassly juxtaposed with the Abdication Crisis and 'war clouds looming over Europe'. Then the scandal of not declaring a business interest to the Commons was dealt with as 'a gross misunderstanding that nevertheless, for the sake of my honour and that of the government, left me with no option but to resign my post'. The subsequent 'freezing out' by Churchill, who he had stuck by earlier, was described, alluding to a sense of hurt and bitterness felt by Thursby. Postwar he becomes the flamboyant backbencher with periodic iconoclastic outpourings from the sidelines. Radio and television appearances. Newspaper columns for the *News of the World* and the *Sunday Illustrated*. The life peerage in 1964. Harsh criticism of Edward Heath's leadership and his disastrous fall from power in 1974. The victorious libel suit against *Private Eye* over allegations of connections with the gangster Harry Starks – 'the worst kind of scandal-mongering from that notorious muck-raking rag'. The last part was all glorious twilight in honourable decline. Thursby's thoughts on politics and statehood, his pious belief in High Church principles. Huge praise for Margaret Thatcher: 'at last, the Tory Party and the nation have a leader who has the courage of her convictions'. An almost fetishised thrill at her unequivocal self-belief and iron will. Last thoughts and reflections, sage-like warnings about the future.

It was an appalling exercise in self-deception. Vacuously empty, a closet without the skeleton. Of course, I could quite understand Teddy's desire to cover everything up. I almost pitied him for it. But I wanted the real story. And, by Christ, I was going to get it.

Johnny was a painter of sorts. He was into graffiti. 'Paint-bombing', he called it. He felt a calling to decorate and add text to any bare wall or empty hoarding he came across. He explained it to Mick when he was showing him some of his work on an underpass near by.

'It gives it meaning,' he said.

'What?' asked Mick.

'You know, everything.' He gestured vaguely at the bleak urban clearway. 'It's like subtitles.'

Mick looked around and smiled. Johnny was right, it was all like some foreign film. But there was only one way he could make sense of it all.

There was another sort of graffiti that Mick noticed. More elaborate, decorative. Not slogans but simple naming, using different aerosols that airbrushed depth and intricate designs around complex lettering. Multicoloured calligraphy that reminded Mick of the fairgrounds.

'That's hip-hop,' Johnny explained.

And Mick got some work through Johnny. Painting and decorating. When the foreman saw how handy Mick was with a paintbrush he offered him more work after the job was finished. Johnny just couldn't work quickly enough, but he didn't seem to mind when Mick was asked to work on a bigger contract instead of him.

He worked on a warehouse in Docklands that was being converted into loft apartments. It was cash in hand, no questions asked. Piece-work. Laying on paint. Not the elaborate decoration that he was used to doing. It was methodical, just laying it on. Blocking it out. There was something calming about it as he went to work with a roller. Covering space. Painting out everything. Making the past a blank surface.

And he found he could earn quite a lot. He worked long hours and started to save up cash. He would need this. Soon he would have enough to get what he required.

He'd get back to the squat late in the evening. It was always in a state of chaos. He spent half the night cleaning up the kitchen. The fading rota on the wall that listed names and household duties didn't look like it had been attended to for months. He added his name to it and ticked one of the boxes.

Nothing was said about whether he could stay or not so he took action himself. He cleaned out an unused room that was full of junk and redecorated it.

Peter always talked about action. He was always occupied with something or other. Meetings, demos, distributing leaflets and newspapers, holding forth about whatever issue was current. Swearing loudly at the television news. Full of a sense of injustice. But despite all of his talk of 'activism' he seemed passive. As if all his actions were a minor distraction from some big event.

'One day,' he'd mutter darkly. 'One day, we'll fucking show them.'

There was a big demonstration outside the new premises of the *Sunday Illustrated* in Docklands. Mick went along with them. It was quite close to where he worked. Peter joined a group of young men who covered their faces and busied themselves hurling missiles at the police lines. Police in riot gear retaliated, but the stone-throwers were behind the main ranks of the protesters and were able to get away. *They're just bloody hooligans, really*, Mick thought. And they'd sing that song again. The Billy Porter song. It sent a shiver down his spine.

Mick would go drinking after work. It helped him to relax after long hours painting. But he was looking for something as well. The whole of the area was being tarted up for big business, but there were still plenty of pubs around where he could find what he wanted. He was cautious. He knew from experience the look of a man that might have what he needed. Or might know someone who did. But he had to be careful in how he made his approach. Someone fencing bent gear. Or drugs. It all seemed to be drugs these days. He bought some speed off a guy in a pub on East Ferry Road because he seemed a likely prospect and he wanted to gain his trust. The speed helped him work the long shifts he'd taken on as well.

There was a meeting in the café on the corner of the square. It was squatted too. It served up cheap veggie food, a gloomy candlelit place. The meeting was about the future of the square. There was a big split between those that wanted just to be squatters and those that thought they should organise themselves into a housing co-op and apply to the Housing Corporation for funding. Peter was, of course, loudly in favour of the former view. Anything else was 'selling out'. Mick realised that all these people were against so many things. Against the state, the police, the rich. Against animal testing, whaling, nuclear weapons, pollution. Against capitalism, Thatcher, Reagan. Against racism, imperialism, fascism, sexism, heterosexism. But, above all, they were against each other. They were always squabbling among themselves. Always arguing about the best course of action but never getting around to doing anything. Mick knew what he had to do. There was no argument about it in his head. He had no choice.

In one of Peter's pamphlets he found a picture of the police file photograph of Billy Porter. The one they had used on the wanted posters. Crudely reproduced into a xeroxed icon. BILLY PORTER, read the rubric, WORKING-CLASS HERO. Mick folded it up and shoved it in his pocket.

He lay on his bed in the evening. Muttley was practising juggling in the room above. Three faded tennis balls made spasmodic ellipses around a bare-bulb sun. Mick heard a soft triple thudding on the ceiling as Muttley lost control of his little solar system. The loneliness of planets, out of orbit, falling from their spheres. It would be soon now, he thought.

29

Operation Daybreak ended in bloody mayhem. In over twenty-five years in the job I'd never seen anything quite so diabolical, and I've seen my share of fuck-ups, that's for sure. The behaviour of the Wiltshire Old Bill and whatever other mutual-aid Police Support Units waded in that day was fucking appalling. If I'd stopped to think about what I had witnessed with my own eyes in England's green and pleasant fucking land I don't know what I'd have done. But the fact was I had one thought and one thought only: I had to find the owner of that coach I had seen in the photograph.

What with the bank-holiday traffic and the roadblocks that the Wiltshire Constabulary had set up I didn't get to the Savernake Forest until nightfall. I could see the Peace Convoy campfires glowing against the brow of a hill. There were police vans everywhere. A helicopter strafed the woods with its searchlight, turning the trees into ghostly white negatives. I parked up on a lay-by and tried to get some sleep.

Just before noon the next day the convoy set off south on the A338 with dozens of reinforced police vans full of riot police in pursuit. The police helicopter clattered above. I started up the motor and gave chase. Soon enough the caravan of brightly coloured hippie vehicles and tooled-up police Transits came to a halt. I got out of my car and made my way to where the convoy was on foot, flashing my warrant card at any woodentop that tried to get in my way.

There was a police roadblock up ahead at a junction with the A303. Some of the convoy vehicles then moved on to this road to get away, only to find another roadblock farther down. It was a trap. I pushed my way through the first roadblock, warrant card held high.

'What the fuck's going on?' I asked the nearest officer.

'We got some unfinished business to deal with,' he replied with a West Country drawl.

By the time I'd passed the line of police vans leading to the convoy it had already kicked off. I heard shouting and jeering. Whole serials of officers in riot gear making low battle cries, drumming truncheons against shields. It was bloody ugly. There was something like evil in the air.

There was the sound of breaking glass as the Wiltshire Constabulary had decided that the best way to enforce High Court injunctions was to smash the windscreens of as many of the travellers' vehicles as they could get to. Riot sticks were jammed into radiators that hissed mournfully as they were broken. Scruffy-looking hippies who hardly looked like dangerous enemies of the state were being dragged out of their vehicles and bludgeoned. I saw one policeman hit a woman who had been shrilly remonstrating with him with a truncheon. As she fell to the ground I noticed she was pregnant. Fucking swedes, I thought. What the fuck do they think they're doing? But, as I said, I had only one priority on my mind at the time: to find that fucking coach.

As I got near to the front of the convoy, the first few buses and vans suddenly started up and turned off the road, crashing through a hedge and a wooden fence into an adjacent field that was planted with beans.

In the hours that followed tragedy and farce seemed inseparable. As the helicopter buzzed overhead, police vans gave chase as what remained of the convoy made circuits of the bean field. It looked absurdly comical at a distance, like some dreadful stock car race, then when it came around close again you could see the ugly maliciousness of it all. At times the convoy vehicles turned to aim themselves at the pursuing riot vans, then veered off, sowing confusion in the police ranks.

Convoy vehicles that had not been completely trashed were commandeered by the Wiltshire force and were being used as battering rams against their quarry. They had some success with this, but when they were used up there was a stalemate. All the PSU vans and riot police regrouped. This was endgame, you could feel it. The helicopter came clattering in low. Its loudspeaker made a metallic announcement:

'Those who wish to leave without trouble should drop their weapons and walk out!'

A few men and women, children and dogs slowly emerged from the battered vehicles. Then hundreds of riot police waded into what remained. It was then that I caught sight of the coach. A whole serial of riot cops boiling into it, pulling out a woman by her hair. There was an orgy of destruction as police smashed up all the vehicles that remained on the bean field. This 'counterculture' Barnes had gone on about was being beaten into submission.

The sun was coming down over the bloody aftermath. A hot summer's day nearly over, the golden hues of the early evening light illuminating what might have been a quaint rural scene. Except that it framed a grotesque tableau of chaos. A churned-up field littered with debris, the remaining travellers being frogmarched away, lines of police trooping back to their vans, visors up, some with helmets removed. A nervous buzz of post-conflict euphoria. Some were smiling, joking and laughing.

'That'll teach the fucking hedge monkeys a lesson,' I heard one officer say.

Others looked shellshocked, battle-fatigued. Wide-eyed at what they had seen, what they had done.

Over 500 arrests were made. Some of the convoy's dogs were destroyed on police orders. It was dark before I managed to track down where the woman who had been in the coach was being held. I had to pull rank and talk to the Assistant Chief Constable to get access to her. He was reluctant at first but when I told him, in confidence, what it was about he complied. Her name was Janis Green. A WPC brought her into the interview room. She looked dazed and disorientated. She had a split lip and a yellowing bruise under one eye.

'Janis?' I asked softly.

She nodded slowly.

'Do you want to sit down?'

She shrugged and scraped the chair out from under the table and slumped in it sullenly. I tried to catch her eye but she turned her head at an angle from my line of vision.

'I'm Detective Chief Superintendent Frank Taylor.'

She looked sidelong at me.

'I want to see a solicitor,' she muttered.

'Look, Janis, this isn't about what you've been charged with. I can get you released, straight away. I just need to ask a few questions.'

'I'm not saying anything until I see a solicitor.'

I sighed.

'Look, if you co-operate with me they'll drop the charges.'

'We weren't doing anything wrong.'

'Well, that's up to the courts to decide, isn't it?'

She scowled.

'Why do you hate us?' she asked.

I couldn't answer that one.

'Look, you won't have to go through any more hassle if you just answer a few questions.'

Janis shrugged.

'Lovely paintwork on your coach,' I went on, casually, like I was making polite conversation or something.

She turned and frowned, looking directly at me for the first time.

'What the fuck has that got to do with anything?'

'Just saying, your coach . . .'

'My coach? My bloody coach? It isn't just a coach, you know. It's my home. It was. You lot . . .' Her voice caught in a sob. 'You fucking destroyed it.'

She was crying now. But at least she was coming out of the shock. Now she might open up. I took out a packet of fags and offered her one. She took it in a trembling hand and I lit it for her. She wiped her battered face and took a deep drag at it.

'Who painted it?'

She looked up, puzzled.

'Was it someone called Mick?'

There was a flash of recognition in her eyes that she couldn't hide.

'What's it to you?'

'I need to find him.'

She took another sharp pull on the cigarette and looked about the room anxiously.

'Just tell me where he is and you can go.'

She chewed at her bloodied lip thoughtfully.

'I don't know,' she replied. 'He got arrested.'

'What, here?'

She shook her head.

'No, not here. A while back. At Molesworth.'

* * *

Thursby's door was opened by a fortyish queen with blond flecks in his hair and a sunbed tan. He kept the chain on, his pinched, leathery face peering out at me.

'Yes?' he hissed.

'I've come to see Teddy.'

'He's not well. Confined to bed.'

'I'm sure he'll want to see me.'

'Whom shall I say is calling?' he asked, petulantly.

I gave him my name. He let me into the hallway.

'Stay there. He's really not up to having visitors, you know.'

The queen trotted upstairs. I could hear his whining voice and Thursby's, deeper and insistent.

'Wait here,' he said when he returned, walking out into the kitchen.

He came back with a tray. There was a cup of tea on it and a bowl of what looked like gruel.

'Take that up to him.'

'What on earth is this?' I asked, taking the tray.

'Complan. He needs feeding up. Don't let him have any drink, mind. I know he's hidden a bottle somewhere. I've got to get off. I can't spend all day looking after his lordship.'

He took a coat off the peg in the hallway and put it on.

'Tell him I'll be back tomorrow,' he said as he went to the door. 'No booze, mind. Doctor's orders.'

I climbed the stairs and, balancing the tray in one hand, knocked softly on the door.

'Come,' groaned Thursby from inside.

I walked in and put the tray on his bedside table. Thursby was propped up in bed with a pile of pillows. He looked ghastly.

'Tony,' he said, with a deathly rictus of a smile. 'How kind of you to visit. I'm sorry about Derek. He can be a bit tetchy. Can't get the staff, you know.'

He picked up the tray and sniffed at it disdainfully.

'Oh, sweet Jesus, will you look at this slop.'

He put it back on the side table.

'Maybe you should eat something,' I suggested.

'No appetite, dear boy. No bloody appetite left. Tell you what I need.'

He smiled again, baring a row of discoloured teeth protruding from receding, puttylike gums.

'I need a drink.'

He breathed the word lovingly.

'Are you sure? Derek said . . .'

'Oh, never mind her,' he snapped. 'I've secreted a bottle of brandy in the cupboard under the stairs. Just for medicinal purposes, you understand. Go and get it and a couple of glasses. Then we can talk.'

I did what he said and poured both of us a large glass. Thursby took a sip.

'Ahh!' he exhaled. 'Almost makes me feel alive. So, my boy, have you looked at the work?'

'Yes,' I replied cautiously, taking a sip myself.

'And what do you think? You'll do it, won't you?'

'Well, I've looked through it all and I can't help thinking that there's something missing.'

Thursby gave a rich low chuckle. His loose and flabby jowls quivered slightly.

'Well, of course, dear boy. There have been some, shall we say, necessary omissions. But you surely understand the need for discretion.'

'Yes, but if I'm going to write all of this up I need to know the whole story. I'd like you to take me into your confidence. You can trust me.'

Thursby's yellowy eyes emitted a faint sparkle.

'Yes,' he said. 'Of course. I mean, that was the deal with Julian. I showed him everything. I need to unburden my soul, Tony. I'd like to let you know it all, I really would. You know, despite the split with Rome, the Anglican Church never got rid of the sacrament of auricular confession. But as with confession I require sanctity. Promise me that. That you'll write the book as planned. Then you can know all the rest.'

I took another mouthful of brandy and thought for a second.

'You say you showed Julian everything.'

'Oh yes.'

'What do you mean, "showed"?'

'The diaries, of course.'

'You kept diaries?'

'Oh yes. Quite comprehensive. You see, they are the source material. The arrangement with Julian was that we would use them as a basis for the book and then . . .'

Thursby shrugged and drained his glass. He let out a fumed sigh.

'And then?'

'And then we'd destroy them.'

Diaries. Teddy Thursby had kept diaries. The thought of it ran through my head as I poured him another brandy. My mind reeled at what they might contain. All that knowledge, an incomparable source of scandal. And Teddy wanted them destroyed and in their stead some tepid form of memoir as his testimony. Christ, that would be like the burning of the library at Alexandria.

Teddy was droning on about something. His rheumy eyes peered up at me. He noticed my distraction.

'Are you paying attention, Tony?' he asked.

'Sorry,' I replied with a slight shake of the head. 'What were you saying?'

'Oh,' he groaned. 'Nothing much. Just how Winston was such a cunt to me. Gave me the cold shoulder after I got into hot water over not declaring a business interest to the House. Not much of a scandal, really. I wasn't that naughty, after all. I mean, look at it now. All these fucking grammar school oiks in the lobby now, their snouts in Ian Greer's trough. Renting themselves out to Arab businessmen. It's a bloody gravy train. My meagre sins rather pale into insignificance.'

'I want the diaries, Teddy,' I suddenly blurted out.

Thursby gave a start. One of his pillows slipped and fell to the side of the bed.

'What?' he spluttered. There was a fearful look on his sallow face.

'I mean,' I went on, softening my tone, 'I want to have a look at them.'

He eyed me suspiciously. I refilled his glass and took another shot myself.

'I can trust you, Tony, can't I?'

He looked up imploringly. He was utterly helpless.

'Of course you can, Teddy. We'll work on the book together. I'll do a proper job of it. Not like Julian.'

'No,' he muttered. 'That useless little shit.'

He drained his glass and held it up for more brandy. I raised the bottle by its neck.

'We appear to have finished this one off, Teddy.'

Thursby gave a little childlike moan.

'I could go and get us another,' I suggested.

His eyes lit up.

'Oh, goody!'

'And while I'm up I could dig out those diaries of yours. Just to have a little look at them. You know, size up the weight of the material we'll be working from.'

He nodded. I took the keys to the flat and went out into the night to find the nearest off-licence. I was quite drunk and glad of the evening air to clear my head of the fetid atmosphere of Thursby's room. I went through it in my mind: how to gain access to his journals. I could contrive to become his literary executor, gain possession of them that way. Then, when he croaked, they'd be mine. There would be all sorts of procedures, paperwork and such. It all seemed unduly complicated. There must be an easier way.

I came back with the brandy rolled up in paper. Teddy raised himself from semi-slumber as I entered. I unwrapped the bottle and held it up like a trophy. Thursby's sunken face beamed into half-life.

'Let's have another snifter,' he wheezed. 'Just a tincture.'

He held up his glass expectantly.

'Uh-uh,' I teased playfully. 'First things first.'

'Oh yes,' he groaned, his visage sunken once more. 'Well, if we must. But remember our agreement.'

'Of course,' I said, filling both our glasses and holding mine up for a toast. 'To the great work,' I proposed, and we clinked receptacles.

'They're in a tin box under the bed,' he instructed.

I put my glass on the side table and crouched down to rummage underneath him. It was filthy down there – scraps of old newspaper and soiled crockery. My hands found the box and I slid it out. I tried the lid. It was jammed.

'I can't open it,' I said tetchily.

'Well, it's locked, of course,' he replied indignantly. 'I'll get the key.'

He fumbled in the side table drawer and handed it over. I turned the lock and opened the treasure chest. There was a pile of bound books inside.

'They're all here?'

'Well . . .' He shrugged. 'A few entries here and there might be missing. Some of the more *outré* stuff that I've already been through with Julian. You know what he was like. Always sniffing around for filth.'

'Well, there's plenty left to be going on with. It'll be quite a job.'

'Oh yes,' he said. 'But let's leave it for now.'

'Of course,' I said, slamming the metal box shut and relocking it. I put the key on the bedside table. 'Another drink?'

'Rather.'

I was getting drunker. I felt a familiar darkness descend on my mind. Teddy was holding forth again. Giving his opinions on the current state of things.

'Ah!' he breathed. I caught a whiff of alcohol and decay. 'The blessed Margaret. She's got a stomach for a fight. Took the fucking miners on and saw them off. Not like the blasted Heath. He was fucking useless. Never had the nerve. She showed them. A real leader.'

I stood above him, looking down at his atrophied form. I could so easily put him out of his misery. He was dying for it anyway. What had he said? *At seventy-five euthanasia should be voluntary, at eighty-five it should be compulsory*. Compulsory. Dying for it. The blackness was beginning to take hold.

'That it had to be' – he sniffed with apparent distaste – 'a woman.'

I looked at the folds of skin in his neck which shuddered like a wattle as he spoke. Revulsion sobered me. Compulsion was tempered by a sense of necessity. I didn't want to touch that rotting flesh, the rank corruption of it. I would take little pleasure in dispatching him. It would not be like the other times. I was in control now, I would be taking a life again but this time I had a logical motive.

'But what a woman, eh? What did that Frenchman say? The mouth of Monroe, the eyes of Caligula, what? Heh, heh.'

He grinned, baring his yellow teeth. I picked up the pillow that had slipped to the side of the bed and plumped it up. He caught my intent stare.

'What?' he said with a mirthless smile.

'Let me make you comfortable,' I suggested.

'No,' he managed to utter.

But I move quickly. *Yes.* I smothered him with the soiled pillow. *Yes.* I held it hard against his face. He put up a bit of a struggle. His left arm reached out blindly to the key on the table and it tinkled to the floor, but he gave in to the dreadful softness of the pillow. Taking a life. I'd got away with it before. This time I was clear-headed about the whole thing. It wasn't even revenge. Well, maybe a bit. But I was doing him a favour, after all. The hand went limp with the rest of him. I released the pressure and there was an awful groan of expiration.

I retrieved the key and claimed what was mine. His diaries. I was taking a life, all right.

Mick worked three days and nights on the trot. The speed kept him going, though he managed to grab a couple of hours' kip here and there. And there was a shower in one of the completed flats that he could use. The gaffer didn't mind. The quicker the work got done the better it was for him. And Mick was a good worker. Didn't say much, mind. But, boy, was he a grafter. He obviously really needed the cash.

Work, work, work. It had been a means in itself for so long. It had fed the restlessness. As the travelling had done all those years. On the run. Now it was a means to an end. A higher purpose. The End. Billy Porter is our friend.

He came back to the squat at the weekend. His heart sank as he wandered into the kitchen. It was a bloody mess as usual. He went to his room and dumped his bag on the bed. He took out something wrapped up in cloth and hid it under a loose floorboard.

Peter, Johnny and Muttley were all sat around the television in the front room. There was a row of beer cans on the wooden pallet on the floor that they used as a coffee table. Mick wanted to say something about the state of the house but they all seemed so intent on the screen. Engrossed in the images that flickered with blue light from the telly.

'Fucking bastards!' Peter was commenting loudly. 'Fucking fascist pigs!'

It was the evening news, and a droning voiceover was accompanied by images of riot police moving in on a line of brightly coloured vans and buses parked by a field.

'Mick,' Johnny called to him as he noticed him enter, 'come and have a look at this. It's your lot, isn't it?'

Mick sat on the edge of the sagging sofa and peered into the television. He couldn't work out at first what he was looking at, then, slowly, it began to take shape. He recognised some of the vehicles. It was the convoy.

'The pigs are on the fucking rampage,' said Peter. 'Just because they wanted to get to Stonehenge. It's a fucking fascist state.'

It all looked so unreal. Mick thought he could see Janis amidst the confusion. But he couldn't be sure. He felt he might be imagining the whole thing.

'Fucking hell, mate,' said Muttley, patting him on the arm.

They all seemed to be looking at him. Like they expected some comment from him. Like he was supposed to say something to contribute to the endless complaining that went on. But he wasn't going to say anything. He wouldn't waste his breath. He was going to do something.

He suddenly felt a wave of confusing feelings wash over him. Guilt about Janis. Relief that he had avoided her fate. A sense of purpose seemed to emerge from the madness of it all. Of things falling. Falling into place.

On the screen they could see the windscreen of a truck being smashed by police truncheons. There was something apocalyptic about it. Something that made Mick feel all the more certain of what he was to do.

'That is fucking outrageous!' Peter shouted.

They had no bloody idea. They would sit around all day and moan on and on. They would never do anything. They were lazy. Peter was always going on about the working classes but he seemed not to have done a day's work in his life. They all signed on. Did a few silly little scams that they thought were so clever. Housing benefit fraud. A bit of shoplifting. Turned the electricity meter upside down to fiddle it. Gas-meter bandits. Less than that. They thought they were Enemies of the State. They couldn't even keep the house tidy.

They were useless. It was up to him. He would have to end it all. Bring things to some sort of conclusion. Not wait for some imagined day of reckoning.

He got up and started to walk silently from the room. Johnny looked up at him.

'Are you all right, Mick?'

He stopped for a second and nodded.

'Yeah,' he said. 'I'm all right.'

He was all right. Everything was going to be all right. He'd got what he needed. After weeks of searching around dodgy pubs he'd found it and had earned enough cash to get it. He would make sense of it all at last.

30

I wasn't officially part of the operational team that was to go in that morning but I wanted to be there. I had to be there. By rights it should have been my arrest. I'd done all the work. Gone and checked with Cambridgeshire. They still had Mick's fingerprints.

'We really should have destroyed these,' the swede arresting officer had said.

Thank Christ they hadn't. They also still had a record of the address of the guy he'd been released with. I'd done a match with the dabs. It was him, for fuck's sake. Him. And he was mine.

Or should have been. Of course, it all had to go by the book. Procedure. The Flying Squad team assigned to it knew me and could hardly refuse me tagging along. I could identify the suspect, after all. And I could pull rank.

The address was in this whole block of squats. Weird rows of houses like some sort of hippy township. We were plotted up for an early morning dig-out. Two Flying Squad cars, one at the front and one covering the back, and a C11 surveillance vehicle. Those in the team with pink cards had drawn firearms, but there was an Armed Response Unit on call as well in an unmarked van. A gunship, they called it. D11, all tooled up and raring to go. Most of them veterans of the Spaghetti House or Balcombe Street. Some of them ex-SPG. I hoped it wouldn't come to that. I wanted him taken quietly and cleanly.

The telephone jolted me into consciousness like an electric shock. I'd slept soundly that night. I'd come home in the early hours and hidden my booty and then gone to bed and dropped off easily, calm in the knowledge of what I had done for once. The bell rang again.

I kept a bowl of water and a flannel by my bed. It was an old trick I'd learned when I'd been a reporter. That way you could wipe your face and clear your head before you picked up the receiver. So no matter how sleepy or drunk or hung over you were you wouldn't make the mistake of having a semiconscious conversation and missing out on some crucial bit of information. It had been quite a while since I'd worked on the paper and might be expecting a call in the middle of the night, but old habits die hard. And I was glad of it. This might be important. I might well have to get my story straight first time. I let the phone ring a couple more times and pressed the cold flannel against my face. The night's brandy had taken its toll but my mind was shaping up. I imagined, of course, that Teddy's body might already have been discovered. So I went through my alibi. It was very simple. Yes, I had been there, I'd left at eleven (this gave me enough leeway with the time of death). No, he didn't look too good but he had a friend coming around the next morning. It would look like natural causes anyway, but one cannot be too sure. I took a breath and picked up the receiver.

'Yes?'

'Tony?'

'Yes?'

'It's Kevin.'

Kevin had been my junior on the crime desk years ago. He was now a senior correspondent on the *Illustrated*. For a second I thought that the press might already have heard about Thursby's death. But it was something else. He had got a tip-off on another story and he wanted my help. I looked at the clock. It was five-thirty. I sighed and dabbed my forehead with the damp cloth.

'All right,' I said.

He gave me an address and I agreed to meet him there in an hour.

He went to the bathroom and shaved off his beard. He swept back his hair from his face. He used some hair gel he found to comb it into the style he had had all those years ago. He looked into the cracked and stained mirror. He was himself again. He was ready now.

He went to his room and lifted the loose floorboard in his bedroom. He carefully took out the wrapped object. He slowly unwound the oil-stained cloth. He rotated the cylinder of the revolver slowly. It clicked gently, satisfying. It was good to have a gun in his hands again. It had been such a long time.

All those years ago on that crisp winter morning when he'd left his wagon to go for a stroll. He'd come back to find Mick holding up the pistol accusingly. He hadn't meant to kill Mick. It was an accident. But he had meant to kill Joe. With Mick gone he could become him. Take his identity, use his driving licence. Joe was just someone he'd hastily put together. So he got rid of him.

Being Mick was risky. He'd had to avoid the fairground circuit and anyone who might have known him. But the hippy travellers were a different world and they were easily taken in by him.

He felt a sudden grief for Mick now that he was finally dead. It had been a good disguise to become the man he had killed. Now Mick was gone for ever. Joe was gone. He was Billy again.

The grief surged through him. Friend. Mick had been his friend. But Billy Porter is our friend. Their friend. He pulled out the cylinder and loaded the gun. This was his friend. His only friend. He felt the weight of it in his hand. He looked down the barrel. The sun was coming up. He was ready.

He went into the upstairs front room and, parting a badly tacked-up curtain, looked out of the window. There was a car in the square. They had come at last. He shoved the revolver into his waistband and went to Peter's room.

Peter felt someone tapping the end of his bed. *What the fuck?* he thought. He blinked out from under the covers. A thin beam of light chinked into the room. Dust motes danced in its pale stream. Someone was in his room.

'Who's that?' he murmured.

'It's me,' came the reply.

Mick, he thought. Mad Mick, as they'd begun to call him behind his back. What the fuck did he want?

'What is it?'

'Come on.' The voice was urgent. 'Get up.'

'What?'

'House meeting.'

'For fuck's sake.'

The curtain was being drawn open. The low dawn light fingered the room. Peter rubbed his face. Mick looked different. Beard gone and hair slicked back. A manic look on his face.

'Come on. They're coming.'

'Mick . . .'

The new face stared down at him.

'I ain't Mick,' it said, and moved in close to his. 'Don't you recognise me?'

'Stop fucking about.'

'Come on. I'm your friend.'

The new face broke into a grin and gave a low chuckle.

'Mick!' Peter shouted. 'You fucking loony!'

'I told you,' the face insisted sternly. 'I ain't Mick.'

Peter felt a quiver of fear at the eyes that stared down at him.

'Who . . .' he stammered. 'Who are you?'

The face laughed again.

'Oh, you know who I am. I'm your friend.'

There had always been something familiar about him. Something he could never quite place. There had always been something different about him. He wasn't just some ageing crustie. What was it? He who had been Mick fumbled in his pocket and pulled out a piece of paper.

'This,' he said. 'Might jog your memory.'

He unfolded it and handed it to him. Peter squinted at it in the gloom of the morning. It was a picture of Billy Porter. WORKING-CLASS HERO. He looked up at the face. Fuck, he thought. Twenty years of ageing but the features were undeniable. It was Billy Porter. He was Billy Porter.

'Jesus,' he muttered.

'Yeah.' Billy nodded. 'Something like that.'

Peter sat up in bed breathing hard. Billy had got something else from his pockets. A gun. He held it up in front of Peter's face.

'Now come on,' he said. 'Get your clothes on. I've got something to show you.'

Peter tried to wrap himself up in his bedclothes and hide but Billy was pointing the revolver at him now.

'Come on,' Billy said. 'Up we come.'

He pulled on his jeans and put on a T-shirt. Billy nodded towards the door and Peter followed him out to the front room. Billy beckoned him to the the window.

'Look,' Billy whispered harshly, holding up the pistol to the vertical, cocking its hammer.

Peter looked out and saw two groups of men getting out of cars and making their way towards the house.

I watched as they made for the door. I was supposed to stay in the car but I couldn't resist getting out to get a better look. This should have been my arrest, for Christ's sake. I closed the door behind me and started to walk up to the house myself.

Suddenly a shot rang out and everyone dived for cover as it ricocheted, a report echoing around the square. Crouched figures started to scuttle away from the house. I kept moving forward. I didn't give a fuck for my own safety. I wanted to be in on it.

Kevin's tip-off had been that the police now knew the whereabouts of Billy Porter and an arrest was about to be made. It was a real coup for Kevin, something he could sell freelance as well as run for the *Illustrated*. The thing was he didn't have time to research all of the back story and he knew that I was the best source of knowledge for that.

I met him on the corner of this square in Vauxhall. He had a photographer with him. Not like the snatch men of old. These guys had huge lenses on their cameras. Like rocket launchers. They could get a clear picture from miles away.

We watched as a group of plainclothes officers approached the house. The photographer was firing away and moving about to get the best angle. I had a horrible empty-stomached hangover. But I was glad to be there. There was a sort of bleary-eyed sense to it. This could be the end of the whole affair. We heard the shot and the confusion that followed.

'Did you get that? Did you get that?' Kevin was panting at the photographer as we all crouched for cover instinctively.

There was a hiatus as the explosion receded. A brief silence and calm, as if the bullet had sucked everything into a vacuum for a moment. Then someone in the house started singing.

Peter stared at the shattered glass of the window through the thin blue haze of smoke from the discharged revolver. He gave a short nervous giggle.

'Fucking hell.'

'This is now,' Billy announced. 'No more waiting.'

'Steady on.'

'This is happening now.' He held up the gun. 'This is this.'

'Take it easy, Mick.'

'The name ain't Mick, is it?'

'No, I mean . . .'

'It's Billy. Billy what?'

'Billy Porter.'

'And what is Billy Porter?'

'Sorry?'

'I said what is Billy Porter?'

Billy was almost shouting.

'What?'

'You know,' he insisted, cocking the hammer of the gun and holding it against Peter's head.

'I don't. Oh, please, I'm sorry. I don't know.'

'You know,' Billy repeated, in a soft voice now.

'Please.'

'The song. You know the song, don't you? Sing it.'

'Billy Porter,' Peter croaked.

'That's it.'

'Is our friend.'

'Go on.'

'Is our friend, is our friend.'

'Louder. Come on, sing out, boy.'

Johnny slept through the whole thing. Muttley heard the commotion and scrambled out of bed. He pulled on a pair of trousers and went down to the front door.

The D11 gunship started up and moved towards the house. Immediate Action Drill. The three-man team checked their weapons as the van screeched to a halt. Flak-jacketed, bristling with equipment, they bundled out and took positions for rapid entry. It was their operation now. The suits had fucked up badly. It was up to them to finish it.

Muttley stumbled out of the front door and found himself surrounded by crouching uniformed figures, their weapons aimed at him.

'On the floor! Now!' they shouted at him.

He hit the deck.

* * *

I was up close to the house now. The D11 team were standing over a prone figure. The door to the house was swinging open. I rushed inside. I could hear the singing coming from the upstairs front room. I tiptoed up the stairs.

'Come on!' came another voice. 'Come and get me, you fuckers!'

It suddenly came to me that this was what he wanted. It was a very public suicide attempt. But I wasn't going to let him have that. Those trigger-happy bastards from D11 would be only too ready to oblige. Christ, we'd got tooled up over the years. Porter himself had been part of that. I'd seen it all. And I was tired of it. Tired. It struck me then that maybe I wanted it all over for myself too. All over. Jeannie, the only woman I'd ever loved. David – I owed him for his father. My best mate. My buck. I wasn't even armed. But I was ready. I felt an exhilarating sense of recklessness.

I walked into the room. There was a spiky-haired boy on his hands and knees. Billy Porter stood over him with a pistol against his temple. He looked up as I entered. His eyes glared at me.

'Hello, Billy,' I said.

I felt calm. Prepared.

'Get back!' he spat out at me. 'Get back or I'll kill this fucker.'

'Please,' groaned the boy.

He wasn't singing any more.

'Why don't you kill me, Billy? Like you killed the others. Like you killed Dave.'

'I'm warning you. Stay back.'

'What's the matter, Billy? Lost your bottle?'

Now. I never felt so alive. So close to death. Everything had led up to this moment. This was now. It all suddenly fell into place. Made sense. Another breath and it would all be over. I put my palms up and edged forward.

'Come on, Billy,' I said. 'It's over.'

'It ain't over. It ain't fucking over.'

There was an awful pain in his eyes. A pain I shared. All the years falling away. We'd both had enough.

'Come on, Billy. Let's go home, eh?'

He closed his eyes for a second and nodded. He brought up the pistol and aimed it at my face. I closed my eyes and waited for the shot. Someone was thundering up the stairs behind me. I felt a blow against my back as someone pushed past me. There was a shot. I thought: this is it. This is the end. As I recovered my balance I saw Billy Porter hurled to the floor by the force of a bullet from the gun of one of the D11 officers who had stormed into the room. He was standing over Porter now. The boy was snivelling at his feet, his nose against his boots. Sobbing in gratitude.

'It's all right, son,' he said, patting the spiky head. 'It's all right.'

The photographer got some good shots of the body-bag being carried out of the squat. Kevin was really animated. He'd got a good story. That's what it was all about. I knew the excitement of that, to be there on the scene and to have something really explosive to file. Front-page stuff. And I'd be able to help him with the background to the whole case. I'd seen it all through. It was Kevin's story, but it was my book. I could do it now. I had all the material. I had the End. It wouldn't take long and it could be rushed into print while the public interest in it was still fresh.

A killer brought to book. All the details pieced together for consumption. And the moral of it all? Well, there didn't seem any moral certainties left. Porter's story hardly had the power to shock any more. Later that year a policeman was hacked to death in a riot on a Tottenham housing estate. Violence escalating, police tactics becoming more brutal. Society seemed in a war of attrition with itself.

As for Thursby's diaries, well, they were another matter. I had to be careful with them; after all, I wasn't exactly their legitimate owner. But they were mine by right of possession and I would guard them jealously. They were a source, a word-hoard of scandal and gossip that I would be able to draw from. I had taken a life, admissions and revelations that could eclipse my own desire for confession. My own misdeeds hidden for ever. The writer, telling all, revealing nothing. I had the power of revenge for all those years of fruitless muck-raking. All the details, the reputations laid bare, the secrets I could use. And I would use them. I wasn't sure how yet. But I would think of something.

JAKE ARNOTT

truecrime

1

ghost writers in the sky

In Newspeak, euphony outweighed every consideration other than exactitude of meaning. Regularity of grammar was always sacrificed to it when it seemed necessary. And rightly so, since what was required, above all for political purposes, were short clipped words of unmistakable meaning which could be uttered rapidly and which roused the minimum of echoes in the speaker's mind. The words of the B vocabulary even gained force from the fact that nearly all these words – goodthink, Minipax, prolefeed, sexcrime, Ingsoc, bellyfeel, thinkpol *and countless others – were words of two or three syllables, with the stress on the first syllable and the last.*

George Orwell, *Nineteen Eighty-Four*,
Appendix: *Principles of Newspeak*

Transcript of taped conversation between Tony Meehan and Eddie Doyle

5/3/95

TM: You OK to start?

ED: Yeah, sure. But look, I do want to talk about how this whole thing is going.

TM: Fine. But let's try and get some ground covered first.

ED: It's just that I'm, well, I'm not happy about some of it, you know?

TM: I understand. It's a difficult process. But if we can just get something on tape.

ED: OK. Yeah. Well, where do you want to start?

TM: I thought we could talk about the Hounslow bullion job. If that's OK.

ED: That (laughs). Right, well, there's some things I can't talk about, you know that, don't you?

TM: I know.

ED: Never saw a penny of my cut. Twelve fucking years. Kept my mouth shut and all. For what?

TM: Let's talk about the events on the day.

ED: That fucking security guard we had on the inside. First whiff of trouble and his arse drops out. Fucking joke. Sorry, you want to talk about the day?

TM: If we can.

ED: Well, let me tell you something about that day. We had no fucking idea what we'd got. How fucking big it was. Maybe if we'd just got what we'd been going for in the first place, if we'd just got the money, well, maybe it wouldn't have turned out so bad.

TM: How do you mean?

ED: Well, it was cursed, you know. That gold. Opening up that vault was like opening up the tomb of Tutankhamun or something. It cursed us, that gold.

TM: You know, that's not a bad angle for the story.

ED: And I'll tell you something else. You know all those films when they open the vault and there's all the gold bars all neatly stacked up and gleaming like fuck? Well, it wasn't like that.

TM: No?

ED: No. They were all in these cardboard boxes with metal tapes around them. Like fucking shoeboxes. We wouldn't have noticed them if we hadn't had trouble getting the safe open. We were going after the money, you see. If only we'd got that safe open. The money, that would have been easy. Used notes, unmarked. Just divvy it up after the job. Instead we end up with all that fucking gold. And that's when the grief started.

TM: What happened with the safe?

ED: Well, we had trouble getting the combinations out of the guards. They were shitting themselves but maybe we'd put the frighteners on them a little too much. They couldn't concentrate, could they?

TM: Well, you had doused their private parts with petrol and threatened to set light to them.

ED: Yeah, well. Hang on.

TM: I'm only going by the trial report.

ED: Yeah, well, let's talk about this.

TM: Yes, let's.

ED: Let me tell you about the petrol. It was watered down. It wouldn't have ignited if you'd put a match to it. There was enough of a smell to make them think that. But that was the point. To scare them into giving us the combinations.

TM: I see.

ED: But this is where it all goes wrong. You know?

TM: I'm not sure I do.

ED: I mean the way you're telling my story. It's like

you're always dwelling on anything nasty and brutal. Like I'm some sort of a thug.

TM: I can assure you I'm not trying to do that, Eddie.

ED: And some of the stuff I've seen. It makes me sound, well, inarticulate. You're supposed to be a writer, for fuck's sake. It all comes across as really trashy, you know?

TM: Well, the public do go for a brusque style.

ED: Fuck the public. I want my story told properly.

TM: We both do, Eddie. Look, it's early days. Once we're at the editing stage we can go through all this. But we really do need to get it all down first.

ED: It's like all you're interested in is the violence and the scandal.

TM: Well, that is what's going to sell copies, you know.

ED: And all the Ruby Ryder stuff.

TM We did talk about that.

ED: Well, I don't know, Tony. I don't know.

TM: It is a crucial selling point of your story. You were married to her, after all.

ED: But she's trying to get her career going again. I know she won't be happy having the past dragged up again.

TM: Look, can we try and get back to the story? We can go over this later.

ED: No. I want to sort this out now.

TM: Eddie . . .

ED: Turn the tape off.

TM: We are behind schedule, you know.

ED: I said turn the fucking tape off . . .

Tape ends

'There.' I pressed the stop button. Eddie looked liked he was about to grab the tape machine. 'It's off.'

'Right.'

Eddie sits back in his chair, folds his arms and gives me that well-practised glare of his. A look I've seen on countless villains and old lags.

'So.' I sigh, trying to soothe the situation. 'Let's talk, then, shall we?'

'Yeah,' he replies with a grudging shrug.

And I knew I was in for another difficult session. But I had to try to get him to talk. Because, well, this is not my story. I'm the 'as told to' or the 'with'.

I'm the ghost. The ghost writer.

Once, when drunk at some dreadful book launch trapped in that soul-destroying 'and what do you do?' small talk, I slurred my nomenclature as 'ghost rider' rather than 'ghost writer'. It conjured up that old country and western song 'Ghostriders in the Sky' where howling echo-chamber cowboys are doomed to chase a spectral herd across the firmament.

Yippy-ay-oh, yippy-ay-eh.

Ghost writers in the sky.

Doomed is right, like the Flying Dutchman or the Ancient fucking Mariner. Tony Meehan, twenty years crime journalist for the *Sunday Illustrated*, erstwhile editor of *Murder Monthly*, author of *Cop Killer: The Billy Porter Story* (remaindered after one edition), I am condemned to ghost-write sickening boastful memoirs of retired villains for the Groombridge Press. And having hacked away my meagre writing talents down the decades, to indulge in childish word games and perverse etymologies.

Though Eddie Doyle seems quite capable of unnecessary semantics himself.

'Thing is,' he says, 'you're supposed to be my ghost writer but I'm the one that feels like a ghost. It just doesn't seem real.'

Christ, a professional criminal getting all existential on me. That's all I bloody need.

'Well,' I reply, 'we just need to get the tone right.'

Get the tone right. Well, we know what that means: lower it. True Crime, what a racket it is. I prefer to rearticulate this term into a lower case composite: *truecrime*. Like George Orwell's newspeak words *thoughtcrime* or *sexcrime*, the coining of the term *truecrime* came to me from that ancient Stalinist logic – the manipulation of vocabulary to ensure correct thought. But this newspeak is imposed not by a totalitarian state but by my publishing dictatorship, the Groombridge Press. True and Crime, words that were once at odds with each other as much as alibi and detection, now conspire to create trashy bestsellers. Another newspeak conjunction, *prolefeed*, comes to mind, but these days, with the decline of the proletariat, it strikes me that, rather than feeding the proles, we are now serving them up for suburban consumption. Fetishised masculinity, the stories of hard men to provide vicarious thrills for the boring lives of white-collar strap-hangers. 'Get the tone right,' that's what Victor Groombridge, my boss, insists is my job as ghost writer. 'Make it sound authentic.' That is to say: make this intelligent, emotionally complex, deviously manipulative, professional villain sound like an engaging thug, a curious monster.

'Yeah, but it's my story,' he almost pleads with me.

'Of course it is,' I say, nodding hopefully.

I mean, Eddie Doyle seemed an easy enough prospect when Victor Groombridge signed him up and passed him over to me for the treatment. Jewel thief, bank robber, known associate of most of the major gangland faces. Got sent down in 1983 for the Hounslow bullion job – twelve years served and he never divulged where all that fifteen or so million went missing. But one of the biggest hooks for his story was that he was Ruby Ryder's husband in the sixties and seventies. Ryder's career has seen more downs than ups but at the moment her kitsch has attained a kind of cult status. Rumour has it that she is in the frame for a major part in a TV soap opera. So, it's all there: gangland iconography, showbiz gossip, heist stories, the lot.

But the problem is Eddie. He has his own ideas, far too many of them. He's been away too long. Years of emptiness filled with nonsense, courtesy of some half-baked liberal prison education scheme. He is far too well read. And he is painfully aware of not being the author of his own memoirs. He's not happy being put through the mill. With most of the villains I've done, they're only too glad to let you do all the work. They're happy to just cough it all up on to the tape recorder and let you hack it out. When the book comes out they're so pleased to see their name on the cover with some suitably menacing picture that they imagine somehow they've written it. A good ghost will never disabuse them of this. It's always their book. You just content yourself with a split in the royalties and everybody's happy and they don't realise about the money until after it's all been sewn up. They don't realise how they've been stitched up until after the game's over. They imagine publishing to be some gentlemanly practice, not realising that they're up against the most heinous form of organised crime, of organised lying, until it's far too late. But even here, Eddie is questioning.

'And what about this advance?' he asks.

'What about it?'

'Well, I've not seen much of it.'

'I told you.'

'You told me twenty grand. I've only seen two and a half thousand.'

'I told you, we don't get it all at once. A quarter on signing. A quarter on delivery. A quarter on hardback. A quarter on paperback.'

The familiar litany, the vagaries of the racket.

'Christ,' seethes Eddie. 'And I thought that I was fucked over by gangsters. But a quarter, that means I'm due five grand on signing, not two fifty.'

'I told you, it's a fifty-fifty split.'

'Jesus. You lot are good. You're fucking lairy.'

'So look, Eddie. Going back to the bullion job. You say the gold was cursed. What do you mean by that?'

'I mean that we weren't up to dealing with it. We were just a team of blaggers. Good ones, mind, South-East London's finest, but blaggers nonetheless. We were after a substantial haul of used notes with no problems. But that gold, I mean, we couldn't believe our luck when we realised what we were sitting on, and we were right, it was luck all right, bloody bad luck. It meant we had to find a way of getting rid of it. And you know what that means, don't you?'

'You tell me.'

'It meant approaching certain people. People who could fence that kind of amount. And that's when the trouble really started. There was so much more at stake than we'd bargained for. Pretty soon all that lovely gold had more than a bit of blood on it.'

'You want to talk about that?'

'Hm. Probably not a good idea, you know.'

'The tape's not running.'

'Look, Tony, I did twelve years and kept my mouth. I'm not going to start yakking now, am I?'

'Well, you wouldn't have to name names.'

'Just tell the story?'

'It sounds like a good one.'

And it did have a ring to it. An archetypal narrative, wealth corrupting those who find it, death coming in the form of gold. Like the Pardoner's Tale.

'Look, I'm serious,' Eddie insists, becoming more agitated. 'I don't want a bullet in the back of my head, you know.'

'Don't worry,' I try to placate him.

'Don't worry?' he cuts in. 'Let me show you something.'

He leads me furtively to a window, standing to one side of it and peering down at the street below. He cocks his head.

'See that parked car – don't get any closer to the window – see it?'

'Yeah.'

'Don't lean forward like that. Come over here. See? That bloke. See him?'

'I'm not sure.'

I try to get a proper look but Eddie pulls me back.

'Don't. Oh, for fuck's sake. Come on, get away from the window.'

'Do you mean to say you're being followed?' I ask him as we sit back down again.

Eddie nods. An intent look on his face. Paranoia, probably.

'Who do you think it is?'

'Don't know. Now that I'm out it could be that certain people are getting a bit jumpy. Might think that I want my money.'

'And do you?'

'What?'

'Want your money.'

Eddie smiles.

'Well, what do you think? But I don't want to get myself killed. I was hoping that I could make some gelt from this racket, you know, selling my story. But I kind of figured that I might get a bit more up front, though. I mean, two and a half grand? Maybe I should stick to what I'm really good at.'

'Well . . .'

Eddie gives a dry laugh.

'Don't worry, Tony, I'm fucking redundant. No one robs banks any more. It's all drugs now. The Hounslow job, well, that was supposed to be my pension. My final coup. And it was all taken away from me.'

'So how are we going to tell the bullion job story?' I ask him.

Eddie sighs.

'Up to when I went away, I guess. I kept my mouth but others didn't. That stupid fucking security guard, our bloody inside man, he starts to bottle it, doesn't he? As soon as he gets a tug he starts coughing.'

'Can I put the tape recorder back on?'

'Yeah, but I ain't saying anything about where the gold went. And I want it told intelligently, not like we were just a bunch of thugs.'

After the session, as I'm coming out of Eddie's flat, I go past the car that he pointed out to me. There's no one in it. Eddie's probably imagining things. It's hard adjusting to the outside world after such a long stretch. But I have a quick scan around. No. Nobody's following me. Some chance.

Ghost life. Make my way back home. *Yippy-ay-oh, yippy-ay-eh*. Nobody knows. I've managed to control myself all these years. I got away with it all.

Get an *Evening Standard* by the Underground. The headline is: *GANGLAND KILLER RONNIE KRAY DIES A PRISONER*. The first paragraph heads, *Notorious gangland killer Ronnie Kray died today in hospital, two days after collapsing in his ward at Broadmoor. Police said 61-year-old Ronnie – the madder and badder of the feared Kray Twins – died at 9.07 a.m.* . . . The Beast is dead, that'll be good for business. I bet Victor is already buying somebody up, some crony or associate to squeeze another drop out of the tired old Kray legend.

Back at the flat I check the tape and go through my existing notes on Eddie Doyle. Somebody else's life. Try to muster some enthusiasm for this book. I like the cursed-treasure angle, something allegorical about that. Victor will, however, want it all done to the *truecrime* formula.

truecrime is a beast with two backs. It has two main forms. There are the nasty murderers, the rippers, the sex killers, the mass murderers: *sexcrime*, if you like. Then there are the gangsters, the villains, the Kray associates. All hoarded together in that furtive corner of the bookshop, a section that is expanding: *truecrime* is booming. Victor Groombridge has done very well out of it. Though this book with Eddie is way behind schedule and he isn't happy with me. I've got lunch with him tomorrow.

I'm not that interested in villains' memoirs but I made a conscious decision to work in that field rather than explore the awful killers. Conscious – well, if you knew my proclivities you'd understand why it seemed safer to be employed in this way. Too much of a temptation for me to indulge myself in the *sexcrime* branch of *truecrime*. I have gone straight, as it were.

I haven't killed anyone for almost ten years. But I thought it best to avoid anything that might arouse my dormant desires.

Besides, that end of the field has the danger of becoming respectable. Gordon Burn, Brian Masters, Gita Sereny. It's this modern thing about psychology. I blame Colin Wilson, this existential obsession with the self. I used to believe in all of that, of course. But that was before I became a killer myself.

Everybody now is obsessed with the 'serial killer'. In my day it was more blunt: mass murderers, that's what we called them. But in the eighties the FBI Behavioral Science Unit asserted a new *truecrime* paradigm. Psychological profiling, offender signatures, victimology. But this new 'science' has a whiff of pulp fiction about it. Robert Ressler, the FBI profiler, claims that he was inspired to coin the term 'serial killer' out of a sense of cheap drama. 'Now that I look back on that naming event,' he is quoted as saying, 'I think that what was also in my mind were the serial adventures we used to see on Saturday at the movies.' The dissatisfaction of the cliff-hanger ending that increases rather than lessens the tension. It's certainly what kept the readership of *Murder Monthly* going. And this new pop psychology approach has an inspiration all of its own. In 1993 a rather dreary psychopath called Colin Ireland picked up masochistic homosexuals at the Colherne leather bar in Earls Court, took them back to their flats and strangled them. JACK THE GRIPPER, the *News of the World* called him. *The Sunday Illustrated* went one better: THE FAIRY LIQUIDATOR. Sid Franks, the news editor in my day, he would have loved that one. I was intrigued, for a while, since his modus operandi seemed so familiar. So similar to the circumstances of that time I throttled a homo back in 1966.

It turned out that the Fairy Liquidator was actually inspired by Ressler's book on serial killers and indeed, along with a useful forensic awareness he had acquired in the execution of his crimes, his very aspiration was simply to join the hallowed ranks himself. Once he had gone past the required score of victims he was ready to retire. 'I have read a lot of books on serial killers,' he declared in a phone call to the police. 'I think it is from four people that the FBI class as serial, so I may stop now I have done five.' Tabloid celebrity secured, he had realised himself, with the help of all that wisdom from *truecrime*. Self-help for serial killers.

But I have been able to control myself. I was never one for getting carried away, after all. And nothing can be traced to me. My crimes are all cold cases now. Indeed, that is what I have become: a cold case. I'm as dead as they are. All my sins remembered but nothing much left inside. I have no desires left to enact except to watch and record. And I console myself with this fact: I am not a serial killer. Neither in inclination nor statistics. Remember, I only killed three. That queen in Earls Court, the whore in Shepherd Market. And Teddy Thursby. And of course the 'victimology' of Lord Thursby of Hartwell-juxta-Mare doesn't really count on the profile. I got no pleasure wringing his flabby neck. Christ, no. No *sexcrime* there. No, the FBI *Crime Classification Manual* clearly defines my opportunistic strangling of Teddy Thursby as: *108.02 Situational Felony Murder. Property crime (robbery, burglary) is the primary motivation for felony murder, with murder the secondary motivation.* I killed him for his diaries. For my own gain. Though in some way the acquisition of them has all the hallmarks of acquiring a 'fetish object from the victim' that all these serial killer books bang on about. I have so much of him in my possession, after all.

Teddy Thursby's diaries, oh yes, quite a treasure is my little wordhoard. Of course, I can never fully exploit them, not publicly, I mean, that would implicate me. But then I'd rather not have them published and pored over by the grubby-fingered masses. They're mine. A wonderful reference work they are too. Incomplete, though. Thursby and Julian, his 'official biographer', destroyed some of the more damaging material when they were working on that dreadful whitewash that was to be his memoirs. But there's still plenty of scandal and ignominy recorded by the poisoned pen of that dirty old peer. Particularly entries in the sixties – Teddy really was feasting with panthers back then. Bits of underworld stuff that could be useful for what I'm working on now, you never know. There's even a reference to the Hounslow bullion job somewhere, I'm sure of it.

Thursby was definitely my last killing, I think I was finally cured of it by suffocating him. It was a means to an end, I wasn't being driven by some frenzied passion, I got no enjoyment from it, in fact it rather disgusted me. No, what really did give me a thrill was taking those diaries. I was taking a life, you see, that's what I'd always wanted to do. With that pile of battered journals in my grasp I realised that I wasn't really a murderer. I was a biographer.

My first book on Billy Porter, the notorious Shepherd's Bush Cop Killer, should have been my big break. It had been my story right from the start. Victor Groombridge commissioned it but we argued for a long time over the manuscript. It was 'over-written', he said, whatever that was supposed to mean. He wanted a brash, sensationalist account but I felt that there was something deeper in the story. Our discussions became quite heated: at one point Victor said: 'I can't believe that you can make this terrific material so boring and drawn out.' We made some compromises in the end and it was published but it didn't sell and Victor blamed me.

And I ended up ghost-writing for him, which is all right, but you don't get that control over the subject that I really want. The book with Eddie started out with some promise – he is intelligent and articulate, at least, not like some of these moronic thugs Victor has had me ghost. Of course, this makes it difficult to come up with the standard Groombridge Press treatment on him. With that and all the other troubles we've been having, I don't know how this book is going to work.

Eddie's tape and my own notes reveal a myriad of theories about what happened to the loot, how it was disposed of – money laundering, dodgy gold dealers, offshore banking fraud, and so on. Some crooked businessmen and gangsters put away for receiving but rumours of a bigger internationally coordinated operation. A number of murders and disappearances associated with the bullion job. Although I like the notion of how wealth destroys and corrupts I'm not sure how I'm going to make it work as a story.

I'm weary of it all. I'm tired of having to eke out a miserable living with all this hack work. Something Eddie Doyle said about the bullion job: *it was to be my final coup, something to retire on*. That's what we all dream of, I suppose, to be at rest. I was looking forward to retirement myself until I found out what the useless pension scheme I had been conned into buying into in the eighties was going to be worth. Absolutely bugger all. I dread to think about being left to the mercies of the state in old age.

I need one more chance to write a proper book. Not just a ghosted memoir, something that will secure my reputation, something that will sell. A *truecrime* classic, something big and definitive like John Pearson's *The Profession of Violence*. That's all I want now, but will I ever get another chance?

Bedtime. Brush my teeth and stare into the looking glass. Ugly old queen. But I'm not a monster. Am I? My crimes were not so bad. The dead don't miss much. I think about all that cursed gold and men dead because of it and it gives me a bit of a thrill. Can't think why. I've kept myself clean all these years, for what? A ghost's life, a monster in captivity, a specimen in the jar. A face in the mirror. All this psychological profiling is a bit like a return to Cesare Lombroso's notion of the criminal type, *L'Uomo delinquente*. Physiognomy, external signs from which we can read guilt. But my face betrays nothing.

I wipe a bit of toothpaste off my chin. Turn the light out.

Lunch with Victor. The publishing world marches on its stomach. Any problem, any issue to discuss, any deadline looming, any problem with a manuscript, they leap into action and sit down to feed. Victor Groombridge had been the gossip columnist on the *Sunday Illustrated* before he set up on his own. He was known for his finesse in buying up people and quickly getting a story out of them. I tell him about my angle on the Eddie Doyle story. He is not impressed.

'The fucking Pardoner's Tale? What are you talking about now?'

'Well, it's a universal story, of how money corrupts. It's like a parable.'

'Do me a favour, Tony, drop all these fucking literary pretensions, will you? We're well behind schedule as it is.'

'I just thought it would give it some shape. He doesn't want to name names on who got rid of the gold so I thought that if we had a sort of moral-to-the-story element, well, that could be the hook.'

Victor sighs and shakes his head.

'He doesn't want to name names on the bullion job, he doesn't want to dish the dirt on Ruby Ryder, just what have you two been talking about all this time?'

'Well, he's not the easiest story I've had to ghost. And I can see his point with the bullion thing. There's been more than one murder connected to that job. But he does want to tell his story. He's just a bit sensitive about how he comes across.'

'Yeah, yeah. Look, much as we'd really like some redemptive, moral-of-the-story angle, how I rehabilitated myself with a sociology degree or whatever, it ain't what's selling. The public want lovable monsters. Unspoiled monsters.'

'Yeah, well.'

'And now that Ronnie Kray's croaked, well, it's just the right time. End of an era and all that bullshit. There must be plenty of old faces to buy up who'll trot out all that nostalgia trip. If it isn't working with Eddie Doyle, well, maybe, I don't know, maybe we should drop him.'

'You mean . . . ?'

'Well, we're way behind and Eddie isn't exactly being cooperative, is he?'

'Well, no, but . . .'

'So, I want something by the end of May or we forget about it.'

I don't know what to say. I want to tell him to fuck off but I need the work. I need the money.

'Victor . . .' I begin.

'Just get on with it, Tony. You fuss around too much. Just hack it out.'

'So, is that all you think I'm good for?'

Victor sighs and shakes his head wearily. We carry on eating for a while without talking.

'Look,' Victor says finally, 'get him to the funeral at least.'

'What?'

'Eddie. Get Eddie to the funeral.'

'What funeral?'

'Ronnie Kray's, of course. I'll get a photographer. It's going to be the social event of the calendar for retired villains. He'll have to be seen there. Get him lined up with a few faces from the sixties. That'll look good. And try to get him to talk about Ruby Ryder.'

So a week later and we were in the press huddle in front of St Matthew's, Bethnal Green. A monster's funeral, the churchyard teeming with old lags and young wannabes. A phalanx of bouncers, the cream of London's doormen, formed a guard of dishonour around the lich-gate. A police helicopter buzzed overhead. The hearse arrived. A black-and-gold glass-sided carriage, drawn by six black-plumed horses. Victoriana kitsch, just as he would have wanted. The Last Empire Hero. Wreaths and flowered tributes to the grand old psychopath: RON and THE COLONEL. One from Reggie, his womb-mate: TO THE OTHER HALF OF ME, like a floral expression of schizophrenia.

I was there with Eddie Doyle, a reluctant mourner. *I never had much truck with the Twins*, he protested. But Victor was insistent: *Get a picture of him with some other celebrity villains. Reputation, that's what it's all about*. And sure enough our smudger Geoff was on hand, patiently setting up a small aluminium stepladder to get a good angle over the crowd.

Also with us was Piers, a young journalist with the Groombridge Press's latest publishing venture, *Sorted* magazine. *Sorted* is aimed at what Victor assures me is a fresh and growing market: the 'New Lad'. I have no idea what this means. Apparently it's all about postmodernism, post-feminism. It's 'ironic', according to Piers. Well, it's all newspeak to me.

And this Piers character, well, he was just full of it. All these hard men giving him a hard-on. His lazy, public-school vowels droned on in my ear, wanting me to put names to faces. Faces. Yeah, I know them. Yes, Piers, that's Mad Frankie Fraser.

He turned his tape recorder on Eddie.

'Can I ask you a question, Eddie?' he said, pointing the little gadget in his direction.

'Uh?' Eddie seemed distracted, looking around, a bit twitchy.

I started to worry about Eddie and his paranoia. He still thinks he's being followed and he's not used to such a big crowd. He did his full stretch in closed conditions, high security. An hour or so a day in the exercise yard or association for twelve years doesn't exactly prepare you for something like this.

'What do you think?' Piers continued. 'It's the end of an era, isn't it?'

'What do you mean?'

'Well, you know, the old school of crime. Codes of honour, that sort of thing.'

Eddie winced and turned to me.

'What's this cunt fannying on about?' he asked me.

Piers gave a nervous little laugh.

'Oh, that's good,' he declared. 'I might well use that.'

Geoff teetered on his perch, screwing a huge lens into his camera.

'Ready when you are, chief,' he told me.

So, the idea was to get Eddie up to the doorway of the church, but he was hesitant, looking out into the crowd.

'Christ,' he muttered. 'Look at all this lot. It's like fucking *Jurassic Park*.'

'Come on, Eddie,' I urged him. 'We need to get you up near the front.'

It had all been sorted, Eddie had got an invite. Flanagan, a blonde-haired ex-Page Three girl, was doing the guest list and his name was on it. All we had to do was get him up by the door, through the crowd, then Geoff could start snapping away. I tapped Eddie on the shoulder.

'Hang on,' he said. 'Look.'

He was looking at somebody in the crowd. I tried to see who but there was just a mass of solemn faces. He nodded at someone.

'There,' he whispered sharply at me.

'What?' I tried not to sound impatient.

I didn't really care who he was looking at. I needed to get him moving.

'Come on, Eddie,' I begged, hoping to encourage him. 'We're on.'

'Wait a minute,' he insisted. 'It's . . .'

I tugged at his sleeve. He was in some sort of trance or something. He turned around, briefly, his face incredulous. I thought I'd got his attention but just at that moment Reggie Kray arrived, handcuffed to a prison warder. The crowd was suddenly roused and started surging forward.

'I don't fucking believe it,' Eddie declared, then looked back. 'It's . . .'

The mob was pushing towards the church, the doormen were holding everyone back, keeping the path clear for Reggie and the other guests. I had to get Eddie up there but he was working his way in the other direction, against the momentum of the masses.

'Eddie!' I called after him.

I watched him make for somebody who was standing stock still in the moving throng. A thickset man, swept-back hair, reminded me of someone but, so I thought at the time, only in the way so many of these dinosaurs do. A face, familiar. But the churchyard was full of them. I remember seeing a granite face break into a smile as he saw Eddie trying to reach him. And then his back turned and he was away. Eddie still tried to barge his way through in pursuit.

Shit.

The funeral party were filing into the church and I was losing sight of Eddie. Geoff called down to me.

'What's happening? Where's our bloke gone?'

'Stay there,' I said, mounting the stepladder. 'I'm coming up.'

'What? Wait a minute, I don't think this thing can hold the both of us.'

'Don't worry. Just hold on.'

I clambered up. The ladder creaked and teetered a bit but I made it to the top and grabbed hold of Geoff.

'Steady on, chief,' he complained.

I scanned the crowd. I could just make out the man Eddie was following. He was dodging around an outside broadcast van on the other side of St Matthew's Row. I pointed him out to Geoff.

'That bloke,' I said.

'Yeah?'

'Get him!'

The stepladder wobbled again as Geoff strained to get a good shot. He suddenly understood my urgency and let fly with a barrage of shots, his camera whirring like an angry cicada. I crouched down to steady the ladder for a second then stood up to see Eddie come into sight, emerging from the throng, looking around. I saw him catch sight of the man he was following and move towards him.

'There's Eddie,' I said to Geoff. 'Try and get them both together.'

The two men stood looking at each other for a moment and Geoff carried on clicking away. Then one of the funeral Daimlers moved slowly between them. When it had passed Eddie was alone. The other man had disappeared. Eddie looked around, then started making his way up towards Bethnal Green Road and we soon lost sight of him as well.

'What was all that about?' Geoff asked.

'I don't know. But it certainly isn't what was planned. Let's get off this thing before we break our necks.'

And we both got down.

'So, what do we do now, chief?' he asked.

I sighed.

'Don't know. Wait until it's over and there's people coming out. Might be able to get something then.'

I didn't have much confidence in that. Victor was going to be furious. The funeral service was in full swing. The strains of Frank Sinatra singing 'My Way' could be heard coming out of the church PA system.

When it was all over and the funeral procession, a vast column of Daimlers packed with recidivists, was on its way to Chingford Mount Cemetery, Eddie staggered back into the churchyard. He looked flustered and scant of breath.

'Well,' I declared, 'there goes our little photo opportunity.'

Eddie just looked at me blankly.

'Are you all right?' Geoff asked, looking up from packing his camera bag.

'Yeah, yeah,' he muttered. 'Look, I'm sorry, chaps.'

'Eddie, what the fuck was all that about?'

With a nod of the head he motioned for me to follow him off a bit, out of the earshot of Geoff and Piers. Eddie caught his breath.

'It was him,' he whispered, as if to himself. 'I'm sure of it.'

'What do you mean?'

'I mean, maybe that's what's been going on. Who's having me followed. It would make sense. He wants to know where all the missing gelt went too.'

'Will you just tell me what the hell you're talking about.'

'That bloke. The one I was chasing. It was Harry.'

'What?'

'Starks,' he hissed, his eyes wide and crazy. 'It was Harry fucking Starks.'

2

camp classic

The old, they say, find little fun in hoping.
Time's what they need, and time begins to press.
But for the young, they say, the gates are open.
They open, so they say, on nothingness.

Bertolt Brecht, *The Good Person of Szechwan*

Little Julie, aged ten, creeping out on to the landing, hearing gruff voices downstairs in the kitchen, thinking: maybe Dad's come back after all. Sitting on the stairs listening . . .

There she is.

There I am. In a dream. Well, not quite dreaming. Halfway between sleep and being awake, lucid but not yet conscious. A memory. I reach out to hold it, to know more, but motion becomes struggle, reverie turns into wilful thought.

And I wake up. Before I can work out what it meant. It was about Dad, that much was for sure.

Dad. I do miss him, even though I can hardly remember him at all. I didn't see much of him. He was away until I was seven. Inside. Visiting time didn't add up to much. Then when he did get out he was soon away again. Spain. *Timeshares*, that's what Mum told me he was doing out there. Not much time to share with me, though. Then he was gone for ever. And there was another little lie Mum had to make up. Another alibi. But I do miss him. And the worst thing is there's so little to hold on to. Just a big gap where he should have been. And all the memories tainted with badness.

You know how you can go through life with all these bad feelings, fears and doubts that you can't quite explain? Insecurities that nag at you and eat away at your confidence. You figure that it's just because you're neurotic. What was it that student counsellor had said? Yeah, you *internalise* all the things that have gone wrong in your life. You turn them in on yourself and make them all your own fault. And that eats away at you until you feel that you have to find out what is really to blame for your unhappiness. The one thing that could make sense of all of these confused emotions. Something you could put a name to.

I'd buried Dad deep for a long time. The only way I had to deal with the shock of it was to pretend it had never happened. Pretending, that's what I did, Mum had always encouraged me to do that. It was her that had got me started with acting in the first place. She was projecting her own ambitions on me but it was also a way of us avoiding the truth. A dreamworld. And that's what I thought it was, like entering a world of other possibilities where you could become other people. Of course, when I went to drama school all of a sudden acting was supposed to be about reality, about channelling real feelings. We did what were called 'sense memory exercises' where you use recalled emotions to give truth to a performance. In one particularly intense session we were supposed, in turn, to relive a traumatic experience of our lives in front of everybody. Well, I couldn't do it. I just froze. I couldn't think about anything else except what I felt like when I found out about Dad and I couldn't go through the lies that I'd always used about what had happened to him. I just walked out of the class. The next day my acting teacher sent for me and went into this lecture about how an actor has to confront their demons in order to be any good. I would have to deal with whatever it was, he insisted, otherwise it would block me as a performer. He spoke to me in such a concerned tone that I was filled with dread, to be honest. When he suggested that I go and see the student counsellor I agreed more to reassure him than anything else. But I didn't tell her the truth either. Instead I used the story Mum had concocted all those years ago. And this counsellor woman talked about *bereavement* and *loss* and *closure* and all these modern words that made no sense to my ancient grief. She mentioned something called *recovered memory syndrome* which I didn't like the sound of at all. I went along with these sessions just to make everybody happy. Except me. Therapy was no good. I mean, where would that get me? But I did learn a new litany of terms that I could use to cover up what I really felt. And from then on I learnt to fake this internal stuff if I ever needed it.

I felt more at ease with the externals of acting, the technical side of things. Voice production particularly interested me at drama school. More than anything I wanted to be able to speak quite differently from Mum, to become quite a different person to the one my background had determined. And when I went about building a character I always approached it from the outside in rather than the other way around.

Maybe this inability to really let go in a part was the reason that I haven't been as successful as I might have been. Though it mostly seemed a matter of chance. Some of my peers went on to do really well after drama school, others hardly got any work at all. I've fallen somewhere in the middle, become what they call a 'jobbing actress', and I seemed quite happy with that. I had a simple sense of purpose, I enjoyed what work I managed to get and I felt in control of my life.

I got depressed from time to time, especially between jobs – 'resting', some people call it, though it never feels like that. I think for a while I blamed Dad for this, or rather the lack of him. Him not being there. One great big negative that made it easier to block things out. But it wasn't his fault, not really. It was someone else. I knew that deep down. I had just spent so much of my life covering it all up.

And that was how I wanted it to be. I had reinvented myself as a confident young woman with middle-class manners. When I'd got enough acting contracts I applied for an Equity card with a new name, a stage name. Julie McCluskey became Julie Kincaid. I felt a bit guilty, getting rid of Dad's name like that, but I wanted to leave the past alone. And for a few years I felt quite free of it all.

Then it all started to come back. Lost memories clicking into place like a ratchet. I started having that dream – well, that half-dream – in the mornings, just as I was coming up to the surface. About being little and hearing voices downstairs, talking about me. And something else happened.

The counsellor at drama school had once told me that traumatic memories could be sometimes triggered by quite unexpected stimuli. Some seemingly harmless detail in day-to-day life could suddenly throw you off balance.

I remember coming out of the Gate cinema in Notting Hill with Jez, I don't know, some time in the spring of 1995. We'd been to see *Pulp Fiction*. Jez was raving about it. It was a *bloody masterpiece*, he announced in that lazy drawl of his. I didn't really like it, but I didn't think that I was much bothered one way or another. But when he asked me what I thought I remember I said:

'I don't really like films with guns and gangsters in.'

I hardly thought about saying it, but once I had I suddenly felt very cold. Jez didn't notice I'd gone quiet. He was still talking about the film. He was never happier than when he was rattling on about a film he liked.

I hadn't been that impressed by it, or so I thought. It was smart and slick, a *bloody masterpiece* all right in that it was modern *grand guignol*. It was the audience's reaction that had been really perturbing. There was a great deal of laughter at the violence displayed. There were groans, too, but they sounded disturbingly like groans of disappointment. As if all the blood had not been enough.

But out in the street I realised that the subject of the movie had made an impact on me. Perhaps because of the very frivolousness of its treatment, which rendered cool something that I had a deep and painful fear of.

Guns and gangsters.

Dad. I'd spent all those years holding it together and now that stupid Tarantino movie had brought it all back. The horror of it all.

'Julie?' I heard Jez say my name, softly. It sounded distant. 'Are you OK?'

I turned and forced a smile. I didn't want Jez to know about it. I'd told him that Dad had been killed in a car crash. Not a hard lie to tell. It had been the official family line for years. What Mum had told me to tell people. I had only been ten at the time. Mum hid the newspapers from me. Told me not to take any notice of what people said. We didn't talk about it, not properly, so a lot of it got mixed up in my mind. Over the years, I'd just about got to believe it myself. But something had clicked, that was for sure. I knew then that I would have to go back over it and work out what had really happened. But I didn't want Jez to know about any of it, not yet.

'What's the matter?'

'I'm fine. Really.'

We were standing in the street looking at each other. There was something sweet in that little frown of concern beneath Jez's mop of blond hair. It meant that I could smile properly and look him in the eye.

'You're coming back to mine?' he asked.

'Yeah,' I replied. 'Sure.'

I'd been seeing Jez for about three months. We'd met on a short, no-budget film I had a part in and he was directing. It was his first real break. His *calling card*, he called it. He loved to think of himself as a struggling Young Turk. The fact was that he had contacts. He had worked as a runner in a film company owned by a friend of his father's. He'd done a few music videos. Now he was trying to get a screenplay together for a feature film but he was having trouble with it.

The strange thing was that Jez was as keen to cover up his background as I was mine. He had started to pick up this wide-boy demeanour, this silly fake cockney accent. He was quite good at it actually. I mean, he was a good mimic. But I knew what hard men were really like and he wasn't it. I think, in a way, that's what endeared me to him. There was something awfully vulnerable about the way he puffed himself up. He seemed utterly harmless and that's just what I wanted in a man. There was a sense of security I felt with him, something safe that I had always longed for.

He made a big thing of the fact that he had left school at sixteen. Public school, that is. While it had been quite a struggle for me to get into drama school. Mum hadn't wanted me to go, she'd thought that stage school was enough but it hadn't really taught me much except all the eyes and teeth show-business stuff. I'd got a speaking part in *Grange Hill* when I was fourteen and she'd been so chuffed, so happy to see me on the telly. But Mum's ambitions were never enough for me. I had wanted to be a proper actress, with classical training and received pronunciation. I didn't want to be stuck with an accent, the voice of my unhappy childhood. I wanted to escape in spite of all the teacher's talk about 'reality'. The real point of acting for me was the opportunity to be someone else. And it had worked, in that I could fool people. I mean, Jez took me for a well-bred girl. And although I hadn't been so lucky with actual jobs since drama school, I'd done small parts in a couple of plays at the Royal Court Upstairs, lots of profit-share fringe work. I'd got away, that was the main thing. I had made a break with my past. The thought of having to go back over it made me feel a bit sick. And frightened.

We got back to Jez's flat, the second storey of a Georgian house just off the Portobello Road. His father had bought it for him. He still had that quizzical look on his face as he opened a bottle of Chardonnay.

'Look,' he said, handing me a glass, 'what's up?'

'It's nothing, really.'

But my brain was bursting. I took a gulp of wine. His pale blue eyes stared into me. I sighed, relieved by the distraction of his prettiness. And he was pretty, much prettier than he was comfortable with. I suddenly felt that if I could summon up an urgent desire for him then I could stop thinking about anything else.

I kissed him on the mouth. My lips were cool, wet. I knew that I looked quite impressive. Long red hair that I'd inherited from Dad. A friend of Mum's once remarked that I looked like Maureen O'Hara. And my height, I got that from Dad too, he had been a big man. I was a couple of inches taller than Jez. He didn't seem to mind me towering over him; in fact, I was pretty sure that was one of the things he liked about me. He always liked me being on top when we had sex.

'What's this?' he said, still curious.

'I want you,' I murmured.

And I did. I wanted him. I wanted to empty my head of all the bad thoughts. To feel a simple bodily desire for life. To be in control of it.

'Yeah?' Jez whispered, his face close to mine.

'Yeah,' I breathed, all husky. 'Right now.'

We went into the bedroom. He let me take off his clothes and push him on to the bed. I stripped off and straddled him. I felt anger mingled with the desire and I clawed at him as I felt a wave of release come over me. Afterwards he touched the marks I had made on his chest. He sucked in a little breath.

'You hurt me,' he moaned.

And yes, there was hurt in those baby blue eyes of his. I smiled with cruel joy.

'I thought that's what you public schoolboys liked,' I taunted him.

'Leave it out,' he complained, sulkily. *Leave it out*, his fake vowels flat. He was such a give-away when he was angry.

And I felt another little jab of meanness inside of me. I was annoyed by how he imagined, in some way, that he was wider than me. I knew more than him and I never let on. I didn't have that weakness, that middle-class guilt. So whenever I felt that Jez was getting close to me, I mean close to finding out about my past, I would go on the offensive. Tease him about his own background.

'So what did you get up to in the dormitory?'

'What do you mean?'

At first I had thought there might be something gay about Jez.

The way that he so desperately wanted to project this exaggerated masculinity. His obsession with hard men even though he was pretty and quite fey really. But it was more complicated than that.

'You know,' I went on, 'you and the other boys.'

Jez sat up in bed.

'Look,' he said, all indignant, 'I never . . .' He trailed off, not knowing the ending.

'Well, it must have gone on.'

'Yeah, well.'

'So didn't you ever . . . I mean, with another boy.'

Jez stared at me. His blue eyes had gone all steely.

'No,' he said, flatly.

'Not ever?'

'No.' He sighed. 'Never.'

It seemed such a definite. Such a definite sadness. Something else in his expression. Resentment. A wistful look suggesting that he had somehow missed out. That he lacked some knowledge, some sense of initiation. It was then that a thought occurred to me that almost made me laugh out loud, though I managed to restrain myself since I didn't want to hurt his feelings *that* much. I thought that maybe Jez was a public schoolboy who had been traumatised because he *hadn't* had a homosexual experience.

He found sleep sooner than I did. I lay there in the darkness, trying to empty my mind. Noises of street life outside harsh and malevolent. Exhaustion finally overwhelmed me but in the morning the half-dream came for me again.

Little Julie, aged ten, creeping out on to the landing, hearing gruff voices downstairs in the kitchen, thinking: maybe Dad's come back after all. Sitting on the stairs, listening. But it's not Dad. It's Dad's friends, those big friendly men who'd come to the house sometimes. Speaking low and soft, trying to calm down Mum who is angry and tearful.

'And what about Julie?' Mum is saying. 'I've had to tell her she can't go to stage school now.'

Little Julie blushing, hearing that they are talking about her. The low voices mutter something consoling. Little Julie gets up and tiptoes down the stairs . . .

* * *

A low thumping noise. Jez was already up and padding around the bedroom clumsily. I groaned.

'Sorry,' Jez whispered. 'Do you want a cup of tea?'

I groaned again and turned over in bed. I thought about the dream, tried to work out what happened next. But it was gone.

I took a shower and got dressed. Jez was in the front room tapping away at his laptop. He looked absorbed.

'You working on the screenplay?' I asked.

He hadn't written anything for weeks. He looked up and grinned, shook his head.

'Nah,' he said. 'I'm starting a new one.'

'What?'

'Yeah. And this time I think I've really got something.'

'Well, that's great.'

I had meant that to sound encouraging but it came out flat and bitter. Jez looked up and frowned.

'What's the matter?' he asked.

I sighed. I didn't want to talk to Jez about what was going on in my head.

'It's nothing. Sorry, I mean it. Everything's great.'

I gave him a big warm fake smile.

'I'll let you get on,' I said.

I went into the bedroom and called my agent. There was an audition for a small theatre company doing a tour with a Brecht play. Equity minimum. I took down the details. Jez was still at it when I came back through.

'Look,' I said, going over to him, 'I'm going to get off.'

'OK,' he replied, hardly looking up.

He looked happy, occupied, his face held in childlike concentration, blue eyes twitching. I smiled for real this time and ruffled his blond hair.

'I'll see you,' I said, and kissed him on the cheek.

I went back to my flat and mooched about. Tried to busy myself. Put my CV up on the computer screen and tried to rearrange it so it looked convincing. After an hour or so it still read like a desperate alibi. I went through a new audition speech. Constance from *King John*. But I could distract myself only for so long. I knew what I had to do. Who I had to talk to.

Mum. I know so little about Dad but far too much about Mum. We know each other all too well. Her thwarted ambition foisted upon me at such an early age. She wanted me to be the person she could have been. If only. Expectations and disappointments were measured out through the years. And yet so little was said. Like there was vowed silence between us.

I knew that it wasn't going to be easy. I phoned to say that I was coming over, hoping that my voice would not betray that something was up. I didn't want her on the defensive.

'How's work?' she asked me, almost before I was through the door.

She always wanted to talk about work, about 'the business'. As long as I can remember this was what we talked about. Or rather, what she talked to me about. Ballet and tap classes almost as soon as I could walk. A fish-finger commercial when I was four, for God's sake. Always telling me to 'have a big smile and lots of personality' or whatever. I found out at stage school that I wasn't alone. Most of the girls there (and some of the boys too) had been propelled into 'the business' by pushy mothers. Frustrated women who'd never made it themselves. I always felt slightly guilty thinking of Mum in this way. She wanted so much for me, after all. And although I somehow knew that she was projecting her own desires on to me, I felt that I was being cruel and ungrateful if I didn't go along with it.

I told her about the audittion for the tour but she wasn't impressed.

'Do you really want to bother with that, darling?' she said. 'Nobody's going to see you in that.'

She was right, of course. A medium-scale tour of studio theatres and community art centres probably. I wasn't sure I wanted to do it myself. But maybe I needed the work more than ever now. Something to focus on that wasn't . . . well, wasn't all this stuff going on in my head about Dad. Acting had always been a refuge for me, I'd never cared much one way or the other about success as long as I could escape.

But she had this unreal notion that somewhere, just around the corner, was my big break. This, for her, meant television or film. In her mind theatre wasn't worth bothering about unless it was West End.

'I saw Ruby the other day,' she announced, proudly.

Ruby Ryder, she meant. I cringed a bit, embarrassed that my

mother couldn't resist name-dropping, even with her own daughter, about someone who was, at best, a C-list celebrity. But they did go back. They'd met in the sixties when Mum had worked as a showgirl in a club in Soho. Well, a stripper really, not that she would ever quite admit to that.

'She's being considered for a big telly part. In a long-running series. It's all a bit hush-hush at the moment. She asked after you. You should go and see her. She might be able to help you, you know, casting directors and that.'

'Look, Mum, I really don't need any help.'

'Baby, you've got to take what breaks you can in this business. I should know.'

I felt an awful sense of panic that we'd end up going over her failed career, the breaks she'd never had. There was something she seemed to relish about her misfortunes, as if they formed some great tragic role for her. She indulged herself in regret. She'd talk about the struggle it had been to put me through stage school. The sacrifice she'd made. And I was supposed to redeem all of this somehow. She'd never seemed to understand what I wanted. I felt resentment and something else. Urgency. I just didn't want us to end up having the same old conversation.

'I want to talk about something else, Mum.'

'What do you mean, something else?'

'I mean something other than the business.'

'Fine,' she said petulantly.

I had wanted to ease gently into this somehow. In the end I couldn't help just blurting it out.

'I want to talk about Dad.'

Her eyes widened. I cursed myself inwardly for being so brusque.

'Oh,' she said, with a sigh of disappointment. 'Oh.'

Oh, the big O. I knew then that I had sod-all chance of getting much out of her. Her face froze over and I went from resentment right back to guilt again. I knew how much she'd suffered. How much she'd had to hold in all these years.

'Sorry, Mum, it's just . . .'

I didn't know what to say. She lit a menthol cigarette and let the smoke sigh out in a long stream.

'Oh, love,' she moaned. 'What do you want to know?'

'Well, you know, about what happened.'

The awkwardness was almost unbearable. This had been a big mistake. Mum's lips trembled. She sucked on the pith of the cigarette hungrily. Smoke hissed in. Out.

'You mean about . . .'

'Yes. About.'

About. It had always been *about*.

'About him being killed,' I said.

There, I'd said it. Mum just stared at me.

'Julie, please,' she chided, as if I'd said something rude.

'It's just we've never really talked about it.'

'But what good . . .'

'Mum.'

'I mean, I'm sorry, I know I should have . . .'

'Don't.'

'I know, I know. But you were so little. I wanted to protect you from it all. I wanted . . .'

There was a catch in her voice. A little forlorn sob. Her eyes brimmed with tears.

'I only . . . only . . .' she stammered, throatily. 'I only wanted the best for you.'

'Mum, please don't cry.'

I got up and went to her, held her as she quivered with grief. I spent the next hour or so calming her down. Eventually she was done and I talked of other things, changed the subject. While I had been comforting her all I could feel was a frustration that she wouldn't talk to me about what I needed to know. But when all of that was done, after all the mascara-streaked smiles and fake happy goodbyes, when I left the house to go back to my flat, my feelings changed into something quite different. A slow-burning anger inside me at how both our lives had been ruined.

Dad. What could I remember myself? Jock McCluskey. 'Big Jock', that's what everyone called him. A big man with a soft rough voice. Smooth and abrasive at the same time, like sandpaper. Singing to me gently as he tucked me in. 'Strangers in the Night' in a thick Glasgow accent. *Do be do be do*.

Away. Inside. Vague memories of prison visits. The smell mostly. And all the clattering noise of confinement. Mum and Dad talking across the table. Him winking at me, calling me 'princess'.

The rest was keeping up appearances. Me and Mum putting on a brave front. Blotting out things even back then.

Then he came out and there was a big party. I do remember that. I was seven so it must have been 1977. The function room above a pub. Tables laden with sandwiches and booze. Me in a party dress with my long red hair up. Lots of well-dressed men with big hands covered in jewellery, smiling down at me.

Uncle Tam down from Glasgow. Feather-cut hair and huge lapels on his suit jacket. CODY tattooed on the knuckles of his right hand.

'Who's Cody?' I asked him.

'Come On Die Young.' He spelled it out, his voice warm and gruff like Dad's, holding up the inked letters on his battered fist for inspection.

Dad out on parole. Straight life. Going out to work during the day. Always coming home late. Sometimes not coming home for days on end. Mum and Dad arguing at night. I thought they were going to split up or something.

But then Spain happened. Dad went away to Spain on business. He came back with pictures of the villa. He went back after only about a week. Dad lives in Spain now, I remember thinking. In a villa in Marbella. Me and Mum went over there in the school holidays. A big white building, a tower with inlaid coloured glass. Pink marble floors and Moroccan wall hangings. A stone fireplace with a driftwood sculpture above it. Wrought-iron gates at the end of the drive. A fairy-tale castle. Blue skies. Happy holiday memories, bright and clear as home-movie colour film. *Dad works in timeshares*, that's what Mum told me. *Timeshare*. Back and forth through Málaga airport. Our place in the sun. It seemed to work out, Mum seemed happy enough. A new routine. A timeshare life.

Diving into the swimming pool. Showing off for Dad. Breaking the still, turquoise water. Feeling the cool silence as I came to the surface in a perfect arc. I loved that swimming pool. The . . . oh Christ, yes. The pool. Diving into the past, falling. I'd forgotten that. No, the swimming pool. Dad falling . . .

The swimming pool. They found Dad face down in it. His blood diffusing from the bullet wounds. Turning the water pink.

We were back home when it happened. Crowds outside the house. Cameras with huge lenses. The press. Mum tried to shield me from it all. Hiding me from it all. Keeping the newspapers from me. But, shit, yes, I remember it now. That headline in the *Sunday Illustrated* that I managed to sneak a glance at: *GANGLAND SLAYING IN SPAIN. 'Big Jock' shot in Marbella*.

It was all too much. Memories after this point are memories of trying to block things out. News hounds and strange messages we got in the post or through the letter box. Anonymous phone calls. *Your dad was a grass*, somebody hissed once when I picked up the receiver. Mum disconnected the phone. And everything else. We moved house. She went through what we were to tell people about ourselves. We rehearsed it, we got our story straight.

Then later on, the night when I heard the voices downstairs. The gruff voices of men like my dad. The dream I keep having. It meant something. And it wasn't just about Dad. It was about Mum too. And me, something about me going to stage school.

I just felt so exhausted. Too many memories flooding back. My head was bursting and I needed to talk to someone. I just couldn't think who.

I still couldn't talk to Jez about it. I still didn't want him to know the truth about my past. I wasn't quite sure why. But I suppose I just wanted to hold it all together for as long as possible. I was scared of what I was now facing up to and there seemed certainty in deception. If I could carry on fooling Jez at least I would be in control of that. And I needed to be sure of something.

The bizarre thing was that Jez was becoming more and more fake wide boy with every passing day. It was all to do with the screenplay he was working on. That Tarantino film had really set him off. A 'classic British gangster movie', that's what he said he was working on, and he'd got a writing partner now, Piers, a journalist friend of his. Piers claimed to have met some real 'faces' in the line of duty. He was a serious coke-head as well so, like most of the London media world, it seemed, he had a recreational link with organised crime. But Jez's research was more corporeal. The barrow-boy voice and the cocky little swagger started to take him over. Though with his cherubic face and, well, his *gentleness*, this was all a bit contradictory. He was trying to toughen himself up, working out at the gym, going to Thai boxing classes, but it couldn't alter the essential fact of himself. That he was a nice, well-brought-up young man. Which is what I loved him for. This yobbishness was all a bit silly, but harmless, playful. I didn't like it when he and Piers started hanging out with a drug dealer friend who took them to dodgy pubs and drinking clubs. For research purposes, Jez insisted, though it was easy to tell that he was excited by it all. Not that I worried about him getting into drugs, Jez was far too clean cut for that. I just didn't want him to get into trouble.

And I would feel a little left out when I was with Piers and Jez. They would go into this routine, repeating lines of dialogue at each other. It could be infuriating but boys will be boys. Once they started bantering about me, calling me a 'posh bird'. Well, I nearly lost it that time.

And I thought, well, that's ironic. Not that I was certain that my predicament conformed to the rules of irony. It was just that word seemed to be everywhere at the time. Piers was always using it. He worked for *Sorted*, a new glossy magazine for men. For the 'new lad', that was the new market niche, apparently. Along with football and fast cars there was the usual timid soft porn. But it was deliberately tacky, Piers insisted, it was 'ironic sexism'. It was a joke, he explained. I didn't get it.

But maybe that was it, my situation was a joke, it was just part of all this 'ironic humour' that was so fashionable. But it didn't feel comic. It felt tragic. Jez was quite different when he was alone with me, sensitive, affectionate, but I couldn't talk to him about what I was going through. Not until I felt strong enough about it myself. But his current obsession didn't exactly help.

I needed to talk to someone. Someone who would have some idea of what I had been through. There was Joe Patterson, an actor I knew from when I'd worked at the Royal Court. Joe's dad had been a serious South London villain. Joe had had a lot of success in the late seventies and early eighties, he'd played the lead in the punk film *Borstal Breakout* in 1979, but he'd not had much work since. There were rumours that he'd been following in the family business. I'd already suggested him to Jez and Piers for their film project. Some of the Royal Court lot loved the fact that he knew real criminals and he'd indulge them with all sorts of stories, but he was always discreet when it came to me. He knew about my past but kept quiet about it, which I appreciated. Joe never really talked to me directly about my dad or anything, he knew that I wanted to keep shtum about that, but I always felt that he understood somehow. I got to know him fairly well but we lost touch after the run. But that's always the way with the acting business. The business and the other business. They had a lot in common in some ways. A lot of people I knew had one foot in each of them.

I'd really messed up with Mum. If only I'd spent more time listening to her instead of jumping in with 'I want to talk about Dad'. She'd wanted to talk, after all. What had she been going on about? Oh yeah, Ruby. Ruby Ryder. Well, there's one for you, I thought. And then I realised that there was someone I could talk to after all. Ruby Ryder.

> *I am not mad: this hair I tear is mine;*
> *My name is Constance; I was Geoffrey's wife;*
> *Young Arthur is my son; and he is lost.*
> *I am not mad; I would to God I were,*
> *For then 'tis like I should forget myself.*
> *O, if I could, what grief should I forget!*

Sometimes you know when you've got them, when the speech you are doing is absolutely captivating them. The most difficult thing about any audition is that you are taking something out of context, a speech that in performance would have the whole play to build up the intensity that it needs. But in an audition you have to do it cold and usually in some God-forsaken church hall at eleven o'clock in the morning. But I wasn't cold. I was burning. I was channelling all the stuff that had been going on in my head the last few days into Constance from *King John*. This was sense memory all right, I had grief down pat. And it was working, I could tell. I had them.

Red Rag was a feminist theatre company that had been set up in the seventies. They had had a good reputation but were now in decline. Their Arts Council grant was due to be cut and they would have to apply to the Lottery instead. Radical theatre was a thing of the past.

They were doing a production of Brecht's *The Good Woman of Szechwan*, three weeks' rehearsal, six months touring. I was tempted to point out that *Der Gute Mensch von Sezuan* translated more correctly as The Good Person (or even the Good Soul) of Szechwan, and that to apply a gender could be misleading. But this could have stirred up some pointless debate about sexual politics, and besides,

I was being very working class with this lot, instinctive rather than intellectual. I knew that would go down well with them (I found myself talking like Mum). But I did know the play. I'd done Brecht at drama school. And I liked it, especially the part I was up for, the lead, a good-natured prostitute, Shen Te, who pretends to be her own ruthless male cousin in order to protect herself from people who take advantage of her kindness.

I somehow had a soft spot for Red Rag too, although they did seem a little ridiculous. Out of date. A bit humourless and worthy, despite their name. Piers would have deemed them an 'irony-free zone'. But they stood for something, which was becoming very unfashionable these days. Maybe it was a sense of a lost cause that I had an affinity with. They told me they'd let me know the next day. Did I want the job? I wasn't sure.

'And what about Julie?' Mum is saying. 'I've had to tell her she can't go to stage school now.'

Little Julie blushing, hearing that they are talking about her. The low voices mutter something consoling. Little Julie gets up and tiptoes down the stairs.

Walking into the kitchen in her pyjamas. Mum and a lot of grim-faced men sitting around the table. They don't notice her at first. Then one of the rough faces lights up.

'Aw,' he goes. 'Here she is.'

'Aww,' they all go, smiling down at her.

Julie does a few ballet steps, lifting up for a pirouette. The men clap and laugh.

I met Ruby Ryder for lunch at Elena's on Charlotte Street. Ruby was half an hour late. She swept in looking a bit wild about the eyes but still managing to radiate charisma. I stood up to greet her.

'I'm sorry, love,' she said, kissing me on both cheeks. 'I've had a hell of a morning.'

Her trademark blonde hair looked immaculate, cut in a simple bob. Probably a wig but you really couldn't tell. She let a waiter take her topcoat. She wore a skirt suit with large pink and black checks. Gold buttons and lots of jewellery.

'Gerry Wilman's croaked,' she explained as she sat down. 'Found him in his flat yesterday. Dead as a doornail. An overdose, apparently.'

Gerald Wilman was a comedian, famous for his long-running radio series *How's Your Father?* and much TV work. Ruby had done a film with him, *A Bird in the Hand*, back in the sixties.

'Had the press and the TV on the phone all morning wanting some fucking eulogy. I'm sorry, love, I'm all wound up by it. I can't even remember what I said.'

The waiter handed her a menu. She stared at it blankly for a moment then looked up again.

'I mean, what is there to say? Gerry, I mean, I loved him to death and everything but he was a bitter old queen really. Sad and lonely. Sorry, I'm in a bit of a state. I've had to say about a hundred times what a marvellous performer he was, a warm person and all that shit. Well, he ain't warm any more.'

She started a chuckle that ended in a groan.

'Maybe this isn't a good time,' I said.

'Don't be stupid. It's lovely to see you.' She looked at the menu again. 'You know what you're having? Good, let's order now then we can talk.'

A smile and a slight nod of her head brought the waiter over. He took our orders and then Ruby leaned across the table slightly.

'So, you working?'

My agent had phoned that morning to say that Red Rag had offered me the tour. I told Ruby about it. I still wasn't sure whether I was going to take it.

'Do you want to do it?'

'I like the part, yeah.'

'Then do it, darling.'

'But I'll be out of London for six months and playing places where no one's going to see me.'

'Then don't do it.'

She grinned at me.

'Sorry, Ruby, I know, I've got to decide myself.'

'I know what it's like, you get to your mid-twenties and nothing's really happened yet and you start to worry. But there's nothing you can do about it. You never know what will come up. All that trashy stuff I did in the sixties, that film with Gerry, that stuff's getting me work now. They're calling it "camp classic".'

She shrugged.

'What goes around, comes around,' she declared, picking up a piece of bread.

'Mum says you're up for a big TV part.'

'Yeah, well, she should have kept her trap shut. It's all touch and go and I'm supposed to keep quiet about it. I think they're worried about my past. My first husband, Eddie, he's out of prison and he's selling his bloody story, isn't he? It's all I bloody need. I tried talking to him but there's something up with him. Seeing ghosts or something. Reckons he saw Harry Starks at Ronnie Kray's funeral—'

Ruby's butter knife clattered to the floor. She sat stock still for a moment, staring.

'Sorry,' she muttered. 'I didn't mean to bring up . . .' She trailed off, slowly gesturing with the piece of bread. '. . . all that.'

That name. I hadn't heard it in years, but I'd always known it. Off by heart. Newspaper reports that Mum tried to hide from me: *Starks, the double murder suspect in the 'Costa del Crime' killings* . . . A name always whispered, just out of earshot. Harry Starks. He was the one that . . .

'Anyway, as I was saying,' Ruby continued nervously.

He was the one that killed Dad.

'No, Ruby, that's just it. That's what I want to talk about.'

'What?'

'The past.'

'The past?' She frowned at me.

Yes, I thought, the past. I want it back. Starks. He was the one that took it all away from me.

'I want to know about Dad,' I said, flatly.

'Jock? He was a lovely fellah. Really lovely. A real gentleman. Some of those stories in the press, you know, they really exaggerated.'

'Please, Ruby,' I broke in.

'What?'

'I don't want a bloody alibi. I know Dad did bad things. But I want to know the truth. So much has been messed around in my head about it. Mum won't talk about it. But it's driving me crazy. I keep having this dream and I can't work it out.'

'Well, you've got a right to know about these things,' Ruby said. 'But be careful, dear. It's all . . .'

'I want to know, Ruby. About all of it. I want my life back.'

'What?' She frowned at me again.

I couldn't explain what I meant.

'Just tell me what you know,' I said.

'Where do you want me to start?' Ruby shrugged.

'I don't know. The beginning, I suppose.'

'Well, Jock was with Harry Starks' firm when your mum was working at the Stardust Club. That was Harry's club. That's how they met.'

'When Mum was a stripper?'

'Yeah, well.' Ruby shrugged. 'It was a revue-style show. It wasn't obscene.'

'And she got pregnant with me and they got married.'

'Well, that's being a bit blunt. Your dad was quite a charmer, you know.'

'But it was all a bit of a rush, wasn't it?'

'Well . . .' Ruby sighed. 'Jock was on remand by then. I remember the wedding. Brixton Register Office. He was handcuffed to the biggest copper they could find from the Serious Crime Squad.'

The sad beginning of my existence, I thought. Barely legitimate. Dad being taken away when I was still *in utero*. Then taken away for good. By him.

'So, why did Harry Starks kill my dad?' I demanded.

Ruby flinched slightly.

'Julie, I . . .'

'I need to know, Ruby.'

'I don't know, love. Business. Your dad was looking after Harry's money through business deals in Spain. Something went wrong.'

'Something went wrong? Business? Christ, Ruby, you make it sound like an administrative error or something.'

Ruby squirmed in her seat a bit.

'Well . . .'

'Just tell me.'

'Harry Starks was very, very heavy. So was your father, for that matter. They were bad times, Julie. Things got messed up. There was this bent copper, Mooney. Now he was a really nasty piece of work. It was horrible.'

She was hunched over now, as if she were going into herself somehow, trembling slightly.

'Ruby?'

A shaky hand came across the table and held on to mine.

'I'm sorry love. I've seen some bad things myself, you know.'

'Tell me.'

'Nah, I can't talk about some of it. Look,' she said, glancing up at me, pulling herself together, 'I don't know what happened between Harry Starks and your dad. I know that something was settled with your mum afterwards.'

'What?'

'I don't know any more. Sorry. I'm in a bit of a state. What with Gerry dying and everything. I'm still in shock.'

She was holding something back, I felt sure of it.

'You know what the worst thing was about Gerry?' she went on, carefully changing the subject. 'He was dead two days before they found him. It was only because a neighbour noticed a funny smell coming from his flat. Isn't that terrible? Him a household name and all.'

I thought about asking her more about Dad's death but I left it at that. It was about as much as I could hope to get out of her for now anyway. And more than enough for me to think about.

'Ladies?'

It was the waiter arriving with our orders. Ruby suddenly had her for-the-public smile. All eyes and teeth.

I left the restaurant with a peculiar sense of relief. The unspeakable had been spoken and maybe I could now start to make sense of things. It was him, he was the answer to it all. Mum would never allow that name to be uttered. It had been a secret word for me, a curse that I'd never completely known the meaning of. I'd spent so much of my life turning hatred on to myself, carrying around an absurd sense of guilt about what had happened to my family. Now I felt the beginnings of a kind of calculation. The deep sense of loss I had always felt, the emptiness, well, I had a name for it now. Harry Starks. This was something to focus my anger on. This could be a way of sorting myself out, dealing with some of my neurotic and insecure feelings. I would have to find out more, remember more. And maybe I could start to work out what the dream meant. Then what? I didn't know.

So other decisions came more easily. I took the Red Rag tour.

I certainly needed something to concentrate on so I wouldn't just explode. I needed to work or I would go crazy.

The first day of rehearsals was the following Monday. I still hadn't told Jez about the job. About the fact that I would be away for six months. After all the introductions, the director gave a short speech about the production then we settled down to the first read-through.

The Good Woman of Szechwan is a parable. The gods come down to earth searching for a truly good person (unless they can find one the world cannot continue to exist), but of all the people of Szechwan, only Shen Te, a prostitute, offers them shelter. She is rewarded with money with which she buys a small tobacco shop.

But when news of her good fortune spreads a whole horde of parasites, would-be relatives and creditors, descend upon the shop. To protect herself, Shen Te assumes the personality of a ruthless male cousin, Shui Ta, a tough and implacable young man who drives away all those who prey on the goodness of Shen Te.

Back as Shen Te, she falls in love with an out-of-work pilot who is only after her money. She loses her money, and him, but it is only when she realises that she is pregnant that she takes action. Back comes the bad cousin Shui Ta to sort things out again, utterly pitiless where Shen Te has been the soul of generosity. When Shui Ta is accused of killing Shen Te (she has been missing for such a long time suspicions are aroused), there is a trial in which the gods act as magistrates. Shen Te finally reveals that the bad Shui Ta and herself are one and the same person. Only under the guise of greed and cruelty can the good person of Szechwan hope to provide for herself and her unborn child. For the good cannot live in our world and stay good.

The gods depart, content that the one good person they found still exists. When Shen Te confronts them they evade the issue; somehow, they insist, she will manage. The epilogue implores the audience to make its own happy ending; a world in which the good cannot survive without becoming bad must be changed.

After the read-through the designer showed us a model of the set we were going to tour with. Then we broke for lunch.

I met up with Jez at the end of the day. He was having a drink with Piers at the Atlantic Bar in Piccadilly. On the way there I remembered something Ruby had said: *something was settled with your mum afterwards*. What the hell could that mean?

I had the play to think about now as well. The good woman Shen Te becoming the bad man Shui Ta, that had a sense of foreboding about it. Memories of the past had made me feel weak and vulnerable. In the future I would have to find strength from somewhere. I would have to become bad, I thought, without really knowing what that could mean.

When I arrived at the bar, Jez and Piers were having martinis. Piers was holding forth, speaking very quickly in a confident manner. Coke talk, obviously. As I joined them and Jez stood up to kiss me, Piers seemed to lose his flow.

'Ah.' He nodded in my direction. 'Julie, we were just . . . what were we talking about?'

Jez laughed and shook his head.

'All right, babe?' he murmured to me.

'Yeah,' I said. 'I've got some good news.'

'That's great,' said Jez.

'Well, good news and bad news.'

Piers stood up.

'Er, just got to powder my nose,' he said, and wandered off.

'He should really go easy, you know,' I told Jez.

'Yeah.' Jez shrugged. 'I guess. So, what's the good news?'

'I've got a job.'

'What?'

'You know, a part.'

'That's fabulous. What is it? TV or film?'

'It's theatre.'

'Oh.'

The conversation suddenly fell flat. Despite Jez's very expensive middle-class education and upbringing he seemed entirely unscathed by bourgeois values. He had absolutely no interest in the theatre. He loved popular culture. That was what he wanted to understand.

'That's really good,' he added quickly, trying to summon up as much enthusiasm as he could.

He smiled and kissed me again. I liked the way he always tried to be sweet to me, tried to show interest, even if there was none. He was the sort of boy you could take home to your mum but I'd never done that. If he met my mum, well, that would give the game away.

Piers re-emerged rubbing at his nose and sniffing. His pupils were like pencil leads. He came up behind Jez.

'I've put money in your pockets,' he announced in a *faux* East End drawl. 'Even when you was out of order. Well, now there's been an eruption!'

Jez poked him in the stomach.

'You're a big man,' he replied. 'But you're out of shape. With me it's a full-time job. Now behave yourself.'

And they both burst into laughter.

When we got back to his flat I felt light hearted. For the whole evening I'd managed to forget about everything. I still had something to tell Jez, though.

'You haven't asked me what the bad news is yet,' I said.

'What?'

'I told you I had good news and bad news. I haven't told you the bad news.'

'Oh.' (I bet he thought that the bad news was that it was a theatre job.) 'What is it?' he asked.

'It's a tour. I'm going to be away for six months.'

'Shit,' he said.

'Yeah, I know.' I shrugged. 'It's work. Come here.'

He moved close to me.

'You won't be getting rid of me yet, you know. We've got three weeks of rehearsal first.'

'Good,' he said, and kissed me on the mouth.

'Hold me,' I said.

He put his arms around me.

'I'll miss you,' he said.

Yeah, I thought, *you will. You'll hardly know me. But just hold me for now.* I felt Jez's body. His muscles were firmer and more defined than when I'd first known him. He was hardening up, on the outside. All that exercise and weight training. But I was hardening up inside.

Little Julie gets up and tiptoes down the stairs.

Walking into the kitchen in her pyjamas. Mum and a lot of grim-faced men sitting around the table. They don't notice her at first. Then one of the rough faces lights up.

'Aw,' he goes. 'Here she is.'

'Aww,' they all go, smiling down at her.

Julie does a few ballet steps, lifting up for a pirouette. The men clap and laugh. Mum turns and smiles. Her eyes are red.

'It's all right, Julie,' she says. 'It's going to be all right.'

'Yeah.' One of the battered faces looms down at her. 'You're gonna be a star, darling.'

I woke up with a start and woke Jez up too.

'What's the matter?' he muttered.

'Nothing,' I said. 'Just a bad dream.'

I sat up in bed and thought about it again. About Dad, about Mum. About me going to stage school. I remembered something.

'Hey,' said Jez, trying to pull me back under the covers.

I pushed him back. I had to think.

'Go back to sleep,' I told him.

After Dad died, Mum had told me that I couldn't go to stage school, that we couldn't afford it now, and I remembered that I'd felt relieved. I knew that I really should have felt disappointed, like Mum was, but I wasn't. I didn't have to take all of that seriously any more, that's what I had felt. I could just be a normal girl, go to a normal school.

I got up, showered and got ready to go to work. I had to think about that now. But I was distracted. *Something was settled with your mum afterwards*, that's what Ruby had said.

The second day of rehearsals and we were going through the Prologue, where the gods have come down to Szechwan and Shen Te has given them refuge. There is a bit of comic business where the gods offer payment to Shen Te for her hospitality. The joke is the embarrassment of the Illustrious Ones being seen giving money to a prostitute. I didn't have any lines but I remember where we were in the script:

> THE FIRST GOD, *awkwardly, to Shen Te:* We understand that you have no money to pay for the rent. We are not poor people, so it is natural that we should pay for our lodging. Here you are. *He gives her money*. But please let nobody know that we paid. It might be misinterpreted.
>
> THE SECOND GOD: Only too easily!

'What do you want me to do?' I asked the director

'Just stand there and take the money,' she said.

So I stood there as the gods went through their exchange and it suddenly hit me. The money. That was what the dream was all about. The money.

It hadn't come from heaven. *They* had paid for me. The gruff-voiced men downstairs. *He* had paid. Starks. The man who had killed my dad. That was what was *settled*. And Mum had taken it. Blood money.

I can't remember much of the rest of the day. I kind of walked through it, in character, thank God. But as soon as it was over I knew what I had to do, who I had to see.

Mum. All that bullshit about 'sacrifice'. All that guilt-tripping, years of betrayal. This time we really would talk.

'Who paid for me to go to stage school?' I demanded almost as soon as we'd sat down.

'What?'

'You heard. Who paid?'

'Well, I did, of course.'

'No you didn't.'

'What do you mean, Julie? I can show you the check stubs if you like.'

'Where did you get the money?'

'Look, Julie, love . . .'

'You took money from them, didn't you?'

'Please.'

'No. I'm sick of being good little Julie. For you. For them. I want to know the truth.'

'OK.'

She lit a cigarette, her nicotine-stained fingers fumbled with the lighter. Her eyes started to well up.

'I'm sorry darling,' she said. 'I just wanted . . .'

'Don't start all this, Mum.'

'What?'

'All this I'm sorry, I only wanted the best for you. I only wanted you to have the breaks I never got. I'm fucking tired of it, Mum. I just want to know. I just want what's mine.'

'What's yours?'

'Yes. Mine. My fucking life.'

'What do you mean, dear?'

'I mean it's all been taken away from me, hasn't it?'

She stared at me, baffled.

'Oh, it doesn't fucking matter,' I snapped. 'Just tell me what happened.'

'Your father didn't leave us with very much when he died. The timeshare business, well, that was just a front. I didn't have any money coming in and I had you to look after.'

'So you took money from the man who killed Dad?'

'Well, not him directly, of course. But some of his, you know, business associates, they . . .'

'You bitch,' I cut in coldly.

'What else was I supposed to do?'

I stood up to leave.

'Julie, please, you've got to understand.'

'You fucking bitch,' I said, and walked out.

Seething, I was seething with rage. I got back to my flat and it was all I could do not to smash the whole place up. *Bitch, bitch, bitch,* went through my head for hours. But that wasn't it. I was seething but it boiled down to something else. It would take me a long time to forgive Mum but I couldn't hate her, I couldn't blame her. In a way what I felt towards her was a sense of release. I was free of any guilt now. And it wasn't her fault. *What else was I supposed to do?* she had said. What she had done wasn't right, but it was for the best, in the only way she could understand. No, my seething boiled down to something else. Someone else. Starks. It was his fault, he had taken away Dad and determined the course of my life, he had paid for me to go through stage school, made me what I had become. I had no choice but then neither had Mum; that was all she knew, after all. I could have been a normal girl. But I wasn't. I was a fucked-up actress full of rage. And it would all turn in on me if I wasn't careful. And I had to get on top of this otherwise it would destroy me. I had to understand it, try to work it through somehow.

I briefly thought about trying therapy or counselling again. Maybe there was a talking cure that could mend some of the damage that had been done to my life. But I was hardly convinced of that. At least I could concentrate on work, on the only thing that I had ever really known, on performance.

I was trying to develop the physicality of my character. Of how Shen Te becomes Shui Ta. A woman becoming a man. Posture, the way she held himself as him. The walk, the gestures, the arrogance.

How a hard man moves. I remembered Joe Patterson, at the Royal Court, talking about 'shaping up', the display of aggression, the assertion of power that is often the defining moment in conflict. I had a long way to go. In rehearsals I'd only managed a kind of comic swagger, which got a few laughs but wasn't what I wanted. I'd tried to move like Dad but ended up looking like Jez. He was another male impersonator, after all. I'd have to do better than that.

And I was too busy to see much of Jez. He was hard at work, too. When we were together he'd tell me about the screenplay and I'd nod and grin. It sounded pretty stupid but I didn't want to be discouraging. I was more concerned about the 'research' he was doing with Piers. Collecting characters and stories that 'had an edge', as they put it, as if reality for them existed *in extremis*. They went on about 'authenticity', whatever that was supposed to mean. They had talked to 'real villains' and believed every word they'd said, which seemed a very foolish policy indeed from what I knew. Of course, I was worried about them getting close to my own past. I would have to tell Jez some time but now, more than ever, I needed to keep it all close to my chest. But I did wish that they would realise how horrible and brutal that world really was. They saw the glamour not the ugliness. And I didn't trust Piers. His cocaine-fuelled bravado would get them out of their depth if they weren't careful.

And I felt compelled now to do my own research on the subject. I found a couple of well-thumbed paperbacks on Jez's desk. *The Profession of Violence: The Rise and Fall of the Kray Twins* and *London Underworld*. True crime books. I picked up *London Underworld* and looked through it. There were photographs in the middle. Blurred black-and-white shots of men like the ones that were in the kitchen in my dream. There was an index. I looked up Dad. *McCluskey, 'Big Jock,' 201, 203, 207*. I looked up the last entry.

> Then, on 5 December 1979, 'Big Jock' McCluskey was found dead in the swimming pool of his villa in Marbella. He had been shot in the chest. The next day, in nearby Llanos de Nagueles, retired Detective Superintendent George Mooney was shot dead on the balcony of his house. A ballistics report indicated that the same gun was used to kill both men. Although both murders remain officially unsolved by the Spanish police the main suspect for them has always been Harry Starks, who is

still on the run after his spectacular escape from Brixton Prison that year.

McCluskey was, of course, part of his firm for many years. George Mooney took early retirement from the Met in 1973 having received numerous commendations during his service, though there were rumours that Mooney was part of the 'firm within a firm' of corrupt police officers . . .

I checked all the other references but Dad was just listed with others, just part of a litany of villains. I dropped the book back on to the desk. It was all laid out with such detachment. My father in this cheap history. Men. Bang bang you're dead. Never mind what happened to their families. It was all here, the 'truth', True Crime in black and white. But there was a surprising amount of information in these kinds of books about Harry Starks. Part of me wanted to obliterate that name from my mind but another part of me was fascinated. I started to study him, I even began making notes. I became obsessed by him, wanting to find out everything I could. Ruby had said that her ex-husband Eddie had seen him recently, at Ronnie Kray's funeral of all places. The thought of his presence made me uneasy. There were simple feelings of fear but something else that I couldn't fathom, a sense of excitement, of expectation.

We were coming up to the last week of rehearsals, getting to that stage when the production starts to crawl, blinking, into the light. It's a nerve-racking time for a company. All the major decisions have been made and if you haven't got something by then it's unlikely that any amount of reworking is going to save it. We did a first run-through. It was laborious but it was coming together. All the elements other than the acting were being put in place. Costumes were being made, the set was being built. Music and songs were worked into the play. It was an ensemble piece and there was an atmosphere of intense collaboration. It gave an illusion of belonging to something and that was comforting in a way.

Part of me remained distant, though, from the rest of the group. I had a selfish sense of concentration on my role. A ruthlessness about it that I felt the other actors must have noticed, though nobody said anything. I had got Shui Ta now. I had broken through the comic effect of a woman pretending to be a man and found something convincingly dangerous. Bits of costume helped, and he now had a manner and deportment of flamboyant callousness. I could understand why Jez and Piers could get obsessed with a person like this. The sense of power, the lack of conscience. I knew who I was playing now, who my subject was. It was him, of course. It was Harry Starks.

I still had a way to go with Shen Te but I was getting there. I found that I had really made a breakthrough with my acting work on this job. I had finally achieved some sort of deep engagement with a character, an emotional truth I had never hitherto thought possible. Of course, it was hardly Brechtian, full of passion and an insistence on empathy that he had always railed against. But I didn't care. I had put something into practice, eked something out of my sad, sorry experience. At times I felt a cold fear that he, Starks, had become my motivation, along with all the other unwarranted menaces he had subjected me to. I couldn't avoid that terrifying fact but I tried not to think about it, intellectualise it or follow any implications from it. It worked, that was all that mattered, and my role could soar above all the fears and doubts I had. It was something I could use.

And there was a sort of happiness in my work. I felt that it was the best thing I'd ever done and I was looking forward to getting into theatres with it. I was even confident enough to bully some casting directors to come and see it when it came back to London.

I'd be out of town for a few months but, looking at the schedule, I figured that I'd be able to make it back for some weekends. And maybe I'd be able to get my career going a bit. I was in control again and had a clear sense of purpose, of calm occupation. Then something awful happened.

I was in bed asleep when I got the phone call. It was about 3 a.m. Saturday morning.

'Er, Jules, um, is that you?'

It was Piers. He sounded out of it as usual. But nervous. I tried to clear my head of sleep.

'What's the matter?' I murmured.

'Look, you better get over here, it's Jez.'

'What's happened. Where are you?'

'Er, Casualty, St Thomas's.'

'Shit. He's had an accident?'

'Yeah, um, something like that. He's going to be all right. Can you come over?'

I got dressed and called a minicab. Piers was outside reception, having a cigarette.

'It's all right,' he said. 'He's being seen to.'

'What do you mean? What the fuck's happened?'

'He's just had to have a few stitches.'

'Oh, Christ. What's he gone and done?'

'Well . . .' He gave a horrible, nervous giggle. 'It was mad. It all happened so quickly. It all just kicked off.'

'You got into a fight?' I asked incredulously.

'Not exactly. It was more of, er, a kind of altercation, really. Then someone came at us with a Stanley knife.'

'What? What have you done?'

'Calm down, Jules. I mean, we didn't mean to start anything. We were just having a laugh. Then it all turned nasty.'

'You wanker. You stupid wanker. I blame you for this, Piers. You think you're so fucking clever.'

Piers was backing away from me. He'd never seen me this fierce nor heard me talk like this. My 'posh bird' voice disappeared and the harsh sound of my past poured out of my mouth at him.

'Oh, Jules, look,' he was protesting. 'I'm sorry. OK?'

'So. Where was he cut?'

'In this club. Well, it was more like a drinking den, really.'

'No. I mean where. On him.'

'Oh. Yeah, heh-heh. No. Um. Well, er, on his face, actually.'

His face. His beautiful face. I saw him come out of the treatment room with a dressing all down the side of his left cheek. He looked dazed, still in shock. We got a cab back to his flat.

I tucked him into bed.

'I'll sleep on the sofa,' I suggested.

'No,' he said softly. 'Don't go.'

'But your face. I don't want to hurt it.'

'Please,' he implored. 'I'm . . . I'm scared.'

I got under the covers and carefully nestled up to him. He was trembling.

'It's all right,' I whispered.

He started to cry. I held on to him and he sobbed away in the darkness.

The next day he was quiet, sullen.

'Do you want to talk about it?' I asked.

He shook his head.

'I want to go home,' he said, like a little child.

'But Jez,' I replied, 'you are home.'

Then I realised what he meant. He wanted to go home to Mum and Dad.

They lived in a big pile out near Chalfont St Giles. Jez hadn't introduced me to his parents before then and this wasn't exactly the best of occasions on which to meet the folks but they were friendly enough. He called them by their first names, which seemed a bit odd to me. Alex was an advertising executive, Caroline had been a successful model in the sixties. They were seriously posh but they had this assumed air of casualness. I realised that this was the key to it. My middle-class act had always been a bit too earnest, too serious.

The mood in the house, though, was a little edgy. Jez had told them that his wound was an accident, that he had fallen on some broken glass. They hardly seemed convinced by that but they didn't say anything. Jez was quiet and brooding and I had to try to make conversation. At one point, when Jez was out of the room, Alex said:

'We're worried about Jez. He is all right, isn't he?'

'We know things have been difficult for him,' Caroline added.

And I tried to reassure them. I held back the feelings of resentment that I had. Jez had misspent his youth and pretended to rebel against privilege but there was always this safety net here for him. I'd walked a tightrope with a sheer drop below all my life, it seemed.

But then I remembered that I did have a wealthy benefactor. Starks. A gangster's trust fund, what a dreadful thought. That any precarious sense of self I might have had was tainted by the influence of his blood money. He had added insult to injury. He was not a benefactor, I reasoned, he was a malefactor.

On Sunday Jez's grandfather came to lunch. He had been a war hero, a major in the marines, decorated for gallantry in a rearguard action at Dunkirk. I was expecting some sort of terrifying old patriarch but he was nothing of the sort. He was a charming old soldier with a mischievous, almost camp manner. Jez was happy to see him; they were obviously very fond of each other.

'Lovely to meet you, Julie,' he said with a twinkle in his eye. 'Lucky old Jeremy, eh?'

He was clearly the only one in the family allowed to call Jez 'Jeremy'.

'Goodness me, Jeremy, you have been in the wars. What?'

'Jez had an accident,' Caroline explained.

'Hm,' the major went on. 'Looks like a bit of rough house to me. I know my old Jeremy. Always getting into scrapes, aren't you, boy?'

'Dad, you really shouldn't encourage him,' Alex complained.

'Nonsense, make a man of him. He'll have quite a duelling scar.'

Jez's mood lightened a bit at this. Later, as we were getting ready for bed, I caught him examining the line of stitches in the bathroom mirror, his blue eyes wide with wonder at his new face. I suddenly thought, maybe this is what he wanted. A war wound. A sign of manhood, of proof. A mark of initiation.

Back in London he was more sullen. He didn't want to go out at all, the noise and the bustle of the streets below seemed to frighten him. He moped about his flat during the day and slept badly at night. I spent as much time with him as I could but I was busy. There was a technical rehearsal, then a dress rehearsal, and we were previewing the play at the end of the week. Jez's wound was starting to heal; he had a cicatrice of scar tissue down the left side of his face. His prettiness now had an edge to it. His expression began to change, becoming colder, saturnine.

By the weekend I was off on tour. I'd felt for some time now that a great change was happening in my life, though I had no real idea what it might be. But I hadn't imagined that Jez might be changing too. I'd hoped that I could rely on the certainties of his life, a sense of stability I felt about him, of balance. Now I wasn't so sure. We said goodbye and made all kinds of promises to each other. But I was scared. I was worried about what we were both becoming.

3

essex comedown

Soma *was served with the coffee. Lenina took two half-grammes and Henry three. At twenty past nine they walked across to the newly opened Westminster Abbey Cabaret. It was a night almost without clouds, moonless and starry; but of this on the whole depressing fact Lenina and Henry were fortunately unaware. The electric sky-signs effectively shut off the outer darkness.* 'CALVIN STOPES AND HIS SIXTEEN SEXOPHONISTS', *from the façade of the new Abbey the giant letters invitingly glared.* 'LONDON'S FINEST SCENT AND COLOUR ORGAN. *ALL THE LATEST SYNTHETIC MUSIC*'.

Aldous Huxley, *Brave New World*

The snow has started to fall. Yes, the weather forecast is right for once: snow is general all over Essex. Watch it through the window. White dots against the black. Like an old telly gone on the blink. Interference. Like the fuzziness in my head.

The phone goes and I sort of jump a bit. I'm so fucking edgy. Pick it up.

'Yeah?'

'Gaz?'

It's Beardsley.

'Yeah. What?'

'The coma girl's dead.'

'Yeah?'

'Yeah.'

'So?'

'Look, Gaz, this isn't good. No. This is very bad. The press are going fucking crazy. This isn't inner-city lowlife. This is middle fucking England. And you know that her old man . . .'

'Yeah, I know. Used to be a cozzer.'

'Well, then. The fucking Essex Constabulary are going to be coming down heavy on all of us. We've got to sort a few things out.'

'Yeah, well, do you think . . .'

'Look, we shouldn't be talking on the phone. I just wanted to let you know, that's all. Let's meet in our usual place.'

'Right.'

Then he's gone. I put the phone down and try to think. I chop out a couple more lines on the coffee table, roll up a note and give it both barrels. More snow. Outside and inside. It's a fucking joke. My head is like a fucking snowstorm. You know, those little plastic domes filled with fluid and these little bits of white in them that swirl and fall tinkle tinkle tinkle when you turn them over.

I try to think. But everything seems blanked out. Like the landscape outside. Pick up the phone again and call Karen.

'Hello,' she says.

'Karen? It's me. Gaz.'

She sighs.

'Look, Gaz. I've got an injunction.'

'I know, I know. Look, you didn't have to do that.'

'Well, it's done.'

'Yeah. I'm sorry. Please. Come home.'

'Gaz, I can't cope with this. I can't cope with you.'

'It won't happen again, babe. I promise.'

'No. I can't trust you. You've got to sort yourself out. You know what? You need help, that's what you need. Professional help.'

'Look, I ain't going to see no shrink.'

'Well, you've got to do something. You've got to change.'

There's a bit of a pause. Can't think what to say.

'How are the girls?'

'Fine.'

'Do they miss their dad?'

'I can't deal with this, Gaz.' Her voice goes into a sob. 'I can't.'

The line goes dead. Hold the dialling tone against my head for a bit. Then put the phone down. Change. She's right. I've become a monster. I didn't mean to lash out. The snow's beginning to settle on the ground outside, white as uncut charlie. Need to talk to someone. Not a fucking shrink, that's for sure. A friend. Someone like Dan. He always seemed to know what was going to happen next. But I haven't seen Dan in five years.

Dan was my oldest and best friend. He'd settled down and I'd just carried on being naughty. It had always been just a bit of a laugh with Dan. Something I guess he always knew he'd grow out of. For me it was always serious.

We grew up together in Stepney. The East End was a shithole back then, don't let anyone tell you any different. Luftwaffe playgrounds. Bombsites that were never cleared with TEMPORARY OPEN SPACE council signs on them. Dad was a docker until he got laid off in the seventies. Worked hard all his life for some poxy redundancy pay-out. Then another job when we moved to Dagenham. Factory robot slave. They'd go on strike every so often to remind themselves they were human. That they could disobey orders. I decided early on that I wasn't going to be a mug like him.

Not that there were that many opportunities. But there were stories and rumours. People who had made something for themselves without ever being told what to do. Villains and gangsters. The Kray Twins. Harry Starks. Flash bastards. Legends.

I wanted to be someone. I wanted that kind of power and respect. I remember going to Madame Tussaud's on a school trip with Dan. I remember being overwhelmed by this idea that if you were famous enough they'd make this life-sized copy of you that people would come to gawp at.

'Fucking amazing, ain't it?' I said to Dan.

'They're only waxworks, Gaz,' he said. 'A bunch of fucking dummies.'

'Well,' I declared, 'I'm going to be in here one day.'

'The only way you're getting in here is when they put you in the Chamber of Horrors. You evil bastard.'

Dan started cackling and I went to give him a smack. But I remember thinking back then that he was probably right. I wanted to be someone. And if it was from doing bad I didn't care. I felt apart from other people. A tearaway, Mum called me. Torn away, more like. Never felt I could fit into a crowd. Never wanted to. A problem child, school called me. Even sent me to this school shrink. Never did any good. Once, when he was out of the room, I took a butcher's at something he'd written down: *Gary Kelly's disruptive behaviour is an obvious ploy to get attention.*

But maybe they were right all along and there is something wrong with me. Maybe Karen's right and I need to have my head examined. I don't know.

The next day I'm driving out to a service station on the M25 to meet Beardsley. Get a paper and a cup of tea and sit in my usual place. On the front page is this picture of the girl that died after banging a pill at a party in Basildon. A tangle of tubes coming out of her face. *LOOK WHAT DRUGS DO*, screams the headline. *The picture her parents want Britain to remember.*

Beardsley arrives. He picks up the paper and looks at it. Shakes his head and sighs.

'Isn't that terrible?'

I nod. He drops the paper on the table. Stares at me.

'You don't look so good yourself, Gaz.'

'I'm all right.'

'You wanna sort yourself out, son.'

'Look, I just had a rough night. OK?'

'OK, OK. So. What do we know about this?'

He points at the paper. I shrug.

'The pill was bought at a club in Basildon. Some people are saying it was contaminated.'

Beardsley shakes his head.

'No. It wasn't a snide one. I've heard that for sure. It was an Apple. You know what that means, don't you?'

Apples were a new batch of Es from Amsterdam. Extra strong, they were. Beardsley had smuggled a load of them in only a couple of weeks before.

'It means they could trace it to us,' I say.

'Yeah, us or Tony Tucker's firm. They were dealing them as well. Look, Essex Old Bill are going to want a body for this and there'll be no peace for the wicked until they find someone.'

'So?'

'So, we keep our heads down until it all blows over. Yeah, and maybe someone should give them a clue. Let Tucker's firm take the blame.'

'You saying we should grass somebody up?'

'Well, it doesn't have to be like that, does it? It could be done, like, indirectly.'

'How?'

'I don't know, do I? We'll think of something, eh?'

'Yeah.'

'One thing is for sure. The happy smiley time is over.'

'Beardsley,' I said. 'The happy smiley time was over long ago.'

I never figured I'd know about fashion, let alone be able to make a lot of money out of one. Fact is, in the past, fashion always caught me out somehow. No, it was Dan that knew about style and that. Right from the start. He'd follow the trends, be up with whatever the thing was that week. Aged twelve and he was a baby skinhead. Orange Ben Sherman, white Sta-Press, braces and cherry-red Astronauts. I wasn't so flash. Monkey boots, jungle greens and a collarless shirt. We were too young for it first time around. We tried following around the older kids but they'd tell us to piss off. One thing I have to say: I fucking loved the music. Ska and bluebeat. Dad would always complain: 'Turn that fucking jungle-bunny music down!' he'd shout. I could get lost in it, the mad skanking rhythm of it.

The fashions moved and Dan moved with them. Always one step ahead of the other kids in our school. The seventies. He grew his hair out. Suedehead then a shoulder-length Smoothie. Had it done in a feather cut. Platform shoes. Oxford bags. Tank tops with silver stars on. He followed the football too. West Ham, of course. The Under Fives. They were like an apprentice firm for kids who wanted to prove themselves and would spy on rival fans for the older hooligans. I used to go along to home matches. But I couldn't really understand it all, you know. I always thought that if you were going to get into trouble it should be for some sort of gain. Hooliganism, vandalism, Paki-bashing, these things were done just for the buzz. There had to be more to it than that.

And I'd started to notice the real villains around my way. The clothes, the gold, the cars. They had got something out of life. Something more than cheap thrills at the weekend and some shitty job for the rest of your days.

Well, we moved to bloody Dagenham. The old man got a job on the assembly line at Ford, building 1600E Cortinas. New school and I had to prove myself. But I was a big lad, even then. I could handle myself. Age fourteen and I was already scaring the teachers. I didn't have Dan around to get me into normal teenage trouble. So the trouble I got into started getting serious.

Next time I saw Dan was five years later, 1979. I'd just got out of Youth Detention for the second time. Burglary. I'd liked the idea of it but I was no good at it. I was a big clumsy fucker. You needed to be light footed and nimble to shin up drainpipes and balance on window ledges. I kept on getting caught, didn't I? Ended up in the juvenile courts. Probation, approved school, borstal, the lot.

After a while Mum and Dad didn't want me back home any more. Can't say I blamed them, I'd caused them enough grief and I wanted to get away from them and all. So I found myself looking for clues back in the East End and that's when I bumped into Dan. It gave me a shock when I saw him, though. It wasn't that I didn't recognise him. It was like he'd become too familiar. The long hair, the lairy big collars, the flared trousers – gone. He'd got a number-one crop, bottle-green Fred Perry, straight-leg Levi's and a pair of Doc Martens. Like all the seventies had been cut away from him and there was just a big version of the little Dan I knew ten years ago. I mean, time plays tricks when you're away inside. Every time you come out you have to try and catch up. New money, new governments. But this was like time had gone backwards. I shook my head.

'What's happened, Dan?'

He gave me this big nutty grin.

'The skinheads are back, Gaz,' he announced.

He played me this new record. It was a version of 'Skinhead Moonstomp' by this local group called Earthquake. *Yeh-yeh-yeh-yeah, yeah, yeaah, yeaah, yeaah, yeaaah.*

I laughed. 'Fuck me. This takes me back.'

He told me that this was the new thing now. Two Tone, they were calling it. Ska bands like The Specials and The Selecter from the Midlands and Earthquake who were from Upton Park. They were playing at the Music Machine in Camden Town that very night.

'Come along,' Dan said. 'It'll be a laugh.'

It seemed a bit odd. A bit too young for it first time around and a bit too old for it now. But then I'd missed out on my youth what with borstal and probation and that. And I'd always loved the music. I grinned at Dan.

'Yeah, all right,' I said.

'Just one thing we've got to sort out.'

I still had long hair, of course. Everybody had it when I'd gone away last. So Dan got his electric clippers out and shaved it all off in the kitchen. Funny, it's a treatment you expect going into Youth Detention, not coming out of it.

So we went to this gig mob handed. All these new skinhead types. West Ham, most of them. The InterCity Firm they were calling themselves these days, on account of the fact that they had started to travel in this fashion to away games instead of on the poxy football specials that were laid on for the plebs. Made it easier to avoid the Old Bill or being ambushed by rival home fans, and it was a helluva lot more flash. And they did like looking flash. The ICF/Earthquake look was boots, red-tag Levi's and tasty-looking green MA1 flight jackets. Lots of familiar and half-familiar faces. Lots of drinks bought for me when Dan told people where I'd just come from. It was more of a homecoming than I got from Ma and Pa, that was for sure. Had a line of sulphate with Dan in the bogs and I was raring to go.

Earthquake took the stage and we all went mental. I felt the speed rush come up as I was bouncing around in this crowd. They played ska dead fast, drums, bass, guitar, organ, saxophone and two guys out front. A white guy who did the singing and this black kid in a porkpie hat and wraparound shades who called out on the rhythm, went *chicka chicka chicka chicka*, or talked his talk over the songs. It's funny, because there was a bit of *sieg-heiling* between numbers from some of the skins. I saw some NF and British Movement badges on the arm pockets of some of the MA1 jackets in the crowd. And when they did 'Skinhead Moonstomp', this black guy, Caleb he called himself, called out, NOW REMEMBER, I'M YOUR BOSS SKINHEAD SPEAKING. HUH? REMEMBER, I'M THE BOSS, and most of the skins cheered but there was some monkey-noise taunting and *sieg-heiling* from the crowd as well. I didn't try to understand this. I just felt the buzz of it all. It was like having my childhood back after being banged up and confined.

Some poxy punk band were on next so we went on the rampage. Scared the fuck out of all of these punk rockers, even though they outnumbered us about four to one. They didn't want to know. Went back to Dan's afterwards. He let me kip on the sofa, said I could stay for a bit, until I found a place of my own. He was working as a plasterer and he said he'd keep a lookout for any labouring work that might be going. Well, I didn't fancy that but I didn't say anything because he was just being a good mate, looking out for me and that. I hung about with his group of friends, brought the gear, went to the Earthquake gigs. It was a bit of a laugh and, I guess, a bit like being in a gang but I didn't think that it was a thing that I really belonged to. But then I met Beardsley.

Earthquake were doing this gig at the Hope and Anchor on Upper Street and some trouble kicked off. There were these North London skins there that were acting like they owned the place. Someone got shoved and a fight broke out. I waded in and started to put it about a bit lively. It was this mob instinct, I guess. Them and us. I can be big and nasty if I want to be, and I was. I led the charge and we ran them out of there.

Afterwards I was standing about having a drink and I was kind of like the centre of attention for a bit, the others standing around me, and it was then that Beardsley came over. The group around me just parted to let him through, lots of respect, that's what Beardsley got, and there he was, suddenly in front of me, looking me up and down. Simon Beardsley was Earthquake's manager. A skinhead legend, he was. Rumour had it that he started the whole thing back in the sixties. He'd only shot a couple of Hell's Angels in the Golden Goose amusement arcade in Piccadilly back then. A real face. A real villain too, in his time. He'd worked with Harry Starks and Jack 'The Hat' McVitie. And he'd done a lot of porridge. He was supposed to be legitimate now but the music business always was a front for all kinds of naughtiness and everybody knew that he'd never really retired. And there he was, shaped up in front of me, staring me out. He gave this little grin – just showing his teeth, mind, the eyes stayed cold.

'Think you're fucking tasty, don't you?' he asked flat, all matter-of-fact.

I shrugged. Nodded.

'Yeah,' I replied.

He smiled, eyes and all this time.

'Good. Want a job, rude boy?'

'What?' I gave a little laugh, surprised at the question. 'What you mean?'

'I mean working for me. Earthquake are going on tour. We're going to need extra security. What you reckon?'

That's how I first teamed up with Beardsley. All that time ago. I've learnt a lot from him over the years. Now he thinks I'm losing it. *You wanna sort yourself out, son.* Yeah, yeah. So everyone's on my fucking case now.

I go home and crash out. Wake up around seven and make myself something to eat. Watch a bit of telly. The news comes on and there's more about the girl that died. Grieving parents. Kind of shakes me up a bit. Think about my daughters. Charlene and Donna. Karen won't let me see them. Pour myself a drink and brood about it. Can't help thinking about the coma girl. What if something like that happened to one of my kids?

Snap out of it. Got to go into Southend tonight. Have a couple of lines to sharpen myself up. Drive to Tiffany's, this Sharon and Tracey club near the seafront that's started doing House and Jungle nights for the last couple of years. I run the doors there, which also means controlling who does the dealing. But it's the legit stuff to sort out tonight. I've got all the invoices so that the doormen can get paid.

Frank, the manager, is out front, expecting me. Friday night is usually busy as fuck but tonight it's a fucking graveyard.

'How's it going, Frank?'

He rolls his eyes.

'This business with this girl,' I say, shaking my head.

'Well,' he replies, 'I think we can forget about our four o'clock licence for a while.'

Frank had applied for an extension at the weekends.

'Speaking of which,' he goes on, 'had a bloke from the council in here earlier. Looking for you. Wants you to phone him.'

He fishes out this business card and hands it to me. *Roger Wilbey*, it says, *Environmental Health Registration Scheme*. This could be hassle over my licence to run doors. There's been complaints against me. Fuck. That's all I fucking need.

I pay off the doormen and have a quick chat with George, the head bouncer. He nods at a bloke over at the bar.

'See him? Well, there's something dodgy about that one.'

I look around slowly. Short ginger hair, lime-green Ted Baker shirt worn on the outside, a pair of dark blue Dockers. Eyes darting about, as if looking for something.

'He's been asking around, wants to "score", apparently.'

'And has he?'

'Nah, I've told everyone to act innocent.'

'Good. What you reckon? Cozzer?'

George frowns.

'Don't think so. Don't know what he is but he just doesn't look right. Shall I chuck him out?'

'No. I'll deal with it.'

I go over and stand beside him at the bar. Now I ain't exactly inconspicuous so he soon notices this big fucker looming over him.

'You sorted?' I ask him.

'Er, no,' he replies.

'Well, I've got Apples. Dead strong. Ten pound each.'

His little eyes light up. He reaches into his pocket.

'Not here,' I tell him. 'Follow me.'

I lead him out to the fire escape at the back, beckon him to go up against the bar on the double doors, then give him a big shove into the alleyway beyond. He tumbles over into this pile of boxes and rubbish. I wave to George to come and close the door after me and I go out myself. I pick this bloke up. He's whimpering a bit.

'Please,' he says. 'Please don't hurt me.'

'Who the fuck are you?'

'Press,' he wheezes.

'What?'

'Journalist,' he goes on, still out of breath. '*Sunday Illustrated*.'

I laugh and let go of him.

'What's the story? How the evil dealers have taken over the clubs?'

'Yeah. Well, something like that.'

Then it hits me. This could be it. Beardsley saying how we need to hand somebody up for that girl dying. Well, this could be the way. Don't have to go to the cozzers. Do it through the papers. I laugh again.

'You want a story?'

He nods.

'Well, I'll give you a story.'

We go back to his hotel room. I say: you can put that fucking tape machine away for a start. Just write it down. You want an exclusive? Well, he goes. No, don't worry about payment. This is a favour (and remember I'll want one back in return). Just get all of this down.

I go through the lot with him. Give him a couple of Tony Tucker's dealers. That should keep the cozzers off our backs for a while. Give him some leads to follow up in time for a big juicy story on Sunday.

Help myself to the minibar. Start to flag after a while and I get the charlie out.

'Fancy a toot?' I ask.

And this little hack, Keith is his name, he sort of looks all wide eyed for a bit and gives this silly little grin that middle-class wankers give when they think they're doing something naughty.

'Oh, yeah, all right, then.'

These media types, they're the fucking worst, if you ask me.

Drugs. The big story. Never thought it would ever get this big. Me and Beardsley thought we could just retire to Essex and live off the fat of the land. But it got so fucking competitive. Villains moving in from everywhere. No one's going to bother with over-the-pavement stuff when you could make so much money dealing. Thing is, we'd been at it for quite a while, Beardsley had been selling uppers way back in the sixties. But we never figured it would get this big.

Back in 1979 when I first worked with him it was just 'extras'. I didn't know what he meant when he'd employed me as a minder for Earthquake. He just said:

'Well, it's a ton a week plus extras.'

So I ended up going around the country with the band in this battered old coach. My job was to look after them. I'd meet up with whoever was organising the stewards for whatever venue we were playing to let them know who I was. It was their job to look after the hall. I'd be with the band backstage and then down the front when they were playing. Then afterwards, when the road crew were getting the stuff out, I'd be about in case there was any trouble. I made sure I was tooled up. A bottle of squirt, ammonia that is, and a Stanley knife.

During a gig it would get pretty mad. Most nights I'd find myself on stage near the end to stop the local crowd storming it. I'd be pretty whizzed up by then and I'd end up doing this funny kind of boot stomp to the music as I pushed or kicked out at any potential interlopers. After a while it became part of the act, me getting up to do this nutty dance. I got known by the hard-core Earthquake followers and they'd chant 'Gaz, Gaz, Gaz' at me. I even ended up being featured on the video for the band's second single, 'Ska Train InterCity'. I liked that. Showing off. Having a bit of recognition.

And I found out soon enough what Beardsley had meant by 'extras'. He had this amphetamine factory somewhere out in Canning Town banging out kilos of speed and he had me look after shifting it to the audience every night. Kevin, one of the roadies, did the dealing and I'd be his minder in case there was any hassle or any rival dealers to be dealt with. Beardsley didn't want the band to know about it or get caught up in it in any way. They already had an 'image problem', as he called it. The NF and British Movement elements of the band's following were doing them no favours at all. There were these stupid press stories calling them 'Nazi Hooligans' and shit like that. So I was to make sure that the speed business was all done discreetly.

It was sweet. I was having fun and making a load of money out of it. There were groupies here and there, too. Girl skins with peroxide fringes around the crop. And with the side racket I was running I had a way into the dodgy side of Beardsley's activities. Something I felt sure would come in handy for the future. I was thinking of the long term, see? After the tour.

We did the North, and the Midlands, then made our way South again. But it was at the Queensway Hall, Dunstable, that's when things kicked off really badly.

There was a big fuss by the front entrance. This mob had arrived who were out to get any NF or BM skins. Now some of them were weedy-looking lefty types, there were some Anti-Nazi League placards and that, but with them were a bunch of real nasty, pikey-looking greasers. One of the Queensway Hall stewards said he thought they were the South-East Outlaws, a local biker gang. This chant had started up, *Fascists out! Fascists out!* Now there wasn't much point in trying to reason with this lot, pointing out that there was a black guy in the group, for fuck's sake. The greeboes were here for a ruck, that was for sure.

The stewards were keeping them out for now, but for how long? I got on the phone to Beardsley and begged him to get some back-up to us. Dan and some of his ICF mates were at the gig so I got him to round up some of the tastier ones among them and get them to tool themselves up with whatever came to hand. Kevin the roadie had equipped himself with a short scaffolding pole. So I assembled my troops and gave them a bit of a pep talk.

Half an hour later, just as the support act was going on stage, there was this banging noise from below. The greasers were kicking at the fire doors in the downstairs foyer, where the cloakroom and the bogs were. We rushed down the stairs mob handed just as they stormed in. Some of the skins who were quick on their toes got caught up in the charge and took a right pasting. I shouted at the others to hold back so that we could make a proper stand.

This ugly bearded greebo was coming forward slowly, a rusty cut-throat in his hand.

'Who wants some?' he taunted, his little eyes gleaming.

Behind him some poor fucker was being kicked about like a rag doll. I looked around. A lot of the skins had bottled out and made for the girls' toilets. Kevin and Dan were beside me and a few others behind.

I took my squirt bottle out and let the cut-throat geezer have it right in the eyes. He started squealing. Another bloke came forward and Kevin whacked him out cold with the scaffolding pole. More and more of them were coming through the fire doors and we moved back to the stairs to get some high ground, lashing out desperately at anything that moved. This biker was swinging a chain about at us, which actually kept back some of his own side, he was going so wildly with it. We were just about holding our ground but it couldn't last.

Then there was this loud boom. A shotgun, no doubt about it. Fuck, I thought, this is it, they've got fucking shotguns. But there was a commotion outside. Someone shouting and the greasers legging it. A whiff of cordite and suddenly Beardsley appeared through the fire doors in a sheepskin coat with some other geezer behind him holding a sawn-off. And the rest of the greeboes scarpered.

After the gig I drove back to London with Beardsley and the bloke with the shotgun, Declan he was called.

'I owe you a drink,' Beardsley had said.

We ended up in an after-hours club he ran in Tottenham. Rock steady music playing in the background.

'So,' he said. 'You fancy some more work once this tour's over?'

'What, with Earthquake?'

'Nah. I don't think there's going to be many more gigs for a while the way things are going. All this trouble that's been kicking off. Bookers don't want to know, to tell you the truth. The band is going to have to clean up its act if they want to go anywhere now. I'm trying to get them to change their image, become more like a comedy band, sort of, you know, music-hall stuff. A novelty record, that would be good. Get a younger following, drop all of this heavy skinhead palaver. It's been bad for business.'

'You mean stop being a ska band?'

He frowned, shrugged. A new track came over the sound system.

'I'm In A Dancing Mood' by Delroy Wilson. Beardsley smiled at it.

'Listen to this,' he said. 'This is the real stuff. Earthquake are just plastic compared to this. Look, I'm as honky as the next guy but white boys just ain't got it. All the music I've ever loved has been spade music. R&B, Tamla Motown, reggae. White kids, well, they try to copy it but they just ain't got the soul. You know what I mean?'

I nodded vaguely. Wasn't quite sure what he was on about to tell you the truth. He'd mentioned work and I wanted us to get back to that subject.

'So,' I said. 'This "work", it wouldn't be with Earthquake?'

'No. I reckon you've done your apprenticeship. I was thinking of something more, well, serious.'

I liked the sound of this.

'Yeah,' I replied, nodding, grinning. 'Sure.'

And so I started doing jobs for him on a regular basis. There was the speed racket that was turning over nicely and Beardsley branched out into coke and hash. There was this bloke who smuggled it into Essex from Amsterdam in this big fuck-off power boat. Beardsley would use me and Declan as minders on meetings when big quantities of drugs and cash were being exchanged.

Beardsley was still officially in the music business. It was a useful front for all the dodgy dealings he was up to. I learnt from him that it was always important to have some sort of legitimate front. Earthquake released their last single at the end of the year. It flopped and they split up but Beardsley carried on doing stuff. 'Management and Promotions', he called it. He also ran various hookey companies, not in his own name, of course. Long-firm frauds that would be set up and then dissolved, with a load of unpaid for goods going missing. These would need front men, 'business associates', he called them, that would sometimes have to take the rap if there was a proper investigation. Sometimes his unfortunate 'partners' would want to tell all about who was behind the scheme when they got a tug from the Old Bill. And that's when me and Declan would be called in to give a little gentle persuasion, as it were. And that's when I got into trouble again.

This bloke, Douggie Kennedy, he was adamant that he wasn't going away for this warehouse load of electrical goods in Wood

Green. So we went around to see him. Well, it got pretty nasty and he ended up hospitalised. Then he grassed us all up. In the end they couldn't get a result on the long firm itself so we would have all been all right if only he'd held his mouth. But me and Declan ended up going down for two counts of making an unwarranted menace and one count of GBH.

So I went away again. It was proper bird this time. Two years. Prison was a real education for me. Approved school, borstal, that had been like O-level stuff. But this was the university. The Royal College of Useful Knowledge.

I did my first couple of months in the Scrubs. This was an allocation period when they work out what category you are and where to put you. An overcrowded Victorian gaol, three to a tiny little cell. A real mix of cons during allocation. I was banged up with some nutter who had been robbing sub post offices and this timid little white-collar bloke who was in for embezzlement. Everybody's trying to front it out in their own way, working out what the pecking order is. You're in with some really horrible people and some proper arseholes too. You learn quick how to look through people, to know whether someone is genuinely dangerous or just full of bullshit.

After about six weeks in the Scrubs I was allocated to Coldingley, this modern nick in Surrey. Electronic doors and cameras everywhere. I got to know some proper faces in there. Tommy Patterson, this South London villain with a real reputation. One of the chaps, as they say. And Chris Lambrianou, who had been on the Kray firm.

I was a bit wary of Chris at first because he was in for being part of the murder of Jack 'The Hat' McVitie, and Beardsley and the Hat had been a team back in the sixties. Prison paranoia – you're always aware that there might be grudges, scores to settle, shit like that. I needn't have worried. Chris had found God and put all of that Kray stuff behind him. He was this big, mild-mannered, born-again Christian who worked in the prison garden. Chris was a clever bloke, wise, I guess you'd call it. He did me a favour once and I thanked him for it. He smiled and said, 'A brother is born to help in time of need.'

But, to be honest, I wasn't after that kind of wisdom. I wasn't ready to be saved, I was up for more villainy once I was out. Tommy Patterson was well connected. He knew Beardsley and some of the other faces I'd got to know on the outside. So I learnt from him.

About how reputations are made and used. How to get to know the right people. And how to get to be known by them. Prison is full of nasty, devious people for the most part. You find out who to trust and who to steer clear of. You get to spot what bad is really like, I mean real bad, not just naughty bad. So when I got to the end of my sentence I thought I was a little bit cleverer than when I had first gone in. I'd done a little bit. Just a little bit of time at the start of my career that could stand me in good stead.

'You know,' I say to this Keith bloke in his hotel room, 'I got loads of stories I could tell you. Tricks of the trade, faces I've known, stuff like that.'

'Yeah,' he replies, nodding. Looks a bit wired.

'I could tell you stories, Keith. Look, fancy another line? Shit. I run out. I could go and get some more.'

'Look, Gaz. I better get some sleep. I need to get on with this story. But I hear what you're saying. I'm always interested in a good story.'

He hands me his card.

'Let's keep in touch,' he says.

Go back to the motor. Freezing night air clears the head a bit. Don't want to go home. Don't want to go back to a poxy empty house. Run out of gear anyway. Christmas lights on everywhere. Feel so fucking lonely. Need to get out of it. Out of my head.

Phone Martin on the mobile. One of our dealers. Come on over, he says. Like I'm welcome somewhere. A semi-detached council house out in Braintree. Martin's been saving up to buy it on the discount. Then maybe sell it on. Get on the property ladder, so he says. Only he's worried about this negative equity thing.

Martin stays up all night watching satellite. Works the night shift drugs-wise. Always reliable like that, and he can afford to charge a little bit extra for the availability. Like those twenty-four-hour Paki grocers.

Of course, I'm a discount customer. But I always give Martin something just for the service. My nights have been so fucked recently I've needed it badly.

Get in the door and he's already talking about the girl that died.

'Leave it out Martin,' I say. 'I've heard enough about her.'

We go in through to the lounge and there's this young bird on the settee. Eyes dark rimmed, filmy and blinking, like little screens reflecting the gloomy light of the telly.

'But it was an Apple, wasn't it? That's what done her, I heard. I've been dealing them myself.'

'Look, Martin, just give it a rest for a bit. I've had enough.'

Martin shrugs, hands up like an apology. Scared of me like most of them. Without being asked he gets the gear out and starts chopping out big long lines of it on the powder-smeared mirror on the coffee table.

I sit down next to this girl. She turns her head slightly and gives me a fucked-up smile.

'Natalie,' says Martin. 'This is Gaz.'

'Hi,' she sighs.

We hoover up the coke. Martin skins up some skunk weed. A bottle of Jack Daniel's. This is good. Feel numb. Warm. It's started snowing again outside. Time goes whizzing past. Grey morning comes. Kids' cartoons on the telly. Natalie giggling on the settee.

We have some ketamine. *Special K for breakfast*, Martin jokes. I'm lying on the floor as the horse tranquilliser takes hold. *I could tell you stories*, I mutter to myself. I feel so heavy, sinking into the stained white shagpile like I weigh a hundred tons. The world is spinning, falling, turning. Body dead. Mind racing. Thinking. Remembering. Coming out of prison that first time.

Coming out, well, you're never prepared for it. Release date is all you ever think about inside but it doesn't make you ready for it. Outside seems extra manic and bright after being in the grey world inside. And there are all these changes, things that have happened to remind you that everything has moved on while you've been standing still. It was June 1982, three million on the dole and there'd been a war with Argentina. But it was the little things that took me by surprise, as per fucking usual.

I was on the Underground, Central Line going east, off to see Dan in Mile End. Now I was wearing what I wore before I went inside. Doc Martens, red-tag Levi's, green MA1 jacket. And I'd just had a number-one crop, almost the first thing I did when I came out. Well, this bloke gets on at Liverpool Street dressed exactly the same, skinhead just like me, and sits opposite. I clock him, thinking maybe he's a face I know, someone from the Earthquake days or one of

Dan's ICF mates. But when I look up: nothing. Don't know him from Adam even though it's kind of like looking in the mirror. He's a big bloke, like me. I sort of give him a slight nod and he nods back slowly. A half-smile on his gob but a cold stare. Like he's saying: *Yeah, I know you*. But I don't know him. And I think: shit, maybe he's Millwall or one of the North London skins I had a row with that time. I look away. I don't want to get into a row with this geezer. I've only just got out, for fuck sake. I look back and he's eyeing me up and down like he's thinking about how he's going to do me. I give him the fiercest eyeballing I can muster but he's screwing me back, still with this stupid smile on his face. I decide to ignore him. I think to myself: I could have this cunt but he's not worth it. It's not worth the bother. Unnecessary aggro. That's one of the things I learnt to avoid inside.

So we get to Mile End and I get up to get off. I give him a last *fuck you* look and step out on to the platform. As I'm going up the steps I glance back to see he's only got off himself, hasn't he. I try to think nothing of it, maybe it's his stop as well. But as I'm going down Burdett Road I look back and there he is. He is definitely following me. I start to get ready for the off. Thinking. Maybe he's tooled up. I haven't got a thing on me. I start looking around, for a brick or something.

I go into the waste ground by Mile End Park and shape up. I am definitely going to have this fucker, I decide. I'm by some manky bushes waiting for him.

'Over here,' I call out to him as he comes by.

He sees me and smiles, walks up to me.

'Isn't this a bit open?' he asks.

It was then I realise that something is wrong. Very, very wrong. His voice doesn't match his clothes. It's soft, a bit posh.

'What do you mean?' I say.

He comes right up close to me. I don't fucking believe this.

'Well, if we're going to, you know . . .'

He is touching me, the fucker is only stroking my fucking leg.

'Get your fucking hands . . .'

I push him away. I shape up to give him an almighty punch but he's still staring with that silly smile on his lips like maybe this was something he was into too. So I draw back. I don't want to touch him.

'Fucking queer!' I shout at him.

But he just carries on smiling. Lets out this queeny sigh.

'Oo, we are upset, aren't we?'

'Look, just fuck off, OK?'

He shrugs and turns to walk away.

'Another time, then,' he calls out.

I was fuming. I felt like going after him and kicking the shit out of him but I knew that would make things worse. I felt dirty. And confused. What was a queer doing dressed up like that?

When I met up with Dan he explained it all to me, as usual. As usual, the fashions had changed while I'd been away. They'd gone fucking haywire.

I mean, now Dan looked like a poof. Floppy hair in a side parting. A pink polo shirt and V-neck golf sweater, for fuck's sake. Slacks and these silly slip-on loafers and white socks. This was what the ICF lot were wearing now, apparently. I told him the story. I was embarrassed, to tell you the truth. Dan just laughed like a drain.

'Well, Gaz, it's only poofs that are wearing stuff like that these days,' he said, pointing at my clobber. 'That and the diehard Nazi lot.'

'You mean homos are dressing like skinheads?'

'Yeah. Crazy, isn't it?'

And all the hooligans were now going for this poncey look. Designer stuff. The casual look, Dan explained. Obsessed with labels. Pringle, Fila, Sergio Tacchini, Diadora, Ellesse, Lacoste. All trying to outdo each other with all this expensive gear. Like a bunch of girls. All with this floppy side-parted hairstyle, the Wedge, they called it.

I don't know, poofs dressed like hooligans, hooligans dressed like poofs. Well, I thought I'd seen it all now. I thought that if I ever went away and came out again fashion would never change in such a crazy way. I was wrong, of course. The next time it would be even weirder, but we'll come to that later.

So, I started wearing this designer stuff, didn't I? Got rid of my old gear. I mean, I didn't want people to think I was a bum-bandit or some NF loony. But I kept the hair short. It suited me. All this label stuff was like a sign of the times. It wasn't just about looking flash, the label showed it cost a lot of money too, it proved you had cash. The East End was changing, all that proud-to-be-working-class stuff was over. The docks were being redeveloped, there was real dosh to be made, legitimate too. Some of Dan's mates even worked in the City, for fuck's sake. It was a funny time. A lot of people were out of pocket while some were flush. There was a lot of selling-off going on and money sloshing about in the trough.

I went back to work for Beardsley. I'd kept my mouth shut and done my time so he owed me work. Business was booming for him too. Though it weren't exactly legit.

He had a new scam. Gold. He was smuggling it into the country and selling it to a reputable dealer. The buyer would be liable to pay VAT, fifteen per cent of the cost price. Of course, Beardsley's 'company' would just be a fake firm with short-let office accommodation with some headed notepaper with a moody VAT number on it that would fold in a couple of months without making any returns. So he could pocket fifteen per cent of all the deals he had made. It was quick money. And simple.

'You mean you're actually collecting tax?' I asked him.

'Yeah,' he said with a big grin. 'On behalf of Her Majesty's Customs and Excise. Except her lot doesn't exactly get to see any of it. Good, ain't it?'

So Beardsley got to know a lot about gold. And when the Hounslow bullion job happened he was well placed to have a bit of it. Fifteen million pounds' worth of gold blagged. The whole of the underworld started buzzing about the bullion and where it might be going. Of course, Beardsley was well placed for a touch but he played it all very carefully. There was a lot at stake and it got a little bit hairy, I can tell you.

I got to work out what was happening by the little things he told me when I was running errands. And I put some of it together myself as well. I knew that the gold had to be resmelted first before it could be sold on. And there was this front man, Solly Blumberg, who ran a jeweller's in Hatton Garden who would do the selling to legitimate gold dealers and fix the paperwork so it looked like it was kosher. Me, Beardsley or someone else on his firm would courier the stuff down to Solly bit by bit.

We'd have to be extra careful because Beardsley figured that there was a lot of surveillance going on. C11, the Met's Criminal Intelligence Unit, or customs investigators. I've never exactly looked inconspicuous so I went for this disguise. I'd dress up like some

Aussie backpacker with a stupid hat on to cover my features and the trademark crop. I'd come out of Farringdon Station with this rucksack on which was, of course, stuffed full of resmelted gold bars. Weighed a fucking ton. I'd walk down to Hatton Garden and into Solly's shop. I'd announce in this stupid accent I'd rehearsed in front of Beardsley that I was looking for an engagement ring for my sheila back in Wogga Wogga. Solly would start showing me trays of stuff and I'd take off the backpack. Then, while we were fannying on, the rucksack would be swapped for an identical one with just clothes and stuff in it.

Solly was a real talker. Never knew what the hell he was on about half the time but he could be dead funny. Always telling these Jewish jokes.

There was this other bloke involved too. Manny Gould, an ancient bent accountant who dealt with the money that was made from selling the bullion. Laundering, offshore banking stuff that was well above my head. Once, I took a whole suitcase of £50 notes down to southern Spain. Fuengirola was the drop, at 'Pete's English Bar', run by a cousin of Beardsley's. There was an international organisation that was running things. I had my own ideas about who might be behind it all but I kept my mouth shut and tried not to think about it too much. It doesn't pay to know too much sometimes.

Anyway, we were raking it in. Beardsley bought this huge mansion in Essex with a swimming pool and everything. And he was paying me a fair whack. But the money I earned during that time soon went. Motors, flash clothes, tarts, a bit of charlie from time to time, gambling, going out and showing off. I knew in my mind that I should be putting some of this gelt aside, investing it or whatever. But in my heart I always felt that it was bad money. Money that had to be spent.

I still kept in touch with Dan. He was doing all right for himself and all. There was a lot of building work going on in Docklands. He'd settled down with this bird Marcia and they'd had a kid together. But the funny thing was he was still running with the ICF at weekends. And they were so fucking organised. Blokes pushing thirty still acting like hooligans. Like military planning how they took on their enemies. They even printed up calling cards to leave on rival fans that they'd done, *Congratulations, you have just met the ICF*, stuff like that. I couldn't understand it given that they weren't making anything out of it.

Then we got some bad news. Beardsley had been doing some surveillance of his own. Apparently Solly had been visited by the Flying Squad at his Hatton Garden premises and had kept shtum about it. Then some gold went missing. Beardsley reckoned that Solly might be making a deal with the cozzers. Returning some of the stuff officially or using it as a bribe. Whatever, it looked bad. If Solly coughed we could all be fucked.

Beardsley and me went round to his shop as he was closing up. Solly acted all jovial and friendly. You could tell he was scared, though.

'Simon,' he greeted Beardsley, his arms raised palms upward. 'And young Gary. I didn't recognise you without your wild colonial boy disguise.'

Beardsley was worried that Solly might be wired up so the conversation was all sort of coded.

'I told them nothing,' Solly insisted.

'Really?' said Beardsley. 'Then why didn't you tell us that you'd had visitors?'

'I didn't want to worry you. This I can deal with myself.'

'Deal? You've made a deal?'

'No, you misunderstand me. No deal. No talk. No nothing.'

'So where's the stuff gone?'

'Well, I had to put it somewhere safe for a while. I can't say right now where it is.'

'You won't say, you mean.'

'No, no. Can't. Some things cannot be said. Or rather they are explained in another way.'

'You're talking in riddles, Solly.'

'Yes. Well, that's it. That's exactly it.'

'Look, Solly. You really shouldn't be fucking us around like this. There's far too much at stake. We need to know where it is.'

'No, please, Simon, try to understand. It's hidden but' – he leaned forward and whispered – 'there's a map.'

'What are you talking about, a map?'

'That's what makes it safe. Just give me some more time.'

'I can't promise you any more time. Sorry, Solly. It's not just down to me, you know. Come on, Gaz.'

'Please, Simon,' Solly begged as we walked out of the shop.

Two days later Solly Blumberg was shot dead as he was opening up his shop in the morning. A motorcycle with a pillion passenger pulled up beside him and three bullets were fired into him.

Beardsley never made any direct comment on whether it had been him that had ordered the hit. 'Shame about poor Solly,' was about the most he'd ever say on the subject.

And after that the bullion thing got really quiet. The missing gold never got found, either by the cozzers or people on our side. Rumours went round about it being hidden somewhere. Buried treasure. Beardsley stopped being involved and tried to make sure that there was nothing that could link him to it. And I tried to forget it all. To deliberately not remember things and to work out all sorts of alibis for that time. Bit by bit a lot of the dodgy businessmen who had been handling the Hounslow bullion got pulled but Beardsley remained in the clear. One thing stayed in my mind, though. Solly had got done. I could get done one day.

So it made me a little edgy. But that's a natural thing, isn't it? I mean, you look at an animal in the wild and their little head is going to be darting about all the time, checking out if some bigger fucker's going to do them. And at the same time they're looking around for something to pounce on themselves.

Open my eyes and I'm looking up at the ceiling. Little swirls of textured paint. Move my head to look around. Natalie asleep on the settee. No sign of Martin. I'm fucking lying on the floor. Weak as a kitten. I try to sit up a little but I'm pinned down, like I'm on a fairground ride, as the whole of Martin's council house goes whizzing around through space. I'm fucking helpless. Anyone could come in and do me.

I look around the lounge. There's a sheath knife under the coffee table. I crawl over and grab it. I've got to get up and get on. But I've got to rest for a bit more. I just need a little more time.

A little more time.

In 1985 I got into trouble again. My flat got spun by the Drugs Squad at seven in the morning. They didn't find what they were looking for but they came across a handgun I kept under a loose floorboard by my bed. So I went away again, this time Parkhurst, on the Isle of Wight. Reggie Kray was there and I got to know him a bit during evening sessions in the gym. I was a bit worried, again because of Beardsley's connection with the Hat. But all these old scores seemed forgotten. Inside it's different, you're more likely to have a grudge with someone over an ounce of snout or a lump of blow.

Reggie seemed very gentle really. Mad keen on weight training, but very soft spoken. He was always going on about this friend of his on his wing.

'He's going to be a star, you know. He's got a terrific voice and he's a fantastic mover. He's won medals for disco dancing.'

It was strange, this famous gangster going on like a schoolgirl. And there was a lot of gossip going around. *It's nothing like that*, said one of the old lags, but with a kind of glint in his eye like you weren't sure whether he was taking the piss or not. It got me thinking. Of course, a lot of *that* went on inside, I knew that. But it wasn't the sex. It was something else. Being close to other people. I mean, I'd always found it hard. Inside you don't have any choice. You can't feel properly alone, just properly lonely. One time, when I got in a row with another con, I was glad to be on chokey block, in isolation for a while. But sooner or later you have to deal with other people.

Outside, who had I been close to? Dan? Yeah, well, I'd never been that close to even him. Birds? Well, tarts I'd paid for. Earthquake groupies, skinhead girls that might as well have been boys the way they looked.

I wouldn't tell anyone but I got to thinking about all sorts of shit on that stretch. Disconnected, that's how I felt. Now I'm swimming, it's that out-of-body feeling, nothing is happening from the neck down or the waist down for that matter. Just thinking. Not knowing fuck-all really. Mind reeling away. The way that queer at Mile End looked at me, like he knew something. I wish I fucking knew.

But I don't. A kind of lovely numbness. A dullness that soothes bad memories. Thank fuck I'm out of there. Out of it.

When you're banged up, wanking away and running out of things to think about, as I said, it ain't just sex, or rather the lack of it, it's coping with being crammed together with all those people. Having to fight for that space around you that you take for granted in normal circumstances. That space that you need to protect yourself. It becomes part of the prison.

Tired.

Curled up. Quiet and warm. Safe.

No.

Feel the floor move slightly. Someone is creeping up on me. Fuck. Grab the handle of the sheath knife. Hope that I can move fast enough.

A hand touches my shoulder and I roll over. Grab at the legs and pull this fucker over. I'm on top of them. Knees on their arms, hand on their face, blade at their throat.

A loud scream. I look down. It's the girl. It's Natalie. I let go of her face and take the knife away from her neck.

'What the fuck are you doing?' I shout at her.

Her mad little eyes staring up in terror at me.

'I, I . . .'

She's trembling. I get off her and stand up. Help her up on to the settee. She lights a fag shakily.

'I was . . . I was just going to wake you up,' she finally says. 'I didn't mean to freak you out.'

'Yeah, well. I thought it was someone else. Sorry.'

She's already scraping a couple of lines together. We both have a bit of a pick-me-up and she puts the kettle on for a cup of tea. It's dark outside again. I haven't seen the light for days. What time is it? I look at the timer on the video but it's just flashing 00:00. Come to think of it: what fucking day is it? I ask Natalie when she comes back through with the tea.

'It's Saturday. It's five o'clock.'

'Where's Martin?'

'He had some business to attend to. Said that I should look after you.'

'Oh yeah?'

She was pretty. Skin and bones, though. And scarcely more than a kid. I got my mobile out and switched it on. Two messages. Both from Beardsley. I played them. Number one: *Gaz, it's Beardsley. Call me.* Number two: *Where the fuck are you? Look, call me. Something's come up.* I start to dial his number. Natalie's come over. Standing right up close to me. Touching me.

'You want a blow job?' she says.

'What?' I scowl at her. Move her hand away from my crotch. 'No,' I say. 'No, no, no, no.'

'Go on. Twenty quid.'

'How old are you?'

She gives this stupid grin.

'Sixteen.'

Look down at her face. Knowing smile marked out in lipstick. Old before its time. Think about that other girl's face in the papers with tubes coming out of it. Think about my girls. Charlene and Donna.

Natalie's walked around me and put the telly on again. I wander out into the kitchen and make that call to Beardsley.

'Where the fuck have you been?'

'I've been busy.'

'Yeah, sure. Busy getting off your face.'

'Look, I've sorted something out. What we talked about.'

'Oh yeah?'

'Yeah.'

'What have you done?'

'Never you mind. Just check out the papers on Sunday.'

A pause. I can tell Beardsley's intrigued. I've caught him on the hop. Thinks I'm fucking useless.

'What is it?'

'No,' I say. 'You tell me.'

'What?'

'You phoned me. So. What is it?'

'Meet me tomorrow night,' says Beardsley. 'I'll let you know where.'

Drive home. There's a letter from this bloke Roger Wilbey from the Environmental Health Registration Scheme informing me of a review of my licence to run doors in the district on Wednesday and requesting my attendance.

I've still got Dan's phone number even though we haven't spoken to each other for all this time. I want to talk to him now. I pick up the phone and dial. For all I know he's moved or changed his number or whatever. It rings six times then an answerphone message. Dan's voice recorded. He's still there. Can't think of what message to leave so I just put the phone down.

* * *

I got out in the summer of 1988. This time I thought I would be ready for whatever lairyness fashion could throw at me. But as I said before, I was wrong. It was a shock, I can tell you, especially after coming out of the most drab and grey place imaginable.

I went to see Dan. He said he wanted to go out and celebrate, as we always did. He looked a right fucking state when he opened the door to me. He was wearing dungarees, for Christ's sake. Some hippy tie-dye T-shirt, a pair of scruffy baseball boots and to top it all a fucking paisley-pattern headscarf.

'Dan, what the fuck is this?' I said.

'It's all right, Gaz,' he said, kind of patting me on the arm, like. 'It's cool.'

We just sat and talked for a while. Tried to catch up with all the years. It was getting late and we'd just had a couple of beers. I was ready for a skinful.

'We ought to be getting ready to go,' I said. 'It's nearly ten.'

'Don't worry,' Dan insisted. 'We're going to this club later.'

I assumed that he meant an after-hours drinking place.

'Ain't you going to get changed?' I asked.

Dan laughed and shook his head.

'You mean, I'm going to have to be seen with you going out like that?'

'Don't worry, Gaz. Some of the old firm will be there.'

Well, we got to this club around midnight. It's a bloody warehouse. A half-derelict dock building on the south side of the river between Southwark Bridge and London Bridge. Weird electronic music with this thumping beat blaring out.

'What the fuck is this?' I ask Dan.

'Don't worry,' he replies, and holds something up between his thumb and forefinger. 'Take this.'

It's a pill. He goes to put it in my mouth.

'Uh-uh,' I say, grabbing his hand.

I take the pill off him and look at it. It's a big white thing.

'What is it? Speed?'

'You'll see,' says Dan.

And so I put it in my gob and swallow it.

We meet up with some old ICF mates of Dan's and some of them look as lairy as he is. They all look really pleased to see me and are dead friendly. All talking to me at once: *Good to see you, Gaz. Nice one, mate. Fucking blinding. Get on one.* And so on. They're all huddled around me. A bit too close really. I put up my hands.

'Easy now,' I say to them.

Dan clocks me looking a bit uneasy and he ushers me through.

'Come on, lads,' he says, laughing. 'Let the dog see the rabbit.'

We walk through the warehouse. It's filling up with kids, young and old. All doing this spastic dance to this thump-thump-thump music.

'You feel it yet, Gaz?' he asks.

'What?'

'You know, the pill.'

I shake my head. We're moving through the crowd and people are letting us through, smiling. Dan seems to know a lot of people here because they're like patting him on the arm as he passes them. People are wearing all kinds of things: smiley-face T-shirts, over-sized jumpers, there's even someone in a fucking poncho. *Can you feel it?* this voice keeps saying on the record. No I fucking can't, I think. Then I see a couple of tasty-looking geezers looking over in our direction. I nudge Dan.

'Dan', I say. 'Those blokes over there.'

'Where?'

I try to nod at them surreptitious, like. But they've already noticed that we've noticed them. They're coming towards us. I get ready to shape up. Dan's just grinning.

'Dan, they're fucking Millwall, aren't they?'

I'm thinking, here we go. I'm looking back to see where the rest of the ICF lot are. But Dan's just going up to these geezers and shaking their hands.

'Gaz,' he says, turning to me. 'Meet Billy and Johnno.'

They both grin at me and I manage a smile back. What the fuck is going on?

'I need a drink, Dan.'

'Stay here, I'll get you one.'

This new record starts. Boom-boom bass drum with harsh high hat. Piano chords. Then: *all right* chanted on the beat. *All right. All right. All right.*

Dan's back and he hands me my drink. I take it off him. It's one of those little bottles of Lucozade. I hold it up.

'What the fuck is this, Dan?'

This is the last straw. I'm livid, or at least I think for a second that's how I feel. Then I start laughing. It's so fucking stupid. Lucozade. What Mum used to give you as a treat when you were sick, I mean really sick, not just bunking off school. I'm grinning like an idiot. Like a kid again. I take a swig from the bottle, all the bubbles rising in my head. Lucozade Aids Recovery, I think, grinning away. *But it's gonna be all right,* says the record. *'Cos the music plays for ever.* And bosh, my head is lifted. All that pressure, that aggro, that loneliness, it just falls away on to the filthy warehouse floor. *On and on and on and on and on.* And, yeah, I know now. What all these silly fuckers were saying. I'm on one.

Shoom! It all happened for me at once then. *All right.* I'm moving like a spastic, too. *All right.* I'm among the crowd, dancing. *All right.* I'm letting go of that solid block of space around me. *All right.* I'm smiling, touching people.

Five o'clock in the morning and we're outside by the river, watching the sun come up, passing a spliff around. I'm sat cross-legged on the floor.

'Look at Gaz,' Dan says. 'He looks like the fucking Buddha.'

I was happy. I ended up hanging around with Dan and his mates for a bit, going to all these different Acid nights. There were plenty of Es around. This bloke Brian was supplying. He was a normal fellah, not a proper dealer or anything. He'd come across the stuff in Ibiza the year before and he'd get hold of enough to sort his mates out. It was good to relax and let go of it all for a bit. Especially after being inside for a while. And I felt that I could connect with people. Feel warm towards them.

But you know what, after a while I thought: so what? Maybe I was getting less of a rush from the pills. Maybe I was just getting bored with being happy. It's not my style, to tell you the truth. It was time to get back to work, I thought. And this scene had given me a few ideas.

I was at this thing called Spectrum on a Monday night. It was in a proper club under the arches at Charing Cross. I'd gone up on the balcony to get away from the crowd for a bit. I remember watching the light show. A green laser fanning out over the crowd, like a thin film of scum on a pool. Hands reached up to break the surface as all the pond life wriggled below. I started to think about how much cash I could make out of all of those happy mugs.

Of course, I'd be lying if I told you that I was first in thinking how much could be made out of this racket. Already people were making their moves. The ICF and other hooligan firms were muscling in to a lot of the clubs that were springing up all over the place. But it was early days and with a bit of organisation someone could make a killing. I knew who I had to go and see.

There's a photo of one of Tony Tucker's dealers on the front page of the *Sunday Illustrated*. *EXCLUSIVE: WE REVEAL MEN QUESTIONED IN ECSTASY DEATH INQUIRY*.

Beardsley is well pleased.

'You have something to do with this?'

'Yeah,' I reply, and tell him about my meeting with Keith.

'Nice one, Gaz. That ought to keep things off our backs for a bit. Which is just as well 'cos I've got other things to worry about.'

'What?'

'Well, a certain face seems to have reappeared. Either that or someone's seeing things.'

I know better than to pry. Just let him rabbit on.

'It's that fucking gold, Gaz,' he says with a pained look. 'I thought we were done with it but . . .'

He lights a fag. I realise he's nervous.

'Remember Solly?' he asks.

I nod.

'I don't know, Gaz.' He sighs. 'We might have made a very big mistake.'

'What's this all about, Beardsley?'

He holds his hand up and shakes his head.

'You keep out of this, son.'

He turns the paper back over.

'Well done with this,' he says, tapping the front page. 'Maybe now's the time for taking Tucker and his friends out of the game for good.'

'What, grassing them up?'

'What you take me for, Gaz? Nah.' He laughs. 'I was thinking of something more permanent.'

Beardsley and Tucker aren't exactly on good terms although they still do bits of business together. There's supposed to be an agreement about how things should be organised but Tucker is always pushing his luck. He has a reputation for fucking people over in drug deals. And now his main partner Pat Tate is out of prison they're getting more and more lairy. Beardsley resents people like Tucker and Tate as opportunists who've jumped on a bandwagon while he has carefully built up his own organisation and avoided trouble or attention being drawn to his activities.

'Easy come,' he says, 'easy go. I should never have let them move in on my racket.'

'Our racket,' I remind him.

'What?'

Beardsley pisses me off sometimes. He's the guvnor and I've never minded that but sometimes he forgets how things were. It was me that got him started in all of this, after all.

I had taken Beardsley along to this club in Charing Cross back then.

'What the fuck is all this?' he said, looking down from the balcony at all the mad ravers waving their hands in the air.

'They're calling it the Second Summer of Love.'

He turned to me with a sour look on his face.

'Well, it's horrible,' he said.

I shrugged.

'It's business,' I told him. 'The Es, the pills these kids are taking, they're twenty quid a throw.'

'Really?'

'Yeah. You want to try one?'

'Not if that's what it does to you,' he said, nodding at the throng below.

'It's a good buzz.'

'I'll take your word for it.'

'Thing is, the dealing is all a bit laid back. There doesn't seem much organisation to it. If we could get a proper supply we could undercut everyone else and clean up.'

Beardsley thought about it for a while.

'I don't know, Gaz. This so-called Second Summer of Love, well, it's going to be over soon. Thank fuck. After that this whole scene might just blow over. Then we'll be left in debt with a load of unsold drugs.'

'I don't think so.'

'No?'

'No.'

'Well, I'll tell you what. Prove it.'

'What?'

'Prove to me you can make some gelt out of this. Then we'll talk. Now, I'm getting out of this place. It's giving me a fucking headache.'

I went around to see Brian with Dan. He was dead friendly, sort of making a show of it. Bringing out the champagne and the charlie and being all cool with it. He was obviously coining it a bit from selling pills but he was dead slack about it. Didn't seem to have any proper back-up and Brian wasn't what you'd call heavy himself. And he'd let far too many people know what he was up to.

I asked him about the pills.

'Well,' he said, 'I only deal to my friends.'

We talked and talked but I couldn't get him to tell me who his supplier was. He wasn't that stupid. In the end I just put it to him straight.

'Could you get me two thousand?'

'That's a lot of friends, Gaz.'

'Yeah, well, I . . . well, we was thinking of having a bit of a party, like.'

'Hm.'

He went a bit quiet. Suddenly out of his depth.

'Well?'

'Yeah, sure,' he said, fronting it all casual. 'Take me a couple of weeks, though.'

'How much?'

'Um, er, fifteen, er, fifteen grand.'

I wondered what the real mark-up was. I'd soon find out.

'Sweet,' I said. 'Let me know when you've got them.'

Ten days later and I got the call. I went around there with Dan again. Brian had the pills.

'There you are, geezer,' he says, all cocky, holding up this bag full of them. 'Yellow Burgers, the best that's around at the moment.'

'Thanks, Brian,' I replied, taking them from him.

'So,' he said with a grin. 'Um . . .'

'What?'

I think he knew then that something was wrong.

'Well . . .' he said.

He was getting very, very edgy. I thought: get it over with. I took out my squirt bottle and did him in the eyes with ammonia. He clutched at his face, with a horrible squeal.

'Sorry about that, Brian,' I said.

'What you do that for?' he moaned, stumbling about the flat.

'I need to know your supplier.'

He was heaving and groaning, panting and wheezing. Cursing.

'Fuck! You fucking bastards!'

'Now, Brian,' I went on, 'you don't want me to hurt you any more. Do you?'

I grabbed him by the hair and got him down on his knees. It didn't take long. Though getting this name and address was a right palaver. Dutch. Luckily Dan was there to do the spelling. We dragged him into the bathroom and put him under the cold tap, phoned an ambulance and got out of there.

'That wasn't very nice,' Dan told me.

'Taught him a lesson. If it hadn't have been me it would have been someone else.'

'But fucking hell, Gaz. You didn't have to.'

'What's the matter with you?'

Dan sighed.

'I don't know, Gaz. I thought you'd calmed down.'

I shrugged. I would have told him that I was calm. That this had been business, not me being out of order. But I knew he wouldn't understand. He wouldn't even take a proper cut from the pills we'd nicked. Silly cunt didn't want to know.

It was then that me and Dan sort of fell out with each other. We didn't have a row or anything, we just stopped spending time together. He had his family and he had stopped all that ICF stuff. And I was getting busy with something.

I set up some guys I'd met in these clubs who I thought I could trust. I sold the pills on to them at a tenner each so I made just about twenty grand. Beardsley was well impressed when I dropped the pile of money on his desk.

'Well, I'm impressed, Gaz,' he said, holding up the money like he was weighing it or something.

I gave him the name and address of Brian's contact but Beardsley said he was planning a trip to Amsterdam to have a word with some of his own friends out there. He went to hand me back the cash. I shook my head and put up my hand.

'Nah,' I said. 'That's an investment. In our new business.'

Beardsley smiled.

'You're learning, son.'

There were a lot of rumours going on at that time about who was running what on the acid scene, as it was called back then. Hooligan firms getting organised, various faces and well-known families wanting to move in. But it was hard to keep track of. Clubs were coming and going. Warehouses would be squatted in for one night and then the promoters would move on. Everybody was talking about this new Acid House thing but no one was quite sure what was going to happen next. Beardsley had his own ideas about what we should be doing.

'It's about power and control,' he said one night when we were having a bit of a coke session.

'Yeah.' I nodded. 'Of course.'

'You know, when I was inside I did a bit of studying.'

Beardsley always started with the clever talk when he'd had a bit of charlie.

'This Roman,' he went on. 'Juvenal, he was called. He said: *quis custodiet ipsos custodes*.'

'Oh yeah?'

I didn't know what the fuck he was on about now.

'You know what it means?'

'Nah.'

'It's Latin. It means, who will guard the guards themselves.'

'Oh,' I said, like I understood what he was fannying on about. 'Yeah.'

'What he meant, Gaz, is that those entrusted with power by the state or whatever, they're the ones that can end up running things. You know, like those African countries where the army takes over the government.'

'Yeah.' I still didn't get what he was on about. 'Right.'

'It's who runs the doors, Gaz. That's what this thing's going to be all about. It doesn't matter who runs the club, who promotes the event or whatever. It's who's in control of security, that's going to be the thing. That way you decide who can bring in drugs and deal inside the place. It's the guards, Gaz, *ipsos custodes*.'

* * *

Custodis Security, that's what I call my door firm now. Sounds classy, doesn't it? And I made sure that it all looks above board. Tax, VAT, national insurance, the fucking lot. When I settled down with Karen the whole idea was that I'd go straight. I didn't want our kids to have a daddy away in prison.

Of course, the business was a legitimate front for lots of naughty things that I've been up to and it's also been a way of laundering money, but I've always been really careful to make it look kosher. Then I get this grief from the council. This Environmental Health Registration Scheme thing. There's been complaints against some of my doormen and me personally about 'using excessive force' and suspicions that my staff have allowed drugs to be brought into premises.

Needless to say this girl dying hasn't helped. It's Wednesday morning and I'm sat in front of them all. A couple of blokes from the Police Licensing Unit, some local councillors, this twat Roger Gilbey who sent me the letter and this woman from Environmental Health who announces that she's chairing the meeting. Kangaroo court, more like.

She starts off droning on in this foreign language about policy and procedure, monitoring and guidelines. I nearly doze off. Another bad night and my head is fucked. I just nod along to it at first. It's them trying to be all reasonable and shit before they start to have a go.

Then the aggro starts. Complaints. Persons assaulted by my doormen. Evidence of drug dealing apparently sanctioned by some of my doormen. The criminal records of some of them. My criminal record. I butt in and say:

'Hang on a minute.'

But this woman stops me and says:

'Mr Kelly, please do not interrupt. You will have your chance to answer these allegations in good time.'

And she looks at me like I'm a fucking naughty schoolboy or something. I try to stay calm. Think about how I can talk my way through this when the time comes. But then it all goes horribly wrong.

'And we understand,' one of these cunts is saying, 'that your wife, Mr Kelly, has served an injunction against you as part of proceedings in a complaint of assault on her person.'

Well, I lose it now, don't I?

I'm shouting. I'm on my feet and I'm shouting at them.

'What the fuck has this got to do with you?'

'Mr Kelly, please calm down.'

'This has got nothing to do with you!'

I've really blown it now. It's funny, part of my brain is taking in this fact, while the rest of me is going ballistic. I'm going to lose my licence and half of Essex knows that I'm a wife-beater. Great. Fucking great. No point taking any more of this shit so I just walk out.

I'm going to lose my licence. There goes my legitimate livelihood. And with Beardsley shutting everything else down what the fuck am I going to do for money? It goes so fucking quickly. The dodgy cash just gets burned up and the clean money I've put through the firm, well, the fucking taxman's going to be after most of that.

The thing that really nags at me is that I'm damn sure they mentioned the injunction Karen got served on me deliberately to wind me up. Get me angry and justify their opinion of me as just a mindless thug. And it was horrible all of that coming out in the open. Embarrassing. Worse than that. Shameful.

I've had a few drinks and I find myself welling up. I'm so fucking sorry. I'm in a fucking sorry state. Got to snap out of it. Have a wash and a shave. It's getting late. A couple of lines and I feel a bit sharper. And it numbs things out a bit, does the old charlie.

Got to go out. Got to prove that I can hold it together. Need to know what's happening too. If Beardsley isn't up for anything maybe I'll just find someone who is. Drive over to the Epping Forest Country Club. Bit of a flash place. Know the guys on the door. Some of them have worked for me. Have a bit of a chat.

Wander in and see a few familiar faces. Cautious nods all round. Everybody wary of each other since this girl dying. Loads of dealers have been busted, clubs raided. Tons of Class As flushed away in panic. Essex Drugs Squad extra proactive. Essex gangland completely paranoid.

Spot Tony Tucker and Pat Tate in the corner. Hard to miss them, they're both fucking huge bastards like me. First thought is: avoid those two, they'll have the hump about that story I fed to the press. Then I think: wait a minute, they don't know it was me, do they? And I don't want to make it look like I'm blanking them.

Send a bottle of champagne over. Kind of flash gesture they'll go for. Get a nod from Tucker and I go over.

'All right, Gaz?' says Tony as I join them. Friendly enough. Bit of an edge.

Pat Tate is gibbering away. Gurning. Off his face obviously.

'We're going to do them,' he's saying. 'Fucking take the cunts.'

'Take it easy, Pat,' Tony mutters.

'All right, mate?' Pat grins at me. 'How's Beardsley?'

'He's fine.'

It doesn't look like they suspect a thing and everything's all right with their arrangement with Beardsley. I stay and have a drink with them. Tate is really hyper. Making up for lost time. Only got out a month ago. He wants to make up for lost time in other ways too. He's talking about how he's missed out on making lots of money because he's been away so much. Looking around and seeing how well some people have done. Know how he feels. Beardsley's got a big mansion and I've got a Barratt home that's worth less than what I paid for it.

Tate's just got back from Holland. Went to get his money back on some bad puff he had smuggled in. Now he's got some cash and him and Tucker are about to do some sort of deal. He's talking far too much. Tony Tucker's quiet. Asking me questions. Obviously wanting to know what me and Beardsley are up to.

'Beardsley's keeping well quiet until this thing with the girl what died calms down a bit,' I tell him.

'And what about you?' Tucker asks.

I shrug. Don't tell them about losing my licence to run doors. What am I going to do? Got to start making money soon. Bills to meet and cash running out. Tax and VAT to pay on the legitimate front of Custodis Security. Don't know what's going to happen with Karen but I want the girls to be properly looked after. So many things to worry about and so much of my money going straight up my nose.

Everybody's taking far too many drugs. Tate especially. His body all pumped up with steroids and all. Pat's got a right reputation in Essex. Back in 1988 he'd got into a row in a Happy Eater and robbed the till. He got arrested and they found a load of gear on him. Two weeks later at a remand hearing at Billericay magistrates' he jumped the dock and made a getaway on a motorbike waiting for him outside. He hid out in Spain for a while but made the mistake of going to Gibraltar and got pulled there. Ended up doing six years for what started as an argument in a cheap restaurant.

He's talking to me later, going on about his plans. Bragging about how much money he's going to make. Flying in consignments of coke from the Continent in a light aircraft.

'Everybody's made a fucking fortune while I've been away,' he's saying. 'Well, now it's my turn. And if you aren't doing anything with Beardsley at the moment, why don't you come in with me?'

'What do you mean?'

'Put some money up. I've got something lined up. You put something up and I could double it.'

'How much?'

'I don't know – say, thirty grand. In a week I could double that for you.'

'I don't know, Pat.'

'Come on, Gaz. You should start making money for yourself. Don't be Beardsley's fucking junior partner all your life.'

'Yeah, well. I'll think about it.'

'Do that. But make it quick. As I said. Something's lined up.'

Drive home. Think about it. Thirty grand turned into sixty. Could buy myself some time. Sort things out with Karen. Get away from all of this for a bit.

Think about what Tate said about me and Beardsley, too. I'm sick of being in his shadow. He's done so much better than me out of all of this yet I was the one that really saw how much could be made out of the rave thing.

It was late on in '88 and I'd gone to this outdoor rave held in this disused aircraft hangar in Kent. It was at a secret location, the precise address was left on a phone bank answering service just a couple of hours before the thing started. A huge convoy of motors all turned up at the appointed hour. 'Paradise', this thing was called, and it was fucking incredible. Flares lining the side road that led to the gig. Dry ice all over the floor and lasers flashing into the night sky with a mammoth sound system throbbing away so hard you could feel it in your bones. There was fairground rides and even a fucking bouncy castle, for Christ sakes. The ravers looked even more lairy than usual, white gloves and goggles, fluorescent face paint, some bloke on stilts wandering about, all holding their hands up in the air like they were worshipping some god. I was coming up on one and feeling well happy. Most of all I was high on the numbers. There must've been near on ten thousand punters at this thing, all of them pilled up. Fifteen quid to get in and fifteen quid a pill – well, my mind was buzzing at the pure mathematics of it all. If we could move into this one we'd be laughing.

I reported back to Beardsley and we spent a bit of time finding out who this Paradise lot were. Turns out it was run by this public schoolboy type called Ben Holroyd-Carter. He was using ex-squaddies as their security, not any London faces, out-of-towners, yokels. We put together an extra-tasty team of heavies together for the takeover. Then we kidnapped him and took him to this lock-up that Beardsley used for such purposes.

We tied him to a chair and knocked him about a bit. Beardsley let him know of the new arrangement. We'd take fifty per cent of the takings and control all the drugs at the raves.

'Well, thank you for your kind offer,' Holroyd-Carter said in his posh voice, trying to act all cool. 'But we've already got our own security arrangements.'

I held my Stanley under his nose.

'How'd you like a permanent smiley face?' I asked him.

Beardsley waved me back. He had this big mobile phone in his hand.

'Look, give me the number and I'll call up your guys. Tell them to come here and you can let them know what's going to happen from now on.'

'Well, they're not going to like this. What if they take it out on me?'

'Don't you worry about that. We can deal with these country bumpkins. One thing is certain, though. If you don't deal with us you're gonna get your throat cut.'

So Holroyd-Carter called them up and they arrived team handed. We had all of our firm there, tooled up to the back teeth. Baseball bats, CS gas, shooters. We outnumbered and outgunned this ex-army lot. They were fronting it out a bit but we had the upper hand.

'Look.' Beardsley was talking to Holroyd-Carter. 'You knew it was only a matter of time before a London firm would take over. You think that every villain in the Smoke hasn't been looking to move in on this racket sooner or later? We can give you proper protection, better than this bunch of fucking swedes. So tell them.'

Holroyd-Carter sighed.

'I'm sorry, boys,' he said to the squaddies. 'I'm going to have to go with these new guys.'

The yokels kind of looked around at us and each other. For a moment it looked like they might make a move. Then suddenly their leader kind of shrugged and said:

'Oh, fuck it, lads. Let's go.'

And they walked out of there.

So Paradise was ours and all through the next year Holroyd-Carter put on all these big fuck-off raves all around the South-East. He was a clever little cunt, was Ben. Beardsley thought that he would have some kind of input, him knowing about music promotion and so on, but he ended up learning from him. He knew about money laundering too. Paradise Incorporated was registered in the Virgin Islands, a nice little tax haven, so the authorities couldn't touch it.

'Never underestimate a rich rid,' Beardsley said to me. 'Business sense, well, they get it in their mother's milk.'

And Ben had a lot of useful friends in high places, clever lawyers to do all the paperwork, moody leases on sites and so on. A lot of the punters reckoned what they were attending was all very anti-Establishment but Holroyd-Carter was a right little Tory.

'It's enterprise culture, Gaz,' he said to me once.

'Yeah, fucking *Starship Enterprise* culture, more like,' I replied, looking around at all these gurning space cadets.

He was clever with technology, too. He used the British Telecom Voice Bank system, which meant he could put loads of phone lines into one answering machine. That meant he could leave a message telling everyone of the location from his mobile phone at the last minute and keep the Old Bill off the trail.

And the M25 had just opened. All the raves were set up somewhere close to it. Because it was a big circular motorway it was harder for the cozzers to set up a roadblock on it. There would be this long convoy of party people on it on the night of the rave, waiting for the signal. 'Keep it orbital' was what Ben would say.

I felt dead clever. There was plenty of money about and this time I was ahead of the game. Fashion had always played tricks with me in the past. Well, now I was getting my own back. I got to learn some of the words that these rave people would use. 'Dibble' for the police, 'cool' for about almost everything, and so on. And I got a nickname of my own. 'Geezer Gaz' was what they called me. At first I thought they were taking the piss but I came to take it as a mark of respect. That I was the top geezer, as it were.

Friday and I've arranged to take out thirty grand from the tax account of Custodis Security. Doesn't leave very much in the balance. Fuck it. Might as well dissolve the company. Put the cash in a sports bag, take it home and stash it. They're burying the girl that died today. Hear about the funeral on a news bulletin on the car radio. The priest groaning on about how she was not to blame but rather the guilt lay with a society that allowed the creeping cancer of drug abuse to destroy so many lives. And so on.

In the afternoon I've got this appointment with the doctor. It's a group practice and I suppose I assume it's going to be a bloke that I'm going to see. But it's not. Dr Hanson turns out to be a woman.

So it's difficult to talk about what the matter is. Embarrassing. What do I say? I've knocked the wife about and she's got an injunction against me and thinks that I've gone psycho and can I have some treatment please?

I start off saying that I've had trouble sleeping and had nightmares and that. I tell her that I've found it hard to control my temper and that there are times that I feel paranoid. And she's just sitting there nodding. In the end she says:

'So, Mr Kelly, what do you think the problem is?'

'Well,' I reply, 'I don't know. You're the doctor.'

'Hm, yes. Do you think it's a medical problem?'

Oh Christ, I think.

'I don't know,' I say.

'Because I could refer you to a community psychiatrist. If that's what you want.'

'A shrink?'

Dr Hanson gives a little laugh.

'Yes, a shrink. Do you want me to do that?'

'Not really.'

'You see, Mr Kelly, there may be many ways of looking at this. You have problems with sleeping, feelings of anxiety, issues with aggression and violence. Would you say that you were a violent person, Mr Kelly?'

She looks up, staring me right in the eyes.

'Yeah,' I say. 'I guess.'

She stands up and goes to a filing cabinet and starts rooting around in it.

'Look,' she's saying, 'there is something. Now, where did I . . . ? Oh yes, here it is.'

She's got a little pamphlet in her hand. She gives it to me.

'MOVE,' she says.

'What?' I almost jump up out of my seat.

'Sorry,' she goes on. 'Men Overcoming Violence in Essex. It's a support group for people in your predicament. It meets every week. Why don't you give it a try?'

Jesus fuck, I'm thinking. A fucking support group. Let's go around the circle and introduce ourselves. 'Hi, my name's Gary and I'm a professional thug.' But I nod and look at this leaflet like I might be interested. Maybe I can convince Karen that I'm doing something to change. Maybe it'll look good if anything goes to court.

Dr Hanson is writing something on a prescription pad.

'I can give you something to help you sleep as well. See how it goes and come back and see me if it doesn't work out.'

Pick up the prescription from the chemist's and drive home. Lots of traffic. Everybody out shopping. Less than four weeks to Christmas. All the houses in my street have got their decorations up. Only our house is dark. Decide to put some fairy lights up around the windows. Don't want burglars to think the house is empty. Don't want neighbours to think that my wife and kids have left me.

Drag the Christmas box from the cupboard under the stairs. Sort through the lights and the decorations. Think: maybe I should get a tree. Think: what's the fucking point? Put the lights up and the effort of it all makes me exhausted for some reason. Depression, I suppose.

Order a takeaway and have a few drinks. Decide to stay off the gear tonight. Get an early one, yeah. Check out the pills the doc gave me. Temazepam. Yeah, I'll have a few of those.

Have a look at this pamphlet. Shit. I don't want to talk about my personal problems with a load of blokes I never seen before. Still, maybe I should tell Karen about it. It was her idea that I should go and see someone, after all.

Phone her up. It rings a couple of times then this recorded voice comes up. *The number you have dialled has not been recognised. Please check and try again.* Shit, must have dialled the wrong number. I phone her again. Same poncey voice telling me I've not been recognised. Fuck. Karen's changed her number.

But I want to talk to her. Not sure what I'll say. That I'm sorry, I guess. That I miss her? Well, we don't really feel very much for each other any more. But it was good once. I miss that. Take another handful of temazepam and stumble off to bed.

It was in the summer of 1989, at one of the raves, that I met her. It was the morning after and the sun was coming up over this field full of lunched-out punters still at it. I was having a walk around, checking up on things. Sometimes people we knew would give us the nod if anyone else was dealing other than our people. Then we'd grab them, chuck them out and nick their drugs so we could sell them on. I was walking around the edge of this field that the rave was on. The birds were making a right old racket like they were competing with the thump of the bass line in the background. I noticed this girl crouched down by the hedge. I thought she might be sick from banging too many or something so I went over.

'Are you all right?' I asked, standing over her.

She looked up with this amazing smile on her face. Green eyes luminous in the low sunlight. Pupils like pinpricks.

'I'm just picking flowers,' she said. 'I ain't done this since I was a kid.'

I sat down next to her. The grass was wet with dew but I didn't care.

'It's nice, ain't it?' she said.

'Yeah,' I said. 'Nice.'

She'd made a daisy chain and she put it over my head like a little crown.

'Leave it out,' I said, laughing.

'No. It suits you.'

'What's your name, love?'

'Karen.'

'Hello, Karen. I'm Gaz. Geezer Gaz.'

She laughed at this then we sort of stared into each other's eyes for a bit, then started kissing. I felt all warm and tingly, buzzing from the pills. 'Loved up', as they say, and at that moment I knew what they meant. It wasn't really sexual. I felt I wanted to be close to this girl, to touch her gently and delicately.

We walked back to the party holding hands. *It's just the sun rising*, went this song. And it was. Me and Karen looked at each other and laughed like we suddenly thought the same thought together at the same time. Like we were connected. A woman's voice wailing these strange notes over the top of the music. Repetitive. Hypnotic. Murmur murmur murmur. *Love is just a state of mind. You leave behind.*

We ended up back at my gaff at about three in the afternoon and went to bed. It was sweaty and clumsy but it was good. It was nice just lying next to each other, both completely knackered. Empty and quiet. Just a little warm buzz to take us into sleep.

Wake up to a cold grey morning. Gloomy. But the temazepam did the trick. Slept through without any bad dreams. Head a bit thick, though.

Get up and make a cup of tea. Letter on the doormat from the Environmental Health Registration Scheme. Have a look at it . . . *officially informing you that after due consideration we have decided to suspend your licence to provide security for entertainment premises forthwith* . . . Chuck it in the bin.

The house is a tip. Try and tidy it up a bit. Phone rings and I pick it up. Little jolt of hope: maybe it's Karen. Stupid. It's Frank, the manager at Tiffany's.

'Gaz, what's going on? I just heard you lost your licence.'

'Yeah, that's right.'

'Well, what am I going to do? Who's doing the door tonight?'

'I don't know, Frank. You'll have to sort it, I guess.'

'But Gaz, it's Saturday night. I mean . . .'

'Well, it's not my problem any more, is it? They've taken away my fucking livelihood, haven't they?'

He's droning on. Doesn't give a fuck about my situation.

'And what do I say to your door staff when they turn up tonight?'

I really don't need this grief.

'I don't know, Frank, and I don't fucking care.'

'But Gaz . . .'

'Look, Frank, you useless cunt, just fuck off and leave me alone, OK?'

Put the phone down and think. Fuck. Every fucker is going to be phoning me up. Club managers, doormen I employ, geezers that pay me to use my company as a front so they've got legit invoices to give to people paying for their services and so on. Well, fuck them. Custodis is going into liquidation. I'll have to have a word with the accountant next week.

Of course, this means we won't be able to control who deals the drugs in all these clubs. Beardsley's not going to fucking like this. Anyway, I've decided, I'm going to make as much money as I can and fuck off out of it. Make a new start somewhere.

Phone Pat Tate and tell him I'm in. Arrange a meet at a café in the Lakeside Shopping Centre in Thurrock. Put the sports bag in the back of the car and drive over there. The sky looks cold and grey and heavy. Looks like it's going to snow again.

I hand over the money.

'How about coming in with us for good, Gaz?' he says.

'I don't know, Pat.'

'Beardsley's got you running around doing his dirty work but what have you got to show for it, eh?'

'Well . . .'

'We're going to be the main firm in Essex. We're going to take over the fucking manor. You want to make sure that you're on the winning side, Gaz.'

I shrug. Don't know what to say. I get up.

'I've got to be going,' I say.

'Think about it,' Tate calls after me as I leave.

Get back and there's a load of messages for me. Ignore all of them except Beardsley. Give him a call. Wants me to go over to his place.

It's dark when I get there. Talk to the intercom and the wrought-iron gates slowly swing open. Crunch up the gravel drive to the front of his huge gaff. Spotlit columns and Greek urns. Beardsley comes to the door with one of his Rottweilers. He looks edgy.

'You on your own?' he asks.

'Yeah, 'course.'

He gets rid of the dog and shows me through to this big lounge with a bar attached. He goes to fix the drinks.

'Cognac all right?'

'Sure,' I say, sitting down on this big white suede settee.

Beardsley comes over and hands me this huge glass. Grabs an armchair.

'So,' he starts, no fucking about. 'What's going on?'

'What?'

'What's this about you losing your licence?'

I sigh.

'It's these fucking Environmental Heath people.'

'So you lost the fucking doors in Southend?'

'Yeah.'

'Great. That's fucking great, Gaz. So what am I going to do now?'

'I don't know.'

'Well, I'm going to have to find someone else to deal with. You're no fucking use to me now.'

'Thanks a fucking lot, Beardsley.'

'It's fucking true. You're no fucking use to anyone these days. You're off your face most of the time. Look, I know you've been having personal problems but I'm running a fucking business here.'

'I thought we were supposed to be laying low what with this girl dying.'

'Yeah, but I didn't mean just to roll over and die. And what's with you getting involved with certain people?'

'What are you talking about?'

'You know what I mean. You're up to something with Tucker and Tate, aren't you?'

'So you been checking up on me?'

'Look, that firm ain't exactly being discreet themselves. They're going to fuck up really badly one of these days. Well, I've had enough.'

'What?'

'It isn't working out any more. You're a fucking mess. And I can't trust you any more.'

That is well out of order.

'You fucking what?' I demand.

'You heard.'

'You cunt. You fucking ungrateful cunt.'

'What?'

'After all I done for you.'

'You done for me?'

'It was me that got us started in this thing. Me. You always made more money than me but it was my idea in the first place. Well, fuck you, Beardsley. Thanks for fuck-all.'

And I walk out of there.

'I picked you out of the gutter when you were just a little hooligan!' he calls after me.

Fuck him, I think. I don't need him. I can take up Tate's offer and go in with them. Drive home and think: fifteen years working for Beardsley and it comes to this. Diabolical. It seemed so easy back then. So simple when we were just doing the big raves. A bit of a laugh.

Everybody came to Paradise. I mean all sorts. From pikey-looking kids who kind of lived the life to yuppie twats who just wanted to get monged out of their skulls every weekend or so. There wasn't any overall style. Sure, there were odd little things some of the hard-core ravers picked up, white gloves, kids' dummies, face masks with Vicks Vap-O-Rub smeared on them which was supposed to boost the buzz, but there didn't seem to be any big fashion thing going on. A lot of the people who came were quite old really. I remember looking out at this mixed crowd with a feeling that something was over, that fashion was over – well, in terms of it being about youth and rebellion and that.

Of course, all these grinning people being happy with each other would no doubt be kicking the shite out of each other if it wasn't for the pills. The music got faster and harder. 'Mental', that's what everyone was doing that summer, 'going mental'. But they were easy enough to keep under control. Docile. We hardly ever had to do much real security work at the raves. Just organise the drugs and keep ready eyed for any rival firms that might want to muscle in.

Beardsley told me that he'd read this book set in the future where the government gave happy drugs to everybody to keep them in order. *Soma*, this stuff was called, and he reckoned it sounded just like E. He said that the state should dole it out on the National Health if they wanted to keep things nice and quiet.

He grinned. ''Course if it was legal we'd be out of a fucking job, wouldn't we?'

The powers that be didn't see Beardsley's point and they were getting a bit edgy. *SMASH THESE EVIL ACID PARTIES* was a typical headline in the press. *Evil dealers openly peddling drugs to the background of mind-bending music and lasers.*

The cozzers started organising themselves so that they could close down the raves. Dibble was getting wise. This special squad was set up to deal with all the raves – the Pay Party Unit, it was called. Now they had to stop the party from actually taking place. I mean, once there was ten or twenty thousand people in some field or warehouse it was going to be bloody difficult to arrest everybody, wasn't it? Undercover officers would go around clubs and record shops and pick up flyers. They'd listen in to pirate radio broadcasts, they even started sending out broadcasts themselves, sending potential punters to the wrong places. They'd have police helicopters buzzing the M25 on the run-up to Saturday night, looking for anything big and suspicious on the move like fairground rides.

Holroyd-Carter was smart but he was running out of luck. One night the Pay Party lot followed Paradise's lighting riggers to this venue and closed it all down at about six o'clock. There was a reserve site, this warehouse in the East End, so everyone made for there. But the cozzers were having a good day because they managed to track that one down too. It was about ten and the Paradise lot had set up and there was about a thousand kids in this building. Suddenly a whole convoy of plod vans turn up, riot police, dogs, the lot. Holroyd-Carter tried to reason with them with his moody paperwork and posh manner but they were having none of it. A bloke with a megaphone told everyone to disperse. Some of the kids tried to steam in but they got beaten back pretty quickly. I had to get out of there because I had a shed-load of Class As on me.

Holroyd-Carter called a meeting with me and Beardsley the next week. It was bad news.

'I'm getting out, I'm afraid,' he told us.

'What do you mean?' I demanded. 'A little bit of trouble and you're getting frightened.'

'Look, I'm under so much surveillance I can hardly fart without them knowing about it. They've got the Tax Inspectorate and the Customs investigating me. I can't afford this much grief.'

'So where does that leave us?' I asked.

'Well, gentlemen, it's been a pleasure doing business with you.'

'How do we know that you're not having us over?' Beardsley cut in sharply.

Ben started to look a little flustered. 'What do you mean?'

'I mean, how do we know you're not going in with another firm or something?'

'Really, I can assure you.'

I grabbed him by his neck and pulled him up out of his chair a bit.

'We ought to do him anyway,' I said to Beardsley.

He was wheezing and going a funny colour. Beardsley started laughing.

'Let him go, Gaz.'

'You sure?'

'Yeah.'

So I dropped him back on his arse.

And that was it. By the end of 1990 it was all over. Most of the other raves closed down about then too. Some people reckoned it was the cozzers and this Pay Party Unit but it was us too. The villains, I mean. It had got all a little heavy for some people. But one thing changed for ever – drugs. Everyone was taking them now. So there would be a lot of money from that up for grabs.

But something really big in my own life was happening. Karen was pregnant.

'Gary is it?'

'Yeah, well, everybody calls me Gaz.'

I'm at this Men Overcoming Violence thing. Dingy community centre, plastic chairs in a circle. Tea and coffee things on a table in the corner. I'm early and it's just me and this guy I spoke to on the phone.

'I'm Bob,' he says.

'You the teacher?'

He sort of laughs at this.

'No, I'm the group facilitator.'

'What does that mean?'

'Well, it's my job to try and get people to talk, to share with each other. MOVE is about men taking responsibility and supporting each other. The group has to belong to the men in it for it to work. I'm just here to get this rolling.'

Fuck me, I think. Bob can tell I ain't too keen.

'It's not easy, Gaz. But remember, one of the hardest things is having the bottle to come to this group in the first place.'

I go and make myself a cup of tea. People are starting to turn up. I look at them all. Wife-beaters probably. Like me. Why don't they just call it Wife-Beaters Anonymous. Oh, fuck. Someone I know. I don't fucking believe this but someone I know has just walked in the door. It's Trevor something or other, used to work as a doorman for me a couple of years back.

'Good to see you, Gaz,' he says to me.

I lean close to him.

'Look,' I say softly, 'this isn't my idea coming here and if anyone finds out about this I will fucking kill you.'

'It's all right, Gaz.'

Then we're all sat in a circle. There's this big pad of paper on a stand next to Bob with GROUND RULES written at the top of it. Bob introduces me and everybody says their name. Then we're supposed to come up with these rules that Bob writes on the chart with a big marker pen. Things like not interrupting each other or making judgements. One of them is called GROUP CONFIDENTIALITY and Bob explains that it means that anything we say in the session is not to be repeated anywhere else, and I make sure that I catch Trevor's eye at this point and give him a bit of a nod and a glare. The last one is BE POSITIVE which Bob underlines twice. I get this horrible queasy feeling.

Now we are all taking turns to talk. Going around the circle. All these confessions. People saying about how they were knocked about as kids and how they were taught to see violence as acceptable. Everyone seems to have worked out why they've done bad things. One bloke going on about it being like an addiction, the adrenalin rush and that. Someone else says he always felt powerless and aggro was a way of asserting himself.

Everybody's yapping away about themselves. It's like those daytime TV shows that Karen likes to watch. I can't understand it, these blokes grassing themselves up, going QE on all the bad things in their lives.

It comes around to me and I don't know what to say.

'I don't know what to say.'

'It's all right, Gaz,' says Bob. 'Just maybe share a few things.'

Shit. *No comment*, that's what I usually say when someone's asking questions. *I ain't saying anything without a brief*. They're all looking at me. Waiting for me to cough something up.

'I don't have an alibi,' I say at last.

There's this pause.

'Go on,' says Bob.

'Well, I don't know why I'm a big nasty bastard, I just am. My old man might have clouted me a few times and my mother certainly did but that didn't make me what I am. I can't blame anybody. I've done some horrible things and I'll probably do some of them again.'

'So why are you here?' This is from one of the blokes in the group.

'Well, I lost it, didn't I?'

'Lost it?'

'Yeah.'

I suddenly feel giddy. The circle turning like a fairground ride. Surrounded by all these faces.

'I lost it completely. I can't remember all of it. Some of that was the drugs. You see, I was off my face. Off my fucking face at four in the afternoon. But I've blanked some of it out as well. It was so fucking horrible. I remember the voices. The kids crying. My wife screaming. And somebody shouting. I remember that. I remember thinking: who's that shouting? Then I realised it was me. And I stopped. And I looked around. Karen on the floor and me over her. And it suddenly went quiet. And she just looked up at me, face all swollen where I'd hit her, all swollen with hatred for me.'

Head spinning. In a cold sweat. Panting like a dog. And now it's quiet in the room. Here. That horrible quiet. Somebody coughs.

'You say you lost it, Gaz,' Bob is saying. 'Is that how you feel? Do you feel lost, Gaz?'

'Yeah,' I croak.

And then the others start talking. Saying things to me. Like they are trying to encourage me and that it's a difficult process and so on. And I'm not really listening, just trying to get my breath back and to get this fucking merry-go-round to slow down a bit. And then somebody else starts talking about their problems and I can relax a bit.

The session ends and I'm out of there as quickly as possible. Bob follows me out into the corridor.

'Gaz,' he says. 'I know that was hard. But I think you made a real breakthrough there. Well done. See you next week, I hope.'

I get to the motor. Well done? That's a good one. I'm still shaking from it all as I drive away. Put the radio on. Weather report: another big freeze expected. *Do you feel lost, Gaz?* I feel lost, all right. Lost in space.

Flashbacks of me beating Karen up. Need to blot it out. Need to stop that video nasty playing in my head. Get hold of Martin on the mobile and head over there.

When I get there him and Natalie have been chasing the dragon. Bacofoil all over the coffee table.

'Fancy some?' asks Martin.

And my first thought is: no, I'm not a fucking junkie. But then I think: why not? No harm in just smoking it.

'Me and Nat just do it from time to time,' says Martin, like he's reading my mind.

'Yeah, all right, then,' I say.

And before you know it I'm sucking up this smoke from this line of smack on the foil as I'm burning it with a lighter underneath.

'Tell Gaz the story,' Martin is saying.

Feel sick. Go and puke up in the downstairs bog. Stomach retching away but I don't feel it. Wash my mouth out in the kitchen and come back through.

'A friend of Nat's heard this story. Go on, tell him.'

I collapse on to the settee. Feel warm, calm. Numb.

'You mean the pizza story?' Natalie is saying.

'Yeah. Listen to this, Gaz, this is the latest on Pat Tate. Tell him, Nat.'

'Well, according to Sharon last night Pat Tate's girlfriend was ordering a pizza from this pizza place in Basildon and she wanted this pizza with different toppings on it.'

'What, different pizzas?' I say.

'No, different toppings on the same pizza, you know, on different slices of it. Anyway, this bloke says they don't do that sort of pizza so Pat Tate grabs the phone and starts shouting at this geezer saying, "Bring us the fucking pizza we want, you cunt, or we'll come and get it," stuff like that, and the bloke puts the phone down on him. Well, then Pat Tate goes fucking mental. He turns up at the shop and throws the till at this bloke. He presses the panic button and Tate jumps the counter and smashes this bloke's face against the draining board in the kitchen, then fucks off before the police arrive.'

Shit. If Tate's been pulled I'm screwed.

'So then what happened?' I ask.

'Well, they can trace the call to Tate's house. But this pizza bloke, a few of his friends let him know who it was that beat him up, you know, what kind of bloke Tate is, and surprise, surprise, by the next day he don't want to press charges.'

Well, thank fuck for that.

Have a couple of lines and decide to go home. It's started to snow again. Get some gear off Martin to keep me going. Some charlie and some K.

'Want a bit of this?' Martin asks, holding up the bag of smack.

I shrug. Nod.

Why not?

It does take away the pain, after all.

Drive home through flurries of snow. Delicate little flakes of it melting on the windscreen. I'm thinking about the fact that I've given thirty grand to a maniac who beats people up because of disagreements over pizza toppings. What the fuck have you gone and done now, Gaz? Still, the drugs keep me calm and numb. I'll think about it tomorrow.

Home. Fairy lights flashing on and off in an empty house. Get inside and put the central heating on. Think about the group tonight. Me saying all those things in front of strangers. Shudder with embarrassment. And all that stuff coming back about what happened.

Have a bit more of the smack. That stuff does the trick, you know. All the things I worry about fade out. Don't care. Don't have to care. Mmm. A yawn goes all tingly inside of me. Put the telly on. Lie on the settee and let it all wash over me.

When Karen was a few months gone she moved back in with her parents in Southend. Then I bought us the house here. I'd put enough money aside to buy it outright. Put it all in Karen's name just to be on the safe side. We were married in July 1990 at Southend Register Office. I'd wanted Dan as my best man but we'd lost touch with each other. So Beardsley did the honours. He'd done really well out of the rave thing, much better than me. But I didn't mind back then. I had more than I'd ever imagined I'd get out of life. My own house, a woman that I loved, money in the bank and, to top it all, on 1 September that year Charlene was born, a beautiful baby daughter weighing in at seven and a half pounds.

The next few months, well, Charlene took up most of our time. It was a steady, uneventful time and for a while I was content with just being a family man. I loved our little daughter so much. It was probably the happiest period of my life.

I set up Custodis Security at the beginning of 1991. I got to learn all the details about running a legitimate business. And the loopholes too. Beardsley was organising the drugs side of things. I was to try and run the doors on as many clubs as I could and that way make sure it was always our drugs and our dealers that operated in those places. But it was much harder than when we were doing the raves. More competition. Lots of little power struggles going on in Essex. Beardsley ended up having a meet with Tony Tucker and they divided up some of the county, a sort of peace agreement. But to be honest things seemed to be getting heavier all the time. Beardsley didn't notice back then but the happy smiley time really had already gone. The music got faster and darker. The drugs got fiercer. Guns got easier to get hold of and loads of wannabes and coked-up chancers were running around Essex with automatic weapons.

And things started to get strained between me and Karen. After Charlene was born sex suddenly disappeared from the agenda to all intents and purposes. I didn't mind that so much but we didn't have very much else to get close to each other with. We didn't have very much in common. I could buy her nice clothes and a car and that but she wanted to be respectable. We'd moved into a fairly middle-class area and Karen wanted to keep up with that. I stuck out like a sore thumb, of course. When they found out that I ran a security firm I got an invitation to come along to the local Neighbourhood Watch scheme meetings but I didn't fancy that. I didn't really fit in with Karen's new friends and I felt that sometimes she was embarrassed about me.

Karen got up the duff again. Must have been that weekend we went away to Paris and left Charlene with the in-laws. I kind of wanted it to be a boy. Don't get me wrong, when Donna was born on 11 March 1992 I wasn't anything but overjoyed. I loved having two daughters. I just felt a little bit outnumbered, that's all.

In the autumn of 1993 I read this article in the local paper about a nine-year-old boy called Darren Tyler who was suffering from a form of leukaemia that could only be treated in America. His family were trying to raise funds for this treatment. Something clicked inside of me and I decided I would help them. I thought that if I could get involved with doing some good people might see that I wasn't just some mindless thug. I figured that some charity work might give me a bit of respectability.

I started writing letters to people, celebrities and public figures, telling them of Darren's plight and asking for help. I wrote to Reggie Kray at Maidstone Prison and he wrote back. He remembered me and said that he was very touched by poor Darren's situation and that he wanted to get involved with some sort of fund-raising event. He sent me a list of contact numbers of friends of his that he thought might want to attend. These were gangland people but also pop stars and actors that he had known. His brother Ron was keen to get involved too and he phoned me from Broadmoor to offer his support.

I was well pleased that I was becoming acquainted with the Kray twins and gaining their respect. I thought that it would do my reputation good. Beardsley was a bit dismissive, though, when I told him. I thought that it might be because he had been involved with Jack 'The Hat' in the past but he denied that.

'It can't be bad being in with people that well known, can it?' I told him.

'Gaz, some of us are trying to avoid being well known. Know what I mean? The Twins always loved getting that attention but it didn't do them much good in the end, did it?'

I ignored that. I knew that like me a lot of people had a good deal of respect for Ronnie and Reggie. After a lot of phone calls and discussions it was decided that we would arrange a charity boxing show and dinner at a leisure centre in Romford. This bloke Harry Fraser got in touch soon after the decision was made saying that he had been appointed by the Krays to act as the promoter for the event. I wasn't entirely happy with this arrangement at first because I assumed that it would be me that would the promoter but I trusted the Twins' judgement and let Fraser get on with it.

The event was to be staged on 26 November, but the week before that unfortunately Darren died. He had been such a brave little fucker and I phoned his mother to offer my sympathies. And to assure her that the event would take place as a tribute to his courage and his memory. But when I next met with Fraser the first thing he said was: 'Well, what do we do with the money now, then?' I felt sick at this. Darren's family were heavily in debt from preliminary trips to the States and from paying for the extra care that their son needed and I told Fraser that all the cash raised should go to them. But I should have known then, from his attitude, that there was something dodgy about Fraser.

Both the twins were very sad at the news and sent tributes to Darren that I read out at the event. We managed to sell over two hundred tickets at £50 a head and there was a raffle for a load of personal mementoes, some of them autographed, that had been donated by various celebrities. Charlie Kray attended, as did Tommy Patterson and his son Joe, the actor, and Ruby Ryder was there too. It was a great night and I was proud to have helped organise something like this. By my reckoning we had raised over ten thousand pounds.

But at the end of the night, when I went to collect the money, Fraser had scarpered. The hire of the leisure centre and the caterers had been paid but Fraser had made off with the rest. Subsequent attempts to contact him got no result. I was livid. I contacted Reg about it but in the end he said it would be best if the whole thing was forgotten. The press would have a field day if the Twins were seen to be associated with a charity rip-off. In the meantime I had to deal with Darren's family. I tried to explain to them what had happened but I got the silent treatment. I think they figured I was the one doing the ripping off.

The whole episode left me feeling bitter. Karen was not very sympathetic. I had been so involved in this charity event I had neglected my own family. It was about that time the rows began.

And the fact was that I had started to take a lot of drugs. It was an occupational hazard. Didn't really think about it much because everybody around me was at it. Nobody thought of themselves as being dependent or anything. People started taking more and more Es, trying to get that buzz you get from the first time you take it. Everybody saying the stuff was much better in the old days. I started taking more and more to sort of balance things out. Booze and puff to chill out. Coke and E to get up and feel confident. Then stuff to bring you back down again, ketamine or prescription drugs like temazepam or rohypnol. I never thought that I was a druggie. Oh no, I was in charge. I could control how I felt. Well, that's what I thought. And I knew it wasn't exactly a healthy lifestyle and I should keep myself fit, so I started to get serious about going to the gym again. That's when I started taking the steroids. I was pushing forty and worried about keeping in shape but now I could train hard and get a really good muscle definition.

My relationship with Karen was getting worse and worse but we both just concentrated on leading our own lives. She had her own friends and my work meant that I was out most nights. I actually thought that I was stable with all the different drugs I was taking, like they were medicine to make me strong, keep me relaxed, get me high, level me off, help me work, help me sleep and so on. But I wasn't stable. I was like a chemical weapon ready to go off. A weapon of mass destruction.

I was on edge all the time. I started to worry about things all the time. I kept thinking that the house was being watched or I was being followed. I began to suspect that Karen was cheating on me. With Charlene at school and Donna at the nursery during the day, Karen started getting out of the house and doing things. An aromatherapy course and exercise classes. I didn't trust her. I felt sure she was having an affair.

I brooded over it for months. Got fixated on it. It got to be not if she was screwing someone else but who that someone else was. Any man she had contact with was a potential suspect as far as I was concerned. I was constantly checking in my mind who she spent time with, names of men she mentioned. Jason from two doors down who she'd got friendly with and was recently divorced, Barry, her step-aerobics instructor, and so on.

Some Saturday nights, if I was working, I might stay on for an all-night session somewhere and not get back home until the day after. This would piss Karen off and it would be another cause of us rowing. It wasn't as if she missed me, it was just that she'd worry something might have happened to me. So I agreed that I'd always let her know in advance if I wasn't coming home that night.

But the next time it happened, the beginning of November it was,

I remember thinking, just as I'd put the phone down to let her know, this little thought: well, she knows the coast is clear now, doesn't she, Gaz? It was like a whisper in my ear. I couldn't get it out of my mind for the whole night. Her humping away while the old man was out.

I thought about going back to the house and catching them at it. Murderous thoughts. But I ended up just getting beasted on drink and drugs. A party at the house of one of the dealers until the early hours. Then some of us drove uptown to this chill-out club in Old Street. Twenty-four-hour party people – it seemed normal enough going on and on and on. It was nearly six o'clock on Sunday evening before I got back to the house.

'Don't know why you bother coming home at all,' Karen said. 'The girls have been wondering where you were.'

Charlene and Donna came through and wanted to play, jumping up and grabbing hold of me. But I was out of it.

'Sorry,' I said to them, pulling them off me. 'Daddy's very tired. He's been working hard.'

'Daddy's very off his face,' Karen hissed at me.

'Yeah, well, maybe Mummy's been having a good time too,' I whispered back.

'What's that supposed to mean?' she said out loud.

'I know what you're fucking up to!'

'Oh, great. Swear in front of the kids, why don't you?'

'Leave me alone.' I pushed past her and hauled myself up the stairs.

The next day it was my turn to pick up Donna from nursery and Charlene from school and then Karen from the sports centre. I'd slept through into the afternoon so I had a bit of charlie to try and perk myself up. Charlene's teacher came out and spoke to me by the school gates. Charlene's behaviour had become an issue for the school this term and the teacher was going on about how it was still a problem, she was being aggressive and disruptive. I hardly took in what she was saying. I felt bleary and irritable. I knew that Karen would blame me for this as well. *You hardly spend any time with them these days*, she was always saying.

Get to the sports centre and wait for Karen to come out. Watch her walking out of the front entrance talking with Barry the instructor. They look happy together. They are laughing.

They are laughing at you, Gaz. That voice whispering to me again.

They say goodbye. Barry holding up a palm, see you. Karen gently pats him on the arm then turns and walks out to the car park. A simple, delicate gesture. A gentle, intimate thing. She is still smiling until she sees where I'm parked and then her face flattens out again. She puts her bag in the boot and gets into the passenger seat.

Then I know. I know that it is him. Barry. That's who she's been fucking. Barry, Barry, Barry, Barry. Bet he preys on them. It's all women in those stupid classes.

Get home and the girls go into the lounge to watch children's TV. I follow Karen into the kitchen. I'm shaking. I'm wiped out from the weekend. Cold sweat running down the backs of my legs. I feel like a fucking zombie. Empty. Like there's nothing inside of me, just a pulse throbbing away, a vein on the side of my head twitching. Blood-red rage pumping into me. Filling me up. It's warm, oh yes, it's warm. *It's him*, says the voice. *Hmmm.*

'It's him,' says my voice. 'Isn't it?'

'What are you talking about?'

'It's Barry, isn't it?'

'What?'

'Is it good, then? With Barry?'

'Gaz, I really don't know what you're talking about.'

'You're fucking him, aren't you?'

'What?'

'Barry.'

She stares at me, green eyes wide, mouth open.

'Barry?' she says.

'Yeah.'

And then she laughs out loud. She's laughing at me. And I lose it. And I hit her. And she goes down. Laughter turning into screaming. And I keep hitting her. And the girls are crying as they come through the hallway hearing all this noise. And I hear this shouting. And that's when I think: who's that shouting? And I realise it's me. It's me shouting my head off.

And I stop.

And it goes quiet.

And Karen is looking up at me.

Her face swollen with hatred.

Christ.

And the girls are cowering together in the corner of the room.

And I stagger out of there. Get into my car and drive. I come back three hours later to an empty house. She's gone and taken the kids to her mum's. I go around there and Karen's mum tells me that Karen doesn't want to see me and I start rowing with her and she threatens to call the police. And the next day Karen gets that injunction thing out on me.

I come to some time in the afternoon. The smack's worn off and my body aches all over. Head's throbbing. The snow has come down heavily again. It's beautiful the way it covers everything and makes it look clean and new. I feel old and dirty. I lie there brooding about all the bad things in my life.

I'm so fucking stupid. I was going to go and do that Barry bloke. I asked around about him and only found out he was gay, didn't I? That's why Karen was laughing at me.

The phone rings. I let it go on to the answerphone. *Gaz?* comes the voice. It's Karen. *Gaz, are you there?* What does she want? She sounds worried. I pick it up.

'Hello.'

'Thank God. You're there.'

'Yeah. What's the matter?'

'There was something on the news. I thought it was you.'

'What was on the news?'

'These blokes that got shot.'

'No, I'm all right.'

'Right. Well, then.'

'Hang on.'

'Look, I was just worried you might be dead. That's all.'

And she puts the phone down. Well, she's worried I might be dead. That's nice. Think about it. These blokes that got shot? What could that mean? Get up and my whole body is groaning at me. Go out and get a local paper.

GANGLAND CLUE TO MEN SHOT DEAD IN RANGE ROVER, is the headline in the *Echo*. Three men were shot in the head as they sat in a car after apparently being lured to a remote farm track in Essex. Fucking hell, I think. Look down the page to see if they say who it is but *their identities have not yet been disclosed*. Beardsley's got a Range Rover. Maybe he's one of them. A shudder goes right through me. Someone walking on my grave.

I'm walking up to my front door when I suddenly notice that someone's got out of a car parked up in front of the house and they're coming up behind me. Fuck, I think. I get my keys out and run for the door.

'Wait,' this bloke calls out. 'It's all right. I'm Old Bill.'

I turn around and this geezer's holding up this fob with a badge on it.

'Detective Sergeant Wilkinson,' he says.

'What do you want?'

'You seem a bit edgy, Mr Kelly. Expecting someone?'

'You got a warrant?'

'Just an informal chat.'

'I ain't letting you in here.'

'We can talk out here. You know what this is about, don't you?'

'No idea.'

'Come on, Gary. The whole of Essex is talking about it. The Range Rover shootings. Who do you think did it?'

'I don't know. I don't even know who it was that got done, do I?'

'Tony Tucker, Pat Tate and a guy called Craig Rolfe.'

This cozzer sees the look of shock on my face and he grins.

'Friends of yours?' he asks.

'Not particularly.'

'Seen your business associate recently?'

'And who would that be?'

'Simon Beardsley. I hear you and him have had a bit of a falling out.'

'I don't know what you're talking about.'

He comes up close to me and looks up and down the street.

'If I had been somebody else, say somebody who had a grudge, do you think you'd have made it indoors before I could have got to you?'

He hands me a card with his name and number on it.

'Think about it, Gary. Get in touch if you want to talk about it.'

Get inside and slam the door behind me. Some fucking clever little cozzer trying to frighten me. The thing is I do feel scared. All the details of the shootings are on the news. Heads nearly blown off with shotguns. Horrible. What if it was Beardsley that did it? Then I am in trouble.

And Pat Tate dead. My thirty grand gone. Shit. What am I going to do? After I've taken the money I gave to him from the Custodis account I've only got about three or four thousand. The phone keeps ringing. People thinking it might have been me shot dead in the Range Rover. And it might have been. I was all ready to go in with that lot. I feel sick. Get off my face again to keep my nerves going haywire. Try to stave off the nightmares but I don't get a good night's sleep.

Next day there's a bit of a thaw. Piles of dirty grey slush everywhere. *POLICE WARN OF GANG WAR AFTER DRUG MURDERS*, says the *Echo*. Maybe Beardsley's done it. What did he say? *Maybe now it's time for taking Tucker and his friends out of the game for good*. Try to stay straight. Clear headed. But by night-time I've got the shakes. I'm in a cold sweat. Feel like shit. Try to sleep but nightmares come. Wake up and I'm full of fear. Keep thinking that they're going to come and do me.

I've got to get away from this fucking place. I drive to the bank and draw out all that's left in all my accounts. Just about three and a half grand. It ain't much but I need every penny I've got. Tiffany's still owe me. I'm paid in arrears so I'm due a couple of weeks' work. I put a combat knife in the back of my trousers and a bottle of squirt in my pocket and head down there.

George is on the door. Looks edgy when he sees me.

'I'd better warn you,' he says. 'Beardsley's in there.'

Fuck, I think. But I ain't going to back down. I go in. Frank comes up to me. Fear in his eyes, sweating like a little pig.

'Gaz,' he says. 'I'm sorry. There's nothing I could do. Beardsley's running the door here now.'

'Never mind that. I want my money. Two weeks' worth.'

'All right, all right,' he stammers. 'I'll go and get it.'

Beardsley's at the bar. Team handed. Lording it over. He spots me and comes over with a couple of his guys in tow. All eyeballing me.

'What do you want, Gaz?' Beardsley snaps at me.

'This is nothing to do with you. I've just got some business with Frank.'

'I run this club now. You walked out of it. Now piss off.'

Frank's back with the money looking like he's about to have a heart attack.

'What's this?' demands Beardsley.

'Er, it's the money I owe Gaz.'

'You don't owe him nothing, Frank. Tell him to fuck off.'

Frank looks at me. Eyes wide. Mouth open.

'Give me the money, Frank,' I say.

He starts to hand it over. Beardsley makes a grab for it and before I even know it I've got the knife out and I'm holding it at Beardsley's throat. I grab his jacket and pull him slowly towards me.

'The money, Frank,' I say.

Frank tucks it into my pocket. Beardsley's men move forward a bit.

'Get back. Or I'll cut his fucking throat.'

'You are dead for this, Gaz,' Beardsley mutters through clenched teeth.

I put my arm around him and keep the point of the knife against his neck and shuffle out of the club with him.

'Steady on,' says George by the door.

'Shut up. I suppose you're working for this cunt now, are you?'

'Don't have much choice, Gaz. I got to eat.'

'Come after me, or mess with me again,' I say to Beardsley, 'and I'll fucking kill you.'

And I give him an almighty shove through the door and leg it to the car.

Get back to the house and put a load of stuff in the car. Leave the fairy lights on and drive off. One last thing to do. Stop by Karen's mum's.

'You're supposed to stay away from me, Gaz,' she says when she comes to the door.

I hand her the keys to the house.

'You can move back in. I'm going.'

'What do you mean, going?'

'I'm getting away. There's nothing for me here any more.'

'Right, so you're just walking out on everything?'

'Well, you don't want me around any more. Do you?'

She looks me up and down. Shakes her head. I must look a right state.

'You're a mess, Gaz.'

'Yeah, well, maybe you're right. Maybe I do need to change. I'm sorry.'

'Bit late for that.'

'I want to see the girls.'

'They're in bed, Gaz.'

'Yeah, but I want to see them. You know, in the future.'

'Yeah, well, we'll see about that. Where you gonna go?'

'Dunno. Back to London, I guess. I'll let you know where I am.'

'Right.'

I try to explain. 'Look. I lost it. I'm completely fucking lost. I've . . . I've got to find it somehow.'

'What the hell is that supposed to mean?'

'I don't know.'

And we just look at each other for a couple of seconds. There's still a bit of bruising on her face where I hit her. I wish that there was something I could say. But I can't think of anything. So I just go:

'See you.'

And she just says:

'Yeah.'

And I turn around and walk back to the car. I start driving west along the A13. Sodium fuzz above the gloomy marshlands. Glad to be away from this fucking county. Out of Essex. London calling, like that song by The Clash. Phone Dan on the mobile. I hope he's in this time.

4

offshore

I got Geoff to develop the film he had shot outside the churchyard and to bring around the contact sheets. I hoped he had no idea what he might have caught that day. I had no idea myself, not really. Eddie could easily have had some sort of hallucination, some manifestation of delusional paranoia.

I looked over the frames with a magnifying glass as nonchalantly as possible while Geoff looked on. All the time thinking: *is it Starks?* Geoff had got a few close-ups of the man's face. I moved the glass over one of them.

I had explained Eddie's erratic behaviour to Geoff by saying he thought that he had spotted somebody that had cuckolded him with his girlfriend while he had been in prison and it had driven him into a rage. I wasn't sure whether Geoff had fallen for that one. I was worried that his press photographer's nose might sniff that he'd inadvertently got something.

I'd had a good look at all the smudges that I had on file of Harry Starks. Police mug shots and celebrity line-ups. Even that one of him taken in 1979 when he was on the run in Marbella. I tried to study every aspect of his physiognomy. Of course, there were rumours that he had had plastic surgery but then Eddie had sworn that he had recognised him. I breathed out and looked down through the lens.

Heavily lined and gaunt featured, the face was crowned with grey hair. An old man. But it was him all right. A half-smile bringing out the scar on his right cheek, the telltale eyebrows that joined in the middle. I nearly laughed out loud. *Got you*, I thought. But I held it all in and feigned disappointment. I sighed and dropped the contact sheet on the table.

'Well, I don't think there's anything we can use here, I'm afraid,' I said.

'Who's this bloke, then?' asked Geoff.

'No idea. Just someone who Eddie thinks has been fucking his bird.'

'Looks familiar, though.'

'Yeah, well, maybe he's been featured on *Crimewatch*.'

Geoff went to pick up the contact sheets.

'Can I keep the contacts? Eddie wants a look at them. It might help to calm him down a bit.'

'Sure. What do I tell Victor?'

'Don't worry. I'll deal with Victor.'

And I knew what I would have to do. I would have to keep Victor away from all of this. I wasn't going to let him have any of it. This was *my* story. This was *truecrime* par fucking excellence.

You know, whenever a really good story came in at the *Sunday Illustrated*, Sid Franks, the news editor, used to shake his head and take in a little hiss of breath. He'd then let out a sigh that seemed part pleasure, part disappointment.

'This story is too good for our readers,' he'd declare. 'They just won't appreciate it.'

And that was exactly how I felt. This story was far too good for Victor. This was mine. This was what I'd been looking for. This could be the book. With Ronnie Kray dead, Starks was now the doyen of ancient gangland mythology. The last of the Old School and still at large. If I could find out where he was hiding, this could be my coup, as Eddie would put it. Something to retire on. The problem was Eddie, though. I would have to find a way to work with him somehow. Maybe he would be able to lead me to Starks. And we'd have to keep all of this to ourselves for the time being.

So I stopped returning Victor's increasingly irate phone calls. It was so soothing to hear his frustration as he ranted away into my answer machine. He repeated his threat to drop Eddie Doyle completely and that suited me fine. All I needed to do now was to sort things out with Eddie.

I had one of the contacts blown up and I showed it to him.

'Well, it is him,' I said. 'But he was taking a hell of a risk showing up like that.'

'Yeah. Maybe he just couldn't resist the occasion.'

'I hope you haven't told anyone else about this.'

'Well . . .'

'What?'

'I did mention it to Ruby.'

'You did what?'

'She phoned me up. She was going on about the book, and it just slipped out.'

'It just slipped out?'

'Look, I'm sorry, Tony. I didn't mean it. We were just talking about old times. I'm not sure she believed me anyway. You're not the only one who thinks I'm paranoid, you know.'

'Well, look, maybe you should try and tell her that your eyes were playing up or something. And you can reassure her about her story. We won't be needing that now we've got this.'

'What do you mean?'

'I mean Harry Starks. Next to finding Lord Lucan this is the biggest story going.'

'Oh,' said Eddie petulantly. 'Thanks a lot.'

'I mean in terms of pure sensationalism, Eddie.'

He frowned at me.

'So what about my story?' he asked.

'Well, we'll get around to it. But we can do it your way, not that trashy tone that Victor wants. If we get this Starks story then we'll be made.'

'You mean work on it together?'

'Yeah. We could renegotiate our contract. Get a proper advance. Or we could go and see another publisher and pitch it to them. Fuck Victor.'

Eddie nodded slowly.

'Yeah, maybe,' he said. 'Maybe we should put the old memoirs on hold. I mean, maybe it's not over yet.'

'What's not over?'

'My story,' he said. 'This is unfinished business, Tony.'

I didn't like the sound of this.

'What do you mean?'

'Look, you want your precious story. I want something too. My fucking portion.'

'Eddie, I don't want to get involved in . . .'

'Don't worry,' he cut in. 'I'll sort that out myself. You want the story? Well, you can get the whole fucking story. And so can I. I want to know what happened to my money. Yeah, we can work together, Tony. We can both get what we want.'

'But . . .'

'It's all connected, Tony, don't you see? Starks, the bullion job, everything.'

'But I thought you didn't want to talk about all that.'

'I don't. You can have the story, Tony. It's all yours. I just want my cut.'

'This is ridiculous, Eddie,' I said, standing up. 'Absolutely ridiculous. To think that I'd get involved with something like this.'

I picked up the contact sheet and put it back in its envelope. I'd walk away, I thought. I'd cut my losses. I'd take the photo of Starks to one of the tabloids. The *Sunday Illustrated* would give me a good price for it and a little story. But I only had the contacts and if I tried to buy the originals off Geoff he'd get suspicious. He might work out what he'd got and sell them himself. So what would I do next? Crawl back to Victor Groombridge with my tail between my legs? Walk away from my last big chance? If I'd had any sense I suppose I would have done. This could get me into trouble. I'd spent decades avoiding acting on dangerous impulses. For what? Maybe it was just my sociopathic tendencies but I felt a sudden surge of childlike wonder. And it was such a good story, more than anything I wanted to find out what happened next.

I hadn't really thought through how I was going to collaborate with Eddie and I certainly hadn't banked on this. But this would have to be it. I felt an odd little thrill run through me. I was going to get into trouble again, I just knew it.

I dropped the envelope on the table and sat down.

'So?' asked Eddie.

'So,' I replied. 'We're both completely crazy.'

Eddie laughed.

'Where do we start?' I asked him.

'When I got put away I left my cut in the hands of people connected with Starks. Manny Gould, Manny the Money, we used to call him, Starks's old accountant. What do the Yanks call it? His fucking *consiglieri*. He was supposed to be running it and some of the old firm were meant to be keeping an eye on things. They used this dodgy Hatton Garden jeweller, Solly Blumberg, to resmelt the stuff. But then a whole load of it goes missing and Solly gets bumped off. So I come out after twelve years with nothing to show for it.'

'And you think that Starks knows where the missing gold is?'

'I don't know. Maybe he's trying to find out himself. Maybe he thinks I know. Maybe it's him who's having me followed. There is one person who'll know what he's up to.'

'Who's that?'

'Manny Gould, of course.'

His offices were in Charlotte Street. *Emmanuel Gould, FCA, FCCA*, read the brass nameplate by the door. Gould was a tubby little man with beetle brows. Hooded, buglike eyes blinked behind thick round spectacles. He shuffled through piles of books and files to show us through to his desk. Scuttling sideways, crablike, scooping up paperwork and moving it to and fro to clear a couple of chairs for us to sit down on.

'Please.' He gestured for us to sit as he clambered around his desk. 'Eddie,' he announced with a little shrug, a placatory gesture of the hands. 'It's been a long time.'

'It has, Manny,' Eddie returned. 'It really has.'

Manny sighed.

'What can I say?'

'I don't know,' said Eddie, leaning forward. 'What *can* you say?'

Manny hunched in his chair a little. He stroked his chin and looked at me.

'You haven't introduced your friend,' he said.

'This is Tony.' Eddie jerked a thumb in my direction. 'He's a writer, a journalist.'

Manny Gould frowned, his eyebrows twitching like antennae.

'Now, Eddie,' he said. 'What's all this about? I mean' – he shrugged, and gave a sour look – 'a journalist.'

'Don't worry, Manny. He's not here to do an exposé on you or anything. We're working on a book together.'

Manny's face opened up into a smile.

'A book, is it?' He shook his head slightly. 'Oy, a book.'

'We're working on Eddie's memoirs,' I said.

Manny stared at me, his eyes goggled in rimless magnification.

'And you are his what? His, what do they call it, his amanuensis? No, his recording angel?'

'He's my ghost writer,' said Eddie.

Manny cackled and with a little clap rubbed his hands together.

'A book, eh? Well, I hope when the account is settled, if you like, nothing seems out of place. Know what I mean?'

'Manny, it's all going to be done with discretion,' said Eddie.

'Discretion, yes, I like that.' He waved his hands, palms upward, at the stacks around him. 'See all of my books? Interesting accounts, I can tell you. There are so many stories here. I go over them sometimes, you know? That may seem preposterous to you but these are my journals. The things I've hidden. You know, it's always a question of balance. Of balancing the books. Sometimes a figure here, a figure there.'

Manny folded the air with his fingers.

'What we want to talk about is all off the record,' I told him.

'Good, good.' He nodded.

'We want to talk about Harry Starks,' said Eddie.

'Tch, Harry Starks.' He sighed. 'Everyone wants to talk about Harry Starks. Are you sure this is not for a book or an article? I've had many people asking me about Mr Starks over the years, you know.'

'We think you might know where he is,' Eddie went on.

'How should I know. He is on the run, Eddie. You know what that means? To be on the move all the time. How should I know where he is?'

'Because I've seen him.'

'Uh?' Manny exclaimed. His mouth hung open and the shutters of his heavy eyelids blinked slowly. 'What are you talking about?' he demanded.

'I saw him, Manny. At Ronnie Kray's fucking funeral. Now what's going on? Someone's having me followed. Is it him?'

'What's going on?' Manny retorted indignantly. 'What's going on? You come in here, with a journalist, asking me all these questions . . .'

'I just want to know.'

'No. I think you should leave, Eddie. I think you and your . . . your official biographer should take these ridiculous stories elsewhere. I think . . .'

Eddie pulled something out of his jacket pocket and reached over the desk to show it to Manny. It took me a moment to register that it was a pistol of some sort.

'Eddie,' I chided him. 'For fuck's sake.'

Manny's eyes bulged at the barrel of the firearm pointed at his face. His mouth formed a perfect O, a bubble of sputum popped from his lips. Then he raised his hands slowly, more in a gesture of supplication than surrender, and tilted his head to one side.

'Now what's all this?' he demanded. 'For goodness' sake.'

'I've fucking had enough!' Eddie spat with sudden vehemence. 'I did all that time for you lot. Now I want some fucking answers.'

'Take it easy,' I implored him.

'You shut up,' Eddie ordered. 'I saw him, Manny. I've been out three months and no one has had the decency to even talk to me about what happened to mine.'

'Eddie.' Manny shrugged. 'I understood that you didn't want . . .'

'Oh yeah,' Eddie cut in. 'Eddie Doyle's going straight. Didn't have much choice, did I? I got to know about it all going missing years back. No chance of me making a deal to get a few years off my sentence, was there? I didn't have anything to fucking give them. So I keep quiet, try and do my time the easy way. Forget about it all. Wipe my mouth and just get on with it. I get out and I'm all ready to retire. Then I notice that someone's having me followed. And then Starks turns up. I want to know what's going on.'

'I don't know anything about you being followed, Eddie.'

'What about Starks?'

Manny grinned.

'Maybe he wanted to pay his last respects to dear old Ronald,' he said.

'I'm serious. Did you know he was in the country?'

'Well, yes.'

'You saw him?'

'No. And he is gone again already. Like the Wandering Jew, you know? Walking the earth, bearing witness to the error of our ways.'

'What's he up to?'

'He is putting his affairs in order.'

'What?'

'That is all I can tell you.'

'And would his affairs include the missing Hounslow bullion?'

'Please . . .' Manny gave a little downward wave with both hands. 'Put the gun down. Ha! "Put the gun down", that sounds like a bit of cheap dialogue.' He turned to me. 'Writer, you should be taking notes, eh?'

Eddie put the pistol back into his pocket. Manny rested his hands on his desk. He sighed.

'Well,' he began. 'Here we have it. So many people want to know where that missing gold went to.'

'Including Starks?'

'Nothing is directly connected to him, you know. His methods of asset protection are necessarily complicated, difficult to trace. That's the point, isn't it? But then when things go wrong and funds start to disappear . . .'

'You mean to say . . . ?'

'All I mean to say is that Harry lost a considerable sum himself from all of this.'

'He lost? He fucking lost? What about the boys that did the job in the first place? All that gold – it was us what had it away, Manny. It was our fucking job.'

'Yes, Eddie, your job. But our business. It's hard to deal with such an amount, as you well know. You know what the Customs people call fencing and money laundering? "Realisation". Good, no? And that's what it is, Eddie, realisation. You have to make it real, make it legitimate. It's like alchemy in reverse, turning all that nice shiny gold into something dull and everyday. Something that doesn't draw attention to itself.'

'Yeah, that's all very clever, but then it all gets fucked up at your end.'

'There was a breakdown in communication. Everyone was getting a bit jumpy. With all that was at stake.'

'Solly Blumberg,' said Eddie.

'Tch, that was a bad business.'

'Did Harry . . . ?'

Eddie let the question hang in the air. Manny drew in a breath and shook his head.

'No,' he replied. 'Not at all. Somebody messed up very badly there. Killing an old man like that. And with him dead no one knows where it went.'

'The gold?'

'Hmm,' mused Manny. 'Or something else.'

'What do you mean?'

'I mean, maybe it had already been turned into something else.'

'And you say Starks lost out on this?'

'Listen,' said Manny. 'I am not under any instruction from Harry on this. But if you are interested in recovering your assets, I could make some enquiries. We could try to find it, if you want.'

'I don't know,' Eddie said, shaking his head.

'If you want something from all of this.'

'Of course I fucking do.'

'Then we must look for it.'

'Yeah, but where do we start?'

'Right here, of course,' Manny declared with an open-palmed gesture. 'I told you, I look at my records, my accounts. There'll be a clue here, I'm sure of it.'

'I don't care about your precious accounts,' Eddie said. 'I just want my fucking money. Everyone seems to have done all right out of this except me.'

'That may be,' Manny said. 'But we do need to find it. And, you know, recirculate it legitimately. You'll need to cover your tracks, Eddie. You can't simply acquire a fortune from nowhere. You say you are being watched? Maybe it is the authorities are following your tracks. We need to be careful.'

'I want something now. Up front.'

Manny sighed.

'You mean you have not received any renumeration at all?'

'Not a fucking penny.'

'Well, that is remiss. Simon Beardsley should have furnished you with something.'

'Beardsley?'

'Yes, he was looking after some of the resmelting back then.'

'That fucking toerag?'

'I can assure you that he is far from being a toerag these days. A little clumsy in his methods maybe. He should be able to let you have something, on account as it were. In the meantime let me consult my archives.'

'Don't fuck me about, Manny.'

'I have no intention of doing so. We'll sort this out. I'll speak with Beardsley. And get in touch with other interested parties. And my books.' Manny rubbed his hands together with relish. 'I'll look through my books.'

As we were leaving Eddie checked the street from the doorway.

'Fuck,' he whispered sharply.

'What?'

'There.'

He nodded towards a car parked on the other side of the road.

'That's the fucker who's been following me. Come on,' he urged.

We raced across the street and into a little alleyway that led into Rathbone Street or Rathbone Place, I can't remember which. I turned back and managed to get a quick glance at the man in the car as he looked up.

'Come on,' he insisted, and I ducked into the alley after him. He zigzagged through the back streets of Fitzrovia, doubling back on himself until he was sure we were not being followed. He slowed down, turned to me and frowned.

'You think I'm paranoid, don't you?'

'No, no,' I panted, out of breath. 'The man in the car. I got a look at him. He reminded me of someone.'

'Who?'

'I can't think.'

'Well, try to remember, for fuck's sake.'

We walked on a little.

'You think Manny was telling the truth?' he asked.

'It's hard to tell.'

'And we still don't really know what Harry Starks is up to, do we?'

I shrugged. I didn't know what to make of it all. We passed a pub.

'Come on,' he said. 'I need a drink.'

Eddie took a sip of his large vodka and tonic. 'Maybe he was just taking the piss. You know, patronising me.' His right hand trembled slightly. He looked up at me, holding my gaze with his. A little of the murderous anger he had taken out on Manny still flickered in his eyes.

'Are you patronising me, Tony?' he demanded.

'Wouldn't dream of it.'

And at that moment I wouldn't have. Eddie's rage had impressed me. It was a reminder that this gaunt, nervous-looking man with grey hair was still something of a hard man. And he was desperate. It was that desperation, that fury and disillusion, which made me feel something for him. A sort of kinship, perhaps. Maybe I had been patronising him in the past when Victor had assigned me to him but he had gained my respect now. And I was intrigued by all that was unfolding. Our relationship had changed, I was no longer merely his ghost. We had embarked on a strange and dangerous partnership. I felt excited by this. But could I trust him?

'What was with the gun, Eddie?' I asked him.

Eddie gave a nervous grin.

'It got results, didn't it?'

'Well, it got Mr Gould talking. But as you said, he didn't tell us everything.'

'Silly fucker. Going on about his books like he's the fount of all knowledge. Yeah, well, we're going to have to be a bit more careful with some of the other people involved in this.'

'I suppose so,' I muttered.

Something came to mind. My vision drifted into the middle distance. The blur of the fruit machine flashing in the corner of the pub.

'What's the matter with you?' Eddie was saying.

I focused back on him.

'I was just thinking.'

'What's the matter? That bloke in the car?'

'No. I've just had an idea.'

'What?'

'Just something I've got to look up, that's all.'

I'd have a look in my own books, my own records. Just as Manny Gould was consulting his accounts for clues, studying columns in ledgers like scripture for meaning, I resolved to do a little reading myself. I dusted down Teddy Thursby's diaries and flipped through the years. There were entries for 1984 that had always fascinated me though they had not made complete sense up until now. I began to read and make footnotes.

Friday, 11 May
Tangier
Arrive at Boukhalef airport at midday & then taxi to Hotel El Minzah. Suite agreeable enough. Me & Julian have lunch at the hotel then set out for a walk. Go up through the Grand Socco into the Medina. Hustlers homing in on us from every direction. Try to politely ignore them but Julian v. tiresomely starts to banter with them. I think somehow he imagines that they are attracted to him because of some great charm that he possesses. Maybe he sees something kindred; after all, he was once quite a little hustler himself. Though his looks have long gone. That petulant little pout of his twisted into an ugly sneer.

Get to the Petit Socco & settle on the terrace of the Café Central for a mint tea. Tangier isn't what it was. All the colourful expats replaced with scruffy backpackers & dreary tourists. We get lumbered with an annoying & totally unnecessary 'guide' called Mohammed who trails after us all around the Kasbah, insisting that we should visit his uncle's carpet shop. Julian hints at all kinds of filthy propositions with this wretched boy, who grins & plays along quite happily. I decide I've had enough of this after a while & paying off the lad with a ten-dirham note shout at J. to stop fucking around & show a bit more discretion.

Get back to the El Minzah quite exhausted. A note left at the desk: *Came around but you had gone out. Meet me in Dean's Bar noon tomorrow, H.*[1]

Read it v. surreptitiously. Julian curious but I haven't told him about this aspect of our jaunt. As far as he knows it's just research for the memoirs & a little holiday. Tried to get some work done this p.m., though J. was his usual lethargic self. Talked through the time I was first here in '21 when Archie Clark-Kerr was Consul-General. Pig-sticking on the Town Beach when my horse bolted & I nearly ran through a French cavalry officer with my spear & travelling south to Marrakesh with Walter Harris, the *Times* correspondent & adventurer. Tremendous fun being young & British back then.

Spot of dinner & a drink in the hotel bar. Julian announced that he was going out for a walk. Know exactly what he is up to & with

[1] 'H' referred to here and elsewhere is clearly H. Starks. See corroborating evidence in note below.

his sense of propriety would not be at all surprised if he ends up left for dead in some alleyway.

Saturday, 12 May.
J. turns up late for breakfast looking unbearably smug. Starts telling me about last night's trade. Becomes petulant when I tell him that I'm not really interested. Says he has to listen to my dreary stories all the time, so I tell him that's what I pay him for.

Consider shaking him off & going to this rendezvous on my own but decide that it will be easier to take him along. Might shut him up for a bit.

It's just a short walk from the El Minzah to Dean's. Trust H. to pick this notorious drinking den for 'a meet', as he'd so succinctly put it. In its heyday in the '50s when Tangier was still an international zone Dean's attracted an extraordinary collection of high and low life. Expat pederasts, Soho bohemia, villains and *contrebandiers*, American beatniks. Dean was quite a character himself, half-caste. Some said that his mother was a Ramsgate landlady and his father a West Indian passing through Kent. Robin Maugham had told me that he had been a gigolo in London before the war and had come to Morocco after being caught up in a scandal involving the death of a Gaiety Girl in Brilliant Chang's opium den in Limehouse. All sorts of extraordinary stories surrounded him which, like H., he did little to play down & often clearly encouraged. H. had some dealings with him, I think. He had been in Tangier back then when he worked for Billy Hill.[2] In fact our paths must have crossed at some time & probably in Dean's Bar.

Dean died back in the early sixties so I had no idea what to expect of what was left of his establishment as we passed through the beaded curtain into the tiny bar. The layout & decor of the place were largely unchanged but the clientele were all rather rough-looking Moroccans. We were the only Westerners in the place and were eyed up with some suspicion as we made our way to the bar. It had become a 'local', I suppose, like so many things in Tangier now that its cosmopolitan days seem over.

[2] Gang boss referred to in Thursby's diaries, 12 February 1965: 'He [Harry Starks] had been in Tangier in the fifties when he'd worked for Billy Hill, the king of the racecourse gangs.'

The piano, where Peter Lacy, former Spitfire pilot & Francis Bacon's lover, used to play all hours to pay off his gambling debts was gone. We got a couple of drinks, all the time being eyed by the sullen natives. Julian smiled & simpered, which didn't seem to help matters. I heard one of the drinkers mutter *maricones* & there were various derisive grunts in our direction. But then the beaded curtain clattered & the assembled eyes shifted to the doorway. H. had arrived.

All at once the atmosphere in the bar changed. As he walked in there were nods and smiles of greeting. He had a handsome and thick set Moroccan in tow. H. stood in front of me for a moment, just grinning. So much older than when I last saw him, though with a healthy tan and looking as charismatic as ever (Christ knows what I must have looked like to him, a warmed-up corpse, I suppose). 'Teddy,' he said finally, holding both my upper arms gently. 'I'm so glad you're here.'

We went through and sat at a table. Drinks & tapas were brought to us. H. nodded towards his companion, who he introduced as Mustapha. After a few drinks & some gossip over old times H. declared it was time to go. 'We need to talk,' he told me. 'I mean seriously. And I haven't got long in Tangier. It isn't safe for me here. It's not like the old days, eh? I've got a place I'm staying on the Mountain. Come back and have a chat.'

Mustapha drove us all up to the hill in the Marshan district to the west of the city that the British expats used to call the Mountain. Remnants of the old colony here & there, twisting lanes, dried-out gardens & disused tennis courts. What Cecil Beaton had once described as 'oriental Cheltenham', mostly faded now. The house that H. was staying at had a marvellous view of the town & the bay from its terrace. H. insisted that we should talk in private. I suggested that Mustapha might show Julian some of the sights of Tangier. 'A little local colour. It'll help to establish a background when you come to write it all up.'

So off they went. H. made us some drinks & we got down to the matter in hand. H. explained that he still used Tangier as a base for some of his smuggling activities, using the rag trade as cover. British companies use sweated labour out here & shift the stuff back by HGV. But he had been, for the most part, hiding out in the Dominican Republic since the extradition treaty with Britain had broken down after the Falklands War. 'The Caribbean is a good place to operate,' he said. 'You can hop from island to island.' 'Like a pirate,' I suggested. 'Funny you should say that, Teddy. I mean, that's sort of what I want to talk to you about.' He leaned towards me, beckoning slightly with one hand. I too lowered my head as if in conspiracy, though there was no one else in the room. 'Buried treasure, Teddy,' he whispered hoarsely.

I couldn't help letting out a deep chuckle. I leant back and took a sip from my glass. Same old H., I thought. He was smiling at me. 'It's true, Teddy. There was this job that was pulled, back in Blighty a year or so ago. Fifteen million in bullion taken.[3] You might have heard about it.'

I nodded. He told me that the gold had been disposed of in various ways and a sort of consortium had been formed. 'Those of us that understood that kind of international finance,' he explained. But inevitably there had been some kind of falling out & a substantial amount had gone missing.

'Of the gold?' I asked. 'That or money realised from it. No one seems to know where it is.'

H. held two fists up then opened his hands. He said that there were details of the missing loot hidden somewhere. 'You mean like a map?' I suggested. 'Maybe,' he sighed. 'Or an audit trail.' 'Fascinating,' I exclaimed, 'just like *Treasure Island*.' He grinned at that but then went on to suggest that I might help him with the recovery of these ill-gotten gains. I demurred but he was quite insistent.

'There're so many people I can't trust in this. The few I can are under surveillance or gone missing,' he said. I didn't like the sound of this. He tried to reassure me. 'Teddy, there's absolutely no risk involved for you. I just need you to pass on some information and maybe bring some back to me here.' He grinned that old shark smile of his and poured me another drink.

Julian & Mustapha arrived back. Later we all went out to a place called Scott's Disco in the Ville Nouvelle. Strange little club, rather tawdry with a mirror ball dangling over a tiny wooden parquet dance floor. Rather charming illustrations of Scottish regiments line the walls & two large oil paintings of beautiful Arab boys in full Highland dress take pride of place above the bar & on the

[3] Clearly a reference to the Hounslow bullion job.

wall opposite. We had a few drinks & the place started to fill up around one. The others started eyeing up the prospects in earnest but I'm really too tired, too old. Left them to it. Arranged to meet H. at Guitta's tomorrow for Sunday lunch. Mustapha drove me back to the El Minzah.

Sunday, 13 May

Go to morning service at St Andrew's, the little Anglican church built in a Moroccan style that nestles by the Grand Socco. The combination of a Moorish decorative style and an English country churchyard evokes some strange melancholy feeling in me. Looking up at its cedar ceiling carved by craftsmen from Fez, the Lord's Prayer scrolled in Arabic above the chancel, I'm moved by some feeling of nostalgia. But for what? God knows. The service itself a little vulgar, not really High Church enough for my liking. Bumped into Freddy Carruthers as I was coming out.

'Goodness, Teddy!' he exclaimed. 'I didn't know you were here. What are you doing in Tangier?'

Felt suddenly furtive, remembering the conversation with H. last night. Muttered something appropriate, though. Freddy came here in the early '50s after he was sent to prison for cottaging & his family couldn't bear the scandal of it all. We had a bit of a wander around the graveyard. They're all here. *Walter Harris, He Loved The Moorish People And Was Their Friend*, & there a cracked & overgrown headstone in the corner: *Dean. Missed by all and sundry.* Freddy asks about England & sniffs a bit as I reply. 'I'm never going back, Teddy,' he says. 'George Greeves[4] is dead, you know.' 'That evil old gossip.' 'Yes,' Freddie sighed wistfully. 'I do miss him.'

We got to the lich-gate & said goodbye. I headed up the Rue de Belgique towards Guitta's. Had a hell of a time finding it. A new mosque has been built opposite & any premises selling alcohol have to be screened from the holy place so a bloody great big wall has been built separating it from the street. Its entrance is now around the corner. Another reminder of how the blasted Islamicists have the run of things here now.

[4] George Greeves (1900–1984), Reuter's Morocco correspondent, notorious pederast and gossip-monger. 'His stories are endless. He keeps up a constant stream of foul-mouthed commentary – life and death, nobody is saved' – Joe Orton.

The place still has some of its old style. Run by an Italian family since the '40s, it is, I suppose, all that is left of the international zone days. A French-style house in an overgrown ornamental garden. Here, in its elegant if rather dilapidated dining room, the old guard come for their Sunday roast. Propped up like lizards in the sun, the dwindling gathering of exiles. H. is waiting by the colonnaded bar. The Moroccan waiter, resplendent in white tuxedo, black bow tie, tasselled fez & bottle-thick glasses, shuffles & wheezes heavily as he leads us to our table. Looks like he could drop dead any minute. 'Christ,' I say to H. when we are seated. 'This really is God's waiting room.'

H. chuckles darkly. I suddenly have an awful vertiginous feeling, lost years falling away yet still farther to drop. An eternity, of course. Can't outstare the void. We have roast lamb & a very passable Côtes du Rhône. H. passes an envelope across the table to me. 'You know who to take this to,'[5] he says, 'and you know you mentioned *Treasure Island* last night.' 'Did I?' 'Yeah. And the funny thing is, it's come up before. It's a clue of some sort.[6] Have a think about it.'

I had no idea what he was talking about. I took the envelope. Suppose I don't have much choice about running this errand for him. After lunch we wandered out. Mustapha was waiting in a car for him. They dropped me off at the hotel. Julian was lounging about by the pool. He's done absolutely no work at all while we've been here. It's been me that has been busy writing things down. Lazy little bastard. I fear he'll never write this bloody biography & I'll be at the mercy of the vultures once I'm gone.

I searched through the rest of the diary to see whether there were any references to what was in the envelope that Starks had given to Teddy Thursby. There were none. I showed the extracts to Eddie. In giving my interpretation to some of the text I hoped that he might be forthcoming with some of his own opinions.

'How did you get your hands on this?' he asked.

'The diaries? Well, I was a friend of his literary executor.'

'So they belong to you now, do they?'

[5] Who is Starks referring to here? Manny Gould?

[6] *Treasure Island* as a clue? What can this mean? Note: reread R.L. Stevenson.

'Er, sort of. Look, never mind about that, have a look at this bit.'

I pointed out the sections that featured Harry Starks.

'Well, he doesn't seem to know where the fucking gold went to either,' was Eddie's only comment.

'What about *Treasure Island* as a clue?' I asked him.

'Well, it's a pretty fucking obvious literary allusion.'

'But could it mean anything specific?'

'You're obsessed with stories, Tony. This isn't a fucking story. What were the dates again?'

I handed him back the diary.

'Well,' he said, 'it's around the time Solly got bumped off, isn't it? That's the key to this whole thing. You know who had him done, don't you?'

I shrugged.

'The word always had it it was Beardsley. We should front him out about that.'

'But if it was him that had Solly Blumberg killed wouldn't that be dangerous?'

Eddie gave a flat laugh.

'I ain't afraid of him,' he snorted. 'I remember him when he was Harry Starks' pet hooligan, just a snot-nosed little Mod kid.'

Eddie was becoming increasingly filled with bravado and derring-do. I found his recklessness frightening but exhilarating as well. As much as he had insisted that 'this isn't a fucking story, Tony', that was how I felt. A wonderful, ridiculous story. An adventure. And I found myself drawn into it.

I felt restless. I spent the whole night reading *Treasure Island*. Stevenson's storytelling is so marvellous, fantastical, yet compelling and strangely touching. Conjuring the childlike wonder with action and danger. But I searched vainly for clues about the bullion robbery. Maybe Eddie was right, it was merely a clumsy literary reference.

A cold, grey dawn arrived and I staggered through the last chapters, my eyes burning with fatigue. Then, coming to the part where the treasure itself is finally uncovered, I came across a passage that seemed to jump out from the page at me and insist upon some sort of universal meaning. The sky began to blush with red a little and, in a manic state of over-tiredness, a crazed somnambulant lucidity, I mumbled the words out loud like an aubade:

> It was a strange collection, like Billy Bone's hoard for diversity of coinage, but so much larger and so much more varied that I think I never had more pleasure than in sorting them. English, French, Spanish, Portuguese, Georges, and Louises, doubloons and double guineas and moidores and sequins, the pictures of all the kings of Europe for the last hundred years, strange Oriental pieces stamped with what looked like wisps of string or bits of spider's web, round pieces and square pieces, and pieces bored through the middle, as if to wear them round your neck – nearly every variety of money in the world must, I think, have found a place in that collection; and for number, I am sure they were like autumn leaves, so that my back ached with stooping and my fingers with sorting them out . . .

As in a trance, or a waking dream where some occult or arcane knowledge is signified, these words and symbols blazoned themselves on my mind like emblems or a chart's legend. As if somewhere in the lines was a key, a map ('or an audit trail,' Starks had said). It was a discourse on the nature of treasure – no, on the nature of money itself. *Every variety of money in the world*, capital, international money markets, loot and possession. Money laundering, 'realisation', Manny Gould had called it, bullion transformed into commodities, treasure hidden in endless and numberless accounts. My mind reeled with labyrinthine exchanges and currencies. For an untransactable moment I had a clear notion of what was conceivable, that unpalpable pulse that throbs with meaning and clarity, only to reverberate into echoing reveries like coins clattering in an uncollectable jackpot. I slept and imagined an unconscious coinage of inscrutable sovereigns, money becoming immaterial, an abstract semantic, oaths in inscription, a future in sterling – *I promise to pay the bearer on demand* – a multiplication of possibilities. Change: I dreamt of coinage, obverse and reverse, treasured memories, a storehouse of properties. Everything suddenly made sense as I swooned into darkness.

I woke with an awful start, my feeble body jerking itself awake in the armchair. The book had fallen from my hands and my head was dull and empty. The illusory clarity faded into a forgotten, ungraspable dream.

We drove out to Simon Beardsley's mansion in Essex. Manny Gould had set up a meeting. Eddie wanted me to come along.

'Why?' I asked him, slightly daunted at the prospect.

'I need someone with me.'

'But why me?'

'Well, who else? The only people I can trust any more are either dead or inside. I can't trust anyone on the outside any more. Things have changed. Drugs, that's what it's all about these days. All these fuckers who made money out of us. This bent lawyer that was looking after Charlie and Ray's bit, you know, the guys who did the job with me, well, he ended up turning two million into five. Property boom, you know, that Docklands thing. I mean, we steal this stuff and yet there's other people who can make even more out of it just by sitting on their arses. Speculation. Of course, they caught up with him in the end. Got twelve years but he was out in five. That's white-collar crime for you. And you can be damn sure he salted some of it away somewhere. No, Tony, I can't trust any of them.'

'But you can trust me?'

'I don't know, Tony, I don't know. Fact is, you're harmless enough. And we're supposed to be working together, right?'

'Right,' I agreed, grudgingly.

'Don't worry,' Eddie said with a smile. 'There'll be no guns this time.'

'I'm very glad to hear it.'

'It's all about front, Tony. Just keep your mouth shut. It's all gonna be very polite and respectful. Face to face, that is.'

Eddie gave a mirthless cackle.

'Then we get done in when we least suspect it,' he said.

Beardsley's place was out in the country just the other side of Braintree. Electrically operated wrought-iron gates opened on to a gravel driveway. A large modern brick house with a ludicrous colonnaded portico. Greek urns and silly statues all over the place.

'Well,' said Eddie as we pulled up in front of this vulgar edifice, 'some people have done all right, haven't they?'

Beardsley was by the front door, holding back two demonic-looking Rottweilers. He nodded towards us and called out:

'Just let me put the dogs away.'

He dragged the slavering hounds into a side room then led us through.

'Good to see you, Eddie,' he said. 'I don't think I've met your friend.'

'This is Tony,' Eddie told him. 'He's a business associate.'

'Nice to meet you, Tony,' said Beardsley as we came into a huge reception room.

Eddie and Beardsley stood facing each other for a second, as if squaring up to one another. Beardsley was a muscular man in his forties with cropped hair, designer sportswear and lots of chunky gold jewellery. Eddie's frame was frail in comparison but there was an attempt at dignity in his deportment which was touching and impressive. Beardsley's head bowed slightly and he grinned to reveal yet more of the yellow metal.

'Eddie,' he said with a shrug. 'What can I say?'

Eddie Doyle smiled back.

'That's what everyone keeps asking,' he said.

'Drink?' asked Beardsley.

'I'd love a cup of tea,' said Eddie.

Beardsley made a pot and brought it through and we all sat down on a white suede three-piece suite. He reached under the glass-topped coffee table and pulled out a plastic carrier bag and handed it over to Eddie.

'What's this?' Eddie demanded.

'It's for you,' replied Beardsley.

Eddie peered inside the bag. He gave a short laugh then looked up at Beardsley.

'Is this a fucking joke?'

'Eddie . . .'

'What's in here? A couple of grand?'

'It's five thousand.'

'Have a fucking whip-round, did we?'

'Look, it's just something to tide you over.'

'Where's the rest of it?'

'That's just it. We don't know, do we. That business with Solly . . .'

'Yeah, well, maybe someone was a little bit hasty there. If Solly was still alive maybe he'd be able to tell us.'

'Or tell certain other people.'

'Did he tell you anything?' Eddie asked.

'What do you mean?'

'I mean before he was done in.'

'Nah. He was going on about having hidden the gold somewhere for safe-keeping. Said something about a map.'

'A map?' Eddie frowned and looked over at me.

'Yeah,' said Beardsley with a little laugh. 'He was really fucking losing it by then. Coming up with any kind of rubbish to buy himself more time.'

'Well, maybe you should have given him some.'

'Look, we didn't have a choice. He was about to grass.'

'That's what you think.'

'We couldn't take the risk. Honestly, Eddie, it all got fucked up and we had to cover our tracks. I don't know if we'll ever find out where the gold went to now.'

'It looks like you and half of Essex are fucking wearing it.'

Beardsley laughed again and with a sovereign-ringed paw toyed with the thick gold chain around his neck.

'You think it's a bit much?'

'I'm serious, Beardsley. And I'm not the only one.'

'What do you mean?'

'I mean I'm not the only one that might be interested in what went missing. Saw an old face recently.'

'Oh yeah?' Beardsley commented as he picked up his teacup.

'Harry Starks,' said Eddie softly.

Beardsley lost his grip on the cup handle and it clattered on to the glass table.

'Shit!' he exclaimed, standing up to avoid the spillage of tea. 'You're joking, aren't you?'

'I told you, I'm serious.'

'Shit,' he repeated, brushing at his trousers.

'A bit nervous, are we, Simon?'

Beardsley forced a smile.

'Just a shock, you know. I mean, Harry fucking Starks.'

'Yeah, and maybe he thinks you were a little hasty too.'

'Look, I can explain about Solly.'

Eddie stood up.

'Come on,' he told me. 'Let's go.'

He picked up the carrier bag.

'We're getting off now,' Eddie told him.

'You only just got here.'

'Well, you know, things to do.'

Beardsley followed us out through the hall.

'You really see Harry?' he asked.

'Large as life.'

'Fuck. Eddie, about Solly, we didn't have any choice. You've got to believe me.'

We were at the door. Eddie turned to Beardsley.

'Doesn't really matter what I believe, does it?' he said. 'So long, Beardsley. Be lucky.'

'You clock the reaction when I mentioned Starks?' Eddie asked me as we drove back to London.

'He was a little flustered.'

'I figure Beardsley's worried because he bumped off the only person who knew for certain where the gold was.'

'So where does that lead us?'

'Don't know. I'll tell you something, though, we're really in trouble now.'

'What do you mean?'

'You know, stirring things up like this. People are starting to get edgy and that's not a good thing.'

'Maybe we should, er, take things easy.'

'Too late for that, Tony.'

I got back to my flat and brooded over the situation. Eddie's attitude was becoming very disconcerting. He was an old man and yet was exhibiting all the recklessness of youth. It was ridiculous. And yet it struck me that maybe his behaviour was in keeping with his age. Why don't we become more desperate as the years advance? Why is it that the less we have to lose the more we cling on to what is left of a meagre existence? I also reflected that it was in Eddie Doyle's nature to take risks, to be always putting all of his energy into one big gamble. He was still a recidivist at heart. Rehabilitation would come only with the grave, it seemed.

And my sedentary life was now disturbed by action. I felt that I was losing control. I was no longer merely recording the facts but becoming part of the story itself. My head throbbed with the insane excitement of it all. I'd not felt so alive for years. I was myself being driven by an unpredictable narrative. Something was happening. And something would happen next. And, of course, I was beginning to lose track of what was the real story and what were plot lines of the imagination.

There was a plethora of references, fact and fable: underworld rumours, endless newspaper articles and *truecrime* accounts of the Hounslow bullion job, Teddy Thursby's chronicles and, in encrypted fiction, some obscure interpretation of *Treasure Island*. I picked the book up from where I had left it, lying on the floor, face down, with a cracked spine. I read the three or four pages that remained. The book's actual ending is somewhat disappointing, the journey home, a return to normality. Even Silver's escape is downplayed and anti-climactic. In its conclusion no words or phrases seemed to testify or offer the clue Starks had alluded to. I noted only that whereas with most fictions concerning treasure it is the loot which is jinxed, in Stevenson's tale it is where the hoard is buried, the island itself, which seems bewitched. In the end Jim Hawkins calls it 'that accursed island' and is only too happy to see the last of it slip from view over the blue curve of the horizon.

Was it the island itself which was of significance, rather than the treasure? Stories of isles, charmed or blessed, have been told since *The Odyssey* and perhaps before, with an ancient insistence that there is meaning and significance in how we navigate them. Symbol of alternative realities from Atlantis to Neverland, the island is also metaphor for the individual (Donne's attempted contradiction merely reminds us of how compelling is this image of isolation). We remember, perhaps, a primal insularity: the foetus a tiny atoll in an amniotic sea.

But if the clue is in the island, what is it? Some sort of code to where the treasure is buried? It all seemed rather fanciful given the brutal realities of the Hounslow job. I carried on reading. Stevenson wrote two appendices to *Treasure Island*. In the first, he explains that the writing of the story was preceded by the drawing of the map; in fact it was drafting an imaginary chart which gave the inspiration for the book itself, a narrative formed out of a prophetic topography. Beardsley had said that Solly had mentioned a map. But what could that mean? Was the tale itself in some way prescient of the treasure we sought? I couldn't see how. I read to the end and found nothing.

Wearily, I went back to the beginning. Not the start of the novel but its introduction, in my volume by a certain Frank Simpson, a professor of American literature. I scanned his little essay with not much enthusiasm until my eyes suddenly alighted on this short passage:

> There has been much scholarly debate as to the location of Stevenson's island. Does his fictional isle have an actual, geographical progenitor? Candidates range from the Isle of Pines off the coast of Cuba to the outline of Edinburgh as seen from the Pentland Hills. The most obvious geographical location is Norman Island in the British Virgin Islands. Overgrown and deserted but for a few wild goats, the largest of the uninhabited islands in the BVI has long been thought to be a site of buried treasure. More important, though, is the cultural placement of the island . . .

I didn't see it at first but then my mind had been island-hopping a whole archipelago of insular notions and deranged cartographies. Then it came into focus, a promontory suddenly visible against the horizon. *Land ho!* I almost said it out loud like a lookout spying *terra incognita*. Land fucking ho. It was so obvious. The British Virgin Islands, a remnant of Empire and a major site for offshore banking and money laundering. Eddie was right, *Treasure Island* was a literary allusion but also an analogy. Just as eighteenth-century pirates had buried their treasure in Caribbean islands, so modern-day equivalents do exactly the same thing but with shell companies and numbered bank accounts. The missing loot was offshore. It was somewhere in the British Virgin Islands.

I told Eddie of my findings but he wasn't convinced.

'Aren't you getting a bit carried away?' he demanded.

'Well, it's worth investigating, wouldn't you say?'

'I don't know. Let's hear what Manny has to say.'

'Can we trust him?'

'Probably not, but he's the expert in all of this. If anyone can put all of this together he can.'

'But what if it's a set-up? What do we do then?'

'I don't know,' said Eddie. 'But we can't afford not to talk to Manny. Let's hear what he says.'

So another meeting was arranged at the good offices of Emmanuel Gould, FCA, FCCA. I told him of my theory. The little accountant frowned across the desk at us; his black brows bristled with thought.

'A reference in Lord Thursby's diaries, you say? A literary clue? A little tenuous, don't you think?'

'That's what I told him,' said Eddie.

'But,' Manny continued, 'it could be offshore. And why not the BVI? My own research has had considerably less poetic licence, I'm afraid, but maybe it does connect with this rather, er, imaginative idea. Solly Blumberg's assets at the time of his death seem to have completely vanished. Liquidated or transferred somewhere. Now, although a substantial amount of the resmelted gold seems to have gone missing, Solly might already have sold it on and hidden the assets away.'

'Offshore?' I asked.

'That would make sense, supposing of course he had disposed of the bullion.'

'And supposing he did? How would that work?' I asked him.

'In terms of laundering it offshore?' Manny asked.

'Yes.'

'Well, there are three major stages in cleaning money. First is placement – you know, finding somewhere to put your assets, a financial system to get the money out of the country. Then what is called "layering", setting up a business, some sort of shell company, so you can disguise these funds as proceeds from legitimate business. Then finally "integration", with a complex web of money transfers, false loan repayments, income from investments. By this time it becomes exceedingly difficult to distinguish between legal and illegal wealth and all of this loot can come back looking squeaky clean. Oh yes, it all makes perfect sense, doesn't it? Only one problem.'

'What's that?' I asked.

'It didn't come back, did it?'

'No, it bloody didn't,' said Eddie.

'And there we have it. Money laundering is deliberately complicated, the audit trail has to be difficult to follow in order to keep the authorities off the trail, but when there's a breakdown in communication among those doing the laundering, well, then huge amounts can go missing, greedy people who are supposed to be involved in asset protection line their own pockets, and that is what might have happened.'

'Might have?'

Manny shrugged.

'We can't be sure. But in the BVI we got burned. There was an investigation. A joint operation, an Anglo-American thing, Scotland Yard and the DEA. This British tax lawyer, Joe Clement, had been salting away funds in the Isle of Man and the BVI. He had contacts with the Florida Mafia too. But he ended up doing a deal with the authorities in exchange for immunity from prosecution. Ended up on a witness protection programme. Assets were frozen, funds were confiscated.'

'Did that include proceeds realised from the Hounslow job?' I asked him.

'Perhaps. Unless they were transferred elsewhere on the island. That could be what this clue of yours is all about. That it's still hidden there somewhere.'

'But how on earth are we going to find it?' asked Eddie.

'We have to be methodical,' Manny announced. 'Try and find an audit trail from Clement's investment trust to another shell company.'

Manny got hold of a list of companies registered in the British Virgin Islands.

'I really don't know where to start,' he protested.

'Let me have a look,' I said.

He handed me the list. I didn't know what I was looking for but I felt that there must be another clue somewhere. And I found it. Flint Investments were listed with an address in Road Town, Tortola.

'You should check this one out,' I told Manny, pointing to it.

'Why's that?' Manny frowned at it, then his eyebrows shot up. 'Oh yes, of course, Flint, of course. Well, we might as well give it a try.'

'What are you two on about?' Eddie demanded.

Manny held up the list.

'See?' he said. 'Flint. Flint was the name of the pirate whose treasure was buried on the island.'

'Oh, for fuck's sake,' Eddie muttered.

But I was right. It took Manny a couple of days to find a link between Clement and Flint Investments and then we had another meeting in his office.

'So what do we do now?' Eddie asked.

'Well, I have taken the liberty of making contact with Mr Starks. He has people in that area who, shall we say, protect his interests, and they can go about attempting to recover whatever assets remain in this company.'

'What about my fucking interests?' Eddie demanded.

'Of course they will be represented too, Eddie.'

'And in the meantime I just sit on my arse while other people divide up my takings, as per fucking usual. Like I spent all my time inside doing.'

'I don't see what else we can do. We don't even know what is in Flint Investments, after all. It will be merely a shell company, maybe an empty shell.'

'All the more reason to find out ourselves.'

'You're not suggesting that we . . .' Manny began.

'No,' Eddie cut him off. 'Not you and me. Me and him.'

Eddie nodded in my direction.

'We'll go there and check things out ourselves.'

'Now, wait a minute,' I complained.

'Come on, Tony. We can't let Starks or anyone else take us for a ride again.'

'Take you for a ride, Eddie. This really isn't my problem.'

'No, but it was your fucking idea, Tony.'

'What?'

'This *Treasure Island* nonsense. Come on, a little holiday. It'll do you good.'

'I don't think so.'

'It'll be a good story. You can be Jim Hawkins and I'll be Long John fucking Silver.'

We flew into Antigua and got a connecting flight to Beef Island in the British Virgins then a taxi to Road Town. The sea was a deep gentian diffusing into the horizon; green hills sloped gently into cliffs and coves. A coastal road took us past clutches of porched wooden houses and one-room shacks. There were bigger houses as well with chain-link fences and concrete driveways.

'Look at some of these fucking mansions,' Eddie declared as we bumped along. 'You know, this is what I always dreamed of. Doing one last coup and retiring to a tropical island. That's what the Hounslow job was supposed to be all about.'

'And would you have done?'

'What?'

'I mean, if you'd got away with it.'

'What?' he said. 'Come away to somewhere like here?'

'Yeah.'

Eddie turned and gave me a look of exasperation or disdain.

'Of course not,' he said. 'It never works out like that.'

'So what will you do if you get some of your money back?'

'I don't know, do I? Look, will you stop spoiling it? I was enjoying myself for a minute there.'

Road Town was a busy little burgh. A boom town. The harbour was crammed with charter yachts, a fat cruise ship was coming in to dock. Amid the ramshackle dwellings, bars and shops were concrete-and-glass office blocks housing all manner of financial services. Herds of four-wheel-drives clogged the dusty streets. The wooded hillsides surrounding the town were studded with tiered condominia.

We checked into the Treasure Isle hotel on Waterfront Drive. Everywhere were tourist traps promoting the islands' glorious seafaring past. Tortola is the biggest sea yacht chartering centre in the world and the town had grown rich from the power of sail. And buried treasure in the form of international business companies and trusts drawn up here because of zero taxation and banking secrecy laws.

Our rooms overlooked the harbour. Eddie studied a guidebook.

'This ain't really Treasure Island, you know, Tony,' he announced.

He gestured out across the bay at a group of islands that rose out of the shimmering silvery sea on the horizon.

'It's out there,' he went on, checking a small map in the guidebook. 'Norman Island. And that little one,' he pointed, 'that's Dead Man's Chest where Blackbeard left fifteen men marooned to settle their differences with a cutlass and a bottle of rum.'

Eddie seemed in good spirits. I began to fear, with growing dread, that he was in a holiday mood.

'So what do we do now?' I asked.

'We wait for somebody to make contact.'

'Great.'

'Relax, Tony.'

Relax. The word always comes in the form of a command, doesn't it? A command that never fails to make me tense up.

'We can get a bit of sun while we're here,' he went on.

But I've never been that keen on bright sunlight. I've always felt that there was something reptilian about lounging about in it all day. And I found the heat oppressive and stupefying.

Eddie, on the other hand, lapped it up. He spent hours by the tiny hotel pool, sunbathing.

'What's the matter with you?' he demanded as I crouched in the shade, nursing a drink. 'It's therapeutic, you know. All this light. All this sky. It's what I missed most about being inside. Not being able to see the sky.'

There were a lot of people of retirement age staying at the hotel so Eddie and I didn't look out of place. There was a lot of ancient flesh on display which I frankly found quite sickening. Bulging out all over the place, flaccid and glabrous, oiled and reddening in the harsh ultraviolet. Eddie himself wasn't in too bad shape, though. His body sagged a little around the middle but his frame retained a taut muscularity. Semi-naked, his body had a jaunty ease in its movement. A quirky animal grace I could only envy.

I spent as much time as I could in my hotel room reading to the drone of the air conditioning. I missed my usual dull routine. I'm not cut out for vacations. I need a sense of order, an illusion of being in control of my surroundings. In the evenings Eddie insisted that we go out and try the local cuisine. Over-spiced fish that gave me heartburn. In one of the restaurants, a converted shack on the waterfront with reggae music throbbing away, I noticed someone at the bar looking over at us. It was the man in the car outside Manny Gould's, I was sure of it. As he saw me looking back at him he turned away, paid his bill and left. I nudged Eddie.

'Over there,' I hissed.

'What?'

He turned. The man had gone. A black youth cleared away a glass and wiped the counter.

'The barman?' Eddie whispered.

'No. There was someone else there a moment ago. The man who was following us back in London.'

'What? Are you sure you're not seeing things?'

'Yes.'

'I mean, the heat's been getting to you.'

'I'm perfectly sure, Eddie.'

Eddie sighed.

'Shit. You said you recognised him. Before.'

'Yeah, but I still can't think who he is.'

The next day Eddie booked us a day trip on a schooner going out to Norman Island. I really didn't want to go.

'Look,' Eddie insisted. 'We've got to make it look like we're holidaymakers. Especially if this bloke is checking up on us out here. Come on. We can go and see the real Treasure Island.'

The other day-trippers were amiable Americans and Canadians. They all seemed to be paired off.

'You notice everybody on this boat is a couple?' I said to Eddie.

'Yeah.'

'Do you wonder if they think that's what we are?'

'What?'

'A couple.'

I grinned at Eddie.

'Fuck off,' he muttered.

But Eddie could easily have passed as an ageing homosexual. Even in shorts and polo shirt he looked immaculately turned out. His neatly cut greying hair and well-kept body bore all the marks of an old queen who looked after himself. I, on the other hand, barely passed muster as human in this company. There was a camaraderie that I shrank from. People introduced themselves with that easy manner that North Americans seem so good at, making little comments about the places they came from. Eddie was outgoing and talkative, telling all manner of lies, no doubt. I retreated to a spot under an awning while the others chatted, slathering their skin with suncream, exposing themselves to the hideous sun.

The boat rolled to and fro as it cut through the water. My stomach lurched horribly. I felt an awful sense of unease, of uncertainty about the movement below me.

We moored off Norman Island. I stayed on board as the others went snorkelling. The only other people remaining apart from the crew were an antique couple from Indiana. The woman droned on incessantly about her ailments and operations in a slow, lazy

Southern drawl. I was sorely tempted to throw the old bitch overboard. Luckily there was plenty to drink.

Eddie emerged later full of wonder at the secrets of the deep.

'It was fantastic, Tony. All these lairy coloured fish. And these spiney things . . .'

He went on, fervently describing a catalogue of grotesque marine biology. I'd begun to feel sick and it gave me no comfort to contemplate all of this gaudy life beneath the surface. But it was on the way back that I became really nauseous. I went below for a while but this only made things worse. It was hot and stuffy down there. The diesel engine was cacophonous, its fumes sickening. And the listing of the boat was more pronounced below the waterline.

I staggered back up top and spewed over the side vigorously. It was humiliating.

'Go on, my son,' Eddie urged. 'Get it all out.'

And the other tourists felt the need to join in with their own jocular encouragements.

When we got back to the hotel there was a message at the front desk. It was simply an address and a time to meet on the morning of the following day.

'Right,' said Eddie. 'This is it.'

The taxi took us to a condominium on one of the steep hillsides overlooking Road Town. The door to the apartment was opened by a dark-haired handsome man in his forties.

'I'm Hector Orosco,' he announced in a Hispanic accent.

'Where's Harry?' Eddie demanded.

'I'm here on Mr Starks' behalf,' Orosco replied.

'You mean he sent you down here to do his dirty work for him?'

'In a manner of speaking, yes.'

'Well, that's fucking typical.'

Hector Orosco grinned and shrugged.

'You know how it is,' he said.

'I certainly do, old son. Now, I hope you don't mind me asking, but who the fuck are you?'

'I'm a Cuban. I grew up with the fucking Revolution but I was not, shall we say, a very good little *comunista*. I got into trouble almost as soon as I could walk. I got sent to a work camp when I was a teenager. Re-education, they called it. Well, that didn't work and later it was jail. In 1980, during the Mariel boat lift – you know, when a whole crowd of people got sanctuary in the Peruvian embassy compound and the Yankees sent down boats to get them out of Cuba? – well, Fidel took the opportunity to throw out some people he didn't want, he insisted that they take the undesirables as well, prisons and mental hospitals were emptied, "anti-social elements", *escoria*, the government called us, you know, scum. So I ended up in Florida. Miami was a great town for somebody like me. But soon enough I get into trouble there and the Feds want to deport me back to fucking Cuba.'

'Yeah, right,' Eddie interjected. 'But what has this got to do with Starks?'

'I was coming to that, man. I left the States in a bit of a hurry. Ended up in the Dominican Republic. That's where I met Harry Starks.'

'When was this?'

'In 1983. Diplomatic links with Britain had been broken off after the Falklands War so it was a good place for him to operate. He had been running a marijuana smuggling operation from Morocco into Spain for some time but here was a chance to do something much, much bigger. For a while it was really beautiful, man. We had these five luxury yachts with uniformed crews and old folks we hired to look like rich retired people on a cruise. We even had this old guy who acted like he was really sick with a nurse who was actually a hooker from Key West. This way we could bring tons of grass from Colombia into Florida. And the sweetest part about it was here. Tortola. The BVI had really just opened up for offshore business. We linked up with this British tax lawyer, Joe Clement, and we could launder all our money through here. You see, nobody knew, nobody suspected. It was a very tight operation. But then the fucking Cuban mafia in Miami got to hear about it and they wanted a piece. Those bastard *gusamos* thought I still owed them. Then Harry got involved in this bullion thing, you know?'

'Yeah, I do,' said Eddie. 'It was my job.'

'Well, no disrespect, señor, but it brought us bad luck, you know. It drew some unwanted attention our way. Harry was trying to launder it through one of Clement's international business companies and before we knew it all of heaven fell down on us. The

DEA were investigating the Florida Mob and the British cops were after the gold. They did a joint fucking operation. Clement, well, he was just a crooked businessman, no fucking *cojones*, you know? He soon broke down under interrogation. Did a deal in return for immunity. We had to finish the operation. But the thing is they never did find two things. The money from the bullion or the records they wanted incriminating the Miami Cubans. So we've got to work fast, you know? If the bloody Cubanos know that we're down here digging up paperwork that could put them away they will not be happy.'

'So what do we do?' Eddie asked.

'I've got the address of the registered agent for Flint Investments. A guy called George Peterson. We go and see him and get the records, find out where this bloody money is. But we have to move fast. So, *vámanos*. Let's go.'

Main Street, Road Town, is not a main street at all but a dusty winding back road. Lined with wooden shacks cheek by jowl with colonial buildings and concrete office blocks. A big-bellied cruise liner had just disgorged its cargo of American tourists and they wandered about Main Street's gaudy gift shops and restaurants, uniformed in baseball cap, shorts and T-shirts. They had a scorched look about them, their ruddy flesh glowing, blotchy and corpulent. Some looked as if they were suffering from a kind of radiation sickness, which indeed they were. More formally attired islanders went about their business with considerably more determination and dignity. A squawking hen led a row of chicks through a puddle in the gutter.

The address that Hector had was on the top of a two-storey wooden building accessed by stairs on the outside. We went up. Hector knocked on the door. A middle-aged black man opened it a crack and peered out into the daylight.

'What you want?' he demanded tersely.

'We're here to see Mr Peterson.'

'Him not here,' the man declared, and made to close the door.

Hector pushed against it with a greater force and the man staggered back into the office. We entered.

'You don't mind if we come in for a moment, do you?' said Hector.

'What you doing?' The man was indignant. 'This is private office. Me not supposed to let anyone in here.'

'Where's Peterson?' Hector asked.

'I tell you, man. Him gone. Now please, leave de premises at once, sir.'

He walked over to a desk and picked up the phone.

'Leave now, please. Or I call de police.'

'I wouldn't do that,' Hector suggested.

He had produced a pistol from somewhere and was pointing it at the man.

'What de bloodclaat?' the man shrieked, his eyes wide with shock.

'Put the phone down,' Hector insisted. 'OK. Now, where's Peterson?'

'Truly, man. Him gone.'

'And who are you?'

'Harrington Miller. Personal assistant to Mr Peterson.'

'OK, Harrington. We're going to search the office.'

But the office was empty of records. It had been cleaned out.

'Where is everything, Harrington?' Hector asked, putting his gun to Harrington Miller's head.

'Please, man . . .'

'All the files have gone. Peterson's gone. He's in some sort of trouble, isn't he?'

'Please.'

'Just leaving poor old Harrington to mind the store.'

'No, man. No trouble. All incorporated businesses correct under island jurisdiction.'

'Oh, I'm sure you're all above board with the local authorities. But maybe it's other jurisdictions that you're in trouble with.'

'I don't know what you mean, man.'

'Other less official jurisdictions, of course.'

'I just work for Mr Peterson. I don't know nothing.'

'And your boss just clears out and leaves you with an empty office. Not a very considerate employer. Where has he moved the files?'

'I don't know, man.'

'Come on, Harrington. You can do better than that.'

He pressed the pistol against Harrington Miller's temple.

'Him . . . him . . .' Harrington stammered. 'Him have a house up in the hills.'

'Give us the address.'

Miller scribbled something on a piece of paper.

'Your boss is up to something. What is it?'

'I don't know.'

'He's scared. Who is he scared of?'

'Please, man,'

'Come on, Harrington. What do you know?'

'I tol' you. Nothing.'

'That's not good enough.' He pressed the gun into his temple again. 'We haven't got much time. So tell us or I'll kill you.'

'Please.'

'Come on.'

Harrington Miller's breath was coming in sharp pants of fear.

'Please. Man. Nothing.'

'Oh, for God's sake. Tell us something. Anything.'

'Anything?'

'Yeah, anything.'

'I don't understand.'

'Tell us . . .' Hector mused. 'Tell us a story.'

'What?'

'You know, a story that you know.'

Hector was smiling.

'Me don't know no story.'

'Yes you do. Everyone knows a story.'

'Hector,' Eddie complained. 'What the fuck are you on about now?'

But Orosco lifted his free hand in a little wave.

'Come on,' he went on. 'Make it a good one and I won't shoot you.'

'Oh, Jesus Christ, man.'

'Harrington.'

'A story?' Harrington Miller asked.

'Yeah.'

'Right.' Miller took a few breaths and tried to concentrate. 'OK, mek me see . . .'

He let out a long sigh. He closed his eyes and his face relaxed, nodding slightly as if remembering something. A little smile played upon his lips. He seemed to go into some sort of trance. He opened his eyes and began:

'Back time in Spanish Town, Jamaica, I knew of dese tree brothers. Bad man, you see? Dem were bad breed roughnecks dat run tings an' nah business fi use fist or knife or gun 'gainst any man. Dem have a sistrin call Bella, an' in all de town she was de prettiest ting you ever see, but you fi see dem bredrin guard she most jealously 'gainst de attentions of any man. An' though so many desire she, Bella was all 'pon her own but for her brothers, wit' no husband, no man.

'But dere come one bwoy call Lawrence, a handsome yout', him have charm an' fine manners. Him a work for dem bredrin as small-time ganja dealer. When Bella see fi him looks and him demeanour it please she so much she heart jump an' she yearn after loving he. Lawrence too did fall for de beauty of she. An' since dem did sweet each other equal, dem were spiteful of de danger dem know an' soon come time when dem do what dem desire de most.

'Long time nobody catch on fi dem secret. Opportunities were many fi dem to spend time in each other's arms but soon come too de recklessness of pleasure an' de brothers did find out dere secret. Hateful of de shame dem felt der sistrin had suffer dey, so dem see it, at de hand of dis Lawrence, it vex dem an' mek dem act most drastically.

'Pretending everything normal, dem joke an' play friendly wit' Lawrence an' drive he out to dere ganja plantation. But dere dem shoot him dead an' bury he in de bush, down an' dirty. Den dem chat 'bout how Lawrence gone America on special business. Bella kep' asking 'bout he an' soon de oldest bredrin get vex an' tell she: "Country woman, why ya keep aksin' 'bout dis yout'? What business ya have wit' he? Aks again an' ya get answer ya deserve. Seen?"

'She come all full of grief an' though she aks no more of de brethren, many time at night she call out to he wit' tears an' lamentation. One night she a bawl so hard that she cry she self to sleep an' in a dream Lawrence come inna form of a duppy.'

'A duppy?' Eddie asked.

'Yeah, man,' said Harrington Miller. 'Duppy. Ya know, a jumbie spirit. A ghost.'

'Right.'

'So Lawrence as a duppy come an' tell she what 'appen. Inna de dream him a chat 'bout de spot where him body was bury and de next day come an' in belief of her vision, she a get she an' go down dere deh. She sweep 'way de dead leaves dem dat cover him in burial an' wit' she own hands dig 'way at de shallow grave. De corpse not decay too much an' when she scrape 'way de earth from de head dere was still de handsome face of the yout' dat she had loved so much. If she de strengt' she would a tek him body 'way fi bury it proper but as she caan't do dat she do take a cutlass an' chop off him beautiful head, wrap it in one claat an' gwan with it.

'She tek it home an' after bathing it wit' de tears of she an' kissing it gently, she a bury it in a big earthenware pot. She den tek some sensimilla seeds an' a plant dem dere, watering dem wit' yet more tears. De plant catch quickly an' because a de richness of de soil from a de decomposing head, de weed dat come from dat vase was de sweetest an' de most mellow smoke dat one could have. She would pluck 'way de leaves nurtured by tears an' dry dem inna de sunlight. At night-time de most fragrant smoke would waft tru de house and though de bredrin were in most strong disapproval of what she a do as she smoke dis most fine ganja weed, dere seem little dat dey could do in dissuading she. Bella draw' way from de worl', come 'way from de eyes of men an' de life in de town. An' she nah business 'cept fi tend she ganja pot. De beauty of she begin fade an' eyes come dark rimmed an' bloodshot. But Bella's one joy was de vase an' de deep green drug dat it bore. She feel dat when she smoke it, though her loved one gone, she a breathe his living thoughts an' drink from de very chalice of him mind. De ganja was sweet, so very sweet, an' it would a inspire de dullest an' most day-to-day of hearts. But Bella was in a state of ecstasy for she a grieve an' it sent she quite mad. De brethren soon get vex by her strange dotage an' as she fall ill dem take de sensimilla pot from de room while she a sleep. Discovering it gone, she a call out for it. Full of fever an' a ravin' in she sick bed she aks for nothing but she pot. De brothers were perplex by she, an' curious too. So dey pour de earth from out a de pot an' uncover de head. It was not so rot 'way an' dem could recognise it. In horror dem see dat it was Lawrence an' dat give dem mortal fear. So much shock an' dread dat all dey boldness at once vanish wit' terror dat dem murder might be discover. Dem bury de head an' swiftly leave town for fear.

'Bella remain behin' still crying out for de vase beloved of she to be return. She nah look so good an' a she wander de streets an' soon de whole town know of de strange yearning of she an' someone wrote a sad song dat's still sung, ya know.'

Miller started to sing a lilting, mournful tune:

'Who dat wicked man,
Him what,
Tief me sensimilla pot.'

Miller had been quite animated as he told his tale but now, as he came to the end, his head became once more conscious of the deadly device pressed against it and it warily stilled itself once more.

'Is that it?' asked Hector.

Harrington Miller nodded very gently.

'Yeah, man.'

'Well,' intoned Hector. 'What do we think, eh, amigos?'

'Yeah,' Eddie enthused. 'Nice one. Reminds me of something, though.'

Hector turned to me, still holding the gun against Miller's head.

'So,' he asked me. 'You're the writer. What do you think?'

I wanted to say that it was a marvellous retelling of the 'Isabella and the Basil Pot' story from Boccaccio's *Decameron*, better even than John Keats' long poem on the theme. But I figured that literary criticism at this moment in time wasn't exactly appropriate. So I just said:

'I think you should put the gun down, Hector.'

'What the fuck was all that about?' Eddie demanded when we were back on the street. 'Getting him to tell a story like that?'

'An interrogation method I learnt from the Revolutionary Police. They would keep us talking, saying anything, just so they could tell whether we were lying or not.'

There was a mischievous smile on Hector's lips.

'You're having us on,' Eddie insisted. 'You were just doing that out of badness.'

Orosco shrugged.

'Anyway,' he said. 'We have the address. We go there tonight, OK?'

Me and Eddie went back to our hotel with time to kill. We went out for an early evening drink. A bit of Dutch courage, Eddie had suggested, and I wasn't in the mood to disagree. We found a waterfront bar and settled down with a couple of rum and Cokes. Our pursuer turned up again. This time he made no attempt at subterfuge but instead started to walk towards our table, a little smile playing across his face.

'Good evening, gentlemen,' he announced. 'Frank Taylor. Mind if I join you?'

'Go ahead,' Eddie muttered with a bemused stare.

And it was then that I remembered who he was. Frank Taylor. A policeman, for God's sake. He had been connected to the Billy Porter case. A friend of his, a former partner, I believe, had been one of the officers killed in the Shepherd's Bush shootings. I had tried to interview him when I was writing the book but he hadn't wanted to talk. Eddie seemed to know who he was as well.

'Flying Squad, right?' he said, pointing a finger.

'Flying Squad, C1, C11, I was all over. But I'm not in the job any more, Eddie. I'm retired.'

'But you've been following me since I came out.'

'I've had you under surveillance, yes. You see I'm working for the insurers that covered the Hounslow job. My employers are interested in securing a return of assets, if you know what I mean. Nothing to do with police business. So we can be civil about this. In the true meaning of the word, if you get me.'

'I don't know what the fuck you're talking about, Frank.'

'Come on, Eddie. Don't take the piss. What are you doing in Road Town, for fuck's sake?'

'We're on holiday. Aren't we, Tony?'

'Yeah, and I'm the Queen of Romania. Look, I was with the Criminal Intelligence operation that tried to trace the way the Hounslow job was being laundered. Your bit of it took us to the Isle of Man and then here to Tortola. We did this joint thing with the DEA, Operation Panther it was called. Bit of a farce, to tell you the truth. The Yanks were lording it over, us lot were pretending to be the best detectives in the world, you know, this Scotland Yard reputation thing, but you know what the Met lads are like when they go abroad – messing about and getting pissed on expenses. And most ridiculous of all was this copper from the Isle of Man, where an investigation into this Clement guy had started, well out of his depth and desperate to make sure that nobody thought that he was a dumb swede. We got Clement to go QE and we managed to nick a few bodies. Good for

PR but everyone knew we'd missed out on getting some of the really big faces.'

'Like Harry Starks?'

'Yeah, but to be honest he was small fry compared to some of the Florida lot. They were seriously heavy. You know their favoured way of disposing of anyone who crossed them? Take them out to sea, zip them up in a sleeping bag and chuck them over the side.'

'Nasty.'

'Yeah. Look, I don't know what exactly you're up to here, Eddie. I don't deal with the financial side of the investigation. Never had any Fraud Squad experience. There's other people looking into that. My job is to keep tabs on you, maybe persuade you to cooperate. And to warn you.'

'Warn me?'

'Yes, Eddie. Have you been listening? All that time you were away, well, things changed. You and me, we're old school, right? Yeah, we're fucking dinosaurs. The Hounslow thing, well, it was a nice touch, Eddie, a fucking coup, but it was the end of an era. It's all drugs now. Drugs and white-collar stuff, all with very nasty people attached. And it's a lot heavier on our side these days too. The Yanks have got this war on drugs crusade, there's the DEA and the FBI, and you know the US Coastguard is bigger than the British Navy now. And even the Brits are getting involved, Customs and Excise, even MI6 now that they don't have to worry about the commies. And on your side, well, you don't really belong to that any more, trust me. There's some really horrible people out there and you don't want to get mixed up with them, believe me.'

'I'm touched by your concern, Frank.'

'I'm fucking serious, Eddie. I'm doing you a favour here, for fuck's sake. For old times' sake. I happen to think you've suffered enough. I'll let you into a little secret. When I was at C11 and we were just set to make a deal with Solly Blumberg, you know, just before he got topped, well, it wasn't for recovery of assets, I'll tell you that. It was for a substantial amount of the gold itself. Yeah. That would have looked so good, you know. The gold from the actual blag turning up. Rumour has it that it wasn't sold on. That it's hidden somewhere. One source claimed that it was buried in a warehouse in the East End but we never managed to find it. So maybe your share isn't out here, Eddie. And even if it is my employer's financial investigators aren't going to let you walk away with it. If they can trace any of their unrecovered assets to you they'll bring a civil action to secure an attachment of earnings for every penny that comes near you, bent or otherwise.'

'So that's what being civil means, does it?' demanded Eddie.

Frank Taylor gave a pained look and shook his head.

'As I said, I'm here to warn you. Go home, Eddie. Or have a bit of a holiday and try and keep out of trouble. And if you do want to cooperate . . .'

Taylor took out his wallet and slipped a business card out of it. He wrote something on the back of it.

'That's the number of my hotel. We can always do a deal, you know.'

'A deal?' Eddie looked incredulous.

'Yeah.'

'Like the old days?'

Taylor laughed.

'Well, not exactly, I'm afraid.'

'Then what do you mean?'

'As I said, my employers are simply concerned with the recovery of assets.'

'You mean I'd get a reward for returning some of the stuff I stole in the first place?'

'Well, we'd have to be fucking discreet about any arrangement we might come to. But let's say there would be room for negotiation. The main thing, of course, is that they'd be off your back. Otherwise, I promise you, they'll be checking up on your affairs for the rest of your life.'

Frank Taylor held out the card. Eddie didn't take it.

'I told you,' he said. 'We're here on holiday.'

Taylor put the card on the table and stood up.

'Suit yourself,' he said. 'But think about it.'

George Peterson's house was high up in the hills overlooking Road Town. I could see the cruise ship in the bay below picked out in a pointillism of lights. Across the vertiginous slopes the dark forest was decorated with condos lit up like jack-o'-lanterns. The night clicked and chirruped with little mechanisms of life. Hector went to the door and knocked. There was no reply.

Eddie had a good look around the house, checking out the security situation.

'So, we break in, no?' asked Hector.

Eddie winked at him.

'Leave this to me, old son,' he said. 'I think I can do this place. There's an upstairs window I should be able to get into.'

'What if there's an alarm?'

'I think I can sort that too. You stay here. I'll let you in.'

And with that Eddie launched himself into action with alacrity, climbing up the side of the house, finding footings somehow. He moved swiftly upwards undaunted by age or gravity. He was inside the house within minutes.

'Incredible,' muttered Hector.

He let us in through the front door.

'Harry Starks said you were a good thief,' Hector told him.

'Yeah, well, it's been a long time. But I've always been a climber at heart. And you never really lose the knack, you know?'

The front room of the house was littered with boxes and a couple of suitcases.

'Looks like this Peterson has been getting ready to move out,' Hector said.

'Yeah,' Eddie agreed. 'Let's have a look through this stuff.'

They quickly found the business records and we started to work our way through the paperwork. Hector started putting some of the files in a pile to one side.

'Jesus,' he said. 'There's over a hundred incorporated international business companies here.'

'And what's all that lot?' asked Eddie, pointing at the pile.

'That, my friend, is evidence. This could provide an audit trail for money laundered from drugs by the Florida Mob.'

'So what are you going to do with it?'

Hector grinned.

'Sell it to them.'

Finally Eddie found the Flint Investments files. He started leafing through them.

'Tony,' he said. 'Come and have a look at this. I don't really understand it.'

I went over.

'It looks like it's just a property,' he went on.

'Well, maybe it is,' I said. 'Plenty of people use offshore businesses to buy property.'

'You mean we come all this fucking way . . .'

'Shh!' hissed Hector.

'What?' Eddie whispered.

'There's a car outside.'

'Shit!' said Eddie softly. 'I hope it's not your friends from Miami.'

'Don't even joke about it, man,' Hector murmured, and took out his gun.

Footsteps. The sound of a group of people coming to the door. Banging.

'Police! Open up!'

'Come on,' Eddie urged. 'Out the back.'

But Hector had started to screw up some sheets of paper and stuff them into the pile of files he had made.

'What the fuck are you doing?' Eddie demanded.

'I've got to burn this, man. If they find out I let the police get hold of all of this I am dead.'

The banging on the door and the shouted commands came again. Hector took out a cigarette lighter and started a small bonfire on the floor.

'Shit,' he said, looking around. He went into the kitchen.

The police had started to break the front door down. Hector came back through with a bottle of something. He poured it over the smouldering pile and it erupted in a sheet of flame.

'Come on, Hector,' Eddie insisted, and we moved through to the back of the house. The police broke through the door but were immediately beaten back by the fire that now had started to take. In the panic and confusion that followed we managed to slip out the back and creep through the woods undetected.

It took hours to get back to Road Town. We had to keep off the main tracks and fumble through dense undergrowth. By the time we got to Waterfront Drive we were all scratched and tattered.

'What happens now?' Eddie asked.

'We get out, man,' said Hector.

'You think Miller went to the police?'

'No. I think it was part of a bigger operation. I think we should fucking get out of this place soon.'

'And George Peterson?'

Hector shrugged. He pointed out to sea.

'I've a feeling he might be out there somewhere.'

We walked down towards the marina.

'I chartered a yacht here,' said Hector. 'I think I know which bar the crew will be in. Gentlemen, I'm sorry.'

Eddie shrugged.

'That's the way it goes,' he said.

I was surprised at how calm Eddie was as we said goodbye to Hector. I was furious.

'Well, this has all been a fucking waste of time,' I said to Eddie back at the hotel.

'Not exactly, Tony.'

'What?'

'I worked it out.'

'Worked what out?'

He pulled something from his pocket.

'There is a map after all, Tony.'

'What?'

'This,' he said, holding up a crumpled piece of paper.

'What is it?'

'A property acquired by Flint Investments on behalf of Solly Blumberg. A warehouse in the East End purchased just a couple of months before Beardsley lost track of where the gold was. Think about it.'

'But why buy the property offshore?'

'Because of the business secrecy laws. He could have this place to stash the stuff and no one would know he owned it or would be able to trace it to him. Besides, it makes good business sense to buy property that way.'

'So what was Solly up to?'

'Maybe he was just have trouble resmelting and selling the stuff on. It was getting too difficult. Maybe Solly figured he'd sit on it for a while until all the fuss died down. Maybe he was about to do a deal with the Old Bill – remember what Frank Taylor said. It was for the gold itself and he mentioned a warehouse in East London.'

'So what are you going to do?'

He shrugged.

'I'm not sure yet,' he said with a grin. 'But I know where it is now.'

5

song of the smoke

For a while touring worked for me, travelling light with a sense of purpose in simply being on the move. It lifted me out of the brooding introspection of the rehearsal room into a line of flight. I could escape the dark thoughts I'd been having; motion freed me from the sense of being trapped. I was running away, of course. But I had this fear that my past was chasing me with some awful unknown destiny. Touring, on the other hand, broke life up into a simple series of destinations, crossing the country in a big red Mercedes van, the get-ins and get-outs, creating a show and then disappearing into the night. The bed-and-breakfast life, spare afternoons in provincial towns – I could breathe a little. I could concentrate on my performance and on being part of a group. And relax into the sense of a journey that was taking me. Taking me from myself.

But as I settled into the routine of the tour, and got that slightly deadening sense of familiarity with a part that comes after a few weeks, I began thinking again about the lack of resolution in my life. I mean, I couldn't go on running from it, or playing through it in performance, but what could I do? The play itself didn't help with this feeling of uncertainty. There is no happy end in *The Good Woman of Szechwan*. The gods ascend to heaven leaving Shen Te to deal with her difficulties on her own. An epilogue exhorts the audience themselves to change society, to consider: *what sort of measure you would recommend/ to help good people to a happy end*. This was the political message of the piece, after all. But it didn't leave much for me. I couldn't change the world. I couldn't even change myself. But there would have to be some sort of reckoning to my life, some sense made of what had happened to me. I felt a horrible, sickening feeling whenever I thought of how Mum had taken that money from the man who had murdered Dad. I felt tainted by this ghastly attempt at atonement, poisoned by it. And as much as I tried not to think about Harry Starks he was always there, lurking in the shadows of my life. But I did try to forget him. I mean, there wasn't anything I could do about it now, was there?

I found myself in a sort of static orbit on tour. Gravity would get me in the end, I feared. At least my relationship with Jez didn't suffer from my being away. In fact, having periods of time apart made it special again. We had to struggle to find time for each other. Weekends together when he'd come up to visit when I was in Manchester or Newcastle or wherever. Time that was precious, unexplained. Sundays when we'd go to the pictures or for a walk together, not talking much about anything, just being with each other. For most of the time we'd be in bed together. The lack of time gave sex an urgency and passion.

Circumstances became romantic. Saying goodbye on railway platforms, brief notes and messages passed between us when I was on the road with simple unsophisticated sentiments, *love you, miss you*, the wonderful little banalities of affection. Jez had become quieter and more moody since the attack. But it was good to see him away from London. He could let go as well, let his guard down. He could drop his faux tough persona and just relax for a while.

When the tour came back to London winter was coming, the city was cold and grey. I felt the dread of return, of coming back down to earth; it felt like falling. We brought the show to the Bloomsbury Theatre for its final week. We got a few good reviews and my agent was pleased because a couple of important people had seen it. I might get some good work from this, he told me. But I was losing any enthusiasm I might have had for that. When the gods ascended for the very last time and I was left on the stage on my own I felt a genuine sense of despair. What the hell was I going to do now? No happy end for me, just a growing sense of doom.

I was able to spend some proper time with Jez but I found myself more distanced from him than when I'd been away. I still wanted to hold on to him, I could feel really secure with him sometimes. But maybe that was just the illusion that having a good-looking boyfriend could prove that I was a normal, desirable person. I couldn't feel good about myself. And I couldn't be totally honest with him. He was busy, he had finished the first draft of his screenplay and was starting on the rewrites. And he had already rewritten some bits of his own story. He became deliberately casual and offhand about how he had got his scar. *I got it in a ruck*, I overheard him telling someone. He talked and behaved in such an affected way now. But then, I suppose, so did I.

Who was I kidding, after all? I'd always carried that nagging fear around with me, that I'd be found out, sooner or later. Now I thought I might be heading for a breakdown, it didn't happen though I almost longed for it. Like Constance, who yearns: *I am not mad; would to God I were, for then 'tis like I should forget myself.* No, I was just crippled with grief and loss and an overwhelming sense of humiliation. I kept having this thought: *I want to get my own back*, without knowing what it could mean. I would have to do something, that was for sure.

And then one day it all just came to me, what I would have to do. I was going to a meeting at the National Theatre. There was a new play going on at the Cottesloe and the director wanted to see me. He'd seen me at the Bloomsbury and apparently had been impressed. This could be the big break, everyone kept telling me. It was a cold and windy day. I'd got the Tube to Waterloo and I was walking up to that big grey concrete building on the South Bank but as I got to the National I suddenly thought: *fuck this, I don't want to do this any more*. So I carried on walking, down to the river and along the Embankment.

My mind was racing but I began to think really clearly about my life. I would give up acting, I decided. I couldn't go on like this, just living through performance, sublimating all my feelings into the work. I'd never had a choice about the matter in the first place, Mum had put me on the stage. But it was him that had really made sure I had become an actress. Starks. It was him that had made me do it really, his blood money that had put me through stage school. He had been controlling me for all this time. He would turn me into a neurotic old woman, if I let him. I would have to stop him for good.

Of course, I still had to think about things in dramatic terms. That was how I had been taught, I couldn't escape that. My life was a drama after all, but what kind? I had to make my own terms now, determine it myself instead of being a passive player in it. I was classically trained, that was the only choice I'd made for myself, maybe because, in some instinctive way, that was the only level on which I could understand what had happened to me. That was all I really knew or trusted. I wasn't a populist like Jez.

This wasn't soap opera or pulp fiction, this was tragedy.

It was fucking Greek.

And then I knew, I suddenly knew, what it had meant when I had thought: *I want my own back*.

This was classical.

This was revenge.

No happy end, just a world where good people have to become bad in order to survive. Starks had made me what I was. And I would become bad. I would get my own back on him.

I had got to Lambeth Bridge, wind-burnt and slightly breathless. The muddy Thames swirled below. Seagulls wheeled above, keening, flying inland from a storm out at sea.

Of course, I had no idea how I was to go about taking my revenge. The decision itself was enough for now, it made sense of things. And little ideas started to form themselves in my head. Ruby had said that Eddie Doyle had seen Starks at Ronnie Kray's funeral. So he had been in the country quite recently, and maybe he could be lured back again by something. It sounded a bit like a B-movie plot but it was a start.

In the meantime I had to deal with the fallout from the other decision I had made. My agent was furious when he heard that I hadn't made the meeting at the National. But when I told him that I was giving up acting altogether it cut him dead. He suddenly went all quiet and concerned, as if someone had died or something.

And Mum found out somehow.

'Sweetie, you can't give up, not now that everything's going so well,' she told me on the phone.

She went on and on about not making such a rash decision. I couldn't help feeling just a little bit guilty. It was an old habit I'd soon get rid of, I hoped, but all her ambitions for me that she'd clung to over the years were going up in smoke.

'You can't just leave the business, baby.'

'It's what I want, Mum.'

'But it's your life. At least think about trying something connected to it, management or casting or something.'

I knew that she desperately wanted to keep some contact with her precious show business through me, so I went along with it to keep her quiet.

'OK, Mum,' I agreed. 'I'll think about it.'

I hadn't told Jez yet. He had finally finished his script and he wanted me to have a look at it. *Scrapyard Bulldog*, it was called. A 'caper movie', Jez explained. It had a deranged sense of plot and character, full of misspellings and outbursts of gratuitous violence. A gang of jewel thieves working for a gangster called Big Lenny lose their haul after a heist that goes wrong because they've been double-crossed. Or something like that. It was one movie cliché after another, full of exaggerated slang, borrowed wisecracks and cartoon-like action. And apart from a female card dealer called Ladyfingers (a nice little touch, I thought at first; turns out it was a direct steal from *The Cincinnati Kid*) no women in it at all.

'I thought you said there was a part in this for me,' I said to him.

Jez looked sheepish.

'Yeah. Well, there was. But she sort of disappeared with the rewrites.'

'Well, thank you very much.'

He sighed.

'Look, I'm really sorry,' he said.

I pretended to sulk. I was toying with him, as I often did, but also testing myself, seeing how manipulative I could be.

'I could go back to an earlier draft and try and rework it in again,' he suggested hesitantly.

'Could you, darling?'

'Well . . .'

He looked awkward and vulnerable. I knew that this was the version of the script he wanted. And it made sense. An absence of women was merely part of the absence of any sense of consequence to the actions in the screenplay. It was a complete parody of what had afflicted my life. Violence rendered as slapstick, tragedy made comic. One big joke, ugly and mocking. But there was something quite brilliant about it as well. It struck me that this was what so many people really thought about men like my dad. Jez had got something. The laughter of cruelty. But I'd have the last laugh, I thought.

'What's so funny?' asked Jez, and I realised I was smiling.

'Don't worry,' I told him.

'What?'

'I don't want a part in your film.'

'Oh.'

'In fact,' I went on, 'I don't want to act any more.'

'What?'

'I'm giving it up, Jez.'

'Why?'

Everyone was going to be asking me this question and I was in no mood to give a truthful answer. I needed an excuse. I remembered how I'd reassured Mum.

'It's too insecure,' I told Jez. 'I still want to be in the business but I thought I'd try to get work on the production side of things, or maybe casting.'

'But you're so good,' he insisted.

That was sweet of him.

'No, really, darling. It's such a bloody struggle. This will be for the best in the long term, believe me.'

'Well, if that's what you want.'

This seemed to satisfy him. He probably liked the idea of his girlfriend being in a more stable profession. And I could tell that his curiosity was already starting to wane. I knew that he wanted to know what I thought of the script. He coughed nervously.

'So, Julie, I know it's probably not your kind of thing but, well, what do you think of it?'

I smiled again and he looked at me edgily. An idea came; this was something I could use, something that could fit into my plot somehow. Hamlet came to mind, the play within the play, the dumb-show that he uses to expose Claudius's guilt. A pretentious and theatrical idea, maybe, but pretentiousness and theatricality were all that I really knew. *Scrapyard Bulldog* was a dumb-show all right, but Jez and Piers had been delving into the very places that I needed to investigate now. They had been making contacts with real villains. If I was involved with this project I could start networking in that way without raising suspicions. I could work with this script, I thought, it would give me a cover story.

'I think you've got something here, Jez. It needs a bit of work but you've got something.'

And what I meant was *I* had got something. I would be using him, of course. But that was how I'd have to operate from now on. Jez looked at me wide eyed.

'You really think so?' he asked incredulously.

'Yeah, it's got a real sense of, um . . .' I struggled to find a word. 'Energy.'

'Thanks.'

'In fact, I'd really like to work on it.'

'What?'

'On the production side, I mean. This could be the beginning of my new career.'

He was frowning.

'Wait a minute, Julie.'

'We could work as a team,' I went on.

'Well, Piers is going to be the producer.'

He looked anxious, suspicious even. I had to reassure him somehow. I had to make him part of my story. I had been going too fast.

'I could do the casting,' I suggested.

'We're not exactly at that stage yet.'

I couldn't be be too pushy. Jez was jealously protective of this little-boy's world that he had created with Piers and he was wary of letting a girl come and spoil the fun. I would have to prove myself useful. In the meantime I had to calm down. I was all wired up and I was making Jez uneasy. Be cool, I thought, be normal. Reassure him.

'Well.' I sighed. 'We should go out. Celebrate.'

'What?'

'This of course,' I said, holding up his script.

I needed to track down Eddie Doyle so I tried to get in touch with Ruby Ryder. But she was out of town rehearsing *Cinderella* at the Theatre Royal Brighton. Christ, I thought, it's panto season already. I tried phoning and I left a couple of messages with the theatre management but in the end I thought that the easiest thing would be to get the train and go down and see her.

I walked through the back of the stalls as Ruby and some TV soap opera star were walking through the dance steps of a number together. Pantomime. I remember Mum putting me on the stage of the Yvonne Arnaud Theatre in Guildford when I was six or maybe seven. *Babes in the Wood*.

As they broke for lunch Ruby spotted me and came down.

'I got your message, darling,' she said. 'Are you all right?'

'I'm fine. I just want a quick word.'

'Well, let's go down to the front. Get some fish and chips, eh?'

We went to a seafood restaurant on the Esplanade. The seafront was empty and windswept. We chatted. Ruby asked about the tour, I asked her about the job.

'Fairy fucking godmother,' she said, wearily. 'I tell you, Julie, things aren't what they used to be in the theatre, you know. No respect for your elders these days. All my experience and these youngsters think I'm just an old has-been.'

I looked across the bleak promenade. The West Pier in the distance; derelict, skeletal.

'Anyway,' Ruby went on, 'you didn't come all the way down here to talk about the business. I know you better than that, Julie. What is it, dear?'

'I want to talk to Eddie Doyle.'

She sighed.

'This is about your dad, isn't it?'

'Well, you said Eddie had seen Harry Starks.'

She shrugged.

'I don't know, Julie. He's only just got out after twelve years. Maybe it's got to him. You know?'

She tapped her temple with a forefinger.

'Well, I'd like to see him.'

'So would I, dear.'

'What?'

'I told you he's writing this book, didn't I? God knows what's going to come out. I nearly got implicated in that bullion job, you know? He used my accountant to bank a load of cash just before he got arrested and they thought I had something to do with it. Nearly got my collar felt. I've been divorced from him for nearly twenty years and he still haunts me. And my career, you know. So, yeah, I want a word with him too, dear.'

'So you don't know where he is?'

'He's just disappeared. Out of the country, apparently.'

'Do you know where?'

'Somewhere in the bloody Caribbean, that's all I know. Look, I've got his home address and a telephone number but I've no idea when he'll be back. Sorry, dear.'

'No. Thanks, Ruby. For taking the time.'

She reached over the table and patted my hand.

'You're like family, dear. It's been hard what you've been through but try not to blame your mum.'

'She spoke to you about me?'

'Yeah, of course. Who else is she going to talk to? Look, it wasn't easy for women in that world back then. I should bloody know, dear. The things that happened, well, they were between men. That's how they lived.'

'And died.'

Ruby gave a little shrug and sighed.

'Yeah. Look, she feels bad about what she did, you know, taking that money, but try not to be too hard on her. She thought it was for the best.'

'I suppose,' I said.

'And she told me that you're getting out of the business. Is that true?'

Ruby was frowning at me but there was no judgement there. I knew, given her own experience, that she was the one person I didn't have to explain myself to.

'Yeah,' I said. 'Well, not out of it altogether. I don't want to act any more, Ruby. I was thinking of going into casting or something.'

'I don't blame you, dear. I mean, look at me, fucking pantomime at my age.'

'There's a chance of this telly series, though, isn't there?'

'Please. Don't ask. But if you do see Eddie, tell him he could fuck it up for me if there's another "Ruby and the Robber" exposé.'

'OK.'

'And good luck with whatever you decide on doing. Anything I can do to help.'

'Thanks.'

She patted my hand again.

'I mean it. Well,' she announced, 'I'd better be getting back.'

It was getting dark as my train came into London. As it clattered across the river by Battersea I turned to look at the lights on Chelsea Bridge. They looked so pretty. My eyes prickled with sadness. I blinked and the lamplight diffused through a film of tears. I felt pity for Mum for a moment. And for Ruby. And for myself. But I knew that I could not afford to feel like this. I'd worked it out and could start to feel a cold certainty about my actions. I wouldn't end up like them. I would become Shui Ta, become ruthless, use anything or anyone to get what I wanted. Use Jez, use Mum, use Ruby. And it suddenly struck me how I might use Ruby. I turned away from the pretty lights and looked over at the other side of the carriage. I caught a hollow reflection of my face in the darkened glass.

I'd arranged to meet Jez at a bar on Ladbroke Grove. When I got there he was with Piers. Piers seemed friendlier than usual towards me.

'Jez tells me you like the script,' he said, with a mischievous look on his face.

'Yeah, I do. And I've just had an idea.'

'Really?' asked Piers.

Jez frowned.

'About casting.'

'Look, Julie,' Jez butted in. 'I told you we're nowhere near casting it yet.'

'Well, let her say what it is,' said Piers. 'I'm interested.'

'It's just a little thing.'

'Go on,' Piers urged.

'Just a cameo really. Ruby Ryder for Ladyfingers the card dealer.'

Jez laughed dismissively. Piers had his hand on his mouth, thinking.

'Wait a minute,' he said. 'Yeah, that's fucking brilliant. You know, that would really work.'

'What are you talking about?' Jez demanded.

'Well, it fits in perfectly with the sixties iconic thing we're going for,' Piers enthused.

'Aren't we getting a bit ahead of ourselves?' said Jez. 'We haven't even got backing for this thing yet.'

'But maybe if we approach some people interested in being cast that might attract some interest. It would be great if we could get one of these rock stars who wants to act, you know, like Sting or someone. They'd bring in capital of their own then. Who else have you thought about?' Piers asked me.

'Well, Joe Patterson for the lead.'

'Who?'

'You know, *Borstal Breakout*.'

'Oh, yeah. What's he been doing since then?'

'His dad's a villain, isn't he?' asked Jez.

'And so was Ruby Ryder's husband,' said Piers. 'Yeah, this is great. There're all these references that we can play with.'

'Joe's an old friend, isn't he?' Jez said, with a slight edge to his voice.

'Yeah,' I retorted. 'So's Ruby.'

'You know Ruby Ryder?' asked Piers, wide eyed.

'She's a friend of the family.'

'That's fantastic! We've got to use her. She's such a camp icon. Authentic villainy meets old school show business. Yeah, we can be really postmodern with this film.'

Jez screwed up his face at this.

'You really talk shit sometimes,' he said to Piers. 'I'm going for a piss.'

'Well, he's got the hump,' Piers said as Jez walked off.

'What's the matter?' I asked.

Piers leaned across the table, confiding in me. 'He takes things so seriously. I mean, the script is great, but you know what? Look, for Christ's sake don't tell Jez I said this but I think it works as a comedy. A black comedy but a comedy nevertheless. Jez has got it into his head that he's written some dark *film noir* thing. And I don't want to disillusion him but I want him to do what he does in his pop promos. I want it to be fast, slick, over-cranked, you know?'

I didn't but I nodded along anyway.

'And I like your ideas about casting, Julie, it could really bring out the intertextualities in the script. Get the retro feel just right.'

'I'd like to get involved,' I said. 'But I think Jez is a bit wary.'

'Well, we need all the help we can get at the moment.'

Jez came back from the toilet and sat down silently.

'What about Big Lenny?' Piers asked me. 'We were thinking about Keith Allen.'

'Keith Allen?' I shook my head. 'Oh no, not him. You want someone with real menace. Someone convincingly scary.'

Piers laughed and nudged Jez.

'She's good, you know. She's really good. You know what?' Piers held up a forefinger in front of his face. 'We should get a real villain to play Lenny.'

'Piers does talk a lot of bullshit,' said Jez when we were in bed together later.

'I'm serious about getting involved with this film.'

'Well, *he* seemed to like your ideas.'

'Are you saying that they were bullshit as well?'

'No.'

'Well?'

'I thought they were good choices. I just don't understand.'

'What?'

'What you're getting out of this.'

'I told you. A career move. Maybe casting is where my real talent lies.'

'But what about acting? You're giving it up just like that?'

'Yeah.'

'But it's been your whole life. There's got to be more to it than that.'

I wanted to tell him: my whole life is based upon a lie. But I didn't. I told him:

'I really do want to find something steadier. Maybe I could get work with a casting agency. Learn the job. But I do want to work on your film too.'

'Yeah, well, we've got to find the backers first.'

'Maybe I could help out there too.'

'You're awfully keen. It's not even your cup of tea.'

Jez was definitely suspicious. I had to be very careful with him now. I was acting out of character in getting enthusiastic about the script. And although I'd managed to keep so much from him he might easily guess that something was wrong from my mood. What I'd feared was happening: he was becoming inquisitive.

'And you never said you knew Ruby Ryder,' he went on.

'Didn't I?'

'A friend of the family?'

'Yeah, I told you, my mum used to work in the business.'

'You don't talk much about your family.'

'Well, you keep yours fairly quiet as well. You don't like people knowing that you're a nice middle-class boy when you're putting on that wide-boy act of yours.'

Usually this sort of attack on Jez's fake persona would shut him up. But he was having none of it this time.

'I'm just having a laugh,' he said. 'With you it seems like there's something that you're seriously trying to hide.'

So I changed tack.

'Well, after Dad died it was difficult.'

I put a little sob in my voice.

'I'm sorry,' said Jez. 'I didn't mean to . . .'

'It's OK. It's just hard to talk about, that's all. The accident tore us apart as a family, I guess.'

Jez slipped his arm around me and held on to me. I was becoming good at this cold, calculating act.

'I don't want to pry,' he whispered. 'But if you do want to talk about it I'm here, you know.'

I probably felt soft and warm in Jez's arms. But I was an impenetrable fortress. He wouldn't know the truth from me. I'd never break under questioning.

I'd put some of my research together. Bits of memory, things that had been said and references in true crime books. The timeshare business was, of course, all a front. He had been laundering money from pornography rackets and business frauds in London. It seemed my father got mixed up with a corrupt policeman called George Mooney who had retired to the Costa del Sol. Harry Starks had escaped from Brixton Prison in 1979. The story was that Dad had double-crossed Starks over money and also by tipping off the police as to where he was hiding out. Starks came to Spain and killed both Dad and the bent copper. And then he disappeared. There were all sorts of rumours as to where he might have gone and some sightings, though none actually confirmed. Eddie Doyle was the last person to have claimed to have seen him. But Eddie was still out of the country.

I went home to Mum's for Christmas and Jez went to his parents. I took Ruby's advice about not being too hard on Mum. I made it up with her. I realised it was a waste of time being confrontational about Dad and what had happened and that I couldn't really blame her for taking the money from Starks. It was just the two of us through to Boxing Day, which sounds a bit lonely, but that was what we were used to. All the times Dad was in prison or away and after he died it had been Mum and me most of the time. There was an intense, unexplained bond between us, which I had broken when I'd been direct with her about Dad but which re-established itself as we prepared Christmas dinner together in her kitchen, singing snatches of show tunes, retelling jokes that only me and her would understand, using private nicknames for things and people. I'd forgotten how close we had been and what a struggle it had been to become independent. It was drama school that had done it – received pronunciation, classical training. That had given me distance from her.

And I'd always known for as long as I can remember that I didn't want to end up like Mum. It was just that now I no longer let myself feel guilty about that. Or about her. Oh, I felt sorry for her in a way. She smoked too much, drank too much. She got depression. Ruby was right, I shouldn't be hard on her. I shouldn't waste my hardness on her.

After we had eaten we sat and watched telly for a while. Mum had a snooze on the sofa. For some reason I took all the old photo albums down from the shelf and leafed through them. Not many pictures of Dad and some pages with glue marks and shreds of paper where photographs had been deliberately taken out. One head-and-shoulders of him, sandy hair swept back, heavy jaw relaxed into a half-smile, a broken-nosed vulnerability about his face. I tore that one out myself and put it in my bag.

There were a lot of photographs of me. Posing for the camera from an early age. Julie in tap shoes and a ribbon in her hair. In a fairy costume, in a party dress, in a tutu. All eyes and teeth, wanting to please, to be seductive. Once I'd have been appalled and embarrassed by these pictures. I might have even felt indignant that Mum had forced all of this approval-seeking behaviour on to me. But I didn't really feel anything about them any more. The little girl in the pictures no longer existed. I gathered up the albums and put them back on the shelf.

Maybe there was a sense of loss, that I'd never get my childhood back, that I'd spent so much of my life putting on an act to hide the grief. I worried about feeling so cold and numb about things. But it felt like I could stand back and see my life for what it really was. After years and years of confusion I finally understood.

And I had something to occupy myself, something that might lead somehow to my purpose. If Jez was cautious about me becoming involved in the film, Piers was encouraging. Him and Jez had very different ideas about how *Scrapyard Bulldog* was going to work but Piers didn't want to get into a conflict about it.

'It's best if he doesn't really know what he's doing,' Piers confided in me. 'The humour in the script will only work if he takes it absolutely seriously.'

He had been hawking the script around film agents, trying to get representation. He hadn't had any luck.

'That cunt Nick Marsten at Curtis Brown said it was illiterate,' Piers said. 'They just don't get it.'

Piers had done most of the running in trying to stir up interest in the project, I think because he was aware of how sensitive to criticism Jez was and wanted to protect him from that. So instead he talked to me. He was using me as a way of mediating his relationship with Jez, but I didn't mind as it suited my plans perfectly.

I had suggested that I might proof-read the script and make it more legible. Jez always made a joke about the fact that he was dyslexic, though I suspected that his real feelings about this ran a little deeper. Piers had been adamant, though, that we shouldn't change a thing.

'It's a masterpiece of inarticulacy,' he declared. 'It's all going to work through the visuals, the references, the soundtrack. We've got to get a fucking solid soundtrack. It's the style of the thing that matters. That's where your boyfriend's genius lies, trust me.'

Piers and I became unlikely allies. He must have thought that I really went along with all his ideas. All these words he bandied about: *postmodernism, knowingness, retro chic* and so on. He thought that he knew what irony was. He really had no idea. And I would go along with it because I really did know what that term could mean. Together we would make sure that this film got made. That it was, in my mind, to be a parody – well, that seemed apt somehow. My plot was a tragedy; the play within the play would be a comedy.

Jez, of course, was completely unaware of this. He was strutting around with his wide-boy act which, in its own way, both me and

Piers agreed, might be useful in stirring up interest in the project. It was amazing how many people seemed to be taken in. The scar helped. People couldn't help but notice it and it seemed to lend a real edge to Jez's tough-guy demeanour, some proof. Like it was written all over his face.

His connections helped too. They were trying to raise private finance and Jez's dad had plenty of contacts in advertising and the film world. They found someone who had directed commercials who was interested and could bring a huge amount of funding to the project, but he wanted to direct the thing himself. Piers had some contacts too; his father had been a successful record producer in the sixties and seventies. Both of them belonged by birth to the media aristocracy. It was a world I knew nothing about but I wanted to learn about it. I also started to look at other ways that one could get funding and finance for feature films.

Though I'd never be able to network the way Piers and Jez could. They knew some seriously rich people and could feel relaxed with them. Piers knew this girl Georgina, the daughter of a fantastically wealthy banker, Albert de Brett. The plan was that he was going to try and persuade her dad to put some money up. A double date was arranged one Friday night at the Met Bar on Park Lane.

Georgina de Brett was blonde and petite. She had a husky posh voice and an insouciant manner. There was an easeful coquettishness in the way she behaved towards the men. The idea was that Piers would lead the charm offensive but it soon became clear that it was Jez she was more interested in.

They had people in common to talk about. Common for them, that is. The famous, the wealthy, the successful. Georgina never dropped names but rather floated them across the room with a lightness of familiarity. I didn't find much to say myself. I was scared of putting my foot in it somehow. All my words seemed leaden. I watched while she flirted with Jez and felt dull. I felt heavy and big boned, awkward.

The evening seemed to go well for them. Georgina promised that she would 'talk to Daddy'. Piers drove her home but she made a big fuss about saying goodnight to Jez. I did my best to hide my indignation. Nothing really matters to these people, I reasoned, and tried to adopt some of that indifference myself.

I worried about appearing useless in this rarefied world but I could prove myself in my knowledge of actors and casting. I'd suggested Joe Patterson for the lead part of Mickey and I'd arranged a meeting, ostensibly to talk about the film. I had my own reasons for getting in touch with Joe. His father Tommy had been a major South London face. He had spent time in Spain before extradition had been restored. Maybe he'd know something about my dad and Starks.

Piers couldn't make the meeting in the end, he had a deadline to meet for *Sorted* magazine, so it was just me and Jez. I'd briefed Joe on the phone beforehand:

'Look, he doesn't know about my past.'

'And you don't want him to?'

'No, so can you please, just . . .'

'Listen, Julie, I know the drill. I'll keep my mouth shut about all of it.'

And he did. He talked a lot about his own underworld connections, though, and Jez lapped it all up. I could see him watching Joe's mannerisms and listening to his vocal intonations for future reference. Jez explained the script to him and Joe nodded impassively.

'Sort of a Tarantino thing, then, is it?'

'Yeah,' said Jez. 'But British, know what I mean? I want an authentic London gangland feel to it.'

Joe gave a flat laugh and sneaked a look across the table at me.

'So, have you done any film work since *Borstal Breakout*?' Jez asked.

'Nah. A bit of telly. Some theatre. But mostly ducking and diving. Know what I mean?'

Jez nodded and affected a knowing laugh.

'Yeah,' he said, standing up. 'Look, I've just got to . . .' He nodded towards the toilets.

'Seems like a nice boy,' said Joe once Jez was out of earshot. 'Bit of a plonker, though. Sorry, Julie, I don't mean . . .'

'It doesn't matter. Look, Joe . . .'

'So when are you going to tell him about "authentic London gangland"?'

'Not yet. I've just got to . . .'

'What are you up to?'

'Nothing, Joe, honest.'

'Are you in some sort of trouble?'

'No. Well.' I looked him in the eye. 'First things first. Have a look at the script. I know it might seem a bit, well, ridiculous, but it could just work. Could be a break, you know?'

Joe frowned, shrugged.

'And?'

'I want to see your dad.'

'You are in trouble, aren't you?'

'No, I just want to ask him some things. That's all.'

'Well, I'm seeing him tonight. There's this book launch we're going to. It's at somewhere called the Tardis Studios on Turnmill Street. I'll put you on the list. Heads up, your boyfriend is coming back. Be there around seven thirty, eight.'

The launch was for a book called *Basher* by Georgie Lewis, bare-knuckle boxing champion and gangland legend. The cover showed a battered physiognomy and a pair of huge sovereign-ringed fists with the strapline: *If I come at you you'll know about it alright!* Lewis himself was on display, having his picture taken in a whole series of line-ups. There were other famous villains present, mingling with journalists and media people. Freddie Foreman, Frankie Fraser, one of the Lambrianou brothers and Tommy Patterson. Nick Reynolds, the son of Bruce the Train Robber, had something to do with Tardis Studios. It struck me that there was a story here, what with me and Joe Patterson as well, about the children of famous criminals. A TV producer was probably already dreaming up a documentary proposal.

Except my story was different. My dad was dead. Joe came over and I was introduced to some of the faces. They knew who I was, they knew the truth about my life. This was the world I had tried to escape from. They were polite and respectful. I've never encountered a stronger sense of etiquette than among the people in this life. But there was a wariness as well. I was the daughter of McCluskey, 'Big Jock', who had died in dubious circumstances. Sins of the father. I remembered that voice on the phone I'd heard as a child: *Your dad was a grass*. But more than anything I think it was the superstition which put a little distance in their protocol. I was bad luck.

I noticed a frisson in the place caused by this roll-call of infamy. The media types were consumed with a hungry fascination for all this well-dressed villainy. An effete desire for brutal mythology. Jez and Piers were not alone, the room was full of gangster groupies, and it struck me then that their film could be a real success, something ugly in the culture that they had tapped into. That, I reasoned, would be their pay-off.

'Joe says you want a word.'

It was Tommy Patterson. Short and on the tubby side in a bespoke suit and designer-framed spectacles, he looked like a banker or a corporate lawyer. He was rumoured to have killed Jimmy Murphy back in the sixties but the body was never found. Legend had it that it ended up in the foundations of the Westway flyover.

'Yeah,' I said. 'Can we find somewhere quiet?'

We walked over to the far corner of the bar. Someone shook his hand and offered a salutation as we made our way through the crowd.

'Quite a circus,' I said.

'Yeah, well, everyone's getting book deals now.'

'You?'

He shrugged and looked a little sheepish.

'There's a real demand for the stuff, apparently.'

We sat down.

'So, what can I do for you, Julie?' Tommy asked.

'My dad,' I began, not quite sure what to say.

Tommy nodded slightly, waiting for more.

'Look,' I went on, 'you were in Spain.'

Shit, I suddenly thought. Maybe Tommy Patterson had something to do with my father's death. His face betrayed nothing, though. His features solid, impassive.

'Julie,' he said, as if reading my thoughts, 'I was on the Costa del Sol after your father was killed. I was there in the eighties up until the bastards deported me and I was dragged back here for a bit more of Her Majesty's pleasure.'

'I just want to know as much as I can about what happened.'

'Well, it was Harry Starks.'

'I know. I just want to, I don't know, put it all together. Part of my life has been blotted out.'

Tommy sighed.

'Maybe that's not such a bad thing. Don't get me wrong, Julie, but some things are best left alone. You know? Really, I mean it's bad what happened to your father. Really bad. But what's the use in going over it again? These days everyone wants to talk, air their problems, tell their story. Daytime telly people arguing with each other about who's to blame, why their lives are in such a mess. In my day we kept our mouths shut and got on with it. It's a better way, trust me.'

This attitude made perfect sense to my way of thinking, but I had to pretend otherwise.

'But you're selling your story, aren't you?' I demanded.

He smiled.

'Yeah. But I ain't exactly going to be telling it like it was. I'll just be giving the public what it wants. It's not even me, anyway, they'll get this writer bloke to do it for me.'

'Harry Starks has been spotted,' I said.

'What?'

'Ruby says Eddie Doyle saw him.'

'What, in the country?'

'Yeah. You know anything about that?'

'Look, Julie, I swear . . .'

'What do you know, Tommy?'

He laughed.

'What is this? I'll be asking for my brief next. Look, I've not had any dealings with Harry Starks since way back. I did see him in Spain a couple of times but I heard he was somewhere in the Caribbean. I don't know anything about him being in the country. Eddie and him, well, rumour had it that Harry was involved in laundering the Hounslow thing, you know, the bullion job.'

Ruby had mentioned the bullion job. Maybe this was what connected Eddie Doyle to Harry Starks. Maybe I could use that, use Eddie. But he was still abroad by all accounts. Tommy had started to eye me up a bit. I felt that he was beginning to get suspicious.

'Look, Julie,' he went on, 'all I know about what happened to Jock is what everybody else knows. I can't tell you anything else. Sorry, love.'

'It's just that I want . . .' I searched for a word. What would sound convincing? Oh, yeah. 'Closure,' I told him.

That was a good one, I thought, play the victim, cover your tracks. Tommy nodded solemnly at this. I got up to go. He stood and clasped both my hands in his.

'Well,' he said, kissing me on both cheeks, 'anything I can do to help.'

I made my way through the crowd to the exit and saw Piers coming in. *Shit*, I thought. He could find out about me. I hadn't even told Jez that I was going to this thing. He spotted me and looked surprised. I went over to him.

'What are you doing here?' I asked him.

'Well, it's work, sort of. It's a Groombridge Press launch. You know, they own *Sorted* magazine. More to the point, what are you doing here?'

'I'm with Joe Patterson.' I looked around for Joe. 'There he is. Let's go over and I can introduce you.'

'Where's Jez?' he asked as we went over.

'Er, he couldn't make it. Joe!' I called out above the dull roar of conversation.

Joe turned around and nodded in our direction.

'Excuse me,' I said, pushing my way through the group around him. 'Joe, meet Piers. He's the producer for *Scrapyard Bulldog*.'

'How you doing?' said Joe, holding out his hand.

'We'd really like you in our film, Joe,' said Piers as he shook Joe's hand. 'Your work, well, it's fantastic.'

Joe shrugged.

'Don't know about that. Few and far between, I'd call it.'

'Well, *Borstal Breakout*, that was a classic, you know?' Piers went on. 'We really want to explore the iconography of Britishness in what we're doing. And you're really part of that, you know?'

'Don't know what you're talking about, pal,' said Joe with a smile.

Piers rattled with laughter.

'Great,' he said with a smirk. '"Don't know what you're talking about, pal", that's great.'

Joe frowned sidelong at me.

'Isn't this great?' Piers went on, looking around the room, his eyes bright with excitement. 'All these famous villains. Look, I'd better go over and say hello to Victor, you know, the boss. And I want to see if I can get an interview with Mad Frankie Fraser for the magazine. I'll see you later.'

And he was gone.

'Well, they're a right pair,' commented Joe. 'Your boyfriend and that one. What is it about nice middle-class boys that makes them so obsessed with the rough side of things?'

'I don't know, Joe. But there's something there to be cashed in on, you've got to admit it.'

'Maybe. But what are you getting out of this?'

'Look, it's just something I've got involved in. I think it could work.'

'Yeah, yeah,' said Joe dismissively. 'Same old Julie.'

'What do you mean?'

'Always playing her cards close to her chest.'

'Look, Joe . . .'

'It's all right. I know the routine. I've kept your secret before, you know. But this time . . .' He sighed. 'Just let me know what you're up to some time. Won't you?'

'Yeah,' I said. 'OK.'

'You speak to the old man?'

'I did. Thanks, Joe. I'm getting off now. Have a look at that script, won't you?'

'Yeah, yeah. I might just do it, you know. To tell you the truth I really need the work at the moment. You know what it's like.'

Piers reckoned that the budget for *Scrapyard Bulldog* could be kept down to a million pounds. Everything would be on a shoestring and the cast would have to agree to perform for deferred payment. It became my job to convince the actors we wanted that we had a potential hit on our hands. Piers was putting together private finance through his and Jez's contacts as well as going begging for donations of film stock and equipment hire. It was going to be a very tight shooting schedule, but Piers was confident that this would bring the best out of Jez. With little room to manoeuvre he would be forced into creating the fast, sharp and uncluttered style he had developed with his promos and advertising work.

Jez was not so sure. There was not much for him to do at this stage except brood over the script and worry about what Piers was turning it into. He became moody and seemed resentful of my enthusiasm. He no longer felt that he had control over the project, I guess. He exaggerated his yobbish act like a sullen child.

But I couldn't help feeling an excitement about how things did actually seem to be moving along. What could have been a tedious round of phone calls, appointments, meetings and lunches was fired up by my sense of a greater purpose. Even Jez had to admit to how good I became at selling this idea to people. But what, exactly, did all of this mean in terms of getting my revenge? I didn't know yet; I just had a gut feeling that I was on the right track.

We were getting close to securing the investment that we needed but there was a shortfall of around £200,000. It was my idea to apply for funding from the National Lottery. But when the form arrived it proved to be a real nightmare. We had to define the aims of our organisation, give a complete breakdown of our budget, determine a cash-flow forecast for the project, identify who would benefit and how from the project, and so on. But the real killer was on page seven: how will the project meet the needs of disabled people?

When I talked to Piers about this question he just laughed.

'Well, can't we just leave that bit blank? It doesn't really apply to us, does it?' he said.

'I'm not sure that's a good idea.'

'Well, we could say that we were raising awareness of disability. Danny the Debt Collector's victims get their legs broken, after all.'

'Piers, we've got to take this seriously. They're not going to hand over the cash unless we meet their equal opportunities criteria.'

'Oh, Christ. Well, I don't know.'

'Look,' I told him, 'I'll see what I can come up with.'

I phoned Sally, who had worked as a fund-raiser for Red Rag. She knew all about funding applications and the right language to use.

'Talk about raising access issues with the venues that are showing your film,' she told me.

'What else?'

'Well, does the theme of the film have anything to do with disability?'

I groaned, thinking about Piers' comment. *Scrapyard Bulldog* was probably going to be one of the least politically correct films ever made.

'There is an obvious thing you can do,' she went on.

'What?'

'Employ a disabled actor.'

I mentioned the idea to Piers. He laughed again.

'Well, you're in charge of casting,' he said. 'Just don't tell Jez. You know what he'll be like.'

Piers did an impression of Jez doing his wide-boy impression: '"I ain't having no fucking raspberry ripple in my film,"' he declared, jerking his shoulders about manically.

I laughed in spite of myself. Suddenly Piers went quiet.

'How is Jez?' he asked.

'What do you mean?'

'Well, he's not much fun these days. Seems to have the hump most of the time.'

'I think he feels that there's not much for him to do until we start shooting.'

'Yeah, but . . .' Piers said, then stopped. 'Look, I ought to mind my own business.'

'What is it?'

'Well, look, Julie, are things OK between you and Jez?'

'Yeah,' I lied quickly. 'Of course.'

'It's just that, well, I don't want to poke my nose in.'

'Get to the point, Piers.'

'I've liked working with you, Julie. I know in the past we didn't always see eye to eye . . .'

'Piers . . .'

'. . . but I'm responsible for making sure that nothing goes wrong with the project. If you two fall out it could bugger things up.'

'I don't know what you're talking about.'

'It's just something that's bugging me.'

'What?'

He sighed. 'That night of the book launch. Jez didn't know anything about it.'

'So?'

'Well, you were there with Joe but you hadn't told Jez. I talked to him about it and he was none the wiser.'

'And you told him I was there?'

'No, I thought it best not.'

'Because you think I'm having a thing with Joe Patterson?'

Piers shrugged.

I laughed out loud, with relief more than anything. For a moment I'd thought that Piers was on to me.

'Certainly not,' I told him.

'Right,' he said.

'It's the most ridiculous thing I ever heard.'

'OK, OK. I'm sorry.'

'So look,' I said, moving the subject on, 'we need to work out what we put in this bit of the form. Maybe we should say that we plan to employ a disabled actor.'

'Can you deal with this bit? I mean, you know all the politically correct stuff from that lesbian theatre company you were in.'

'It wasn't a lesbian theatre company, you little faggot.'

'Well, you know what I mean. I'm absolutely useless at this sort of thing. And besides, I've got a really big job on for *Sorted*.'

'Oh yeah?'

'Yeah. One of the main features for our "Cool Britannia" edition.'

This 'Cool Britannia' thing was everywhere. People talked about BritPop and BritArt, about 'Swinging London Mark II'. *Sorted*'s cover for May 1996 was a big-breasted girl in a Union Jack bikini.

Piers was convinced that all of this was going to make *Scrapyard Bulldog* a great success.

'We're in tune with the *zeitgeist*,' he announced.

He showed Jez and me the layouts for his features. LONDON CALLING TO THE UNDERWORLD, it was entitled. There were pieces on classic British genre celluloid: *The Italian Job*, *Get Carter*, *The Sweeney*, and so on. Photo shoots of real villains and wannabe gangsters who were signed up on the Groombridge Press payroll. An over-excited prose style, peppered with mockney patois, ran through the text and the captions. The Kray Twins' generation were served up as heritage culture. There was even a fashion spread.

'We've got to get the look right,' Piers insisted to Jez, pointing out some of the photographs of suited and booted male models.

Jez shrugged, unconvinced.

'It looks like just another Mod revival to me,' he said.

'Yeah, well,' Piers went on. 'It's an up-to-date retro chic. We need to get it in the clothes, the set design, the locations, everything.'

'I thought we were on a tight budget,' said Jez.

'Well, we should look into sponsorship, product placement, stuff like that. We can really sell this thing.'

'I don't know,' Jez muttered.

Piers turned to me.

'You see what I mean, don't you, Julie?'

'Yeah,' I agreed. 'Sure.'

We both looked at Jez. He shrugged again and gave a little grunt of resentment.

Later, when we were walking back to his flat, he complained to me:

'Piers just thinks this film's one big advert.'

'He just wants to get it made, Jez. We've got to think of every angle.'

'Maybe he thinks that's all I'm good for.'

'What?'

'Making adverts. He doesn't take me seriously. He doesn't take the script seriously.'

'Yes he does. It's just that he has to think about the more superficial aspects of production at the moment. Once we start filming, well, you'll be in control.'

'Yeah,' said Jez, smiling a little. 'I guess. Look, Julie . . .'

He gazed at me imploringly.

'You take me seriously, don't you?' he demanded.

And I felt a sudden stab of anger. He was constantly wanting reassurance. This spoilt little child that I had given so much to and yet was still demanding. The past few months I'd spent all my time helping him get this stupid film made and I'd done nothing for myself. And I still had no idea of how I was to get what I wanted. My plans had gone nowhere so far.

'Oh, for fuck's sake!' I spat out at him.

Jez looked shocked.

'What's the matter?'

'It's always you we've got to be worrying about, isn't it?'

'I don't understand this, Julie.'

'Do you ever wonder how I'm feeling?'

'That's not fair.'

'Not fair?'

'No, it's bloody not fair,' he complained. 'You never tell me anything. If I ask you about yourself you just cut me off.'

'Well . . .'

'And then you accuse me of not being interested. That's fucking out of order.'

I didn't have anything to say to this. He was right, I guess. We walked for a while in silence.

'Sorry,' I said to him as we were coming up to his flat.

'I'm sorry too. I do go on, I know. The truth is I'm really nervous about the film.'

We were at the front of the house. Jez started up the front steps.

'Jez.'

He turned.

'What?'

'I'm not coming in.'

'What?'

'I think I need some time on my own.'

'Julie . . .'

He came down and tried to hold me. I turned away.

'I'm sorry,' I said.

'Julie, for God's sake, talk to me.'

I started to walk away. He called after me. But that was what I was afraid of: that I might talk to him. Tell him everything.

Next morning I felt bad about the way things had gone. I was so overcritical of Jez. He couldn't help the way he was and he did care about me in his own way. Maybe I could talk to him about myself a bit more. Not the truth, obviously, but I could share some of my feelings with him.

I really didn't have any idea of how I might do this. I didn't want to talk on the phone so I just went over to his place. I was walking down his street when I noticed somebody coming out of his front door. It was a woman. She turned to kiss Jez goodbye on the front steps. I came a little closer. As she skipped down the steps I could see that it was Georgina de Brett.

I stepped back. I didn't want her to see me as she sauntered across the road. And I wandered back to the Tube station in an angry daze.

I turned most of this anger on to myself, of course. I felt such a failure, a fraud. So much of what had attracted me to Jez in the first place was his class. That being with him could make real my own pathetic aspirations. But I was fooling myself. I could never be like this Georgina girl. I could never have her easy sophistication. And I realised with an awful bitterness that I was jealous of what she was as much as anything.

It was no use trying to escape what I was. I needed to confront it head on and destroy what had ruined my life, but I'd made no actual progress. I'd spent all this time working on the film but I still had no real idea of what I was going to do. Then Ruby phoned.

'Hello, darling,' she said. 'I've seen the script.'

'What do you think?'

'It isn't much of a part, dear.'

'Well, it's a cameo, isn't it.'

'Yeah, I suppose. Look, I'll do it.'

'Thanks, Ruby.'

'My agent isn't happy about this deferred payment thing, you know.'

'I'll talk to him.'

'Another thing.'

'What?'

'You still want to talk to Eddie Doyle?'

'Yes.'

'Well, he's back. And if you do go and see him . . .'

'Uh-huh.'

'Can you say to him that if he is selling his story can he spare me any more grief.'

'Won't that be better coming from you?'

'I can't go through it all again, Julie. It's all too much. We'll just end up having a row or something. I just want him to know, that's all. If I arrange a meeting with him, will you do that for me, darling? Tell him that I've spoken to my lawyers.'

We met in the afternoon, in a pub in New Cross. Eddie was tall and thin. He wore a blue suit with an open-necked shirt. His face was lined and hollowed out from prison but he was still handsome in a gaunt sort of a way.

'So you're Jock McCluskey's girl,' he said.

'Yes.'

'Pleased to meet you, darling. Last time I saw you you were about this high.'

He patted an imaginary girl on the head then held out his hand. As he shook mine his grey-blue eyes took me in. His head shook a little, thinking of all the years maybe, all the sentences passed down. We sat.

'Ruby said you wanted to meet me.'

'Ruby's not happy about the book, Eddie.'

Eddie sighed.

'Is this what this is all about?'

'Well, not just that. But Ruby wanted me to tell you.'

'Ruby could have come herself. I don't know why she's getting so high and mighty.'

'She's serious, Eddie. She's seen a lawyer.'

'Oh, for Christ's sake.' He leaned forward. 'Well, look, tell her she doesn't have to worry. It's all done with.'

'Right.'

'So,' he went on tersely. 'Is that it?'

'No, look, Eddie, I'm sorry. We haven't really started out very well, have we? I just wanted to get that out of the way. I promised Ruby I'd tell you.'

Eddie sat back in his chair and looked me up and down again.

'What do you want, darling?'

'I want to talk.'

'About your dad?'

'Yeah. You knew him, didn't you?'

'Yeah.'

'What did you think of him?'

'What did I think?'

He smiled.

'What's so funny?'

'Well, to be honest with you, darling, Jock scared the shit out of me.'

And I laughed too. Out of relief, really, that someone could be honest about my dad.

'Hard as nails, your dad,' Eddie went on. 'A lot of London firms used Glaswegians back then. They had a reputation, see.' He gave a little chuckle. 'No one wanted to mess with your old man.'

'But somebody did.'

Eddie's smile suddenly dropped.

'Yeah,' he muttered. 'Well.'

He couldn't think of anything to say but he slid a hand across the table and patted mine gently. 'Those were bad times, darling. It must have been hard for you.'

'People say he was a grass.'

'Well, people say lots of things. You don't want to listen to most of them.'

'But I want to know what happened.'

Eddie sighed.

'There's not much I can tell you, love.'

I could feel the conversation coming to a dead end. No one wanted to talk about my dad's murder. It was bad business. So I resolved to keep Eddie drinking. Keep him drinking, keep him talking. He told a couple of anecdotes about my father. He asked about my work and I told him about the film. He had some ideas about some of the technical details in the heist part of the script. He was on his fourth vodka and orange when I got back to the matter in hand.

'Ruby says that you saw Harry Starks.'

'What?'

He frowned at me. His voice slightly blurred with the booze.

'Well, did you?'

'Look, Julie . . .' He looked nervously around the half-empty pub. 'Let's not talk about that, not here.'

'I want to know where he is, Eddie.'

'I wish I knew that, darling. I really do.' Eddie looked down and muttered: 'That bastard owes me.'

I shook him by the arm.

'Well, he fucking owes me too!' I hissed.

Eddie stared at me, shocked out of the slight stupor of the alcohol. He touched my hand, which was still clawing at his arm.

'Steady on, girl,' he whispered.

'We've got something in common, then, haven't we? What do you mean, he owes you?'

'Well, it's the same old story, isn't it?' He looked around the room again. 'You know what we used to call people like Starks? Thieves' ponces, that's what we called them. People like me would take all the risks and the gangsters, the heavies, they'd always want their cut.'

I remembered what Ruby had told me.

'You mean like the bullion job?' I asked him.

He put a finger to his lips.

'Not here, darling. We can't talk about that here.'

'Where, then?'

Eddie drained his drink and slammed it clumsily on the table. He sighed.

'What do you want, Julie?'

'I want what's mine.'

He nodded slowly. I think he thought I meant money.

'Come back to the flat,' he said. 'We can talk there.'

It was still a bright sunny day as we walked up to Deptford to where Eddie lived. He started to tell me a story on the way.

'A long time ago, and I mean a long time, late fifties, I used to do big houses in the country with a couple of other fellas. It was easier back then, not so much security as you get nowadays, and I was fit enough to shin up the drainpipes. Anyway, we'd sized up this place in Surrey. Big stately pile, it was. There'd been this photo spread about it and the guy that owned it in the *Tatler*. I always kept up with the society pages back then, my "trade publications", I'd call them. Very nouveau this bloke was so we figured there'd be plenty of tom, you know, jewellery, and all the other trappings of conspicuous wealth. The main problem, though, was dogs. He had four really nasty Dobermans loose in the grounds at night. Now I'd read somewhere that what dogs were really scared of was the smell of tigers or lions because they're like their natural predators. So what I did was I got talking to one of the keepers at London Zoo, took him for a drink and persuaded him to let me have a bag of lion shit. Can't remember for the life of me what I told him I wanted it for but I do remember that we negotiated a price and decided that the going rate for lion shit was three quid a pound. Not a bad little earner for a zookeeper back then. Anyway, he meets me after work the next day with a big bag of the stuff and I pay him off. So, when we get to this house we've got the ladder against the wall and I'm up at the top of it waiting for these vicious dogs to turn up. And sure enough, just as soon as my head's over the wall, there they all are, the hounds of hell, teeth bared, growling, eyes all fiery and full of murder. I duck back down and get the bag and sling the contents over the wall at them. Suddenly it all goes quiet and I stick my head over again, hoping to see the dogs fleeing as they get a whiff of this fearsome lion scent. But instead they're merrily rolling about in it like it's the sweetest stuff in the world. And I realised that although this trick might work with dogs in Africa where they know what a lion smells like it ain't going to be much use here where they've never had so much as a whiff of one.'

We got to his flat. It was on the second floor of a concrete-and-brick low-rise block. A lot of the other dwellings were boarded up.

'Well, this isn't exactly stately,' he said as he turned the key in the lock. 'Come in and see how crime pays.'

I followed him through into the kitchen. He put the kettle on.

'Cup of tea?' he asked.

I nodded. He picked up a mug from the draining board and peered into it.

'We could join forces,' I said.

'What are you talking about?'

'We could both get our own back on Starks.'

'What?'

'There must be a way. He's come into the country before. Perhaps we can find a way so he does it again.'

He put the cup down and turned to me. He held on to both my arms. His bony hands shuddered a little at the contact.

'You don't want to know about this.'

'Yes I do.'

'Look, girl, he's dangerous.'

'I know that.'

'Do you? Do you really know?'

'What do you mean?'

'I mean, I know what a lion smells like.'

'What?'

'That story I told you. I know what to fear. I know the smell of it.'

He let go and dropped his arms by his sides. He shrugged and said:

'I've had lion shit all my life.'

A thin smile, milky blue eyes staring at me once more. I reached out and touched his chest. He shivered.

'You don't want to get involved,' he said. 'Trust me.'

And I knew then what I needed to do. I needed to involve myself with him, manipulate him, like all the others. I touched his face. I kissed him gently on the lips. His breath came in little sobs.

'What? What is this?'

'Come on,' I murmured, drawing closer to him.

'Please, don't.'

He tried to pull away from me but he needed to be held so much he couldn't resist. His thin body quivered against mine.

'It's just been so long,' he hissed. 'So bloody long. Look, I don't think I know how to do this any more.'

'Don't worry,' I said, and led him into the bedroom.

I was gentle with him. He wanted to be touched more than anything else. And to touch. After we had made love he buried his face in my breasts and cried for a bit. Then he rolled off me and lay on his back. His face was wet and slack with relief. I stroked his greying hair gently.

'Tell me,' I told him softly. 'Tell me everything.'

A car horn sounded in the street below. The minicab that Eddie had called for me. I left his flat just before midnight. He shuffled to the door to see me out in a sort of trance. His brittle frame yielded a little, softened with booze and sex and talk.

'Goodnight, Julie,' he said hoarsely.

I kissed him on the lips.

'I'll phone you soon,' I told him. 'I've got some ideas.'

'Julie . . .'

'No, Eddie. I'm in on this. We've going to do this together. You promised.'

He blinked slowly. His tired face nodded.

'OK,' he whispered.

'I'll phone you,' I repeated, and turned to leave, to clatter down the stairwell into the dark blue night.

'McCluskey?' asked the minicab driver.

Eddie had given him my real name.

'Yeah,' I said, and got into his car. I gave him my address and we pulled away. I had a plan now.

This involved getting Piers and Jez to agree to have Eddie as a technical consultant on the film. I suggested it to Piers first.

'Eddie Doyle, eh?' he said. 'Well, you are well connected.'

'Not really. I know him through Ruby.'

'And Tommy Patterson too.'

'Well, that's because of Joe.'

He gave a flat little laugh.

'It's hard to know where crime ends and showbiz begins, or should that be the other way around? So postmodern and ironic, isn't it? It's hard to know whether somebody is acting or not.'

His voice had suddenly got an edge to it.

'What do you mean?'

'I mean, it's hard to know whether somebody has actually stopped acting or not. Or if they're just acting all the time.'

'Piers, what the fuck are you getting at?'

'I'm getting at you, Julie. I've got it, you see.'

'Got what?'

'You. I've got you. I know who you are, darling. I know all about you.'

I stared at him. He laughed again.

'It's incredible. It's quite a story, Jules. Big Jock McCluskey's daughter.'

'Piers, listen . . .'

'I thought something was up at that book launch. I thought you were cheating on Jez, that has why you were so cagey. Then, when I phoned up Frankie Fraser to get a quote for the "London Underworld" piece for *Sorted* and mentioned that I met him there, he says, "I didn't expect to see Jock McCluskey's daughter." That's you, isn't it? He'd noticed you, you see. Your dad was a gangster. You've kept this quiet.'

'I can explain.'

'And in a way you have been cheating on Jez, haven't you? I mean, he knows nothing about this, does he?'

'No, but . . .'

'That's out of order, Jules. This is all fucked up.'

'Just let me explain.'

Piers folded his arms and tipped his head back slightly.

'Go on, then.'

'You've done your homework so you know all about my father, right?'

'Right.'

'Then you know what happened. I was ten years old when he was murdered, Piers. Just a little girl. Think of the effect of that. I was made to feel guilty and ashamed all the time as I was growing up. I had to tell lies about my past. I got used to that, Piers. I always wanted to get away from the badness in my life. I wanted to be a nice middle-class girl. People like you and Jez, you don't know what it's like not to have that sort of security in your life. To always feel that there's something wrong with you. That's why I covered things up.'

'Yeah, but . . .'

'Everyone likes to pretend. I mean, you and Jez with the wide-boy act.'

Pier gave a little laugh.

'Yeah, well, it is funny that all the while you were pretending, we were . . .'

'But with me . . .' I went on.

'I mean it's, you know . . .'

'Don't say it.'

'What?'

'That fucking word.'

Piers shrugged.

'What I mean to say is,' I continued, 'that I needed to pretend. That's why I started acting.'

'And Jez never guessed anything?'

'Well, you know how self-obsessed he is.'

'I suppose. Still, it must be difficult if you're having a relationship with someone and keeping all of this a mystery.'

'Piers, I've been doing it all my life. Even before my father died. What do you think I told kids at school?'

He frowned.

'I still don't get it.'

'What?'

'Well, wanting to keep that part of your life covered up and then getting involved with the film. I mean, doesn't it just bring up bad memories?'

'I'm just coming to terms with things. The film, well, it's like part of that. It's, you know . . .' I searched for the right word. 'Cathartic.'

'Hmm.' He nodded. 'I guess.'

I could tell that he wasn't altogether convinced.

'So, are you going to tell Jez?'

'I will. I just need a bit more time. I want things to work out between us. You won't tell him, will you? Not yet.'

'He's my best friend, Julie. It's going to be hard keeping something like this from him. It puts me in a difficult situation.'

I thought about telling Piers about Jez and Georgina de Brett. But that would only complicate things.

'Just give me some time,' I said. 'Let's get this film into production first. We don't want to mess anything up, do we?'

'No, we don't. But look, I want something in return.'

'What?'

'I want your input on the script. It still needs a polish.'

'What?'

'Look, *Scrapyard Bulldog* is really going to work if it plays with gritty reality and a sort of knowing surface. Strikes me you'd be an expert.'

'You're a calculating bastard.'

'And you're a clever bitch. A good working combination, if you ask me. You want me to keep quiet, then that's the deal.'

'But how am I going to be able to do it without Jez knowing?'

'Well, you said about using Eddie Doyle as a consultant. It can be done through that, can't it? I mean, I'm sure Eddie has some suggestions himself, but it's your ideas I'd be interested in. So, what do you say?'

6
double jeopardy

Well, the East End had really fucking changed. Dan was working in Shoreditch and Hoxton, turning old warehouses into plush apartments, artists' studios, galleries. All those grotty old buildings were turning into desirable properties. I couldn't believe it. And Dan was coining it.

I kipped at his for a few days. He had this big Victorian house in Mile End that he had converted himself. It was lovely. Really sophisticated. He had Marcia, his wife, two teenage kids, his own business. Dan was pretty well fixed. All very grown up and respectable now. It was like he'd got all his badness out of his system. All his naughtiness. Me, well, I was back to square one, wasn't I?

I told Dan about my marriage breaking up. I didn't go into the gory details, though.

'Maybe you're having a mid-life crisis, Gaz,' he said.

'I don't like the sound of that.'

'It could be a good thing. You know, a chance to change.'

'Change? What's so good about change? The way things are going I'll be asking for it. You know, like a fucking beggar.'

'You'll be all right, Gaz. You just need to sort yourself out.'

He was right there. I did some labouring for him, which came in handy. There was plenty of work about. A big property boom around the corner, Dan was sure of it. I found a flat for myself above a shop on the Roman Road and set about thinking what I was going to do next. Dan offered me a regular job with his firm but I said no. I knew that it wasn't my style. I didn't have a trade and I was too old to learn one now.

Christmas was coming up. A depressing time if you're on your own. A couple of days before it in a supermarket I saw this pensioner with half a chicken and a packet of mince pies in her basket. All she could afford, I guess. It's a hateful fucking time if you've got no one.

Karen let me come over Christmas Day morning to give the girls their presents. Charlene was giving me the silent treatment. Donna was shy of me at first then got all playful when the presents came out. Karen was coldly polite. She put on a bit of a show so as not to upset the kids. When we were alone together in the kitchen I tried to have a word. She didn't want to know.

'I've spoken to a solicitor,' she said.

Well, a Merry Christmas to you too, dear, I thought.

I drove back to London at midday. The city was quiet. Dead. Everyone stuffing themselves, getting pissed and having a double dose of *EastEnders*. Dan had invited me over to his for Christmas dinner. I couldn't face that somehow. I made up some excuse. I didn't want him to know I was all on my tod. I didn't want anybody's pity but my own.

No work about so I spent the next week on my own watching telly and getting off my face on booze. I'd decided to stay off drugs for a bit, but I just ended up drinking like a fish. I mooched about this little flat, hardly going out. I didn't bother to wash or shave for days. I kept churning things around in my head, but none of it seemed to make any sense any more. I started to think that maybe Dan was right and I was having some sort of a breakdown. Maybe I was just losing my bottle. I had horrible moments of panic and paranoia. Nightmares. The booze helped blot it out but I'd get the shakes in the mornings and start to worry about things again.

Dan came around and it was embarrassing. The place was in a right fucking state. I didn't want to let him in at first but he just barged past me at the door.

'Jesus Christ, Gaz,' he said, looking at me and around the flat. 'What's the fuck's the matter with you?'

I sighed.

'I don't know, Dan,' I said. 'I guess I've just fucking lost it.'

'Come on, Gaz. Don't talk like that.'

'No, it's fucking true.'

'Look, Gaz, you can pull it together. I know you can. You're just going through a bad patch.'

He patted me on the arm. He was being so nice to me I almost couldn't bear it. I felt all choked up as if I was going to start crying or something. Like that time at that MOVE meeting. Part of me wanted to let go but I was scared. I was worried that I might just fall apart completely.

But it was all right. I was able to hold it all together. I wanted to tell Dan how much I appreciated him as a friend and how much I took for granted all the times he had stood by me, been there when I'd come out after a sentence and all that. I wanted to say sorry for that time that we didn't speak to each other. But I didn't know how to. So I just patted him on the arm back and managed to croak:

'Thanks, mate.'

'Look. Smarten yourself up and come out with us tonight. That's what I came round for.'

'Tonight?'

'Yeah. Of course. It's New Year's Eve, isn't it?'

I didn't even know. I really had hit rock bottom. But suddenly I thought: well, maybe I can't get any lower, maybe it's time to start coming back up again. A new start.

'Yeah,' I said. 'All right.'

'We're going to this place south of the river. The Groove Corporation, it's called. One of these new super-clubs. It's supposed to be the dog's bollocks.'

We got to this club just before midnight and there was this huge queue even though Dan had got tickets. I went up to the door and sure enough there was someone I knew there, by the crash barriers. It was Jason, who had worked for me back in the rave days. I had a quick chat with him and he waved us through.

The Groove Corporation was a converted warehouse but not like those warehouse venues of the past. It had all been tarted up, with different levels with bars and dance floors on. It was huge and someone had spent a fortune on it. I had a wander around. I was staying sober so I noticed how most people were off their faces, pilled or coked up, as usual. But there was something different about the atmosphere of the place, something cold and calculated like some sort of institution. A big fun palace but one that was carefully controlled and regulated. There was a separate VIP area with a balcony that overlooked the main dance area. I saw somebody standing on their own with a glass in their hand, not looking down but out across the whole building. I recognised him. It was Ben Holroyd-Carter.

I went to the entrance of the VIP area. There were two doormen there. Nobody I knew and as I clocked them I knew that they didn't know me from Adam neither. No flicker of recognition or anything. I was known by a lot of doormen but not these two, it seemed. But I did have a reputation.

'Gaz Kelly,' I said.

One of the blokes looked at the clipboard.

'Sorry, mate,' he said.

'I'm with Ben Holroyd-Carter,' I tried.

Clipboard laughed and turned to his partner.

'Sure you are, mate,' he said. 'We all are.'

'You know who I mean?'

'You having a laugh? You mean our boss, don't you? The bloke what owns this place.'

So Holroyd-Carter ran this gaff. Always wondered what happened to him. Clipboard shook his head slowly and turned to the other one again.

'You think they'd try something a little more subtle, wouldn't you, Dave?'

I tried not to get riled by this. I took a breath.

'Look, mate, I ain't taking the piss. I'm an old friend of your guvnor's. Just tell him I'm here and he'll want to see me.'

This bloke stared at me for a second then shrugged.

'OK,' he said. 'I'll have a word. Who was it again?'

'Gaz.'

'Gaz? Gaz who?'

I don't think Holroyd-Carter ever knew my second name.

'Geezer Gaz,' I said. 'Tell him Geezer Gaz is here.'

He was off and back in five minutes with a stupid smile on his face.

'Go on through,' he said.

I wandered into this poncey party that was going on. The VIP lounge was all big sofas, glass tables and lairy light fixtures. There were fit birds everywhere and I recognised someone off the telly in a loud suit. Holroyd-Carter was in the corner surrounded by people, holding court, like. I sort of hovered, not wanting to interrupt the group, who were all yakking and laughing away. I felt a right cunt. Suddenly I was spotted.

'Gaz!' he called out, and waved to me. '*Geezer* Gaz.'

I walked over. He was taking the piss, I thought. Everybody turned around to look at me. Gawping, like I was some strange animal or something.

'Now, Piers,' he continued, turning to somebody next to him. 'You'll be interested in Gaz, here. He's the geezer. Aren't you, Gaz?'

I tensed up. I felt like giving him a slap.

'You want to watch your fucking mouth, Ben,' I told him.

And the group all burst into laughter, like this was a comedy routine or something.

'See what I mean, Piers?' Everyone was hanging off his every fucking word. He turned to me. 'Piers here is a writer. He'll be after you for material.' He turned back to Piers. 'Gaz here was one of my . . . well, let's say associates, when I used to run the Paradise raves.'

'All double-barrelled names and double-barrelled shotguns back then, wasn't it?' this Piers bloke says.

'Yes, very funny. Thinks he's got a way with words. You write anything about my nefarious past I'll fucking sue you for every penny.'

Laughter. Holroyd-Carter came closer to me.

'All legitimate now, you see, Gaz,' he said. 'So, how are you, Geezer? Happy New Year. Old acquaintance be forgot and all that, what?'

'Don't take the piss out of me,' I hissed at him.

His eyes flashed some of their old fear for a second. But only for a second.

He sighed. 'Gaz, I wouldn't dream . . .' He trailed off. 'Look. Let me show you something.'

He led me through the lounge and up some stairs. We ended up in this huge office, like a big glass cage suspended in the roof of the building. There was a bank of television monitors, you could see every part of the club.

'Welcome to the Groove Corporation,' he said.

'Well, you've done all right, haven't you?'

'Oh yes. Of course, you're a part of it, Gaz.'

'What do you mean?'

'I mean, well, I learnt so much from people like you. About exploitation. Of course, your methods were a little primitive. Look,

Gaz, I'm not taking the piss. What I mean is, well, how have I got all this? Legitimately, mind, completely legitimately. You want to know?'

I shrugged.

'Yeah, I guess.'

He led me over to one of the windows. He pointed.

'It's about exploiting the market. Yeah, you had some good ideas about that. But I have to say you lacked finesse. There's about two and a half thousand bodies down there. There's a finite number of people we can physically get into the club, but you see the Groove Corporation isn't just a club. It's a brand.'

He walked over to a desk. There was a pile of stuff on it. He started picking things up and throwing them across the room.

'The *Groove Corporation Club Mix* CD. The *Ibiza Club Mix*. Groove Corporation T-shirts. *In the Groove* magazine. We can sell it in so many ways. Franchising, sponsorship. It's a bloody gravy train, Gaz. More than you ever imagined. What do you do? You squeeze every last drop out of them. Look, here's a really simple example.'

He led me over to one of the monitors. He pointed to the screen that showed the doors.

'See those people queuing? Why are they queuing, Gaz?'

'To get into the club.'

'No. They're queuing because I want them to queue. We could get them into this place much quicker, you know. But I want a queue. You know why? Well, it's sort of an advertisement for the club, makes the place look like it's popular. But also because in weather like this you're going to need a coat if you're standing around. And a coat means you've got to use the cloakroom. That's five thousand every weekend just keeping the queue slow. It's the little things, Gaz. Oh, and in case you're wondering about who runs the door here, well, that is something I learnt off you. I keep rotating companies, I make sure that no one firm gets too entrenched here. And sure, they can run their dealers, but only as long as they are very, very discreet about it. This is a respectable business, Gaz.'

'I can see that.'

'You still working for Beardsley?'

'Well, not exactly.'

'Sounds like it's pretty heavy in Essex.'

'That's why I've moved back to the Smoke.'

'Well, it's all happening here. People are calling it "Swinging London" again, you know, like back in the sixties.'

'Who are?'

'You know, the media. It's a boom time, Gaz. And the Groove Corporation is the *zeitgeist*.'

'The what?'

'The spirit of the times, Gaz. Cool Britannia rules the waves and all that shit.'

I didn't try to follow what Holroyd-Carter was fannying on about at this point. But what he had explained about his business operation was clear enough. He'd got it all sewn up nicely. All above board. And he was too big for the likes of me to threaten any more.

'Don't suppose you'd consider using me to run security here, would you?'

Well, it was worth a try. Holroyd-Carter smiled.

'Times have changed, Gaz.' He rubbed his chin. 'Still, something might come up. Something that might require your particular talents. You know?'

'Oh yeah?'

'You never know. Here.' He handed me his business card.

'See you, then, Ben.'

'Keep in touch, Gaz,' he called after me, and I went back to find Dan and Marcia.

My New Year's resolutions were: come off the drugs and the booze for a bit; start going to the gym again regular but keep off the steroids; get back in business somehow. There were bits of door work and debt collecting here and there but I'd lost all the contacts I'd had through Beardsley. Word had got around about our falling out. And people kept asking about the Range Rover shootings. All sorts of theories about who done it. Funny, but some faces and some firms would like to give the impression that they had something to do with it. Stick their own names up, as it were. Not to the police, of course, but to other villains. It was like claiming a bit of clout. And what with all the double-crosses and rip-offs that were going on it might be useful for people to think that you'd wiped out those three. And it kind of made sense to me. A bit of moody respect could come in handy.

I heard that Essex Constabulary still wanted to have a word with me about it. But I was staying away from that manor. I wanted to keep my head down and find some sort of earner. Something a bit more easy going. I thought about Charlene and Donna. I wanted to provide for them but I wanted them to grow up with a father they could be proud of. To be honest I was tired of the life I had led. But what could I do?

Dan reckoned I should invest in property.

'Do a conversion. Buy up some empty warehouse space in EC2 and I could do it up as a loft apartment. It would suit you for now and you could sell it on in a couple of years and make a fortune.'

'You reckon?'

'I'm telling you, Gaz, prices are set to go right up around here.'

'But why would anyone want to live in fucking Shoreditch? When you and me were growing up everyone wanted to get away from the East End. If they had any sense.'

'Well, it's central enough. And it's fashionable, Gaz. It's become a fashionable area.'

'But what am I going to buy property with? I'm boracic at the moment.'

'Well, you could remortgage your house in Essex, couldn't you?'

I'd have to sort this out with Karen. She'd moved back into it but it shouldn't be a problem. I phoned her up and told her about the idea.

'Well, there's a few things we need to sort out, Gaz,' she said. 'Give me your address, there's something I need to send you.'

I told her where I was staying.

'How are the girls?'

'They're OK, Gaz.'

'I really want to see them.'

'Look, I've got to go.'

Then something turned up. I was doing this door job at a club in the West End and this doorman called Sean said that there was some film work going out at Shepperton Studios. They were looking for big, evil-looking blokes and he reckoned I'd be just the ticket. We went out there and sure enough I got the job. I was one of the extras in this American action film called *Red Mercury*. Our scene was set in a Russian nuclear power plant and we played the henchmen of a mad ex-KGB colonel who have surrounded the hero, played by Hollywood star Rick Sanchez. He offs us all single-handedly, of course. It was three weeks' work at a hundred pounds a day plus overtime. I couldn't believe at first that it would take so long to shoot something that would last just a few minutes in the actual film. But everything took so long. Most of the time we were standing around waiting for the film crew to set things up. So I got talking to people. There was a lot of work around. The stunt men were on a good whack but I wouldn't fancy that. All that bravado was never my cup of tea. The proper actors didn't tend to mix with the extras and the stars sort of lived in a world of their own, in trailers or on chairs with their names on. Sean had been an extra in loads of films. 'Noddy work', he called it.

'Just keep your head down, Gaz,' he told me.

I wasn't quite sure what he meant by that.

But I really liked it. It was a piece of piss. An early start usually, picked up in a minibus from Charing Cross Station. We'd arrive just as the caterers were setting out breakfast. Then make-up and wardrobe. We waited to be called on to the set and Phil, the assistant director, would tell us what to do. Then it would be action, lots of takes, then more waiting as the camera was moved or whatever. The film crew themselves seemed a bit aloof. There was this pecking order among them that I couldn't quite figure out but it had something to do with that list of credits at the end of a film when all those strange names like 'best boy' and 'key grip' come up on the screen.

Then, on the fourth day that I'd been working on the film, I found out what Sean had meant. There was a close-up scene between Rick Sanchez and a couple of the henchmen who were actual actors and had some lines to say. We were on the set as background. Phil came over to us from the huddle he'd been in with the director and the cameraman.

'We need somebody to be in the next shot,' he said.

I didn't want to push myself forward really, but all the other guys were backing off for some reason. I looked at Sean and he sort of nodded at me but I couldn't work out what he meant.

'I'll do it,' I said to Phil, and I followed him over.

'Right,' said the director to me. 'Just stand there and look dangerous. That's fantastic.'

I'll tell you something. I've seen Ricky Sanchez in a couple of films but I didn't realise he was that short. Nice bloke, though. Friendly. He made these little jokes in between takes and said 'Thanks a lot, guys' to us when we finished.

I was dead chuffed at the end of the day. I was actually going to be recognisable in this film. But when I saw Sean in Wardrobe when we were getting changed he shook his head at me.

'What's the matter?' I asked.

A runner had come in with the call sheets for the next day's shooting and my name wasn't on it.

'Sorry, Gaz,' said Sean. 'But I told you to keep your head down, didn't I?'

'I don't understand.'

'Well, look. You're an extra, right? You end up in shot in one scene, they can't use you in another, can they?'

'Why not?'

'Because if you turn up in another scene the audience will be thinking, "That geezer who was killed a couple of minutes ago seems to have come back to life." It's called continuity.'

I felt such an idiot on the minibus back to London. But sort of pleased as well. I was actually going to be on-screen in this film, even if it was just for a few seconds. Charlene and Donna would be able to see their dad in a Hollywood movie. Though with all the violence in this film they couldn't go to the pictures to see it for a fair while. Maybe I'd get it for them when it came out on video.

'Don't worry, Gaz,' Sean told me. 'There'll be other work. Look, I could have a word with my agent, if you like.'

'You got an agent?'

'Yeah. He just does extra work, walk-ons and modelling. Strong characters are his speciality. Heavies, you know. Bodybuilders and big ugly-looking geezers like you and me.'

The David Merriman Agency was run from a mansion flat on Streatham High Road. The door was opened by this sullen-looking bloke with dyed blond hair. He showed me through to a large living room stuffed full of furniture and poncey ornaments.

'David will be with you in a minute,' said this bloke, and he disappeared.

Sean had given me the SP on David Merriman.

'He's gay and he goes for the big butch types. So, you know, use that to your advantage.'

'What do you mean?' I'd asked him.

'You know. Play along.'

Play along. I didn't like the sound of that. I had a shufti around the room. It was like *Antiques* bloody *Roadshow* or something. Little fucking china figurines everywhere. The door opened and this podgy little queen swanned in with a fixed smile on his gob and a little sausage dog waddling after him. He had an orange suntan and his hair seemed to be perched on his round face like a bird's nest. Probably a wig, I thought.

'Hello,' he said, all sing-song like. 'David Merriman.'

He held out his hand and I shook it. Limp and clammy it was.

'Gaz Kelly.'

His watery blue eyes glared at me like he was sizing me up.

'You're a friend of Sean's.'

'That's right.'

The little dog started yapping at me.

'Quiet, Portia,' he said, patting it on the head. 'She gets jealous of anybody else getting the attention, you know. Well, Sean was certainly right about you. Big lad, aren't you.'

He looked me up and down.

'Good body?'

'Sorry?'

'Your body, it's in good shape?'

'Yeah,' I said. 'I guess.'

And I reckoned it was. I'd been to the gym every day since New Year.

'Well, let's have a look at it, then.'

'What?'

'For purely professional reasons, Gary. After all, I can't take you on unless I know what I'm representing.'

The fixed smile widened. I felt like punching the fucker but I remember what Sean had said. *Play along*.

'What, here?'

'Don't worry, we won't be interrupted.'

So I got my kit off. He asked me whether I'd done much work and I told him about *Red Mercury*. He pursed his lips.

'Well, we don't do much extra work. A bit of modelling. Walk-ons and small parts.'

I was down to my underpants.

'But in your case, well, who knows?'

His greedy little eyes were staring.

'Let's have a little look at that, shall we?'

I coughed.

'You don't mind, do you?'

'Of course not,' I lied, and pulled them off as well.

'Oh yes, very nice.'

The dog barked again.

'Portia, stop it!'

He slapped her on the back, all the time ogling me.

He sighed. 'Well, put your clothes back on and we'll have a little chat.'

I sat with him on this leather settee and he went through all sorts of things that I needed to do. I needed to get some photographs done. And I needed an Equity card.

'How do I get one of those?'

'Well, cabaret is the best way. Do you have an act of any sort? Any special skills?'

'Er, no.'

'Can you sing?'

'Not really.'

'Well, you could try stripping, you know. That's how Sean got his. Have a word with him.'

'You never told me about that,' I said to Sean when I saw him next.

'Well, you didn't ask, did you? It was a long time ago.'

'You don't do it any more, then?'

'Nah,' he said, slapping his belly. 'Not exactly in shape for it now, am I?'

'Well, I don't fancy it. Can't you just join this fucking union?'

'Nah. You need contracts, you need to prove that you're a professional.'

'Can't that be fixed?'

'Yeah, I guess. It wouldn't be the first time.'

'You know anyone who could straighten it for me?'

'I'll ask around.'

And I started thinking about it myself. Beardsley would have known someone probably. Then I suddenly thought about Fat

Wally, who'd been an associate of his back in the old days. Walter Peters had been a big player in the Soho porn rackets in the past but he now ran the Comedy Club, which had started out at the Stardust, Harry Starks' old place, and had now moved to Leicester Square. Wally had done eighteen months for assisting a fugitive when Starks had escaped from Brixton Prison and gone on the run in the late seventies. I knew he still ran a few shops and peep shows around Brewer Street, so I headed up there.

LIVE NUDE GIRLS, said one of the signs. This tart trying to hustle up trade outside.

'Only five quid, love, lots of lovely girls,' she says.

'Are you sure they're live?'

'Oh, a comedian. Come on, darling, you want to see a show? It's starting any minute.'

'I want to see Fat Wally.'

'Fat Wally? Who's he?'

'You know.'

'And who might you be?'

'I'm a friend of his.'

She shrugged her bare shoulders and cocked her head towards an alleyway farther up the street.

'He's in the shop at Walker's Court.'

There was a big sign that said PRIVATE SHOP. In the window were displays of fetish gear and pictures of half-dressed birds gaping away. I went through the multi-coloured plastic fly screen into this dimly lit place and saw Wally, his fat arse perched on a stool at the back of the shop. I went over. He was flipping through a copy of *Loot*.

'Wally,' I said.

He looked up from the paper. Frowned at me.

'It's Gaz. A friend of Beardsley's,' I lied, hoping he hadn't heard about what had happened.

He squinted, then nodded. We'd only met a couple of times.

'Oh yeah,' he said. 'Gaz. What can I do for you, Gaz?'

'Well, I wondered if you could fix something for me.'

Wally's eyes darted about the shop dramatically. There was only one sad fucker in the corner but he leaned forward and spoke out of the side of his mouth.

'Let's go to my office,' he whispered.

He hopped off the stool with surprising agility for a man of his size.

'Oi! Marcello!' he called down into the basement. 'Come up here and mind the store. I've got some business to attend to.'

Wally's office was above the shop. He sat on the edge of his desk. He lit a cigarette and puffed at it manically.

'How's Beardsley?'

'He's all right.'

'So, what can I do you for?'

'I want an Equity card.'

Wally burst into laughter at this. His huge belly heaving and bouncing up and down on the desk.

'I'm serious. I've heard that I can apply as a variety artist if I have enough contracts. You could fix the contracts for me. I'll make it worth your while.'

'So you're going into acting, Gaz?'

'Yeah.'

Wally chuckled a bit more, then stopped. He looked me up and down.

'Well, you'd be good for playing heavies, you know. You look the part.'

'That's what I was thinking. I've already done this film out in Shepperton.'

'Can you do stand-up?'

'What?'

'You know, stand-up comedy.'

'No. Look, what I was meaning was fixing it to look like I did, not actually doing it.'

'Don't worry, it's a piece of piss. All these cunts that play my club, they're always whining on about how hard stand-up is. Wankers. All it takes is bottle. I reckon you'd be a natural.'

'What are you talking about, Wally?'

'I need a compère for Tuesday nights. The cunt I had down for it has gone and got a telly job. It's an open mike, like the old days. A try-out spot for anyone who wants a go. Can get a bit rowdy. You'd be just right for it. All you'd have to do is introduce the acts and keep the punters in order. Then you'd get an Equity card legit.'

'I don't know, Wally.'

Wally slammed a palm against the desk.

'I got it!' he declared. 'You could be like a comedy bouncer. It would be like you were running a door. Look, give it a try.'

'Well . . .'

'I tell you, Gaz, a lot of people get their big break from doing stand-up.'

I liked the sound of that.

'Yeah,' I said. 'All right.'

'Nice one.'

'So,' I went on, curious, 'how is the comedy business?'

'It's doing all right. Just opened another club up in Manchester. Got plans to open them all over. You know, university towns, students love this shit. Got a live TV series lined up: *Friday Night at the Comedy Club*.'

'You still running the sex shops and peep shows, though?'

Wally heaved a deep sigh.

'Ah, Gaz, Soho is not what it was,' he lamented. 'What we used to rake in from that business in the old days you would not believe.'

He slipped off the desk and went to a grime-caked window. You could just make out the lights of Brewer Street below.

'No,' he went on. 'Soho is all being cleaned up now. I've got a couple of shops, a basement cinema, a peep show. They tick over but there's not the demand that there once was. You know what I hear? People are making pornography themselves. You know how cheap video equipment is these days. Or this new computer thing, you know, this fucking Internet. Diabolical. It's putting the retail trade out of business. And you know what? We actually get raided for the hard-core stuff, I mean really raided. Taken to court and everything. Can't do deals with the Old Bill any more. It's terrible. Have you seen Old Compton Street?'

I shrugged. He was going into one.

'It's become fucking fashionable. Full of poofy coffee bars. It's horrible.'

He went on like this for a bit longer. And I thought about this stand-up thing. I'd never figured on doing comedy. I was thinking about hard-man roles and so on. Me and Wally agreed to meet at the club the following day and sort out what I would be doing.

As it turned out Geezer Gaz, the Comedy Bouncer, was a great success. I wanted to use 'doorman' instead of 'bouncer' because no self-respecting doorman would ever call himself a bouncer, but Wally said that that was what the punters called us and besides it had a better ring to it. I'd come on in all the gear, black leather coat, big gold chain, wraparound sunglasses, headset and clipboard. I'd announce the acts like they were on the guest list, and when they got booed off I'd come and escort them off the stage like I was chucking them out.

I have to admit I was nervous at first. There was a lot of heckling. Wally gave me some put-down lines but in the end I generally just said shut it or I'd threaten them like I would if I *was* running a door. They seemed to like that. Afterwards Wally told me that it had worked. Staying in character, he called it. The fact was I wasn't expected to be funny, just to bring these sad fuckers onstage and take them off again. I could make the odd joke or comment but being the compère was like an authority role and the humour was in going over the top a bit about how I kept the audience in check. They enjoyed being ordered about by me and then they would take it out on the next poor bastard who was up on stage.

So I got a provisional Equity card and I started to get work. Walk-ons mostly. I was a builder in the caff in *EastEnders*, a soldier in the English Civil War in a BBC2 costume drama, a doorman in a Channel 4 comedy sketch show. David Merriman got me a lot of work. As Sean had said, he had a soft spot for big muscular guys, so the thing to do was to keep in his good books. I would go around to see him every week. He was lonely really. Just little yapping Portia for company. He offered to teach me how to speak lines and that and I thought it would be silly to refuse. He even got me singing, saying it was a good way of developing the voice. He'd get a bit queeny with me, making all these queeny-type comments and suggestions, and I'd go all stern with him. Which he seemed to like. It was like a silly little game. No harm in that if it could get me work.

And it paid off. He put me up for a small part in *The Bill*. Playing a villain, of course. I got to be in three scenes and I worked out OK. I was dead nervous but it wasn't that difficult really. I was playing myself, after all. And I had remembered what Merriman had told me about acting for the screen, about not doing too much but concentrating on what was going on in the character's head.

And I was dead chuffed. Charlene and Donna would be able to see their dad on the telly. But that was all they would see of him. I hadn't had any contact with them in months. I'd tried to send Karen money and stay in touch with her but it just hadn't turned out that way. The fact was that I wasn't making very much out of this acting lark, most of the time I was between jobs.

And Dan had found this place for me just off Old Street. A 'shell', he called it. Just a unit in a disused warehouse. A big open space with cast-iron pillars and a loading bay. We went around it with an estate agent.

'It's got a lot of character,' this spotty kid in a cheap suit and too much hair gel was saying. 'Lots of original industrial features.'

'Is that a good thing?' I whispered to Dan. He nodded.

Industrial features? I remember thinking. Why would anyone want industrial features?

They wanted ninety thousand for it.

'You can probably knock them down to eighty,' Dan told me.

'It's a lot of cash for a bit of an old warehouse.'

'I'm telling you, Gaz, give it a year or so and it will have doubled in value. If you can get hold of a big cash deposit, twenty or thirty grand, you can get an unsecured mortgage and you're laughing.'

Christ, I wish I hadn't blown that thirty large on that stupid deal with Pat Tate. I mean, it looked like you could make more money these days dealing property than dealing drugs. I'd have to try and mortgage the house. Or sell it. I tried to get hold of Karen. I left a message on her mobile.

Then something came through the post from her. Or rather, her solicitors. So that was why she wanted my address. It was a divorce petition. The grounds she gave were unreasonable behaviour and desertion. She wanted full custody of the kids. I phoned her up.

'Gaz, I want this done through the solicitors. I don't want to talk to you about it.'

'Karen . . .'

'And you'll want to get a solicitor yourself. If you're going to contest it.'

'Well, of course I'm going to contest it.'

'What, "unreasonable behaviour"? Good luck, Gaz.'

'But what about desertion? You left me, remember.'

'Yeah, but I'm back in the house now. And you've been gone since Christmas.'

'Yeah, but I had to get out of Essex, didn't I?'

'Why don't you tell the court all about that? I'm sure they'll be most impressed.'

'Karen, please. Don't stop me seeing the girls. Please.'

'Gaz, don't you see it's for the best? I don't want them to grow up around people like you. I want them to have a proper start in life.'

'There's someone else, isn't there?'

'That's got nothing to do with it. Gaz, I want this sorted out all proper and legal. I'm not going to argue with you about it any more.'

'Karen, wait.'

'I'm going to put the phone down.'

'Wait. There is something we need to talk about.'

'What?'

'The house. We need to sort out selling it.'

'Why?'

'So we can divide up the money from it. Half and half. That would be fair, wouldn't it?'

'Why would I want to do that, Gaz?'

'Well, if we're splitting things up, you know.'

'But why would I want to sell my house?'

'What? You mean our house.'

'No, Gaz. I mean my house. It's all in my name, remember?'

'But I bought it.'

'Yeah, with whose money?'

'My money, of course.'

'But that wasn't your money, was it, Gaz?'

'What are you talking about?'

'You stole it. Or got it from selling drugs. That's why you put it in my name.'

'Karen, for fuck's sake.'

'No, you listen now. I'm taking what I can. I can't trust you to pay maintenance, can I? I can't trust you to stay out of prison. So I want something I can be sure of for me and the girls. So I'm taking the house.'

'You bitch.'

'Goodbye, Gaz.'

So everything was fucked up. It was my fortieth birthday in a week's time and what did I have to show for it? I had nothing to my name except the motor, and I figured the way things were going I'd have to sell that. All that money that had passed through my hands, where had it all gone? Where had all the time gone?

Dan had got a nice house and a family, everything that had been taken away from me. He'd made it all legitimately too. But I didn't have the mentality for that. Working, it's always seemed like a mug's game. That's why this acting seemed like a good thing. A way of making lots of money without too much slog. But it just hadn't worked out like that. And I thought it might be a way of proving to Karen and the kids that I could go straight, but she just didn't take me seriously any more.

I'd got to do something, I thought. A little job or two to get enough cash to buy property like Dan had suggested. Then I'd have something, at least. I brooded about all of these things as the big four zero loomed. I didn't want to do anything on the day, I mean, what the fuck was there to celebrate? But Dan remembered and he wanted him and Marcia to take me out for a meal or something. I know he meant well but I didn't want him to be treating me again. It would just be a reminder of how down on my luck I was. So I said it was my turn to take them out. I wanted to feel flash again. It was my fucking birthday and I wanted it to be like I still was somebody. And I suddenly thought of Holroyd-Carter's club, the Groove Corporation. I could get us into the VIP room and maybe arrange it so we were treated like honoured guests and that. I phoned up Holroyd-Carter. He sounded pleased to hear from me and he put us all on the guest list.

On the night it felt good to be walking past the queue on the main door and having that little rope thing unhooked for us so we could walk into the VIP lounge. That's all I've ever wanted really, to feel special. A waitress brought over a bottle of champagne for us.

'With the compliments of Mr Holroyd-Carter,' she said.

I looked over at him in the far corner of the room. He caught my eye and raised his glass.

'I'm just going to go over,' I told Dan and Marcia.

Holroyd-Carter was talking to this bloke in a suit and a red tie.

'Happy birthday, Gaz,' he said. 'This is Paul.'

'All right.' I nodded to him.

'Pleased to meet you.'

'Gaz here is one of your floating voters, Paul. A real Essex man.'

Holroyd-Carter was taking the piss again.

'I ain't from Essex,' I said.

'Paul works for the Labour Party, you see.'

'I thought you supported the other lot, Ben,' I said.

'Well, they're on their way out. And Labour's a party of free enterprise now, isn't it, Paul?'

'Free enterprise and social justice,' this bloke Paul declared.

'What do you think of that, Gaz?' asked Holroyd-Carter.

'Sounds great,' I said.

'I've really got to get off now, Ben,' Paul said. 'So I'll tell Peter that you're interested.'

'You do that, Paul. And give him my regards.'

Holroyd-Carter nodded towards Paul as he left.

'Good to get in with the new bosses. Know what I mean, Gaz?'

'Yeah,' I said. 'I suppose.'

'They want to be young and groovy, well, I can help them with that. And you know what they say? A favour for a favour. So how are you?'

'All right. I guess.'

'How does it feel? To be forty?'

'I don't fucking know.'

To be honest I felt like a failure but I wasn't going to tell him that.

'And how's business?' he asked.

'I'm trying to go straight, Ben.'

'Yeah? And how's that going?'

'Well, you know.'

'Maybe you could do with a bit of capital.'

'What do you mean?'

'Well, you remember I said that something might come up?'

'Yeah.'

'A friend of mine wants a job doing.'

'What sort of job?'

'A little delivery.'

'I don't know.'

One of the club staff came over. Holroyd-Carter nodded towards him.

'You'll have to excuse me, Gaz. Think about it, though, won't you?'

I went back to Dan and Marcia. Marcia was having a good time. She'd just talked to someone who was in *EastEnders*. Dan started talking about property again.

'You want to put an offer in for that place we saw soon, Gaz,' he told me.

'Yeah,' I muttered.

I looked around the room. Everyone was having a good time. Acting flash. At the end of the night I found Holroyd-Carter.

'I'll do it,' I told him.

He handed me a little piece of paper.

'Phone this number,' he said.

Two weeks later and it was all set up. It seemed simple enough. Deliver a package, collect some money and that was that. But there was something about it that didn't seem right. I couldn't really afford not to do it, though. There was a couple of grand in it for me. I decided to cover myself a bit, just in case.

I got the driver to pick me up at half past ten in the evening at the Elephant and Castle. Beforehand I'd gone in to the Groove Corporation and made sure that the CCTV cameras had got me on tape by the main entrance. It would be an alibi if I needed it. The video would show the time and the date on it. I would come back later and make sure I was filmed leaving so I could say I'd been in the club all evening. I made my way through the premises and left by a fire exit and went to the rendezvous to be picked up.

We got to the place just before eleven. It was a ground-floor flat in a terraced house in Tottenham. I went up to the front door but when I knocked it swung a little. It had been left open. Well, I should have just got right out of there but I was curious. Stupid, more like. I went in and tiptoed along the front hall. I could hear the TV turned up loud in the front room. I tapped on this door. Nothing. I barged in there. This bloke was lying sprawled on the settee, his eyes wide open. It was Beardsley. It was fucking Simon Beardsley staring up at me. I thought at first that he must be stoned or something. He didn't move or flinch or anything. Then I realised that he wasn't looking at me at all. He wasn't looking at anything. He was dead. There were these patches of blood on his chest and loads more of it all down the settee and on the floor.

I couldn't work this one out at first. Then I heard police sirens coming closer. Then I knew the whole thing had been a set-up with me as the fucking mug punter. Time to go. I dropped the package on the floor. Then I picked it up again. It would have my dabs all over it.

A squad car was coming around the corner as I made it on to the pavement. The driver had fucked off, of course, so I started to leg it and ran straight into this old bloke.

'Oi!' he shouted. 'Watch it!'

The police car was squealing up the street behind me. This old fellah's bony hands gripped my arms.

'What's going on?' he said.

'Sorry, sir,' I told him. 'I'm a police officer. We're after someone.'

He let go and I pushed past him and ran as fast as I could. As I turned the corner at the end of the street I could hear car doors slamming and voices shouting into the night. A pub up ahead was crowded with closing-time traffic. I lost myself in the drunken mob as another squad car came shooting past. An Asian bloke next to a battered motor nodded at me.

'You want cab?' he asked.

I was out of breath. I nodded and got into the back. I got him to take me back to the Elephant, back to the Groove Corporation. I wiped down the package and chucked it out of the window. When I got to the club I thought about finding Holroyd-Carter. I felt like killing the little fucker. But that wouldn't do me much good. I knew what I had to do was to fix my alibi, so I just crept in there and made sure I was on tape leaving the club at about 2 a.m.

I was arrested a couple of days later. They asked me all of these questions that I just went 'no comment' to. Then I was put on an identity parade. The bloke I'd nearly knocked down had got a look at me but it had been dark. I was in a line with a load of other big bald-headed blokes. Must have been fun for the cozzers to round up that lot. I just hoped that the old fellah would point out one of the other skinheads by mistake.

I was put back in the cell and had plenty of time to think. I needed to work out what they might have on me. An ID perhaps. They'd done a forensic check on all of my clothes but I should have been clean. The main thing was the motive. I was well in the frame there. It was common knowledge that me and Beardsley had a grudge against each other. Someone had topped Beardsley and wanted a fall guy. Holroyd-Carter had fingered me for them, the bastard. Finally they dragged me out to an interview room again.

'Well, Gary,' this detective said with a big smug smile on his chops. 'We have a positive identification of you at the scene of the murder. Do you have anything to say about that?'

'No comment.'

'I draw your attention to the fact that if you refuse to answer or make comment at this time it may prejudice any other evidence you give at your trial. Do you understand?'

'No comment.'

'You were a business associate of Simon Beardsley's, were you not?'

'No comment.'

'Up until last December, that is. I understand you had something of a dispute concerning security arrangements at Tiffany's nightclub in Southend. Do you want to tell us anything about that?'

'No comment.'

'All right, Gary, let me jog your memory a little. We have a statement here from Frank Whitehead, the manager of the aforementioned club. I won't read it all out now but simply draw your attention to the fact that he says that on the ninth of December 1995 a serious argument occurred between you and Mr Beardsley at the club. Do you want to give us your version of the events of that evening?'

'No comment.'

'Right. Well, according to Mr Whitehead's statement the argument culminated in you saying to Simon Beardsley, and I quote: "Come after me, or mess with me again, and I'll fucking kill you." Anything to say about that, Gary?'

'No comment.'

'OK. The time by my watch is 2325 hours and I am now charging you with the murder of Simon Beardsley. Do you wish to say anything?'

Of course, I could have told him I'd been set up but they'd hardly believe that. Even if I told them the whole story of how Holroyd-Carter had put me in touch with these people they'd never believe that I hadn't actually done the killing. It would just have got me further into the shit. I had to prove that I hadn't been there at all. What I did have was the CCTV alibi but I had to be a bit clever with that. The tapes were in Holroyd-Carter's possession and if he knew about them he might fuck about with them or get them mysteriously wiped or something.

'No comment,' I said.

I was remanded in custody and sent to Belmarsh. I got into the papers this time because the episode of *The Bill* with me in it had been broadcast the same week and some clever journalist picked up on it. TV VILLAIN CHARGED WITH MURDER, was the headline. The kind of publicity I could do without, I thought at the time.

They made me a Double A Category prisoner, which was like letting me and the rest of the world know that they considered me a really dangerous hitman. The Double A Cat Unit at Belmarsh is like a prison within a prison, and it's meant for those who the state consider to be the most dangerous prisoners in the system. In there with me were some very big serious villains, a couple of major Yardie faces, some IRA blokes and a lot of other nutters: a hijacker, an animal rights activist and some fellah who threatened to put anthrax in the water supply. So I had hit the big time, criminal-wise. I almost felt privileged. But having that much security around you can only be prejudicial to the trial process. The jury's going to see you coming in and out of court being treated like you're Public Enemy No. 1 – well, it ain't a good start to the proceedings, is it?

There was surveillance everywhere in the unit. My cell was bare and sterile. Stainless-steel sink, stainless-steel mirror, stainless-steel table, stainless-steel seat. Like a bloody cage. You get to know who'll stick by you pretty quickly when you're inside. I remember one old con telling me that at the end of the year he'd count his Christmas cards and he'd know how many friends he had left. He'd done five years and at the last count he'd had four cards. Dan came to visit and kept in touch, which I really appreciated.

Strangely enough my agent, David Merriman, came to see me. I thought he'd want to drop me like a stone once I'd been charged but he was very supportive. I think he got a bit of a thrill coming on visits, to tell you the truth. The thought of all those dangerous men banged up probably gave him the horn.

My committal hearing came up. I got taken through to the magistrates' court attached to the prison. The police presented their evidence, which was being identified at the scene of the crime and a bit of forensic. They'd found this particle that related to the firearm used in the murder in the pocket of my jacket when they'd arrested me. My brief seemed confident that we could challenge both of these bits of evidence. But the main thing was my alibi. I'd kept shtum up until now, but I had only seven days to file a notice of alibi to be submitted to the trial when it went to the crown court.

I had to get the tapes, but if we applied to Holroyd-Carter for them he might fuck about with them. I realised that I had to make some sort of deal with him. It's bloody difficult to get messages in or out of Belmarsh because they monitor everything. In the end I used David Merriman as a go-between. I got him to tell Holroyd-Carter that if he fucked about with the tapes I'd start telling the whole story of what really happened. But if he just handed them over I'd keep quiet and if I walked I wouldn't take any revenge on him.

When Merriman came to see me we had this code when we talked about the CCTV evidence. We called it the 'show reel', which is what actors call a tape they have of clips of them in whatever they've been in. So if anyone was listening in they'd think that we were talking about my acting career.

'The show reel's ready, Gary,' he told me.

And we were on. I submitted the tapes as evidence and a trial date was set. I started writing letters to the celebrities and public figures I'd contacted when I'd done that charity event for that kid with leukaemia, Darren Tyler. Some of them remembered me and sent back messages of support. Dan and some other friends started this 'Gary Kelly Is Innocent' campaign. David Merriman was telling lots of his friends in high places that he reckoned that I was being fitted up. So there was going to be quite a lot of publicity buzzing around my trial.

But just as I was beginning to feel a little bit confident and determined about my situation I got the decree nisi of my divorce sent to me. I'd been expecting it but it still came as a blow. It took the wind right out of me, to tell you the truth. It was like everyone was out to get me. I'd been set up by Holroyd-Carter or whoever, fitted up by the police over the forensics, and now I was being stitched up by my own fucking wife, for Christ's sake. It nearly sent me loopy. Talk about paranoia. I nearly gave up. I thought about ducking my nut and changing to a guilty plea. Get it over with. Darker days, I thought about topping myself. Almost impossible in Double A Cat in Belmarsh. There's nothing you can get hold of to do yourself in and you're being watched nearly every minute of the day. It was like someone was taking the piss with my life. I felt like the whole world's mug punter.

7

london calling

When we got back from Tortola we lay low for a while. Things had got quite out of hand out there and Eddie said that he needed time to think about what to do next.

'I've got to act very carefully now,' he said.

'Yes, but you know where the gold is now, don't you?'

'Where it might be. Look, certain people might be watching me. Waiting to see what I do next. I don't want to lead anybody to where it is, do I?'

Weeks passed and nothing happened. I began to suspect that he was avoiding me or, worse than that, had forgotten me altogether. After all I had done for him this really annoyed me. Indifference is the worst insult of all. He was up to something, I was sure of that, and he was excluding me.

And I had become quite attached to him. It's never been an easy thing for me to do, to connect with someone. I feel a sort of autism towards the world in general, but I had found myself drawn to Eddie Doyle. He was the opposite of me in so many ways. He was a man of action, full of blood and passion. Maybe it was that I could feel and engage with things vicariously through him. Maybe I really had become his ghost in a way that I could not have foreseen.

Then the news came of Beardsley's murder. I had a meeting with Eddie. I expected him to be edgy, another person connected to the Hounslow job had been killed, but he seemed calm and collected.

'Right,' he said. 'I know what I'm going to do now.'

'And do you mind letting me know what that might be?'

'All in good time, Tony. First up we go and see Manny.'

'What's the matter with you?' I demanded.

'What do you mean? There's nothing the matter with me. I'm in a good mood, Tony.'

'Well, that's just it. This Beardsley fellow has just been bumped off and you don't seem rattled at all. Wait a minute, you didn't have anything to do with it, did you?'

'Of course not, Tony. What do you take me for?'

'You don't seem worried by it.'

'I'll watch my back. Don't worry, everything's going to plan.'

Something was up. And I had no idea what it might be. Eddie was acting strangely, that was for sure. Something about him had changed since we'd got back to England. He seemed relaxed, his usual agitation and paranoia gone somehow, his manner and demeanour apparently carefree, jocular even. He seemed untroubled, which was unlike the Eddie Doyle I knew, and that perplexed me. If I didn't know better about human nature I would have said that he was happy.

Manny Gould, on the other hand, was in an entirely different mood.

'I expected that you gentlemen might have come to see me sooner.'

'Sorry, Manny,' Eddie retorted. 'We were just getting over the merry dance your client has been leading us.'

'Well, it was a complex situation, granted, but weren't you supposed to bring some paperwork for me to have a look at?'

'It wasn't there, Manny. Solly never sent the assets from the gold that went missing out there. It was never smelted down. It's still here, somewhere in London. And you know that. So does Starks.'

'We were never completely sure. It was, shall we say' – he shrugged – 'a process of elimination.'

'Elimination, yeah, that's a good one, Manny. That's what it's been about all along, hasn't it? Except that it's been people that have been eliminated. What's this with Beardsley?'

Manny shrugged again.

'I really don't know. This Essex business, I believe. It's like the Wild West out there.'

'Are you sure your esteemed client didn't have a hand in it?'

'Of course I'm sure.'

'Well, Beardsley certainly had the wind up about Harry.'

'He had nothing to do with it.'

'Whatever. The good news is I might just know where it is now.'

Manny's eyes goggled.

'Where?' he demanded.

'Not so fast, my old son. We play these things my way this time. You tell your boss that he can have it all, for the right price.'

'How much is there?'

'We don't know yet. Ask him how much he's prepared to gamble and he can have the lot. A fixed price. I just want to walk away from all of this with a bit of cash for once.'

Manny nodded cautiously.

'All right. I'll make some enquiries.'

'And tell him I want to meet him there. Where it's hidden.'

'What?'

'You heard. I'll let him know the time and the place when I'm ready.'

'You really don't expect that Harry will just come into the country at your beck and call, do you?'

'That's exactly what I expect.'

'But he'd be taking a hell of a risk doing that.'

'Well, we've all been taking risks. He's done it before. Tell him I want him alone, too.'

'I don't understand,' I told Eddie when we left Manny's offices. 'Why do you want to bring Starks in on this? You could take the gold yourself, couldn't you?'

'And be stuck with the stuff again, Tony? Do me a favour.'

'And what about Frank Taylor? What are you going to do about him?'

'I can sort him out. Do a deal. Like the old days. In the meantime I'm sorting out cover for the operation.'

'Let me get this straight. You're going to deal with Starks and Taylor. That doesn't make sense.'

Eddie laughed.

'I'm going to do the right thing, Tony.'

I didn't like the sound of this.

'I don't understand, Eddie.'

'It'll all come clear in the end. You'll get the big scoop on Starks, don't you worry. You want your story, don't you? Well, you'll get it all right.'

I tried to work out what Eddie was playing at but I was baffled by it all. I soon found out what his 'cover' was, though. He was working as a consultant for a film company called Cutthroat Productions, advising them on some gangster movie called *Scrapyard Bulldog*. I went to see him in their small run-down office in Soho.

He was going over a section of dialogue with a young man I vaguely recognised.

'Hello, Tony,' said Eddie. 'You remember Piers, don't you?'

I tried to place him.

'All right, mate?' said the youngster. 'We met at Ronnie Kray's funeral.'

Then it came back to me. He had worked on *Sorted*, Groombridge's infantile lad magazine.

'How's Victor?' I asked, shaking his hand.

Piers chuckled.

'He's well pissed off with you, mate.'

The use of *mate* rankled. No bloody respect. As did the reminder that my so-called career was on its uppers. This youth probably saw me as some pathetic washed-up old hack.

'So, what are you up to, Eddie?' I asked.

'Eddie's our consultant on this film we're making,' Piers interjected. 'We want to get the details right, you know, the authenticity of the piece.'

'They're paying me for my expertise,' said Eddie.

'Yeah,' said Piers. 'Eddie's the real thing.'

'Isn't he just,' I muttered.

Just then a couple came into the office. A tall red-headed woman and a blond-haired man.

'We could always build a set of the warehouse,' Blond was saying.

'It'll cost too much,' Redhead replied. 'Look, we've gone through this before. It'll be easier and cheaper to find a place and do it on location.'

'Yeah, you keep saying this but you haven't found anywhere, have you?' said Blond.

'Well, it's where the main part of the action happens, you want it to be right, don't you?' said Redhead.

'Of course I want it to be right.'

'Well then, it might take a bit of time to find the right location.'

'But if we built it we wouldn't have to worry, would we?'

'I've told you, we can't afford it. We've got to keep the budget down.'

Blond sighed.

'I shouldn't have to worry about this, you know,' he complained. 'Just find somewhere soon, can't you? I want to know how I'm going to shoot this bloody thing.'

'Here's the happy couple,' Piers announced.

'Who's this?' Blond demanded.

'He's a friend of Eddie's,' Piers explained. 'Tony, meet Jez Scott, he's the director. And Julie Kincaid, my co-producer.'

'All right, mate?' Jez said, cocking his head back a little to show a scar on his right cheek.

'Pleased to meet you,' said Julie.

I tried to meet her eye and noticed her shoot an anxious glance at Eddie.

'Welcome to Cutthroat Productions,' said Piers. 'You've met all the staff now.'

'Yeah, well,' said Jez. 'Eddie, if you'll excuse us we need to have a meeting.'

'You want me in on it?' asked Eddie.

'No, just me, Piers and Julie. You can go for lunch if you want.'

'What do you say, Tony? I'll buy you lunch, put it on my expenses for once.'

As we were leaving the office Eddie had a quick exchange with the red-headed girl. It was something about an arrangement to meet up and talk about something in the script. The other two men were already engaged in some deep conversation of their own and they paid no heed to a strange sort of casual intensity between Eddie and this woman Julie. It wasn't in the words that they said to one another but rather the intimacy of space between them. I saw Eddie touch her ever so lightly on the shoulder as he took his leave.

'Well, you have fallen in with a young crowd,' I said to Eddie in the restaurant.

'Yeah,' he replied. 'I guess.'

'And that Jez and Julie, they're a couple?'

'Yeah.'

'Quite a family business, isn't it?'

'What's that supposed to mean?' Eddie snapped.

'Nothing,' I replied.

I hit a nerve there, I thought. Eddie poured himself some more wine.

'So you worked it out, then?' he asked.

I sighed.

'This warehouse location is the place where the gold's buried.'

'Yeah.' He grinned. 'Good, isn't it?'

'Brilliant.'

'Gives me time to find out if it really is there. And if the film company approaches the estate agents managing the property about renting it as a location there's no suspicion about what we might be up to and nothing that can get traced back to me.'

'And everybody thinks that it's just being used to make a film.'

'Yeah, it's a low-budget number. You know they got lottery money for it?'

'Really?'

'Yeah. Imagine that. Lottery money for some stupid B-movie.'

'And that's what it is?'

'*Scrapyard Bulldog*? Yeah, it's a bit silly to tell you the truth. Imagine all those people wasting their money on scratch cards for something like that. I'm supposed to be putting the realistic criminal element into it.'

'Well, you're certainly doing that.'

Eddie laughed.

'And they have no idea how realistic?' I asked.

'No. What do you think I am, stupid?'

'Well, the girl seemed very keen on using the warehouse.'

'Yeah,' said Eddie, a little cagily. 'She's a bright kid.'

'Not too bright, I hope.'

Eddie put his glass down.

'What are you getting at?'

'Nothing, Eddie. It seems you've got everything sewn up. I'm just not sure how I fit into this any more.'

'You'll get your story, don't worry.'

'Yeah, you already said that, but how?'

'You'll find out soon enough.'

'You seem very confident, Eddie.'

'I am.'

'Yeah. You seem, I don't know, happy.'

'I am, Tony.'

'Something's happened.'

Eddie smiled.

'Don't be so suspicious. Can't a fellah be happy?'

No, I thought to myself, he can't. He must be up to something. I had time on my hands so I decided to find out what was really going on. Eddie's guard was down now. He wasn't an easy person to follow, his instincts were sharp. But I managed to tail him driving out to the warehouse in East London that Solly had the deeds for. The red-headed girl Julie was with him. Location hunting, I suppose, is what these film people would call it. And Eddie was setting up his 'cover', as he called it. But there was something wrong about how the pair of them behaved with each other. Something playful, mischievous.

There was no sign of Frank Taylor shadowing him so perhaps Eddie had done some sort of deal with him. Taylor hadn't exactly been incorruptible during his time on the job, after all. I started watching Eddie's flat. I saw the girl Julie arrive at it late at night and leave early in the morning. So this was what it was all about. There was something going on between them. And this was why he seemed so happy. The poor old fool was in love.

And I felt an odd sense of betrayal. Of jealousy even. It was pathetic, I know, but it seemed to mock the loneliness and desolation of my life. I felt left out. I thought about confronting Eddie about this new dalliance of his but decided to wait. I wanted to find out as much as I could for myself. I wanted to outwit him, to outflank him.

I got in touch with Piers. We arranged to meet for a drink. I told him that I wanted his advice on how I might get back with Victor. He must have seen me as a charity case. He said he'd have a word, whatever that meant. The conversation moved on to his project fairly swiftly. People always want to talk up what they're doing. I asked him about the director, Jez. It turned out they were old pals, they had gone to school together. Then I brought up Julie.

'Yeah,' Piers explained. 'She used to be an actress, then she wanted to get involved in casting and stuff on this film. I wasn't sure it was going to work but she's been great. Bit of a dark horse, really.'

'You can say that again.'

Piers frowned at me. He'd had quite a lot to drink by then.

'You mean, you know about her?' he mumbled.

I didn't know where this was leading so I just shrugged and nodded.

'Shit,' he went on. 'Well, you would, wouldn't you?'

I smiled and pretended I knew what he was talking about.

'Of course you would. I mean, you were a crime journalist, after all.'

What did this mean? I let him carry on.

'I told her people were going to find out. The thing is . . .' He sighed. 'Well, Jez doesn't know and she really wants to keep it a secret from him.'

'Well, I suppose she would.'

'But I can't see why. He's going to know sooner or later. Eddie knows.'

I laughed.

'Well, he would, wouldn't he?' I said.

'What's so funny?' Piers demanded.

And then I realised that he was talking about something else altogether. But what? I got Piers another drink. A large one.

'So what did she tell you about it?' I fished.

'Well, just that she'd tell Jez in her own time. Look, I really shouldn't be talking about this. I promised Julie. You won't tell anyone, will you? I mean, anyone who doesn't know already. I think she's always wanted to put it all behind her, you know. It must have been a tough time.'

'Yeah, I guess so,' I agreed, without any idea with what.

I thought about letting Piers know about Julie and Eddie's affair. That would really stir things up. But I decided against it. I had the advantage of knowing something that he didn't and nearly knowing something that he did. There would be time enough to find out what it was.

In the meantime I prepared myself for the big story. I had a thick file on Harry Starks and loads of old clippings. I had done him for *Murder Monthly* back in the '80s. Then there were all the references in Teddy Thursby's diaries. Some of the real meat had been hacked out of the journals when he and Julian had been working on the official biography, but there was plenty of stuff that I could use. I just had to find a way of incorporating it without revealing its source.

I would go to Victor with it. I didn't really want to deal with Groombridge again but I still owed him for the advance on Eddie's book and I was still technically under contract with him. But I knew that I could renegotiate something really sweet for a book this big. I began to muse about serialisation rights, film and television options.

Eddie had promised me the Starks story. I had no idea how he was going to deliver but I'd make sure he kept his side of the bargain somehow. I'd lost a lot of trust in Eddie. Since he'd been seeing this wretched girl I'd been completely cut out of things. It struck me that maybe she was the key to what Eddie was planning. Something about her nagged at me but I couldn't work out what.

Maybe I was just haunted by the loss of Eddie's companionship. Not that we'd become friends or anything. But there had been a semblance of contact with a fellow being. I felt foolish and resentful at this weakness.

My life had been a series of timid adjustments to loneliness. But I'd managed never to let anyone get to me. I had been utterly ruthless in the past. I had repressed my desires. I had murdered them. Now all that was left was the slow surcease of feeling. Vigilance, that was all that was left for me now. To be able to watch.

So I reverted to my dull world of calm and morbid preoccupation. All these adventures, this senseless running around, were not really my style at all. I'd given up on real life, after all. It was an argument that I'd lost years ago. I found that I preferred the ghost life. Controlling events in the way they are recorded. This was my own *truecrime.*

The genre at large was growing. A turgid swelling in the publishing market. As Victor had prophesied, all sorts of Kray associates and hangers-on had come out of the woodwork since Ronnie's death. The Groombridge Press seemed to be issuing hagiographies of small-time crooks with an almost religious fervour. Every week another simple soul endowed with miraculous physical prowess would be staring out of the shelves of WH Smith's. Each cover photo an icon of brutality along with some charming aphorism of violence. *Basher: The Story of a Bare-Knuckle King: 'If I come at you you'll know about it alright!'*. These were Victor's Unspoiled Monsters.

And news came that the man held for Simon Beardsley's murder had been released after police evidence had fallen apart at his trial. It was suggested by the defence that forensics could have been contaminated as one of the arresting officers had been present at the crime scene, a positive identification of the suspect was in some doubt, and the defendant was able to supply an alibi in the form of a CCTV tape of him attending a nightclub at the time of the crime. The case got most attention in the media for a comment made by the defendant on leaving the dock. Gary Kelly had announced to the waiting press pack outside, presumably thinking that he was now protected by the double jeopardy rule: 'Yeah, I done it.' The *Sunday Illustrated* ran an exclusive interview with TV VILLAIN GAZ KELLY (apparently he had found time to do some acting between his nefarious activities) in which he spouted no end of ghastly braggadocio.

I felt strangely envious of this ridiculous thug. He could admit to his crimes. He could boast of noble savagery, claim a revenge on the modern world that we all secretly long for. I couldn't admit to mine, could I? And who would be interested? My sordid little secrets. I hadn't been a particularly successful psychopath. I'd got away with it, that was all.

And I had a job to do. I was *truecrime*'s faithful amanuensis, recording the sins of others. I would judge the readers' thirst for evil by the dryness of my own palate. I still had a taste for it. As I researched Harry Starks' story, the secret of what Eddie was up to with this girl Julie, what Piers had alluded to, nagged at me. Then it came to me quite by chance. I'd spent all day at the Newspaper Library in Colindale checking a few facts, near snow-blind from hours spent straining my eyes in the white light from the microfilm reading machine. I was looking at the reports on the Costa del Sol murders and there was a photograph in the *Daily Mirror*, a snatch shot of Jock McCluskey's wife and daughter coming out of their house. The wife was covering her face but the daughter had been caught with her full face into the lens, looking bewildered but with a half-smile on her face as if unable to stop herself posing for the camera. A ten-year-old girl stared out at me. The picture quality was poor but there was something about that face. The caption gave her name as Julie.

It's a complicated process confirming somebody's real name with their stage name. Equity has a register but they have rules of confidentiality. I knew someone from my *Sunday Illustrated* days who specialised in this sort of thing. It took him a couple of days but I was sure now that Eddie and this girl really were up to something: Julie Kincaid and Julie McCluskey were the same person.

I'd arranged to have another drink with Piers. I wanted to pitch the Starks book to Victor and I thought that he might be a good go-between since relations between me and Groombridge had completely broken down.

Piers had just come from a casting session when we met. He seemed possessed by some intense manic energy that was quite disturbing. Some sort of horrible animation. Pop-eyed with pinprick pupils, his mandible mechanically clenching and twitching. Cocaine, I concluded. The drug for ventriloquists' dummies.

They had just hired this goon Kelly to play a heavy in this moronic film of theirs.

'It's great, Tony,' he jabbered gleefully. 'We've got a real villain playing a villain.'

'And I don't suppose all of this publicity over the murder case will do any harm.'

'No. Not at all. Quite the reverse, I reckon. I've already got him doing a column for *Sorted*. He's got a lot of great stories.'

'Well, I've got a really good story, Piers. I want you to let Victor know that I've got something big for him.'

'Yeah, yeah.' He nodded. 'Sure.'

He grinned like an idiot. His mouth an awful rictus. I could tell that he wasn't really listening.

'Of course,' I went on, 'your co-producer, Julie Kincaid, well, she's got a really good story, don't you think?'

'Not half.'

He looked around, his burnt-out eyes scanning the room distractedly.

'I mean what with her father being murdered.'

'Yeah.' He continued chewing. 'Terrible.'

'Don't you think that you could use that?' I asked him.

'Well, I've been trying, on the quiet, mind. It would be a terrific angle. But you know what women are like.'

'No,' I said emphatically.

'What?'

His face froze into a frown for a second.

'I have *no* idea what women are like,' I insisted.

He broke into a spasmodic giggle.

'No,' he squealed. 'Neither do I.'

It was time to confront Eddie. We met for lunch at an Italian restaurant in Frith Street.

'You've been avoiding me, Eddie,' I said as we made our way through the main course.

'Now, now, Tony,' he chided me. 'I've been busy. You know that.'

'You certainly have, Eddie. So have I.'

He put his knife and fork down and glared at me.

'What the fuck are you on about now?' he demanded.

'I know,' I said.

'You know what, exactly?'

'I know about you and this girl.'

'You . . .'

'And I know who she is.'

'Let me tell you something.'

'It's quite a story, Eddie.'

'You don't know nothing, Tony.'

'Oh, I don't blame you. A young attractive girl like that.'

'Just shut up!' he hissed.

'And her old man done in by our friend Mr Starks.'

Eddie drew himself up suddenly. His chair scraped back, cutlery clattered, a wineglass tipped over. The room was alerted to the commotion and turned as one in our direction. A waiter came over.

'Is everything all right, sir?' he demanded.

Eddie slowly sat back down.

'Yeah,' he muttered. 'No problem.'

He looked at me across the table. Nostrils flared slightly. Blue-grey eyes full of contempt. I shrugged.

'I'm sorry,' I said. 'I just want to know what's going on, that's all.'

'What do you get out of all this?'

'You've lost me now, Eddie.'

'Snooping around. It's just another story to you, isn't it?'

'Well, that is the general idea, Eddie, yes.'

'There are other kinds of stories, you know. Good stories.'

'Oh yes. Happy ever after. All that. Spare me the details. You promised me an ending of a different sort. I want to know what it is now.'

'You're sick, you know that?'

'Yes I do, actually.'

'What?'

'I'm not a normal person, Eddie. I've never had a normal feeling in my life. I've led a vicarious life. Always watching. Never taking part.'

'What are you talking about?'

'I'm trying to explain. I'm sorry if I'm a little insensitive to this, um, affair with this girl. It's just that I don't . . .' I sighed. 'Well, I've never . . .'

I made a futile gesture with my hands. Eddie stared at me.

'You've never . . .' He frowned. 'You've never had a relationship?'

I laughed out loud.

'A relationship? Isn't that a wonderful word? No, not in the way that you mean.'

'I don't believe you. You must have.'

'Oh, I've tried to, you know.' My mind flashed memories of those awful moments. 'I did some things in the past but you couldn't call them normal.'

Eddie shook his head sadly.

'That's . . .'

'Tragic? No. It's a joke. My whole life's a fucking joke. I don't want your pity, Eddie. I've enjoyed your company. It's been exhilarating. But it's been an arrangement. That's all I can deal with really. Arrangements. And if an arrangement gets broken, well, it really upsets my world. Don't you see?'

Eddie sighed. Shrugged.

'I guess.'

'Now, you're up to something with this Julie. Let me rephrase that. You have made some sort of arrangement with her. Yes?'

'I'm in love with her, Tony.'

'Hmm.' I nodded, trying my hardest to look understanding.

'You know what happened to her dad. Well, she wants justice for that.'

'Really?'

'So the plan is that we arrange a meet with Starks to collect the gold and he gets handed over to the police.'

'He's a dangerous man, Eddie.'

'I know that. I can handle him.'

'And the gold?'

'I've made a deal with Frank Taylor. It's going back. The lot of it.'

'You really are in love with her, aren't you?'

'Yeah. And I'm sick of the bullion. It's destroyed too many people's lives. So you can be there, Tony. When they take Starks. You can have your story after all.'

8
the night shoot

I fell in love with Eddie though I hadn't really meant to. It took me by surprise, which is what it should do, I suppose. All my life had seemed foretold up until this point, determined by a fixed narrative. But love is a random event. At first he was just part of the plan, just another person I was using, another player in the drama. Then it happened. I found out that I really did like being in his company, I could relax with him. I think Eddie was the first person in my life I could truly be myself with. There had been so much deception in the past, I'd always had to put on such a front to the outside world. But when we were together, just me and Eddie, it was like we were hiding from them, not from each other. I felt safe with him. Safe enough to be me.

We tried to tell each other everything, and we both had a lot to let go of. All those years in prison had taken their toll on Eddie. But it was like we had both been released. So many things that I'd never said to anyone. So many issues I could talk through, just as I was supposed to have done in those counselling sessions. But this wasn't therapy. This was love.

And I really didn't want to think about me and him in these modern analytical terms. I knew how some professional might see it, you know, that my affection for Eddie was the need for a sort of father substitute or something. But it wasn't that. Besides, Eddie was nothing like Dad. There was something familial between us, we were connected to each other's pasts in a way. And I mean, Ruby had been like an aunt to me. But I saw nothing incestuous in how I felt about Eddie. My Electra complex was classical, not Freudian. I simply wanted revenge for my father. I wasn't looking for any other kind of motivation, but it bothered me, I'd made no allowances for something like this happening. And when I found myself wanting him I was scared. Scared of some twisted psychology inside of me maybe, but mostly scared of weakness. I didn't want to let go of my anger. I needed it. And I didn't want to feel that I was somehow making up for the absence of Dad. There was only one thing that could do that.

But I gave in to Eddie. He loved me with such a passion. It was overwhelming at first, then I felt it fire something inside of me. Something real. I'd never felt like this before. Love had been about superficial attraction, determined desire for what I felt I should feel. It had made sense. I had wanted Jez because he was the sort of boy I had wanted to want. I didn't want to want Eddie. It didn't make sense. It just happened.

And it wasn't only emotional love. I found I desired Eddie physically as well. Jez had a commodity of good looks but there was something bland and milk-fed about him. A gym-toned body, the inevitable musculature of repetitious exercise. His physical hardness meant nothing, a duplication of images from *GQ* or *Men's Health* magazines. Even his scar had healed into a perfect ellipse, like a design feature. Eddie really was hard but his body was soft and lithe. He was peppered with marks, scribbled with lines, pushing sixty but still in good shape. Prison had kept him thin, there was a sprightliness about him, an agility retained from his cat-burglaring days. A sad smile in his gauntly handsome face that could break my heart. And he had style, not flashness, not this new-lad affectation, but a sombre elegance, an *éminence grise*.

But with me he was self-conscious about his body, about his age. He recoiled from my touch sometimes, drew in to himself. But I wanted to see him. To know him.

One night after we had made love I put on the light and drew back the sheets.

'What are you doing?' he asked.

'Let me look at you.'

'Julie . . .'

I traced my fingers along his weathered skin. Marbled with broken veins and liver spots.

'For Christ sakes, girl, I'm an old man.'

I brushed my lips along the contours of his ribcage.

'You're my old man,' I said.

'I'm your lucky old man.'

'Tell me a story,' I urged him.

'I'm tired, babe.'

'Go on.'

'I don't know. I've told you all my best ones.'

'Then make something up.'

'Well . . .' He sighed.

'What?'

'Put the light out, darling. It's hurting my eyes.'

I found the switch. The room went back to near-darkness. Just a milky wash from the street lights outside.

'I was thinking about something,' Eddie went on.

'What?'

'A story. I only remember the beginning bit.'

'Tell me.'

'It's in *The Thousand and One Nights*. I only know the start of it. This fisherman finds a bottle, right? He opens it up and whoosh! This bloody great genie comes out of it. And this genie says: "Right, you're done for, little man," and the fisherman goes: "Please don't kill me! How come you want to kill me when I've just released you from this bottle?" And the genie explains that he's been trapped in the bottle for three hundred years. And he says that in the first hundred years he vowed that whoever set him free he would give eternal riches to. A hundred years passed and no one came. In the second hundred years of his imprisonment the genie promised that he would open up all the buried treasures of the earth to the person who would free him. Still no one came. Then after three hundred years this genie had had enough. He was full of rage and anger. He said: "Fuck this! I'm going to kill the first fucker who sets me free." So . . .'

Eddie paused. A siren wailed in the distance.

'Yeah?' I whispered.

'Well, that's it.'

'What happened to the fisherman?'

'I don't remember. I was just thinking about the first bit of the story. About what happens to the genie when he's trapped in that bottle all those years. It just reminds me of being inside. At first you can kid yourself it's OK. I can do the time, you think. I can do five, no problem. Then you get a parole knock-back. Then another. All your optimism about life gets burned out of you. By the time you get out you're just full of bitterness and hatred about everybody. It's like it's too late, you know, your release date never really comes. All your feelings are still banged up. The time to feel good about things has gone.'

'And is that how you feel?'

'It's how I used to feel, Julie. I scarcely even knew how much anger I had inside of me. It was like it had gone solid or something. I never thought that I'd feel properly happy again. Until . . .' There was a catch in his voice. He swallowed. 'Until I met you.'

He reached out to me in the darkness. I touched his face. It was wet with tears.

'You let me out,' he said. 'You set me free proper.'

He kissed me.

'And I want to give you all the buried treasures of the earth for that.'

'You don't want to kill me, then?' I asked.

Eddie laughed.

'No, I don't,' he said. Then his voice went flat and cold all of a sudden. 'I want to kill someone else.'

'Shh,' I said, holding him close to me.

There was something that I wasn't telling him. I didn't tell him that I meant to kill Harry Starks. I really didn't want to keep anything from Eddie but I knew that I couldn't tell him that. He would try to stop me. Or worse. He would try to do it himself. Another spell in prison would kill him. What would I get? Life with a recommendation to serve fifteen, at the worst. Life, that's what I'd be getting. My own life back. It didn't matter if I had to spend some of it in Holloway.

But I knew this would upset Eddie. He might not go along with the plan at all if he knew how it would all end. And I needed to get to Starks. So we agreed that the plan was to hand over Starks once we had lured him back into the country. And it was all nearly set up now. We had found the place, the warehouse where the gold was hidden. Eddie had done a deal with the retired policeman who was working for the insurers. All we had to do was convince Jez to use it as a location.

My relationship with Jez held together all through this time. I had to make it work, somehow. I couldn't afford to let it fall apart, not now. Everything had to run smoothly. So I had to be very secretive and arrange things carefully. Piers was suspicious, which didn't help at all, but Jez was busy covering up his own infidelity and struggling to keep up the façade. He was never as good at lying as I was.

We still had sex. And it was good in an efficient, workout sort of way. I detected something competitive about it now. Maybe it had always been there and I'd just not noticed it before. I still ended up on top, though. Jez would put up a fight but I knew that was what he liked. I suspected that frail little Georgina didn't quite indulge him like this.

Eddie didn't like the fact that I was still sleeping with Jez. I tried to talk about it with him but it didn't help things. I couldn't explain to Eddie that what we had was deeper and more real than what passed between me and Jez. It was about understanding, but I couldn't put it into words. Then it came to me: the way that in the Bible 'to know' is used to describe sex. That was how I felt with Eddie. It was pure knowledge. It was something that he and nobody else could give to me. I'd been knowing all my life, I'd had to be. But now I was known. It was wonderful to be known.

And I wanted to talk to Jez, he had a right to know about me too. I resolved that as soon as I could I would tell him. It wouldn't be long now. In the meantime we carried on with the happy deceptions of many a young couple. I still found affection for him and he still needed me, for support more than anything else. Not just all the practical stuff but emotional support as well. He had all sorts of anxieties and doubts about the film and we were coming up to the time when it would be up to him to come up with the goods. I got the impression that this girl of his was a little too demanding of him. You know, I actually worried that she wasn't right for him.

Finally I had got to understand Jez properly. I suppose I felt detached and less annoyed with him than I had in the past. When I'd gone through the script again, as Piers had suggested, it struck me how often the insults in it had to do with sexuality. It was full of men calling each other 'faggots' or 'poofs'; at one point a character talked of ''aving me pants pulled down'. At first I simply thought, well, public school homophobia, what a dead give-away. But then I realised it made sense in relation to this 'crisis of masculinity' and the 'feminisation of culture' some of the broadsheet pundits had been going on about. It was something Piers could vaguely articulate, though he much preferred to pretend to enjoy talking about football or the semiotics of action movies. I had thought that this crisis in masculinity was all a bit of a joke. I thought of Dad's generation, his world – they could have done with some of that. It would have seemed a luxury.

But Jez didn't intellectualise, he was an instinctive embodiment of these contemporary ideas. Maybe that was where the heart of his talent really lay. I got to know that he acted hard because of a crushing sensitivity that he had to hide from the world. In the time leading up to shooting he opened up to me about his schooldays. He'd been a nervous, pretty little teenager. Because of his dyslexia he'd had to attend special classes. Other boys called him 'spaz' or 'Special Needs Scott'. Even the teachers had made jokes at his expense. All the arrogance of the working class over-achiever that I was had meant that I had failed to see that he'd had a hard time too. And *Scrapyard Bulldog* was to be his revenge as well as mine. Revenge against all of the people who had taunted him and put him down. Revenge of the middle-class thick kid.

We went to see the warehouse. Me, Jez, Piers and Eddie. I was really nervous that Jez wouldn't like it. He didn't say anything for a long time. He walked about the place, looking at it from different angles. He stared up at the light that streamed in from the broken skylights, diffusing through the motes of dust that hung in the air. He stood in the middle of it and looked around once more. He nodded slowly.

'It's great,' he declared.

'Isn't it just?' muttered Eddie wryly.

'We can do at least three of the main interior set-ups in here,' Jez was telling Piers.

I caught Eddie's eye. He saw the look of relief on my face and gave me a wink.

'So, what's the deal on this place?' Jez asked.

'Well . . .' Eddie shrugged. 'We've approached the agents managing it. Cutthroat Productions could get it for a very reasonable rent.'

'Yeah?'

'Yeah. So what do you think?'

Eddie looked across at me nervously.

'I think we use it,' said Jez.

I winked at Eddie. Jez was still in his own world, walking around, lining up shots.

'It's fantastic,' he said, his blue eyes twitching with ideas.

We were nearly ready to shoot and he had come alive after months of brooding. I was happy for him.

Scrapyard Bulldog started filming on 2 September 1996. The first action to be shot was a poker game scene. This was Ruby Ryder's cameo as the card dealer Ladyfingers. The set was in the warehouse and it was not much more than a huge green baize table with lampshades suspended above it.

There was a real buzz on-set when Ruby arrived. She'd never been a big star but she had this very British sort of fame. She was an icon of sorts, and I knew that I had been right in suggesting her for the part. She could bring just the right sort of charisma to the film. Some of the cast and crew came up to her during lunch asking for autographs. She joked about it.

'I'm a cult,' she announced loudly in that camp way of hers. 'I'm a complete cult.'

A handsome but nervous young man was escorting her when she arrived. His name was Greg. She got me to look after him.

'Met him doing panto,' she explained to me.

'He seems nice.'

She sighed.

'Oh, he is, darling. Too nice. He's a sweet, sensitive boy. It was lovely when we first started seeing each other but it's hard for him. He has to deal with this larger-than-life persona of mine. He hasn't been getting the work lately and you know what that can do to your confidence at the best of times. I'm worried that I'm cutting his balls off. It doesn't help Eddie being here either.'

'You knew he was a consultant on the film.'

'Yeah, but I didn't know he was going to be on the set, did I?'

Ruby and Eddie cautiously approached each other. Little signals, polite nods and tentative greetings. Then Eddie broke into a huge grin, threw his arms open wide and with a hug kissed her on both cheeks.

'You look fantastic, Ruby,' he said.

Ruby tensed a little in his embrace then smiled and let her shoulders drop.

'Yeah, yeah,' she said. 'Mind the make-up.'

I must confess I felt a tiny twinge of jealousy seeing them both laughing together. I'd seen photographs of them as a couple back in the sixties. They had both looked so glamorous back then.

The set was lit and a smoke machine started up.

'Oh, this is atmospheric,' enthused Ruby, then hissed out of the side of her mouth at me: 'Ain't exactly big-budget, is it?'

But she never complained out loud. She was a professional of the old school. Always smiling, never being difficult or superior.

A real card sharp was used to do the close-ups of the fanning and shuffling of the cards in the scene. This dealer was a man but his hands had been made up and dagger-sharp bright pink false nails applied to the ends of his fingers. Ruby came off the set and we chatted together.

'Well, Eddie looks happy,' she said.

'Yes, I suppose so.'

'No, I mean really. I've never seen him so happy. Not since . . .'

She looked me in the eye.

'What's going on?' she asked.

'What do you mean?'

'I mean, I saw the way he looked at you earlier. And it reminded me of something. I remember he once looked at me like that.'

Just at that moment Piers came over.

'We've got a problem with the dealer,' he told me.

'What?'

'We need to shave his forearms.'

'What?'

'They're too hairy.'

Ruby giggled.

'Well, get them shaved, then,' I said.

'Yeah, but . . .'

'What?'

'Well, I haven't asked him yet. I wonder if you could.'

'Oh, for Christ's sake.'

'I just thought it would be be better coming from you.'

I sighed.

'OK,' I agreed. 'I'll be over in a minute.'

'And try and make sure he doesn't ask for extra for it,' Piers called out as he walked away.

'Ruby,' I muttered.

'Look, I should mind my own business. But something's going on, isn't it?'

I shrugged, nodded.

'Well, he's still a charmer.'

Yes, I thought. *But it was me that charmed him.*

'He's trouble, you know,' she said.

No he's not. I'm trouble.

We wrapped around eight that evening. It had been a good day's work and a good start to the film. Ruby's presence had really lifted everyone's spirits. There was a sense of occasion about the shoot. A strange feeling that we could actually be on to something.

Jez congratulated Ruby as she was leaving the set. He looked awe-struck.

'Thank you so much, Ruby,' he said. 'You were fantastic.'

His voice was all polite and posh for once; he really looked quite sweet.

I walked her and Greg out to their car.

'Look, dear,' she said to me as Greg walked on ahead. 'I didn't mean to pry.'

'It's all right.'

'I mean, I'm one to talk with my toyboy here.' She nodded at Greg, who was out of earshot. 'He's thirty-two, you know. Looks younger, doesn't he?'

'Ruby . . .'

'Yes, dear.'

'Don't tell Mum. Not yet.'

'I wouldn't dream of it, darling. Just you be careful with that one, that's all.'

'Of course I will,' I lied.

Scrapyard Bulldog was shot on a tight schedule. Everyone involved on it was working hard for little money and few creature comforts. Early mornings and occasional night shoots at the warehouse. Jez was using all sorts of special effects and state-of-the-art camera tricks he'd learned from doing adverts and pop promos, over-cranked and under-cranked steadicam shots. Most of the action seemed either to be speeded up or in slow motion, gaudy colours awash with a dirty brown filter. Characters were established by freeze-frame and voice-over. The dialogue pattered in staccato cross-over, like music-hall routine. Piers had been right, it was shaping up as a knockabout comedy with glossy slapstick ultra-violence. But it moved along with a twitchy, juvenile exuberance that made up for what it lacked in substance with pure flash.

The acting, such as there was any, was of variable quality. Joe Patterson's performance had a gravitas that was unfortunately entirely out of place with everything around him. There was far too much naturalism in what he was doing, it looked like a real character had found himself in the middle of a cartoon. I suspected that his heart wasn't really in it. I watched him struggle with the script, vainly trying to find something that he could believe in. Most of the rest of the cast looked like male models on a particularly frenetic fashion shoot with guns as designer accessories. Resplendent in Crombies, suits and Gabicci polo shirts that never seemed to get messed up despite all the mayhem around them. Again Piers was right – this look was tailor made for the new-lad audience the film would be courting. A paean to power dressing and male grooming, they would see more glamorous versions of themselves on-screen, it would be sexy for them, a swaggering advertisement for their deep dreams of sartorial brutality.

But the real surprise of the film was Gaz Kelly, who played the heavy. When we looked at the rushes something astonishing came across in his portrayal of Big Lenny. There was a luminosity in his presence, as if he was lit from within. A real coruscating rage that leapt out of the celluloid at you. It was a stylised performance but instinctive too. A heightened super-realism, an exaggerated choreography of menace that was somehow persuasive and convincing, like Cagney or something. He wasn't great at delivering lines but his physicality drew your attention like a magnet.

There had been some worries about casting Kelly. He had a real criminal past and had only just been released from prison after being acquitted on a murder charge. But Piers was sure that this could only be good publicity for the film. 'Authenticity,' he insisted, for the millionth time.

Eddie was less convinced by Gaz's villainous credentials.

'He ain't really one of the chaps,' he commented. 'Talks himself up. More of a wannabe, if you ask me.'

'Maybe that's it,' I said, suddenly knowing why Gaz worked so well on screen. 'He's been playing at it all his life. That's why he comes across so well.'

Eddie and I didn't have much time to be together during the filming at the warehouse. And we had to concentrate on the plan. He had found where he thought the gold was buried. There was a mismatched patch of cement on part of the floor that he had gone over with a metal detector one night when the warehouse was deserted. Once the shooting was finished we'd meet with Starks there and dig it up.

We were rapidly approaching what Jez would call the denouement.

Jez was absorbed in his work, walking around in almost a trance state. I found myself being close to him throughout. We had become used to each other and could work side by side with a quiet unspoken understanding. But I wanted to settle my account with him somehow, I owed him that much.

After the final day's filming at the warehouse I went back with him. We were burned out and over-tired but ended up having energetic sex until the small hours. There was a sense of release, a feeling of abandonment, of letting go.

'I need to tell you something,' I said afterwards.

'I'm really tired, babe,' he groaned.

'This is important,' I insisted. 'I'll get you a drink. You're going to need it.'

I got a bottle of wine from the fridge and poured us both a glass. I sat on the edge of the bed.

'You know my real name's McCluskey,' I began.

'Yeah.'

'You ever wonder who my father was?'

'You never really talk about him, just the car accident.' He sat up in the bed. 'What's all this about, Julie?'

'My dad was from Glasgow.'

I sighed. I didn't know how to tell this story. I didn't really want to, to be honest, I just wanted Jez to know. So I picked up the true crime book *London Underworld* from the side of his bed, found the reference to Dad and handed it to him.

'That's my dad,' I told him, pointing at the relevant passage.

Jez read slowly, tracing each word with a finger, frowning at the text.

'It's all there,' I said. '"Big Jock" McCluskey. Like one of your bloody characters. No mention of me or Mum, of course. But no one's very much interested in that, are they?'

Jez looked up from the book, his face agape with wonder and curiosity.

'You?'

'Yeah, me.'

'Why didn't you tell me before?'

'I might have done if things had been different. I've been trying to get away from this darkness all my life. Then I find that my nice middle-class boyfriend is obsessed with it. It's hardly reassuring for a girl, you know.'

'But you said you liked the film. You got involved in it, for Christ's sake.'

'*Scrapyard Bulldog* doesn't exactly bear much relation to reality, Jez.'

'You don't think it's any good?'

I laughed. It was so typical of him to be thinking about his stupid movie even at this moment.

'It's not the real thing,' I told him. 'But who on earth would be interested in the real thing? I wanted you to succeed, Jez, that's why I helped out. And I think you will. They'll all fall for it just like you have.'

I started to get dressed.

'There's something I need to do now. I'm going to go.'

Jez sat up in bed.

'I worried about you, you know,' he said.

'I know you did.'

'I knew something was up. But you never talked to me. I wish you'd talked to me.'

'I'm sorry.'

He pouted sulkily.

'It's not nice to be lied to.'

'Well, we haven't exactly been telling the truth to each other for a while, have we? I know about Georgina.'

'What?'

'Oh yeah.'

'I can explain about that.'

'Please, Jez. It doesn't matter. I don't blame you. Though I don't think she's right for you, somehow. A nice posh bird like I used to want to be. But a bit drippy. You need a strong woman in your life. Someone older maybe.'

As I got ready to leave Jez followed me about the flat in a bewildered state.

'So,' he said. 'So, what happens now?'

'I told you. I'm leaving. This is goodbye, Jez. Good luck with it all.'

I got to the door and turned to look at him one last time. Blue eyes staring helplessly. Little boy lost.

'You'll be all right, Jez,' I said, and kissed him on the cheek.

On the way over to Eddie's I thought: that's it, I'm saying goodbye to people. I thought about Mum, about explaining things to her. But she would understand, I reasoned. I was doing this partly for her, after all, but then my stomach sank suddenly and I realised I was scared. But this was a useful fear, like stage fright. It would keep me focused.

```
INT. A WAREHOUSE. NIGHT.
P.O.V. from above. EDDIE is standing in a pool of
light. Sound of warehouse door opening, footsteps.
We see a shadow of a man at first, then HARRY STARKS
enters, stepping into the light.
                        HARRY
        Well, this is atmospheric, isn't it?
```

I can't help seeing it like this. I accused Jez of a lack of realism and here I am losing it myself. I've got to concentrate. I'm hidden in the darkness, up above on a gantry by a loading bay. The set hasn't been completely dismantled yet and we've used one of the film lights to illuminate the building. So the place does look theatrical, cinematic. I'm waiting in the wings. Waiting for my cue. I feel I should be meditating clearly on the matter at hand, not lost in the illusion of it. Maybe it's all this time I've been spending on this bloody film. It's got to me. But maybe that's how I'm going to cope with this. A sense of detachment so that I can go through with it . . .

'Yeah,' Eddie replied. 'We've been using this place for a film.'

'Was that the cover, then?'

'Something like that.'

'I've parked the van outside. Is it here, then?'

'Well, we'll soon find out, won't we?'

Eddie had marked out a rectangle on the mismatched patch of cement where the metal detector indicated the gold might be. He lifted a pickaxe.

'We're going to have to do it by hand, I'm afraid,' he said. 'You want to start?'

Starks shrugged. Eddie handed him the pickaxe.

'About time you got your hands dirty,' he said.

They set to work, digging. Taking it in turns to break up the cement with the pickaxe. Pulling out chunks of it by hand. When the hole was big enough they went at it with a spade as well. I don't know how much time passed but finally Eddie stopped and called out.

'Hold up!'

He lay on the ground and reached into the hole. He pulled at something. It wouldn't budge. He got up again and pointed at a certain part of the excavations.

'Give that bit another whack,' he said.

And Starks swung the pickaxe down. This time Eddie reached down and pulled what looked like a brick at first.

'Shit,' he groaned. 'I'd forgotten how much these things weighed.'

He brushed the dust off it and it gleamed as it caught the light.

'Fuck me,' Starks gasped.

They set to work pulling out the rest of it.

'Nobody else knows about this, do they?' Starks asked.

Eddie shook his head.

'They're all dead, Harry.'

'Is that the lot?'

'Looks like it.'

'Right. Well, let's get it loaded up in the van.'

When they had finished Starks brought a hold-all into the warehouse and dropped it on the floor.

'You want to count it?' he asked Eddie.

'I'll have a look,' he replied.

He crouched down, unzipped the bag and had a rummage inside.

'Looks about right,' he said.

Starks grinned.

'All in a day's work. Well, Eddie, that's about it, then.'

He moved towards Eddie with his hand out. Eddie pulled out his gun and pointed it at him.

'Not quite, Harry.'

'What the fuck?'

His hands instinctively went up in front of him.

'Keep those hands up.'

'Stop fucking around.'

'I'm quite serious, Harry.'

Starks sighed and shook his head.

'Oh, Eddie. We're both too old for this carry-on.'

Eddie reached into the front of Starks' jacket. He pulled out a pistol.

'Well, we both came prepared, didn't we, Harry?' he said, backing slowly away from him.

'Look, let's talk this through.'

'Now the keys, Harry.'

'You what?'

'The van keys. Throw them over here.'

Starks tossed them over and they chimed on the concrete floor.

'You're making a big mistake, Eddie. You won't get away with this.'

'I don't plan to.'

'What?'

'You'll find out. There's someone here who wants a word.'

That was my cue. I came down the stairs and walked towards the light. I got my first good look at Starks. From above, with thick shadow framing him, he had seemed impressive. Close up under the light's glare he looked worn out. He hadn't aged as well as Eddie. His face had sagged and gone puffy around the eyes. There was a haunted look about him. I'd been ready to meet a monster but here I was face to face with just a sad old man.

'This is Julie,' Eddie announced. 'Julie McCluskey.'

'Oh yeah?'

I had to clear my mind of any feelings of sympathy or empathy. I had to concentrate on how ruthless he had been.

'You don't even know who I am, do you?' I demanded. 'I don't suppose you remember.'

'Sorry, love, I haven't had the pleasure. Look, Eddie, can you tell me what the fuck is going on?'

Eddie handed me Starks' gun and fished in his pocket for his mobile phone. He started to call up the ex-cop Taylor and this journalist Tony I'd met at the offices that time to tell them we were ready. I pointed the pistol at Starks. It would be good to kill him with his own gun, I thought.

'Look, darling, do you mind not pointing that thing at me?'

'Shut up,' I said, feeling the weight of it, steadying it with both hands. 'I want you to think very carefully. I want you to remember what you did.'

'I don't know what you're talking about, darling,' he said.

'Well, just have a think, eh?'

He frowned at me. Eddie had finished talking into the phone. He switched it off and put it back in his pocket.

'They're on their way,' he said.

'Who are? Some team you've got waiting to have me over? I didn't think that was your style, Ed.'

'This is even less like my style. You see, I'm handing the gold back.'

'Back? What do you mean back?'

'To who it belongs to.'

'You silly cunt. What do you want to go and do that for?'

'Just doing the right thing for once.'

Starks started laughing.

'Oh, fuck me, Eddie, now you really are having a laugh.'

'Yeah. And here's something even funnier. We're going to hand you up and all.'

'Now wait a minute . . .'

'You see, this is Julie McCluskey. You know, Jock's daughter?'

Starks went wide eyed and open mouthed for a second. He stared at me.

'Fuck,' he rasped under his breath.

'Yeah,' I said. 'Just another of your victims. I've had to live all my life under the shadow of what you did to my father. I want you to think about that.'

'And you're going to hand me up for that? Well, listen . . .'

'No,' I said. 'You listen. We're not going to hand you up.' I steadied the gun again, pointing it at his incredulous face. 'I'm going to kill you.'

'Julie!' Eddie exclaimed.

'Just like you did Dad.'

'Julie,' said Eddie. 'Wait a second.'

I knew that with every moment of delay it would become harder to pull the trigger. But I wanted him to know what he had done before I killed him.

'I want you to think about it. You ruined my life, Harry Starks.'

'Put the gun down, Julie,' Eddie was saying.

'No. This is how it's done, isn't it? No going to the police or worrying about the implications of killing another human being. This was the way it was done, wasn't it?'

'Julie, they're going to be here any minute,' Eddie went on. 'Put the gun down, for Christ's sake.'

'Oh, I don't worry about being caught. I don't mind going to prison for this. I just want him to know what he did and why he's going to die for it.'

At that moment Starks lunged forward. Eddie turned and kicked his legs from under him. Starks tumbled to the floor on all fours.

'Sorry about that, Harry,' said Eddie. 'Julie, please, don't do this.'

'Shut up, Eddie. I want my fucking own back.' I pointed the gun at the crawling figure on the ground. 'You stay down there,' I told him.

'Jesus fucking Christ!' Starks spat out, looking up at me. 'Look, girl, I didn't fucking do it!'

I needed him to admit what he had done. I needed to hear it from his own lips.

'Liar!' I shouted. 'You took my life away from me. Now you're going to pay for it.'

Starks rocked back on to his knees and rubbed his hands. He shook his head.

'Well, go on, then, girl. Shoot me,' he said with a shrug.

'Julie, please,' Eddie implored.

I aimed the pistol at his head. *Shoot him*, I thought. But I wanted him to break down and confess and he wasn't doing that.

'But I'm not the one that killed your dad,' Starks went on.

'I don't believe you.'

'Then shoot me. Get it over with. I'm a dead man anyway.'

I started to imagine what it would be like to shoot somebody. Would it be like a Tarantino film or those weird violent Japanese gangster movies Jez was so keen on? It would be easier imagining it like that than facing the real horror of it. But then I'd be doing just what I had criticised Jez for, glorifying violence. Was that what I was doing? No, no, I thought, I musn't start to feel doubt now. Just do it, not think about it, just get it over with. Just then Taylor and Tony came into the warehouse.

'What the fuck's going on here?' the ex-cop demanded with a shocked look on his face.

The journalist stood by with a bemused smile.

'She wants to kill me,' Starks announced.

'Things have got a bit out of hand,' Eddie explained.

'I just want you to admit it,' I said to Starks.

'But I wouldn't be telling the truth, darling.'

Taylor edged his way towards me.

'Now steady on, girl,' he said. 'Admit what, exactly?'

'That he killed my father.'

'Who?'

'Jock McCluskey.'

'I didn't do it,' Starks insisted.

'Big Jock?' the ex-cop demanded. 'You're Big Jock's daughter?'

'Yeah,' I said. 'Have a big gawp, the lot of you. I'm Little Julie. I'm the one that was robbed of a dad and paid off with stage school fees. What was that about?'

'It was what your mother wanted.'

'What was it? Guilt? Compensation for what you did?'

'Wait a minute,' Taylor said.

'It was nothing like that. Jock was on the firm. It was like a responsibility.'

'Responsibility? You don't know the meaning of the word.'

'Hold on,' Taylor went on.

'I want you to understand what responsibility is. Admit it.'

'He didn't kill your dad,' said Taylor.

'What?' I demanded.

'Just calm down a second and let me explain.'

'Who the fuck are you anyway?' Starks asked.

'Frank Taylor. I used to be in the Job. Remember? We met a couple of times.'

Starks squinted at him.

'You worked for Vic Sayles?'

'Yeah. And I was part of the team that put you away in '69.'

'Thanks a lot.'

'My pleasure. Got a commendation for that.'

'Sorry to interrupt the reunion, gentlemen,' I said. 'But you say he didn't kill my father. How do you know?'

'Well, I worked with George Mooney, too. He was the retired detective that got killed about the same time as your father.'

'Yeah, I know about him. Go on.'

'I worked with him on an internal investigation into corruption amongst officers in South London. The Operation Skeleton inquiry. It was a cover-up, we wanted to avoid more widespread hookiness being brought out into the open, you know, this "firm within a firm" thing, and we managed to restrict the inquiry to three detectives low down the scale who were going to take the fall for it. Thing is, there was this one guy, a detective sergeant called O'Neill. He didn't want to duck his nut and threatened to start coughing up all sorts of nasty stories. So Mooney organised him being paid off to skip the country. Ended up in Morocco for a while then the Costa del Sol when the extradition was dropped. Did a bit of business with Mooney when he went out there on retirement. Anyway, O'Neill comes back in the eighties and gives himself up. Did a bit of bird. He had all sorts of stories. And one of them was that it was Mooney that had Jock McCluskey killed and pinned it on Harry here.'

'How do you know he was telling the truth?'

Taylor shrugged.

'Well, he did have a grudge against the Met, that was for sure, but certain details he gave us, that no one else could have known about, tallied with the investigation done by the Spanish police. But no one wanted to dig it all up again, it wouldn't have looked good. So we stuck to the official line, that Starks had done it.'

'Thanks a lot,' muttered Starks.

'Well, you did kill Mooney, after all,' said Taylor.

'I didn't even do that, mate.'

'Really? Then who . . . ?'

'You would never believe me if I told you.'

'That's enough!' I shouted. 'I don't believe this. I won't believe it.'

I lined up the gun again. My hands were trembling. Starks held his hands up in supplication. He looked like a demented holy martyr kneeling on the floor.

'Then shoot me,' he said. 'You might be doing me a favour.'

They were trying to take this away from me. I had to do it now. My finger quivered against the trigger.

'I'm a dead man anyway.'

'You said that before. What do you mean?'

'I got cancer. Inoperable. I got a year. Two maybe. It ain't going to be a pretty end. Might as well get it over with.' He sighed. 'To tell you the truth I'm sick of running. Always fancied dying on my native soil. I was born just up the road from here, you know.'

I started to shake.

'Julie,' Eddie said softly.

I let my arms drop. It wasn't fair. There would be no revenge now. No restitution. No meaning to it all. Just another unsolved crime. Another unsolved life.

'Why?' I started to sob. 'Why can't you be the man I want to kill?'

Tears came. Eddie walked over and put an arm around me.

'Shh,' he whispered. 'It's all right now.'

'No it's not!' I wailed. 'I can't be. It'll never be all right now.'

Harry Starks got up off the floor and brushed himself down. Eddie turned and pointed his gun at him.

'So what happens now? You want to take me in?' asked Starks.

'Julie?' Eddie asked.

'I just want you to go away,' I said to Starks.

'Frank?'

'I'm retired, Eddie. I don't need another commendation. I do want the gold, though.'

Eddie crouched down and picked up the van keys. He handed them to Taylor.

'Move the van somewhere else, could you? You know, so it can be officially recovered somewhere away from here. Don't want anyone implicated.'

'Right,' he said. 'Thanks, Eddie. See you, Harry.'

And he walked out.

'Well,' said Starks, making for the bag. 'I'll just get my things and be off.'

'Uh-uh.' Eddie held the gun up. 'I think that's mine.'

'Oh, be reasonable, Eddie.'

'I think I deserve it after all I've been through.'

Starks stood there, thinking for a minute. He shrugged.

'Well, let me have a little back. I'm a bit short, to tell you the truth.'

Eddie motioned with the pistol.

'Go on, then. Help yourself.'

Starks grabbed a couple of bundles of cash and stuffed them in his pockets.

'I had a set-up with the gold that could have tied me over until the end,' he said. 'Now all my Caribbean contacts are burned. I'm diving for scraps, if you want to know.'

'Where are you going to go now?' Eddie asked.

'Northern Cyprus, I guess. No extradition there. Look, Julie,' he said to me. 'I'm . . . I'm really sorry about your dad but . . .'

'It was all a long time ago.'

'What?'

'That was what you were going to say, wasn't it? That's what everyone says, don't they? It was all a long time ago. A lifetime. My lifetime.'

I looked at him. He had the weary look of a hunted man. But there was something about the eyes. They still burned with some kind of energy, the charm everybody had spoken of. But no, I wasn't going to fall for this. He might not have killed Dad but he'd certainly killed other people's fathers.

'Look, what I mean is . . .' he began.

'Please,' I cut in. 'Just go.'

'Right, then,' he said.

'Wait a minute,' Tony suddenly announced. 'You're not going to let him get away, are you?'

'Who's this fucker?' Starks demanded.

'What about my story?'

'He's a writer,' said Eddie.

Starks burst out laughing.

'A writer? That's a good one. Well, you've had a good story here tonight. Shame no one's going to believe you.'

He started to walk out. The clatter of the van starting up could be heard in the distance.

'Wait,' said Tony.

'Be lucky!' Starks called out as he left.

'Eddie?' Tony demanded.

'What are you going to do? Go after him?'

'But . . .'

'Leave it, Tony. It's over.'

Eddie took Starks' gun from me and put it in the bag. He zipped it up.

'Come on, sweetheart,' he said.

I wiped my face.

'What?'

'Let's go.'

'Go? Where am I going to go now?'

'Give me your gun, Eddie,' Tony was saying.

'What?'

'Give me the gun now and I'll be able to catch him. There's still time.'

'Don't be so ridiculous.'

I heard them argue behind me as I walked out of the warehouse. Nothing made sense any more. Where would I go now? I didn't know. I just started to walk. A purple dawn streaked the sky above the back streets of the East End. The morning star burned bright and low over the city.

'Julie!' Eddie called out after me.

But I just kept walking. I felt like a ghost, empty, lost in the yawning emptiness of the morning. What I'd imagined as tragedy had turned out as farce. A bad joke that echoed hollow with the pitiless laughter of comedy. I'd been so stupid. There was no ending, no resolution, no denouement. I thought that I was being so bloody clever but I'd ended up acting out what I thought I'd despised. I'd deluded myself that my life was some great classical drama and it had merely become like a scene in a cheap gangster movie.

I'd thought I'd had some answer, that I'd found a name for my pain. And now that had been taken away and only the pain remained. A rage had burned away inside me and it hadn't left much behind. What the hell was I supposed to do now?

I'd got to Victoria Park by the time Eddie caught up with me, carrying the bag. The sun was coming up behind the tower blocks of Hackney.

'Julie,' he panted, out of breath. 'Wait a minute.'

For a while we just walked together in silence.

'Hang on,' he said, after a while. 'Just got to do something.'

He went over to the canal and dumped the guns in the muddy water.

'Look,' he said when he came back. 'I don't expect you to feel . . .'

'Please, Eddie, not now.'

'I just want you to know that I love you.'

I didn't know what to say. I didn't know what I could feel about another person any more. And what could my feelings towards Eddie mean now? Maybe that was part of the problem, too, maybe it was just me clinging to the past I thought I wanted to escape from, maybe that was why I, too, had wanted some of this stupid 'authenticity'.

'There's a fair bit of cash here, babe. We could maybe, you know, make a new start somewhere.'

'A start?'

'Yeah, you know.'

'I can't make any plans, Eddie. My life isn't just going to start somewhere. I don't know who I am any more or what I'm going to do, for God's sake.'

'I'm sorry. You want me to go?'

'I don't even know that, Eddie.'

'Right,' he said, and we fell into silence once more.

London was waking up. Joggers and dog walkers were making their way around the park. It was just another day and all over the city people were getting ready for it. People with their own private grief and damaged childhoods, with their own lonely little feelings of despair.

'There is something we can do, you know,' Eddie said.

'Please . . .'

'No, nothing heavy, darling, honest. I was just thinking.'

'What?'

'We could go and get breakfast somewhere,' he said with a sad smile. 'I don't know about you but I'm starving.'

[illegible]

[illegible]

[illegible] you know that [illegible]

[illegible]

[illegible]

9

the voice of society

I hadn't planned to say what I did to the press after my trial, it just sort of happened. I was relieved to be getting off, that was for sure, but I still felt angry about it all. And there was this huddle of press outside. All these microphones and cameras being shoved in my face. Not that I minded all that attention but I thought: *It's my turn now, you fuckers.* I'd been fucked around so much in the last few months. It was my turn to do the fucking around. So when some cunt asked me what I thought of the judgement I just said:

'It's fine by me because I done it.'

And there was a bit of an uproar at this.

'You mean to say you admit to the murder of Simon Beardsley?' someone else asked.

Well, I know you can't be tried twice for something you've been acquitted for. That's the double jeopardy rule. And I thought: *Yeah, this will give them something to chew on.*

'Yeah,' I said. 'I done it.'

The press had a field day over that. I was all over the papers. There was even a question asked in the House, apparently. The *Sunday Illustrated* ran a big two-page exclusive interview. It was with this guy Keith who I'd fed that story to back in Essex. There was a big photo spread, like a hall of infamy. There were pictures of me at that charity thing I'd organised, lined up with a few tasty faces. There was one of me next to Tony Tucker and Pat Tate taken at the Epping Forest Country Club. A blurred photo of me with Reggie Kray that I'd had done surreptitiously when I'd visited him at Maidstone Prison one time. They even dug up an old picture of me as a skinhead back in the Earthquake days. I was presented as a dangerous and well-connected gangster. Of course, they had to condemn me and all that. But that only made it better. I'd become notorious, a celebrity villain.

And all for something I hadn't actually done.

The police requested an informal interview with me. I didn't have anything to lose so I went along. It was weird, all these cozzers with this pained look on their faces. That I'm-not-angry-I'm-disappointed look I used to get in the headmaster's study. Only I wasn't bending over this time.

'We can't see why you did it, Gary,' said one. 'I mean, it makes everyone look bad.'

'No, mate,' I told him. 'I reckon it makes me look fucking great.'

There was a lot of shaking of heads and tut-tutting. A senior officer went on to say, in no uncertain terms, that from now on they would be on my case, checking my every move and so on. My card was marked, right? He fannied on about the 'public interest' and all that. One thing was clear: I'd have to watch myself. I'd thought about getting back at that little toerag Holroyd-Carter but I'd have to go easy on that score. Bide my time, maybe. But when they were finished with me I couldn't resist one last crack at their expense.

'Well,' I said, 'I know I don't have any statement to sign or anything, but do any of you gentlemen want my autograph?'

And David Merriman was well pleased with me. All these offers started to come in. He told me that this poofy writer Oscar Wilde once said that there wasn't any such thing as bad publicity. I got a small part in this BBC drama playing a drug dealer. The Channel 4 sketch show that had used me as this doorman character did this series of scenes with me in this mocked-up prison cell, ranting away. Then a part in a feature film came up.

Merriman wasn't so sure about *Scrapyard Bulldog* at first. It was low-budget and they were only offering what they called deferred payments, which meant that if it went tits up we could end up with fuck-all. In the end he negotiated a tiny percentage of the gross takings, which turned out to be a very clever move on his part.

My role in the film wasn't very big. But it was a good one. I had a couple of key scenes and my character sort of dominated the film. I was playing this big nasty evil bastard called Big Lenny. And everyone on the film seemed well pleased with the way I came across.

It was touch and go during the shooting. Because it was so low-budget it had to be shot from week to week. Sometimes we'd have the weekend off because there wasn't enough money to film on the Saturday. There were times when most people thought it just wasn't going to happen. But the director, this young guy Jez Scott, he just had so much drive. A real sense of self-belief which I respected.

The film had a real struggle to get a distribution deal at first. Then this buzz started going around about it. *Scrapyard Bulldog* was released in the spring of 1997. The premiere was a real event, loads of stars turned up at it. I could hardly believe it. There were these famous actors coming up to me afterwards, congratulating me. The reviews were pretty mixed but a lot of them, even some of the bad ones, said that I was the best thing in it.

Then things really started to kick off. I was everywhere. I already had this little column in *Sorted* magazine, 'A Word from the Geezer'. I didn't actually write it. I just sat down with this journalist every month and talked about the old times, stuff about the naughtiness in my past, stories from the rave scene days, things like that. Then bingo! My column would appear with a fearsome-looking byline photo.

Scrapyard Bulldog became a big hit, it grossed over £12 million at the box office with video sales to come. So I was going to be in pocket what with this percentage point thing. And everyone wanted a piece of me. I did photo shoots for *Esquire* magazine and *GQ*. Interviews with *Arena* and *Maxim*. I even got on the telly on *TFI Friday* with Chris Evans. Offers come in all the time for advertisements and promotions.

I got to go over to the States for the American premiere. The film didn't go down as well over there but things look good for the video market. The main thing was that I got to meet some of the influential casting agents from Hollywood. I've had meetings about a part in a new action movie called *Hotwire*. There are no lines as such but it's a featured role and as David Merriman pointed out: 'It's your strength of character they're after.'

Back home I've got a theatre show lined up, a cabaret thing called *An Evening with the Geezer*. And Merriman keeps going on about this new thing called 'reality TV'. I don't know what it is but he reckons I'd be good for it.

* * *

So now I'm a celebrity. I'm in the VIP lounge of life. The best thing about success is that all your failures become part of it too. Like they were just part of your struggle to get to the top of your game.

And being pretty well fixed financially means that I've been able to make a proper settlement with Karen. She can't stop me seeing the kids now. And even if I don't see as much of them as I'd like to, they'll grow up knowing who I am because I'm famous now. They've got a dad they can look up to and be proud of. Some of that fame stuff even rubs off on Karen, and though she'd never admit it in a million years I reckon she doesn't mind that one bit.

And I've got to look the part too. I go for style rather than fashion. These days it's Versace suits, silk shirts with the collars worn outside the jacket and lots of personal jewellery. Tasteful, though. It's not showing off how much you got that's important, it's having a sense of refinement. I always say you can't buy class, you can only buy flash.

The thing about being a celebrity is that you get to meet a lot of other celebrities. And at first it throws you because there you are standing right next to someone famous. Then you get used to it. You realise that you're in the same boat. You're not like some fan gawping at them from a distance. You belong there. You can have a proper conversation with them. They're as surprised to see you as you are them. And you get respect. Just for being famous. It doesn't seem to matter too much these days what you're famous for. It's just celebrity, and everyone wants it.

And it's funny being recognised, in the street or out and about somewhere. You get used to that too. It becomes a pain sometimes when someone always wants to stop you and say something or come over to say hello. Even being looked at all the time gets to be like a drain on your energy or something. Your life becomes public. That's where you exist now. Where you become real. But I tell you what, you worry most when you don't get noticed. It sets off a little fear, deep down inside, that you might just suddenly become invisible again.

I still think about the bad times now and then. It gives me the fear, to tell you the truth. I'm lucky to have got out when I did. Now I've got the lifestyle of a top-class villain with none of the danger. So I hope. I still keep looking over my shoulder. Plenty of faces out there with grudges to bear. Cozzers on the lookout to fit me up for something. I think of those boys shotgunned to death in the Range Rover. I see Beardsley's face staring out at nothing, lying in a pool of his own blood.

And I'm not the big, bad gangster that I'm made out to be. Nowhere near it really, never was. But I talk it up for public consumption. I ain't the baddest, but for the mugs, the punters, I'm the best bad guy they're ever going to get. And they love it.

I sometimes wonder why. I'm like the voice of something that they're frightened of but want to hear at the same time. I'm living the dream because I'm living their nightmare. And they can sleep easily in their beds knowing that I'm playing it out for them.

That's why I have people coming up to me all familiar. Normal, boring, straight-life people want to shake my hand, touch me, because I'm real to them. More real than their own lives. The Geezer has no doubts, no fears, no day-to-day worries, according to them. They have all these frustrations. Something goes wrong, hassle from the bank manager, a row with the boss, and they dream about how someone like me would deal with it. And everyone seems to want to act like a geezer these days. For most of these blokes mouthing off in these poncey bars that have sprung up all over London, the Geezer is their deepest fear and their biggest fantasy.

Some people come on with this anti-authority thing. But I don't buy that. I ain't anti-authority. Christ, authority was my job description when I was working the doors or collecting debts. That's what a gangster is, an authority figure. No, some people have this Robin Hood idea about villainy. Wealth distribution or something. That's bollocks. I've never known a proper villain to operate like that. I ain't exactly sure that old Robin Hood himself had that MO. I mean, in all the films and that you don't see much of him divvying up the swag with the peasants, do you? What did he do, have a fucking means test or something? No, it's just another alibi. And a useful one too. It keeps people from remembering that all the really big crime – not the petty stuff, mind, but what I was into – it's about trying to get rich and powerful, and most victims of crime are poor.

Everyone likes the idea of getting hold of something for nothing. The cash, the loot, the bling-bling. But there's something more to it. I remember that trip to Madame Tussaud's with Dan when we were kids and him joking about me ending up in the Chamber of

Horrors. Well, it didn't end up like that. Instead it's like I'm one of the guides, showing them around. Except the Chamber is that little room in their heads where all the bad stuff is stored. I give people permission to have those nasty thoughts. Ambitious, greedy thoughts. Thoughts of violence. I'm the voice for them.

Everything changed for me in 1997. So many things happened. But there were all sorts of things going on around me too. Tony Blair came to power and invited all these fashionable people to Downing Street. Rock stars and comedians and what have you. No, I didn't get an invite, but guess who I saw a picture of in the paper, standing next to the new PM with a glass of champagne in his hand and a smug grin on his face? Ben Holroyd-Carter, that's who. I guess he's become too well connected and powerful to touch now. Not that I've really seriously thought about if for a while anyway.

But I still think about Beardsley's murder. Was Holroyd-Carter directly involved in it? Was it some Essex firm or was it about the Hounslow bullion job? I guess we'll never know now. The missing gold did turn up in the end. It was recovered by the police from this abandoned van in the East End just after we finished shooting *Scrapyard Bulldog*. Funny that.

Harry Starks surrended himself to British justice in September. He's terminally ill with cancer. He had been hiding out in northern Cyprus but he he didn't fancy the health service there once he started to get really ill. He said he wanted to die on British soil, so he gave himself up. He's currently in the hospital wing of Belmarsh Prison, ready to croak his last words.

Dan was right about the property boom. It's crazy what they're asking for somewhere in the East End these days. He's become quite rich now and we're proper friends again after all this time. He still takes the piss out of me but he says I need it. He reckons there's far too many people telling me what a great bloke I am.

I've become quite good friends with Jez Scott too. I went on a shooting weekend with him and some of the other guys from the film the other week. Turns out he's pretty handy with a shotgun, not a sawn-off, mind, but, you know, these proper sporting models. I had a great time on this pheasant shoot. It was a proper weekend in the country, great food and plenty of booze in this big old mansion. And blasting away at these birdies is a great laugh, I can tell you.

Doesn't seem legal to have that much fun with a firearm. Jez is getting ready to make another film with a proper budget this time. I'm lined up for a part.

And to top it all, I'm writing a book. Yeah, that's right, a fucking book. Gaz Kelly, chucked out of school at fifteen without even a CSE to his name, is going to become a fucking author. I can't wait for it to come out and I can show all those teachers who thought I was an illiterate yobbo.

Of course, there's going to have to be a writer involved. I've been a bit concerned over this, about how it's going to work out. But my publisher, Victor Groombridge, has set me straight.

'Don't worry about the writer,' he told me. 'Writers aren't important. Two-a-penny hacks, most of them. No, Gaz, it's the subject that's important. And let me tell you, you are a fantastic subject.'

Which has put my mind at rest. You see, I want my story told the right way. I want to be in control of my material, you know what I mean? Certain things that happened in my life, well, I'd sooner skirt around some of them. The marriage break-up, for example, especially that business with the court injunction. The stuff about me cracking up on drugs, some of my criminal activities that haven't been taken into account, and that. And I want it played so that the violence was always against people who had it coming to them.

And Victor sees it my way. I've got a nice little advance on the book. It's going to be called *The Geezer*. The art department have already done a mock-up of the cover. A big photo of me looking fierce in all my shaven-headed glory in a tasty white sharkskin suit I had made recently.

So he arranges a meeting with the writer I'm going to work with at the Groombridge Press. I arrive a little early and I wait outside Victor's office while he has a quick chat with this bloke. I can just hear their voices so I go up to the door to listen in. Old habits die hard. I can hear their conversation.

'Let me do the Starks book, Victor.'

'I told you, no.'

'But he's about to die, for God's sake. I could get it done quickly. We could have it in print in time for the funeral.'

'I can just imagine your God-awful over-wrought prose style. Like that Porter book that never sold any copies. You're better at ghosting, Tony, trust me.'

'But I've got stuff that nobody else knows about. Stuff you'd never believe.'

'I've heard it all before. Anyway, I've already got somebody working on a Starks book. No, you do this. You fucked me about, Tony. Now you pay for it. You still owe me an advance, you know.'

'I know, Victor. But please, not this.'

'Think of it as penance.'

'But *The Geezer*. It's like that other one of yours, *Basher*. They sound like comic-book titles.'

'I get very tired of your superior attitude, you know? I mean, you're hardly some great literary talent youself, are you? And do you know how many copies of *Basher* we sold? In hardback? Over a hundred fucking thousand. And *The Geezer* is going to be even bigger. I'm cleaning up in the true crime market, Tony. And I'm offering you a chance to be part of it.'

'Why?'

'Because of your gutter press instincts. You have all these pathetic pretentions but this is what you're good at. I suspect you'll make a good job of it. Oh, you'll hate it, of course. But that'll be good for your soul. Maybe you'll learn a little humility.'

'And if I say no?'

'You'll have a solicitor's letter in the morning concerning the recovery of an outstanding advance.'

'I see.'

'Then we're agreed, then. Here. Go on, shake my hand. There. Isn't publishing a civilised business? Well, I'll just go and fetch our noble subject.'

I hear him coming to the door so I go and sit down again. The door opens.

'Ah, Gaz,' says Victor. 'Please. Come in.'

This writer bloke stands up as I enter.

'Gaz,' Victor continues. 'This is Tony Meehan, your ghost writer.'

He gives this little smile as he shakes my hand but he doesn't look too happy.

'I was thinking that maybe you two could get acquainted,' says Victor. 'Have a sort of preliminary session. You can use the boardroom. Then we can all go for lunch somewhere.'

So me and Tony go through to this room with a long table a
chairs around it. It looks like he's not been having a good day so I start telling him a few things to try to cheer him up. You know, little jokes and asides that I think might work well with the book. He nods and smiles, so I know I'm on the right track. It's got to have a sense of humour, after all. One of the publicity girls brings some coffee through and we finally get sat down at the end of the table. Tony gets out a notepad and a little tape recorder.

He sighs, switching it on. 'Right, let's get started, shall we?'

So me and Tony go through to this room with a long table and chairs around it. It looks like he's not been having a good day so I start telling him a few things to try to cheer him up. You know, little jokes and asides that I think might work well with the book. He nods and smiles, so I know I'm on the right track. It's got to have a sense of humour, after all. One of the publicity girls brings some coffee through and we finally get sat down at the end of the table. Tony gets out a notepad and a little tape recorder.

He sighs, switching it on. 'Right, let's get started, shall we?'